'The very personification of SF [Arthur C. Clarke] writes always with lucidity and candour, often with grace, some times with a cold, sharp evocativeness that has produced some of the most memorable images in SF'
The Encyclopedia of Science Fiction

'The most popular English SF writer in the world'
David G. Hartwell

'One of the colossi of SF'
John Clute

'More than any other SF author, Clarke has been faithful to a boyhood vision of science as a saviour of mankind, and of mankind as a race of potential gods destined for the stars. If Stapledon has successors, Clarke is the foremost . . . [*Rendezvous With Rama* is] memorable and at times magical . . . it is Clarke's ability to evoke in us a true sense of wonder at unfolding marvels which enlivens the work'
Brian W Aldiss

Also by Arthur C. Clarke

SF MASTERWORKS

Rendezvous with Rama

ARTHUR C. CLARKE

This edition first published in Great Britain in 2023 by Gollancz
an imprint of the Orion Publishing Group Ltd
Carmelite House, 50 Victoria Embankment
London EC4Y 0DZ

An Hachette UK Company

1 3 5 7 9 10 8 6 4 2

A CIP catalogue record for this book
is available from the British Library.

(Paperback) ISBN 978 1 399 61717 8
(eBook) ISBN 978 0 575 08800 9

Typeset by Deltatype Ltd, Birkenhead, Merseyside

Printed in Great Britain by Clays Ltd, Elcograf S.p.A.

www.sfgateway.com
www.gollancz.co.uk

to Sri Lanka
where I climbed
the Stairway of the Gods

1
Spaceguard

Sooner or later, it was bound to happen. On 30 June 1908, Moscow escaped destruction by three hours and four thousand kilometres – a margin invisibly small by the standards of the universe. Again, on 12 February 1947, yet another Russian city had a still narrower escape, when the second great meteorite of the twentieth century detonated less than four hundred kilometres from Vladivostok, with an explosion rivalling that of the newly invented uranium bomb.

In those days, there was nothing that men could do to protect themselves against the last random shots in the cosmic bombardment that had once scarred the face of the Moon. The meteorites of 1908 and 1947 had struck uninhabited wilderness; but by the end of the twenty-first century, there was no region left on Earth that could be safely used for celestial target practice. The human race had spread from pole to pole. And so, inevitably ...

At 09.46 GMT on the morning of 11 September, in the exceptionally beautiful summer of the year 2077, most of the inhabitants of Europe saw a dazzling fireball appear in the eastern sky. Within seconds it was brighter than the sun, and as it moved across the heavens – at first in utter silence – it left behind it a churning column of dust and smoke.

Somewhere above Austria it began to disintegrate, producing a series of concussions so violent that more than a million people had their hearing permanently damaged. They were the lucky ones.

Moving at fifty kilometres a second, a thousand tons of rock and metal impacted on the plains of northern Italy, destroying in a few flaming moments the labour of centuries. The cities of Padua and Verona were wiped from the face of the earth; and the last glories of Venice sank forever beneath the sea as the waters of the Adriatic came thundering landwards after the hammer-blow from space.

Six hundred thousand people died, and the total damage was more than a trillion dollars. But the loss to art, to history, to science – to the whole human race, for the rest of time – was beyond all computation. It was as if a great war had been fought and lost in a single morning; and few could draw much pleasure from the fact that, as the dust of destruction slowly settled, for months the whole world witnessed the most splendid dawns and sunsets since Krakatoa.

After the initial shock, mankind reacted with a determination and a unity that no earlier age could have shown. Such a disaster, it was realised, might not occur again for a thousand years – but it might occur tomorrow. And the next time, the consequences could be even worse.

Very well; *there would be no next time.*

A hundred years earlier a much poorer world, with far feebler resources, had squandered its wealth attempting to destroy weapons launched, suicidally, by mankind against itself. The effort had never been successful, but the skills acquired then had not been forgotten. Now they could be used for a far nobler purpose, and on an infinitely vaster stage. No meteorite large enough to cause catastrophe would ever again be allowed to breach the defences of Earth.

So began Project SPACEGUARD. Fifty years later – and in a way that none of its designers could ever have anticipated – it justified its existence.

2
Intruder

By the year 2130, the Mars-based radars were discovering new asteroids at the rate of a dozen a day. The SPACEGUARD computers automatically calculated their orbits, and stored away the information in their enormous memories, so that every few months any interested astronomer could have a look at the accumulated statistics. These were now quite impressive.

It had taken more than a hundred and twenty years to collect the first thousand asteroids, since the discovery of Ceres, largest of these tiny worlds, on the very first day of the nineteenth century. Hundreds had been found and lost and found again; they existed in such swarms that one exasperated astronomer had christened them 'vermin of the skies'. He would have been appalled to know that SPACEGUARD was now keeping track of half a million.

Only the five giants – Ceres, Pallas, Juno, Eunomia and Vesta – were more than two hundred kilometres in diameter; the vast majority were merely oversized boulders that would fit into a small park. Almost all moved in orbits that lay beyond Mars; only the few that came far enough sunwards to be a possible danger to Earth were the concern of SPACEGUARD. And not one in a thousand of these, during the entire future history of the solar system, would pass within a million kilometres of Earth.

The object first catalogued as 31/439, according to the year and the order of its discovery, was detected while still outside the orbit of Jupiter. There was nothing unusual about its location;

many asteroids went beyond Saturn before turning once more towards their distant master, the sun. And Thule II, most far-ranging of all, travelled so close to Uranus that it might well have been a lost moon of that planet.

But a first radar contact at such a distance was unprecedented; clearly, 31/439 must be of exceptional size. From the strength of the echo, the computers deduced a diameter of at least forty kilometres; such a giant had not been discovered for a hundred years. That it had been overlooked for so long seemed incredible.

Then the orbit was calculated, and the mystery was resolved – to be replaced by a greater one. 31/439 was not travelling on a normal asteroidal path, along an ellipse which it retraced with clockwork precision every few years. It was a lonely wanderer between the stars, making its first and last visit to the solar system – for it was moving so swiftly that the gravitational field of the sun could never capture it. It would flash inwards past the orbits of Jupiter, Mars, Earth, Venus and Mercury, gaining speed as it did so, until it rounded the sun and headed out once again into the unkown.

It was at this point that the computers started flashing their 'Hi there! We have something interesting' sign, and for the first time 31/439 came to the attention of human beings. There was a brief flurry of excitement at SPACEGUARD Headquarters, and the interstellar vagabond was quickly dignified by a name instead of a mere number. Long ago, the astronomers had exhausted Greek and Roman mythology; now they were working through the Hindu pantheon. And so 31/439 was christened Rama.

For a few days, the news media made a fuss of the visitor, but they were badly handicapped by the sparsity of information. Only two facts were known about Rama – its unusual orbit, and its approximate size. Even this was merely an educated guess, based upon the strength of the radar echo. Through the telescope, Rama still appeared as a faint, fifteenth magnitude star – much too small to show a visible disc. But as it plunged in towards the heart of the solar system, it would grow brighter and larger, month by month; before it vanished forever, the orbiting observatories would be able to gather more precise information about its shape and size. There was plenty of time, and perhaps during the next few years some spaceship on its ordinary business might be routed close enough to get good photographs. An actual rendezvous was most unlikely; the energy cost would be far too great to permit physical contact with an object cutting across the orbits of the planets at more than a hundred thousand kilometres an hour.

So the world soon forgot about Rama; but the astronomers did not. Their excitement grew with the passing months, as the new asteroid presented them with more and more puzzles.

First of all, there was the problem of Rama's light curve. It didn't have one.

All known asteroids, without exception, showed a slow variation in their brilliance, waxing and waning within a period of a few hours. It had been recognised for more than two centuries that this was an inevitable result of their spin, and their irregular shape. As they toppled end over end along their orbits the reflecting surfaces they presented to the sun were continually changing, and their brightness varied accordingly.

Rama showed no such changes. Either it was not spinning at all or it was perfectly symmetrical. Both explanations seemed equally unlikely.

There the matter rested for several months, because none of the big orbiting telescopes could be spared from their regular job of peering into the remote depths of the universe. Space astronomy was an expensive hobby, and time on a large instrument could easily cost a thousand dollars a minute. Dr William Stenton would never have been able to grab the Farside two-hundred-metre reflector for a full quarter of an hour, if a more important programme had not been temporarily derailed by the failure of a fifty cent capacitor. One astronomer's bad luck was his good fortune.

Bill Stenton did not know what he had caught until the next day, when he was able to get computer time to process his results. Even when they were finally flashed on his display screen, it took him several minutes to understand what they meant.

The sunlight reflected from Rama was not, after all, absolutely constant in its intensity. There was a very small variation – hard to detect, but quite unmistakable, and extremely regular. Like all the other asteroids, Rama was indeed spinning. But whereas the normal 'day' for an asteroid was several hours, Rama's was only four *minutes*.

Dr Stenton did some quick calculations, and found it hard to believe the results. At its equator, this tiny world must be spinning at more than a thousand kilometres an hour; it would be rather unhealthy to attempt a landing anywhere except at the poles. The centrifugal force at Rama's equator must be powerful enough to flick any loose objects away from it at an acceleration of almost one gravity. Rama was a rolling stone that could never have gathered any cosmic moss; it was surprising that such a body had managed to hold itself together, and had not long ago shattered into a million fragments.

An object forty kilometres across, with a rotation period of only four minutes – where did that fit into the astronomical scheme of things? Dr Stenton was a somewhat imaginative man, a little too prone to jump to conclusions. He now jumped to one which gave him a very uncomfortable few minutes indeed.

The only specimen of the celestial zoo that fitted this description was a collapsed star. Perhaps Rama was a dead sun – a madly spinning sphere of neutronium, every cubic centimetre weighing billions of tons ...

At this point, there flashed briefly through Dr Stenton's horrified mind the memory of that timeless classic, H. G. Wells' *The Star*. He had first read it as a very small boy, and it had helped to spark his interest in astronomy. Across more than two centuries of time, it had lost none of its magic and terror. He would never forget the images of hurricanes and tidal waves, of cities sliding into the sea, as the other visitor from the stars smashed into Jupiter and then fell sunwards past the Earth. True, the star that old Wells described was not cold, but incandescent, and wrought much of its destruction by heat. That scarcely mattered; even if Rama was a cold body, reflecting only the light of the sun, it could kill by gravity as easily as by fire.

Any stellar mass intruding into the solar system would completely distort the orbits of the planets. The Earth had only to move a few million kilometres sunwards – or starwards – for the delicate balance of climate to be destroyed. The Antarctic icecap could melt and flood all low-lying land; or the oceans could freeze and the whole world be locked in an eternal winter. Just a nudge in either direction would be enough ...

Then Dr Stenton relaxed and breathed a sigh of relief. This was all nonsense; he should be ashamed of himself.

Rama could not possibly be made of condensed matter. No star-sized mass could penetrate so deeply into the solar system without producing disturbances which would have betrayed it long ago. The orbits of all the planets would have been affected; that, after all, was how Neptune, Pluto and Persephone had been discovered. No, it was utterly impossible for an object as massive as a dead sun to sneak up unobserved.

In a way, it was a pity. An encounter with a dark star would have been quite exciting.

While it lasted ...

3
Rama and Sita

The extraordinary meeting of the Space Advisory Council was brief and stormy. Even in the twenty-second century, no way had yet been discovered of keeping elderly and conservative scientists from occupying crucial administrative positions. Indeed, it was doubted if the problem ever would be solved.

To make matters worse, the current Chairman of the SAC was Professor (Emeritus) Olaf Davidson, the distinguished astrophysicist. Professor Davidson was not very much interested in objects smaller than galaxies, and never bothered to conceal his prejudices. And though he had to admit that ninety per cent of his science was now based upon observations from space-borne instruments, he was not at all happy about it. No less than three times during his distinguished career, satellites specially launched to prove one of his pet theories had done precisely the opposite.

The question before the Council was straightforward enough. There was no doubt that Rama was an unusual object – but was it an important one? In a few months it would be gone forever, so there was little time in which to act. Opportunities missed now would never recur.

At rather a horrifying cost, a space-probe soon to be launched from Mars to beyond Neptune could be modified and sent on a high-speed trajectory to meet Rama. There was no hope of a rendezvous; it would be the fastest fly-by on record, for the two bodies would pass each other at two hundred thousand kilometres an hour. Rama would be observed intensively for only a few minutes – and in real closeup for less than a second. But with the right instrumentation, that would be long enough to settle many questions.

Although Professor Davidson took a very jaundiced view of the Neptune probe, it had already been approved and he saw no point in sending more good money after bad. He spoke eloquently on the follies of asteroid-chasing, and the urgent need for a new high-resolution interferometer on the Moon to prove the newly-revived Big Bang theory of creation, once and for all.

That was a grave tactical error, because the three most ardent supporters of the Modified Steady State Theory were also members of the Council. They secretly agreed with Professor Davidson that asteroid-chasing was a waste of money; nevertheless ...

He lost by one vote.

Three months later the space-probe, rechristened Sita, was launched from Phobos, the inner moon of Mars. The flight time was seven weeks, and the instrument was switched to full power only five minutes before interception. Simultaneously, a cluster of camera pods was released, to sail past Rama so that it could be photographed from all sides.

The first images, from ten thousand kilometres away, brought to a halt the activities of all mankind. On a billion television screens, there appeared a tiny, featureless cylinder, growing rapidly second by second. By the time it had doubled its size, no one could pretend any longer that Rama was a natural object.

Its body was a cylinder so geometrically perfect that it might have been turned on a lathe – one with centres fifty kilometres apart. The two ends were quite flat, apart from some small structures at the centre of one face, and were twenty kilometres across; from a distance, when there was no sense of scale, Rama looked almost comically like an ordinary domestic boiler.

Rama grew until it filled the screen. Its surface was a dull, drab grey, as colourless as the Moon, and completely devoid of markings except at one point. Halfway along the cylinder there was a kilometre-wide stain or smear, as if something had once hit and splattered, ages ago.

There was no sign that the impact had done the slightest damage to Rama's spinning walls; but this mark had produced the slight fluctuation in brightness that had led to Stenton's discovery.

The images from the other cameras added nothing new. However, the trajectories their pods traced through Rama's minute gravitational field gave one other vital piece of information – the mass of the cylinder.

It was far too light to be a solid body. To nobody's great surprise, it was clear that Rama must be hollow.

The long-hoped-for, long-feared encounter had come at last. Mankind was about to receive its first visitor from the stars.

4
Rendezvous

Commander Norton remembered those first TV transmissions, which he had replayed so many times, during the final minutes of the rendezvous. But there was one thing no electronic image could possibly convey – and that was Rama's overwhelming size.

He had never received such an impression when landing on a natural body like the Moon or Mars. Those were worlds, and one expected them to be big. Yet he had also landed on Jupiter VIII, which was slightly larger than Rama – and that had seemed quite a small object.

It was very easy to resolve the paradox. His judgement was wholly altered by the fact that this was an artifact, millions of times heavier than anything that Man had ever put into space. The mass of Rama was at least ten million million tons; to any spaceman, that was not only an awe-inspiring, but a terrifying thought. No wonder that he sometimes felt a sense of insignificance, and even depression, as that cylinder of sculptured, ageless metal filled more and more of the sky.

There was also a sense of danger here, that was wholly novel to his experience. In every earlier landing he had known what to expect; there was always the possibility of accident, but never of surprise. With Rama, surprise was the only certainty.

Now *Endeavour* was hovering less than a thousand metres above the North Pole of the cylinder, at the very centre of the slowly turning disc. This end has been chosen because it was the one in sunlight; as Rama rotated, the shadows of the short enigmatic structures near the axis swept steadily across the metal plain. The northern face of Rama was a gigantic sundial, measuring out the swift passage of its four-minute day.

Landing a five-thousand-ton spaceship at the centre of a spinning disc was the least of Commander Norton's worries. It was no different from docking at the axis of a large space-station; *Endeavour*'s lateral jets had already given her a matching spin, and he could trust Lieutenant Joe Calvert to put her down as gently as a snowflake, with or without the aid of the nav computer.

'In three minutes,' said Joe, without taking his eyes from the display, 'we'll know if it's made of anti-matter.'

Norton grinned, as he recalled some of the more hair-raising theories about Rama's origin. If that unlikely speculation was true, in a few seconds there would be the biggest bang since the solar system was formed. The total annihilation of ten thousand tons would, briefly, provide the planets with a second sun.

Yet the mission profile had allowed even for this remote contingency; *Endeavour* had squirted Rama with one of her jets from a safe thousand kilometres away. Nothing whatsoever had happened when the expanding cloud of vapour arrived on target – and a matter-anti-matter reaction involving even a few milligrams would have produced an awesome firework display.

Norton, like all space commanders, was a cautious man. He had looked long and hard at the northern face of Rama, choosing the point of touchdown. After much thought, he had decided to avoid the obvious spot – the exact centre, on the axis itself. A clearly marked circular disc, a hundred metres in diameter, was centred on the Pole, and Norton had a strong suspicion that this must be the outer seal of an enormous airlock. The creatures who had built this hollow world must have had some way of taking their ships inside. This was the logical place for the main entrance, and Norton thought it might be unwise to block the front door with his own vessel.

But this decision generated other problems. If *Endeavour* touched down even a few metres from the axis, Rama's rapid spin would start her sliding away from the pole. At first, the centrifugal force would be very weak, but it would be continuous and inexorable. Commander Norton did not relish the thought of his ship slithering across the polar plain, gaining speed minute by minute until it was slung off into space at a thousand kilometres an hour when it reached the edge of the disc.

It was possible that Rama's minute gravitational field – about one thousandth of Earth's – might prevent this from happening. It would hold *Endeavour* against the plain with a force of several tons, and if the surface was sufficiently rough the ship might stay near the Pole. But Commander Norton had no intention of balancing an unknown frictional force against a quite certain centrifugal one.

Fortunately, Rama's designers had provided an answer. Equally spaced around the polar axis were three low, pill-box shaped structures, about ten metres in diameter. If *Endeavour* touched down between any two of these, the centrifugal drift would fetch her up against them and she would be held firmly in place, like a ship glued against a quayside by the incoming waves.

'Contact in fifteen seconds,' said Joe. As he tensed himself above the duplicate controls, which he hoped he would not have to touch, Commander Norton became acutely aware of all that had come to focus on this instant of time. This, surely, was the most momentous landing since the first touchdown on the Moon, a century and a half ago.

The grey pill-boxes drifted slowly upwards outside the control port. There was the last hiss of a reaction jet, and a barely perceptible jar.

In the weeks that had passed, Commander Norton had often

wondered what he would say at this moment. But now that it was upon him, History chose his words, and he spoke almost automatically, barely aware of the echo from the past:

'Rama Base. *Endeavour* has landed.'

As recently as a month ago, he would never have believed it possible. The ship had been on a routine mission, checking and emplacing asteroid warning beacons, when the order had come. *Endeavour* was the only spacecraft in the solar system which could possibly make a rendezvous with the intruder before it whipped round the sun and hurled itself back towards the stars. Even so, it had been necessary to rob three other ships of the Solar Survey, which were now drifting helplessly until tankers could refuel them. Norton feared that it would be a long time before the skippers of *Calypso, Beagle* and *Challenger* would speak to him again.

Even with all this extra propellant, it had been a long hard chase; Rama was already inside the orbit of Venus when *Endeavour* caught up with her. No other ship could ever do so; this privilege was unique, and not a moment of the weeks ahead was to be wasted. A thousand scientists on Earth would have cheerfully mortgaged their souls for this opportunity; now they could only watch over the TV circuits, biting their lips and thinking how much better *they* could do the job. They were probably right, but there was no alternative. The inexorable laws of celestial mechanics had decreed that *Endeavour* was the first, and the last, of all Man's ships that would ever make contact with Rama.

The advice he was continually receiving from Earth did little to alleviate Norton's responsibility. If split-second decisions had to be made, no one could help him; the radio time-lag to Mission Control was already ten minutes, and increasing. He often envied the great navigators of the past, before the days of electronic communications, who could interpret their sealed orders without continual monitoring from headquarters. Why *they* made mistakes, no one ever knew.

Yet at the same time, he was glad that some decisions could be delegated to Earth. Now that *Endeavour*'s orbit had coalesced with Rama's they were heading sunwards like a single body; in forty days they would reach perihelion, and pass within twenty million kilometres of the sun. That was far too close for comfort; long before then, *Endeavour* would have to use her remaining fuel to nudge herself into a safer orbit. They would have perhaps three weeks of exploring time, before they parted from Rama forever.

After that, the problem would be Earth's. *Endeavour* would be virtually helpless, speeding on an orbit which could make her the first ship to reach the stars – in approximately fifty thousand years. There was no need to worry, Mission Control had promised. Somehow, regardless of cost, *Endeavour* would be refuelled – even if it proved necessary to send tankers after her, and abandon them in space once they had transferred every gramme of propellant. Rama was a prize worth any risk, short of a suicide mission.

And, of course, it might even come to that. Commander Norton had no illusions on this score. For the first time in a hundred years an element of total uncertainty had entered human affairs. Uncertainty was one thing that neither scientists nor politicians could tolerate. If that was the price of resolving it, *Endeavour* and her crew would be expendable.

5
First EVA

Rama was as silent as a tomb – which, perhaps, it was. No radio signals, on any frequency; no vibrations that the seismographs could pick up, apart from the micro-tremors undoubtedly caused by the sun's increasing heat; no electrical currents; no radioactivity. It was almost ominously quiet; one might have expected that even an asteroid would be noisier.

What did we expect? Norton asked himself. A committee of welcome? He was not sure whether to be disappointed or relieved. The initiative, at any rate, appeared up to him.

His orders were to wait for twenty-four hours, then to go out and explore. Nobody slept much that first day; even the crew members not on duty spent their time monitoring the ineffectually probing instruments, or simply looking out of the observation ports at the starkly geometrical landscape. Is this world alive? they asked themselves, over and over again. Is it dead? Or is it merely sleeping?

On the first EVA, Norton took only one companion – Lieut-Commander Karl Mercer, his tough and resourceful life-support officer. He had no intention of getting out of sight of the ship, and if there was any trouble it was unlikely that a larger party would be safe. As a precaution, however, he had two more crew members, already suited up, standing by in the airlock.

The few grammes of weight that Rama's combined gravitational and centrifugal fields gave them were neither help nor hindrance; they had to rely entirely on their jets. As soon as possible, Norton told himself, he would string a cat's-cradle of guide ropes between the ship and the pill-boxes, so that they could move around without wasting propellants.

The nearest pill-box was only ten metres from the airlock, and Norton's first concern was to check that the contact had caused no damage to the ship. *Endeavour*'s hull was resting against the curving wall with a thrust of several tons, but the pressure was evenly distributed. Reassured, he began to drift around the circular structure, trying to determine its purpose.

Norton had travelled only a few metres when he came across an interruption in the smooth, apparently metallic wall. At first, he thought it was some peculiar decoration, for it seemed to serve no useful function. Six radial grooves, or slots, were deeply recessed in the metal, and lying in them were six crossed bars like the spokes of a rimless wheel, with a small hub at the centre. But there was no way in which the wheel could be turned, as it was embedded in the wall.

Then he noticed, with growing excitement, that there were deeper recesses at the ends of the spokes, nicely shaped to accept a clutching hand (claw? tentacle?). If one stood *so*, bracing against the wall, and pulled on the spoke so ...

Smooth as silk, the wheel slid out of the wall. To his utter astonishment – for he had been virtually certain that any moving parts would have become vacuum-welded ages ago – Norton found himself holding a spoked wheel. He might have been the captain of some old wind-jammer standing at the helm of his ship.

He was glad that his helmet sunshade did not allow Mercer to read his expression.

He was startled, but also angry with himself; perhaps he had already make his first mistake. Were alarms now sounding inside Rama, and had his thoughtless action already triggered some implacable mechanism?

But *Endeavour* reported no change; its sensors still detected nothing but faint thermal crepitations and his own movements.

'Well, Skipper – are you going to turn it?'

Norton thought once more of his instructions. 'Use your own discretion, but proceed with caution.' If he checked every single move with Mission Control, he would never get anywhere.

'What's your diagnosis, Karl?' he asked Mercer.

'It's obviously a manual control for an airlock – probably an emergency back-up system in case of power failure. I can't imagine *any* technology, however advanced, that wouldn't take such precautions.'

'And it would be fail-safe,' Norton told himself. 'It could only be operated if there was no possible danger to the system ...'

He grasped two opposing spokes of the windlass, braced his feet against the ground, and tested the wheel. It did not budge.

'Give me a hand,' he asked Mercer. Each took a spoke; exerting their utmost strength, they were unable to produce the slightest movement.

Of course, there was no reason to suppose that clocks and corkscrews on Rama turned in the same direction as they did on Earth ...

'Let's try the other way,' suggested Mercer.

This time, there was no resistance. The wheel rotated almost effortlessly through a full circle. Then, very smoothly, it took up the load.

Half a metre away, the curving wall of the pill-box started to move, like a slowly opening clamshell. A few particles of dust, driven by wisps of escaping air, streamed outwards like dazzling diamonds as the brilliant sunlight caught them.

The road to Rama lay open.

6
Committee

It had been a serious mistake, Dr Bose often thought, to put the United Planets Headquarters on the Moon. Inevitably, Earth tended to dominate the proceedings – as it dominated the landscape beyond the dome. If they *had* to build here, perhaps they should have gone to the Farside, where that hypnotic disc never shed its rays ...

But, of course, it was much too late to change, and in any case there was no real alternative. Whether the colonies liked it or not, Earth would be the cultural and economic overlord of the solar system for centuries to come.

Dr Bose had been born on Earth, and had not emigrated to Mars until he was thirty, so he felt that he could view the political situation fairly dispassionately. He knew now that he would never return to his home planet, even though it was only five hours away by shuttle. At 115, he was in perfect health, but he could not face the reconditioning needed to accustom him to three times the gravity he had enjoyed for most of his life. He was exiled forever from the world of his birth; not being a sentimental man, this had never depressed him unduly.

What did depress him sometimes was the need for dealing, year after year, with the same familiar faces. The marvels of medicine were all very well, and certainly he had no desire to put back the clock – but there were men around this conference table with whom he had worked for more than half a century. He knew exactly what they would say and how they would vote on any given subject. He wished that, some day, one of them would do something totally unexpected – even something quite crazy.

And probably they felt exactly the same way about him ...

The Rama Committee was still manageably small, though doubtless that would soon be rectified. His six colleagues – the UP representatives for Mercury, Earth, Luna, Ganymede, Titan and Triton – were all present in the flesh. They had to be; electronic diplomacy was not possible over solar system distances. Some elder statesmen, accustomed to the instantaneous communications which Earth had long taken for granted, had never reconciled themselves to the fact that radio waves took minutes, or even hours, to journey across the gulfs between the planets. 'Can't you scientists do something about it?' they had been heard to complain bitterly, when told that face-to-face conversation was impossible between Earth and any of its remoter children. Only the Moon had that barely acceptable one-and-a-half-second delay – with all the political and psychological consequences which it implied. Because of this fact of astronomical life, the Moon – and *only* the Moon – would always be a suburb of Earth.

Also present in person were three of the specialists who had been co-opted to the Committee. Professor Davidson, the astronomer, was an old acquaintance; today, he did not seem his usual irascible self. Dr Bose knew nothing of the infighting that had preceded the launch of the first probe to Rama, but the Professor's colleagues had not let him forget it.

Dr Thelma Price was familiar through her numerous television appearances, though she had first made her reputation fifty years ago during the archaeological explosion that had followed the draining of that vast marine museum, the Mediterranean.

Dr Bose could still recall the excitement of that time, when the lost treasures of the Greeks, Romans and a dozen other civilizations were restored to the light of day. That was one of the few occasions when he was sorry to be living on Mars.

The exobiologist, Carlisle Perera, was another obvious choice; so was Dennis Solomons, the science historian. Dr Bose was slightly less happy about the presence of Conrad Taylor, the celebrated anthropologist, who had made his reputation by uniquely combining scholarship and eroticism in his study of puberty rites in late twentieth-century Beverley Hills.

No one, however, could possibly have disputed the right of Sir Lewis Sands to be on the Committee. A man whose knowledge was matched only by his urbanity, Sir Lewis was reputed to lose his composure only when called the Arnold Toynbee of his age.

The great historian was not present in person; he stubbornly refused to leave Earth, even for so momentous a meeting as this. His stereo image, indistinguishable from reality, apparently occupied the chair to Dr Bose's right; as if to complete the illusion, someone had placed a glass of water in front of him. Dr Bose considered that this sort of technological *tour de force* was an unnecessary gimmick, but it was surprising how many undeniably great men were childishly delighted to be in two places at once. Sometimes this electronic miracle produced comic disasters; he had been at one diplomatic reception where somebody had tried to walk through a stereogram – and discovered, too late, that it was the real person. And it was even funnier to watch projections trying to shake hands ...

His Excellency the Ambassador for Mars to the United Planets called his wandering thoughts to order, cleared his throat, and said: 'Gentlemen, the Committee is now in session. I think I am correct in saying that this is a gathering of unique talents, assembled to deal with a unique situation. The directive that the Secretary-General has given us is to evaluate that situation, and to advise Commander Norton when necessary.'

This was a miracle of over-simplification, and everyone knew it. Unless there was a real emergency, the Committee might never be in direct contact with Commander Norton – if, indeed, he ever heard of its existence. For the Committee was a temporary creation of the United Planets' Science Organisation, reporting through its Director to the Secretary-General. It was true that the Space Survey was part of the UP – but on the *Operations*, not the Science side. In theory, this should not make much difference; there was no reason why the Rama Committee – or anyone else for that matter – should not call up Commander Norton and offer helpful advice.

But Deep Space Communications are expensive. *Endeavour* could be contacted only through PLANETCOM, which was an autonomous corporation, famous for the strictness and efficiency of its accounting. It took a long time to establish a line of credit with PLANETCOM; somewhere, someone was working on this; but at the moment, PLANETCOM's hard-hearted computers did not recognize the existence of the Rama Committee.

'This Commander Norton,' said Sir Robert Mackay, the Ambassador for Earth. 'He has a tremendous responsibility. What sort of person is he?'

'I can answer that,' said Professor Davidson, his fingers flying over the keyboard of his memory pad. He frowned at the screenful of information, and started to make an instant synopsis.

'William Tsien Norton, Born 2077, Brisbane, Oceana. Educated Sydney, Bombay, Houston. Then five years at Astrograd, specialising in propulsion. Commissioned 2102. Rose through usual ranks – Lieutenant on the Third Persephone expedition, distinguished himself during fifteenth attempt to establish base on Venus ... um ... um ... exemplary record ... dual citizenship, Earth and Mars ... wife and one child in Brisbane, wife and *two* in Port Lowell, with option on third ...'

'Wife?' asked Taylor innocently.

'No, child of course,' snapped the Professor, before he caught the grin on the other's face. Mild laughter rippled round the table, though the overcrowded terrestrials looked more envious than amused. After a century of determined effort, Earth had still failed to get its population below the target of one billion ...

'... appointed commanding officer Solar Survey Research Vessel *Endeavour*. First voyage to retrograde satellites of Jupiter ... um, that was a tricky one ... on asteroid mission when ordered to prepare for this operation ... managed to beat deadline ...'

The Professor cleared the display and looked up at his colleagues.

'I think we were extremely lucky, considering that he was the only man available at such short notice. We might have had the usual run-of-the-mill captain.' He sounded as if he was referring to the typical peg-legged scourge of the spaceways, pistol in one hand and cutlass in the other.

'The record only proves that he's competent,' objected the Ambassador from Mercury (population: 112,500 but growing). 'How will he react in a wholly novel situation like this?'

On Earth, Sir Lewis Sands cleared his throat. A second and a half later, he did so on the Moon.

'Not exactly a novel situation,' he reminded the Hermian, 'even though it's three centuries since it last occurred. If Rama is dead, or unoccupied – and so far all the evidence suggests that it is – Norton is in the position of an archaeologist discovering the ruins of an extinct culture.' He bowed politely to Dr Price, who nodded in agreement. 'Obvious examples are Schliemann at Troy or Mouhot at Angkor Vat. The danger is minimal, though of course accident can never be completely ruled out.'

'But what about the booby-traps and trigger mechanisms these Pandora people have been talking about?' asked Dr Price.

'Pandora?' asked the Hermian Ambassador quickly. 'What's that?'

'It's a crackpot movement,' explained Sir Robert, with as much embarrassment as a diplomat was ever likely to show, 'which is convinced that Rama is a grave potential danger. A box that shouldn't be opened, you know.' He doubted if the

Hermian *did* know: classical studies were not encouraged on Mercury.

'Pandora – paranoia,' snorted Conrad Taylor. 'Oh, of course, such things are *conceivable*, but why should any intelligent race went to play childish tricks?'

'Well, even ruling out such unpleasantness,' Sir Robert continued, 'we still have the much more ominous possibility of an active, inhabited Rama. Then the situation is one of an encounter between two cultures – at very different technological levels. Pizzaro and the Incas. Peary and the Japanese. Europe and Africa. Almost invariably, the consequences have been disastrous – for one or both parties. I'm not making any recommendations: I'm merely pointing out precedents.'

'Thank you, Sir Robert,' replied Dr Bose. It was a mild nuisance, he thought, having two 'Sirs' on one small committee; in these latter days knighthood was an honour which few Englishmen escaped. 'I'm sure we've all thought of these alarming possibilities. But if the creatures inside Rama are – er – malevolent – will it really make the slightest difference what we do?'

'They might ignore us if we go away.'

'What – after they've travelled billions of miles and thousands of years?'

The argument had reached the take-off point, and was now self-sustaining. Dr Bose sat back in his chair, said very little, and waited for the consensus to emerge.

It was just as he had predicted. Everyone agreed that, once he had opened the first door, it was inconceivable that Commander Norton should not open the second.

7
Two Wives

If his wives ever compared his videograms, Commander Norton thought with more amusement than concern, it would involve him in a lot of extra work. Now, he could make one long 'gram and dupe it, adding only brief personal messages and endearments before shooting the almost identical copies off to Mars and Earth.

Of course, it was highly unlikely that his wives ever would do such a thing; even at the concessionary rates allowed to spacemen's families, it would be expensive. And there would be no point in it; his families were on excellent terms with each other, and exchanged the usual greetings on birthdays and anniversaries. Yet, on the whole, perhaps it was just as well that the girls had never met, and probably never would. Myrna had been born on Mars and so could not tolerate the high gravity of Earth. And Caroline hated even the twenty-five minutes of the longest possible terrestrial journey.

'Sorry I'm a day late with this transmission,' said the Commander after he had finished the general-purpose preliminaries, 'but I've been away from the ship for the last thirty hours, believe it or not ...

'Don't be alarmed – everything is under control, going perfectly. It's taken us two days, but we're almost through the airlock complex. We could have done it in a couple of hours, if we'd known what we do now. But we took no chances, sent remote cameras ahead, and cycled all the locks a dozen times to make sure they wouldn't seize up behind us – *after* we'd gone through ...

'Each lock is a simple revolving cylinder with a slot on one side. You go in through this opening, crank the cylinder round a hundred and eighty degrees – and the slot then matches up with another door so that you can step out of it. Or float, in this case.

'The Ramans really made sure of things. There are three of these cylinder-locks, one after the other just inside the outer hull and below the entry pill-box. I can't imagine how even one would fail, unless someone blew it up with explosives, but if it did, there would be a second back-up, and then a third ...

'And *that's* only the beginning. The final lock opens into a straight corridor, almost half a kilometre long. It looks clean and tidy, like everything else we've seen; every few metres there are small ports that probably held lights, but now everything is completely black and, I don't mind telling you, scary. There are also two parallel slots, about a centimetre wide, cut in the walls and running the whole length of the tunnel. We suspect that some kind of shuttle runs inside these, to tow equipment – or people – back and forth. It would save us a lot of trouble if we could get it working ...

'I mentioned that the tunnel was half a kilometre long. Well, from our seismic soundings we knew that's about the thickness of the shell, so obviously we were almost through it. And at the end of the tunnel we weren't surprised to find another of those cylindrical airlocks.

'Yes, *and* another. *And* another. These people seem to have done everything in threes. We're in the final lock chamber now, awaiting the OK from Earth before we go through. The interior of Rama is only a few metres away. I'll be a lot happier when the suspense is over.

'You know Jerry Kirchoff, my Exec, who's got such a library of *real* books that he can't afford to emigrate from Earth? Well,

Jerry told me about a situation just like this, back at the beginning of the twenty-first – no, twentieth century. An archaeologist found the tomb of an Egyptian king, the first one that hadn't been looted by robbers. His workmen took months to dig their way in, chamber by chamber, until they came to the final wall. Then they broke through the masonery, and he held out a lantern and pushed his head inside. He found himself looking into a whole roomful of treasure – incredible stuff, gold and jewels ...

'Perhaps this place is also a tomb; it seems more and more likely. Even now, there's still not the slightest sound, or hint of any activity. Well, tomorrow we should know.'

Commander Norton switched the record to HOLD. What else, he wondered, should he say about the work before he began the separate personal messages to his families? Normally, he never went into so much detail, but these circumstances were scarcely normal. This might be the last 'gram he would ever send to those he loved; he owed it to them to explain what he was doing.

By the time they saw these images, and heard these words, he would be inside Rama – for better or for worse.

8
Through the Hub

Never before had Norton felt so strongly his kinship with that long dead Egyptologist. Not since Howard Carter had first peered into the tomb of Tutankhamen could any man have known a moment such as this – yet the comparison was almost laughably ludicrous.

Tutankhamen had been buried only yesterday – not even four thousand years ago; Rama might be older than mankind. That little tomb in the Valley of the Kings could have been lost in the corridors through which they had already passed, yet the space that lay beyond this final seal was at least a million times greater. And as for the treasure it might hold – that was beyond imagination.

No one had spoken over the radio circuits for at least five minutes; the well-trained team had not even reported verbally when all the checks were complete. Mercer had simply given him the OK sign and waved him towards the open tunnel. It was as if everyone realised that this was a moment for History, not to be spoiled by unnecessary small-talk. That suited Commander Norton, for at the moment he too had nothing to say. He flicked on the beam of his flashlight, triggered his jets, and drifted slowly down the short corridor, trailing his safety line behind him. Only seconds later, he was inside.

Inside *what*? All before him was total darkness; not a glimmer of light was reflected back from the beam. He had expected this, but he had not really believed it. All the calculations had shown that the far wall was tens of kilometres away; now his eyes told him that this was indeed the truth. As he drifted slowly into that darkness, he felt a sudden need for the reassurance of his safety line, stronger than any he had ever experienced before, even on his very first EVA. And that was ridiculous; he had looked out across the light-years and the megaparsecs without vertigo; why should he be disturbed by a few cubic kilometres of emptiness?

He was still queasily brooding over this problem when the momentum damper at the end of the line braked him gently to a halt, with a barely perceptible rebound. He swept the vainly-probing beam of the flashlight down from the nothingness ahead, to examine the surface from which he had emerged.

He might have been hovering over the centre of a small crater, which was itself a dimple in the base of a much larger one. On either side rose a complex of terraces and ramps – all geometrically precise and obviously artificial – which extended for as far as the beam could reach. About a hundred metres away he could see the exit of the other two airlock systems, identical with this one.

And that was all. There was nothing particularly exotic or alien about the scene: in fact, it bore a considerable resemblance to an abandoned mine. Norton felt a vague sense of disappointment; after all this effort, there should have been some dramatic, even transcendental revelation. Then he reminded himself that he could see only a couple of hundred metres. The darkness beyond his field of view might yet contain more wonders than he cared to face.

He reported briefly to his anxiously-waiting companions, then added: 'I'm sending out the flare – two minutes delay. Here goes.'

With all his strength, he threw the little cylinder straight upwards – or outwards – and started to count seconds as it dwindled along the beam. Before he had reached the quarter minute it was out of sight; when he had got to a hundred he shielded his eyes and aimed the camera. He had always been good a estimating time; he was only two seconds off when the world exploded with light. And this time there was no cause for disappointment.

Even the millions of candlepower of the flare could not light up the whole of this enormous cavity, but now he could see enough to grasp its plan and appreciate its titanic scale. He was at one end of a hollow cylinder at least ten kilometres wide, and of indefinite length. From his viewpoint at the central axis he could see such a mass of detail on the curving walls surrounding him that his mind could not absorb more than a minute fraction of it; he was looking at the landscape of an entire world by a single flash of lightning, and he tried by a deliberate effort of will to freeze the image in his mind.

All round him, the terraced slopes of the 'crater' rose up until they merged into the solid wall that rimmed the sky. No – that impression was false; he must discard the instincts both of earth and of space, and reorientate himself to a new system of coordinates.

He was not at the lowest point of this strange, inside-out world, but the highest. From here, all directions were *down*, not up. If he moved away from this central axis, towards the curving wall which he must no longer think of as a wall, gravity would steadily increase. When he reached the inside surface of the cylinder, he could stand upright on it at any point, feet towards the stars and head towards the centre of the spinning drum. The concept was familiar enough; since the earliest dawn of space-flight, centrifugal force had been used to simulate gravity. It was only the scale of this application which was so overwhelming, so shocking. The largest of all spacestations, Syncsat Five, was less than two hundred metres in diameter. It would take some little while to grow accustomed to one a hundred times that size.

The tube of landscape which enclosed him was mottled with areas of light and shade that could have been forests, fields, frozen lakes or towns; the distance, and the fading illumination of the flare, made identification impossible. Narrow lines that could be highways, canals, or well-trained rivers formed a faintly visible geometrical network; and far along the cylinder, at the very limit of vision, was a band of deeper darkness. It formed a complete circle, ringing the interior of this world, and Norton suddenly recalled the myth of Oceanus, the sea which, the ancients believed, surrounded the Earth.

Here, perhaps, was an even stranger sea – not circular, but *cylindrical*. Before it became frozen in the inter-stellar night, did it have waves and tides and currents – and fish?

The flare guttered and died; the moment of revelation was over. But Norton knew that as long as he lived these images would be burned on his mind. Whatever discoveries the future might bring, they could never erase this first impression. And History could never take from him the privilege of being the first of all mankind to gaze upon the works of an alien civilization.

9
Reconnaissance

'We have now launched five long-delay flares down the axis of the cylinder, and so have a good photo-coverage of its full length. All the main features are mapped; though there are very few than we can identify, we've given them provisional names.

'The interior cavity is fifty kilometres long and sixteen wide. The two ends are bowl-shaped, with rather complicated geometries. We've called ours the Northern Hemisphere and are establishing our first base here at the axis.

'Radiating away from the central hub, a hundred and twenty degrees apart, are three ladders that are almost a kilometre long. They all end at a terrace or ring-shaped plateau, that runs right round the bowl. And leading on from *that*, continuing the direction of the ladders, are three enormous stairways, which go all the way down to the plain. If you imagine an umbrella with only three ribs, equally spaced, you'll have a good idea of this end of Rama.

'Each of those ribs is a stairway, very steep near the axis and then slowly flattening out as it approaches the plain below. The stairways – we've called them Alpha, Beta, Gamma – aren't continuous, but break at five more circular terraces. We estimate there must be between twenty and thirty thousand steps … presumably they were only used for emergencies, since it's inconceivable that the Ramans – or whatever we're going to call them – had no better way of reaching the axis of their world.

'The Southern Hemisphere looks quite different; for one

thing, it has no stairways, and no flat central hub. Instead, there's a huge spike – kilometres long – jutting along the axis, with six smaller ones around it. The whole arrangement is very odd, and we can't imagine what it means.

'The fifty-kilometre-long, cylindrical section between the two bowls we've called the Central Plain. It may seem crazy to use the word "plain" to describe something so obviously curved, but we feel it's justified. It will appear flat to us when we get down there – just as the interior of a bottle must seem flat to an ant crawling round inside it.

'The most striking feature of the Central Plain is the ten-kilometre-wide dark band running completely round it at the half-way mark. It looks like ice, so we've christened it the Cylindrical Sea. Right out in the middle there's a large oval island, about ten kilometres long and three wide, and covered with tall structures. Because it reminds us of Old Manhattan, we've called it New York. Yet I don't think it's a city; it seems more like an enormous factory or chemical processing plant.

'But there are some cities – or at any rate, towns. At least six of them; if they were built for human beings, they could each hold about fifty thousand people. We've called them Rome, Peking, Paris, Moscow, London, Tokyo … They are linked with highways and something that seems to be a rail system.

'There must be enough material for centuries of research in this frozen carcass of a world. We've four thousand square kilometres to explore, and only a few weeks to do it in. I wonder if we'll ever learn the answer to the two mysteries that have been haunting me ever since we got inside; who were they – *and what went wrong*?'

The recording ended. On Earth and Moon, the members of the Rama Committee relaxed, then started to examine the maps and photographs spread in front of them. Though they had already studied these for many hours, Commander Norton's voice added a dimension which no pictures could convey. He had actually been there – had looked with his own eyes across this extraordinary inside-out world, during the brief moments while its age-long night had been illuminated by the flares. And he was the man who would lead any expedition to explore it.

'Dr Perera, I believe you have some comments to make?'

Ambassador Bose wondered briefly if he should have first given the floor to Professor Davidson, as senior scientist and the only astronomer. But the old cosmologist still seemed to be in a mild state of shock, and was clearly out of his element. All his professional career he had looked upon the universe as an arena for the titanic impersonal forces of gravitation, magnetism, radiation; he had never believed that life played an important role in the scheme of things, and regarded its appearance on Earth, Mars and Jupiter as an accidental aberration.

But now there was proof that life not only existed outside the solar system, but had scaled heights far beyond anything that man had achieved, or could hope to reach for centuries to come. Moreover, the discovery of Rama challenged another dogma that Professor Olaf had preached for years. When pressed, he would reluctantly admit that life probably did exist in other star systems – but it was absurd, he had always maintained, to imagine that it could ever cross the interstellar gulfs …

Perhaps the Ramans had indeed failed, if Commander Norton was correct in believing that their world was now a tomb. But at least they had attempted the feat, on a scale which indicated a high confidence in the outcome. If such a thing had happened once, it must surely have happened many times in this Galaxy of a hundred thousand million suns … and someone, somewhere, would eventually succeed.

This was the thesis which, without proof but with considerable arm-waving, Dr Carlisle Perera had been preaching for years. He was now a very happy man, though also a most frustrated one. Rama had spectacularly confirmed his views – but he could never set foot inside it, or even see it with his own eyes.

If the devil had suddenly appeared and offered him the gift of instantaneous teleportation, he would have signed the contract without bothering to look at the small print.

'Yes, Mr Ambassador, I think I have some information of interest. What we have here is undoubtedly a "Space Ark". It's an old idea in the astronautical literature; I've been able to trace it back to the British physicist J. D. Bernal, who proposed this method of interstellar colonization in a book published in 1929 – yes, two hundred years ago. And the great Russian pioneer Tsiolkovski put forward somewhat similar proposals even earlier.

'If you want to go from one star system to another you have a number of choices. Assuming that the speed of light is an absolute limit – and that's *still* not completely settled, despite anything you may have heard to the contrary' – there was an indignant sniff, but no formal protest from Professor Davidson – 'you can make a fast trip in a small vessel, or a slow journey in a giant one.

'There seems no technical reason why spacecraft cannot reach ninety per cent, or more, of the speed of light. That would mean a travel time of five to ten years between neighbouring stars – tedious, perhaps, but not impracticable, especially for creatures whose life spans might be measured in centuries. One can imagine voyages of this duration, carried out in ships not much larger than ours.

'But perhaps such speeds are impossible, with reasonable payloads; remember, you have to carry the fuel to slow down at the end of the voyage, even if you're on a one-way trip. So it may make more sense to take your time – ten thousand, a hundred thousand years ...

'Bernal and others thought this could be done with mobile worldlets a few kilometres across, carrying thousands of passengers on journeys that would last for generations. Naturally, the system would have to be rigidly closed, recycling all food, air and other expendables. But, of course, that's just how the Earth operates – on a slightly larger scale.

'Some writers suggested that these Space Arks should be built in the form of concentric spheres; others proposed hollow, spinning cylinders so that centrifugal force could provide artificial gravity – exactly what we've found in Rama—'

Professor Davidson could not tolerate this sloppy talk.

'No such thing as centrifugal *force*. It's an engineer's phantom. There's only inertia.'

'You're quite right, of course,' admitted Perera, 'though it might be hard to convince a man who'd just been slung off a carousel. But mathematical rigour seems unnecessary—'

'Hear, hear,' interjected Dr Bose, with some exasperation. 'We all know what you mean, or think we do. Please don't destroy our illusions.'

'Well, I was merely pointing out that there's nothing conceptually novel about Rama, though its size is startling. Men have imagined such things for two hundred years.

'Now I'd like to address myself to another question. Exactly how long has Rama been travelling through space?

'We now have a very precise determination of its orbit and its velocity. Assuming that it's made no navigational changes, we can trace its position back for millions of years. We expected that it would be coming from the direction of a nearby star – but that isn't the case at all.

'It's more than *two hundred thousand years* since Rama passed near any star, and that particular one turns out to be an irregular variable – about the most unsuitable sun you could imagine for an inhabited solar system. It has a brightness range of over fifty to one; any planets would be alternately baked and frozen every few years.'

'A suggestion,' put in Dr Price. 'Perhaps that explains everything. Maybe this was once a normal sun and became unstable. That's why the Ramans had to find a new one.'

Dr Perera admired the old archaeologist, so he let her down lightly. But what would *she* say, he wondered, if he started pointing out the instantly obvious in her own speciality ...

'We did consider that,' he said gently. 'But if our present theories of stellar evolution are correct, this star could *never* have been stable – could never have had life-bearing planets. So Rama has been cruising through space for at least two hundred thousand years, and perhaps for more than a million.

'Now it's cold and dark and apparently dead, and I think I know why. The Ramans may have had no choice – perhaps they were indeed fleeing from some disaster – but they miscalculated.

'No closed ecology can be one hundred per cent efficient; there is always waste, loss – some degradation of the environment, and build-up of pollutants. It may take billions of years to poison and wear out a planet – but it will happen in the end. The oceans will dry up, the atmosphere will leak away ...

'By our standards, Rama is enormous – yet it is still a very tiny planet. My calculations, based on the leakage through its hull, and some reasonable guesses about the rate of biological turnover, indicate that its ecology could only survive for about a thousand years. At the most, I'll grant ten thousand ...

'That would be long enough, at the speed Rama is travelling, for a transit between the closely-packed suns in the heart of the Galaxy. But not out here, in the scattered population of the spiral arms. Rama is a ship which exhausted its provisions before it reached its goal. It's a derelict, drifting among the stars.

'There's just one serious objection to this theory, and I'll raise it before anybody else does. Rama's orbit is aimed so accurately at the solar system that coincidence seems ruled out. In fact, I'd say it's now heading much too close to the sun for comfort: *Endeavour* will have to break away long before perihelion, to avoid overheating.

'I don't pretend to understand this. Perhaps, there may be

some form of automatic terminal guidance still operating, steering Rama to the nearest suitable star ages after its builders are dead.

'And they *are* dead; I'll stake my reputation on that. All the samples we've taken from the interior are absolutely sterile – we've not found a single micro-organism. As for the talk you may have heard about suspended animation, you can ignore it. There are fundamental reasons why hibernation techniques will only work for a very few centuries – and we're dealing with time spans a thousand-fold longer.

'So the Pandorans and their sympathizers have nothing to worry about. For my part, I'm sorry. It would have been wonderful to have met another intelligent species.

'But at least we have answered one ancient question. We are not alone. The stars will never again be the same to us.'

10
Descent into Darkness

Commander Norton was sorely tempted – but as captain his first duty was to his ship. If anything went badly wrong on this initial probe, he might have to run for it.

So that left his second officer, Lieut-Commander Mercer, as the obvious choice. Norton willingly admitted that Karl was better suited for the mission.

The authority on life-support systems, Mercer had written some of the standard textbooks on the subject. He had personally checked out unnumerable types of equipment, often under hazardous conditions, and his biofeedback control was famous. At a moment's notice he could cut his pulse-rate by fifty per cent, and reduce respiration to almost zero for up to ten minutes. These useful little tricks had saved his life on more than one occasion.

Yet despite his great ability and intelligence, he was almost wholly lacking in imagination. To him the most dangerous experiments or missions were simply jobs that had to be done. He never took unnecessary risks, and had no use at all for what was commonly regarded as courage.

The two mottoes on his desk summed up his philosophy of life. One asked WHAT HAVE YOU FORGOTTEN? The other said HELP STAMP OUT BRAVERY. The fact that he was widely regarded as the bravest man in the Fleet was the only thing that ever made him angry.

Given Mercer, that automatically selected the next man – his inseparable companion Lt Joe Calvert. It was hard to see what the two had in common; the lightly-built, rather highly strung navigating officer was ten years younger than his stolid and imperturbable friend, who certainly did not share his passionate interest in the art of the primitive cinema.

But no one can predict where lightning will strike, and years ago Mercer and Calvert had established an apparently stable liaison. That was common enough; much more unusual was the fact that they also shared a wife back on Earth, who had borne each of them a child. Commander Norton hoped that he could meet her one day; she must be a very remarkable woman. The triangle had lasted for at least five years, and still seemed to be an equilateral one.

Two men were not enough for an exploring team; long ago it had been found that three was the optimum – for if one man was lost, two might still escape where a single survivor would be doomed. After a good deal of thought, Norton had chosen Technical Sergeant Willard Myron. A mechanical genius who could make anything work – or design something better if it wouldn't – Myron was the ideal man to identify alien pieces of equipment. On a long sabbatical from his regular job as Associate Professor at Astrotech, the Sergeant had refused to accept a commission on the grounds that he did not wish to block the promotion of more deserving career officers. No one took this explanation very seriously and it was generally agreed that Will rated zero for ambition. He might make it to Space Sergeant, but would never be a full professor. Myron, like countless NCOs before him, had discovered the ideal compromise between power and responsibility.

As they drifted through the last airlock and floated out along the weightless axis of Rama, Lt Calvert found himself, as he so often did, in the middle of a movie flashback. He sometimes wondered if he should attempt to cure himself of this habit, but he could not see that it had any disadvantages. It could make even the dullest situations interesting and – who could tell? – one day it might save his life. He would remember what Fairbanks or Connery or Hiroshi had done in similar circumstances ...

This time, he was about to go over the top, in one of the early-twentieth-century wars; Mercer was the sergeant leading a three-man patrol on a night raid into no-man's land. It was not too difficult to imagine that they were at the bottom of an immense shell-crater, though one that had somehow become neatly tailored into a series of ascending terraces. The crater was flooded with light from three widely-spaced plasma-arcs, which gave an almost shadowless illumination over the whole interior. But beyond that – over the rim of the most distant terrace – was darkness and mystery.

In his mind's eye, Calvert knew perfectly well what lay there. First there was the flat circular plain over a kilometre across. Trisecting it into three equal parts, and looking very much like broad railroad tracks, were three wide ladders, their rungs recessed into the surface so that they would provide no obstruction to anything sliding over it. Since the arrangement was completely symmetrical, there was no reason to choose one ladder rather than another; that nearest to Airlock Alpha had been selected purely as a matter of convenience.

Though the rungs of the ladders were uncomfortably far apart, that presented no problem. Even at the rim of the Hub, half a kilometre from the axis, gravity was still barely one thirtieth of Earth's. Although they were carrying almost a hundred kilos of equipment and life-support gear, they would still be able to move easily hand-over-hand.

Commander Norton and the back-up team accompanied them along the guide ropes that had been stretched from Airlock Alpha to the rim of the crater; then, beyond the range of the floodlights, the darkness of Rama lay before them. All that could be seen in the dancing beams of the helmet lights was the first few hundred metres of the ladder, dwindling away across a flat and otherwise featureless plain.

And now, Karl Mercer told himself, I have to make my first decision. Am I going *up* that ladder, or *down* it?

The question was not a trivial one. They were still essentially in zero gravity, and the brain could select any reference system it pleased. By a simple effort of will, Mercer could convince himself that he was looking out across a horizontal plain, or up the face of a vertical wall, or over the edge of a sheer cliff. Not a few astronauts had experienced grave psychological problems by choosing the wrong coordinates when they started on a complicated job.

Mercer was determined to go head-first, for any other mode of locomotion would be awkward; moreover, this way he could more easily see what was in front of him. For the first few hundred metres, therefore, he would imagine he was climbing upwards; only when the increasing pull of gravity made it impossible to maintain the illusion would be switch his mental directions one hundred and eighty degrees.

He grasped the first rung and gently propelled himself along the ladder. Movement was as effortless as swimming along the seabed – more so, in fact, for there was no backward drag of water. It was so easy that there was a temptation to go too fast, but Mercer was much too experienced to hurry in a situation as novel as this.

In his earphones, he could hear the regular breathing of his two companions. He needed no other proof that they were in good shape, and wasted no time in conversation. Though he was tempted to look back, he decided not to risk it until they had reached the platform at the end of the ladder.

The rungs were spaced a uniform half metre apart, and for the first portion of the climb Mercer missed the alternate ones. But he counted them carefully, and at around two hundred noticed the first distinct sensations of weight. The spin of Rama was starting to make itself felt.

At rung four hundred, he estimated that his apparent weight was about five kilos. This was no problem, but it was now getting hard to pretend that he was climbing, when he was being firmly dragged *upwards*.

The five hundredth rung seemed a good place to pause. He could feel the muscles in his arms responding to the unaccustomed exercise, even though Rama was now doing all the work and he had merely to guide himself.

'Everything OK, Skipper,' he reported. 'We're just passing the halfway mark. Joe, Will – any problems?'

'I'm fine – what are you stopping for?' Joe Calvert answered.

'Same here,' added Sergeant Myron. 'But watch out for the Coriolis force. It's starting to build up.'

So Mercer had already noticed. When he let go of the rungs he had a distinct tendency to drift off to the right. He knew perfectly well that this was merely the effect of Rama's spin, but it seemed as if some mysterious force was gently pushing him away from the ladder.

Perhaps it was time to start going feet-first, now that 'down' was beginning to have a physical meaning. He would run the risk of a momentary disorientation.

'Watch out – I'm going to swing round.'

Holding firmly on to the rung, he used his arms to twist himself round a hundred and eighty degrees, and found himself momentarily blinded by the lights of his companions. Far above them – and now it really *was* above – he could see a fainter glow along the rim of the sheer cliff. Silhouetted against it were the figures of Commander Norton and the back-up team, watching him intently. They seemed very small and far away, and he gave them a reassuring wave.

He released his grip, and let Rama's still feeble pseudo-gravity take over. The drop from one rung to the next required more than two seconds; on Earth, in the same time, a man would have fallen thirty metres.

The rate of fall was so painfully slow that he hurried things up a trifle by pushing with his hands, gliding over spans of a dozen rungs at a time, and checking himself with his feet whenever he felt he was travelling too fast.

At rung seven hundred, he came to another halt and swung the beam of his helmet-lamp downwards; as he had calculated, the beginning of the stairway was only fifty metres below.

A few minutes later, they were on the first step. It was a strange experience, after months in space, to stand upright on a solid surface, and to feel it pressing against one's feet. Their weight was still less than ten kilogrammes, but that was enough to give a feeling of stability. When he closed his eyes, Mercer could believe that he once more had a real world beneath him.

The ledge or platform from which the stairway descended was about ten metres wide, and curved upwards on each side until it disappeared into the darkness. Mercer knew that it formed a complete circle and that if he walked along it for five kilometres he would come right back to his starting-point, having circumnavigated Rama.

At the fractional gravity that existed here, however, real walking was impossible; one could only bound along in giant strides. And therein lay danger.

The stairway that swooped down into the darkness, far below the range of their lights, would be deceptively easy to descend. But it would be essential to hold on to the tall handrail that flanked it on either side; too bold a step might send an incautious traveller arching far out into space. He would hit the surface again perhaps a hundred metres lower down; the impact would be harmless, but its consequences might not be – for the spin of Rama would have moved the stairway off to the left. And so a falling body would hit against the smooth curve that swept in an unbroken arc to the plain almost seven kilometres below.

That, Mercer told himself, would be a hell of a toboggan ride; the terminal speed, even in this gravity, could be several hundred kilometres an hour. Perhaps it would be possible to apply enough friction to check such a headlong descent; if so, this might even be the most convenient way to reach the inner surface of Rama. But some very cautious experimenting would be necessary first.

'Skipper,' reported Mercer, 'there were no problems getting down the ladder. If you agree, I'd like to continue towards the next platform. I want to time our rate of descent on the stairway.'

Norton replied without hesitation.

'Go ahead.' He did not need to add, 'Proceed with caution.'

It did not take Mercer long to make a fundamental discovery. It was impossible, at least at this one-twentieth-of-a-gravity level, to walk down the stairway in the normal manner. Any attempt to do so resulted in a slow-motion dream-like movement that was intolerably tedious; the only practical way was to ignore the steps, and to use the handrail to pull oneself downwards.

Calvert had come to the same conclusion.

'This stairway was built to walk *up*, not down!' he exclaimed. 'You can use the steps when you're moving against gravity, but they're just a nuisance in this direction. It may not be dignified, but I think the best way down is to slide along the handrail.'

'That's ridiculous,' protested Sergeant Myron. 'I can't believe the Ramans did it this way.'

'I doubt if they ever used this stairway – it's obviously only for emergencies. They must have had some mechanical transport system to get up here. A funicular, perhaps. That would explain those long slots running down from the Hub.'

'I always assumed they were drains – but I suppose they could be both. I wonder if it ever rained here?'

'Probably,' said Mercer. 'But I think Joe is right, and to hell with dignity. Here we go.'

The handrail – presumably it *was* designed for something like hands – was a smooth, flat, metal bar supported on widely-spaced pillars a metre high. Commander Mercer straddled it, carefully gauged the braking power he could exert with his hands, and let himself slide.

Very sedately, slowly picking up speed, he descended into the darkness, moving in the pool of light from his helmet-lamp. He had gone about fifty metres when he called the others to join him.

None would admit it, but they all felt like boys again, sliding down the banisters. In less than two minutes, they had made a kilometre descent in safety and comfort. Whenever they felt they were going too fast, a tightened grip on the handrail provided all the braking that was necessary.

'I hope you enjoyed yourselves,' Commander Norton called when they stepped off at the second platform. 'Climbing back won't be quite so easy.'

'That's what I want to check,' replied Mercer, who was walking experimentally back and forth, getting the feel of the increased gravity. 'It's already a tenth of a gee here – you really notice the difference.'

He walked – or, more accurately, glided – to the edge of the platform, and shone his helmet-light down the next section of the stairway. As far as his beam could reach, it appeared identical with the one above – though careful examination of photos had shown that the height of the steps steadily decreased with the rising gravity. The stair had apparently been designed so that the effort required to climb it was more or less constant at every point in its long curving sweep.

Mercer glanced up towards the Hub of Rama, now almost two kilometres above him. The little glow of light, and the tiny figures silhouetted against it, seemed horribly far away. For the first time, he was suddenly glad that he could not see the whole length of this enormous stairway. Despite his steady nerves and lack of imagination, he was not sure how he would react if he could see himself like an insect crawling up the face of a vertical saucer more than sixteen kilometres high – and with the upper half overhanging above him. Until this moment, he had regarded the darkness as a nuisance; now he almost welcomed it.

'There's no change of temperature,' he reported to Commander Norton. 'Still just below freezing. But the air-pressure is up, as we expected – around three hundred millibars. Even with this low oxygen content, it's almost breathable; further down there will be no problems at all. That will simplify exploration enormously. What a find – the first world on which we can walk without breathing gear! In fact, I'm going to take a sniff.'

Up on the Hub, Commander Norton stirred a little uneasily. But Mercer, of all men, knew exactly what he was doing. He would already have made enough tests to satisfy himself.

Mercer equalized pressure, unlatched the securing clip of his helmet, and opened it a crack. He took a cautious breath; then a deeper one.

The air of Rama was dead and musty, as if from a tomb so ancient that the last trace of physical corruption had disappeared ages ago. Even Mercer's ultra-sensitive nose, trained through years of testing life-support systems to and beyond the point of disaster, could detect no recognisable odours. There was a faint metallic tang, and he suddenly recalled that the first men on the Moon had reported a hint of burnt gunpowder when they repressurised the lunar module. Mercer imagined that the moon-dust-contaminated cabin on *Eagle* must have smelled rather like Rama.

He sealed the helmet again, and emptied his lungs of the alien air. He had extracted no sustenance from it; even a mountaineer acclimatised to the summit of Everest would die quickly here. But a few kilometres further down, it would be a different matter.

47

What else was there to do here? He could think of nothing, except the enjoyment of the gentle, unaccustomed gravity. But there was no point in growing used to that, since they would be returning immediately to the weightlessness of the Hub.

'We're coming back, Skipper,' he reported. 'There's no reason to go further – until we're ready to go *all* the way.'

'I agree. We'll be timing you, but take it easy.'

As he bounded up the steps, three or four at a stride, Mercer agreed that Calvert had been perfectly correct; these stairs were built to be walked *up*, not down. As long as one did not look back, and ignored the vertiginous steepness of the ascending curve, the climb was a delightful experience. After about two hundred steps, however, he began to feel some twinges in his calf muscles, and decided to slow down. The others had done the same; when he ventured a quick glance over his shoulder, they were considerably further down the slope.

The climb was wholly uneventful – merely an apparently endless succession of steps. When they stood once more on the highest platform, immediately beneath the ladder, they were barely winded, and it had taken them only ten minutes. They paused for another ten, then started on the last vertical kilometre.

Jump – catch hold of a rung – jump – catch – jump – catch … it was easy, but so boringly repetitious that there was danger of becoming careless. Halfway up the ladder they rested for five minutes: by this time their arms as well as their legs had begun to ache. Once again, Mercer was glad that they could see so little of the vertical face to which they were clinging; it was not too difficult to pretend that the ladder only extended just a few metres beyond their circle of light, and would soon come to an end.

Jump – catch a rung – jump – then, quite suddenly, the ladder *really* ended. They were back at the weightless world of the axis, among their anxious friends. The whole trip had taken under an hour, and they felt a sense of modest achievement.

But it was much too soon to feel pleased with themselves. For all their efforts, they had traversed less than an eighth of that cyclopean stairway.

11
Men, Women and Monkeys

Some women, Commander Norton had decided long ago, should not be allowed aboard ship; weightlessness did things to their breasts that were too damn distracting. It was bad enough when they were motionless; but when they started to move, and sympathetic vibrations set in, it was more than any warm-blooded male should be asked to take. He was quite sure that at least one serious space accident had been caused by acute crew distraction, after the transit of a well-upholstered lady officer through the control cabin.

He had once mentioned this theory to Surgeon-Commander Laura Ernst, without revealing who had inspired his particular train of thought. There was no need; they knew each other much too well. On Earth, years ago, in a moment of mutual loneliness and depression, they had once made love. Probably they would never repeat the experience (but could one ever be *quite* sure of that?) because so much had changed for both of them. Yet whenever the well-built Surgeon oscillated into the Commander's cabin, he felt a fleeting echo of an old passion, she knew that he felt it, and everyone was happy.

'Bill,' she began, 'I've checked our mountaineers, and here's my verdict. Karl and Joe are in good shape – all indications normal for the work they've done. But Will shows signs of exhaustion and body-loss – I won't bother about the details. I don't believe he's been getting all the exercise he should, and he's not the only one. There's been some cheating in the centrifuge;

if there's any more, heads will roll. Please pass the word.'

'Yes, Ma'am. But there's some excuse. The men have been working very hard.'

'With their brains and fingers, certainly. But not with their bodies – not *real* work in kilogramme-metres. And that's what we'll be dealing with, if we're going to explore Rama.'

'Well, can we?'

'Yes, if we proceed with caution. Karl and I have worked out a very conservative profile – based on the assumption that we can dispense with breathing gear below Level Two. Of course, that's an incredible stroke of luck, and changes the whole logistics picture. I still can't get used to the idea of a world with oxygen … So we only need to supply food and water and thermosuits, and we're in business. Going down will be easy; it looks as if we can slide most of the way, on that very convenient banister.'

'I've got Chips working on a sled with parachute braking. Even if we can't risk it for crew, we can use it for stores and equipment.'

'Fine; *that* should do the trip in ten minutes; otherwise it will take about an hour.

'Climbing up is harder to estimate; I'd like to allow six hours, including two one-hour periods. Later, as we get experience – *and* develop some muscles – we may be able to cut this back considerably.'

'What about psychological factors?'

'Hard to assess, in such a novel environment. Darkness may be the biggest problem.'

'I'll establish searchlights on the Hub. Besides its own lamps, any party down there will always have a beam playing on it.'

'Good – that should be a great help.'

'One other point: should we play safe and send a party only halfway down the stair – and back – or should we go the whole way on the first attempt?'

'If we had plenty of time, I'd be cautious. But time is short, and I can see no danger in going all the way – and looking around when we get there.'

'Thanks, Laura – that's all I want to know. I'll get the Exec working on the details. And I'll order all hands to the centrifuge – twenty minutes a day at half a gee. Will that satisfy you?'

'No. It's point six gee down there in Rama, and I want a safety margin. Make it three quarters—'

'Ouch!'

'– for ten minutes—'

'I'll settle for that—'

'– *twice* a day.'

'Laura, you're a cruel, hard woman. But so be it. I'll break the news just before dinner. That should spoil a few appetites.'

It was the first time that Commander Norton had ever seen Karl Mercer slightly ill at ease. He had spent the fifteen minutes discussing the logistics problem in his usual competent manner, but something was obviously worrying him. His captain, who had a shrewd idea of what it was, waited patiently until he brought it out.

'Skipper,' Karl said at length, 'are you *sure* you should lead this party? If anything goes wrong, I'm considerably more expendable. And I've been further inside Rama than anyone else – even if only by fifty metres.'

'Granted. But it's time the commander led his troops, and we've decided that there's no greater risk on this trip than on the last. At the first sign of trouble, I'll be back up that stairway fast enough to qualify for the Lunar Olympics.'

He waited for any further objections, but none came, though Karl still looked unhappy. So he took pity on him and added gently: 'And I bet Joe will beat me to the top.'

The big man relaxed, and a slow grin spread across his face. 'All the same, Bill, I wish you'd taken someone else.'

'I wanted *one* man who'd been down before, and we can't

both go. As for Herr Doktor Professor Sergeant Myron, Laura says he's still two kilos overweight. Even shaving off that moustache didn't help.'

'Who's your number three?'

'I still haven't decided. That depends on Laura.'

'She wants to go herself.'

'Who doesn't? But if she turns up at the top of her own fitness list, I'll be very suspicious.'

As Lieut-Commander Mercer gathered up his papers and launched himself out of the cabin, Norton felt a brief stab of envy. Almost all the crew – about eighty-five per cent, by his minimum estimate – had worked out some sort of emotional accommodation. He had known ships where the captain had done the same, but that was not his way. Though discipline aboard the *Endeavour* was based very largely on the mutual respect between highly trained and intelligent men and women, the commander needed something more to underline his position. His responsibility was unique, and demanded a certain degree of isolation, even from his closest friends. Any liaison could be damaging to morale, for it was almost impossible to avoid charges of favouritism. For this reason, affairs spanning more than two degrees of rank were firmly discouraged; but apart from this, the only rule regulating shipboard sex was 'So long as they don't do it in the corridors and frighten the simps'.

There were four superchimps aboard *Endeavour*, though strictly speaking the name was inaccurate, because the ship's non-human crew was not based on chimpanzee stock. In zero gravity, a prehensile tail is an enormous advantage, and all attempts to supply these to humans had turned into embarrassing failures. After equally unsatisfactory results with the great apes, the Superchimpanzee Corporation had turned to the monkey kingdom.

Blackie, Blondie, Goldie and Brownie had family trees whose branches included the most intelligent of the Old and New

World monkeys, plus synthetic genes that had never existed in nature. Their rearing and education had probably cost as much as that of the average spaceman, and they were worth it. Each weighed less than thirty kilos and consumed only half the food and oxygen of a human being, but each could replace 2.75 men for house-keeping, elementary cooking, tool-carrying and dozens of other routine jobs.

That 2.75 was the Corporation's claim, based on innumerable time-and-motion studies. The figure, though surprising and frequently challenged, appeared to be accurate, for simps were quite happy to work fifteen hours a day and did not get bored by the most menial and repetitive tasks. So they freed human beings for human work; and on a spaceship, that was a matter of vital importance.

Unlike the monkeys who were their nearest relatives *Endeavour*'s simps were docile, obedient and uninquisitive. Being cloned, they were also sexless, which eliminated awkward behavioural problems. Carefully house-trained vegetarians, they were very clean and didn't smell; they would have made perfect pets, except that nobody could possibly have afforded them.

Despite these advantages, having simps on board involved certain problems. They had to have their own quarters – inevitably labelled 'The Monkey House'. Their little mess-room was always spotless, and was well-equipped with TV, games equipment and programmed teaching machines. To avoid accidents, they were absolutely forbidden to enter the ship's technical areas; the entrances to all these were colour-coded in red, and the simps were conditioned so that it was psychologically impossible for them to pass the visual barriers.

There was also a communications problem. Though they had an equivalent IQ of sixty, and could understand several hundred words of English, they were unable to talk. It had proved impossible to give useful vocal chords either to apes or monkeys, and they therefore had to express themselves in sign language.

The basic signs were obvious and easily learned, so that everyone on board ship could understand routine messages. But the only man who could speak fluent Simpish was their handler – Chief Steward McAndrews.

It was a standing joke that Sergeant Ravi McAndrews *looked* rather like a simp – which was hardly an insult, for with their short, tinted pelts and graceful movements they were very handsome animals. They were also affectionate, and everyone on board had his favourite; Commander Norton's was the aptly-named Goldie.

But the warm relationship which one could so easily establish with simps created another problem, often used as a powerful argument against their employment in space. Since they could only be trained for routine, low-grade tasks, they were worse than useless in an emergency; they could then be a danger to themselves and to their human companions. In particular, teaching them to use spacesuits had proved impossible, the concepts involved being quite beyond their understanding.

No one liked to talk about it, but everybody knew what had to be done if a hull was breached or the order came to abandon ship. It had happened only once; then the simp handler had carried out his instructions more than adequately. He was found with his charges, killed by the same poison. Thereafter the job of euthing was transferred to the chief medical officer, who it was felt would have less emotional involvement.

Norton was very thankful that this responsibility, at least, did not fall upon the captain's shoulders. He had known men he would have killed with far fewer qualms than he would Goldie.

12
The Stairway of the Gods

In the clear, cold atmosphere of Rama, the beam of the searchlight was completely invisible. Three kilometres down from the central Hub, the hundred-metre wide oval of light lay across a section of that colossal stairway. A brilliant oasis in the surrounding darkness, it was sweeping slowly towards the curved plain still five kilometres below; and in its centre moved a trio of ant-like figures, casting long shadows before them.

It had been, just as they had hoped and expected, a completely uneventful descent. They had paused briefly at the first platform, and Norton had walked a few hundred metres along the narrow, curving ledge before starting the slide down to the second level. Here they had discarded their oxygen gear, and revelled in the strange luxury of being able to breathe without mechanical aids. Now they could explore in comfort, freed from the greatest danger that confronts a man in space, and forgetting all worries about suit integrity and oxygen reserve.

By the time they had reached the fifth level, and there was only one more section to go, gravity had reached almost half its terrestrial value. Rama's centrifugal spin was at last exerting its real strength; they were surrendering themselves to the implacable force which rules every planet, and which can exert a merciless price for the smallest slip. It was still very easy to go downwards; but the thought of the return, up those thousands upon thousands of steps, was already beginning to prey upon their minds.

The stairway had long ago ceased its vertiginous downward plunge and was now flattening out towards the horizontal. The gradient was now only about one in five; at the beginning, it had been five in one. Normal walking was now both physically, and psychologically, acceptable; only the lowered gravity reminded them that they were not descending some great stairway on Earth. Norton had once visited the ruins of an Aztec temple, and the feelings he had then experienced came echoing back to him – amplified a hundred times. Here was the same sense of awe and mystery, and the sadness of the irrevocably vanished past. Yet the scale here was so much greater, both in time and space, that the mind was unable to do it justice; after a while, it ceased to respond. Norton wondered if, sooner or later, he would take even Rama for granted.

And there was another respect in which the parallel with terrestrial ruins failed completely. Rama was hundreds of times older than any structure that had survived on Earth – even the Great Pyramid. *But everything looked absolutely new; there was no sign of wear and tear.*

Norton had puzzled over this a good deal, and had arrived at a tentative explanation. Everything that they had so far examined was part of an emergency back-up system, very seldom put to actual use. He could not imagine that the Ramans – unless they were physical fitness fanatics of the kind not uncommon on Earth – ever walked up and down this incredible stairway, or its two identical companions completing the invisible Y far above his head. Perhaps they had only been required during the actual construction of Rama, and had served no purpose since that distant day. That theory would do for the moment, yet it did not feel right. There was something wrong, somewhere ...

They did not slide for the last kilometre but went down the steps two at a time in long, gentle strides; this way, Norton decided, they would give more exercise to muscles that would soon have to be used. And so the end of the stairway came upon them almost unawares; suddenly, there were no more steps – only a flat plain, dull grey in the now weakening beam of the Hub searchlight, fading away into the darkness a few hundred metres ahead.

Norton looked back along the beam, towards its source up on the axis more than eight kilometres away. He knew that Mercer would be watching through the telescope, so he waved to him cheerfully.

'Captain here,' he reported over the radio. 'Everyone in fine shape – no problems. Proceeding as planned.'

'Good,' replied Mercer. 'We'll be watching.'

There was a brief silence; then a new voice cut in. 'This is the Exec, on board ship. Really, Skipper, this isn't good enough. You know the news services have been screaming at us for the last week. I don't expect deathless prose, but can't you do better than that?'

'I'll try,' Norton chuckled. 'But remember there's nothing to see yet. It's like – well, being on a huge, darkened stage, with a single spotlight. The first few hundred steps of the stairway rise out of it until they disappear into the darkness overhead. What we can see of the plain looks perfectly flat – the curvature's too small to be visible over this limited area. And that's about it.'

'Like to give any impressions?'

'Well, it's still very cold – below freezing – and we're glad of our thermosuits. And *quiet* of course, quieter than anything I've ever known on Earth, or in space, where there's always some background noise. Here, every sound is swallowed up; the space around us is so enormous that there aren't any echoes. It's weird, but I hope we'll get used to it.'

'Thanks, Skipper. Anyone else – Joe, Boris?'

Lt Joe Calvert, never at a loss for words, was happy to oblige.

'I can't help thinking that this is the first time – *ever* – that we've been able to walk on another world, breathing its natural atmosphere – though I suppose "natural" is hardly the word you can apply to a place like this. Still, Rama must resemble the world of its builders; our own spaceships are all miniature earths. Two examples are damned poor statistics, but does this mean that all intelligent life-forms are oxygen eaters? What we've seen of their work suggests that the Ramans were humanoid, though perhaps about fifty per cent taller than we are. Wouldn't you agree, Boris?'

Is Joe teasing Boris? Norton asked himself. I wonder how he's going to react? . . .

To all his shipmates, Boris Rodrigo was something of an enigma. The quiet, dignified communications officer was popular with the rest of the crew, but he never entered fully into their activities and always seemed a little apart – marching to the music of a different drummer.

As indeed he was, being a devout member of the Fifth Church of Christ, Cosmonaut. Norton had never been able to discover what had happened to the earlier four, and he was equally in the dark about the Church's rituals and ceremonies. But the main tenet of its faith was well known: it believed that Jesus Christ was a visitor from space, and had constructed an entire theology on that assumption.

It was perhaps not surprising that an unusually high proportion of the Church's devotees worked in space in some capacity or other. Invariably, they were efficient, conscientious and absolutely reliable. They were universally respected and even liked, especially as they made no attempt to convert others. Yet there was also something slightly spooky about them; Norton could never understand how men with advanced scientific and technical training could possibly believe some of the things he had heard Christers state as incontrovertible facts.

As he waited for Lt Rodrigo to answer Joe's possibly loaded question, the commander had a sudden insight into his own hidden motives. He had chosen Brois because he was physically fit, technically qualified, and completely dependable. At the same time, he wondered if some part of his mind had not selected the lieutenant out of an almost mischievous curiosity. How could a man with such religious beliefs react to the awesome reality of Rama? Suppose he encountered something that confounded his theology ... or, for that matter, confirmed it?

But Boris Rodrigo, with his usual caution, refused to be drawn.

'They were certainly oxygen breathers, and they *could* be humanoid. But let's wait and see. With any luck, we should discover what they were like. There may be pictures, statues – perhaps even bodies, over in those towns. If they are towns.'

'And the nearest is only eight kilometres away,' said Joe Calvert hopefully.

Yes, thought the commander, but it's also eight kilometres back – and then there's that overwhelming stairway to climb again. Can we take the risk?

A quick sortie to the 'town' which they had named Paris had been among the first of his contingency plans, and now he had to make his decision. They had ample food and water for a stay of twenty-four hours; they would always be in full view of the back-up team on the Hub, and any kind of accident seemed virtually impossible on this smooth, gently curving, metal plain. The only foreseeable danger was exhaustion; when they got to Paris, which they could do easily enough, could they do more than take a few photographs and perhaps collect some small artefacts, before they had to return?

But even such a brief foray would be worth it; there was so little time, as Rama hurtled sunwards towards a perihelion too dangerous for *Endeavour* to match.

In any case, part of the decision was not his to make. Up in the ship, Dr Ernst would be watching the outputs of the bio-telemetering sensors attached to his body. If she turned thumbs-down, that would be that.

'Laura, what do you think?'

'Take thirty minutes' rest, and a five hundred calorie energy module. Then you can start.'

'Thanks, Doc,' interjected Joe Calvert. 'Now I can die happy. I always wanted to see Paris. Montmartre, here we come.'

13

The Plain of Rama

After those interminable stairs, it was a strange luxury to walk once more on a horizontal surface. Directly ahead, the ground was indeed completely flat; to right and left, at the limits of the floodlit area, the rising curve could just be detected. They might have been walking along a very wide, shallow valley; it was quite impossible to believe that they were really crawling along the inside of a huge cylinder, and that beyond this little oasis of light the land rose up to meet – no, to *become* – the sky.

Though they all felt a sense of confidence and subdued excitement, after a while the almost palpable silence of Rama began to weigh heavily upon them. Every footstep, every word, vanished instantly into the unreverberant void; after they had gone little more than half a kilometre, Lt Calvert could stand it no longer.

Among his minor accomplishments was a talent now rare, though many thought not rare enough – the art of whistling. With or without encouragement he could reproduce the themes from most of the movies of the last two hundred years. He started appropriately with Heigh-ho, heigh-ho, 'tis off to work we go, found that he couldn't stay down comfortably in the bass with Disney's marching dwarfs, and switched quickly to River Kwai. Then he progressed, more or less chronologically, through half a dozen epics, culminating with the theme from Sid Krassman's famous late-twentieth-century *Napoleon*.

It was a good try, but it didn't work, even as a morale-builder. Rama needed the grandeur of Bach or Beethoven or Sibelius or Tuan Sun, not the trivia of popular entertainment. Norton was on the point of suggesting that Joe save his breath for later exertions, when the young officer realised the inappropriateness of his efforts. Thereafter, apart from an occasional consultation with the ship, they marched on in silence. Rama had won this round.

On his initial traverse, Norton had allowed for one detour. Paris lay straight ahead, halfway between the foot of the stairway and the shore of the Cylindrical Sea, but only a kilometre to the right of their track was a very prominent, and rather mysterious, feature which had been christened the Straight Valley. It was a long groove or trench, forty metres deep and a hundred wide, with gently sloping sides; it had been provisionally identified as an irrigation ditch or canal. Like the stairway itself, it had two similar counterparts, equally spaced around the curve of Rama.

The three valleys were almost ten kilometres long, and stopped abruptly just before they reached the Sea – which was strange, if they were intended to carry water. And on the other side of the Sea the pattern was repeated: three more ten-kilometre-trenches continued on to the South Polar region.

They reached the end of the Straight Valley after only fifteen minutes' comfortable walking, and stood for a while staring thoughtfully into its depths. The perfectly smooth walls sloped down at an angle of sixty degrees; there were no steps or foot-holds. Filling the bottom was a sheet of flat, white material that looked very much like ice. A specimen could settle a good many arguments; Norton decided to get one.

With Calvert and Rodrigo acting as anchors and paying out a safety rope, he rapelled slowly down the steep incline. When he reached the bottom, he fully expected to find the familiar slippery feel of ice underfoot, but he was mistaken. The friction was too great; his footing was secure. This material was some kind of glass or transparent crystal; when he touched it with his fingertips, it was cold, hard and unyielding.

Turning his back to the searchlight and shielding his eyes from its glare, Norton tried to peer into the crystalline depths, as one may attempt to gaze through the ice of a frozen lake. But he could see nothing; even when he tried the concentrated beam of his own helmet-lamp, he was no more successful. This stuff was translucent, but not transparent. If it was a frozen liquid, it had a melting-point very much higher than water.

He tapped it gently with the hammer from his geology kit; the tool rebounded with a dull, unmusical 'clunk'. He tapped harder, with no more result, and was about to exert his full strength when some impulse made him desist.

It seemed most unlikely that he could crack this material; but what if he did? He would be like a vandal, smashing some enormous plate-glass window. There would be a better opportunity later, and at least he had discovered valuable information. It now seemed more unlikely than ever that this was a canal; it was simply a peculiar trench that stopped and started abruptly, but led nowhere. And if at any time it had carried liquid, where were the stains, the encrustations of dried-up sediment, that one would expect? Everything was bright and clean, as if the builders had left only yesterday ...

Once again he was face to face with the fundamental mystery of Rama, and this time it was impossible to evade it. Commander Norton was a reasonably imaginative man, but he would never have reached his present position if he had been liable to the wilder flights of fancy. Yet now, for the first time, he had a sense – not exactly of foreboding, but of anticipation. Things were not what they seemed; there was something very, very odd about a place that was simultaneously brand new – and a million years old.

Very thoughtfully, he began to walk slowly along the length of the little valley, while his companions, still holding the rope that was attached to his waist, followed him along the rim. He did not expect to make any further discoveries, but he wanted to let his curious emotional state run its course. For something else was worrying him; and it had nothing to do with the inexplicable newness of Rama.

He had walked no more than a dozen metres when it hit him like a thunderbolt.

He knew this place. *He had been here before.* Even on Earth, or some familiar planet, that experience is disquieting, though it is not particularly rare. Most men have known it at some time or other, and usually they dismiss it as the memory of a forgotten photograph, a pure coincidence – or, if they are mystically inclined, some form of telepathy from another mind, or even a flashback from their own future.

But to recognise a spot which *no* other human being can possibly have seen – that is quite shocking. For several seconds, Commander Norton stood rooted to the smooth crystalline surface on which he had been walking, trying to straighten out his emotions. His well-ordered universe had been turned upside down, and he had a dizzying glimpse of those mysteries at the edge of existence which he had successfully ignored for most of his life.

Then, to his immense relief, common sense came to the rescue. The disturbing sensation of *déjà-vu* faded out, to be replaced by a real and identifiable memory from his youth.

It was true – he had once stood between such steeply sloping walls, watching them drive into the distance until they seemed to converge at a point indefinitely far ahead. But they had been covered with neatly trimmed grass; and underfoot had been broken stone, not smooth crystal.

It had happened thirty years ago, during a summer vacation in England. Largely because of another student (he could remember her face – but he had forgotten her name) he had taken a course of industrial archaeology, then very popular among science and engineering graduates. They had explored abandoned coal-mines and cotton mills, climbed over ruined

65

blast-furnaces and steam-engines, goggled unbelievingly at primitive (and still dangerous) nuclear reactors, and driven priceless turbine-powered antiques along restored motor roads.

Not everything that they saw was genuine; much had been lost during the centuries, for men seldom bother to preserve the commonplace articles of everyday life. But where it was necessary to make copies, they had been reconstructed with loving care.

And so young Bill Norton had found himself bowling along, at an exhilarating hundred kilometres an hour, while he furiously shoveled precious coal into the firebox of a locomotive that looked two hundred years old, but was actually younger than he was. The thirty-kilometre stretch of the Great Western Railway, however, was quite genuine, though it had required a good deal of excavating to get it back into commission.

Whistle screaming, they had plunged into a hillside and raced through a smoky, flame-lit darkness. An astonishingly long time later, they had burst out of the tunnel into a deep, perfectly straight cutting between steep grassy banks. The long-forgotten vista was almost identical with the one before him now.

'What is it, Skipper?' called Lt Rodrigo. 'Have you found something?'

As Norton dragged himself back to present reality, some of the oppression lifted from his mind. There was mystery here – yes; but it might not be beyond human understanding. He had learned a lesson, though it was not one that he could readily impart to others. At all costs, he must not let Rama overwhelm him. That way lay failure – perhaps even madness.

'No,' he answered, 'there's nothing down here. Haul me up – we'll head straight to Paris.'

14
Storm Warning

'I've called this meeting of the Committee,' said His Excellency the Ambassador of Mars to the United Planets, 'because Dr Perera has something important to tell us. He insists that we get in touch with Commander Norton right away, using the priority channel we've been able to establish after, I might say, a good deal of difficulty. Dr Perera's statement is rather technical, and before we come to it I think a summary of the present position might be in order; Dr Price has prepared one. Oh yes – some apologies for absence. Sir Lewis Sands is unable to be with us because he's chairing a conference, and Dr Taylor asks to be excused.'

He was rather pleased about that last abstention. The anthropologist had rapidly lost interest in Rama, when it became obvious that it would present little scope for him. Like many others, he had been bitterly disappointed to find that the mobile wordlet was dead; now there would be no opportunity for sensational books and viddies about Raman rituals and behavioural patterns. Others might dig up skeletons and classify artifacts; *that* sort of thing did not appeal to Conrad Taylor. Perhaps the only discovery that would bring him back in a hurry would be some highly explicit works of art, like the notorious frescoes of Thera and Pompeii.

Thelma Price, the archaelogist, took exactly the opposite point of view. She preferred excavations and ruins uncluttered by inhabitants who might interfere with dispassionate, scientific studies. The bed of the Mediterranean had been ideal – at least until the city planners and landscape artists had started getting in the way. And Rama would have been perfect, except for the maddening detail that it was a hundred million kilometres away and she would never be able to visit it in person.

'As you all know,' she began, 'Commander Norton has completed one traverse of almost thirty kilometres, without encountering any problems. He explored the curious trench shown on your maps as the Straight Valley; its purpose is still quite unknown, but it's clearly important as it runs the full length of Rama – except for the break at the Cylindrical Sea – and there are two other identical structures a hundred and twenty degrees apart round the circumference of the world.

'Then the party turned left – or East, if we adopt the North Pole convention – until they reached Paris. As you'll see from this photograph, taken by a telescope camera at the Hub, it's a group of several hundred buildings, with wide streets between them.

'Now *these* photographs were taken by Commander Norton's group when they reached the site. If Paris is a city, it's a very peculiar one. Note that none of the buildings have windows, or even doors! They are all plain rectangular structures, an identical thirty-five metres high. And they appear to have been extruded out of the ground – there are no seams or joints – look at this close-up of the base of a wall – there's a smooth transition into the ground.

'My own feeling is that this place is not a residential area, but a storage or supply depot. In support of that theory, look at this photo ...

'These narrow slots or grooves, about five centimetres wide, run along all the streets, and there's one leading to every building – going straight into the wall. There's a striking resemblance to the street-car tracks of the early twentieth century; they are obviously part of some transport system.

'We've never considered it necessary to have public transport direct to every house. It would be economically absurd – people can always walk a few hundred metres. But if these buildings are used for the storage of heavy materials, it would make sense.'

'May I ask a question?' said the Ambassador for Earth.

'Of course, Sir Robert.'

'Commander Norton couldn't get into a single building?'

'No; when you listen to his report, you can tell he was quite frustrated. At one time he decided that the buildings could only be entered from underground; then he discovered the grooves of the transport system, and changed his mind.'

'Did he try to break in?'

'There was no way he could, without explosives or heavy tools. And he doesn't want to do that until all other approaches have failed.'

'I have it!' Dennis Solomons suddenly interjected. 'Cocooning!'

'I beg your pardon?'

'It's a technique developed a couple of hundred years ago,' continued the science historian. 'Another name for it is mothballing. When you have something you want to preserve, you seal it inside a plastic envelope, and then pump in an inert gas. The original use was to protect military equipment between wars; it was once applied to whole ships. It's still widely used in museums that are short of storage space; no one knows what's inside some of the hundred-year-old cocoons in the Smithsonian basement.'

Patience was not one of Carlisle Perera's virtues; he was aching to drop his bombshell, and could restrain himself no longer.

'*Please*, Mr Ambassador! This is all very interesting, but I feel my information is rather more urgent.'

'If there are no other points – very well, Dr Perera.'

The exobiologist, unlike Conrad Taylor, had not found Rama

a disappointment. It was true that he no longer expected to find life – but sooner or later, he had been quite sure, some remains would be discovered of the creatures who had built this fantastic world. The exploration had barely begun, although the time available was horribly brief before *Endeavour* would be forced to escape from her present sun-grazing orbit.

But now, if his calculations were correct, Man's contact with Rama would be even shorter than he had feared. For one detail had been overlooked – because it was so large that no one had noticed it before.

'According to our latest information,' Perera began, 'one party is now on its way to the Cylindrical Sea, while Commander Norton has another group setting up a supply base at the foot of Stairway Alpha. When that's established, he intends to have at least two exploratory missions operating at all times. In this way he hopes to use his limited manpower at maximum efficiency.

'It's a good plan, but there may be no time to carry it out. In fact, I would advise an immediate alert, and a preparation for total withdrawal at twelve hours' notice. Let me explain ...

'It's surprising how few people have commented on a rather obvious anomaly about Rama. It's now well inside the orbit of Venus – yet the interior is still frozen. But the temperature of an object in direct sunlight at this point is about five hundred degrees!

'The reason of course, is that Rama hasn't had time to warm up. It must have cooled down to near absolute zero – two hundred and seventy below – while it was in interstellar space. Now, as it approaches the sun, the outer hull is already almost as hot as molten lead. But the inside will stay cold, until the heat works its way through that kilometre of rock.

'There's some kind of fancy dessert with a hot exterior and ice-cream in the middle – I don't remember what it's called—'

'Baked Alaska. It's a favourite at UP banquets, unfortunately.'

'Thank you, Sir Robert. That's the situation in Rama at the moment, but it won't last. All these weeks, the solar heat has been working its way through, and we expect a sharp temperature rise to begin in a few hours. *That's* not the problem; by the time we'll have to leave anyway, it will be no more than comfortably tropical.'

'Then what's the difficulty?'

'I can answer in one word, Mr Ambassador. *Hurricanes.*'

15
The Edge of the Sea

There were now more than twenty men and women inside Rama – six of them down on the plain, the rest ferrying equipment and expendables through the airlock system and down the stairway. The ship itself was almost deserted, with the minimum possible staff on duty; the joke went around that *Endeavour* was really being run by the four simps and that Goldie had been given the rank of Acting-Commander.

For these first explorations, Norton had established a number of ground-rules; the most important dated back to the earliest days of man's space-faring. Every group, he had decided, must contain one person with prior experience. But not *more* than one. In that way, everybody would have an opportunity of learning as quickly as possible.

And so the first party to head for the Cylindrical Sea, though it was led by Surgeon-Commander Laura Ernst, had as its one-time veteran Lt Boris Rodrigo, just back from Paris. The third member, Sergeant Pieter Rousseau, had been with the back-up teams at the Hub; he was an expert on space reconnaissance instrumentation, but on this trip he would have to depend on his own eyes and a small portable telescope.

From the foot of Stairway Alpha to the edge of the Sea was just under fifteen kilometres – or an Earth-equivalent of eight under the low gravity of Rama. Laura Ernst, who had to prove that she lived up to her own standards, set a brisk pace. They stopped for thirty minutes at the mid-way mark, and made the whole trip in a completely uneventful three hours.

It was also quite monotonous, walking forward in the beam of the searchlight through the anechoic darkness of Rama. As the pool of light advanced with them, it slowly elongated into a long, narrow ellipse; this foreshortening of the beam was the only visible sign of progress. If the observers up on the Hub had not given them continual distance checks, they could not have guessed whether they had travelled one kilometre, or five, or ten. They just plodded onwards through the million-year-old night, over an apparently seamless metal surface.

But at last, far ahead at the limits of the now weakening beam, there was something new. On a normal world, it would have been a horizon; as they approached, they could see that the plain on which they were walking came to an abrupt stop. They were nearing the edge of the Sea.

'Only a hundred metres,' said Hub Control. 'Better slow down.'

That was hardly necessary, yet they had already done so. It was a sheer straight drop of fifty metres from the level of the plain to that of the Sea – if it was a sea, and not another sheet of that mysterious crystalline material. Although Norton had impressed upon everyone the danger of taking anything for granted in Rama, few doubted that the Sea was really made of ice. But for what conceivable reason was the cliff on the southern shore five hundred metres high, instead of the fifty here?

It was as if they were approaching the edge of the world; their oval of light, cut off abruptly ahead of them, became shorter and shorter. But far out on the curved screen of the Sea their monstrous foreshortened shadows had appeared, magnifying and exaggerating every movement. Those shadows had been their companions every step of the way, as they marched down the beam, but now that they were broken at the edge of the cliff they no longer seemed part of them. They might have been creatures of the Cylindrical Sea, waiting to deal with any intruders into their domain.

Because they were now standing on the edge of a fifty-metre cliff, it was possible for the first time to appreciate the curvature of Rama. But no one had ever seen a frozen lake bent upwards into a cylindrical surface; that was distinctly unsettling, and the eye did its best to find some other interpretation. It seemed to Dr Ernst, who had once made a study of visual illusions, that half the time she was really looking at a *horizontally* curving bay, not a surface that soared up into the sky. It required a deliberate effort of will to accept the fantastic truth.

Only in the line directly ahead, parallel to the axis of Rama, was normalcy preserved. In this direction alone was there agreement between vision and logic. Here – for the next few kilometres at least – Rama looked flat, and *was* flat ... And out there, beyond their distorted shadows and the outer limit of the beam, lay the island that dominated the Cylindrical Sea.

'Hub Control,' Dr Ernst radioed, 'please aim your beam at New York.'

The night of Rama fell suddenly upon them, as the oval of light went sliding out to sea. Conscious of the now invisible cliff at their feet, they all stepped back a few metres. Then, as if by some magical stage transformation, the towers of New York sprang into view.

The resemblance to old-time Manhattan was only superficial; this star-born echo of Earth's past possessed its own unique identity. The more Dr Ernst stared at it, the more certain she became that it was not a city at all.

The real New York, like all of Man's habitations, had never been finished; still less had it been designed. *This* place, however, had an overall symmetry and pattern, though one so complex that it eluded the mind. It had been conceived and planned by some controlling intelligence – and then it had been completed, like a machine devised for some specific purpose. After that, there was no possibility of growth or change.

The beam of the searthlight slowly tracked along those distant towers and domes and interlocked spheres and criss-crossed tubes. Sometimes there would be a brilliant reflection as some flat surface shot the light back towards them; the first time this happened, they were all taken by surprise. It was exactly as if, over there on that strange island, someone was signaling to them ...

But there was nothing that they could see here that was not already shown in greater detail on photographs taken from the Hub. After a few minutes, they called for the light to return to them, and began to walk eastwards along the edge of the cliff. It had been plausibly theorized that, somewhere, there must surely be a flight of steps, or a ramp, leading down to the Sea. And one crewman, who was a keen sailor, had raised an interesting conjecture.

'Where there's a sea,' Sergeant Ruby Barnes had predicted, 'there must be docks and harbours – and ships. You can learn everything about a culture by studying the way it builds boats.' Her colleagues thought this a rather restricted point of view, but at least it was a stimulating one.

Dr Ernst had almost given up the search, and was preparing to make a descent by rope, when Lt Rodrigo spotted the narrow stairway. It could easily have been over-looked in the shadowed darkness below the edge of the cliff, for there was no guard-rail or other indication of its presence. And it seemed to lead no-where; it ran down the fifty-metre vertical wall at a steep angle, and disappeared below the surface of the Sea.

They scanned the flight of steps with their helmet-lights, could see no conceivable hazard, and Dr Ernst got Commander Norton's permission to descend. A minute later, she was cautiously testing the surface of the Sea.

Her foot slithered almost frictionlessly back and forth. The material felt exactly like ice. It *was* ice.

When she struck it with her hammer, a familiar pattern of cracks radiated from the impact point, and she had no difficulty in collecting as many pieces as she wished. Some had already melted when she held up the sample holder to the light; the liquid appeared to be slightly turbid water, and she took a cautious sniff.

'Is that safe?' Rodrigo called down, with a trace of anxiety.

'Believe me, Boris,' she answered, 'if there are any pathogens around here that have slipped through my detectors, our insurance policies lapsed a week ago.'

But Boris had a point. Despite all the tests that had been carried out, there was a very slight risk that this substance might be poisonous, or might carry some unknown disease. In normal circumstances, Dr Ernst would not have taken even this minuscule chance. Now, however, time was short and the stakes were enormous. If it became necessary to quarantine *Endeavour*, that would be a very small price to pay for her cargo of knowledge.

'It's water, but I wouldn't care to drink it – it smells like an algae culture that's gone bad. I can hardly wait to get it to the lab.'

'Is the ice safe to walk on?'

'Yes, solid as a rock.'

'Then we can get to New York.'

'Can we, Pieter? Have you ever tried to walk across four kilometers of ice?'

'Oh – I see what you mean. Just imagine what Stores would say, if we asked for a set of skates! Not that many of us would know how to use them, even if we had any aboard.'

'And there's another problem,' put in Boris Rodrigo. 'Do you realize that the temperature is already above freezing? Before long, that ice is going to melt. How many spacemen can swim four kilometres? Certainly not this one ...'

Dr Ernst rejoined them at the edge of the cliff, and held up the small sample bottle in triumph.

'It's a long walk for a few cc's of dirty water, but it may teach us more about Rama than anything we've found so far. Let's head for home.'

They turned towards the distant lights of the Hub, moving with the gentle, loping strides which had proved the most comfortable means of walking under this reduced gravity. Often they looked back, drawn by the hidden enigma of the island out there in the centre of the frozen sea.

And just once, Dr Ernst thought she felt the faint suspicion of a breeze against her cheek.

It did not come again, and she quickly forgot all about it.

16
Kealakekua

'As you know perfectly well, Dr Perera,' said Ambassador Bose in a tone of patient resignation, 'few of us share your knowledge of mathematical meteorology. So please take pity on our ignorance.'

'With pleasure,' answered the exobiologist, quite unabashed. 'I can explain it best by telling you what is going to happen inside Rama – very soon.

'The temperature is now about to rise, as the solar heat pulse reaches the interior. According to the latest information I've received, it's already above freezing point. The Cylindrical Sea will soon start to thaw; and unlike bodies of water on Earth, it will melt from the bottom upwards. That may produce some odd effects; but I'm much more concerned with the atmosphere.

'As it's heated, the air inside Rama will expand – and will attempt to rise towards the central axis. And this is the problem. At ground level, although it's apparently stationary, it's actually sharing the spin of Rama – over eight hundred kilometres an hour. As it rises towards the axis it will try to retain that speed – and it won't be able to do so, of course. The result will be violent winds and turbulence; I estimate velocities of between two and three hundred kilometres an hour.

'Incidentally, very much the same thing occurs on Earth. The heated air at the Equator – which shares the Earth's sixteen-hundred-kilometres-an-hour spin – runs into the same problem when it rises and flows north and south.'

'Ah, the Trade Winds! I remember that from my geography lessons.'

'Exactly, Sir Robert. Rama will have Trade Winds, with a vengeance. I believe they'll last only a few hours, and then some kind of equilibrium will be restored. Meanwhile, I should advise Commander Norton to evacuate – as soon as possible. Here is the message I propose sending.'

With a little imagination, Commander Norton told himself, he could pretend that this was an improvised night camp at the foot of some mountain in a remote region of Asia or America. The clutter of sleeping pads, collapsible chairs and tables, portable power plant, lighting equipment, electrosan toilets, and miscellaneous scientific apparatus would not have looked out of place on Earth – especially as there were men and women working here without life support systems.

Establishing Camp Alpha had been very hard work, for everything had had to be man-handled through the chain of airlocks, sledded down the slope from the Hub, and then retrieved and unpacked. Sometimes, when the braking parachutes had failed, a consignment had ended up a good kilometre away out on the plain. Despite this, several crew members had asked permission to make the ride; Norton had firmly forbidden it. In an emergency, however, he might be prepared to reconsider the ban.

Almost all this equipment would stay here, for the labour of carrying it back was unthinkable – in fact, impossible. There were times when Commander Norton felt an irrational shame at leaving so much human litter in this strangely immaculate place. When they finally departed, he was prepared to sacrifice some of their precious time to leave everything in good order. Improbable though it was, perhaps millions of years hence, when Rama shot through some other star system, it might have visitors again. He would like to give them a good impression of Earth.

Meanwhile, he had a rather more immediate problem. During the last twenty-four hours he had received almost identical messages from both Mars and Earth. It seemed an odd coincidence; perhaps they had been commiserating with each other, as wives who lived safely on different planets were liable to do under sufficient provocation. Rather pointedly, they had reminded him that even though he was now a great hero, he still had family responsibilities.

The Commander picked up a collapsible chair, and walked out of the pool of light into the darkness surrounding the camp. It was the only way he could get any privacy, and he could also think better away from the turmoil. Deliberately turning his back on the organised confusion behind him, he began to speak into the recorder slung around his neck.

'Original for personal file, dupes to Mars and Earth. Hello, darling – yes, I know I've been a lousy correspondent, but I haven't been aboard ship for a week. Apart from a skeleton crew, we're all camping inside Rama, at the foot of the stairway we've christened Alpha.

'I have three parties out now, scouting the plain, but we've made disappointingly slow progress, because everything has to be done on foot. If only we had some means of transport! I'd be very happy to settle for a few electric bicycles ... they'd be perfect for the job.

'You've met my medical officer, Surgeon-Commander Ernst—' He paused uncertainly; Laura had met *one* of his wives, but which? Better cut that out—

Erasing the sentence, he began again.

'My MO, Surgeon-Commander Ernst, led the first group to reach the Cylindrical Sea, fifteen kilometres from here. She found that it was frozen water, as we'd expected – but you wouldn't want to drink it. Dr Ernst says it's a dilute organic soup, containing traces of almost any carbon compound you care to name, as well as phosphates and nitrates and dozens of metallic salts. There's not the slightest sign of life – not even any dead micro-organisms. So we still know nothing about the bio-chemistry of the Ramans ... though it was probably not wildly different from ours.'

Something brushed lightly against his hair; he had been too busy to get it cut, and would have to do something about that before he next put on a space-helmet ...

'You've seen the viddies of Paris and the other towns we've explored on this side of the Sea ... London, Rome, Moscow. It's impossible to believe that they were ever built for anything to *live* in. Paris looks like a giant storage depot. London is a collection of cylinders linked together by pipes connected to what are obviously pumping stations. Everything is sealed up, and there's no way of finding what's inside without explosives or lasers. We won't try these until there are no alternatives.

'As for Rome and Moscow—'

'Excuse me, Skipper. Priority from Earth.'

What now? Norton asked himself. Can't a man get a few minutes to talk to his families?

He took the message from the Sergeant, and scanned it quickly, just to satisfy himself that it was not immediate. Then he read it again, more slowly.

What the devil was the Rama Committee? And why had he never heard of it? He knew that all sorts of associations, soci-eties, and professional groups – some serious, some completely crackpot – had been trying to get in touch with him; Mission Control had done a good job of protection, and would not have forwarded this message unless it was considered important.

'Two-hundred-kilometre winds – probably sudden onset.' – well, that was something to think about. But it was hard to take it too seriously, on this utterly calm night; and it would be ridiculous to run away like frightened mice, when they were just starting effective exploration.

Commander Norton lifted a hand to brush aside his hair,

which had somehow fallen into his eyes again. Then he froze, the gesture uncompleted.

He *had* felt a trace of wind, several times in the last hour. It was so slight that he had completely ignored it; after all, he was the commander of a *space*ship, not a sailing ship. Until now the movement of air had not been of the slightest professional concern. What would the long-dead captain of that earlier *Endeavour* have done in a situation such as this?

Norton had asked himself that question at every moment of crisis in the last few years. It was his secret, which he had never revealed to anyone. And like most of the important things in life, it had come about quite by accident.

He had been captain of *Endeavour* for several months before he realised that it was named after one of the most famous ships in history. True, during the last four hundred years there had been a dozen *Endeavours* of sea and two of space, but the ancestor of them all was the 370-ton Whitby collier that Captain James Cook, RN, had sailed round the world between 1768 and 1771.

With a mild interest that had quickly turned to an absorbing curiosity – almost an obsession – Norton had begun to read everything he could find about Cook. He was now probably the world's leading authority on the greatest explorer of all time, and knew whole sections of the *Journals* by heart.

It still seemed incredible that one man could have done so much, with such primitive equipment. But Cook had been not only a supreme navigator, but a scientist and – in an age of brutal discipline – a humanitarian. He treated his own men with kindness, which was unusual; what was quite unheard of was that he behaved in exactly the same way to the often hostile savages in the new lands he discovered.

It was Norton's private dream, which he knew he would never achieve, to retrace at least one of Cook's voyages around the world. He had made a limited but spectacular start, which would certainly have astonished the Captain, when he once flew a polar orbit directly above the Great Barrier Reef. It had been early morning on a clear day, and from four hundred kilometres up he had had a superb view of that deadly wall of coral, marked by its line of white foam along the Queensland coast.

He had taken just under five minutes to travel the whole two thousand kilometres of the Reef. In a single glance he could span weeks of perilous voyaging for that first *Endeavour*. And through the telescope, he had caught a glimpse of Cooktown and the estuary where the ship had been dragged ashore for repairs, after her near-fatal encounter with the Reef.

A year later, a visit to the Hawaii Deep-Space Tracking Station had given him an even more unforgettable experience. He had taken the hydrofoil to Kealakekua Bay, and as he moved swiftly past the bleak volcanic cliffs, he felt a depth of emotion that had surprised and even disconcerted him. The guide had led his group of scientists, engineers and astronauts past the glittering metal pylon that had replaced the earlier monument, destroyed by the Great Tsunami of '68. They had walked on for a few more yards across black, slippery lava to the small plaque at the water's edge. Little waves were breaking over it, but Norton scarcely noticed them as he bent down to read the words:

NEAR THIS SPOT
CAPTAIN JAMES COOK
WAS KILLED
14 FEBRUARY, 1779
ORIGINAL TABLET DEDICATED 28 AUGUST, 1928
BY COOK SESQUICENTENNIAL COMMISSION
REPLACED BY TRICENTENNIAL COMMISSION
14 FEBRUARY, 2079

That was years ago, and a hundred million kilometres away. But at moments like this, Cook's reassuring presence seemed very close. In the secret depths of his mind, he would ask: 'Well, Captain – what is *your* advice?' It was a little game he played, on occasions when there were not enough facts for sound judgement, and one had to rely on intuition. That had been part of Cook's genius; he always made the right choice – until the very end, at Kealakekua Bay.

The Sergeant waited patiently, while his Commander stared silently out into the night of Rama. It was no longer unbroken, for at two spots about four kilometres away, the faint patches of light of exploring parties could be clearly seen.

In an emergency, I can recall them within the hour, Norton told himself. And that, surely, should be good enough.

He turned to the Sergeant, 'Take this message. Rama Committee, care of Spacecom. Appreciate your advice and will take precautions. Please specify meaning of phrase "sudden onset". Respectfully, Norton, Commander, *Endeavour*.'

He waited until the Sergeant had disappeared towards the blazing lights of the camp, then switched on his recorder again. But the train of thought was broken, and he could not get back into the mood. The letter would have to wait for some other time.

It was not often that Captain Cook came to his aid when he was neglecting his duty. But he suddenly remembered how rarely and briefly poor Elizabeth Cook had seen her husband in sixteen years of married life. Yet she had borne him six children – and outlived them all.

His wives, never more than ten minutes away at the speed of light, had nothing to complain about ...

17
Spring

During the first 'nights' on Rama, it had not been easy to sleep. The darkness and the mysteries it concealed were oppressive, but even more unsettling was the silence. Absence of noise is not a natural condition; all human senses require some input. If they are deprived of it, the mind manufactures its own substitutes.

And so many sleepers had complained of strange noises – even of voices – which were obviously illusions, because those awake had heard nothing. Surgeon-Commander Ernst had prescribed a very simple and effective cure; during the sleeping period, the camp was now lulled by gentle, unobtrusive background music.

This night, Commander Norton found the cure inadequate. He kept straining his ears into the darkness, and he knew what he was listening for. But though a very faint breeze did caress his face from time to time, there was no sound that could possibly be taken for that of a distant, rising wind. Nor did either of the exploring parties report anything unusual.

At last, around Ship's midnight, he went to sleep. There was always a man on watch at the communications console, in case of any urgent messages. No other precautions seemed necessary.

Not even a hurricane could have created the sound that did wake him, and the whole camp, in a single instant. It seemed that the sky was falling, or that Rama had split open and was tearing itself apart. First there was a rending crack, then a long-drawn-out series of crystalline crashes like a million glass-houses being demolished. It lasted for minutes, though it seemed like hours; it was still continuing, apparently moving away into the distance, when Norton got to the message centre.

'Hub Control! What's happened?'

'Just a moment, Skipper. It's over by the Sea. We're getting the light on it.'

Eight kilometres overhead, on the axis of Rama, the searchlight began to swing its beam out across the plain. It reached the edge of the Sea, then started to track along it, scanning around the interior of the world. A quarter of the way round the cylindrical surface, it stopped.

Up there in the sky – or what the mind still persisted in calling the sky – something extraordinary was happening. At first, it seemed to Norton that the Sea was boiling. It was no longer static and frozen in the grip of an eternal winter; a huge area, kilometers across, was in turbulent movement. And it was changing colour; a broad band of white was marching across the ice.

Suddenly a slab perhaps a quarter of a kilometre on a side began to tilt upwards like an opening door. Slowly and majestically, it reared into the sky, glittering and sparkling in the beam of the searchlight. Then it slid back and vanished underneath the surface, while a tidal wave of foaming water raced outwards in all directions from its point of submergence.

Not until then did Commander Norton fully realize what was happening. *The ice was breaking up.* All these days and weeks, the Sea had been thawing, far down in the depths. It was hard to concentrate because of the crashing roar that still filled the world and echoed round the sky, but he tried to think of a reason for so dramatic a convulsion. When a frozen lake or river thawed on Earth, it was nothing like this ...

But of course! It was obvious enough, now that it had happened. The Sea was thawing from *beneath* as the solar heat seeped through the hull of Rama. And when ice turns into water, it occupies less volume ...

So the Sea had been sinking below the upper layer of ice, leaving it unsupported. Day by day the strain had been building up; now the band of ice that encircled the equator of Rama was collapsing, like a bridge that had lost its central pier. It was splintering into hundreds of floating islands, that would crash and jostle into each other until they too melted. Norton's blood ran suddenly cold, when he remembered the plans that were being made to reach New York by sledge ...

The tumult was swiftly subsiding; a temporary stalemate had been reached in the war between ice and water. In a few hours, as the temperature continued to rise, the water would win and the last vestiges of ice would disappear. But in the long run, ice would be the victor, as Rama rounded the sun and set forth once more into the interstellar night.

Norton remembered to start breathing again; then he called the party nearest the Sea. To his relief, Lieutenant Rodrigo answered at once. No, the water hadn't reached them. No tidal wave had come sloshing over the edge of the cliff. 'So now we know,' he added very calmly, 'why there *is* a cliff.' Norton agreed silently; but that hardly explains, he thought to himself, why the cliff on the southern shore is ten times higher ...

The Hub searchlight continued to scan round the world. The awakened Sea was steadily calming, and the boiling white foam no longer raced outwards from capsizing ice-floes. In fifteen minutes, the main disturbance was over.

But Rama was no longer silent; it had awakened from its sleep, and ever and again there came the sound of grinding ice as one berg collided with another.

Spring had been a little late, Norton told himself, but winter had ended.

And there was that breeze again, stronger than ever. Rama had given him enough warnings; it was time to go.

As he neared the halfway mark, Commander Norton once again

felt gratitude to the darkness that concealed the view above – and below. Though he knew that more than ten thousand steps still lay ahead of him, and could picture the steeply ascending curve in his mind's eye, the fact that he could see only a small portion of it made the prospect more bearable.

This was his second ascent, and he had learned from his mistakes on the first. The great temptation was to climb too quickly in this low gravity; every step was so easy that it was very hard to adopt a slow, plodding rhythm. But unless one did this, after the first few thousand steps strange aches developed in the thighs and calves. Muscles that one never knew existed started to protest, and it was necessary to take longer and longer periods of rest. Towards the end he had spent more time resting than climbing, and even then it was not enough. He had suffered painful leg-cramps for the next two days, and would have been almost incapacitated had he not been back in the zero-gravity environment of the ship.

So this time he had started with almost painful slowness, moving like an old man. He had been the last to leave the plain, and the others were strung out along the half-kilometre of stairway above him; he could see their lights moving up the invisble slope ahead.

He felt sick at heart at the failure of his mission, and even now hoped that this was only a temporary retreat. When they reached the Hub, they could wait until any atmospheric disturbances had ceased. Presumably, it would be a dead calm there, as at the centre of a cyclone, and they could wait out the expected storm in safety.

Once again, he was jumping to conclusions, drawing dangerous analogies from Earth. The meteorology of a whole world, even under steady-state conditions, was a matter of enormous complexity. After several centuries of study, terrestrial weather-forecasting was still not absolutely reliable. And Rama was not merely a completely novel system; it was also undergoing rapid changes, for the temperature had risen several degrees in the last few hours. Yet still there was no sign of the promised hurricane, though there had been a few feeble gusts from apparently random directions.

They had now climbed five kilometres, which in this low and steadily diminishing gravity was equivalent to less than two on Earth. At the third level, three kilometres from the axis, they rested for an hour, taking light refreshments and massaging leg muscles. This was the last point at which they could breathe in comfort; like old-time Himalayan mountaineers, they had left their oxygen supplies here, and now put them on for the final ascent.

An hour later, they had reached the top of the stairway – and the beginning of the ladder. Ahead lay the last, vertical kilometre, fortunately in a gravity field only a few per cent of Earth's. Another thirty-minute rest, a careful check of oxygen, and they were ready for the final lap.

Once again, Norton made sure that all his men were safely ahead of him, spaced out at twenty-metre intervals along the ladder. From now on, it would be a slow, steady haul, extremely boring. The best technique was to empty the mind of all thoughts and to count the rungs as they drifted by – one hundred, two hundred, three hundred, four hundred …

He had just reached twelve hundred and fifty when he suddenly realised that something was wrong. The light shining on the vertical surface immediately in front of his eyes was the wrong colour – and it was much too bright.

Commander Norton did not even have time to check his ascent, or to call a warning to his men. Everything happened in less than a second.

In a soundless concussion of light, dawn burst upon Rama.

18
Dawn

The light was so brilliant that for a full minute Norton had to keep his eyes clenched tightly shut. Then he risked opening them, and stared through barely-parted lids at the wall a few centimetres in front of his face. He blinked several times, waited for the involuntary tears to drain away, and then turned slowly to behold the dawn.

He could endure the sight for only a few seconds; then he was forced to close his eyes again. It was not the glare that was intolerable – he could grow accustomed to that – but the awesome spectacle of Rama, now seen for the first time in its entirety.

Norton had known exactly what to expect; nevertheless the sight had stunned him. He was seized by a spasm of uncontrollable trembling; his hands tightened round the rungs of the ladder with the violence of a drowning man clutching at a lifebelt. The muscles of his forearms began to knot, yet at the same time his legs – already fatigued by hours of steady climbing – seemed about to give way. If it had not been for the low gravity, he might have fallen.

Then his training took over, and he began to apply the first remedy for panic. Still keeping his eyes closed and trying to forget the monstrous spectacle around him, he started to take deep, long breaths, filling his lungs with oxygen and washing the poisons of fatigue out of his system.

Presently he felt much better, but he did not open his eyes until he had performed one more action. It took a major effort of will to force his right hand to open – he had to talk to it like a disobedient child – but presently he manoeuvred it down to his waist, unclipped the safety belt from his harness, and hooked the buckle to the nearest rung. Now, whatever happened, he could not fall.

Norton took several more deep breaths; then – still keeping his eyes closed – he switched on his radio. He hoped his voice sounded calm and authoritative as he called: 'Captain here. Is everyone OK?'

As he checked off the names one by one, and received answers – even if somewhat tremulous ones – from everybody, his own confidence and self-control came swiftly back to him. All his men were safe, and were looking to him for leadership. He was the commander once more.

'Keep your eyes closed until you're quite sure you can take it,' he called. 'The view is – overwhelming. If anyone finds that it's too much, keep on climbing without looking back. Remember, you'll soon be at zero gravity, so you can't possibly fall.'

It was hardly necessary to point out such an elementary fact to trained spacemen, but Norton had to remind himself of it every few seconds. The thought of zero-gravity was a kind of talisman, protecting him from harm. Whatever his eyes told him, Rama could not drag him down to destruction on the plain eight kilometres below.

It became an urgent matter of pride and self-esteem that he should open his eyes once more and look at the world around him. But first, he had to get his body under control.

He let go of the ladder with *both* hands, and hooked his left arm under a rung. Clenching and unclenching his fists, he waited until the muscle cramps had faded away; then, when he felt quite comfortable, he opened his eyes and slowly turned to face Rama.

His first impression was one of blueness. The glare that filled the sky could not have been mistaken for sunlight; it might have been that of an electric arc. So Rama's sun, Norton told himself, must be hotter than ours. That should interest the astronomers ...

And now he understood the purpose of those mysterious trenches, the Straight Valley and its five companions; they were nothing less than gigantic strip-lights. Rama had six linear suns, symmetrically ranged around its interior. From each, a broad fan of light was aimed across the central axis, to shine upon the far side of the world. Norton wondered if they could be switched alternately to produce a cycle of light and darkness, or whether this was a planet of perpetual day.

Too much staring at those blinding bars of light had made his eyes hurt again; he was not sorry to have a good excuse to close them for a while. It was not until then, when he had almost recovered from this initial visual shock, that he was able to devote himself to a much more serious problem.

Who, or what, had switched on the lights of Rama?

This world was sterile, by the most sensitive tests that man could apply to it. But now something was happening that could not be explained by the action of natural forces. There might not be life here, but there could be consciousness, awareness; robots might be waking after a sleep of aeons. Perhaps this outburst of light was an unprogrammed, random spasm – a last dying gasp of machines that were responding wildly to the warmth of a new sun, and would soon lapse again into quiescence, this time for ever.

Yet Norton could not believe such a simple explanation. Bits of the jigsaw puzzle were beginning to fall into place, though many were still missing. The absence of all signs of wear, for example – the feeling of *newness*, as if Rama had just been created ...

These thoughts might have inspired fear, even terror. Somehow, they did nothing of the sort. On the contrary, Norton felt a sense of exhilaration – almost of delight. There was far more here to discover than they had ever dared to hope. 'Wait,' he said to himself, 'until the Rama Committee hears about *this!*'

Then, with a calm determination, he opened his eyes again and began a careful inventory of everything he saw.

First, he had to establish some kind of reference system. He was looking at the largest enclosed space ever seen by man, and needed a mental map to find his way around it.

The feeble gravity was very little help, for with an effort of will he could switch Up and Down in any direction he pleased. But some directions were psychologically dangerous; whenever his mind skirted these, he had to vector it hastily away.

Safest of all was to imagine that he was at the bowl-shaped bottom of a gigantic well, sixteen kilometres wide and fifty deep. The advantage of this image was that there could be no danger of falling further; nevertheless, it had some serious defects.

He could pretend that the scattered towns and cities, and the differently coloured and textured areas, were all securely fixed to the towering walls. The various complex structures that could be seen hanging from the dome overhead were perhaps no more disconcerting than the pendent candelabra in some great concert-hall on Earth. What was quite unacceptable was the Cylindrical Sea ...

There it was, halfway up the well-shaft – a band of water, wrapped completely round it, with no visible means of support. There could be no doubt that it *was* water; it was a vivid blue, flecked with brilliant sparkles from the few remaining ice-floes. But a vertical sea forming a complete circle twenty kilometres up in the sky was such an unsettling phenomenon that after a while he began to seek an alternative.

That was when his mind switched the scene through ninety degrees. Instantly, the deep well became a long tunnel, capped at either end. 'Down' was obviously in the direction of the ladder and the stairway he had just ascended; and now with this perspective, Norton was at last able to appreciate the true vision of the architects who had built this place.

He was clinging to the face of a curving sixteen-kilometre-high cliff, the upper half of which overhung completely until it merged into the arched roof of what was now the sky. Beneath him, the ladder descended more than five hundred metres, until it ended at the first ledge or terrace. There the stairway began, continuing almost vertically at first in this low-gravity regime, then slowly becoming less and less steep until, after breaking at five more platforms, it reached the distant plain. For the first two or three kilometres he could see the individual steps, but thereafter they had merged into a continuous band.

The downward swoop of that immense stairway was so overwhelming that it was impossible to appreciate its true scale. Norton had once flown round Mount Everest, and had been awed by its size. He reminded himself that this stairway was as high as the Himalayas, but the comparison was meaningless.

And no comparison at all was possible with the other two stairways, Beta and Gamma, which slanted up into the sky and then curved far out over his head. Norton had now acquired enough confidence to lean back and glance up at them – briefly. Then he tried to forget that they were there ...

For too much thinking along those lines evoked yet a third image of Rama, which he was anxious to avoid at all costs. This was the viewpoint that regarded it once again at a vertical cylinder or well – but now he was at the *top*, not the bottom, like a fly crawling upside down on a domed ceiling, with a fifty-kilometre drop immediately below. Every time Norton found this image creeping up on him, it needed all his willpower not to cling to the ladder again in mindless panic.

In time, he was sure, all these fears would ebb. The wonder and strangeness of Rama would banish its terrors, at least for men who were trained to face the realities of space. Perhaps no one who had never left Earth, and had never seen the stars all around him, could endure these vistas. But if any men could accept them, Norton told himself with grim determination, it would be the captain and crew of *Endeavour*.

He looked at his chronometer. This pause had lasted only two minutes, but it had seemed a lifetime. Exerting barely enough effort to overcome his inertia and the fading gravitational field, he started to pull himself slowly up the last hundred metres of the ladder. Just before he entered the airlock and turned his back upon Rama, he made one final swift survey of the interior.

It had changed, even in the last few minutes; a mist was rising from the Sea. For the first few hundred metres the ghostly white columns were tilted sharply forward in the direction of Rama's spin; then they started to dissolve in a swirl of turbulence, as the uprushing air tried to jettison its excess velocity. The Trade Winds of this cylindrical world were beginning to etch their patterns in its sky; the first tropical storm in unknown ages was about to break.

19
A Warning from Mercury

It was the first time in weeks that every member of the Rama Committee had made himself available. Professor Solomons had emerged from the depths of the Pacific, where he had been studying mining operations along the mid-ocean trenches. And to nobody's surprise, Dr Taylor had reappeared, now that there was at least a possibility that Rama held something more newsworthy than lifeless artifacts.

The Chairman had fully expected Dr Carlisle Perera to be even more dogmatically assertive than usual, now that his prediction of a Raman hurricane had been confirmed. To His Excellency's great surprise, Perera was remarkably subdued, and accepted the congratulations of his colleagues in a manner as near to embarrassment as he was ever likely to achieve.

The exobiologist, in fact, was deeply mortified. The spectacular break-up of the Cylindrical Sea was a much more obvious phenomenon than the hurricane winds – yet he had completely overlooked it. To have remembered that hot air rises, but to have forgotten that hot ice contracts, was not an achievement of which he could be very proud. However, he would soon get over it, and revert to his normal Olympian self-confidence.

When the Chairman offered him the floor, and asked what further climatic changes he expected, he was very careful to hedge his bets.

'You must realise,' he explained, 'that the meteorology of a world as strange as Rama may have many other surprises. But if my calculations are correct, there will be no further storms, and conditions will soon be stable. There will be a slow temperature rise until perihelion – and beyond – but that won't concern us, as *Endeavour* will have had to leave long before then.'

'So it should soon be safe to go back inside?'

'Er – probably. We should certainly know in forty-eight hours.'

'A return is imperative,' said the Ambassador for Mercury. 'We have to learn everything we possibly can about Rama. The situation has now changed completely.'

'I think we know what you mean, but would you care to elaborate?'

'Of course. Until now, we have assumed that Rama is lifeless – or at any rate uncontrolled. But we can no longer pretend that it is a derelict. Even if there are no life-forms aboard, it may be directed by robot mechanisms, programmed to carry out some mission – perhaps one highly disadvantageous to us. Unpalatable though it may be, we must consider the question of self-defence.'

There was a babble of protesting voices, and the Chairman had to hold up his hand to restore order.

'Let His Excellency finish!' he pleaded. 'Whether we like the idea or not, it should be considered seriously.'

'With all due respect to the Ambassador,' said Dr Conrad Taylor in his most disrespectful voice, 'I think we can rule out as naïve the fear of malevolent intervention. Creatures as advanced as the Ramans must have correspondingly developed morals. Otherwise, they would have destroyed themselves – as we nearly did in the twentieth century. I've made that quite clear in my new book *Ethos and Cosmos*. I hope you received your copy.'

'Yes, thank you, though I'm afraid the pressure of other matters has not allowed me to read beyond the introduction. However, I'm familiar with the general thesis. We may have no malevolent intentions towards an ant-heap. But if we want to build a house on the same site …'

'This is as bad as the Pandora Party! It's nothing less than interstellar xenophobia!'

'Please, *gentlemen*! This is getting us nowhere. Mr Ambassador, you still have the floor.'

The Chairman glared across three hundred and eighty thousand kilometres of space at Conrad Taylor, who reluctantly subsided, like a volcano biding its time.

'Thank you,' said the Ambassador for Mercury. 'The danger may be unlikely, but where the future of the human race is involved, we can take no chances. And, if I may say so, we Hermians may be particularly concerned. We may have more cause for alarm than anyone else.'

Dr Taylor snorted audibly, but was quelled by another glare from the Moon.

'Why Mercury, more than any other planet?' asked the Chairman.

'Look at the dynamics of the situation. Rama is already inside our orbit. It is only an assumption that it will go round the sun and head on out again into space. Suppose it carries out a braking manoeuvre? If it does so, this will be at perihelion, about thirty days from now. My scientists tell me that if the entire velocity change is carried out there, Rama will end up in a circular orbit only twenty-five million kilometres from the sun. From there, it could dominate the solar system.'

For a long time nobody – not even Conrad Taylor – spoke a word. All the members of the Committee were marshalling their thoughts about those difficult people the Hermians, so ably represented here by their Ambassador.

To most people, Mercury was a fairly good approximation of Hell; at least, it would do until something worse came along. But the Hermians were proud of their bizarre planet, with its days longer than its years, its double sunrises and sunsets, its rivers of molten metal ... By comparison, the Moon and Mars had been almost trivial challenges. Not until men landed on Venus (if they ever did) would they encounter an environment more hostile than that of Mercury.

And yet this world had turned out to be, in many ways, the key to the solar system. This seemed obvious in retrospect, but the Space Age had been almost a century old before the fact was realised. Now the Hermians never let anyone forget it.

Long before men reached the planet, Mercury's abnormal density hinted at the heavy elements it contained; even so, its wealth was still a source of astonishment, and had postponed for a thousand years any fears that the key metals of human civilisation would be exhausted. And these treasures were in the best possible place, where the power of the Sun was ten times greater than on frigid Earth.

Unlimited energy – unlimited metal; *that* was Mercury. Its great magnetic launchers could catapult manufactured products to any point in the solar system. It could also export energy, in synthetic transuranium isotopes or pure radiation. It had even been proposed that Hermian lasers would one day thaw out gigantic Jupiter, but this idea had not been well received on the other worlds. A technology that could cook Jupiter had too many tempting possibilities for interplanetary blackmail.

That such a concern had ever been expressed said a good deal about the general attitude towards the Hermians. They were respected for their toughness and engineering skills, and admired for the way in which they had conquered so fearsome a world. But they were not liked, and still less were they completely trusted.

At the same time, it was possible to appreciate their point of view. The Hermians, it was often joked, some times behaved as if the Sun was their personal property. They were bound to it in an intimate love-hate relationship – as the Vikings had once been linked to the sea, the Nepalese to the Himalayas, the Eskimos to the Tundra. They would be most unhappy if something came between them and the natural force that dominated and controlled their lives.

At last, the Chairman broke the long silence. He still remembered the sun of India, and shuddered to contemplate the sun of Mercury. So he took the Hermians very seriously indeed, even though he considered them uncouth technological barbarians.

'I think there is some merit in your argument, Mr Ambassador,' he said slowly. 'Have you any proposals?'

'Yes, sir. Before we know what action to take, we must have the facts. We know the geography of Rama – if one can use that term – but we have no idea of its capabilities. And the key to the whole problem is this: does Rama have a propulsion system? *Can it change orbit?* I'd be very interested in Dr Perera's views.'

'I've given the subject a good deal of thought,' answered the exobiologist. 'Of course, Rama must have been given its original impetus by some launching device, but that could have been an external booster. If it does have onboard propulsion, we've found no trace of it. Certainly there are no rocket exhausts, or anything similar, anywhere on the outer shell.'

'They could be hidden.'

'True, but there would seem little point in it. And where are the propellant tanks, the energy sources? The main hull is solid – we've checked that with seismic surveys. The cavities in the northern cap are all accounted for by the airlock systems.

'That leaves the southern end of Rama, which Commander Norton has been unable to reach, owing to that ten-kilometre-wide band of water. There are all sorts of curious mechanisms and structures up on the South Pole – you've seen the photographs. What they are is anybody's guess.

'But I'm reasonably sure of this. If Rama does have a propulsion system, it's something completely outside our present knowledge. In fact, it would have to be the fabulous "Space Drive" people have been talking about for two hundred years.'

'You wouldn't rule that out?'

'Certainly not. If we can prove that Rama has a Space Drive – even if we learn nothing about its mode of operation – that would be a major discovery. At least we'd know that such a thing is possible.'

'What *is* a Space Drive?' asked the Ambassador for Earth, rather plaintively.

'Any kind of propulsion system, Sir Robert, that doesn't work on the rocket principle. Anti-gravity – if it is possible – would do very nicely. At present, we don't know where to look for such a drive, and most scientists doubt if it exists.'

'It doesn't,' Professor Davidson interjected. 'Newton settled *that*. You can't have action without reaction. Space Drives are nonsense. Take it from me.'

'You may be right,' Perera replied with unusual blandness. 'But if Rama doesn't have a Space Drive, it has no drive at all. There's simply no room for a conventional propulsion system, with its enormous fuel tanks.'

'It's hard to imagine a whole world being pushed around,' said Dennis Solomons. 'What would happen to the objects inside it? Everything would have to be bolted down. Most inconvenient.'

'Well, the acceleration would probably be very low. The biggest problem would be the water in the Cylindrical Sea. How would you stop that from ...'

Perera's voice suddenly faded away, and his eyes glazed over. He seemed to be in the throes of an incipient epileptic fit, or even a heart attack. His colleagues looked at him in alarm; then he made a sudden recovery, banged his fist on the table and shouted: 'Of course! That explains everything! The southern cliff – *now* it makes sense!'

'Not to me,' grumbled the Lunar Ambassador, speaking for all the diplomats present.

'Look at this longitudinal cross-section of Rama,' Perera continued excitedly, unfolding his map. 'Have you got your copies? The Cylindrical Sea is enclosed between two cliffs, which completely circle the interior of Rama. The one on the north is only fifty metres high. The southern one, on the other hand, is almost half a kilometre high. Why the big difference? No one's been able to think of a sensible reason.

'But suppose Rama *is* able to propel itself – accelerating so that the northern end is forward. The water in the Sea would tend to move back; the level at the south would rise – perhaps hundreds of metres. Hence the cliff. Let's see—'

Perera started scribbling furiously. After an astonishingly short time – it could not have been more than twenty seconds – he looked up in triumph.

'Knowing the height of those cliffs, we can calculate the maximum acceleration Rama can take. If it was more than two per cent of a gravity, the Sea would slosh over into the southern continent.'

'A fiftieth of a gee? That's not very much.'

'It is – for a mass of ten million megatons. And it's all you need for astronomical manoeuvring.'

'Thank you very much, Dr Perera,' said the Hermian Ambassador. 'You've given us a lot to think about. Mr Chairman – can we impress on Commander Norton the importance of looking at the South Polar region?'

'He's doing his best. The Sea is the obstacle, of course. They're trying to build some kind of raft – so that they can at least reach New York.'

'The South Pole may be even more important. Meanwhile, I am going to bring these matters to the attention of the General Assembly. Do I have your approval?'

There were no objections, not even from Dr Taylor. But just as the Committee members were about to switch out of circuit, Sir Lewis raised his hand.

The old historian very seldom spoke; when he did, everyone listened.

'Suppose we do find that Rama is – *active* – and has these capabilities. There is an old saying in military affairs that capability does not imply intention.'

'How long should we wait to find what its intentions are?' asked the Hermian. 'When we discover them, it may be far too late.'

'It is already too late. There is nothing we can do to affect Rama. Indeed, I doubt if there ever was.'

'I do not admit that, Sir Lewis. There are many things we can do – if it proves necessary. But the time is desperately short. Rama is a cosmic egg, being warmed by the fires of the sun. It may hatch at any moment.'

The Chairman of the Committee looked at the Ambassador for Mercury in frank astonishment. He had seldom been so surprised in his diplomatic career.

He would never have dreamed that a Hermian was capable of such a poetic flight of imagination.

20
Book of Revelation

When one of his crew called him 'Commander', or, worse still 'Mister Norton', there was always something serious afoot. He could not recall that Boris Rodrigo had ever before addressed him in such a fashion, so this must be doubly serious. Even in normal times, Lieut-Commander Rodrigo was a very grave and sober person.

'What's the problem, Boris?' he asked when the cabin door closed behind them.

'I'd like permission, commander, to use Ship Priority for a direct message to Earth.'

This *was* unusual, though not unprecedented. Routine signals went to the nearest planetary relay – at the moment, they were working through Mercury – and even though the transit time was only a matter of minutes, it was often five or six hours before a message arrived at the desk of the person for whom it was intended. Ninety-nine per cent of the time, that was quite good enough; but in an emergency more direct, and much more expensive, channels could be employed, at the captain's discretion.

'You know, of course, that you have to give me a good reason. All our available bandwidth is already clogged with data transmissions. Is this a personal emergency?'

'No, Commander. It is much more important than *that*. I want to send a message to the Mother Church.'

Uh-uh, said Norton to himself. How do I handle this?

'I'd be glad if you'll explain.'

It was not mere curiosity that prompted Norton's request – though that was certainly present. If he gave Boris the priority he asked, he would have to justify his action.

The calm, blue eyes stared into his. He had never known Boris to lose control, to be other than completely self-assured. All the Cosmo-Christers were like this; it was one of the benefits of their faith, and it helped to make them good spacemen. Sometimes, however, their unquestioning certainty was just a little annoying to those unfortunates who had not been vouch-safed the Revelation.

'It concerns the purpose of Rama, Commander. I believe I have discovered it.'

'Go on.'

'Look at the situation. Here is a completely empty, lifeless world – yet it is suitable for human beings. It has water, and an atmosphere we can breathe. It comes from the remote depths of space, aimed precisely at the solar system – something quite incredible, if it was a matter of pure chance. And it appears not only new; *it looks as if it has never been used.*'

We've all been through this dozens of times, Norton told himself. What could Boris add to it?

'Our faith has told us to expect such a visitation though we do not know exactly what form it will take. The Bible gives hints. If this is not the Second Coming, it may be the Second Judgement; the story of Noah describes the first. I believe that Rama is a cosmic Ark, sent here to save – those who are worthy of salvation.'

There was silence for quite a while in the Captain's cabin. It was not that Norton was at a loss for words; rather, he could think of too many questions, but he was not sure which ones it would be tactful to ask.

Finally he remarked, in as mild and non-committal a voice as he could manage: 'That's a very interesting concept, and though

I don't go along with your faith, it's a tantalisingly plausible one.' He was not being hypocritical or flattering; stripped of its religious overtones, Rodrigo's theory was at least as convincing as half a dozen others he had heard. Suppose some catastrophe was about to befall the human race, and a benevolent higher intelligence knew all about it? That would explain everything, very neatly. However, there were still a few problems ...

'A couple of questions, Boris. Rama will be at perihelion in three weeks; then it will round the sun and leave the solar system just as fast as it came in. There's not much time for a Day of Judgement, or for shipping across those who are, er, selected – however *that's* going to be done.'

'Very true. So when it reaches perihelion, Rama will have to decelerate and go into a parking orbit – probably one with aphelion at Earth's orbit. There it might make another velocity change, and rendezvous with Earth.'

This was disturbingly persuasive. If Rama wished to remain in the solar system, it was going the right way about it. The most efficient way to slow down was to get as close to the sun as possible, and carry out the braking manoeuvre there. If there was any truth in Rodrigo's theory – or some variant of it – it would soon be put to the test.

'One other point, Boris. What's controlling Rama now?'

'There is no doctrine to advise on that. It could be a pure robot. Or it could be – a spirit. That would explain why there are no signs of biological life-forms.'

The Haunted Asteroid; why had that phrase popped up from the depths of memory? Then he recalled a silly story he had read years ago; he thought it best not to ask Boris if he had ever run into it. He doubted if the other's tastes ran to that sort of reading.

'I'll tell you what we'll do, Boris,' said Norton, abruptly making up his mind. He wanted to terminate this interview before it got too difficult, and thought he had found a good compromise.

'Can you sum up your ideas in less than – oh, a thousand bits?'

'Yes, I think so.'

'Well, if you can make it sound like a straightforward scientific theory, I'll send it, top priority, to the Rama Committee. Then a copy can go to your Church at the same time, and everyone will be happy.'

'Thank you, Commander, I really appreciate it.'

'Oh, I'm not doing this to save my conscience. I'd just like to see what the Committee makes of it. Even if I don't agree with you all along the line, you may have hit on something important.'

'Well, we'll know at perihelion, won't we?'

'Yes. We'll know at perihelion.'

When Boris Rodrigo had left, Norton called the bridge and gave necessary authorisation. He thought he had solved the problem rather neatly; besides, just suppose that Boris *was* right.

He might have increased his chances of being among the saved.

21
After the Storm

As they drifted along the now familiar corridor of the Alpha Airlock complex, Norton wondered if they had let impatience overcome caution. They had waited aboard *Endeavour* for forty-eight hours – two precious days – ready for instant departure if events should justify it. But nothing had happened; the instruments left in Rama had detected no unusual activity. Frustratingly, the television camera on the Hub had been blinded by a fog which had reduced visibility to a few metres and had only now started to retreat.

When they operated the final airlock door, and floated out into the cat's-cradle of guide-ropes around the Hub, Norton was struck first by the change in the light. It was no longer harshly blue, but was much more mellow and gentle, reminding him of a bright, hazy day on Earth.

He looked outwards along the axis of the world – and could see nothing except a glowing, featureless tunnel of white, reaching all the way to those strange mountains at the South Pole. The interior of Rama was completely blanketed with clouds, and nowhere was a break visible in the overcast. The top of the layer was quite sharply defined; it formed a smaller cylinder inside the larger one of this spinning world, leaving a central core, five or six kilometers wide, quite clear except for a few stray wisps of cirrus.

The immense tube of cloud was lit from underneath by the six artificial suns of Rama. The locations of the three on this

Northern continent were clearly defined by diffuse strips of light, but those on the far side of the Cylindrical Sea merged together into a continuous, glowing band.

What is happening down beneath those clouds? Norton asked himself. But at least the storm, which had centrifuged them into such perfect symmetry about the axis of Rama, had now died away. Unless there were some other surprises, it would be safe to descend.

It seemed appropriate, on this return visit, to use the team that had made the first deep penetration into Rama. Sergeant Myron – like every other member of *Endeavour*'s crew – now fully met Surgeon-Commander Ernst's physical requirements; he even maintained, with convincing sincerity, that he was never going to wear his old uniforms again.

As Norton watched Mercer, Calvert and Myron 'swimming' quickly and confidently down the ladder, he reminded himself how much had changed. That first time they had descended in cold and darkness; now they were going towards light and warmth. And on all earlier visits, they had been confident that Rama was dead. That might yet be true, in a biological sense. But something was stirring; and Boris Rodrigo's phrase would do as well as any other. The spirit of Rama was awake.

When they had reached the platform at the foot of the ladder and were preparing to start down the stairway, Mercer carried out his usual routine test of the atmosphere. There were some things that he never took for granted; even when the people around him were breathing perfectly comfortably, without aids, he had been known to stop for an air check before opening his helmet. When asked to justify such excessive caution, he had answered: 'Because human senses aren't good enough, that's why. You may think you're fine, but you could fall flat on your face with the next deep breath.'

He looked at his meter, and said 'Damn!'

'What's the trouble?' asked Calvert.

'It's broken – reading too high. Odd; I've never known that to happen before. I'll check it on my breathing circuit.'

He plugged the compact little analyser into the test point of his oxygen supply, then stood in thoughtful silence for a while. His companions looked at him with anxious concern; anything that upset Karl was to be taken very seriously indeed.

He unplugged the meter, used it to sample the Rama atmosphere again, then called Hub Control.

'Skipper! Will you take an O_2 reading?'

There was a much longer pause than the request justified. Then Norton radioed back: 'I think there's something wrong with my meter.'

A slow smile spread across Mercer's face.

'It's up fifty per cent, isn't it?'

'Yes, what does that mean?'

'It means that we can all take off our masks. Isn't that convenient?'

'I'm not sure,' replied Norton, echoing the sarcasm in Mercer's voice. 'It seems too good to be true.' There was no need to say any more. Like all spacemen, Commander Norton had a profound suspicion of things that were too good to be true.

Mercer cracked his mask open a trifle, and took a cautious sniff. For the first time at this altitude, the air was perfectly breathable. The musty, dead smell had gone; so had the excessive dryness, which in the past had caused several respiratory complaints. Humidity was now an astonishing eighty per cent; doubtless the thawing of the Sea was responsible for this. There was a muggy feeling in the air, though not an unpleasant one. It was like a summer evening. Mercer told himself, on some tropical coast. The climate inside Rama had improved dramatically during the last few days ...

And why? The increased humidity was no problem; the startling rise in oxygen was much more difficult to explain.

As he recommended the descent, Mercer began a whole series of mental calculations. He had not arrived at any satisfactory result by the time they entered the cloud layer.

It was a dramatic experience, for the transition was very abrupt. At one moment they were sliding downwards in clear air, gripping the smooth metal of the handrail so that they would not gain speed too swiftly in this quarter-of-a-gravity region. Then, suddenly, they shot into a blinding white fog, and visibility dropped to a few metres. Mercer put on the brakes so quickly that Calvert almost bumped into him – and Myron *did* bump into Calvert, nearly knocking him off the rail.

'Take it easy,' said Mercer. 'Spread out so we can just see each other. And don't let yourself build up speed, in case I have to stop suddenly.'

In eerie silence, they continued to glide downwards through the fog. Calvert could just see Mercer as a vague shadow ten metres ahead, and when he looked back, Myron was at the same distance behind him. In some ways, this was even spookier than descending in the complete darkness of the Raman night; then, at least, the searchlight beams had shown them what lay ahead. But *this* was like diving in poor visibility in the open sea.

It was impossible to tell how far they had travelled, and Calvert guessed they had almost reached the fourth level when Mercer suddenly braked again. When they had bunched together, he whispered: 'Listen! Don't you hear something?'

'Yes,' said Myron, after a minute. 'It sounds like the wind.'

Calvert was not so sure. He turned his head back and forth, trying to locate the direction of the very faint murmur that had come to them through the fog, then abandoned the attempt as hopeless.

They continued the slide, reached the fourth level, and started on towards the fifth. All the while the sound grew louder – and more hauntingly familiar. They were half-way down the fourth stairway before Myron called out: 'Now do you recognise it?'

They would have identified it long ago, but it was not a sound they would ever have associated with any world except Earth. Coming out of the fog, from a source whose distance could not be guessed, was the steady thunder of falling water.

A few minutes later, the cloud ceiling ended as abruptly as it had begun. They shot out into the blinding glare of the Raman day, made more brilliant by the light reflected from the low-hanging clouds. There was the familiar curving plain – now made more acceptable to mind and senses, because its full circle could no longer be seen. It was not too difficult to pretend that they were looking along a broad valley, and that the upward sweep of the Sea was really an *outward* one.

They halted at the fifth and penultimate platform, to report that they were through the cloud cover and to make a careful survey. As far as they could tell, nothing had changed down there on the plain; but up here on the Northern dome, Rama had brought forth another wonder.

So there was the origin of the sound they had heard. Descending from some hidden source in the clouds three or four kilometres away was a waterfall, and for long minutes they stared at it silently, almost unable to believe their eyes. Logic told them that on this spinning world no falling object could move in a straight line, but there was something horribly unnatural about a curving waterfall that curved sideways, to end many kilometres away from the point directly below its source ...

'If Galileo had been born in this world,' said Mercer at length, 'he'd have gone crazy working out the laws of dynamics.'

'I thought I knew them,' Calvert replied, 'and I'm going crazy anyway. Doesn't it upset you, Prof?'

'Why should it?' said Sergeant Myron. 'It's a perfectly straightforward demonstration of the Coriolis Effect. I wish I could show it to some of my students.'

Mercer was staring thoughtfully at the globe-circling band of the Cylindrical Sea.

'Have you noticed what's happened to the water?' he said at last.

'Why – it's no longer so blue. I'd call it pea-green. What does that signify?'

'Perhaps the same thing that it does on Earth. Laura called the Sea an organic soup waiting to be shaken into life. Maybe that's exactly what's happened.'

'In a couple of days! It took millions of years on Earth.'

'Three hundred and seventy-five million, according to the latest estimate. So *that's* where the oxygen's come from. Rama's shot through the anerobic stage and has got to photosynthetic plants – in about forty-eight hours. I wonder what it will produce tomorrow?'

22
To Sail the Cylindrical Sea

When they reached the foot of the stairway, they had another shock. At first, it appeared that something had gone through the camp, overturning equipment, even collecting smaller objects and carrying them away. But after a brief examination, their alarm was replaced by a rather shame-faced annoyance.

The culprit was only the wind; though they had tied down all loose objects before they left, some ropes must have parted during exceptionally strong gusts. It was several days before they were able to retrieve all their scattered property.

Otherwise, there seemed no major changes. Even the silence of Rama had returned, now that the ephemeral storms of spring were over. And out there at the edge of the plain was a calm sea, waiting for the first ship in a million years.

'Shouldn't one christen a new boat with a bottle of champagne?'

'Even if we had any on board, I wouldn't allow such a criminal waste. Anyway, it's too late. We've already launched the thing.'

'At least it does float. You've won your bet, Jimmy. I'll settle when we get back to Earth.'

'It's got to have a name. Any ideas?'

The subject of these unflattering comments was now bobbing beside the steps leading down into the Cylindrical Sea. It was a small raft, constructed from six empty storage drums held together by a light metal framework. Building it, assembling it at

Camp Alpha and hauling it on demountable wheels across more than ten kilometres of plain had absorbed the crew's entire energies for several days. It was a gamble that had better pay off.

The prize was worth the risk. The enigmatic towers of New York, gleaming there in the shadowless light five kilometres away, had taunted them ever since they had entered Rama. No one doubted that the city – or whatever it might be – was the real heart of this world. If they did nothing else, they must reach New York.

'We still don't have a name. Skipper – what about it?'

Norton laughed, then became suddenly serious.

'I've got one for you. Call it *Resolution*.'

'Why?'

'That was one of Cook's ships. It's a good name – may she live up to it.'

There was a thoughtful silence; then Sergeant Barnes, who had been principally responsible for the design, asked for three volunteers. Everyone present held up a hand.

'Sorry – we only have four life-jackets. Boris, Jimmy, Pieter – you've all done some sailing. Let's try her out.'

No one thought it in the least peculiar that an Executive Sergeant was now taking charge of the proceedings. Ruby Barnes had the only Master's Certificate aboard, so that settled the matter. She had navigated racing trimarans across the Pacific, and it did not seem likely that a few kilometres of dead-calm water could present much of a challenge to her skills.

Ever since she had set eyes upon the Sea, she had been determined to make this voyage. In all the thousands of years that man had had dealings with the waters of his own world, no sailor had ever faced anything remotely like this. In the last few days a silly little jingle had been running through her mind, and she could not get rid of it. 'To sail the Cylindrical Sea ...' Well, that was precisely what she was going to do.

Her passengers took their places on the improvised bucket

115

seats, and Ruby opened the throttle. The twenty-kilowatt motor started to whirr, the chain-drives of the reduction gear blurred, and *Resolution* surged away to the cheers of the spectators.

Ruby had hoped to get fifteen kph with this load, but would settle for anything over ten. A half-kilometre course had been measured along the cliff, and she made the round trip in five and a half minutes. Allowing for turning time, this worked out at twelve kph; she was quite happy with that.

With no power, but with three energetic paddlers helping her own more skilful blade, Ruby was able to get a quarter of this speed. So even if the motor broke down, they could get back to shore in a couple of hours. The heavy-duty power cells could provide enough energy to circumnavigate the world; she was carrying two spares, to be on the safe side. And now that the fog had completely burned away, even such a cautious mariner as Ruby was prepared to put to sea without a compass.

She saluted smartly as she stepped ashore.

'Maiden voyage of *Resolution* successfully completed, Sir. Now awaiting your instructions.'

'Very good ... Admiral. When will you be ready to sail?'

'As soon as stores can be loaded aboard, and the Harbour Master gives us clearance.'

'Then we leave at dawn.'

'Aye, aye, Sir.'

Five kilometres of water does not seem very much on a map; it is very different when one is in the middle of it. They had been cruising for only ten minutes, and the fifty-metre cliff facing the Northern Continent already seemed a surprising distance away. Yet, mysteriously, New York hardly appeared much closer than before ...

But most of the time they paid little attention to the land; they were still too engrossed in the wonder of the Sea. They no longer made the nervous jokes that had punctuated the start of the voyage; this new experience was too overwhelming.

Every time, Norton told himself, he felt that he had grown accustomed to Rama, it produced some new wonder. As *Resolution* hummed steadily forward, it seemed that they were caught in the trough of a gigantic wave – a wave which curved up on either side until it became vertical – then overhung until the two flanks met in a liquid arch sixteen kilometres above their heads. Despite everything that reason and logic told them, none of the voyagers could for long throw off the impression that at any minute those millions of tons of water would come crashing down from the sky.

Yet despite this, their main feeling was one of exhilaration; there was a sense of danger, without any *real* danger. Unless, of course, the Sea itself produced any more surprises.

That was a different possibility, for as Mercer had guessed, the water was now alive. Every spoonful contained thousands of spherical, single-celled micro-organisms, similar to the earliest forms of plankton that had existed in the oceans of Earth.

Yet they showed puzzling differences; they lacked a nucleus, as well as many of the other minimum requirements of even the most primitive terrestrial life-forms. And although Laura Ernst – now doubling as research scientist as well as ship's doctor – had proved that they definitely generated oxygen, there were far too few of them to account for the augmentation of Rama's atmosphere. They should have existed in billions, not mere thousands.

Then she discovered that their numbers were dwindling rapidly, and must have been far higher during the first hours of the Raman dawn. It was as if there had been a brief explosion of life, recapitulating on a trillion-fold swifter time-scale the early history of Earth. Now, perhaps, it had exhausted itself; the drifting micro-organisms were disintegrating, releasing their stores of chemicals back into the Sea.

'If you have to swim for it,' Dr Ernst had warned the mariners, 'keep your mouths closed. A few drops won't matter – if you spit them out right away. But all those weird organo-metallic salts add up to a fairly poisonous package, and I'd hate to have to work out an antidote.'

This danger, fortunately, seemed very unlikely. *Resolution* could stay afloat if any two of her buoyancy tanks were punctured. (When told of this, Joe Calvert had muttered darkly: 'Remember the *Titanic!*') And even if she sank, the crude but efficient life-jackets would keep their heads above water. Although Laura had been reluctant to give a firm ruling on this, she did not think that a few hours' immersion in the Sea would be fatal; but she did not recommend it.

After twenty minutes of steady progress, New York was no longer a distant island. It was becoming a real place, and details which they had seen only through telescopes and photo-enlargements were now revealing themselves as massive, solid structures. It was now strikingly apparent that the 'city', like so much of Rama, was triplicated; it consisted of three identical, circular complexes or super-structures, rising from a long, oval foundation. Photographs taken from the Hub also indicated that each complex was *itself* divided into three equal components, like a pie sliced into 120-degree portions. This would greatly simplify the task of exploration; presumably they had to examine only one ninth of New York to have seen the whole of it. Even this would be a formidable undertaking; it would mean investigating at least a square kilometre of buildings and machinery, some of which towered hundreds of metres into the air.

The Ramans, it seemed, had brought the art of triple-redundancy to a high degree of perfection. This was demonstrated in the airlock system, the stairways at the Hub, the artificial suns. And where it really mattered, they had even taken the next step. New York appeared to be an example of triple-triple redundancy.

Ruby was steering *Resolution* towards the central complex,

where a flight of steps led up from the water to the very top of the wall or levee which surrounded the island. There was even a conveniently-placed mooring post to which boats could be tied; when she saw this, Ruby became quite excited. Now she would never be content until she found one of the craft in which the Ramans sailed their extraordinary sea.

Norton was the first to step ashore; he looked back at his three companions and said: 'Wait here on the boat until I get to the top of the wall. When I wave, Pieter and Boris will join me. You stay at the helm, Ruby, so that we can cast off at a moment's notice. If anything happens to me, report to Karl and follow his instructions. Use your best judgement – but no heroics. Understood?'

'Yes, Skipper. Good luck!'

Commander Norton did not really believe in luck; he never got into a situation until he had analysed all the factors involved and had secured his line of retreat. But once again Rama was forcing him to break some of his cherished rules. Almost every factor here was unknown – as unknown as the Pacific and the Great Barrier Reef had been to his hero, three and a half centuries ago ... Yes, he could do with all the luck that happened to be lying around.

The stairway was a virtual duplicate of the one down which they had descended on the other side of the Sea; doubtless his friends over there were looking straight across at him through their telescopes. And 'straight' was now the correct word; in this one direction, parallel to the axis of Rama, the Sea was indeed completely flat. It might well be the only body of water in the universe of which this was true, for on all other worlds, every sea or lake must follow the surface of a sphere, with equal curvature in all directions.

'Nearly at the top,' he reported, speaking for the record and for his intently listening second-in-command, five kilometres away, 'still completely quiet – radiation normal. I'm holding the meter above my head, just in case this wall is acting as a shield for anything. And if there are any hostiles on the other side, they'll shoot that first.'

He was joking, of course. And yet – why take any chances, when it was just as easy to avoid them?

When he took the last step, he found that the flat-topped embankment was about ten metres thick; on the inner side, an alternating series of ramps and stairways led down to the main level of the city, twenty metres below. In effect, he was standing on a high wall which completely surrounded New York, and so was able to get a grandstand view of it.

It was a view almost stunning in its complexity, and his first act was to make a slow panoramic scan with his camera. Then he waved to his companions and radioed back across the Sea: 'No sign of any activity – everything quiet. Come on up – we'll start exploring.'

23
NY, Rama

It was not a city; it was a machine. Norton had come to that conclusion in ten minutes, and saw no reason to change it after they had made a complete traverse of the island. A city – whatever the nature of its occupants – surely had to provide some form of accommodation: there was nothing here of that nature, unless it was underground. And if that was the case, where were the entrances, the stairways, the elevators? He had not found anything that even qualified as a simple door ...

The closest analogy he had ever seen to this place on Earth was a giant chemical processing plant. However, there were no stockpiles of raw materials, or any indications of a transport system to move them around. Nor could he imagine where the finished product would emerge – still less what that product could possibly be. It was all very baffling, and more than a little frustrating.

'Anybody care to make a guess?' he said at last, to all who might be listening. 'If this is a factory, what does it make? And where does it get its raw materials?'

'I've a suggestion, Skipper,' said Karl Mercer, over on the far shore. 'Suppose it uses the Sea. According to Doc, that contains just about anything you can think of.'

It was a plausible answer, and Norton had already considered it. There could well be buried pipes leading to the Sea – in fact, there *must* be, for any conceivable chemical plant would require large quantities of water. But he had a suspicion of plausible answers; they were so often wrong.

'That's a good idea, Karl; but what does New York *do* with its seawater?'

For a long time, nobody answered from ship, Hub or Northern plain. Then an unexpected voice spoke.

'That's easy, Skipper. But you're all going to laugh at me.'

'No, we're not, Ravi. Go ahead.'

Sergeant Ravi McAndrews, Chief Steward and Simp Master, was the last person on this ship who would normally get involved in a technical discussion. His IQ was modest and his scientific knowledge was minimal, but he was no fool and had a natural shrewdness which everyone respected.

'Well, it's a factory all right, Skipper, and maybe the Sea provides the raw material ... after all, that's how it all happened on Earth, though in a different way ... I believe New York is a factory for making – Ramans.'

Somebody, somewhere, snickered, but became quickly silent and did not identify himself.

'You know, Ravi,' said his commander at last, 'that theory is crazy enough to be true. And I'm not sure if I want to see it tested ... at least, until I get back to the mainland.'

This celestial New York was just about as wide as the island of Manhattan, but its geometry was totally different. There were few straight thoroughfares; it was a maze of short, concentric arcs, with radial spokes linking them. Luckily, it was impossible to lose one's bearings inside Rama; a single glance at the sky was enough to establish the north-south axis of the world.

They paused at almost every intersection to make a panoramic scan. When all these hundreds of pictures were sorted out, it would be a tedious but fairly straightforward job to construct an accurate scale model of the city. Norton suspected that the resulting jigsaw puzzle would keep scientists busy for generations.

It was even harder to get used to the silence here than it had been out on the plain of Rama. A city-machine should make some sound; yet there was not even the faintest of electric hums, or the slightest whisper of mechanical motion. Several times Norton put his ear to the ground, or to the side of a building, and listened intently. He could hear nothing except the pounding of his own blood.

The machines were sleeping: they were not even ticking over. Would they ever wake again, and for what purpose? Everything was in perfect condition, as usual. It was easy to believe that the closing of a single circuit, in some patient, hidden computer, would bring all this maze back to life.

When at last they had reached the far side of the city, they climbed to the top of the surrounding levee and looked across the southern branch of the Sea. For a long time Norton stared at the five-hundred-metre cliff that barred them from almost half of Rama – and, judging from their telescopic surveys, the most complex and varied half. From this angle, it appeared an ominous, forbidding black, and it was easy to think of it as a prison wall surrounding a whole continent. Nowhere along its entire circle was there a flight of stairways or any other means of access.

He wondered how the Ramans reached their southern land from New York. Probably there was an underground transport system running beneath the Sea, but they must also have aircraft as well; there were many open areas here in the city that could be used for landing. To discover a Raman vehicle would be a major accomplishment – especially if they could learn to operate it. (Though could any conceivable power-source still be functioning, after several hundred thousand years?) There were numerous structures that had the functional look of hangars or garages, but they were all smooth and windowless, as if they had been sprayed with sealant. Sooner or later, Norton had told himself grimly, we'll be forced to use explosives, and laser beams. He was determined to put off this decision to the last possible moment.

His reluctance to use brute force was based partly on pride, partly on fear. He did not wish to behave like a technological barbarian, smashing what he could not understand. After all, he was an uninvited visitor in this world, and should act accordingly.

As for his fear – perhaps that was too strong a word; apprehension might be better. The Ramans seemed to have planned for everything; he was not anxious to discover the precautions they had taken to guard their property. When he sailed back to the mainland, it would be with empty hands.

24
Dragonfly

Lieutenant James Pak was the most junior officer on board *Endeavour*, and this was only his fourth mission into deep space. He was ambitious, and due for promotion; he had also committed a serious breach of regulations. No wonder, therefore, that he took a long time to make up his mind.

It would be a gamble; if he lost, he could be in deep trouble. He could not only be risking his career; he might even be risking his neck. But if he succeeded, he would be a hero. What finally convinced him was neither of these arguments; it was the certainty that, if he did nothing at all, he would spend the rest of his life brooding over his lost opportunity. Nevertheless, he was still hesitant when he asked the Captain for a private meeting.

What is it *this* time? Norton asked himself, as he analysed the uncertain expression of the young officer's face. He remembered his delicate interview with Boris Rodrigo; no, it wouldn't be anything like that. Jimmy was certainly not the religious type; the only interests he had ever shown outside his work were sport and sex, preferably combined.

It could hardly be the former, and Norton hoped it was not the latter. He had encountered most of the problems that a commanding officer could encounter in this department – except the classical one of an unscheduled birth during a mission. Though this situation was the subject of innumerable jokes, it had never happened yet; but such gross incompetence was probably only a matter of time.

'Well, Jimmy, what is it?'

'I have an idea, Commander. I know how to reach the southern continent – even to the South Pole.'

'I'm listening. How do you propose to do it?'

'Er – by flying there.'

'Jimmy, I've had at least five proposals to do that – more if you count crazy suggestions from Earth. We've looked into the possibility of adapting our spacesuit propulsors, but air drag would make them hopelessly inefficient. They'd run out of fuel before they could go ten kilometres.'

'I know that. But I have the answer.'

Lt Pak's attitude was a curious mixture of complete confidence and barely suppressed nervousness. Norton was quite baffled; what was the kid worried about? Surely he knew his commanding officer well enough to be certain that no reasonable proposal would be laughed out of court.

'Well, go on. If it works, I'll see your promotion is retroactive.'

That little half-promise, half-joke didn't go down as well as he had hoped. Jimmy gave a rather sickly smile, made several false starts, then decided on an oblique approach to the subject.

'You know, Commander, that I was in the Lunar Olympics last year.'

'Of course. Sorry you didn't win.'

'It was bad equipment; I know what went wrong. I have friends on Mars who've been working on it, in secret. We want to give everyone a surprise.'

'Mars? But I didn't know …'

'Not many people do – the sport's still new there; it's only been tried in the Xante Sportsdome. But the best aerodynamicists in the solar system are on Mars; if you can fly in *that* atmosphere, you can fly anywhere.

'Now, my idea was that if the Martians could build a good

machine, with all their know-how, it would *really* perform on the Moon – where gravity is only half as strong.'

'That seems plausible, but how does it help us?'

Norton was beginning to guess, but he wanted to give Jimmy plenty of rope.

'Well, I formed a syndicate with some friends in Lowell City. They've built a fully aerobatic flyer with some refinements that no one has ever seen before. In lunar gravity, under the Olympic dome, it should create a sensation.'

'And win you the gold medal.'

'I hope so.'

'Let me see if I follow your train of thought correctly. A sky-bike that could enter the Lunar Olympics, at a sixth of a gravity, would be even more sensational inside Rama, with no gravity at all. You could fly it right along the axis, from the North Pole to the South – and back again.'

'Yes – easily. The one-way trip would take three hours, non-stop. But of course you could rest whenever you wanted to, as long as you kept near the axis.'

'It's a brilliant idea, and I congratulate you. What a pity sky-bikes aren't part of regular Space Survey equipment.'

Jimmy seemed to have some difficulty in finding words. He opened his mouths everal times, but nothing happened.

'All right, Jimmy. As a matter of morbid interest, and purely off the record, how did you smuggle the thing aboard?'

'Er – "Recreational Stores".'

'Well, you weren't lying. And what about the weight?'

'It's only twenty kilogrammes.'

'*Only!* Still, that's not as bad as I thought. In fact, I'm astonished you can build a bike for that weight.'

'Some have been only fifteen, but they were too fragile and usually folded up when they made a turn. There's no danger of *Dragonfly* doing that. As I said, she's fully aerobatic.'

'*Dragonfly* – nice name. So tell me just how you plan to use her; then I can decide whether a promotion or a court martial is in order. Or both.'

25
Maiden Flight

Dragonfly was certainly a good name. The long, tapering wings were almost invisible, except when the light struck them from certain angles and was refracted into rainbow hues. It was as if a soap-bubble had been wrapped round a delicate tracery of aerofoil sections; the envelope enclosing the little flyer was an organic film only a few molecules thick, yet strong enough to control and direct the movements of a fifty-kph air flow.

The pilot – who was also the powerplant and the guidance system – sat on a tiny seat at the centre of gravity, in a semi-reclining position to reduce air resistance. Control was by a single stick which could be moved backwards and forwards, right and left; the only 'instrument' was a piece of weighted ribbon attached to the leading edge, to show the direction of the relative wind.

Once the flyer had been assembled at the Hub, Jimmy Pak would allow no one to touch it. Clumsy handling could snap one of the single-fibre structural members, and those glittering wings were an almost irresistible attraction to prying fingers. It was hard to believe that there was *really* something there ...

As he watched Jimmy climb into the contraption, Commander Norton began to have second thoughts. If one of those wire-sized struts snapped when *Dragonfly* was on the other side of the Cylindrical Sea, Jimmy would have no way of getting back – even if he was able to make a safe landing. They were also breaking one of the most sacrosanct rules of space exploration;

a man was going *alone* into unknown territory, beyond all possibility of help. The only consolation was that he would be in full view and communication all the time; they would know exactly what had happened to him, if he did meet with disaster.

Yet this opportunity was far too good to miss; if one believed in fate or destiny, it would be challenging the gods themselves to neglect the only chance they might ever have of reaching the far side of Rama, and seeing at close quarters the mysteries of the South Pole. Jimmy knew what he was attempting, far better than anyone in the crew could tell him. This was precisely the sort of risk that had to be taken; if it failed, that was the luck of the game. You couldn't win them all ...

'Now listen to me carefully, Jimmy,' said Surgeon-Commander Ernst. 'It's very important not to over-exert yourself. Remember, the oxygen level here at the axis is still very low. If you feel breathless at any time, stop and hyperventilate for thirty seconds – but no longer.'

Jimmy nodded absentmindedly as he tested the controls. The whole rudder-elevator assembly, which formed a single unit on an outrigger five metres behind the rudimentary cockpit, began to twist around; then the flap-shaped ailerons, halfway along the wing, moved alternately up and down.

'Do you want me to swing the prop?' asked Joe Calvert, unable to suppress memories of two-hundred-year-old war movies. 'Ignition! Contact!' Probably no one except Jimmy knew what he was talking about, but it helped to relieve the tension.

Very slowly, Jimmy started to move the foot-pedals. The flimsy, broad fan of the airscrew – like the wing, a delicate skeleton covered with shimmering film – began to turn. By the time it had made a few revolutions, it had disappeared completely; and *Dragonfly* was on her way.

She moved straight outwards from the Hub, moving slowly along the axis of Rama. When she had travelled a hundred metres, Jimmy stopped pedalling; it was strange to see an obviously aerodynamic vehicle hanging motionless in mid-air. This must be the first time such a thing had ever happened, except possibly on a very limited scale inside one of the larger space-stations.

'How does she handle?' Norton called.

'Response good, stability poor. But I know what the trouble is – no gravity. We'll be better off a kilometre lower down.'

'Now wait a minute – is that safe?'

By losing altitude, Jimmy would be sacrificing his main advantage. As long as he stayed precisely on the axis, he – and *Dragonfly* – would be completely weightless. He could hover effortlessly, or even go to sleep if he wished. But as soon as he moved away from the central line around which Rama spun, the pseudo-weight of centrifugal force would reappear.

And so, unless he could maintain himself at this altitude, he would continue to lose height – and at the same time, *to gain weight*. It would be an accelerating process, which could end in catastrophe. The gravity down on the plain of Rama was twice that in which *Dragonfly* had been designed to operate. Jimmy might be able to make a safe landing; he could certainly never take off again.

But he had already considered all this, and he answered confidently enough: 'I can manage a tenth of a gee without any trouble. And she'll handle more easily in denser air.'

In a slow, leisurely spiral, *Dragonfly* drifted across the sky, roughly following the line of Stairway Alpha down towards the plain. From some angles, the little sky-bike was almost invisible; Jimmy seemed to be sitting in mid-air pedalling furiously. Sometimes he moved into spurts of up to thirty kilometres an hour; then he would coast to a halt, getting the feel of the controls, before accelerating again. And he was always very careful to keep a safe distance from the curving end of Rama.

It was soon obvious that *Dragonfly* handled much better at lower altitudes; she no longer rolled around at any angle, but stabilized so that her wings were parallel to the plain seven kilometres below. Jimmy completed several wide orbits, then started to climb upwards again. He finally halted a few metres above his waiting colleagues and realised, a little belatedly, that he was not quite sure how to land this gossamer craft.

'Shall we throw you a rope?' Norton asked half-seriously.

'No, Skipper – I've got to work this out myself. I won't have anyone to help me at the other end.'

He sat thinking for a while, then started to ease *Dragonfly* towards the Hub with short bursts of power. She quickly lost momentum between each, as air drag brought her to rest again. When he was only five metres away, and the sky-bike was still barely moving, Jimmy abandoned ship. He let himself float towards the nearest safety line in the Hub webwork, grasped it, then swung around in time to catch the approaching bike with his hands. The manoeuvre was so neatly executed that it drew a round of applause.

'For my *next* act—' Joe Calvert began.

Jimmy was quick to disclaim any credit.

'That was messy,' he said. 'But now I know how to do it. I'll take a sticky-bomb on a twenty-metre line; then I'll be able to pull myself in wherever I want to.'

'Give me your wrist, Jimmy,' ordered the Doctor, 'and blow into this bag. I'll want a blood sample, too. Did you have any difficulty in breathing?'

'Only at this altitude. Hey, what do you want the blood for?'

'Sugar level; then I can tell how much energy you've used. We've got to make sure you carry enough fuel for the mission. By the way, what's the endurance record for sky-biking?'

'Two hours twenty-five minutes three point six seconds. On the Moon, of course – a two kilometre circuit in the Olympic Dome.'

'And you think you can keep it up for six hours?'

'Easily, since I can stop for a rest at any time. Sky-biking on the Moon is at least twice as hard as it is here.'

'OK Jimmy – back to the lab. I'll give you a Go-No-Go as soon as I've analysed these samples. I don't want to raise false hopes – but I think you can make it.'

A large smile of satisfaction spread across Jimmy Pak's ivory-hued countenance. As he followed Surgeon-Commander Ernst to the airlock, he called back to his companions: 'Hands off, *please*! I don't want anyone putting his fist through the wings.'

'I'll see to that, Jimmy,' promised the Commander. '*Dragonfly* is off limits to *everybody* – including myself.'

26

The Voice of Rama

The real magnitude of his adventure did not hit Jimmy Pak until he reached the coast of the Cylindrical Sea. Until now, he had been over known territory; barring a catastrophic structural failure, he could always land and walk back to base in a few hours.

That option no longer existed. If he came down in the Sea, he would probably drown, quite unpleasantly, in its poisonous waters. And even if he made a safe landing in the southern continent, it might be impossible to rescue him before *Endeavour* had to break away from Rama's sunward orbit.

He was also acutely aware that the foreseeable disasters were the ones most unlikely to happen. The totally unknown region over which he was flying might produce any number of surprises; suppose there were flying creatures here, who objected to his intrusion? He would hate to engage in a dog-fight with anything larger than a pigeon. A few well-placed pecks could destroy *Dragonfly*'s aerodynamics.

Yet, if there were no hazards, there would be no achievement – no sense of adventure. Millions of men would gladly have traded places with him now. He was going not only where no one had ever been before – but where no one would ever go again. In all of history, he would be the only human being to visit the southern regions of Rama. Whenever he felt fear brushing against his mind, he could remember that.

He had now grown accustomed to sitting in mid-air, with the world wrapped around him. Because he had dropped two kilometres below the central axis, he had acquired a definite sense of 'up' and 'down'. The ground was only six kilometres below, but the arch of the sky was ten kilometres overhead. The 'city' of London was hanging up there near the zenith; New York, on the other hand, was the right way up, directly ahead.

'*Dragonfly*,' said Hub Control, 'you're getting a little low. Twenty-two hundred metres from the axis.'

'Thanks,' he replied. 'I'll gain altitude. Let me know when I'm back at twenty.'

This was something he'd have to watch. There was a natural tendency to lose height – and he had no instruments to tell him exactly where he was. If he got too far away from the zero-gravity of the axis, he might never be able to climb back to it. Fortunately, there was a wide margin for error, and there was always someone watching his progress through a telescope at the Hub.

He was now well out over the Sea, pedalling along at a steady twenty kilometres an hour. In five minutes, he would be over New York; already the island looked rather like a ship, sailing for ever round and round the Cylindrical Sea.

When he reached New York, he flew a circle over it, stopping several times so that his little TV camera could send back steady, vibration-free images. The panorama of buildings, towers, industrial plants, power stations – or whatever they were – was fascinating but essentially meaningless. No matter how long he stared at its complexity, he was unlikely to learn anything. The camera would record far more details than he could possibly assimilate; and one day – perhaps years hence – some student might find in them the key to Rama's secrets.

After leaving New York, he crossed the other half of the Sea in only fifteen minutes. Though he was not aware of it, he had been flying fast over water, but as soon as he reached the south coast he unconsciously relaxed and his speed dropped by several kilometres an hour. He might be in wholly alien territory – but at least he was over land.

As soon as he had crossed the great cliff that formed the Sea's southern limit, he panned the TV camera completely round the circle of the world.

'Beautiful!' said Hub Control. 'This will keep the map-makers happy. How are you feeling?'

'I'm fine – just a little fatigue, but no more than I expected. How far do you make me from the Pole?'

'Fifteen point six kilometres.'

'Tell me when I'm at ten; I'll take a rest then. And make sure I don't get low again. I'll start climbing when I've five to go.'

Twenty minutes later the world was closing in upon him; he had come to the end of the cylindrical section, and was entering the southern dome.

He had studied it for hours through the telescopes at the other end of Rama, and had learned its geography by heart. Even so, that had not fully prepared him for the spectacle all around him.

In almost every way the southern and northern ends of Rama differed completely. Here was no triad of stairways, no series of narrow, concentric plateaux, no sweeping curve from hub to plain. Instead, there was an immense central spike, more than five kilometres long, extending along the axis. Six smaller ones, half this size, were equally spaced around it; the whole assembly looked like a group of remarkable symmetrical stalactites, hanging from the roof of a cave. Or, inverting the point of view, the spires of some Cambodian temple, set at the bottom of a crater ...

Linking these slender, tapering towers, and curving down from them to merge eventually in the cylindrical plain, were flying buttresses that looked massive enough to bear the weight of a world. And this, perhaps, was their function, if they were indeed the elements of some exotic drive units, as some had suggested.

Lieutenant Pak approached the central spike cautiously,

stopped pedalling while he was still a hundred metres away, and let *Dragonfly* drift to rest. He checked the radiation level, and found only Rama's very low background. There might be forces at work here which no human instruments could detect, but that was another unavoidable risk.

'What can you see?' Hub Control asked anxiously.

'Just Big Horn – it's absolutely smooth – no markings – and the point's so sharp you could use it as a needle. I'm almost scared to go near it.'

He was only half joking. It seemed incredible that so massive an object should taper to such a geometrically perfect point. Jimmy had seen collections of insects impaled upon pins, and he had no desire for his own *Dragonfly* to meet a similar fate.

He pedalled slowly forward until the spike had flared out to several metres in diameter, then stopped again. Opening a small container, he rather gingerly extracted a sphere about as big as a baseball, and tossed it towards the spike. As it drifted away, it played out a barely visible thread.

The sticky-bomb hit the smoothly curving surface – and did not rebound. Jimmy gave the thread an experimental twitch, then a harder tug. Like a fisherman hauling in his catch, he slowly wound *Dragonfly* across to the tip of the appropriately christened 'Big Horn', until he was able to put out his hand and make contact with it.

'I suppose you could call this some kind of touchdown,' he reported to Hub Control. 'It feels like glass – almost friction-less, and slightly warm. The sticky-bomb worked fine. Now I'm trying the mike … let's see if the suction pad holds as well … plugging in the leads … anything coming through?

There was a long pause from the Hub; then Control said disgustedly: 'Not a damn thing, except the usual thermal noises. Will you tap it with a piece of metal? Then at least we'll find if it's hollow.'

'OK. Now what?'

'We'd like you to fly along the spike, making a complete scan every half-kilometre, and looking out for anything unusual. Then, if you're sure it's safe, you might go across to one of the Little Horns. But only if you're certain you can get back to zero gee without any problems.'

'Three kilometres from the axis – that's slightly above lunar gravity. *Dragonfly* was designed for that. I'll just have to work harder.'

'Jimmy, this is the Captain. I've got second thoughts on that. Judging by your pictures, the smaller spikes are just the same as the big one. Get the best coverage of them you can with the zoom lens. I don't want you leaving the low-gravity region ... unless you see something that looks very important. Then we'll talk it over.'

'OK, Skipper,' said Jimmy, and perhaps there was just a trace of relief in his voice. 'I'll stay close to Big Horn. Here we go again.'

He felt he was dropping straight downwards into a narrow valley between a group of incredibly tall and slender mountains. Big Horn now towered a kilometre above him, and the six spikes of the Little Horns were looming up all around. The complex of buttresses and flying arches which surrounded the lower slopes was approaching rapidly; he wondered if he could make a safe landing somewhere down there in that Cyclopean architecture. He could no longer land on Big Horn itself, for the gravity on its widening slopes was now too powerful to be counteracted by the feeble force of the sticky-bomb.

As he came even closer to the South Pole, he began to feel more and more like a sparrow flying beneath the vaulted roof of some great cathedral – though no cathedral ever built had been even one hundredth the size of this place. He wondered if it was indeed a religious shrine, or something remotely analogous, but quickly dismissed the idea. Nowhere in Rama had there been any trace of artistic expression; everything was purely functional. Perhaps the Ramans felt that they already knew the ultimate secrets of the universe, and were no longer haunted by the yearnings and aspirations that drove mankind.

That was a chilling thought, quite alien to Jimmy's usual not-very-profound philosophy; he felt an urgent need to resume contact, and reported his situation back to his distant friends.

'Say again, *Dragonfly*,' replied Hub Control. 'We can't understand you – your transmission is garbled.'

'I repeat – I'm near the base of Little Horn number Six, and am using the sticky-bomb to haul myself in.'

'Understand only partially. Can you hear me?'

'Yes, perfectly. Repeat, perfectly.'

'Please start counting numbers.'

'One, two, three, four ...'

'Got part of that. Give us beacon for fifteen seconds, then go back to voice.'

'Here it is.'

Jimmy switched on the low-powered beacon which would locate him anywhere inside Rama, and counted off the seconds. When he went over to voice again he asked plaintively: 'What's happening? Can you hear me now?'

Presumably Hub didn't, because the controller then asked for fifteen seconds of TV. Not until Jimmy had repeated the question twice did the message get through.

'Glad you can hear us OK, Jimmy. But there's something very peculiar happening at your end. Listen.'

Over the radio, he heard the familiar whistle of his own beacon, played back to him. For a moment it was perfectly normal; then a weird distortion crept into it. The thousand-cycle whistle became modulated by a deep, throbbing pulse so low that it was almost beneath the threshold of hearing; it was a kind of *basso-profundo* flutter in which each individual vibration could be heard. And the modulation was itself modulated; it rose and fell, rose and fell with a period of about five seconds.

Never for a moment did it occur to Jimmy that there was something wrong with his radio transmitter. This was from outside; though what it was, and what it meant, was beyond his imagination.

Hub Control was not much wiser, but at least it had a theory.

'We think you must be in some kind of very intense field – probably magnetic – with a frequency of about ten cycles. It may be strong enough to be dangerous. Suggest you get out right away – it may only be local. Switch on your beacon again, and we'll play it back to you. Then you can tell when you're getting clear of the interference.'

Jimmy hastily jerked the sticky-bomb loose and abandoned his attempt to land. He swung *Dragonfly* round in a wide circle, listening as he did so to the sound that wavered in his earphones. After flying only a few metres, he could tell that its intensity was falling rapidly; as Hub Control had guessed, it was extremely localized.

He paused for a moment at the last spot where he could hear it, like a faint throbbing deep in his brain. So might a primitive savage have listened in awestruck ignorance to the low humming of a giant power transformer. And even the savage might have guessed that the sound he heard was merely the stray leakage from colossal energies, fully controlled, but biding their time . . .

Whatever this sound meant, Jimmy was glad to be clear of it. This was no place, among the overwhelming architecture of the South Pole, for a lone man to listen to the voice of Rama.

27
Electric Wind

As Jimmy turned homewards, the northern end of Rama seemed incredibly far away. Even the three giant stairways were barely visible, as a faint Y etched on the dome that closed the world. The band of the Cylindrical Sea was a wide and menacing barrier, waiting to swallow him up if, like Icarus, his fragile wings should fail.

But he had come all this way with no problems, and though he was feeling slightly tired he now felt that he had nothing to worry about. He had not even touched his food or water, and had been too excited to rest. On the return journey, he would relax and take it easy. He was also cheered by the thought that the homeward trip could be twenty kilometres shorter than the outward one, for as long as he cleared the Sea, he could make an emergency landing anywhere in the northern continent. That would be a nuisance, because he would have a long walk – and much worse, would have to abandon *Dragonfly* – but it gave him a very comforting safety margin.

He was now gaining altitude, climbing back towards the central spike; Big Horn's tapering needle still stretched for a kilometre ahead of him, and sometimes he felt it was the axis on which this whole world turned.

He had almost reached the tip of Big Horn when he became aware of a curious sensation; a feeling of foreboding, and indeed of physical as well as psychological discomfort, had come over him. He suddenly recalled – and this did nothing at all to help

– a phrase he had once come across: '*Someone is walking over your grave.*'

At first he shrugged it off, and continued his steady pedalling. He certainly had no intention of reporting anything as tenuous as a vague malaise to Hub Control, but as it grew steadily worse he was tempted to do so. It could not possibly be psychological; if it was, his mind was much more powerful than he realised. For he could, quite literally, feel his skin beginning to crawl ...

Now seriously alarmed, he stopped in mid-air and began to consider the situation. What made it all the more peculiar was the fact that this depressed heavy feeling was not completely novel; he had known it before, but could not remember where.

He looked around him. Nothing had changed. The great spike of Big Horn was a few hundred metres above, with the other side of Rama spanning the sky beyond that. Eight kilometres below lay the complicated patchwork of the Southern continent, full of wonders that no other man would ever see. In all the utterly alien yet now familiar landscape, he could find no cause for his discomfort.

Something was tickling the back of his hand; for a moment, he thought an insect had landed there, and brushed it away without looking. He had only half-completed the swift motion when he realised what he was doing and checked himself, feeling slightly foolish. Of course, no one had ever seen an insect in Rama ...

He lifted his hand, and stared at it, mildly puzzled because the tickling sensation was still there. It was then that he noticed that every individual hair was standing straight upright. All the way up his forearm it was the same – and so it was with his head, when he checked with an exploring hand.

So *that* was the trouble. He was in a tremendously powerful electric field; the oppressed, heavy sensation he had felt was that which sometimes precedes a thunderstorm on Earth.

The sudden realisation of his predicament brought Jimmy

very near to panic. Never before in his life had he been in real physical danger. Like all spacemen, he had known moments of frustration with bulky equipment, and times when, owing to mistakes or inexperience, he had wrongly believed he was in a perilous situation. But none of these episodes had lasted more than a few minutes, and usually he was able to laugh at them almost at once.

This time there was no quick way out. He felt naked and alone in a suddenly hostile sky, surrounded by titanic forces which might discharge their furies at any moment. *Dragonfly* – already fragile enough – now seemed more insubstantial than the finest gossamer. The first detonation of the gathering storm would blast her to fragments.

'Hub Control,' he said urgently. 'There's a static charge building up around me. I think there's going to be a thunderstorm at any moment.'

He had barely finished speaking when there was a flicker of light behind him; by the time he had counted ten, the first crackling rumble arrived. Three kilometres – that put it back around the Little Horns. He looked towards them and saw that every one of the six needles seemed to be on fire. Brush discharges, hundreds of metres long, were dancing from their points, as if they were giant lightning conductors.

What was happening back there could take place on an even larger scale near the tapering spike of Big Horn. His best move would be to get as far as possible from this dangerous structure, and to seek clear air. He started to pedal again, accelerating as swiftly as he could without putting too great a strain on *Dragonfly*. At the same time he began to lose altitude; even though this would mean entering the region of higher gravity, he was now prepared to take such a risk. Eight kilometres was much too far from the ground for his peace of mind.

The ominous black spike of Big Horn was still free of visible discharges, but he did not doubt that tremendous potentials were building up there. From time to time the thunder still reverberated behind him, rolling round and round the circumference of the world. It suddenly occurred to Jimmy how strange it was to have such a storm in a perfectly clear sky; then he realised that this was not a meteorological phenomenon at all. In fact, it might be only a trivial leakage of energy from some hidden source, deep in the southern cap of Rama. But why *now*? And, even more important – *what next*?

He was now well past the tip of Big Horn, and hoped that he would soon be beyond the range of any lightning discharges. But now he had another problem; the air was becoming turbulent, and he had difficulty in controlling *Dragonfly*. A wind seemed to have sprung up from nowhere, and if conditions became much worse the bike's fragile skeleton would be endangered. He pedalled grimly on, trying to smooth out the buffeting by variations in power and movements of his body. Because *Dragonfly* was almost an extension of himself, he was partly successful; but he did not like the faint creaks of protest that came from the main spar, nor the way in which the wings twisted with every gust.

And there was something else that worried him – a faint rushing sound, steadily growing in strength, that seemed to come from the direction of Big Horn. It sounded like gas escaping from a valve under pressure, and he wondered if it had anything to do with the turbulence which he was battling. Whatever its cause, it gave him yet further grounds for disquiet.

From time to time he reported these phenomena, rather briefly and breathlessly, to Hub Control. No one there could give him any advice, or even suggest what might be happening; but it was reassuring to hear the voices of his friends, even though he was now beginning to fear that he would never see them again.

The turbulence was still increasing. It almost felt as if he was entering a jet stream – which he had once done, in search of a record, while flying a high-altitude glider on Earth. But what could possible create a jet stream inside Rama?

He had asked himself the right question; as soon as he had formulated it, he knew the answer.

The sound he had heard was the electric wind carrying away the tremendous ionisation that must be building up around Big Horn. Charged air was spraying out along the axis of Rama, and more air was flowing into the low-pressure region behind. He looked back at that gigantic and now doubly threatening needle, trying to visualise the boundaries of the gale that was blowing from it. Perhaps the best tactic would be to fly by ear, getting as far as possible away from the ominous hissing.

Rama spared him the necessity of choice. A sheet of flame burst out behind him, filling the sky. He had time to see it split into six ribbons of fire, stretching from the tip of Big Horn to each of the Little Horns. Then the concussion reached him.

28
Icarus

Jimmy Pak had barely time to radio: 'The wing's buckling – I'm going to crash – I'm going to crash!' when *Dragonfly* started to fold up gracefully around him. The left wing snapped cleanly in the middle, and the outer section drifted away like a gently falling leaf. The right wing put up a more complicated performance. It twisted round at the root, and angled back so sharply that its tip became entangled in the tail. Jimmy felt that he was sitting in a broken kite, slowly falling down the sky.

Yet he was not quite helpless; the airscrew still worked, and while he had power there was still some measure of control. He had perhaps five minutes in which to use it.

Was there any hope of reaching the Sea? No – it was much too far away. Then he remembered that he was still thinking in terrestrial terms; though he was a good swimmer, it would be hours before he could possibly be rescued, and in that time the poisonous waters would undoubtedly have killed him. His only hope was to come down on land; the problem of the sheer southern cliff he would think about later – if there was any 'later'.

He was falling very slowly, here in this tenth-of-a-gravity zone, but would soon start to accelerate as he got further away from the axis. However, air-drag would complicate the situation, and would prevent him from building up too swift a rate of descent. *Dragonfly*, even without power, would act as a crude parachute. The few kilogrammes of thrust he could still provide might make all the difference between life and death; that was his only hope.

Hub had stopped talking; his friends could see exactly what was happening to him and knew that there was no way their words could help. Jimmy was now doing the most skilful flying of his life; it was too bad, he thought with grim humour, that his audience was so small, and could not appreciate the finer details of his performance.

He was going down in a wide spiral, and as long as its pitch remained fairly flat his chances of survival were good. His pedalling was helping to keep *Dragonfly* airborne, though he was afraid to exert maximum power in case the broken wings came completely adrift. And every time he swung southwards, he could appreciate the fantastic display that Rama had kindly arranged for his benefit.

The streamers of lightning still played from the tip of Big Horn down to the lesser peaks beneath, but now the whole pattern was rotating. The six-pronged crown of fire was turning against the spin of Rama, making one revolution every few seconds. Jimmy felt that he was watching a giant electric motor in operation, and perhaps that was not hopelessly far from the truth.

He was halfway down to the plain, still orbiting in a flat spiral, when the firework display suddenly ceased. He could feel the tension drain from the sky and knew, without looking, that the hairs on his arms were no longer straining upright. There was nothing to distract or hinder him now, during the last few minutes of his fight for life.

Now that he could be certain of the general area in which he must land, he started to study it intently. Much of this region was a checkerboard of totally conflicting environments, as if a mad landscape gardener had been given a free hand and told to exercise his imagination to the utmost. The squares of the checkerboard were almost a kilometre on a side, and though most of them were flat he could not be sure if they were solid, their colours and textures varied so greatly. He decided to wait until the last possible minute before making a decision – if indeed he had any choice.

When there were a few hundred metres to go, he made a last call to the Hub.

'I've still got some control – will be down in half a minute – will call you then.'

That was optimistic, and everyone knew it. But he refused to say goodbye; he wanted his comrades to know that he had gone down fighting, and without fear.

Indeed, he felt very little fear, and this surprised him, for he had never thought of himself as a particularly brave man. It was almost as if he was watching the struggles of a complete stranger, and was not himself personally involved. Rather, he was studying an interesting problem in aerodynamics, and changing various parameters to see what would happen. Almost the only emotion he felt was a certain remote regret for lost opportunities – of which the most important was the forthcoming Lunar Olympics. One future at least was decided; *Dragonfly* would never show her paces on the Moon.

A hundred metres to go; his ground speed seemed acceptable, but how fast was he falling? And here was one piece of luck – the terrain was completely flat. He would put forth all his strength in a final burst of power, starting – NOW!

The right wing, having done its duty, finally tore off at the roots. *Dragonfly* started to roll over, and he tried to correct by throwing the weight of his body against the spin. He was looking directly at the curving arch of landscape sixteen kilometres away when he hit.

It seemed altogether unfair and unreasonable that the sky should be so hard.

29
First Contact

When Jimmy Pak returned to consciousness, the first thing he became aware of was a splitting headache. He almost welcomed it; at least it proved that he was still alive.

Then he tried to move, and at once a wide selection of aches and pains brought themselves to his attention. But as far as he could tell, nothing seemed to be broken.

After that, he risked opening his eyes, but closed them at once when he found himself staring straight into the band of light along the ceiling of the world. As a cure for headache, that view was not recommended.

He was still lying there, regaining his strength and wondering how soon it would be safe to open his eyes, when there was a sudden crunching noise from close at hand. Turning his head very slowly towards the source of the sound, he risked a look – and almost lost consciousness again.

Not more than five metres away, a large crab-like creature was apparently dining on the wreckage of poor *Dragonfly*. When Jimmy recovered his wits he rolled slowly and quietly away from the monster, expecting at every moment to be seized by its claws, when it discovered that more appetizing fare was available. However, it took not the slightest notice of him; when he had increased their mutual separation to ten metres, he cautiously propped himself up in a sitting position.

From this greater distance, the thing did not appear quite so formidable. It had a low, flat body about two metres long and one wide, supported on six triple-jointed legs. Jimmy saw that he was mistaken in assuming that it had been eating *Dragonfly*; in fact, he could not see any sign of a mouth. The creature was actually doing a neat job of demolition, using scissor-like claws to chop the sky-bike into small pieces. A whole row of manipulators, which looked uncannily like tiny human hands, then transferred the fragments to a steadily growing pile on the animal's back.

But *was* it an animal? Though that had been Jimmy's first reaction, now he had second thoughts. There was a purposeful-ness about its behaviour which suggested fairly high intelligence; he could see no reason why any creature of pure instincts should carefully collect the scattered pieces of his sky-bike – unless, perhaps, it was gathering material for a nest.

Keeping a wary eye on the crab, which still ignored him completely, Jimmy struggled to his feet. A few wavering steps demonstrated that he could still walk, though he was not sure if he would outdistance those six legs. Then he switched on his radio, never doubting that it would be operating. A crash that *he* could survive would not even have been noticed by its solid-state electronics.

'Hub Control,' he said softly. 'Can you receive me?'

'Thank God! Are you OK?'

'Just a bit shaken. Take a look at this.'

He turned his camera towards the crab, just in time to record the final demolition of *Dragonfly*'s wing.

'What the devil is it – and why is it chewing up your bike?'

'Wish I knew. It's finished with *Dragonfly*. I'm going to back away, in case it wants to start on me.'

Jimmy slowly retreated, never taking his eyes off the crab. It was now moving round and round in a steadily widening spiral, apparently searching for fragments it might have overlooked, and so Jimmy was able to get an overall view of it for the first time.

Now that the initial shock had worn off, he could appreciate that it was quite a handsome beast. The name 'crab' which he had automatically given it was perhaps a little misleading; if it had not been so impossibly large, he might have called it a beetle. Its carapace had a beautiful metallic sheen; in fact, he would almost have been prepared to swear that it *was* metal.

That was an interesting idea. Could it be a robot, and not an animal? He stared at the crab intently with this thought in mind, analysing all the details of its anatomy. Where it should have had a mouth was a collection of manipulators that reminded Jimmy strongly of the multi-purpose knives that are the delight of all red-blooded boys; there were pinchers, probes, rasps and even something that looked like a drill. But none of this was decisive. On Earth, the insect world had matched all these tools, and many more. The animal-or-robot question remained in perfect balance in his mind.

The eyes, which might have settled the matter, left it even more ambiguous. They were so deeply recessed in protective hoods that it was impossible to tell whether their lenses were made of crystal or jelly. They were quite expressionless, and of a startlingly vivid blue. Though they had been directed towards Jimmy several times, they had never shown the slightest flicker of interest. In his perhaps biased opinion, that decided the level of the creature's intelligence. An entity – robot or animal – which could ignore a human being could not be very bright.

It had now stopped its circling, and stood still for a few seconds, as if listening to some inaudible message. Then it set off, with a curious rolling gait, in the general direction of the Sea. It moved in a perfectly straight line at a steady four or five kilometres an hour, and had already travelled a couple of hundred metres before Jimmy's still slightly-shocked mind registered the fact that the last sad relics of his beloved *Dragonfly* were being carried away from him. He set off in a hot and indignant pursuit.

His action was not wholly illogical. The crab was heading towards the Sea – and if any rescue was possible, it could only be from this direction. Moreover, he wanted to discover what the creature would do with its trophy; that should reveal something about its motivation and intelligence.

Because he was still bruised and stiff, it took Jimmy several minutes to catch up with the purposefully-moving crab. When he had done so, he followed it at a respectful distance, until he felt sure that it did not resent his presence. It was then that he noticed his water-flask and emergency ration pack among the debris of *Dragonfly*, and instantly felt both hungry and thirsty.

There, scuttling away from him at a remorseless five kilometres an hour, was the only food and drink in all this half of the world. Whatever the risk, he had to get hold of it.

He cautiously closed in on the crab, approaching from right rear. While he kept station with it, he studied the complicated rhythm of its legs, until he could anticipate where they would be at any moment. When he was ready, he muttered a quick 'Excuse *me*,' and shot swiftly in to grab his property. Jimmy had never dreamed that he would one day have to exercise the skills of a pickpocket, and was delighted with his success. He was out again in less than a second, and the crab never slackened its steady pace.

He dropped back a dozen metres, moistened his lips from the flask, and started to chew a bar of meat concentrate. The little victory made him feel much happier; now he could even risk thinking about his sombre future.

While there was life, there was hope; yet he could imagine no way in which he could possibly be rescued. Even if his colleagues crossed the Sea, how could he reach them, half a kilometre below? 'We'll find a way down *somehow*,' Hub Control had promised. 'That cliff can't go right round the world, without a break anywhere.' He had been tempted to answer 'Why not?', but had thought better of it.

One of the strangest things about walking inside Rama was that you could always see your destination. Here, the curve of the world did not hide – it *revealed*. For some time Jimmy had been aware of the crab's objective; up there in the land which seemed to rise before him was a half-kilometre-wide pit. It was one of three in the southern continent; from the Hub, it had been impossible to see how deep they were. All had been named after prominent lunar craters, and he was approaching Copernicus. The name was hardly appropriate, for there were no surrounding hills and no central peaks. This Copernicus was merely a deep shaft or well, with perfectly vertical sides.

When he came close enough to look into it, Jimmy was able to see a pool of ominous, leaden-green water at least half a kilometre below. This would put it just about level with the Sea, and he wondered if they were connected.

Winding down the interior of the well was a spiral ramp, completely recessed into the sheer wall, so that the effect was rather like that of rifling in an immense gun-barrel. There seemed to be a remarkable number of turns; not until Jimmy had traced them for several revolutions, getting more and more confused in the process, did he realise that there was not one ramp but *three*, totally independent and 120 degrees apart. In any other background than Rama, the whole concept would have been an impressive architectural *tour de force*.

The three ramps led straight down into the pool and disappeared beneath its opaque surface. Near the waterline Jimmy could see a group of black tunnels or caves; they looked rather sinister, and he wondered if they were inhabited. Perhaps the Ramans were amphibious …

As the crab approached the edge of the well, Jimmy assumed that it was going to descend one of the ramps – perhaps taking the wreckage of *Dragonfly* to some entity who would be able to evaluate it. Instead, the creature walked straight to the brink, extended almost half its body over the gulf without any sign of hesitation, though an error of a few centimetres would have been disastrous – and gave a brisk shrug. The fragments of *Dragonfly* went fluttering down into the depths; there were tears in Jimmy's eyes as he watched them go. So much, he thought bitterly, for *this* creature's intelligence.

Having disposed of the garbage, the crab swung around and started to walk towards Jimmy, standing only about ten metres away. Am I going to get the same treatment? He wondered. He hoped the camera was not too unsteady as he showed Hub Control the rapidly approaching monster. 'What do you advise?' he whispered anxiously, without much hope that he would get a useful answer. It was some small consolation to realise that he was making history, and his mind raced through the approved patterns for such a meeting. Until now, all of these had been purely theoretical. He would be the first man to check them in practice.

'Don't run until you're sure it's hostile', Hub Control whispered back at him. Run where? Jimmy asked himself. He thought he could out-distance the thing in a hundred metre sprint, but had a sick certainty that it could wear him down over the long haul.

Slowly, Jimmy held up his outstretched hands. Men had been arguing for two hundred years about this gesture; would every creature, everywhere in the universe, interpret this as 'See – no weapons?' But no one could think of anything better.

The crab showed no reaction whatsoever, nor did it slacken its pace. Ignoring Jimmy completely, it walked straight past him and headed purposefully into the south. Feeling extremely foolish, the acting representative of *Homo sapiens* watched his First Contact stride away across the Raman plain, totally indifferent to his presence.

He had seldom been so humiliated in his life. Then Jimmy's sense of humour came to his rescue. After all, it was no great matter to have been ignored by an animated garbage truck.

It would have been worse if it had greeted him as a long-lost brother ...

He walked back to the rim of Copernicus, and stared down into its opaque waters. For the first time, he noticed that vague shapes – some of them quite large – were moving slowly back and forth beneath the surface. Presently one of them headed towards the nearest spiral ramp, and something that looked like a multi-legged tank started on the long ascent. At the rate it was going, Jimmy decided, it would take almost an hour to get here; if it was a threat, it was a very slow-moving one.

Then he noticed a flicker of much more rapid movement, near those cave-like openings down by the waterline. Something was travelling very swiftly along the ramp, but he could not focus clearly upon it, or discern any definite shape. It was as if he was looking at a small whirlwind or 'dust-devil', about the size of a man ...

He blinked and shook his head, keeping his eyes closed for several seconds. When he opened them again, the apparition was gone.

Perhaps the impact had shaken him up more than he had realised; this was the first time he had ever suffered from visual hallucinations. He would not mention it to Hub Control.

Nor would he bother to explore those ramps, as he had half-thought of doing. It would obviously be a waste of energy.

The spinning phantom he had merely imagined seeing had nothing to do with his decision.

Nothing at all; for, of course, Jimmy did not believe in ghosts.

30
The Flower

Jimmy's exertions had made him thirsty, and he was acutely conscious of the fact that in all this land there was no water that a man could drink. With the contents of his flask, he could probably survive a week – but for what purpose? The best brains of Earth would soon be focused on his problem; doubtless Commander Norton would be bombarded with suggestions. But he could imagine no way in which he could lower himself down the face of that half-kilometre cliff. Even it he had a long rough rope, there was nothing to which he could attach it.

Nevertheless, it was foolish – and unmanly – to give up without a struggle. Any help would have to come from the Sea, and while he was marching towards it he could carry on with his job as if nothing had happened. No one else would ever observe and photograph the varied terrain through which he must pass, and that would guarantee a posthumous immortality. Though he would have preferred many other honours, that was better than nothing.

He was only three kilometres from the Sea as poor *Dragonfly* could have flown, but it seemed unlikely that he could reach it in a straight line; some of the terrain ahead of him might prove too great an obstacle. That was no problem, however, as there were plenty of alternative routes. Jimmy could see them all, spread out on the great curving map that swept up and away from him on either side.

He had plenty of time; he would start with the most interesting scenery, even if it took him off his direct route. About a kilometre away towards the right was a square that glittered like cut glass – or a gigantic display of jewellery. It was probably this thought that triggered Jimmy's footsteps. Even a doomed man might reasonably be expected to take some slight interest in a few thousand square metres of gems.

He was not particularly disappointed when they turned out to be quartz crystals, millions of them, set in a bed of sand. The adjacent square of the checkerboard was rather more interesting, being covered with an apparently random pattern of hollow metal columns, set very close together and ranging in height from less than one to more than five metres. It was completely impassable; only a tank could have crashed through that forest of tubes.

Jimmy walked between the crystals and the columns until he came to the first crossroads. The square on the right was a huge rug or tapestry made of woven wire; he tried to prise a strand loose, but was unable to break it.

On the left was a tessellation of hexagonal tiles, so smoothly inlaid that there were no visible joints between them. It would have appeared a continuous surface, had the tiles not been coloured all the hues of the rainbow. Jimmy spent many minutes trying to find two adjacent tiles of the same colour, to see if he could then distinguish their boundaries, but he could not find a single example of such coincidence.

As he did a slow pan right around the crossroads, he said plaintively to Hub Control: 'What do *you* think this is? I feel I'm trapped in a giant jigsaw puzzle. Or is this the Raman Art Gallery?'

'We're as baffled as you, Jimmy. But there's never been any sign that the Ramans go in for art. Let's wait until we have some more examples before we jump to any conclusions.'

The two examples he found at the next crossroads were not much help. One was completely blank – a smooth, neutral grey, hard but slippery to the touch. The other was a soft sponge, perforated with billions upon billions of tiny holes. He tested it with his foot, and the whole surface undulated sickeningly beneath him like a barely stabilised quicksand.

At the next cross-roads he encountered something strikingly like a ploughed field – except that the furrows were a uniform metre in depth, and the material of which they were made had the texture of a file or rasp. But he paid little attention to this, because the square adjacent to it was the most thought-provoking of all that he had so far met. At last there was something that he could understand; and it was more than a little disturbing.

The entire square was surrounded by a fence, so conventional that he would not have looked at it twice had he seen it on Earth. There were posts – apparently of metal – five metres apart, with six strands of wire strung taut between them.

Beyond this fence was a second, identical one – and beyond that, a third. It was another typical example of Raman redundancy; whatever was penned inside this enclosure would have no chance of breaking out. There was no entrance – no gates that could be swung open to drive in the beast, or beasts, that were presumably kept here. Instead, there was a single hole, like a smaller version of Copernicus, in the centre of the square.

Even in different circumstances, Jimmy would probably not have hesitated, but now he had nothing to lose. He quickly scaled all three fences, walked over to the hole, and peered into it.

Unlike Copernicus, this well was only fifty metres deep. There were three tunnel exits at the bottom, each of which looked large enough to accommodate an elephant. And that was all.

After staring for some time, Jimmy decided that the only thing that made sense about the arrangement was for the floor down there to be an elevator. But *what* it elevated he was never likely to know; he could only guess that it was quite large, and possibly quite dangerous.

During the next few hours, he walked more than ten kilometres along the edge of the Sea, and the checkerboard squares had begun to blur together in his memory. He had seen some that were totally enclosed in tent-like structures of wire mesh, as if they were giant bird-cages. There were others which seemed to be pools of congealed liquid, full of swirl-patterns; however, when he tested them gingerly, they were quite solid. And there was one so utterly black that he could not even see it clearly; only the sense of touch told him that anything was there.

Yet now there was a subtle modulation into something he could understand. Ranging one after the other towards the south was a series of – no other word would do – *fields*. He might have been walking past an experimental farm on Earth; each square was a smooth expanse of carefully levelled earth, the first he had ever seen in the metallic landscapes of Rama.

The great fields were virgin, lifeless – waiting for crops that had never been planted. Jimmy wondered what their purpose could be, since it was incredible that creatures as advanced as the Ramans would engage in any form of agriculture; even on Earth, farming was no more than a popular hobby and a source of exotic luxury foods. But he could swear that these were potential farms, immaculately prepared. He had never seen earth that looked so clean; each square was covered with a great sheet of tough, transparent plastic. He tried to cut through it to obtain a sample, but his knife would barely scratch the surface.

Further inland were other fields, and on many of them were complicated constructions of rods and wires, presumably intended for the support of climbing plants. They looked very bleak and desolate, like leafless trees in the depths of winter. The winter they had known must have been long and terrible indeed, and these few weeks of light and warmth might be only a brief interlude before it came again.

Jimmy never knew what made him stop and look more closely into the metal maze to the south. Unconsciously, his mind must have been checking every detail around him; it had noticed, in this fantastically alien landscape, something even more anomalous.

About a quarter of a kilometre away, in the middle of a trellis of wires and rods, glowed a single speck of colour. It was so small and inconspicuous that it was almost at the limit of visibility; on Earth, no one would have looked at it twice. Yet undoubtedly one of the reasons he had noticed it now was because it reminded him of Earth ...

He did not report to Hub Control until he was sure that there was no mistake, and that wishful thinking had not deluded him. Not until he was only a few metres away could he be completely sure that life as he knew it had intruded into the sterile, aseptic world of Rama. For blooming here in lonely splendour at the edge of the southern continent was a flower.

As he came closer, it was obvious to Jimmy that something had gone wrong. There was a hole in the sheathing that, presumably, protected this layer of earth from contamination by unwanted life-forms. Through this break extended a green stem, about as thick as a man's little finger, which twined its way up through the trellis-work. A metre from the ground it burst into an efflorescence of bluish leaves, shaped more like feathers than the foliage of any plant known to Jimmy. The stem ended, at eye-level, in what he had first taken to be a single flower. Now he saw, with no surprise at all, that it was actually three flowers tightly packed together.

The petals were brightly coloured tubes about five centimetres long; there were at least fifty in each bloom, and they glittered with such metallic blues, violets and greens, that they seemed more like the wings of a butterfly than anything in the vegetable kingdom. Jimmy knew practically nothing about botany, but he was puzzled to see no trace of any structures resembling petals or stamens. He wondered if the likeness to terrestrial flowers might be a pure coincidence; perhaps this was something more akin to a coral polyp. In either case, it would seem to imply the

160

existence of small, airborne creatures to serve either as fertilizing agents – or as food.

It did not really matter. Whatever the scientific definition, to Jimmy this was a flower. The strange miracle, the un-Raman-like accident of its existence here reminded him of all that he would never see again; and he was determined to possess it.

That would not be easy. It was more than ten metres away, separated from him by a lattice-work made of thin rods. They formed a cubic pattern, repeated over and over again, less than forty centimetres on either side. Jimmy would not have been flying sky-bikes unless he had been slim and wiry, so he knew he could crawl through the interstices of the grid. But getting out again might be quite a different matter; it would certainly be impossible for him to turn around, so he would have to retreat backwards.

Hub Control was delighted with his discovery, when he had described the flower and scanned it from every available angle. There was no objection when he said: 'I'm going after it.' Nor did he expect there to be; his life was now his own, to do with as he pleased.

He stripped off all his clothes, grasped the smooth metal rods, and started to wriggle into the framework. It was a tight fit; he felt like a prisoner escaping through the bars of his cell. When he had inserted himself completely into the lattice he tried backing out again, just to see if there were any problems. It was considerably more difficult, since he now had to use his outstretched arms for pushing instead of pulling, but he saw no reason why he should get helplessly trapped.

Jimmy was a man of action and impulse, not of introspection. As he squirmed uncomfortably along the narrow corridor of rods, he wasted no time asking himself just why he was performing so quixotic a feat. He had never been interested in flowers in his whole life, yet now he was gambling his last energies to collect one.

It was true that this specimen was unique, and of enormous scientific value. But he really wanted it because it was his last link with the world of life and the planet of his birth.

Yet when the flower was in his grasp, he had sudden qualms. Perhaps it was the only flower that grew in the whole of Rama; was he justified in picking it?

If he needed any excuse, he could console himself with the thought that the Ramans themselves had not included it in their plans. It was obviously a freak, growing ages too late – or too soon. But he did not really require an excuse, and his hesitation was only momentary. He reached out, grasped the stem, and gave a sharp jerk.

The flower came away easily enough; he also collected two of the leaves, then started to back slowly through the lattice. Now that he had only one free hand, progress was extremely difficult, even painful, and he soon had to pause to regain his breath. It was then that he noticed that the feathery leaves were closing, and the headless stem was slowly unwinding itself from its supports. As he watched with a mixture of fascination and dismay, he saw that the whole plant was steadily retreating into the ground, like a mortally injured snake crawling back into its hole.

I've murdered something beautiful, Jimmy told himself. But then Rama had killed him. He was only collecting what was his rightful due.

31
Terminal Velocity

Commander Norton had never yet lost a man, and he had no intention of starting now. Even before Jimmy had set off for the South Pole, he had been considering ways of rescuing him in the event of accident; the problem, however, had turned out to be so difficult that he had found no answer. All that he had managed to do was to eliminate every obvious solution.

How does one climb a half-kilometre vertical cliff; even in reduced gravity? With the right equipment – and training – it would be easy enough. But there were no piton-guns aboard *Endeavour*, and no one could think of any other practical way of driving the necessary hundreds of spikes into that hard, mirror surface.

He had glanced briefly at more exotic solutions, some frankly crazy. Perhaps a simp, fitted with suction pads, could make the ascent. But even if this scheme was practical, how long would it take to manufacture and text such equipment – and to train a simp to use it? He doubted if a man would have the necessary strength to perform the feat.

Then there was more advanced technology. The EVA propulsion units were tempting, but their thrust was too small, since they were designed for zero-gee operation. They could not possibly lift the weight of a man, even against Rama's modest gravity.

Could an EVA thrust be sent up on automatic control, carrying only a rescue line? He had tried out this idea on Sergeant

Myron, who had promptly shot it down in flames. There were, the engineer pointed out, severe stability problems; they might be solved, but it would take a long time – much longer than they could afford.

What about balloons? There seemed a faint possibility here, if they could devise an envelope and a sufficiently compact source of heat. This was the only approach that Norton had not dismissed, when the problem suddenly ceased to be one of theory, and became a matter of life and death, dominating the news in all the inhabited worlds.

While Jimmy was making his trek along the edge of the Sea, half the crackpots in the solar system were trying to save him. At Fleet Headquarters, all the suggestions were considered, and about one in a thousand was forwarded to *Endeavour*. Dr Carlisle Perera's arrived twice – once via the Survey's own network, and once by PLANETCOM, RAMA PRIORITY. It had taken the scientist approximately five minutes of thought and one millisecond of computer time.

At first, Commander Norton thought it was a joke in very poor taste. Then he saw the sender's name and the attached calculations, and did a quick double-take.

He handed the message to Karl Mercer.

'What do you think of this?' he asked, in as non-committal a tone of voice as he could manage.

Karl read it swiftly, then said, 'Well I'm damned! He's right, of course.'

'Are you *sure*?'

'He was right about the storm, wasn't he? We should have thought of this; it makes me feel a fool.'

'You have company. The next problem is – how do we break it to Jimmy?'

'I don't think we should ... until the last possible minute. That's how I'd prefer it, if I was in his place. Just tell him we're on the way.'

*

Though he could look across the full width of the Cylindrical Sea, and knew the general direction from which *Resolution* was coming. Jimmy did not spot the tiny craft until it had already passed New York. It seemed incredible that it could carry six men – and whatever equipment they had brought to rescue him.

When it was only a kilometre away, he recognised Commander Norton, and started waving. A little later the skipper spotted him, and waved back.

'Glad to see you're in good shape, Jimmy,' he radioed. 'I promised we wouldn't leave you behind. Now do you believe me?'

Not quite, Jimmy thought; until this moment he had still wondered if this was all a kindly plot to keep up his morale. But the Commander would not have crossed the Sea just to say goodbye; he must have worked out *something*.

'I'll believe you, Skipper,' he said, 'when I'm down there on the deck. *Now* will you tell me how I'm going to make it?'

Resolution was now slowing down, a hundred metres from the base of the cliff; as far as Jimmy could tell, she carried no unusual equipment – though he was not sure what he had expected to see.

'Sorry about that, Jimmy – but we didn't want you to have too many things to worry about.'

Now *that* sounded ominous; what the devil did he mean?

Resolution came to a halt, fifty metres out and five hundred below; Jimmy had almost a bird's-eye view of the Commander as he spoke into his microphone.

'This is it, Jimmy. You'll be perfectly safe, but it will require nerve. We know you've got plenty of that. *You're going to jump.*'

'Five hundred metres!'

'Yes, but at only half a gee.'

'So – have you ever fallen two hundred and fifty on Earth?'

'Shut up, or I'll cancel your next leave. You should have worked this out for yourself … it's just a question of terminal velocity. In this atmosphere, you can't reach more than ninety kilometres an hour – whether you fall two hundred or two thousand metres. Ninety's a little high for comfort, but we can trim it some more. This is what you'll have to do, so listen carefully …'

'I will,' said Jimmy. 'It had better be good.'

He did not interrupt the Commander again, and made no comment when Norton had finished. Yes, it made sense, and was so absurdly simple that it would take a genius to think of it. And, perhaps, someone who did not expect to do it himself …

Jimmy had never tried high-diving, or made a delayed parachute drop, which would have given him some psychological preparation for this feat. One could tell a man that it was perfectly safe to walk a plank across an abyss – yet even if the structural calculations were impeccable, he might still be unable to do it. Now Jimmy understood why the Commander had been so evasive about the details of the rescue. He had been given no time to brood, or to think of objections.

'I don't want to hurry you,' said Norton's persuasive voice from half a kilometre below. 'But the sooner the better.'

Jimmy looked at his precious souvenir, the only flower in Rama. He wrapped it very carefully in his grimy handkerchief, knotted the fabric, and tossed it over the edge of the cliff.

It fluttered down with reassuring slowness, but it also took a very long time getting smaller, and smaller, and smaller, until he could no longer see it. But then *Resolution* surged forward, and he knew that it had been spotted.

'Beautiful!' exclaimed the Commander enthusiastically. 'I'm sure they'll name it after you. OK – we're waiting …

Jimmy stripped off his shirt – the only upper garment anyone ever wore in this now tropical climate – and stretched it thoughtfully. Several times on his trek he had almost discarded it; now it might help to save his life.

For the last time, he looked back at the hollow world he alone had explored, and the distant, ominous pinnacles of the Big and Little Horns. Then, grasping the shirt firmly with his right hand, he took a running jump as far out over the cliff as he could.

Now there was no particular hurry; he had a full twenty seconds in which to enjoy the experience. But he did not waste any time, as the wind strengthened around him and *Resolution* slowly expanded in his field of view. Holding his shirt with both hands, he stretched his arms above his head, so that the rushing air filled the garment and blew it into a hollow tube.

As a parachute, it was hardly a success; the few kilometres an hour it subtracted from his speed was useful, but not vital. It was doing a much more important job – keeping his body vertical, so that he would arrow straight into the sea.

He still had the impression that he was not moving at all, but that the water below was rushing up towards him. Once he had committed himself, he had no sense of fear; indeed, he felt a certain indignation against the skipper for keeping him in the dark. Did he *really* think that he would be scared to jump, if he had to brood over it too long?

At the very last moment, he let go of his shirt, took a deep breath, and grabbed his mouth and nose with his hands. As he had been instructed, he stiffened his body into a rigid bar, and locked his feet together. He would enter the water as cleanly as a falling spear ...

'It will be just the same,' the Commander had promised, 'as stepping off a diving board on Earth. Nothing to it – *if* you make a good entry.'

'And if I don't?' he had asked.

'Then you'll have to go back and try again.'

Something slapped him across the feet – hard, but not viciously. A million slimy hands were tearing at his body; there was a roaring in his ears, a mounting pressure – and even though his eyes were tightly closed, he could tell that darkness was falling as he arrowed down into the depths of the Cylindrical Sea.

With all his strength, he started to swim upwards towards the fading light. He could not open his eyes for more than a single blink; the poisonous water felt like acid when he did so. He seemed to have been struggling for ages, and more than once he had a nightmare fear that he had lost his orientation and was really swimming downwards. Then he would risk another quick glimpse, and every time the light was stronger.

His eyes were still clenched tightly shut when he broke water. He gulped a precious mouthful of air, rolled over on his back, and looked around.

Resolution was heading towards him at top speed; within seconds, eager hands had grabbed him and dragged him aboard.

'Did you swallow any water?' was the Commander's anxious question.

'I don't think so.'

'Rinse out with this, anyway. That's fine. How do you feel?'

'I'm not really sure. I'll let you know in a minute. Oh … thanks, everybody.' The minute was barely up when Jimmy was only too sure how he felt.

'I'm going to be sick,' he confessed miserably. His rescuers were incredulous.

'In a dead calm – on a flat sea?' protested Sergeant Barnes, who seemed to regard Jimmy's plight as a direct reflection on her skill.

'I'd hardly call it *flat*,' said the Commander, waving his arm around the band of water that circled the sky. 'But don't be ashamed – you may have swallowed some of that stuff. Get rid of it as quickly as you can.'

Jimmy was still straining, unheroically and unsuccessfully, when there was a sudden flicker of light in the sky behind them. All eyes turned towards the South Pole, and Jimmy instantly forgot his sickness. The Horns had started their firework display again.

There were the kilometre-long streamers of fire, dancing from the central spike to its smaller companions. Once again they began their stately rotation, as if invisible dancers were winding their ribbons around an electric maypole. But now they began to accelerate, moving faster and faster until they blurred into a flickering cone of light.

It was a spectacle more awe-inspiring than any they had yet seen here, and it brought with it a distant crackling roar which added to the impression of overwhelming power. The display lasted for about five minutes; then it stopped as abruptly as if someone had turned a switch.

'I'd like to know what the Rama Committee make of *that*.' Norton muttered to no one in particular. 'Has anyone here got any theories?'

There was no time for an answer, because at that moment Hub Control called in great excitement.

'*Resolution!* Are you OK? Did you feel that?'

'Feel *what*?'

'We think it was an earthquake – it must have happened the minute those fireworks stopped.'

'Any damage?'

'I don't think so. It wasn't really violent – but it shook us up a bit.'

'We felt nothing at all. But we wouldn't, out here in the Sea,'

'Of course, silly of me. Anyway, everything seems quiet now … until next time.'

'Yes, until the next time,' Norton echoed. The mystery of Rama was steadily growing; the more they discovered about it, the less they understood.

There was a sudden shout from the helm.

'Skipper – look – up there in the sky!'

Norton lifted his eyes, swiftly scanning the circuit of the Sea.

He saw nothing, until his gaze had almost reached the zenith, and he was staring at the other side of the world.

'My God,' he whispered slowly, as he realised that the 'next time' was already almost here.

A tidal wave was racing towards them, down the eternal curve of the Cylindrical Sea.

32
The Wave

Yet even in that moment of shock, Norton's first concern was for his ship.

'*Endeavour!*' he called. 'Situation report!'

'All OK, Skipper,' was the reassuring answer from the Exec. 'We felt a slight tremor, but nothing that could cause any damage. There's been a small change of attitude – the bridge says about point two degrees. They also think the spin rate has altered slightly – we'll have an accurate reading on that in a couple of minutes.'

So it's beginning to happen, Norton told himself, and a lot earlier than we expected; we're still a long way from perihelion, and the logical time for an orbit change. But some kind of trim was undoubtedly taking place – and there might be more shocks to come.

Meanwhile, the effects of this first one were all too obvious, up there on the curving sheet of water which seemed perpetually falling from the sky. The wave was still about ten kilometres away, and stretched the full width of the Sea from northern to southern shore. Near the land, it was a foaming wall of white, but in deeper water it was a barely visible blue line, moving much faster than the breakers on either flank. The drag of the shoreward shallows was already bending it into a bow, with the central portion getting further and further ahead.

'Sergeant,' said Norton urgently. 'This is *your* job. What can we do?'

Sergeant Barnes had brought the raft completely to rest and was studying the situation intently. Her expression, Norton was relieved to see, showed no trace of alarm – rather a certain zestful excitement, like a skilled athlete about to accept a challenge.

'I wish we had some soundings,' she said. 'If we're in deep water, there's nothing to worry about.'

'Then we're all right. We're still four kilometres from shore.'

'I hope so, but I want to study the situation.'

She applied power again, and swung *Resolution* around until it was just under way, heading directly towards the approaching wave. Norton judged that the swiftly moving central portion would reach them in less than five minutes, but he could also see that it presented no serious danger. It was only a racing ripple a fraction of a metre high, and would scarcely rock the boat. The walls of foam lagging far behind it were the real menace.

Suddenly, in the very centre of the Sea, a line of breakers appeared. The wave had clearly hit a submerged wall, several kilometres in length, not far below the surface. At the same time, the breakers on the two flanks collapsed, as they ran into deeper water.

Anti-slosh plates, Norton told himself. Exactly the same as in *Endeavour's* own propellant tanks – but on a thousand-fold greater scale. There must be a complex pattern of them all around the Sea, to damp out any waves as quickly as possible. The only thing that matters now is: are we right on top of one?

Sergeant Barnes was one jump ahead of him. She brought *Resolution* to a full stop and threw out the anchor. It hit bottom at only five metres.

'Haul it up!' she called to her crewmates. 'We've got to get away from here!'

Norton agreed heartily; but in which direction? The Sergeant was headed full speed *towards* the wave, which was now only five kilometres away. For the first time, he could hear the sound of its approach – a distant, unmistakable roar which he had never expected to hear inside Rama. Then it changed in intensity; the central portion was collapsing once more – and the flanks were building up again.

He tried to estimate the distance between the submerged baffles, assuming that they were spaced at equal intervals. If he was right, there should be one more to come; if they could station the raft in the deep water between them, they would be perfectly safe.

Sergeant Barnes cut the motor, and threw out the anchor again. It went down thirty metres without hitting bottom.

'We're OK,' she said, with a sigh of relief. 'But I'll keep the motor running.'

Now there were only the lagging walls of foam along the coast; out here in the central Sea it was calm again, apart from the inconspicuous blue ripple still speeding towards them. The Sergeant was just holding *Resolution* on course towards the disturbance, ready to pour on full power at a moment's notice.

Then, only two kilometres ahead of them, the Sea started to foam once more. It humped up in white-maned fury, and now its roaring seemed to fill the world. Upon the sixteen-kilometre-high wave of the Cylindrical Sea, a smaller ripple was superimposed, like an avalanche thundering down a mountain slope. And that ripple was quite large enough to kill them.

Sergeant Barnes must have seen the expressions on the faces of her crewmates. She shouted above the roar: 'What are you scared about? I've ridden bigger ones than this.' That was not quite true; nor did she add that her earlier experience had been in a well-built surf-boat, not an improvised raft. 'But if we *have* to jump, wait until I tell you. Check your life-jackets.'

She's magnificent, thought the Commander – obviously enjoying every minute, like a Viking warrior going into battle. And she's probably right – unless we've miscalculated badly.

The wave continued to rise, curving upwards and over. The slope above them probably exaggerated its height, but it looked enormous – an irresistible force of nature that would overwhelm everything in its path.

Then, within seconds, it collapsed, as if its foundations had been pulled out from underneath it. It was over the submerged barrier, in deep water again. When it reached them a minute later *Resolution* merely bounced up and down a few times before Sergeant Barnes swung the raft around and set off at top speed towards the north.

'Thanks, Ruby – that was splendid. But will we get home before it comes round for the second time?'

'Probably not; it will be back in about twenty minutes. But it will have lost all its strength then; we'll scarcely notice it.'

Now that the wave had passed, they could relax and enjoy the voyage – though no one would be completely at ease until they were back on land. The disturbance had left the water swirling round in random eddies, and had also stirred up a most peculiar acidic smell – 'like crushed ants', as Jimmy aptly put it. Though unpleasant, the odour caused none of the attacks of sea-sickness that might have been expected; it was something so alien that human physiology could not respond to it.

A minute later, the wave front hit the next underwater barrier, as it climbed away from them and up the sky. This time, seen from the rear, the spectacle was unimpressive and the voyagers felt ashamed of their previous fears. They began to feel themselves masters of the Cylindrical Sea.

The shock was therefore all the greater when, not more than a hundred metres away, something like a slowly rotating wheel began to rear up out of the water. Glittering metallic spokes, five metres long, emerged dripping from the sea, spun for a moment in the fierce Raman glare, and splashed back into the water. It was as if a giant starfish with tubular arms had broken the surface.

At first sight, it was impossible to tell whether it was an animal or a machine. Then it flopped over and lay half-awash, bobbing up and down in the gentle aftermath of the wave.

Now they could see that there were nine arms, apparently jointed, radiating from a central disc. Two of the arms were broken, snapped off at the outer joint. The others ended at a complicated collection of manipulators that reminded Jimmy very strongly of the crab he had encountered. The two creatures came from the same line of evolution – or the same drawing-board.

At the middle of the disc was a small turret, bearing three large eyes. Two were closed, one open – and even that appeared to be blank and unseeing. No one doubted that they were watching the death-throes of some strange monster, tossed up to the surface by the submarine disturbance that had just passed.

Then they saw that it was not alone. Swimming round it, and snapping at its feebly moving limbs, were two small beasts like overgrown lobsters. They were efficiently chopping up the monster, and it did nothing to resist, though its own claws seemed quite capable of dealing with the attackers.

Once again, Jimmy was reminded of the crab that had demolished *Dragonfly*. He watched intently as the one-sided conflict continued, and quickly confirmed his impression.

'Look, Skipper,' he whispered. 'Do you see – they're not eating it. They don't even have any mouths. *They're simply chopping it to pieces.* That's exactly what happened to *Dragonfly.*'

'You're right. They're dismantling it – like – like a broken machine.' Norton wrinkled his nose. 'But no dead machine ever smelled like that!'

Then another thought struck him.

'My God – suppose they start on us! Ruby, get us back to shore as quickly as you can!'

Resolution surged forward with reckless disregard for the life of her power cells. Behind them, the nine spokes of the great starfish – they could think of no better name for it – were clipped steadily shorter, and presently the weird tableau sank back into the depths of the Sea.

There was no pursuit, but they did not breathe comfortably again until *Resolution* had drawn up to the landing stage and they had stepped thankfully ashore. As he looked back across that mysterious and now suddenly sinister band of water, Commander Norton grimly determined that no one would ever sail it again. There were too many unknowns, too many dangers ...

He looked back upon the towers and ramparts of New York, and the dark cliff of the continent beyond. They were safe now from inquisitive man.

He would not tempt the gods of Rama again.

33
Spider

From now on, Norton had decreed, there would always be at least three people at Camp Alpha, and one of them would always be awake. In addition, all exploring parties would follow the same routine. Potentially dangerous creatures were on the move inside Rama, and though none had shown active hostility, a prudent commander would take no chances.

As an extra safeguard, there was always an observer up on the Hub, keeping watch through a powerful telescope. From this vantage point, the whole interior of Rama could be surveyed, and even the South Pole appeared only a few hundred metres away. The territory round any group of explorers was to be kept under regular observation; in this way, it was hoped to eliminate any possibility of surprise. It was a good plan – and it failed completely.

After the last meal of the day, and just before the 22.00 hour sleep period, Norton, Rodrigo, Calvert and Laura Ernst were watching the regular evening news telecast specially beamed to them from the transmitter at Inferno, Mercury. They had been particularly interested in seeing Jimmy's film of the Southern continent, and the return across the Cylindrical Sea – an episode which had excited all viewers. Scientists, news commentators, and members of the Rama Committee had given their opinions, most of them contradictory. No one could agree whether the crab-like creature Jimmy had encountered was an animal, a machine, a genuine Raman – or something that fitted none of these categories.

They had just watched, with a distinctly queasy feeling, the giant starfish being demolished by its predators when they discovered that they were no longer alone. There was an intruder in the camp.

Laura Ernst noticed it first. She froze in sudden shock, then said: 'Don't move, Bill. Now look slowly to the right.'

Norton turned his head. Ten metres away was a slender-legged tripod surmounted by a spherical body no larger than a football. Set around the body were three large, expressionless eyes, apparently giving 360 degrees of vision, and trailing beneath it were three whiplike tendrils. The creature was not quite as tall as a man, and looked far too fragile to be dangerous, but that did not excuse their carelessness in letting it sneak up on them unawares. It reminded Norton of nothing so much as a three-legged spider, or daddy-long-legs, and he wondered how it had solved the problem – never challenged by any creature on Earth – of tripedal locomotion.

'What do you make of it, Doc?' he whispered, turning off the voice of the TV newscaster.

'Usual Raman three-fold symmetry. I don't see how it could hurt us, though those whips might be unpleasant – and they could be poisonous, like a coelenterate's. Sit tight and see what it does.'

After regarding them impassively for several minutes, the creature suddenly moved – and now they could understand why they had failed to observe its arrival. It was *fast*, and it covered the ground with such an extraordinary spinning motion that the human eye and mind had real difficulty in following it.

As far as Norton could judge – and only a high-speed camera could settle the matter – each leg in turn acted as a pivot around which the creature whirled its body. And he was not sure, but it also seemed to him that every few 'steps' it reversed its direction of spin, while the three whips flickered over the ground like lightning as it moved. Its top speed – though this also was very hard to estimate – was at least thirty kilometres an hour.

It swept swiftly round the camp, examining every item of equipment, delicately touching the improvised beds and chairs and tables, communication gear, food containers, Electrosans, cameras, water tanks, tools – there seemed to be nothing that it ignored, except the four watchers. Clearly, it was intelligent enough to draw a distinction between humans and their inanimate property; its actions gave the unmistakable impression of an extremely methodical curiosity or inquisitiveness.

'I wish I could examine it!' Laura exclaimed in frustration, as the creature continued its swift pirouette. 'Shall we try to catch it?'

'How?' Calvert asked, reasonably enough.

'You know – the way primitive hunters bring down fast-moving animals with a couple of weights whirling around at the end of a rope. It doesn't even hurt them.'

'That I doubt,' said Norton. 'But even if it worked, we can't risk it. We don't know how intelligent this creature is – and a trick like that could easily break its legs. Then we would be in real trouble – from Rama, Earth and everyone else.'

'But I've got to have a specimen!'

'You may have to be content with Jimmy's flower – unless one of these creatures cooperates with you. Force is out. How would you like it if something landed on Earth and decided that *you* would make a nice specimen for dissection?'

'I don't want to dissect it,' said Laura, not at all convincingly. 'I only want to examine it.'

'Well, alien visitors might have the same attitude towards you, but you could have a very uncomfortable time before you believed them. We must make no move that could possibly be regarded as threatening.'

He was quoting from Ship's Orders, of course, and Laura

knew it. The claims of science had a lower priority than those of space-diplomacy.

In fact, there was no need to bring in such elevated considerations; it was merely a matter of good manners. They were all visitors here, and had never even asked permission to come inside ...

The creature seemed to have finished its inspection. It made one more high-speed circuit of the camp, then shot off at a tangent – towards the stairway.

'I wonder how it's going to manage the steps?' Laura mused. Her question was quickly answered; the spider ignored them completely, and headed up the gently sloping curve of the ramp without slackening its speed.

'Hub Control,' said Norton. 'You may have a visitor shortly; take a look at the Alpha Stairway Section Six. And incidentally, thanks a lot for keeping such a good watch on us.'

It took a minute for the sarcasm to sink in; then the Hub observer started to make apologetic noises.

'Er – I can just see *something*, Skipper, now you tell me it's there. But what is it?'

'Your guess is as good as mine,' Norton answered, as he pressed the *General Alert* button. 'Camp Alpha calling all stations. We've just been visited by a creature like a three-legged spider, with very thin legs, about two metres high, small spherical body, travels very fast with a spinning motion. Appears harmless but inquisitive. It may sneak up on you before you notice it. Please acknowledge.'

The first reply came from London, fifteen kilometres to the east.

'Nothing unusual here, Skipper.'

The same distance to the west, Rome answered, sounding suspiciously sleepy.

'Same here, Skipper. Uh, just a moment ...'

'What is it?'

'I put my pen down a minute ago – it's gone! What – oh!'

'Talk sense!'

'You won't believe this, Skipper. I was making some notes – you know I like writing, and it doesn't disturb anybody – I was using my favourite ball-point, it's nearly two hundred years old – well, now it's lying on the ground, about five metres away! I've got it – thank goodness – it isn't damaged.'

'And how do you suppose it got there?'

'Er – I may have dozed off for a minute. It's been a hard day.'

Norton sighed, but refrained from comment; there were so few of them, and they had so little time in which to explore a world. Enthusiasm could not always overcome exhaustion, and he wondered if they were taking unnecessary risks. Perhaps he should not split his men up into such small groups, and try to cover so much territory. But he was always conscious of the swiftly passing days, and the unsolved mysteries around them. He was becoming more and more certain that something was about to happen, and that they would have to abandon Rama even before it reached perihelion – the moment of truth when any orbit change must surely take place.

'Now listen, Hub, Rome, London – everyone,' he said. 'I want a report at every half-hour through the night. We must assume that from now on we may expect visitors at any time. Some of them may be dangerous, but at all costs we have to avoid incidents. You all know the directives on this subject.'

That was true enough; it was part of their training – yet perhaps none of them had ever really believed that the long-theorised 'physical contact with intelligent aliens' would occur in their lifetimes – still less that they would experience it themselves.

Training was one thing, reality another; and no one could be sure that the ancient, human instincts of self-preservation would not take over in an emergency. Yet it was essential to give every entity they encountered in Rama the benefit of the doubt, up to the last possible minute – and even beyond.

Commander Norton did not want to be remembered by history as the man who started the first interplanetary war.

Within a few hours there were hundreds of the spiders, and they were all over the plain. Through the telescope, it could be seen that the southern continent was also infested with them – but not, it seemed, the island of New York.

They took no further notice of the explorers, and after a while the explorers took little notice of them – though from time to time Norton still detected a predatory gleam in his Surgeon-Commander's eye. Nothing would please her better, he was sure, than for one of the spiders to have an unfortunate accident, and he would not put it past her to arrange such a thing in the interests of science.

It seemed virtually certain that the spiders could not be intelligent; their bodies were far too small to contain much in the way of brains, and indeed it was hard to see where they stored all the energy to move. Yet their behaviour was curiously purposeful and coordinated; they seemed to be everywhere, but they never visited the same place twice. Norton frequently had the impression that they were *searching* for something. Whatever it was, they did not seem to have discovered it.

They went all the way up to the central Hub, still scorning the three great stair ways. How they managed to ascend the vertical sections, even under almost zero gravity, was not clear; Laura theorised that they were equipped with suction pads.

And then, to her obvious delight, she got her eagerly desired specimen. Hub Control reported that a spider had fallen down the vertical face and was lying, dead or incapacitated, on the first platform. Laura's time up from the plain was a record that would never be beaten.

When she arrived at the platform, she found that, despite the low velocity of impact, the creature had broken all its legs. Its eyes were still open, but it showed no reactions to any external tests. Even a fresh human corpse would have been livelier, Laura decided; as soon as she got her prize back to *Endeavour*, she started to work with her dissecting kit.

The spider was so fragile that it almost came to pieces without her assistance. She disarticulated the legs, then started on the delicate carapace, which split along three great circles and opened up like a peeled orange.

After some moments of blank incredulity – for there was nothing that she could recognise or identify – she took a series of careful photographs. Then she picked up her scalpel.

Where to start cutting? She felt like closing her eyes, and stabbing at random, but that would not have been very scientific.

The blade went in with practically no resistance. A second later, Surgeon-Commander Ernst's most unlady-like yell echoed the length and breadth of *Endeavour*.

It took an annoyed Sergeant McAndrews a good twenty minutes to calm down the startled simps.

34
His Excellency Regrets

'As you are all aware, gentlemen,' said the Martian Ambassador, 'a great deal has happened since our last meeting. We have much to discuss – and to decide. I'm therefore particularly sorry that our distinguished colleague from Mercury is not here.'

That last statement was not altogether accurate. Dr Bose was not particularly sorry that HE the Hermian Ambassador was absent. It would have been much more truthful to say that he was worried. All his diplomatic instincts told him that something was happening, and though his sources of information were excellent, he could gather no hints as to what it might be.

The Ambassador's letter of apology had been courteous and entirely uncommunicative. His Excellency had regretted that urgent and unavoidable business had kept him from attending the meeting, either in person or by video. Dr Bose found it very hard to think of anything more urgent – or more important – than Rama.

'Two of our members have statements to make. I would first like to call on Professor Davidson.'

There was a rustle of excitement among the other scientists on the Committee. Most of them had felt that the astronomer, with his well-known cosmic viewpoint, was not the right man to be Chairman of the Space Advisory Council. He sometimes gave the impression that the activities of intelligent life were an unfortunate irrelevance in the majestic universe of stars and galaxies, and that it was bad manners to pay too much attention to it. This had not endeared him to exobiologists such as Dr Perera, who took exactly the opposite view. To them, the only purpose of the Universe was the production of intelligence, and they were apt to talk sneeringly about purely astronomical phenomena. 'Mere dead matter' was one of their favourite phrases.

'Mr Ambassador,' the scientist began, 'I have been analysing the curious behaviour of Rama during the last few days, and would like to present my conclusions. Some of them are rather startling.'

Dr Perera looked surprised, then rather smug. He strongly approved of anything that startled Professor Davidson.

'First of all, there was the remarkable series of events when that young lieutenant flew over to the Southern hemisphere. The electrical discharges themselves, though spectacular, are not important; it is easy to show that they contained relatively little energy. But they coincided with a change in Rama's rate of spin, and its attitude – that is, its orientation in space. *This* must have involved an enormous amount of energy; the discharges which nearly cost Mr – er Pak his life were merely a minor by-product – perhaps a nuisance that had to be minimised by those giant lightning conductors at the South Pole.

'I draw two conclusions from this. When a spacecraft – and we must call Rama a spacecraft, despite its fantastic size – makes a change of attitude, that usually means it is about to make a change of orbit. We must therefore take seriously the views of those who believe that Rama may be preparing to become another planet of our sun, instead of going back to the stars.

'If this is the case. *Endeavour* must obviously be prepared to cast off – is that what spaceships do? – at a moment's notice. She may be in very serious danger while she is still physically attached to Rama. I imagine that Commander Norton is already well aware of this possibility, but I think we should send him an additional warning.'

'Thank you very much, Professor Davidson. Yes – Dr Solomons?'

'I'd like to comment on that,' said the science historian. 'Rama seems to have made a change of spin *without* using any jets or reaction devices. This leaves only two possibilities, it seems to me.

'The first one is that it has internal gyroscopes, or their equivalent. They must be enormous; where are they?

'The second possibility – which would turn all our physics upside down – is that it has a reactionless propulsion system. The so-called Space Drive, which Professor Davidson doesn't believe in. If this is the case, Rama may be able to do almost anything. We will be quite unable to anticipate its behaviour, even on the gross physical level.'

The diplomats were obviously somewhat baffled by this exchange, and the astronomer refused to be drawn. He had gone out on enough limbs for one day.

'I'll stick to the laws of physics, if you don't mind, until I'm forced to give them up. If we've not found any gyroscopes in Rama, we may not have looked hard enough, or in the right place.'

Ambassador Bose could see that Dr Perera was getting impatient. Normally, the exobiologist was as happy as anyone else to engage in speculation; but now, for the first time, he had some solid facts. His long-impoverished science had become wealthy overnight.

'Very well – if there are no other comments – I know that Dr Perera has some important information.'

'Thank you, Mr Ambassador. As you've all seen, we have at last obtained a specimen of a Raman life-form, and have observed several others at close quarters. Surgeon-Commander Ernst, *Endeavour*'s medical officer, has sent a full report on the spider-like creature she dissected.

'I must say at once that some of her results are baffling, and in any other circumstances I would have refused to believe them.

'The spider is definitely organic, though its chemistry differs from ours in many respects – it contains considerable quantities of light metals. Yet I hesitate to call it an animal, for several fundamental reasons.

'In the first place, it seems to have no mouth, no stomach, no gut – no method of ingesting food! Also no air intakes, no lungs, no blood, no reproductive system …

'You may wonder what it *has* got. Well, there's a simple musculature, controlling its three legs and the three whip-like tendrils or feelers. There's a brain – fairly complex, mostly concerned with the creature's remarkably developed triocular vision. But eighty per cent of the body consists of a honeycomb of large cells, and this is what gave Dr Ernst such an unpleasant surprise when she started her dissection. If she'd been luckier she might have recognised it in time, because it's the one Raman structure that *does* exist on Earth – though only in a handful of marine animals.

'Most of the spider is simply a battery, very much like that found in electric cells and rays. But in this case, it's apparently not used for defence. *It's the creatures source of energy*. And that is why it has no provisions for eating and breathing; it doesn't need such primitive arrangements. And incidentally, this means that it would be perfectly at home in a vacuum …

'So we have a creature which, to all intents and purposes, is nothing more than a mobile eye. It has no organs of manipulation; those tendrils are much too feeble. If I had been given its specifications, I would have said it was merely a reconnaissance device.

'Its behaviour certainly fits that description. All the spiders ever do is to run around and look at things. That's all they *can* do …

'But the other animals are different. The crab, the starfish, the sharks – for want of better words – can obviously manipulate their environment and appear to be specialised for various functions. I assume that they are also electrically powered since, like the spider, they appear to have no mouths.

'I'm sure you'll appreciate the biological problems raised by all this. Could such creatures evolve naturally? I really don't think so. They appear to be *designed* like machines, for specific jobs. If I had to describe them, I would say that they are robots – biological robots – something that has no analogy on Earth.

'If Rama is a spaceship, perhaps they are part of its crew. As to how they are born – or created – that's something I can't tell you. But I can guess that the answer's over there in New York. If Commander Norton and his men can wait long enough, they may encounter increasingly more complex creatures, with unpredictable behaviour. Somewhere along the line they may meet the Ramans themselves – the real makers of this world.

'And when *that* happens, gentlemen, there will be no doubt about it all ...'

35
Special Delivery

Commander Norton was sleeping soundly when his personal communicator dragged him away from happy dreams. He had been holidaying with his family on Mars, flying past the awesome, snow-capped peak of Nix Olympica – mightiest volcano in the solar system. Little Billie had started to say something to him; now he would never know what it was.

The dream faded; the reality was his executive officer, up on the ship.

'Sorry to wake you, Skipper,' said Lieutenant-Commander Kirchoff. 'Triple A priority from Headquarters.'

'Let me have it,' Norton answered sleepily.

'I can't. It's in code – Commander's Eyes Only.'

Norton was instantly awake. He had received such a message only three times in his whole career, and on each occasion it had meant trouble.

'Damn!' he said. 'What do we do now?'

His Exec did not bother to answer. Each understood the problem perfectly; it was one that Ship's Orders had never anticipated. Normally, a commander was never more than a few minutes away from his office and the code book in his personal safe. If he started now, Norton might get back to the ship – exhausted – in four or five hours. That was not the way to handle a Class AAA Priority.

'Jerry,' he said at length. 'Who's on the switchboard?'

'No one; I'm making the call myself.'

'Recorder off?'

'By an odd breach of regulations, yes.'

Norton smiled. Jerry was the best Exec he had ever worked with. He thought of everything.

'OK. You know where my key is. Call me back.'

He waited as patiently as he could for the next ten minutes, trying – without much success – to think of other problems. He hated wasting mental effort; it was very unlikely that he could out-guess the message that was coming, and he would know its contents soon enough. *Then* he would start worrying effectively.

When the Exec called back, he was obviously speaking under considerable strain.

'It's not really *urgent* Skipper – an hour won't make any difference. But I prefer to avoid radio. I'll send it down by messenger.'

'But *why*— Oh, very well – I trust your judgement. Who will carry it through the airlocks?'

'I'm going myself; I'll call you when I reach the Hub.'

'Which leaves Laura in charge.'

'For one hour, at the most. I'll get right back to the ship.'

A medical officer did not have the specialised training to be acting commander, any more than a commander could be expected to do an operation. In emergencies, both jobs had sometimes been successfully switched; but it was not recommended. Well, one order had already been broken tonight ...

'For the record, you never leave the ship. Have you woken Laura?'

'Yes. She's delighted with the opportunity.'

'Lucky that doctors are used to keeping secrets. Oh – have you sent the acknowledgement?'

'Of course, in your name.'

'Then I'll be waiting.'

Now it was quite impossible to avoid anxious anticipations. 'Not *really* urgent – but I prefer to avoid radio ...'

One thing was certain. The Commander was not going to get much more sleep this night.

36
Biot Watcher

Sergeant Pieter Rousseau knew why he had volunteered for this job; in many ways, it was a realisation of a childhood dream. He had become fascinated by telescopes when he was only six or seven years old, and much of his youth had been spent collecting lenses of all shapes and sizes. These he had mounted in cardboard tubes, making instruments of ever-increasing power until he was familiar with the moon and planets, the nearer space-stations, and the entire landscape within thirty kilometres of his home.

He had been lucky in his place of birth, among the mountains of Colorado; in almost every direction, the view was spectacular and inexhaustible. He had spent hours exploring, in perfect safety, the peaks which every year took their toll of careless climbers. Though he had seen much, he had imagined even more; he had liked to pretend that over each crest of rock, beyond the reach of his telescope, were magic kingdoms full of wonderful creatures. And so for years he had avoided visiting the places his lenses brought to him, because he knew that the reality could not live up to the dream.

Now, on the central axis of Rama, he could survey marvels beyond the wildest fantasies of his youth. A whole world lay spread out before him – a small one, it was true, yet a man could spend an entire lifetime exploring four thousand square kilometres, even when it was dead and changeless.

But now life, with all its infinite possibilities, had come to

Rama. If the biological robots were not living creatures, they were certainly very good imitations.

No one knew who invented the word 'biot'; it seemed to come into instant use, by a kind of spontaneous generation. From his vantage point on the Hub, Pieter was Biot-Watcher-in-Chief, and he was beginning – so he believed – to understand some of their behaviour patterns.

The Spiders were mobile sensors, using vision – and probably touch – to examine the whole interior of Rama. At one time there had been hundreds of them rushing around at high speed, but after less than two days they had disappeared; now it was quite unusual to see even one.

They had been replaced by a whole menagerie of much more impressive creatures; it had been no minor task, thinking of suitable names for them. There were the Window Cleaners, with large padded feet, who were apparently polishing their way the whole length of Rama's six artificial suns. Their enormous shadows, cast right across the diameter of the world, sometimes caused temporary eclipses on the far side.

The crab that had demolished *Dragonfly* seemed to be a Scavenger. A relay chain of identical creatures had approached Camp Alpha and carried off all the debris that had been neatly stacked on the outskirts; they would have carried off everything else if Norton and Mercer had not stood firm and defied them. The confrontation had been anxious but brief; thereafter, the Scavengers seemed to understand what they were allowed to touch, and arrived at regular intervals to see if their services were required. It was a most convenient arrangement, and indicated a high degree of intelligence – either on the part of the Scavengers themselves, or some controlling entity elsewhere.

Garbage disposal on Rama was very simple; everything was thrown into the Sea, where it was, presumably, broken down into forms that could be used again. The process was rapid; *Resolution* had disappeared overnight, to the great annoyance of Ruby Barnes. Norton had consoled her by pointing out that it had done its job magnificently – and he would never have allowed anyone to use it again. The Sharks might not be as discriminating as the Scavengers.

No astronomer discovering an unknown planet could have been happier than Pieter when he spotted a new type of biot and secured a good photo of it through his telescope. Unfortunately, it seemed that all the interesting species were over at the South Pole, where they were performing mysterious tasks round the Horns. Something that looked like a centipede with suction pads could be seen from time to time exploring Big Horn itself, while round the lower peaks Pieter had caught a glimpse of a burly creature that could have been a cross between a hippopotamus and a bulldozer. And there was even a double-necked giraffe, which apparently acted as a mobile crane.

Presumably, Rama, like any ship, required testing, checking and repairing after its immense voyage. The crew was already hard at work; when would the passengers appear?

Biot classifying was not Pieter's main job; his orders were to keep watch on the two or three exploring parties that were always out, to see that they did not get into trouble, and to warn them if anything approached. He alternated every six hours with anyone else who could be spared, though more than once he had been on duty for twelve hours at a stretch. As a result, he now knew the geography of Rama better than any man who would ever live. It was as familiar to him as the Colorado mountains of his youth.

When Jerry Kirchoff emerged from Airlock Alpha, Pieter knew at once that something unusual was happening. Personnel transfers never occurred during the sleeping period, and it was now past midnight by Mission Time. Then Pieter remembered how short-handed they were, and was shocked by a much more startling irregularity.

'Jerry – who's in charge of the ship?'

'*I* am,' said the Exec coldly, as he flipped open his helmet. 'You don't think I'd leave the bridge while I'm on watch, do you?'

He reached into his suit carry-all, and pulled out a small can still bearing the label: CONCENTRATED ORANGE JUICE: TO MAKE FIVE LITRES.

'You're good at this Pieter. The skipper is waiting for it.'

Pieter hefted the can, then said, 'I hope you've put enough mass inside it – sometimes they get stuck on the first terrace.'

'Well, you're the expert.'

That was true enough. The Hub observers had had plenty of practice, sending down small items that had been forgotten or were needed in a hurry. The trick was to get them safely past the low-gravity region, and then to see that the Coriolis effect did not carry them too far away from the Camp during the eight-kilometre roll downhill.

Pieter anchored himself firmly, grasped the can, and hurled it down the face of the cliff. He did not aim directly towards Camp Alpha, but almost thirty degrees away from it.

Almost immediately, air resistance robbed the can of its initial speed, but then the pseudo-gravity of Rama took over and it started to move downwards at a constant velocity. It hit once near the base of the ladder, and did a slow-motion bounce which took it clear of the first terrace.

'It's OK now,' said Pieter. 'Like to make a bet?'

'No,' was the prompt reply. 'You know the odds.'

'You're no sportsman. But I'll tell you now – it will stop within three hundred metres of the Camp.'

'That doesn't sound very close.'

'You might try it some time. I once saw Joe miss by a couple of kilometres.'

The can was no longer bouncing; gravity had become strong enough to glue it to the curving face of the North Dome. By the time it had reached the second terrace it was rolling along at twenty or thirty kilometres an hour, and had reached very nearly the maximum speed that friction would allow.

'Now we'll have to wait,' said Pieter, seating himself at the telescope, so that he could keep track of the messenger. 'It will be there in ten minutes. Ah, here comes the skipper – I've got used to recognising people from this angle – now he's looking up at us.'

'I believe that telescope gives you a sense of power.'

'Oh, it does. I'm the only person who knows everything that's happening in Rama. At least, I *thought* I did,' he added plaintively, giving Kirchoff a reproachful look.

'If it will keep you happy, the skipper found he'd run out of toothpaste.'

After that, conversation languished; but at last Pieter said: 'Wish you'd taken that bet ... he's only got to walk fifty metres ... now he sees it ... mission complete.'

'Thanks, Pieter – a very good job. Now you can go back to sleep.'

'Sleep! I'm on watch until 0400.'

'Sorry – you *must* have been sleeping. Or how else could you have dreamed all this?'

SPACE SURVEY HQ TO COMMANDER SSV ENDEAVOUR. PRIORITY AAA. CLASSIFICATION YOUR EYES ONLY. NO PERMANENT RECORD.

SPACE GUARD REPORTS ULTRA HIGH SPEED VEHICLE APPARENTLY LAUNCHED MERCURY TEN TO TWELVE DAYS AGO ON RAMA INTERCEPT. IF NO ORBIT CHANGE ARRIVAL PREDICTED DATE 322 DAYS 15 HOURS. MAY BE NECESSARY YOU EVACUATE BEFORE THEN. WILL ADVISE FURTHER.

C IN C

Norton read the message half a dozen times to memorise the

date. It was hard to keep track of time inside Rama; he had to look at his calendar watch to see that it was now Day 315. That might leave them only one week ...

The message was chilling, not only for what it said, but for what it implied. The Hermians had made a clandestine launch – that in itself a breach of Space Law. The conclusion was obvious; their 'vehicle' could only be a missile.

But *why*? It was inconceivable – well, almost inconceivable – that they would risk endangering *Endeavour*, so presumably he would receive ample warning from the Hermians themselves. In an emergency, he could leave at a few hours' notice, though he would do so only under extreme protest, at the direct orders of the Commander-in-Chief.

Slowly, and very thoughtfully, he walked across to the improvised life-support complex and dropped the message into an electrosan. The brilliant flare of laser light bursting out through the crack beneath the seat-cover told him that the demands of security were satisfied. It was too bad, he told himself, that all problems could not be disposed of so swiftly and hygienically.

37
Missile

The missile was still five million kilometres away when the glare of its plasma braking jets became clearly visible in *Endeavour*'s main telescope. By that time the secret was already out, and Norton had reluctantly ordered the second and perhaps final evacuation of Rama; but he had no intention of leaving until events gave him no alternative.

When it had completed its braking manoeuvre, the unwelcome guest from Mercury was only fifty kilometres from Rama, and apparently carrying out a survey through its TV cameras. These were clearly visible – one fore and one aft – as were several small omni-antennas and one large directional dish, aimed steadily at the distant star of Mercury. Norton wondered what instructions were coming down that beam, and what information was going back.

Yet the Hermians could learn nothing that they did not already know; all that *Endeavour* had discovered had been broadcast throughout the solar system. This spacecraft – which had broken all speed records to get here – could only be an extension of its makers' will, an instrument of their purpose. That purpose would soon be known, for in three hours the Hermian Ambassador to the United Planets would be addressing the General Assembly.

Officially, the missile did not yet exist. It bore no identification marks, and was not radiating on any standard beacon frequency. This was a serious breach of law, but even SPACEGUARD had not yet issued a formal protest. Everyone was waiting, with nervous impatience, to see what Mercury would do next.

It had been three days since the missile's existence – and origin – had been announced; all that time, the Hermians had remained stubbornly silent. They could be very good at that, when it suited them.

Some psychologists had claimed that it was almost impossible to understand fully the mentality of anyone born and bred on Mercury. Forever exiled from Earth by its three-times-more-powerful gravity, Hermians could stand on the Moon and look across the narrow gap to the planet of their ancestors – even of their own parents – but they could never visit it. And so, inevitably, they claimed that they did not want to.

They pretended to despise the soft rains, the rolling fields, the lakes and seas, the blue skies – all the things that they could know only through recordings. Because their planet was drenched with such solar energy that the day time temperature often reached six hundred degrees, they affected a rather swaggering roughness that did not bear a moment's serious examination. In fact, they tended to be physically weak, since they could only survive if they were totally insulated from their environment. Even if he could have tolerated the gravity, a Hermian would have been quickly incapacitated by a hot day in any equatorial country on Earth.

Yet in matters that really counted, they *were* tough. The psychological pressures of that ravening star so close at hand, the engineering problems of tearing into a stubborn planet and wrenching from it all the necessities of life – these had produced a Spartan and in many ways highly admirable culture. You could rely on the Hermians; if they promised something, they would do it – though the bill might be considerable. It was their own joke that, if the sun ever showed signs of going nova, they would contract to get it under control – once the fee had been settled. It was a non-Hermian joke that any child who showed signs of interest in art, philosophy or abstact mathematics was ploughed straight back into the hydroponic farms. As far as criminals and psychopaths were concerned, this was not a joke at all. Crime was one of the luxuries that Mercury could not afford.

Commander Norton had been to Mercury once, had been enormously impressed – like most visitors – and had acquired many Hermian friends. He had fallen in love with a girl in Port Lucifer, and had even contemplated signing a three-year contract, but parental disapproval of anyone from outside the orbit of Venus had been too strong. It was just as well.

'Triple A message from Earth, Skipper,' said the bridge. 'Voice and back-up text from Commander-in-Chief. Ready to accept?'

'Check and file text; let me have the voice.'

'Here it comes.'

Admiral Hendrix sounded calm and matter-of-fact, as if he was issuing a routine fleet order, instead of handling a situation unique in the history of space. But then, he was not ten kilometres from the bomb.

'C-in-C to Commander, *Endeavour*. This is a quick summary of the situation as we see it now. You know that the General Assembly meets at fourteen hundred hours and you'll be listening to the proceedings. It is possible that you may then have to take action immediately, without consultation; hence this briefing.

'We've analysed the photos you have sent us; the vehicle is a standard space-probe, modified for high-impulse and probably laser-riding for initial boost. Size and mass are consistent with fusion bomb in the five hundred to one thousand megaton range; the Hermians use up to one hundred megatons routinely in their mining operations, so they would have had no difficulty in assembling such a warhead.

'Our experts also estimate that this would be the minimum size necessary to assure destruction of Rama. If it was detonated against the thinnest part of the shell – underneath the Cylindrical Sea – the hull would be ruptured and the spin of the body would complete its disintegration.

'We assume that the Hermians, if they are planning such an act, will give you ample time to get clear. For your information, the gamma-ray flash from such a bomb could be dangerous to you up to a range of a thousand kilometres.

'But that is not the most serious danger. The fragments of Rama, weighing tons and spinning off at almost a thousand kilometres an hour, could destroy you at an *unlimited* distance. We therefore recommend that you proceed along the spin axis, since no fragments will be thrown off in that direction. Ten thousand kilometres should give an adequate safety margin.

'This message cannot be intercepted; it is going by multiple-pseudo-random routing, so I can talk in clear English. Your reply may not be secure, so speak with discretion and use code when necessary. I will call you immediately after the General Assembly discussion. Message concluded. C-in-C, out.'

38
General Assembly

According to the history books – though no one could really believe it – there had been a time when the old United Nations had 172 members. The United planets had only seven; and that was sometimes bad enough. In order of distance from the Sun, they were Mercury, Earth, Luna, Mars, Ganymede, Titan and Triton.

The list contained numerous omissions and ambiguities which presumably the future would rectify. Critics never tired of pointing out that most of the United Planets were not planets at all, but satellites. And how ridiculous that the four giants, Jupiter, Saturn, Uranus and Neptune were not included ...

But no one lived on the Gas Giants, and quite possibly no one ever would. The same might be true of the other major absentee, Venus. Even the most enthusiastic of planetary engineers agreed that it would take centuries to tame Venus; meanwhile the Hermians kept their eyes on her, and doubtless brooded over long-range plans.

Separate representation for Earth and Luna had also been a bone of contention; the other members argued that it put too much power in one corner of the solar system. But there were more people on the Moon than all the other worlds except Earth itself – and it *was* the meeting place of the UP. Moreover, Earth and Moon hardly every agreed on anything, so they were not likely to constitute a dangerous bloc.

Mars held the asteroids in trust – except for the Icarian group (supervised by Mercury) and a handful with perihelions beyond Saturn – and thus claimed by Titan. One day the larger asteroids, such as Pallas, Vesta, Juno and Ceres, would be important enough to have their own ambassadors, and membership of the UP would then reach two figures.

Ganymede represented not only Jupiter – and therefore more mass than all the rest of the solar system put together – but also the remaining fifty or so Jovian satellites, if one included temporary captures from the asteroid belt (the lawyers were still arguing over this). In the same way, Titan took care of Saturn, its rings and the other thirty-plus satellites.

The situation for Triton was even more complicated. The large moon of Neptune was the outermost body in the solar system under permanent habitation; as a result, its ambassador wore a considerable number of hats. He represented Uranus and its eight moons (none yet occupied); Neptune and its other three satellites; Pluto and its solitary moon; and lonely, moonless Persephone. If there were planets beyond Persephone, they too would be Triton's responsibility. And as if that was not enough, the Ambassador for the Outer Darkness, as he was sometimes called, had been heard to ask plaintively: 'What about comets?' It was generally felt that this problem could be left for the future to solve.

And yet, in a very real sense, that future was already here. By some definitions, Rama *was* a comet; they were the only other visitors from the interstellar deeps, and many had travelled on hyperbolic orbits even closer to the Sun than Rama's. Any space-lawyer could make a very good case out of that – and the Hermian Ambassador was one of the best.

'We recognise His Excellency the Ambassador for Mercury.'

As the delegates were arranged counter-clockwise in order of distance from the sun, the Hermian was on the President's extreme right. Up to the very last minute, he had been interfacing with his computer; now he removed the synchronizing spectacles which allowed no one else to read the message on the display screen. He picked up his sheaf of notes, and rose briskly to his feet.

'Mr President, distinguished fellow delegates, I would like to begin with a brief summary of the situation which now confronts us.'

From some delegates, that phrase 'a brief summary' would have evoked silent groans among all listeners; but everyone knew that Hermians meant exactly what they said.

'The giant spaceship, or artificial asteroid, which has been christened Rama was detected over a year ago, in the region beyond Jupiter. At first it was believed to be a natural body, moving on a hyperbolic orbit which would take it round the sun and on to the stars.

'When its true nature was discovered, the Solar Survey Vessel *Endeavour* was ordered to rendezvous with it. I am sure we will all congratulate Commander Norton and his crew for the efficient way in which they have carried out their unique assignment.

'At first, it was believed that Rama was dead – frozen for so many hundreds of thousands of years that there was no possibility of revival. This may still be true, in a strictly biological sense. There seems general agreement, among those who have studied the matter, that no living organism of any complexity can survive more than a very few centuries of suspended animation. Even at absolute zero, residual quantum effects eventually erase too much cellular information to make revival possible. It therefore appeared that, although Rama was of enormous archaeological importance, it did not present any major astro-political problems.

'It is now obvious that this was a very naïve attitude, though even from the first there were some who pointed out that Rama was too precisely aimed at the Sun for pure chance to be involved.

'Even so, it might have been argued – indeed, it was argued – that here was an experiment that had failed. Rama had reached the intended target, but the controlling intelligence had not survived. This view also seems very simple-minded; it surely underestimates the entities we are dealing with.

'What we failed to take into account was the possibility of *non*-biological survival. If we accept Dr Perera's very plausible theory, which certainly fits all the facts, the creatures who have been observed inside Rama did not exist until a short time ago. Their patterns, or templates, were stored in some central information bank, and when the time was ripe they were manufactured from available raw materials – presumably the metallo-organic soup of the Cylindrical Sea. Such a feat is still somewhat beyond our own ability, but does not present any theoretical problems. We know that solid state circuits, unlike living matter, can store information without loss, for indefinite periods of time.

'So Rama is now in full operating condition, serving the purpose of its builders – whoever they may be. From our point of view, it does not matter if the Ramans themselves have all been dead for a million years, or whether they too will be re-created, to join their servants, at any moment. With or without them, their will is being done – and will continue to be done.

'Rama has now given proof that its propulsion system is still operating. In a few days, it will be at perihelion, where it would logically make any major orbit change. We may therefore soon have a new planet – moving through the solar space over which my government has jurisdiction. Or it may, of course, make additional changes and occupy a final orbit at any distance from the sun. It could even become a satellite of a major planet – such as Earth …

'We are therefore, fellow delegates, faced with a whole spectrum of possibilities, some of them very serious indeed. It is foolish to pretend that these creatures *must* be benevolent and will not interfere with us in any way. If they come to our solar system, they need something from it. Even if it is only scientific knowledge – consider how that knowledge may be used ...

'What confronts us now is a technology hundreds – perhaps thousands – of years in advance of ours, and a *culture* which may have no points of contact whatsoever. We have been studying the behaviour of the biological robots – the biots – inside Rama, as shown on the films that Commander Norton has relayed, and we have arrived at certain conclusions which we wish to pass on to you.

'On Mercury we are perhaps unlucky in having no indigenous life-forms to observe. But, of course, we have a complete record of terrestrial zoology, and we find in it one striking parallel with Rama.

'This is the termite colony. Like Rama, it is an artificial world with a controlled environment. Like Rama, its functioning depends upon a whole series of specialised biological machines – workers, builders, farmers – *warriors*. And although we do not know if Rama has a queen, I suggest that the island known as New York serves a similar function.

'Now, it would obviously be absurd to press this analogy too far; it breaks down at many points. But I put it to you for this reason.

'What degree of cooperation or understanding would ever be possible between human beings and termites? When there is no conflict of interest, we tolerate each other. But when either needs the other's territory or resources, no quarter is given.

'Thanks to our technology and our intelligence, we can always win, if we are sufficiently determined. But sometimes it is not easy, and there are those who believe that, in the long run, final victory may yet go to the termites ...

'With this in mind, consider now the appalling threat that Rama may – I do not say *must* – present to human civilisation. What steps have we taken to counter it, if the worst eventuality should occur? None whatsoever; we have merely talked and speculated and written learned papers.

'Well, my fellow delegates, Mercury has done more than this. Acting under the provisions of Clause 34 of the Space Treaty of 2057, which entitled us to take any steps necessary to protect the integrity of our solar space, we have dispatched a high-energy nuclear device to Rama. We will indeed be happy if we never have to utilise it. But now, at least, we are not helpless – as we were before.

'It may be argued that we have acted unilaterally, without prior consultation. We admit that. But does anyone here imagine – with all respect, Mister President – that we could have secured any such agreement in the time available? We consider that we are acting not only for ourselves, but for the whole human race. All future generations may one day thank us for our foresight.

'We recognised that it would be a tragedy – even a crime – to destroy an artifact as wonderful as Rama. If there is any way in which this can be avoided, *without risk to humanity*, we will be very happy to hear of it. We have not found one, and time is running out.

'Within the next few days, before Rama reaches perihelion, the choice will have to be made. We will, of course, give ample warning to *Endeavour* – but we would advise Commander Norton always to be ready to leave at an hour's notice. It is conceivable that Rama may undergo further dramatic transformations at any moment.

'That is all, Mister President, fellow delegates. I thank you for your attention. I look forward to your cooperation.'

39
Command Decision

'Well, Rod, how do the Hermians fit into your theology?'

'Only too well, Commander,' replied Rodrigo with a humour-less smile. 'It's the age-old conflict between the forces of good and the forces of evil. And there are times when men have to take sides in such a conflict.'

I thought it would be something like that, Norton told himself. This situation must have been a shock to Boris, but he would not have resigned himself to passive acquiescence. The Cosmo-Christers were very energetic, competent people. Indeed, in some ways they were remarkably like the Hermians.

'I take it you have a plan, Rod.'

'Yes, Commander. It's really quite simple. We merely have to disable the bomb.'

'Oh, And how do you propose to do that?'

'With a small pair of wire-cutters.'

If this had been anyone else, Norton would have assumed that they were joking. But not Boris Rodrigo.

'Now just a minute! It's bristling with cameras. Do you suppose the Hermians will just sit and watch you?'

'Of course; that's all they *can* do. When the signal reaches them, it will be far too late. I can easily finish the job in ten minutes.'

'I see. They certainly *will* be mad. But suppose the bomb is booby-trapped so that interference sets it off?'

'That seems very unlikely; what would be the purpose? This

bomb was built for a specific deep-space mission, and it will be fitted with all sorts of safety devices to prevent detonation *except* on a positive command. But that's a risk I'm prepared to take – and it can be done without endangering the ship. I've worked everything out.'

'I'm sure you have,' said Norton. The idea was fascinating – almost seductive in its appeal; he particularly liked the idea of the frustrated Hermians, and would give a good deal to see their reactions when they realised – too late – what was happening to their deadly toy.

But there were other complications, and they seemed to multiply as Norton surveyed the problem. He was facing by far the most difficult, and the most crucial, decision in his entire career.

And that was a ridiculous understatement. He was faced with the most difficult decision *any* commander had ever had to make; the future of the entire human race might well depend upon it. For just suppose the Hermians were right?

When Rodrigo had left, he switched on the DO NOT DISTURB sign; he could not remember when he had last used it, and was mildly surprised that it was working. Now, in the heart of his crowded, busy ship, he was completely alone – except for the portrait of Captain James Cook, gazing at him down the corridors of time.

It was impossible to consult with Earth; he had already been warned that any messages might be tapped – perhaps by relay devices on the bomb itself. That left the whole responsibility in his hands.

There was a story he had heard somewhere about a President of the United States – was it Roosevelt or Perez? – who had a sign on his desk saying 'The buck stops here'. Norton was not quite certain what a buck was, but he knew when one had stopped at his desk.

He could do nothing, and wait until the Hermians advised him to leave. How would that look in the histories of the future? Norton was not greatly concerned with posthumous fame or infamy, yet he would not care to be remembered for ever as the accessory to a cosmic crime – which it had been in his power to prevent.

And the plan was flawless. As he had expected, Rodrigo had worked out every detail, anticipated every possibility, even the remote danger that the bomb might be triggered when tampered with. If that happened, *Endeavour* could still be safe, behind the shield of Rama. As for Lieutenant Rodrigo himself, he seemed to regard the possibility of instant apotheosis with complete equanimity.

Yet, even if the bomb was successfully disabled, that would be far from the end of the matter. The Hermians might try again – unless some way could be found of stopping them. But at least weeks of time would have been bought; Rama would be far past perihelion before another missile could possibly reach it. By then, hopefully, the worst fears of the alarmists might have been disproved. Or the reverse ...

To act, or not to act – that was the question. Never before had Commander Norton felt such a close kinship with the Prince of Denmark. Whatever he did, the possibilities for good and evil seemed in perfect balance. He was faced with the most morally difficult of all decisions. If his choice was wrong, he would know very quickly. But if he was correct – he might never be able to prove it ...

It was no use relying any further on logical arguments and the endless mapping of alternative futures. That way, one could go round and round in circles for ever. The time had come to listen to his inner voices.

He returned the calm, steady gaze across the centuries.

'I agree with you, Captain,' he whispered. 'The human race

has to live with its conscience. Whatever the Hermians argue, survival is not everything.'

He pressed the call button for the bridge circuit and said slowly, 'Lieutenant Rodrigo – I'd like to see you.'

Then he closed his eyes, hooked his thumbs in the restraining straps of his chair, and prepared to enjoy a few moments of total relaxation.

It might be some time before he would experience it again.

40
Saboteur

The scooter had been stripped of all unnecessary equipment; it was now merely an open framework holding together propulsion, guidance and life-support systems. Even the seat for the second pilot had been removed, for every kilogramme of extra mass had to be paid for in mission time.

That was one of the reasons, though not the most important, why Rodrigo had insisted on going alone. It was such a simple job that there was no need for any extra hands, and the mass of a passenger would cost several minutes of flight time. Now the stripped-down scooter could accelerate at over a third of a gravity; it could make the trip from *Endeavour* to the bomb in four minutes. That left six to spare; it would be sufficient.

Rodrigo looked back only once when he had left the ship; he saw that, as planned, it had lifted from the central axis and was thrusting gently away across the spinning disc of the North Face. By the time he reached the bomb, it would have placed the thickness of Rama between them.

He took his time, flying over the polar plain. There was no hurry here, because the bomb's cameras could not yet see him, and he could therefore conserve fuel. Then he drifted over the curving rim of the world – and there was the missile, glittering in sunlight fiercer even than that shining on the planet of its birth.

Rodrigo had already punched in the guidance instructions. He initiated the sequence; the scooter spun on its gyros, and came up to full thrust in a matter of seconds. At first the sensation of weight seemed crushing; then Rodrigo adjusted to it. He had, after all, comfortably endured twice as much inside Rama – and had been born under three times as much on Earth.

The huge, curving exterior wall of the fifty-kilometre cylinder was slowly falling away beneath him as the scooter aimed itself directly at the bomb. Yet it was impossible to judge Rama's size, since it was completely smooth and featureless – so featureless, indeed, that it was difficult to tell that it was spinning.

One hundred seconds into the mission; he was approaching the halfway point. The bomb was still too far away to show any details, but it was much brighter against the jet-black sky. It was strange to see no stars – not even brilliant Earth or dazzling Venus; the dark filters which protected his eyes against the deadly glare made that impossible. Rodrigo guessed that he was breaking a record; probably no other man had ever engaged in extra-vehicular work so close to the sun. It was lucky for him that solar activity was low.

At two minutes ten seconds the flip-over light started flashing, thrust dropped to zero, and the scooter spun through a hundred and eighty degrees. Full thrust was back in an instant, but now he was decelerating at the same mad rate of three metres per second squared – rather better than that, in fact, since he had lost almost half his propellent mass. The bomb was twenty-five kilometres away; he would be there in another two minutes. He had hit a top speed of fifteen hundred kilometres an hour – which, for a space-scooter, was utter insanity, and probably another record. But this was hardly a routine EVA, and he knew precisely what he was doing.

The bomb was growing; and now he could see the main antenna, holding steady on the invisible star of Mercury. Along that beam, the image of his approaching scooter had been flashing at the speed of light for the last three minutes. There were still two to go, before it reached Mercury.

What would the Hermians do, when they saw him? There would be consternation, of course; they would realise instantly that he had made a rendezvous with the bomb several minutes before they even knew he was on the way. Probably some stand-by observer would call higher authority – that would take more time. But even in the worst possible case – even if the officer on duty had authority to detonate the bomb, and pressed the button immediately – it would take another five minute for the signal to arrive.

Though Rodrigo was not gambling on it – Cosmo-Christers *never* gambled – he was quite sure that there would be no such instantaneous reaction. The Hermians would hesitate to destroy a reconnaissance vehicle from *Endeavour*, even if they suspected its motives. They would certainly attempt some form of communication first – and that would mean *more* delay.

And there was an even better reason; they would not waste a gigaton bomb on a mere scooter. Wasted it would be, if it was detonated twenty kilometres from its target. They would have to move it first. Oh, he had plenty of time … but he would still assume the very worst.

He would act as if the triggering impulse would arrive in the shortest possible time – just five minutes.

As the scooter closed in across the last few hundred metres, Rodrigo quickly matched the details he could now see with those he had studied in the photographs taken at long range. What had been only a collection of pictures became hard metal and smooth plastic – no longer abstract, but a deadly reality.

The bomb was a cylinder about ten metres long and three in diameter – by a strange coincidence, almost the same proportions as Rama itself. It was attached to the framework of the carrier vehicle by an open lattice-work of short I-beams. For some reason, probably to do with the location of the centre of mass, it was supported at *right angles* to the axis of the carrier, so that it conveyed an appropriately sinister hammer-head impression. It was indeed a hammer, one powerful enough to smash a world.

From each end of the bomb, a bundle of braided cables ran along the cylindrical side and disappeared through the lattice-work into the interior of the vehicle. All communication and control was here; there was no antenna of any kind on the bomb itself. Rodrigo had only to cut those two sets of cables and there would be nothing here but harmless, inert metal.

Although this was exactly what he had expected, it still seemed a little too easy. He glanced at his watch; it would be another thirty seconds before the Hermians, even if they had been watching when he rounded the edge of Rama, could know of his existence. He had an absolutely certain five minutes for uninterrupted work – and a ninety-nine per cent probability of much longer than that.

As soon as the scooter had drifted to a complete halt, Rodrigo grappled it to the missile framework so that the two formed a rigid structure. That took only seconds; he had already chosen his tools, and was out of the pilot's seat at once, only slightly hampered by the stiffness of his heavy-insulation suit.

The first thing he found himself inspecting was a small metal plate bearing the inscription:

DEPARTMENT OF POWER ENGINEERING
Section D,
47, Sunset Boulevard,
Vulcanopolis, 17464
For information apply to Mr Henry K. Jones

Rodrigo suspected that, in a very few minutes, Mr Jones might be rather busy.

The heavy wire-cutters made short work of the cable. As the first strands parted, Rodrigo gave scarcely a thought to the fires of hell that were pent up only centimetres away; if his actions triggered them, he would never know.

He glanced again at his watch; this had taken less than a minute, which meant that he was on schedule. Now for the back-up cable – and then he could head for home, in full view of the furious and frustrated Hermians.

He was just beginning to work on the second cable assembly when he felt a faint vibration in the metal he was touching. Startled, he looked back along the body of the missile.

The characteristic blue-violet glow of a plasma thruster in action was hovering round one of the attitude control jets. The bomb was preparing to move.

The message from Mercury was brief, and devastating. It arrived two minutes after Rodrigo had disappeared around the edge of Rama.

COMMANDER ENDEAVOUR FROM MERCURY SPACE CONTROL, INFERNO WEST. YOU HAVE ONE HOUR FROM RECEIPT OF THIS MESSAGE TO LEAVE VICINITY OF RAMA. SUGGEST YOU PROCEED MAXIMUM ACCELERATION ALONG SPIN AXIS. REQUEST ACKNOWLEDGEMENT. MESSAGE ENDS.

Norton read it with sheer disbelief, then anger. He felt a childish impulse to radio back that all his crew were inside Rama, and it would take hours to get everyone out. But that would achieve nothing – except perhaps to test the will and nerve of the Hermians.

And why, several days before perihelion, had they decided to act? He wondered if the mounting pressure of public opinion was becoming too great, and they decided to present the rest of the human race with a *fait accompli*. It seemed an unlikely explanation; such sensitivity would have been uncharacteristic.

There was no way in which he could recall Rodrigo, for the scooter was now in the radio shadow of Rama and would be out of contact until they were in line of sight again. That would not be until the mission was completed – or had failed.

He would have to wait it out; there was still plenty of time – a full fifty minutes. Meanwhile, he had decided on the most effective answer to Mercury.

He would ignore the message completely, and see what the Hermians did next.

Rodrigo's first sensation, when the bomb started to move, was not one of physical fear; it was something much more devastating. He believed that the universe operated according to strict laws, which not even God Himself could disobey – much less the Hermians. No message could travel faster than light; he was five minutes ahead of anything that Mercury could do.

This could only be a coincidence – fantastic, and perhaps deadly, but no more than that. By chance, a control signal must have been sent to the bomb at about the time he was leaving *Endeavour*; while he was travelling fifty kilometres, it had covered eighty million.

Or perhaps this was only an automatic change of attitude, to counter over-heating somewhere in the vehicle. There were places where the skin temperature approached fifteen hundred degrees, and Rodrigo had been very careful to keep in the shadows as far as possible.

A second thrusters started to fire, checking the spin given by the first. No, this was *not* a mere thermal adjustment. The bomb was re-orientating itself, to point towards Rama ...

Useless to wonder *why* this was happening at this precise moment in time. There was one thing in his favour; the missile was a low acceleration device. A tenth of a gee was the most that it could manage. He could hang on.

He checked the grapples attaching the scooter to the bomb

framework, and re-checked the safety line on his own suit. A cold anger was growing in his mind, adding to his determination. Did this manoeuvre mean that the Hermians were going to explode the bomb without warning, giving *Endeavour* no chance to escape? That seemed incredible – an act not only of brutality but of folly, calculated to turn the rest of the solar system against them. And what would have made them ignore the solemn promise of their own Ambassador?

Whatever their plan, they would not get away with it.

The second message from Mercury was identical with the first, and arrived ten minues later. So they had extended the deadline – Norton still had one hour. And they had obviously waited until a reply from *Endeavour* could have reached them before calling him again.

Now there was another factor; by this time they must have seen Rodrigo, and would have had several minutes in which to take action. Their instructions could already be on the way. They could arrive at any second.

He should be preparing to leave. At any moment, the sky-filling bulk of Rama might become incandescent along the edges, blazing with a transient glory that would far outshine the sun.

When the main thrust came on, Rodrigo was securely anchored. Only twenty seconds later, it cut off again. He did a quick mental calculation; the delta vee could not have been more than fifteen kilometres an hour. The bomb would take over an hour to reach Rama; perhaps it was only moving in close to get a quicker reaction. If so, that was a wise precaution; but the Hermians had left it too late.

Rodrigo glanced at his watch, though by now he was almost aware of the time without having to check. On Mercury, they would now be seeing him heading purposefully towards the bomb, and less than two kilometres away from it. They could have no doubt of his intentions, and would be wondering if he had already carried them out.

The second set of cables went as easily as the first; like any good workman, Rodrigo had chosen his tools well. The bomb was disarmed; or, to be more accurate, it could no longer be detonated by remote command.

Yet there was one other possibility, and he could not afford to ignore it. There were no external contact fuses, but there might be internal ones, armed by the shock of impact. The Hermians still had control over their vehicle's movements, and could crash it into Rama whenever they wished. Rodrigo's work was not yet completely finished.

Five minutes from now, in that control room somewhere on Mercury, they would see him crawling back along the exterior of the missile, carrying the modestly-sized wire-cutters that had neutralized the mightiest weapon ever built by man. He was almost tempted to wave at the camera, but decided that it would seem undignified; after all, he was making history, and millions would watch this scene in the years to come. Unless, of course, the Hermians destroyed the recording in a fit of pique; he would hardly blame them.

He reached the mounting of the long-range antenna, and drifted hand-over-hand along it to the big dish. His faithful cutters made short work of the multiplex feed system, chewing up cables and laser wave guides alike. When he made the last snip, the antenna started to swing slowly around; the unexpected movement took him by surprise, until he realised that he had destroyed its automatic lock on Mercury. Just five minutes from now, the Hermians would lose all contact with their servant. Not only was it impotent; now it was blind and deaf.

Rodrigo climbed slowly back to the scooter, released the shackles, and swung it round until the forward bumpers were pressing against the missile, as close as possible to its centre of mass. He brought thrust up to full power, and held it there for twenty seconds.

Pushing against many times its own mass, the scooter responded very sluggishly. When Rodrigo cut the thrust back to zero, he took a careful reading of the bomb's new velocity vector.

It would miss Rama by a wide margin– and it could be located again with precision at any future time. It was, after all, a very valuable piece of equipment.

Lieutenant Rodrigo was a man of almost pathological honesty. He would not like the Hermians to accuse him of losing their property.

41
Hero

'Darling,' began Norton, 'this nonsense has cost us more than a day, but at least it's given me a chance to talk to you.

'I'm still in the ship, and she's heading back to station at the polar axis. We picked Rod up an hour ago, looking as if he'd just come off duty after a quiet watch. I suppose neither of us will ever be able to visit Mercury again, and I'm wondering if we're going to be treated as heroes or villains when we get back to Earth. But *my* conscience is clear; I'm sure we did the right thing. I wonder if the Ramans will ever say "thank you".

'We can stay here only two more days; unlike Rama, we don't have a kilometre-thick skin to protect us from the sun. The hull's already developing dangerous hotspots and we've had to put out some local screening. I'm sorry – I didn't want to bore you with my problems ...

'So there's time for just one more trip into Rama, and I intend to make the most of it. But don't worry – I'm not taking any chances.'

He stopped the recording. That, to say the least, was stretching the truth. There was danger and uncertainty about every moment inside Rama; no man could ever feel really at home there, in the presence of forces beyond his understanding. And on this final trip, now that he knew they would never return and that no future operations would be jeopardized, he intended to press his luck just a little further.

'In forty-eight hours, then, we'll have completed this mission.

What happens then is still uncertain; as you know, we've used virtually all our fuel getting into this orbit. I'm still waiting to hear if a tanker can rendezvous with us in time to get back to Earth, or whether we'll have to make planet-fall at Mars. Anyway, I should be home by Christmas. Tell Junior I'm sorry I can't bring a baby biot; there's no such animal ...

'We're all fine, but we're very tired. I've earned a long leave after all this, and we'll make up for lost time. Whatever they say about me, you can claim you're married to a hero. How many wives have a husband who saved a world?'

As always, he listened carefully to the tape before duping it, to make sure that it was applicable to both his families. It was strange to think that he did not know which of them he would see first; usually, his schedule was determined at least a year in advance, by the inexorable movements of the planets themselves.

But that was in the days before Rama; now nothing would ever be the same again.

42
Temple of Glass

'If we try it,' said Karl Mercer, 'do you think the biots will stop us?'

'They may; that's one of the things I want to find out. Why are you looking at me like that?'

Mercer gave his slow, secret grin, which was liable to be set off at any moment by a private joke he might or might not share with his shipmates.

'I was wondering, Skipper, if you think you own Rama. Until now, you've vetoed any attempt to cut into buildings. Why the switch? Have the Hermians given you ideas?'

Norton laughed, then suddenly checked himself. It was a shrewd question, and he was not sure if the obvious answers were the right ones.

'Perhaps I have been ultra-cautious – I've tried to avoid trouble. But this is our last chance; if we're forced to retreat we won't have lost much.'

'Assuming that we retreat in good order.'

'Of course. But the biots have never shown hostility; and except for the Spiders, I don't believe there's anything here that can catch us – if we do have to run for it.'

'*You* may run, Skipper, but I intend to leave with dignity. And incidentally, I've decided why the biots are so polite to us.'

'It's a little late for a new theory.'

'Here it is, anyway. They think we're Ramans. They can't tell the difference between one oxy-eater and another.'

'I don't believe they're *that* stupid.'

'It's not a matter of stupidity. They've been programmed for their particular jobs, and we simply don't come into their frame of reference.'

'Perhaps you're right. We may find out – as soon as we start to work on London.'

Joe Calvert had always enjoyed those old bank-robbery movies, but he had never expected to be involved in one. Yet this was, essentially, what he was doing now.

The deserted streets of 'London' seemed full of menace, though he knew that was only his guilty conscience. He did not *really* believe that the sealed and windowless structures ranged all around them were full of watchful inhabitants, waiting to emerge in angry hordes as soon as the invaders laid a hand on their property. In fact, he was quite certain that this whole complex – like all the other towns – was merely some kind of storage area.

Yet a second fear, also based on innumerable ancient crime dramas, could be better grounded. There might be no clanging alarm bells and screaming sirens, but it was reasonable to assume that Rama would have some kind of warning system. How otherwise did the biots know when and where their services were needed?

'Those without goggles, turn your backs,' ordered Sergeant Myron. There was a smell of nitric oxides as the air itself started to burn in the beam of the laser torch, and a steady sizzling as the fiery knife sliced towards secrets that had been hidden since the birth of man.

Nothing material could resist this concentration of power, and the cut proceeded smoothly at a rate of several metres a minute. In a remarkable short time, a section large enough to admit a man had been sliced out.

As the cut-away section showed no signs of moving, Myron

tapped it gently – then harder – then banged on it with all his strength. It fell inwards with a hollow, reverberating crash.

Once again, as he had done during that very first entrance into Rama, Norton remembered the archaeologist who had opened the old Egyptian tomb. He did not expect to see the glitter of gold; in fact, he had no preconceived ideas at all, as he crawled through the opening, his flashlight held in front of him.

A Greek temple made of glass – that was his first impression. The building was filled with row upon row of vertical crystalline columns, about a metre wide and stretching from floor to ceiling. There were hundreds of them, marching away into the darkness beyond the reach of his light.

Norton walked towards the nearest column and directed his beam into its interior. Refracted as through a cylindrical lens, the light fanned out on the far side to be focused and refocused, getting fainter with each repetition, in the array of pillars beyond. He felt that he was in the middle of some complicated demonstration in optics.

'Very pretty,' said the practical Mercer, 'but what does it mean? Who needs a forest of glass pillars?'

Norton rapped gently on one column. It sounded solid, though more metallic than crystalline. He was completely baffled, and so followed a piece of useful advice he had heard long ago: 'When in doubt, say nothing and move on.'

As he reached the next column, which looked exactly like the first, he heard an exclamation of surprise from Mercer.

'I could have sworn this pillar was empty – now there's something inside it.'

Norton glanced quickly back.

'Where?' he said. 'I don't see anything.'

He followed the direction of Mercer's pointing finger. It was aimed at nothing; the column was still completely transparent.

'You can't see it?' said Mercer incredulously. 'Come around this side. Damn – now I've lost it!'

'What's going on here?' demanded Calvert. It was several minutes before he got even the first approximation to an answer.

The columns were not transparent from every angle or under all illuminations. As one walked around them, objects would suddenly flash into view, apparently embedded in their depths like flies in amber – and would then disappear again. There were dozens of them, all different. They looked absolutely real and solid, yet many seemed to occupy the identical volume of space.

'Holograms,' said Calvert. 'Just like a museum on Earth.'

That was the obvious explanation, and therefore Norton viewed it with suspicion. His doubts grew as he examined the other columns, and conjured up the images stored in their interiors.

Hand-tools (though for huge and peculiar hands), containers, small machines with keyboards that appeared to have been made for more than five fingers, scientific instruments, startlingly conventional domestic utensils, including knives and plates which apart from their size would not have attracted a second glance on any terrestrial table ... they were all there, with hundreds of less identifiable objects, often jumbled up together in the same pillar. A museum, surely, would have some logical arrangement, some segregation of related items. This seemed to be a completely random collection of hardware.

They had photographed the elusive images inside a score of the crystal pillars when the sheer variety of items gave Norton a clue. Perhaps this was not a collection, but a *catalogue*, indexed according to some arbitrary but perfectly logical system. He thought of the wild juxtapositions that any dictionary or alphabetized list will give, and tried the idea on his companions.

'I see what you mean,' said Mercer. 'The Ramans might be equally surprised to find us putting – ah– camshafts next to cameras.'

'Or books beside boots', added Calvert, after several seconds' hard thinking. One could play this game for hours, he decided, with increasing degrees of impropriety.

'That's the idea,' replied Norton. 'This may be an indexed catalogue for 3-D images – templates – solid blue-prints, if you like to call them that.'

'For what purpose?'

'Well, you know the theory about the biots ... the idea that they don't exist until they're needed and then they're created – synthesised – from patterns stored somewhere?'

'I see,' said Mercer slowly and thoughtfully. 'So when a Raman needs a left-handed blivet, he punches out the correct code number, and a copy is manufactured from the pattern in here.'

'Something like that. But please don't ask me about the practical details.'

The pillars through which they had been moving had been steadily growing in size, and were now more than two metres in diameter. The images were correspondingly larger; it was obvious that, for doubtless excellent reasons, the Ramans believed in sticking to a one-to-one scale. Norton wondered how they stored anything *really* big, if this was the case.

To increase their rate of coverage, the four explorers had now spread out through the crystal columns and were taking photographs as quickly as they could get their cameras focused on the fleeting images. This was an astonishing piece of luck, Norton told himself, though he felt that he had earned it; they could not possibly have made a better choice than this Illustrated Catalogue of Raman Artifacts. And yet, in another way, it could hardly have been more frustrating. There was nothing actually *here*, except impalpable patterns of light and darkness; these apparently solid objects did not really exist.

Even knowing this, more than once Norton felt an almost irresistible urge to laser his way into one of the pillars, so that he could have something material to take back to Earth. It was the same impulse, he told himself wryly, that would prompt a monkey to grab the reflection of a banana in a mirror.

He was photographing what seemed to be some kind of optical device when Calvert's shout started him running through the pillars.

'Skipper – Karl – Will – look at *this*!'

Joe was prone to sudden enthusiasms, but what he had found was enough to justify any amount of excitement.

Inside one of the two-metre columns was an elaborate harness, or uniform, obviously made for a vertically-standing creature, much taller than a man. A very narrow central metal band apparently surrounded the waist, thorax or some division unknown to terrestrial zoology. From this rose three slim columns, tapering outwards and ending in a perfectly circular belt, an impressive metre in diameter. Loops equally spaced along it could only be intended to go round upper limbs or arms. *Three* of them ...

There were numerous pouches, buckles, bandoliers from which tools (or weapons?) protruded, pipes and electrical conductors, even small black boxes that would have looked perfectly at home in an electronics lab on Earth. The whole arrangement was almost as complex as a spacesuit, though it obviously provided only partial covering for the creature wearing it.

And was that creature a Raman? Norton asked himself. We'll probably never know; but it must have been intelligent – no mere animal could cope with all that sophisticated equipment.

'About two and a half metres high,' said Mercer thoughtfully, 'not counting the head – whatever *that* was like.'

'With three arms – and presumably three legs. The same plan as the Spiders, on a much more massive scale. Do you suppose that's a coincidence?'

'Probably not. We design robots in our own image; we might expect the Ramans to do the same.'

Joe Calvert, unusually subdued, was looking at the display with something like awe.

'Do you suppose they know we're here?' he half-whispered

'I doubt it,' said Mercer. 'We've not even reached their threshold of consciousness – though the Hermians certainly had a good try.'

They were still standing there, unable to drag themselves away, when Pieter called from the Hub, his voice full of urgent concern.

'Skipper – you'd better get outside.'

'What is it – biots heading this way?'

'No – something much more serious. *The lights are going out.*'

43
Retreat

When he hastily emerged from the hole they had lasered, it seemed to Norton that the six suns of Rama were as brilliant as ever. Surely, he thought, Pieter must have made a mistake … that's not like him at all …

But Pieter had anticipated just this reaction.

'It happened so slowly,' he explained apologetically, 'that it was a long time before I noticed any difference. But there's no doubt about it – I've taken a meter reading. The light level's down forty per cent.'

Now, as his eyes readjusted themselves after the gloom of the glass temple, Norton could believe him. The long day of Rama was drawing to it close.

It was still as warm as ever, yet Norton felt himself shivering. He had known this sensation once before, during a beautiful summer day on Earth. There had been an inexplicable weakening of light as if darkness was falling from the air, or the sun had lost its strength – though there was not a cloud in the sky. Then he remembered; a partial eclipse was in progress.

'This is it,' he said grimly. 'We're going home. Leave all the equipment behind – we won't need it again.'

Now, he hoped, one piece of planning was about to prove its worth. He had selected London for this raid because no other town was so close to a stairway; the foot of Beta was only four kilometers away.

They set off at the steady, loping trot which was the most

comfortable mode of travelling at half a gravity. Norton set a pace which, he estimated, would get them to the edge of the plain without exhaustion, and in the minimum of time. He was acutely aware of the eight kilometers they would still have to climb when they had reached Beta, but he would feel much safer when they had actually started the ascent.

The first tremor came when they had almost reached the stairway. It was very slight, and instinctively Norton turned towards the south, expecting to see another display of fireworks around the Horns. But Rama never seemed to repeat itself exactly; if there were any electrical discharges above those needle-sharp mountains, they were too faint to be seen.

'Bridge,' he called, 'did you notice that?'

'Yes, Skipper – very small shock. Could be another attitude change. We're watching the rate gyro – nothing yet. Just a minute! Positive reading! Can just detect it – less than a microradian per second, but holding.'

So Rama was beginning to turn, though with almost imperceptible slowness. Those earlier shocks might have been a false alarm – but this, surely, was the real thing.

'Rate increasing – five microrad. Hello, did you feel *that* shock?'

'We certainly did. Get all the ship's systems operational. We may have to leave in a hurry.'

'Do you expect an orbit change already? We're still a long way from perihelion.'

'I don't think Rama works by our textbooks. Nearly at Beta. We'll rest there for five minutes.'

Five minutes was utterly inadequate, yet it seemed an age. For there was now no doubt that the light was failing, and failing fast.

Though they were all equipped with flashlights, the thought of darkness here was now intolerable; they had grown so psychologically accustomed to the endless day that it was hard to remember the conditions under which they had first explored this world. They felt an overwhelming urge to escape – to get out into the light of the Sun, a kilometre away on the other side of these cylindrical walls.

'Hub Control!' called Norton. 'Is the searchlight operating? We may need it in a hurry.'

'Yes, Skipper. Here it comes.'

A reassuring spark of light started to shine eight kilometers above their heads. Even against the now fading day of Rama, it looked surprisingly feeble; but it had served them before, and would guide them once again if they needed it.

This, Norton was grimly aware, would be the longest and most nerve-wracking climb they had ever done. Whatever happened, it would be impossible to hurry; if they over-exerted themselves, they would simply collapse somewhere on that vertiginous slope, and would have to wait until their protesting muscles permitted them to continue. By this time, they must be one of the fittest crews that had ever carried out a space mission; but there were limits to what flesh and blood could do.

After an hour's steady plodding they had reached the fourth section of the stairway, about three kilometres from the plain. From now on, it would be much easier; gravity was already down to a third of Earth value. Although there had been minor shocks from time to time, no other unusual phenomena had occurred, and there was still plenty of light. They began to feel more optimistic, and even to wonder if they had left too soon. One thing was certain, however; there was no going back. They had all walked for the last time on the plain of Rama.

It was while they were taking a ten-minute rest on the fourth platform that Joe Calvert suddenly exclaimed:

'What's that noise, Skipper?'

'Noise! – I don't hear anything.'

'High-pitched whistle – dropping in frequency, you *must* hear it.'

'Your ears are younger than mine – oh, now I do.'

The whistle seemed to come from everywhere. Soon it was loud, even piercing, and falling swiftly in pitch. Then it suddenly stopped.

A few seconds later it came again, repeating the same sequence. It had all the mournful, compelling quality of a lighthouse siren sending out its warnings into the fog-shrouded night. There was a message here, and an urgent one. It was not designed for their ears, but they understood it. Then, as if to make doubly sure, it was reinforced by the lights themselves.

They dimmed almost to extinction, then started to flash. Brilliant beads, like ball lightning, raced along the six narrow valleys that had once illuminated this world. They moved from both Poles towards the Sea in a synchronized, hypnotic rhythm which could have only one meaning. 'To the Sea!' the lights were calling. 'To the Sea!' And the summons was hard to resist; there was not a man who did not feel a compulsion to turn back, and to seek oblivion in the water of Rama.

'Hub Control!' Norton called urgently. 'Can you see what's happening?'

The voice of Pieter came back to him; he sounded awed, and more than a little frightened.

'Yes, Skipper. I'm looking across at the Southern continent. There are still scores of biots over there – including some big ones. Cranes, Bulldozers – lots of Scavengers. And they're all rushing back to the Sea faster than I've ever seen them move before. There goes a Crane – right over the edge! Just like Jimmy, but going down a lot quicker ... it smashed to pieces when it hit ... and here come the Sharks – they're tearing into it ... ugh; it's not a pleasant sight ...

'Now I'm looking at the plain. Here's a Bulldozer that seems to have broken down ... it's going round and round in circles. Now a couple of Crabs are tearing into it, pulling it to pieces ... Skipper, I think you'd better get back right away.'

'Believe me,' Norton said with deep feeling, 'we're coming just as quickly as we can.'

Rama was battening down the hatches, like a ship preparing for a storm. That was Norton's overwhelming impression, though he could not have put it on a logical basis. He no longer felt completely rational; two compulsions were warring in his mind – the need to escape, and the desire to obey those bolts of lightning that still flashed across the sky, ordering him to join the biots in their march to the sea.

One more section of stairway – another ten-minute pause, to let the fatigue poisons drain from his muscles. Then on again – another two kilometres to go, but let's try not to think about that—

The maddening sequence of descending whistles abruptly ceased. At the same moment, the fireballs racing along the slots of the Straight Valleys stopped their seaward strobing; Rama's six linear suns were once more continuous bands of light.

But they were fading fast, and sometimes they flickered, as if tremendous jolts of energy were being drained from waning power sources. From time to time, there were slight tremors underfoot; the bridge reported that Rama was still swinging with imperceptible slowness, like a compass needle responding to a weak magnetic field. This was perhaps reassuring; it was when Rama *stopped* its swing that Norton would really begin to worry.

All the biots had gone, so Pieter reported. In the whole interior of Rama, the only movement was that of human beings, crawling with painful slowness up the curving face of the north dome.

Norton had long since overcome the vertigo he had felt on that first ascent, but now a new fear was beginning to creep into his mind. They were so vulnerable here, on this endless climb from plain to Hub. Suppose that, when it had completed its attitude change, Rama started to accelerate?

Presumably its thrust would be along the axis. If it was in the northward direction, that would be no problem; they would be held a little more firmly against the slope which they were ascending. But if it was towards the south, they might be swept off into space, to fall back eventually on the plain far below.

He tried to reassure himself with the thought that any possible acceleration would be very feeble. Dr Perera's calculations had been most convincing; Rama could not possibly accelerate at more than a fiftieth of a gravity, or the Cylindrical Sea would climb the southern cliff and flood an entire continent. But Perera had been in a comfortable study back on Earth, not with kilometres of overhanging metal apparently about to crash down upon his head. And perhaps Rama was designed for periodic flooding—

No, that was ridiculous. It was absurd to imagine that all these trillions of tons could suddenly start moving with sufficient acceleration to shake him loose. Nevertheless, for all the remainder of the ascent, Norton never let himself get far from the security of the handrail.

Lifetimes later, the stairway ended; only a few hundred metres of vertical, recessed ladder were left. It was no longer necessary to climb this section since one man at the Hub, hauling on a cable, could easily hoist another against the rapidly diminishing gravity. Even at the bottom of the ladder a man weighed less than five kilos; at the top, practically zero.

So Norton relaxed in the sling, grasping a rung from time to time to counter the feeble Coriolis force still trying to push him off the ladder. He almost forgot his knotted muscles, as he had his last view of Rama.

It was about as bright now as a full moon on Earth; the overall scene was perfectly clear, but he could no longer make out the finer details. The South Pole was now partially obscured by a glowing mist; only the peak of Big Horn protruded through it – a small, black dot, seen exactly head-on.

The carefully-mapped but still unknown continent beyond the Sea was the same apparently random patchwork that it had always been. It was too foreshortened, and too full of complex detail, to reward visual examination, and Norton scanned it only briefly.

He swept his eyes round the encircling band of the Sea, and noticed for the first time a regular pattern of disturbed water, as if waves were breaking over reefs set at geometrically precise intervals. Rama's manoeuvring was having some effect, but a very slight one. He was sure that Sergeant Barnes would have sailed forth happily under these conditions, had he asked her to cross the Sea in her lost *Resolution*.

New York, London, Paris, Moscow, Rome ... he said farewell to all the cities of the northern continent, and hoped the Ramans would forgive him for any damage he had done. Perhaps they would understand that it was all in the cause of science.

Then, suddenly, he was at the Hub, and eager hands reached out to grab him, and to hurry him through the airlocks. His overstrained legs and arms were trembling so uncontrollably that he was almost unable to help himself, and he was content to be handled like a half-paralysed invalid.

The sky of Rama contracted above him, as he descended into the central crater of the Hub. As the door of the inner airlock shut off the view for ever, he found himself thinking: 'How strange that night should be falling, now that Rama is closest to the sun!'

44
Space Drive

A hundred kilometres was an adequate safety margin, Norton had decided. Rama was now a huge black rectangle, exactly broadside-on, eclipsing the sun. He had used this opportunity to fly *Endeavour* completely into shadow, so that load could be taken off the ship's cooling systems and some overdue maintenance could be carried out. Rama's protective cone of darkness might disappear at any moment, and he intended to make as much use of it as he could.

Rama was still turning; it had now swung through almost fifteen degrees, and it was impossible to believe that some major orbit change was not imminent. On the United Planets, excitement had now reached a pitch of hysteria, but only a faint echo of this came to *Endeavour*. Physically and emotionally, her crew was exhausted; apart from a skeleton watch, everyone had slept for twelve hours after take-off from the North Polar Base. On doctor's orders, Norton himself had used electro-sedation; even so, he had dreamed that he was climbing an infinite stairway.

The second day back on ship, everything had almost returned to normal; the exploration of Rama already seemed part of another life. Norton started to deal with the accumulated office work and to make plans for the future; but he refused the requests for interviews that had somehow managed to insinuate themselves into the Survey and even SPACEGUARD radio circuits. There were no messages from Mercury, and the

UP General Assembly had adjourned its session, though it was ready to meet again at an hour's notice.

Norton was having his first good night's sleep, thirty hours after leaving Rama, when he was rudely shaken back to consciousness. He cursed groggily, opened a bleary eye at Karl Mercer – and then, like any good commander, was instantly wide awake.

'It's stopped turning?'

'Yes. Steady as a rock.'

'Let's go to the bridge.'

The whole ship was awake; even the simps knew that something was afoot, and made anxious, meeping noises until Sergeant McAndrews reassured them with swift hand-signals. Yet as Norton slipped into his chair and fastened the restraints round his waist, he wondered if this might be yet another false alarm.

Rama was now foreshortened into a stubby cylinder, and the searing rim of the sun had peeked over one edge. Norton jockeyed *Endeavour* gently back into the umbra of the artificial eclipse, and saw the pearly splendour of the corona reappear across a background of the brighter stars. There was one huge prominence, at least half a million kilometres high, that had climbed so far from the sun that its upper branches looked like a tree of crimson fire.

So now we have to wait, Norton told himself. The important thing is not to get bored, to be ready to react at a moment's notice, to keep all the instruments aligned and recording, no matter how long it takes ...

That was strange. The star field was shifting, almost as if he had actuated the Roll thrusters. But he had touched no controls, and if there had been any real movement, he would have sensed it at once.

'Skipper!' said Calvert urgently from the Nav position, 'we're rolling – look at the stars! *But I'm getting no instrument readings!*'

'Rate gyros operating?'

'Perfectly normal – I can see the zero jitter. But we're rolling several degrees a second!'

'That's impossible!'

'Of course it is – but look for yourself ...'

When all else failed, a man had to rely on eyeball instrumentation. Norton could not doubt that the star field was indeed slowly rotating – there went Sirius, across the rim of the port. Either the universe, in a reversion of pre-Copernican cosmology, had suddenly decided to revolve around *Endeavour*; or the stars were standing still, and the ship was turning.

The second explanation seemed rather more likely, yet it involved apparently insoluble paradoxes. If the ship was really turning at this rate, he would have *felt* it – literally by the seat of his pants, as the old saying went. And the gyros could not all have failed, simultaneously and independently.

Only one answer remained. Every atom of *Endeavour* must be in the grip of some force – and only a powerful gravitational field could produce this effect. At least, no other *known* field ...

Suddenly, the stars vanished. The blazing disc of the sun had emerged from behind the shield of Rama, and its glare had driven them from the sky.

'Can you get a radar reading? What's the Doppler?'

Norton was fully prepared to find that this too was inoperative, but he was wrong.

Rama was under way at last, accelerating at the modest rate of 0.015 gravities. Dr Perera, Norton told himself, would be pleased; he had predicted a maximum of 0.02. And *Endeavour* was somehow caught in its wake like a piece of flotsam, whirling round and round behind a speeding ship ...

Hour after hour, that acceleration held constant; Rama was falling away from *Endeavour* at steadily increasing speed. As its distance grew, the anomalous behaviour of the ship slowly ceased; the normal laws of inertia started to operate again. They could only guess at the energies in whose backlash they had been briefly caught, and Norton was thankful that he had stationed *Endeavour* at a safe distance before Rama had switched on its drive.

As to the nature of that drive, one thing was now certain, even though all else was mystery. There were no jets of gas, no beams of ions or plasma thrusting Rama into its new orbit. No one put it better than Sergeant-Professor Myron when he said, in shocked disbelief: 'There goes Newton's Third Law.'

It was Newton's Third law, however, upon which *Endeavour* had to depend the next day, when she used her very last reserves of propellent to bend her own orbit outwards from the sun. The change was slight, but it would increase her perihelion distance by ten million kilometres. That was the difference between running the ship's cooling system at ninety-five per cent capacity – and a certain fiery death.

When they had completed their own manoeuvre, Rama was two hundred thousand kilometres away, and difficult to see against the glare of the sun. But they could still obtain accurate radar measurements of its orbit; and the more they observed, the more puzzled they became.

They checked the figures over and over again, until there was no escaping from the unbelievable conclusion. It looked as if all the fears of the Hermians, the heroics of Rodrigo, and the rhetoric of the General Assembly, had been utterly in vain.

What a cosmic irony, said Norton as he looked at his final figures, if after a million years of safe guidance Rama's computers had made one trifling error – perhaps changing the sign of an equation from plus to minus.

Everyone had been so certain that Rama would lose speed, so that it could be captured by the sun's gravity and thus become a new planet of the solar system. It was doing just the opposite.

It was gaining speed – and in the worst possible direction.

Rama was falling ever more swiftly into the sun.

45
Phoenix

As the details of its new orbit became more and more clearly defined, it was hard to see how Rama could possibly escape disaster. Only a handful of comets had ever passed as close to the sun; at perihelion, it would be less than half a million kilometres above that inferno of fusing hydrogen. No solid material could withstand the temperature of such an approach; the tough alloy that comprised Rama's hull would start to melt at ten times that distance.

Endeavour had now passed its own perihelion, to everyone's relief, and was slowly increasing its distance from the sun. Rama was far ahead on its closer, swifter orbit, and already appeared well inside the outermost fringes of the corona. The ship would have a grandstand view of the drama's final stage.

Then, five million kilometres from the sun, and still accelerating, Rama started to spin its cocoon. Until now, it had been visible under the maximum power of *Endeavour*'s telescopes as a tiny bright bar; suddenly it began to scintillate, like a star seen through horizon mists. It almost seemed as if it was disintegrating; when he saw the image breaking up, Norton felt a poignant sense of grief at the loss of so much wonder. Then he realised that Rama was still there, but that it was surrounded by a shimmering haze.

And then it was gone. In its place was a brilliant, star-like object, showing no visible disc – as if Rama had suddenly contracted into a tiny ball.

It was some time before they realised what had happened. Rama had indeed disappeared: it was now surrounded by a perfectly reflecting sphere, about a hundred kilometres in diameter. All that they could now see was the reflection of the sun itself, on the curved portion that was closest to them. Behind this protective bubble, Rama was presumably safe from the solar inferno.

As the hours passed, the bubble changed its shape. The image of the sun became elongated, distorted. The sphere was turning into an ellipsoid, its long axis pointed in the direction of Rama's flight. It was then that the first anomalous reports started coming in from the robot observatories, which, for almost two hundred years, had been keeping a permanent watch on the sun.

Something was happening to the solar magnetic field, in the region around Rama. The million-kilometre-long lines of force that threaded the corona, and drove its wisps of fiercely ionized gas at speeds which sometimes defied even the crushing gravity of the sun, were shaping themselves around that glittering ellipsoid. Nothing was yet visible to the eye, but the orbiting instruments reported every change in magnetic flux and ultra-violet radiation.

And presently, even the eye could see the changes in the corona. A faintly-glowing tube or tunnel, a hundred thousand kilometres long, had appeared high in the outer atmosphere of the sun. It was slightly curved, bending along the orbit which Rama was tracing, and Rama itself – or the protective cocoon around it – was visible as a glittering head racing faster and faster down that ghostly tube through the corona.

For it was still gaining speed; now it was moving at more than two thousand kilometres a second, and there was no question of it ever remaining a captive of the sun. Now, at last, the Raman strategy was obvious; they had come so close to the sun merely to tap its energy at the source, and to speed themselves even faster on the way to their ultimate unknown goal ...

And presently it seemed that they were tapping more than

energy. No one could ever be certain of this, because the nearest observing instruments were thirty million kilometres away, but there were definite indications that matter was flowing from the sun *into Rama itself*, as if it was replacing the leakages and losses of ten thousand centuries in space.

Faster and faster Rama swept around the sun moving now more swiftly than any object that had ever travelled through the solar system. In less than two hours, its direction of motion had swung through more than ninety degrees, and it had given a final, almost contemptuous proof of its total lack of interest in all the worlds whose peace of mind it had so rudely disturbed.

It was dropping out of the Ecliptic, down into the southern sky, far below the plane in which all the planets move. Though that, surely, could not be its ultimate goal, it was aimed squarely at the Greater Magellanic Cloud, and the lonely gulfs beyond the Milky Way.

46
Interlude

'Come in,' said Commander Norton absentmindedly at the quiet knock on his door.

'Some news for you, Bill. I wanted to give it first, before the crew gets into the act. And anyway, it's my department.'

Norton still seemed far away. He was lying with his hands clasped under his head, eyes half shut, cabin light low – not really drowsing, but lost in some reverie or private dream.

He blinked once or twice, and was suddenly back in his body.

'Sorry Laura – I don't understand. What's it all about?'

'Don't say you've forgotten!'

'Stop teasing, you wretched woman. I've had a few things on my mind recently.'

Surgeon-Commander Ernst slid a captive chair across in its slots and sat down beside him.

'Though interplanetary crises come and go, the wheels of Martian bureaucracy grind steadily away. But I suppose Rama helped. Good thing you didn't have to get permission from the Hermians as well.'

Light was dawning.

'Oh – Port Lowell has issued the permit!'

'Better than that – it's already being acted on.' Laura glanced at the slip of paper in her hand. 'Immediate,' she read. 'Probably right now, your new son is being conceived. Congratulations.'

'Thank you. I hope he hasn't minded the wait.'

Like every astronaut, Norton had been sterilized when he entered the service; for a man who would spend years in space, radiation-induced mutation was not a risk – it was a certainty. The spermatozoon that had just delivered its cargo of genes on Mars, two hundred million kilometres away, had been frozen for thirty years, awaiting its moment of destiny.

Norton wondered if he would be home in time for the birth. He had earned rest, relaxation – such normal family life as an astronaut could ever know. Now that the mission was essentially over, he was beginning to unwind, and to think once more about his own future, and that of both his families. Yes, it would be good to be home for a while, and to make up for lost time – in many ways …

'This visit,' protested Laura rather feebly, 'was purely in a professional capacity.'

'After all these years,' replied Norton, 'we know each other better than that. Anyway, you're off duty now.'

'*Now* what are you thinking?' demanded Surgeon-Commander Ernst, very much later. 'You're not becoming sentimental, I hope.'

'Not about us. About Rama. I'm beginning to miss it.'

'Thanks very much for the compliment.'

Norton tightened his arms around her. One of the nicest things about weightlessness, he often thought, was that you could really hold someone all night, without cutting off the circulation. There were those who claimed that love at one gee was so ponderous that they could no longer enjoy it.

'It's a well-known fact, Laura, than men, unlike women, have *two*-track minds. But seriously – well, *more* seriously – I do feel a sense of loss.'

'I can understand that.'

'Don't be so clinical; that's not the only reason. Oh, never mind.' He gave up. It was not easy to explain, even to himself.

He had succeeded beyond all reasonable expectation; what his men had discovered in Rama would keep scientists busy for decades. And, above all, he had done it without a single casualty.

But he had also failed. One might speculate endlessly, but the nature and the purpose of the Ramans was still utterly unkown. They had used the solar system as a refueling stop – as a booster station – call it what you will, and had then spurned it completely, on their way to more important business. They would probably never even know that the human race existed; such monumental indifference was worse than any deliberate insult.

When Norton had glimpsed Rama for the last time, a tiny star hurtling outwards beyond Venus, he knew that part of his life was over. He was only fifty-five, but he felt he had left his youth down there on the curving plain, among mysteries and wonders now receding inexorably beyond the reach of man. Whatever honours and achievements the future brought him, for the rest of his life he would be haunted by a sense of anticlimax, and the knowledge of opportunities missed.

So he told himself; but even then, he should have known better.

And on far-off Earth, Dr Carlisle Perera had as yet told no one how he had woken from a restless sleep with the message from his subconscious still echoing in his brain:

The Ramans do everything in threes.

ABOUT THE AUTHOR

ARTHUR C. CLARKE was born in Minehead in 1917. During the Second World War he served as an RAF radar instructor, rising to the rank of Flight-Lieutenant. After the war he won a B.Sc. in physics and mathematics with first class honours from King's College, London. One of the most respected of all science fiction writers, he also won the Kalinga Prize, the Aviation Space-Writers' Prize and the Westinghouse Science Writing Prize. He also shared an Oscar nomination with Stanley Kubrick for the screenplay of *2001: A Space Odyssey*, which was based on his story 'The Sentinel'. He lived in Sri Lanka from 1956 until his death in 2008.

"Finn." The prince's voice snapped her out of the memory's choke hold.

She sucked her teeth. "I grew up in a world where watching bad things happen to others and not lifting a finger was how you survived, if not doing some bad things yourself. It's how I've lived my life for a long time."

The prince tilted his head. "But not today?"

Finn looked away from him and picked at her nails. "No, not today."

"Why?"

"Because whatever monster you released looks like it could end the maldito world if it feels like it. I need to fix this, so that the world keeps spinning and I have more chances to say, 'Not today.'" She held his gaze. "Understand, Prince?"

NOCTURNA

MAYA MOTAYNE

BALZER + BRAY

An Imprint of HarperCollins*Publishers*

Library of Congress Control Number: 2018968471
ISBN 978-0-06-284274-9

Typography by Jenna Stempel-Lobell
20 21 22 23 24 PC/LSCH 10 9 8 7 6 5 4 3 2 1
❖

First paperback edition, 2020

To my friends, who believed in me before I did.

MUNDO

The Lost Ocean

Bei Hua

MIRAI

The Jade Sea

Cape Abuja

The Pinch

The Bash

The Brim

The Bow

The Crown

The City of
SAN CRISTÓBAL

NOCTURNA

THE PRINCE WITHOUT A FUTURE

A prince always comes home.

Alfie's mother had told him that when he'd boarded his ship three months ago, leaving San Cristóbal behind to be swallowed by the horizon. And now, as the same ship eased back into the port it had departed from, Alfie's shadow gathered around his feet in a tight spiral of nerves.

He was home.

The rings of the capital city bloomed before him, from the slouching taverns that braced against the sea breeze in the Pinch to the stately haciendas with stained glass windows and sloped adobe roofs deeper inland in the Bow. Mountains swelled in the far distance. If he squinted, he could spot the surrounding sugarcane fields, swaying in the breeze, ripe for harvest. And, of course, rising against the horizon like a second sun was the palace.

Alfie's fingers curled tight around the railing of the ship, the flap of the scarlet sails quieting around him as the crew readied to dock. The shops and taverns of the port were lined with lanterns enchanted to burn all night long to welcome incoming sailors. Even after everything that had happened, the city was so strangely unchanged. But that was the trick of home, he supposed. It stayed the same even when you didn't.

Alfie wanted nothing more than to shout for the captain to head back to open sea. His pounding heart urged him to sail away and not let his feet touch the ground of this place.

"Prince Alfehr," the captain said, pulling Alfie from his thoughts. "Your carriage has arrived."

Alfie took a deep breath, his eyes clinging to the clear blue sea. From the deck he could spot colorful fish darting about in schools, unbothered by the boat gliding over them. As soon as the ship had slid from the choppy foreign ocean into the soft embrace of the Suave, the waters of his homeland, Alfie's stomach began to twist with anxiety. He'd known then that he was getting too close to home. Now there was no turning back.

Like everyone else, he was born with an affinity for one of the four elements—his was water. He wasn't the most skilled water charmer; like most nobles, he hadn't focused much on elemental study, but he still wanted to whip his arms through the air and push waves against the boat, steering the ship far from here. Instead he said, "Thank you, Bastien, for your service." When the captain gave a bow and turned to leave, Alfie spoke again. "Espérate."

"Yes, Your Grace."

"Do I look . . ." Alfie glanced at him furtively. "Do I look all right?"

Bastien gave him a knowing glance. "You look just fine, Prince

Alfie. And even if you did not, your family would be happy to see you. In any condition."

Alfie nodded gratefully as the captain left him to his thoughts. For the last week he'd stopped his drinking and late-night reading of every text of illegal magic he could get his hands on, in hopes of getting rid of the dark circles under his eyes. During his time on board the ship, the drink left him too bold to hide how lost he felt, searching for meaning in his grief only to find anger. The crew knew it all too well, but he didn't want his mother to see who he'd become during these months away. Still, the flask of tequila sat hidden at his hip, an anchor dragging him down into its numbing embrace.

Alfie walked the shifting gangplank to the dock. As his feet touched solid ground it was strange to feel that terrible stillness again, as if hands had sprung out of the earth to hold him here in this place full of memories he'd tried to forget. With gritted teeth, he ground his heels to get his shadow to stop skittering back toward the ship. He was home now. He had an image to uphold. With his head held high, he strode toward the waiting carriage.

People working on the docks, citizens of the kingdom he would wrongfully inherit, began to gather in a wide ring about the carriage, whispering.

"Is that really him?"

"Crown Prince Alfie has returned!"

Their words fell on his shoulders like slabs of stone. The title of crown prince belonged to his brother, Dezmin, not him. Alfie walked faster. A squadron of guards in red capes bearing the insignia of Castallan formed a barrier around the carriage.

A man wearing a brimmed hat raised his son onto his shoulders to get a better look. "Mira, Mijo! It's the prince!"

Alfie couldn't bear it. They all had such hope in their eyes. His heart beating in his throat, he finally reached the coach. But before he could step in, one voice rang out over the others, snapping against him like a whip.

"Your loss is our loss, Prince Alfehr! May Prince Dezmin rest in peace!"

Alfie's smile slipped and fell. The man's condolences held a grain of truth—Dez's absence truly was their loss. They'd been robbed of a real leader and were left with Alfie instead. But the man was wrong about one thing—Dez wasn't dead. Alfie had returned home to find him. For these people who deserved a true king, he had returned. He would make things right.

His throat burning with the effort of holding his grief at bay, he looked at the crowd and said, "Thank you."

His voice was wooden, hollow. But he supposed that was better than sounding broken.

As the carriage drew away from the port and the palace's silver gates rose in the distance, a knot of dread twisted in his stomach. The ride had been too short. People spoke of how time sprinted during the best of moments, but it dashed just as quickly when something unwanted was on the horizon.

The silver gates pulled open and the carriage rolled onto the lush royal grounds. Ahead, the palace sat at the center of a sprawling lake. Its domes, each a patchwork of colored glass, caught gleams of moonlight, reflecting rays of scarlet, azure, and jade.

There was no strip of land to connect the palace to the

surrounding grounds. At least not a permanent one. As the coach reached the water's edge, the stone carvers stationed before the lake raised their arms in unison and a path of stone rose out of the water. As a child, Alfie would stick his head out the window and watch the stone bridge descend back into the lake as the carriage rolled forward. Now he just stared straight ahead.

The driver pulled the horses to a halt before the palace and Alfie stepped out, feeling small before his towering home. A servant stationed at the bottom of the stone stairs bowed as Alfie approached.

"Welcome home, Your Highness," he said. "The king and queen have requested—"

"—that I wait for them in the library," Alfie said, finishing the servant's sentence. It was where his parents always went when there was something important to talk about. The servant nodded at him. "I'll go straightaway. Gracias."

Alfie trudged up the stairs, his half cape flowing behind him in the night breeze. As he approached the doors they swung inward and he was hit with the familiar scent of home—the cinnamon incense his mother loved to burn and the smell of freshly washed linen. His shoes clattered against the hand-painted tiles of the palace floor, the sound echoing through the halls. Swaths of richly colored fabric were draped across the ceiling, bringing a touch of warmth to the looming corridors. The walls were tiled just as the floor was, forming mosaics of bright color—swirls of burnt orange, rosy red, and summer yellows. As he walked, servants stopped their work to bow, and Alfie inclined his head, his discomfort growing with each look of deference he received.

Alfie hurried on to the library. If he and his parents were going to talk, he needed to get it over with quickly. Tonight, he had a game to attend and win.

He turned into a sweeping corridor where a servant no older than twelve meticulously dusted the portraits of past kings and queens that lined the walls in their gilded frames. With a word of magic, the boy floated his feather duster up to clean a gargantuan painting of Alfie's great-grandfather. The servants were taught simple forms of spoken magic, as necessary for their jobs—spellwork to clean and organize. Alfie didn't recognize the boy; he must've been new. He could see the glint of a silver earring in the boy's right lobe. He certainly was new if the head of staff hadn't caught him wearing that. Alfie made to hurry past him unnoticed, but the boy spotted him, his eyes wide. His mouth opened and closed soundlessly, like a fish on a hook.

"Prince Alfehr!" He turned away from the wall of paintings and dropped into a low bow. With his concentration broken, the duster came careening down.

Alfie outstretched his hand. "*Parar!*" With a word of magic the duster froze, hanging suspended just above the boy's head.

A flush crept up the boy's face as he sheepishly plucked it from the air.

Alfie hurried on, leaving the boy to stare after him. He looked at him with too much hope, just like the people at the port.

Alfie dashed down the hall and darted through the dark wood doors of the library. He let the silence of the room swaddle him. The library was cavernous, with a domed ceiling of colored glass. Wheeled ladders leaned against the shelves upon shelves of books that lined the walls. The sweeping room was outfitted with desks and plush armchairs to sink into with a good book. No matter how many talks of legacy and responsibility he'd endured here, there would always be something soothing about the library.

Alfie walked to the nearest bookshelf, where a ladder scarcely taller than he was stood. He looked up. The rows of books stretched all the way to the ceiling. Above, painted on the domed, stained glass ceiling was a mural of the history of the Castallan Kingdom rendered in a starburst of color.

Alfie stepped onto the first rung of the ladder.

"*Alargar*," he said. The ladder stretched upward until it reached the top shelves. His shadow squirmed uncomfortably where it clung to the bookshelves before him. He must have been at least twenty men high. But he wasn't much afraid. Any bruxo worth his salt knew the magic to slow a fall, soften a landing. And being up this high was infinitely better than waiting on the ground to be lectured for turning his back on his responsibilities for three months.

Alfie pushed away those thoughts and ran his hand over the books' leather spines. He stood surrounded by tomes on all types of magic. Books on elemental magic, an art grounded in the inborn ability to manipulate one of the four elements via physical move-ment and instinct; books of written and spoken spellwork, both based on the careful study of the language of magic; there were even books on the least common branch of magic, *propio*—per-sonal magical abilities that were unique to each bruxo. Those born with *propio* were considered blessed with a greater connection to the art of magic. Each form drew upon an energy within the bruxos who called upon it, the principle of balance and exchange between man and magic—man providing his body and energy to house and power the magic, and magic offering its wonders to man.

But no matter how much he read on the subject, no book could describe how it *felt* to use magic, to interact with a living force so powerful that it overwhelmed and humbled you all at once. Magic could not speak, yet interacting with it felt like a conversation, a dance, a story shared with a friend with the ending left up to interpretation. To Alfie, magic was a bit like a stray dog. If you advanced on it with arrogance, it would snap at you. If you approached it too desperately, it would skitter away. But if you came to it with an open heart and respect, it might let you stroke its fur and scratch behind its ears.

He tilted his head back and looked up at the ceiling mural. Alfie concentrated, letting his mind fall quiet until he felt in tune with the magic flowing through the world, through him—a meditative focus that had taken years of study. When he reached this state, it was as if the magic threading through this world had a pulse, a heartbeat, and he could feel it thrumming through the air, slowing down or speeding up to match his own.

As the currents of magic washed over him, Alfie spoke the word he needed: "*Contar.*"

At his command the mural moved with life, swirling above his head in bursts of color. The magic poured life into the images, showing his people swathed in bright colors, prospering and using magic freely. Then the mural slowly darkened as Englassen conquerors appeared on the shores. They chained his people, and Alfie watched the enchanted chains glow as his people's magic was drained from them and transferred to their Englassen masters so that they could perform more magic. The Englassen regime destroyed all the tomes of their language, forcing them to forget the tongue that connected them to their heritage—to their magic. Then came the rebellion, with the enslaved breaking free of their shackles and rising against the conquerors and rediscovering their language. The story finished with a great bird shattering the chains attached to its claws and stretching its wings victoriously, the very image on the Castallan flag. Just below the bird were the words of Castallan: *Magia Para Todos.*

Magic for all.

Alfie dropped his hand and the mural became static once more. He'd tried that spellwork long before he'd left home, and he hadn't been able to perform it. Now he couldn't help but shout "Wépa!" in excitement, his voice echoing throughout the library. At the sound of his lone echo, Alfie's smile fell.

When he was little, Alfie and Dez used to sneak into the library to stage grand duels with their blunt practice swords.

When he'd asked Dez why they always play fought in the library, Dez had shrugged and said, "It's big and dramatic. In the books you always have to have a sword fight in a big, dramatic place. And when you shout the whole room echoes."

At that, Dez gave a loud holler, his voice ricocheting off the cavernous ceiling. Alfie followed his lead, his own shout sounding like a chirp in comparison.

"See," Dez had said, smiling. "You always need a good echo."

Alfie pressed his forehead to a rung of the ladder. The whole palace whispered of Dez. There wasn't a single room where he could be free of his fear that he wouldn't be able to find his brother after all. That he truly was dead, like everyone said.

"Alfehr," a voice sounded from below, shattering the silence. It was a voice that spoke of the rumble of thunder before a flash of lightning. It was the voice of a king.

Alfie started, gripping the ladder with both hands. King Bolívar and Queen Amada stood beside the ladder, staring up at him, their expressions inscrutable from so high up. Where Alfie was tall and lanky, his father was broadly built. Dez had looked much more like him. Alfie took after his mother, with more delicate features.

"Ven acá." Her voice shook with emotion—though whether it was anger or relief, Alfie didn't know.

"Sí, Mother," Alfie called down. He took a deep breath and said, "*Acortar.*" The ladder shrank down slowly until Alfie was just hovering above the ground. He stepped off and turned to his parents. His mother's hands were bunched in her ruffled, violet gown. Her dark eyes were wide, as if she wasn't certain that he was actually standing before her.

He looked down, avoiding their gazes for a long moment. "I'm sorry I took so long to—"

Before Alfie could finish, the queen stepped forward and pulled him into a fierce embrace. The king wrapped his arms around both of them with a gentleness Alfie seldom saw from his father. Alfie's back stiffened in shock.

"Mijo," the king said, his voice soft.

Alfie's eyes stung. "I came back."

Queen Amada pulled away from the embrace, her gaze tender as she placed a hand on Alfie's cheek. "No, you came *home.* You have been missed."

Guilt wormed its way through Alfie. He wouldn't even be here if not for the game tonight. But they'd been waiting for him since the moment he'd left. And now they were looking at him with faith in their eyes, faith that Alfie hardly deserved.

But it would be worth it if there was even the smallest chance that what he found at the game tonight could help him find Dez.

"I shouldn't have stayed away for so long," Alfie said, his voice thick.

"It's all right, my son," the king said, moving toward a quartet of plush armchairs. He sat, motioning for Alfie and his mother to do so as well. "All men grieve in different ways. The important thing is that you're home."

While away, Alfie had worried that Dez had been the glue that held his father and him together. That with Dez gone, whatever was between them would crumble to nothing but filial duty. But he'd been wrong. The love he'd felt in his father's embrace was just as true as he'd remembered and so much more painful without Dez here to share in it.

When they sat, the queen looked over Alfie's shoulder toward the library doors, her eyes beseeching. "Luka, please. Don't you want to say hello?"

At the mention of his cousin and best friend, Alfie jumped out of his seat. They'd been raised in the palace together and only ever referred to each other as brother. His childhood was colored with memories of Luka, himself, and Dez leaving a trail of mayhem in the palace corridors. He hadn't noticed Luka standing at the library doors, but now his presence was unmistakable, and uncharacteristically cold. Luka leaned against the doors, his arms crossed and his eyes hard. Alfie's stomach tightened. To see Luka without a smile on his face was rare enough, but to see him looking so angry didn't feel right.

"Alfie," Luka said, his voice curt. He turned his gaze back to the queen. "I've acknowledged him. May I be excused now?"

The queen extended a hand toward him. "Luka . . ."

Luka narrowed his eyes. "Why should I say hello when he didn't bother to say goodbye?"

Alfie flinched and stepped forward, but Luka raised his chin as if daring him to come any closer.

The king rose and squeezed Alfie's shoulder, giving him a stern look that said, *Leave it*.

"Luka, you may be excused."

"Gracias," Luka said, his eyes ghosting over Alfie as he nodded at the king and queen in deference before turning on his heel and disappearing out the library doors.

Alfie took another step forward, intending to follow, but his father held him back.

"Give him time to cool off," the king said. "He took your leaving quite hard." He gave Alfie a pointed look. "That situation is yours to remedy, but first we must talk."

When Alfie's mother nodded in agreement, Alfie sat back down, his eyes still trained on the doors. Knowing that Luka would try to stop him from leaving, Alfie had taken the coward's way out and boarded his ship without a word. He knew he deserved Luka's anger, but the hurt in his eyes still stung Alfie like a slap to the face.

The king's voice pulled Alfie out of his reverie. "There is so much to say, so much we must do to prepare you for the throne."

Alfie bristled. This was not the first time his parents had spoken of preparing him to become king. It's what had driven him onto his ship and away from home. Still, each time they mentioned him replacing Dez, it was a new wound, raw and stinging.

"We have not forgotten about Dezmin. We never will." The queen turned away from Alfie, her voice catching. Alfie's chest ached at the sight, but then she met his gaze again with a blazing look. "But we must put our people before our grief. You have taken your time away, but now you must prepare. You are the crown prince, first in line for the throne. You must accept this. For your kingdom's sake, if not your brother's, entiendes?"

Alfie gritted his teeth and forced himself to say, "I understand."

"We are on the verge of making history. In only a few months we will meet with our greatest enemy for the first time in generations and make peace," the king said, motioning up at the mural. "Putting the feud between Englass and Castallan to rest and becoming allies will prove that we have risen from the ashes of this kingdom's past of slavery to become an unquestioned world power. But Dez's death," the king said, his eyes shining. "It has made us appear unstable, unable to protect our own. It raises questions about our political standing and what we offer as an ally. So we must prepare you and present you as a prince who is ready to become king. First to Castallan and then to the world. We will begin in two days' time by hosting a dinner party with the highest nobility of Castallan in honor of your return. The Equinox Festival is four days from today and, as always, we will host a ball to celebrate—the perfect opportunity to present yourself to the entire kingdom as its future ruler."

Alfie's heart clenched like a fist at the thought of being presented as Dez's replacement. Even if Dez were truly gone, the world would surely laugh at a prince without a future being responsible for the future of an entire kingdom. Why couldn't they see that he could not do this?

"But, Father," Alfie finally said, wringing his hands in his lap. "My mind has not changed. I still believe that Dez may be alive. We do not know for sure if—"

"*Alfehr!*" his father thundered. Alfie's spine straightened against his chair. The queen put a hand on her husband's shoulder while the king took in a shuddering breath. "I will not have you entertaining these fantasies. You cannot continue to ignore the truth and your responsibilities in favor of a delusion."

"But—" Alfie began, but his father silenced him with a look.

"Those who were discovered to be part of the coup that took Dez from us have been apprehended and imprisoned in cells in the Clock Tower for the rest of their despicable lives. The families of the three who led the operation—Marco Zelas, Alonso Marquez, and Maria Villanueva—have all sworn fealty and renounced their kin who went against the crown. There is no stone left to turn. No route left to explore. *Por favor*," he said, his voice so beseeching that it hurt to hear it. "Let your brother rest in peace."

Alfie looked down at his lap and gritted his teeth again to stop himself from arguing. His fingers twitched, wanting to reach for the flask of tequila hidden at his hip, to mute the turmoil burning in his chest. He was the only one who'd been with Dez when he had been taken. They had been in the Blue Room, a parlor in the east wing of the palace, discussing how to best ask their parents about taking a long trip abroad with Luka for Dez's twenty-third birthday, before his time would be swallowed by learning the ways of a king.

As they strategized, the double doors of the room flew open and a girl who looked barely older than Alfie stepped in. Her name was Xiomara Santoro, he'd learned after his brother was lost to him forever, and it was a name Alfie could never forget. Behind her, two guards were slain on the floor, blood pouring from their open necks. Dez pushed Alfie behind him, protecting him, until the very end.

In the space of a breath, the girl raised her hand and splayed her fingers. The ground beneath Dez opened into a darkness so complete that it seemed unnatural, unreal. Alfie had watched Dez fall into the hole, his eyes full of fear, his hands reaching up to Alfie and Alfie reaching down a moment too late. Before he could leap in after Dez, the hole closed. By then, a group of guards had the girl pinned to the ground while Alfie fell to his knees, speaking every word of magic he could to break open the floor and find that dark void the girl had conjured with her monstrous *propio*. But it came to nothing. Under interrogation the girl had admitted the names of those who'd enlisted her to kill the royal family. His brother was gone because a group of nobles had wanted to take the throne for themselves. The whole kingdom wore its grief like a veil. The marketplace was full of paintings and baubles in memory of the fallen Prince Dezmin. Nobles from every corner of the kingdom were lining up to prove their loyalty to the royal family, afraid to be sent to languish in the Clock Tower with those found guilty of treason. Castallan had become a raw, exposed nerve, flinching at the slightest touch, raising its hackles at any sign of trouble.

Still, he could not give up hope. Something within him knew that Dez was still there, waiting to be found.

"I'm sorry," Alfie said, the lie acrid on his tongue. "I will not speak of it again."

The queen reached over and took Alfie's hand in hers before giving the king a pointed look. "You look tired," she said. "Would you like to rest and discuss this tomorrow?"

His throat dry, Alfie rose from his chair. "Sí, I would."

"Mijo, remember this," the king said before Alfie could speedily leave the room. "My great-grandfather was the first free king of Castallan. In time, you will be the fifth. You are the grandson of men who lived in chains, men who were not allowed to learn the language of magic. Do not disappoint them."

Alfie's shadow curled nervously at his feet. "I won't. I'll make things right, I promise."

Queen Amada gave a resolute nod, her eyes still wet. "We know you will."

And he would, but not in the way his parents were hoping.

THE THIEF WITHOUT A PESO

Finn had never been a fan of puppet shows. Just the thought of them made her shadow twitch at her feet.

Yet in the boisterous maze of the marketplace, something had drawn her to this one. She stood behind the crowd of children watching, her arms crossed. The show had everything she remembered from the ones she'd seen as a child—a villain swathed in black with a deep, booming voice, a princess in a sparkling dress with sweeping eyelashes glued to her too-large eyes, a valiant prince vowing to save her.

Even as a child, before everything had happened, the idea of strings digging into joints, of painted smiles and unblinking eyes, of a grinning master just behind the curtain wielding all the power made fear trickle down her spine. She'd wanted nothing more than to race up to the stage and hack at the strings, watch the puppets collapse and fall still. Better never to move at all than to move at the will of someone else. Maybe, even then, she'd had the foresight to know what was coming for her, to know what master was lurking just behind the curtain, waiting to bind her with his strings.

Don't you miss it, Mija? a voice in her head purred. *Don't you miss your father? You're not faring too well without me, are you? Maybe you were better off strung up. . . .*

Finn shook her head free of the voice, every syllable digging under her skin. She couldn't get swept away by memories. Ignacio wasn't here to twist her with his words until she couldn't tell the difference between his demands and her own thoughts. He wasn't here to tell her to listen, to obey like a dutiful daughter, to thank him for taking her in when she had no one. Her life was her own now.

"Out of the way!"

Before her a boy shoved a small girl who'd been standing on her tiptoes in front of him trying to watch the show. The girl fell, her knees hitting the ground with a sad thunk. But she didn't cry, rise, and hit the boy back as Finn expected. No, she stayed on the ground silent for a long moment before finally standing and shuffling to the side, away from the boy's view. The girl folded her thin arms around her middle, as if trying to make herself smaller. As if she'd been knocked to the ground so many times that it was where she belonged. Finn knew that feeling all too well.

She'd never been a fan of it either.

Finn slid through the crowd of children and crouched in front of the boy, blocking his view.

"You want a closer look at the show?" she hissed with a smile. He opened his mouth to protest, revealing rows of gapped, chocolate-stained teeth, but Finn was too quick for him. She passed her hands over her face and transformed herself into the villain of the puppet show—a monstrous man with a red, sinister mouth too wide for his face and eyes as black as ash.

"Close enough for you?" she asked with a tilt of her head.

The boy gave a strangled yelp and ran away. As he turned, Finn pulled the pouch of pesos out of the back pocket of his trousers. She didn't usually steal from children—even she had her limits—but by the spotless soles of his shoes and the crisp cut of his clothes she knew his parents would replace it without batting an eye.

Finn passed her hands over her face again, returning it to its previous state. The little girl with the scuffed knees stared at Finn, mouth open. Unlike the boy, she hadn't screamed at the sight of the transformation.

"Well," Finn said to her. "You're braver than you look, muchacha."

Finn took in the shabby state of the girl's clothes, the thinness of her arms, the dirt under her fingernails. Or maybe this girl had seen more than her fair share of monstrous things already. Finn could understand that. Finn winked at her before rising and putting her hands on the girl's narrow shoulders. With a gentle push, she moved the girl to where the boy had stood.

"Aquí, front and center, where you belong."

Finn began to walk away, but then stopped, thinking better of it. Though her empty stomach protested, she took the girl's hand and dropped the stolen coin purse into it. "Get yourself something sweet."

As the girl gazed at the purse with a look of wonder, Finn stepped back and melted into the crowds ambling through the marketplace of the Brim.

The Pinch and the Bash—the poorer, outermost rings of the city—were porous, the divide between the two arbitrary and silently understood. After all, the poor hardly needed a distinction between one level of misfortune and the next. The Brim was the third of the city's five rings, a bridge between poverty and luxury. People of all classes met to spend their pesos here, from sauntering noblewomen in long, belted, ruffled skirts and brightly colored silken blouses to dirt-dusted farmhands in their patched trousers.

The next ring, the Bow, however, was a ring where nobles lived just beyond the Brim. The adobe brick barrier had gated entry points where guards stood sentry to keep out the riffraff. Past the Bow was the final ring of the city—the Crown. Beyond its towering walls, the verdant palace grounds sprawled and rolled, a cocoon of greenery surrounding the palace of colored glass where the royal family lived their lavish lives. Finn sucked her teeth at the thought of those pampered rulers with their silk parasols. She'd much rather be here in the Brim where all the action was.

Finn walked on, passing a stall of jewel-toned gowns and skirts. She watched a woman tug a dress over her clothes. When she twirled, it changed from bloodred to a rich blue.

"For that price you get three colors, you want more the price doubles!" the vendor said.

Finn grimaced as happy shoppers stumbled in and out of her path, making it difficult to move through the market as easily as usual. It was a bit too crowded and jolly tonight, with the air of a festival. Earlier she'd even seen water charmer performers dancing in the streets, winding ribbons of dyed water through the air like bolts of colored silk. Something was going on.

When she saw a vendor handing out free flowers to every passerby, she was done guessing. What kind of fool would hand out for free what you could sell for pesos?

"What the hell is going on tonight? Why are you giving out freebies?" she asked, coming to a stop before his stall.

The old man only smiled before pressing a white moon blossom into her hand. As soon as the white bud emerged from the cloth parasol canopying his stall, it bloomed to drink in the moonlight.

"Haven't you heard?" he asked, his eyes alight.

Finn squinted at the useless flower in her hand, but the man's excitement made her think twice about letting it fall to the ground. "No. Clearly."

"The prince!" he said. "The prince has finally returned!"

Finn gave a snort at that. "The dead prince?"

The old man's eyes widened. He blinked twice before answering. "No . . ."

"Then it's not that interesting of a story, is it? Keep your flowers and your sanity, old man."

When she tried to hand him back the flower, he waved her off with a smile, his mood irritatingly undampened. With the blossom in hand, Finn turned on her heel and followed the throng. That was the annoying thing about the capital city. People here were obsessed with the royal family. The prince coming home wasn't going to fill their bellies or get them somewhere warm to sleep, yet the whole city was aflutter. So what if some pampered pretty boy came home? It wasn't as if a prince could survive out in the real world for long. Of course he'd come running back home to his mamá.

"Stupid, maldito prince," Finn cursed.

And wasn't this the prince without a future? No usual announcement when the prince turned five of "The diviner has spoken. He will make a fine leader *blah blah blah*" nonsense like the other royals. The diviner hadn't seen a maldito thing about this boy. So if these pendejos thought this prince was anything to celebrate, they were out of their minds.

As she moved through the marketplace, her stomach gave a persistent growl. The pouch of pesos she'd given that little girl surely could have bought her a meal or two.

"Shut up," she said to her cramping belly, as if admitting the mistake would appease it. But it only ached more. "I know it was stupid of me."

But then again, she preferred going into a job on an empty stomach. It made her sharper. She'd been spending too many pesos lately. But once she pulled off tonight's thieving and sold the goods, she'd be set for another month or two.

So long as she pulled it off.

She dropped those nervous thoughts in the well inside her where she kept her fears, her anxieties—all the things she couldn't afford to feel if she wanted to survive.

"Focus," she mumbled to herself. Worrying was for people who weren't as good at this as she was. She would nail it tonight, like she always did.

Her mind abuzz with doubt, she let herself get distracted by two kids, flame casters, blowing streams of fire from their mouths, trying to see who could keep it going the longest. After a long moment, the taller one bent over, his hands on his knees as he gasped, sweat rolling down his face. Finn couldn't help but smile as they bickered about who was better, the losing boy arguing that he'd skipped lunch so he didn't have the energy to properly compete.

Overhead, the two-faced clock chimed from its tower, a sonorous reminder to every child that they ought to be tucked into bed by now. Finn glanced up at the great timepiece, its hands ticking in an endless procession of time lost and time to be gained. The stone tower held two clocks, one above the other. The scarlet clock face spoke of time in hours and minutes, its hands a glimmering gold. The one of blue-tinted glass charted the movement of the sun and the moon, its silver hands ticking ever closer to the upcoming equinox when night and day would share time equally, like a pair of lovers would share dessert.

The Equinox Festival was the most celebrated holiday of the year. Finn could hardly wait. Ever since she was a child she'd wanted to experience the wonder of it in the capital city. She'd heard tales of fireworks that flew through the air in the shape of great birds spreading flaming wings, each spark manipulated by the finest flame casters in the kingdom. There would be music booming through the rings, bachatas and merengues that made it impossible to stand still. The bakeries would overflow with every manner of pastry she'd ever wanted to taste. It was why she'd decided to stay in the city for this past month instead of just passing through as she always did. She wanted to witness the spectacle, just this once.

Plus, the festival meant fiestas, fiestas meant tequila, and tequila meant there would be plenty of people to pickpocket with ease. After the holiday ended, they would march onward to winter with its shortened days and longer, cooler nights. She'd make sure to hop on a ship to a warmer location well before then. Maybe the islands off the eastern coast? She'd never been there before. She'd heard their paella was too delicious to describe, and their seafood was so fresh that when you bit into the fried squid it sprayed you with ink.

At that, her stomach gave another loud protest. "Cállate," she murmured, but it wouldn't shut up. Maybe she'd made a mistake spending her pesos on a room at an inn instead of saving it for food.

Her stomach gnawing on itself, Finn passed a stand where a young man roasted skewers of adobo-spiced pork. He took in a deep breath and blew a steady stream of flame from his mouth to crisp the tender meat. Finn's stomach roared. Her lips curled into a smirk.

Then again, it was always easier to improvise when it came to getting a quick meal than finding a safe place to sleep.

Finn slipped close to his side and tucked the moon blossom into the pocket of his shirt. He looked up at her, his brown cheeks reddening.

"Tonight's a special night. You ought to look your best, don't you think?" She winked.

"Oh," he said, his mouth drawn into a perfect circle. "Th-thank you." He looked down at the moon blossom as it tilted sideways, leaning away from him in search of moonlight.

When he looked up, two skewers were missing and the thief was nowhere to be found.

THE FOX AND THE DRAGON

As the palace and those within it drifted to sleep, Alfie's shadow zoomed excitedly about his feet like a dog fresh from the bath.

That was the one disadvantage of having *propio* magic—your moving shadow betrayed your feelings. When Alfie dreaded something, his shadow slogged behind him, resistant and stubborn as a child woken early for lessons. When he was happy, it zipped about energetically. It even turned a pale gray when he was ill. Tonight, with his shadow surging about on the ground, Alfie's thoughts were far from a good night's rest.

He rose from his perch on the edge of his canopied bed and walked to the set of drawers, pulling open the lowest drawer and feeling about for the latch to the secret compartment. Within it, he found what he needed—a fox mask and a colorful doorknob of stained glass.

Alfie put the mask on, tying the silk string around the back of his head. It revealed nothing but his mouth and jaw. All players attending these games were to come masked. When it came to card games for illegal goods, anonymity was key.

Especially for a prince.

While he was away from home, searching high and low for the magic to rescue Dez, he'd heard tell of games where the stakes were high, but the winnings were higher still. Without a moment's hesitation, he'd paid the steep entry fee and showed up wherever the black, gold-trimmed invitations instructed. The games took place in different cities and even once on a different continent. But Alfie never missed a single one, and he felt in his bones that tonight's would be the most important game he'd ever partake in.

Tonight's prizes weren't just any illegal goods. They were books of forbidden magic that could help Alfie find Dez, alive and well and ready to take the throne. Dez was out there still, he knew it. Just because his brother had been swallowed by that eerie darkness didn't mean he was gone. Alfie just needed the right magic to find him.

Anticipation thrilled through Alfie as he grabbed the leather satchel from his bed and pulled it onto his shoulder over his dark blue cloak. There was no time to waste. Rayan seldom let players in late. Alfie walked to the wall beside his bed and tossed the glass doorknob at the wall. It didn't bounce off and fall to the ground as it should have. Instead, it spun like a dropped peso before settling and sinking into the stone.

Alfie stepped forward and gripped the doorknob under his palm. He let his magic change from its usual royal blue to a bright orange—the color that would take him where he needed to go. He need only turn the knob and say the word.

Each person's *propio* was unique, some with one singular gift while others had *propios* that branched into multiple abilities over time. Alfie had heard of a noble from Englass whose *propio* was manipulating friction—with a single look he could make the ground beneath your feet as slippery as ice; likewise he could make himself frictionless and travel miles in moments. A girl he'd met in Uppskala could bend light to her will, plunging a room into darkness as easily as she could fill it with light. The abilities that Alfie's *propio* granted him were all related to the color of magic. Alfie could see magic in all its hues, change the color of his own magic to match any shade, and use his ability to make pathways of color to travel by within the network of magic that lived around him.

Alfie turned his doorknob once to the left. "*Voy*," he said.

The wall gave way to a multicolored tunnel that Alfie could see, thanks to his *propio*—the very network that stitched the world together. He'd been taught from a young age that magic was the foundation of this world, the threads that bound men to each other and to the land they lived on. With his *propio* Alfie could use those threads of magic to move from one place to another.

When he'd first discovered his ability, the vastness of the network of magic around him was startling, and he felt like a tiny paddleboat lost in an endless sea. He needed a way to make his ability feel smaller, more accessible. And so he'd come to use a doorknob as a way of focusing his *propio* and seeing his ability as opening doors in the vast expanse of magic that hummed with life around him. He could do it without the doorknob, but it felt less safe, like dashing down a steep staircase when you could walk instead, with your hand on the banister.

He stepped into the magic and let the current carry him away from his bedroom and his legacy.

When Alfie walked back into the world, he did so through a wall between two stately haciendas in the second ring of the city—the Bow. Here, the streets were of cobbled stone and the haciendas were grand, painted in rich, vibrant colors with stained glass windows. Alfie pulled the hood of his cloak over his masked face and walked down the road to Rayan's hacienda. The dark wood door stood before him, tall and imposing. He hesitated. The mask suddenly felt uncomfortably tight as his parents' disappointed faces appeared in his mind's eye. What kind of king would he be if he spent his nights looking for things he shouldn't?

He sat wedged between his parents' worry and his hope for his brother's return, the pressure on both sides great enough to transform a stone into a diamond. He didn't know how much longer he could bear it.

This will be my last try, he thought to himself. *If I don't find what I need tonight, then I'll give up this quest to return Dez and focus on becoming king. Once and for all.*

He swallowed. The finality of the ultimatum gave him a sense of control, an end to the tug-of-war inside him. Yet the possibility of becoming king still stung. He pushed that thought away. He would not need to become king because he was going to win this game and get what he needed to find Dez. Alfie grabbed the knocker and rapped soundly against the door.

A burly servant opened it, his wide frame filling the doorway. "You're late. Señor Rayan does not appreciate tardiness," he said before beginning to close the door.

Alfie jammed his foot between the door and its frame. His shadow darted about the door frantically until Alfie pressed his heels into the ground to make it fall still. The servant eased the door open again, shooting Alfie a look of annoyance.

"Wait, *please*." He reached into his satchel and pulled out a handful of gold pesos. "Señor Rayan does not appreciate tardiness, but I'm more interested in what you appreciate, entiendes?"

A cordial smile unfurled on the man's face. "Have you an invitation?"

Alfie handed him the pesos and spoke the words that granted him entry into one too many of these dangerous games. "A fox does not wait for an invitation, he waits for an opening."

The man stepped aside, and Alfie stepped forward into yet another night of trouble.

The woman Finn was stalking through the Bow was clearly running late.

Late was good. Late meant she would be too busy rushing to look up and notice Finn jumping lithely from rooftop to rooftop to keep pace with her. The haciendas here were stately and grand with gently sloped roofs, perfect for hopping from one to the next. Though each estate was nearly six men high, years of filling in for acrobats in the circuses she'd worked in had stripped her of any fear of heights. If she'd ever had it to begin with.

The warm breeze whistling through her curly hair as she hopped from roof to roof, the patter of her footsteps, and the rustle of her bag against her side were the only sounds tonight. The cobbled streets were empty and the colorful haciendas were silent, their occupants asleep.

Even the name of this ring of the city made her roll her eyes.

The Bow. Something gossamer and cute to fasten around the neck of a kitten. The name suited it, with its delicately built haciendas, manicured gardens, and burbling fountains. There was a quiet calm in the Bow that made Finn itch. A kind of calm afforded by those who were born rich and would die richer. Finn preferred the Pinch and the Bash. Sure, they were dirtier, cramped, and at any given moment you were seconds away from being pickpocketed, but they would still be bursting with life at this hour.

Right now there would be street performers strumming languid bachatas on their guitars and food vendors hawking bowls of pernil, beans and rice, and sweet plantains. Her stomach growled at the thought, but Finn forced herself to focus on the task at hand. She needed to take this woman's place at the game, get the goods, and pawn them off. Then she'd have money for a full belly and a ticket onto the next ship out of here and onto her next adventure.

When Finn had first arrived a month ago, she'd set out to learn San Cristóbal's secrets—the seedy underbelly that would lead her to thievery that'd fetch a fine price—and it was always the noblewomen who were keepers of such knowledge. After days of snooping in the Bow, Finn was hardly surprised to hear about a game where illegal goods were the prizes.

The woman Finn was following ducked into a thin pass between two haciendas—the perfect place for Finn to descend on her. Finn crouched at the edge of the roof, her shadow winding around her feet excitedly as she watched. A bar of moonlight illuminated what the woman pulled out of her bag—a red dragon mask, the required attire for the game. Finn grinned. That was what she was looking for.

Finn raised her hand and made a swift motion, as if she were pulling a knot tight. Coils of stone from the hacienda wall wrapped around the woman's ankles and wrists, pinning her where she stood. The woman dropped her bag and mask. Before she could shout, Finn made another swiping motion, willing a coil of rock to wrap around her mouth, pulling her head back against the wall.

From above, Finn gave a low whistle. The woman looked up. Finn waved at her with one hand and picked at her teeth with the now-empty pork skewer she'd stolen with the other.

"Don't go anywhere," she said, her lips curled into a smirk. "I'll be right down."

The woman struggled against her bonds as Finn tossed the skewer over her shoulder and leisurely climbed down the side of the hacienda. At her touch, the stone of the wall curved outward into handholds and footholds for her to latch onto. As a child she'd wished she were a water charmer, since she'd loved to swim, but damn did being a stone carver come in handy when scaling haciendas. She dropped to the ground between the haciendas in a crouch, her palm braced against the stone floor for balance.

"I know what you're thinking." She grabbed the terrified woman's bag off the ground. "You're thinking, what did I do to deserve this?" Finn dug through the bag and pocketed the pesos she found. "I'm here to reassure you that, as far as I know, you did nothing to deserve this. I'm sure you're a saint. You're just in the wrong place at the wrong time, is all." Finn dropped the bag and picked up the dragon mask next. "And you happen to have something that I want."

The woman's eyes narrowed.

Finn held the mask out before her. It was red, the eyeholes

slanted and rimmed in white. "And in my favorite color too." She ran her fingers over its curved panes. "Lucky me."

Finn lifted the mask to her face and saw that her mouth and jaw would still be visible. "I guess I should match my face to yours, then, and my body too just to be safe, don't you think?"

The woman only stared at Finn in confusion. Like most Castallanos, she had brown skin, dark eyes, and thick brows. Her lips were full and her nose had an aquiline arch to it.

Finn held the mask between her knees and pulled a simple hand mirror out of her own satchel. "This is probably the most interesting thing you'll see all night, so pay attention."

Finn gazed at her reflection, taking one last look at her current face—amber skin, round, full cheeks, and a sharp chin surrounded by a shoulder-length halo of curly hair. It was a face she'd thrown on a few days ago without much thought and she wasn't sorry to see it go.

Finn raised her free hand to her face and molded it like clay as the woman watched, eyes wide. Magic was a mask Finn had slipped over her head so many times, she'd almost forgotten what her own face looked like. But that was just how she liked it.

And tonight there was a new identity to thieve and a prize that would fetch her a hefty price if she played her cards right. Literally.

With the tips of her fingers she reshaped her nose, reversing the upturned bridge into an aquiline one. She ran a finger over each eyebrow and watched them thicken at her touch. She passed her thumb over her chin, rounding it out. Finn rubbed her eyes as if she were sleepy. When her hand dropped, her eyes were larger and darker than before. She ran her hand over her curly hair and felt it smoothen to straight tresses that fell past her shoulders. This was slower work than when she'd scared the spoiled boy at the puppet show. This had to be exact.

With her face done, it was time to change her body to match the woman's as well. To make jumping from rooftop to rooftop easier, Finn had lengthened her body, making her limbs long and agile, but this woman shared her natural body type. So Finn shrank herself back down to her natural height, redistributing so her hips, thighs, and chest became fuller again.

When Finn looked in the mirror she saw no difference between herself and the woman before her.

The woman stared at her in shock. She'd even stopped squirming. Then her eyes flickered down to the ground, where Finn's shadow wound about her feet.

"Sí," Finn said, answering the unspoken question. "It's my *propio*."

Finn had been able to change her appearance since she was eight. It was a useful skill for anyone, let alone a thief, and it came in handy when she found herself parentless on the street.

"Now, I could kill you," Finn said to the woman. She pulled a dagger out of her bag and picked her nails with its point. The woman's breaths came faster, her nostrils flared.

"But I don't see why I need to." Finn shrugged. "You're stuck here, and come morning one of the nice families in this neighborhood will help you. But know this." Finn leaned forward so close that their now-identical noses were nearly brushing. "If you get free and decide to make trouble, every crime I commit from this day on, I will commit with your face on. It won't be much fun having to explain to the guards that you didn't do it, that some girl who can change faces did it instead. Won't take long for the red capes to stop believing you. Blink twice if you understand."

The woman blinked twice.

"All right, then." Finn pulled the mask on and tied its silk ribbon around the back of her head. She usually sketched the new faces she donned in her journal before doing a job, to keep track of all the faces she'd worn and the crimes attached to each one. But she was running late tonight. She'd have to do it later. Finn pulled a handkerchief and a tiny stoppered bottle of blue liquid out of her bag. She soaked the handkerchief in the sleeping draught. The woman began to squirm, making a muffled plea. Finn clucked her tongue. "Cálmate."

She held the handkerchief over the woman's nose. Her eyes slid closed as she fell asleep.

With that done, Finn sauntered out of the alley. She jogged the last of the distance to the hacienda where the games were held. Unlike other haciendas on this boring street, lanterns still burned bright within this one, casting colored reflections through the stained glass windows.

As she approached the hacienda she could see a man at the door arguing with a servant. One moment the servant was trying to shut the door on the man, the next he was stepping aside with a polite smile on his face. As the door began to close again, Finn rushed forward and shoved her foot in. The servant opened it, looking annoyed.

"You're—"

"Late. I know. And so was the other guy," she said, her gaze locked on his.

After a long moment he sighed. "Fine," he said, resigned. "Have you an invitation?"

Finn looked up at him and spoke the words she'd watched the woman say for weeks. "A dragon knows nothing of invitations. She roosts where she pleases."

He stepped aside and Finn strode in, smirking as if she'd owned this face for a lifetime.

CAMBIÓ

The stranger seated across from Alfie was not a good man.

He could tell by the way the magic flowed through him. The man wore a tiger mask, his thin body a puzzle of sharp angles. With his *propio* engaged, Alfie saw that the man's magic was a steely gray. It crept through him, quick and sharp. Predatory. Every movement deliberate. Alfie knew he would have to tread carefully.

To be fair, he would have to tread carefully around everyone in this room. As he sat in the octagonal parlor and looked around the table of masked players, Alfie could see nothing but colored magic that moved through them with dark intentions.

The voice of Paloma, his boyhood tutor, rang in his head: *Magic is a pure force that flows through this world, but it needs a conduit, a home. We are those conduits, the vessels for magic to grow in. One cannot survive without the other. We give it life, purpose, and, in your eyes, color. And when we are done, we return the magic to the ether for another to borrow.*

Paloma was a dueña, a philosopher who studied magic in all its forms and worked in the development and creation of spells. While most dueños chose to only work in spell creation and intensive magical study, others opted to share their knowledge by teaching the craft of magic to children. Paloma had taught him since he was a young boy, training him until he passed his examinations to become a bruxo—a certified practitioner of magic. She had sowed in him a love and respect for magic that had only grown as he did, from boy to man. Thanks to his *propio*, Alfie had spent much of his life watching free magic, colorless and shimmering, flow through the air only to be taken into the human body and given color. He focused and engaged his *propio* to watch the shades of magic in the four players.

Beside the Tiger sat a colossal man wearing a bear mask. Within him swirled a green magic, repulsive and hulking, like mucus. He drummed his thick knuckles on the wooden table as they waited for Rayan to bring tonight's prizes.

A maid placed chilled glasses of sangria before each player. The Tiger took a sip and grinned at Alfie, his teeth splashed red.

The Bear waved his hand at the woman. His hand was the size of her head. "Tequila," he growled. The maid hurriedly left the room and returned with a shot glass and a bottle. The Bear promptly snatched the bottle from her hand, snorting at the shot glass as if it was an insult.

When she placed a glass of sangria before Alfie, he didn't touch it, even though the consequences of not finding what he needed tonight made his fingers itch for a drink. Alcohol made his shadow sway. He needed it to keep still if he didn't want to attract any unwanted attention. Controlling your shadow's movements was like trying to control your facial expressions during a conversation with someone you hated. When he focused, he could keep his shadow from moving just as he could train his facial expression into one of politeness, but the stronger the emotion, the more difficult it was. Tonight it was crucial that his shadow lie still.

Generally, those with *propio* were revered for their deeper connection with magic. But he didn't want anyone to suspect that his *propio* could help him cheat to win the books.

Which was exactly what he planned to do.

He focused on the players and watched the magic run through them once more.

Next to the Bear sat a woman wearing a dragon mask. When he looked at her magic, Alfie's spine straightened in confusion. Hers was red, but it wasn't one shade like the rest of the magic he'd spent his life watching. Hers was a constantly shifting patchwork of reds, darkening and deepening before brightening once more. A gradient of scarlets, crimsons, and burgundies. He must've been seeing things. She cocked her head at him, a smirk curving her lips.

"Got something to say, Fox?" She lounged in her chair as if they were waiting for dinner instead of a chance at illegal goods. "Or should I grip you by the scruff and shake it out of you?"

The other players snickered. Alfie scrambled for a clever retort, but he was saved by Rayan walking into the parlor and shutting the door behind him.

"Welcome, lady and gentlemen," Rayan said. His short nose widened when he grinned. Like most ludicrously wealthy men Alfie knew, Rayan was eccentric and bored, which was why he held these games and procured the illegal prizes that made them so enticing.

In Rayan's arms was a stack of four black-spined books—tonight's prize. Rayan took a seat in the high-backed, gilded chair at the head of the table. He had a flair for the dramatic.

"Are you all ready for a game?" he asked.

The players nodded. A tense silence coiled around them.

Rayan stacked the books neatly at the center of the table. Alfie's heart leaped in his chest—a beat for each word on each page of each book. The risk of Rayan's games was that you never knew what game he would choose. If you wanted the prize badly enough, you paid the steep entry fee and found out. And these were not just any prize; some of these books were from Englass—and like all Englassen goods, they were completely illegal in Castallan.

Though he knew that what Englass had done to his people, using siphoning spellwork to steal their magic away, was foul beyond words, Alfie could hardly stop himself from snatching the books off the table and making a run for it. One of these books might have the kind of spell Alfie had been desperately searching for—the magic that could help him find Dez. If there was any place that would study the spellwork necessary to pull *propio* from one body to another, it'd be Englass. The girl who'd disappeared Dez into that black void had done so with her maldito *propio*, so if he could find a way to pull her *propio* into his body, then he could open the void and go rescue Dez himself. It was his only chance, he knew it.

With his focus gone and his thoughts knotted around the books, Alfie's *propio* fell away. The hues of magic coloring the players disappeared.

"Tonight's game, lady and gentlemen," Rayan said with a flourish, "is cambió."

There was a frustrated murmur around the table, but Alfie could barely stifle a smile. He and Luka had spent too many nights playing cambió. It was a timed game that was equal parts luck, strategy, and, of course, magic. While the hourglass ran, players drew cards from the deck or could even pluck a card from the player to their left in hopes of getting the strongest hand.

Then there were the charmed cards.

At the start of the game, each player was given five cards to charm with their magic. Then the charmed cards were shuffled back into the deck and distributed among the players. Cards could be charmed favorably or unfavorably. A charmed card could ruin your hand, changing your emperor card to a jester before your eyes. Or the opposite could happen and a charmed card could help you. When the hourglass ran out, the best hand took home the prize.

"Clean or dirty?" the Tiger asked. His voice was too cool, calculated. He sounded like someone who lurked behind dark corners, waiting for his prey to pass a little too close.

"Dirty," Rayan said with a smile.

Anticipation surged through the table. Alfie's eyebrows rose beneath his mask. Rayan wouldn't make the game dirty unless the players knew enough spoken magic to play properly. These people must be more educated than the usual sorts he invited. Probably wealthy merchants and nobles looking to add something rare and illegal to their collections. Even so, Alfie hadn't expected Rayan to allow a game of dirty cambió, with the risk of a player dying on his property. Now each player was in more danger than they had been just a moment ago.

Well, everyone except Alfie.

"Wépa!" The boy in the monkey mask to Alfie's right gave a crow of excitement, his wiry body jolting with anticipation. He drummed his fingers on the table as if the game couldn't start soon enough. He hadn't had the chance to observe this boy's magic. Alfie focused on him. His magic was a lemony yellow, energetic and surging. Alfie watched the boy's twitching fingers. He was someone who could barely sit still, let alone win a game of cambió. No one to worry about.

With a flourish, Rayan pulled the deck of cards out of its small, ornate box.

"*Mezclar*," he commanded. As if they were carried by a whirlwind, the cards spun around each other until he called them back to his hand. With another word of magic from Rayan, five cards floated to each masked player. "You all know the rules; charm the cards as you see fit. Be as cruel as you like. It is dirty cambió, after all." A glimmer of mischief lit Rayan's eyes.

Alfie watched the other players hunch over their cards, whispering words of magic. In dirty cambió there were no rules when it came to charming cards. Alfie hoped that they wouldn't use any lethal magic. They were here for rare books, not to leave the game with blood on their hands.

But as he looked around the table, each mask more menacing than the last, he feared that the players had no qualms about a bit more blood caked on their hands.

Alfie did a few simple charms on his five cards. One that would turn emperors into jesters, as well as confounding magic to put them off their game, confuse them. He wanted the books, but he wasn't going to hurt anyone. Not if he could help it.

"You're all done, then." Rayan clapped his hands. "*Regresar*."

The charmed cards flew back into his hands and shuffled into the deck.

"Let's get started!" With another word from Rayan, the cards flew among the players, each person receiving seven. A fat deck to draw from sat at the center of the table.

A moment of silence washed over the players, as if waiting for a charmed card to take its effect. Alfie ran his fingers over his cards and focused; he could see no magic running through them. He didn't have to deflect any charmed cards just yet. Even better, he had a decent hand.

He was safe. Everyone appeared to be safe. Maybe this game wouldn't end in blood.

"The smallest animal always starts first. Monkey." Rayan nodded at the boy in the monkey mask to Alfie's right before turning the hourglass over. "You begin the game."

The Monkey bit the inside of his cheek, his fingers drumming ever faster on the table. Then he reached toward Alfie's hand, his fingers grazing Alfie's emperor card.

Don't take it, don't take it, Alfie willed in his head.

Alfie forced himself to quirk his lips in a barely perceptible smirk, as if he were glad the boy was going to take that card.

It worked. At the last moment, the monkey-masked boy pulled his hand back, sucking his teeth in annoyance. Alfie stopped himself from looking too relieved. The boy reached for the deck instead, drew a card, and returned one of his own to the deck.

For a long moment the boy said nothing. His fingers stopped drumming on the table. An explosion of wheezing coughs erupted from his mouth, blood spattering the table before him. In the space of a breath his eyes had gone glassy and bloodshot. He clutched at his throat.

Alfie started in his seat and grasped the boy's shoulder, unsure of what to do. "Help him! He needs help!" Blood-tinged foam poured over the boy's lips as he fell forward, his head flopping on the table. The monkey-masked boy fell still, his mouth open against the wood.

Rayan softly clapped his hands, his ringed fingers clicking. "Eso! A poisoning card already!"

Alfie stared at Rayan, his heart pounding in his chest. He had underestimated the depravity of these games. He should have known better.

Rayan rang a small silver bell. Two men walked into the room and silently carried the body by the arms and legs out of the parlor. The smell of the boy's blood cut through the air like a scythe. Alfie felt sick to his stomach.

The man seated across from him in the bear mask gave a deep, low chuckle as he eyed Alfie in amusement. The woman in the dragon mask was the only other player who also sat stock-still. He looked at her, searching her body language for the shock he felt in his chest, hammering in his heart. But when she noticed his gaze on her, her body relaxed into nonchalance. She crossed her arms, unfazed. These people were monsters.

Alfie focused on the now bloodstained card that the boy had drawn; within it swirled a vile green magic—the Bear's. Alfie glared at him. The Bear cocked his head at him, as if inviting him to say something, but Alfie could only grip his cards so tightly his fingers ached.

All the while, Rayan shuffled the dead boy's cards back into the

deck and went on as if nothing had happened. A maid came to scrub
the flecks of blood from the polished wood table.

Rayan nodded at Alfie expectantly. "Well then, now that that's
over with. Fox, proceed."

But Alfie couldn't move. The smell of blood still laced through
the air. He could barely look at his glass of sangria without gagging.

"Onward, little fox," the Bear said, his voice as gruff and slow
as his magic.

Alfie glowered at him and took in a breath. He focused, looking at the deck. The top card was charmed by the steely gray magic
of the Tiger. Before picking up the card, Alfie engaged his *propio*
and let the magic flowing through him change color from his own
royal blue to the man's gray. A charmed card wouldn't affect the one
who'd charmed it. Alfie had nothing to fear so long as he matched
his magic to the card before touching it. It would see him as its master and not harm him.

Alfie added the new card to his hand and discarded one of his
lower ones. He rubbed his thumb on the card's face and found the
magic within. He nearly snorted; it was a drunkening card—one
magicked to make the player who touched it become piss drunk at
first contact.

Nice try, Alfie thought as he smirked at the tiger-masked man.
Across the table, the man's shoulders stiffened, and Alfie felt a rush
run through him. He was not as ruthless as these players and he did
not want to be, but he could outsmart them just fine.

Rayan sat at the head of the table, elated by the tension cresting
between Alfie and the tiger-masked man. "And the Fox outfoxes the
deck! For now. . . . Go on, Tiger. The turn is yours."

The Tiger reached for the Bear's hand. As his fingers lingered over a card, the Bear's jaw clenched. With a smirk, the Tiger plucked the card from his deck.

The bear-masked man slammed his fists on the table and stood.

"He cheated!" he roared, spittle flying from his mouth. "He looked at my maldito hand! I know it!" With a curl of his fingers, a globe of flame hovered above the Bear's palm. All the players shot out of their seats. Alfie rose last, unsure of what to do. Sweat on his forehead was making his mask slip. Were they all going to kill each other before the cards did?

The Tiger flexed his fingers in a quick, beckoning motion, and the sangria swirled out of his cup to hover before him. He closed his fist and froze it into a blade of red ice before plucking it from the air and holding it at the ready. He was a water charmer, like Alfie. The Dragon flexed her fingers and seemed to pull a dagger from thin air. Alfie only watched them all, his hand gripping his chair behind him. They stood silent, their bodies coiled tight with tension while Rayan sat in his chair, his arms crossed.

"Cálmate, Bear," Rayan said, sounding bored. He rang the bell. A group of muscular men filed into the room—men he had hired to protect him on the nights that he hosted his games. "Either the cards kill you, or they do. Entiendes?"

The flame quivered above the Bear's hand. The Tiger cocked his head at him, a smirk of amusement on his face.

"Fine," the Bear groused, sitting down. Rayan waved his hand and the men walked silently out of the room. The rest of the players slowly sank back into their seats. The Dragon's dagger disappeared back up her sleeve. With a flick of his wrist, the Tiger liquefied the frozen sangria and guided it back into his glass. Alfie sat down slowly, his cards held tight in his shaking hands. When he caught the dragon-masked girl staring at him, he took a deep breath and forced his sweaty hands to fall still.

"Carry on." Rayan crossed one leg over the other. Alfie could see the low heel in Rayan's gilded shoe. That shoe, like many things in Castallan, was a holdover from Englassen occupation. Englassen people tended to be taller than Castallanos. During Englass's reign, the more you looked like them, the more privilege and respect you had. So the people of Castallan had worn heeled shoes to appear taller, more Englassen. The trend still carried on today.

Enslavement was strange that way. Though his parents always spoke about what had been taken from them during Englass's reign—their autonomy, their magic, their culture, their pride—to Alfie, it wasn't so much about how much Englass had taken from them, but about how little of themselves Castallan had taken back after expelling their conquerors. If they'd truly rid themselves of Englass's influence and returned to their roots, why were they still donning heeled shoes?

"Fox," Rayan said, his voice jarring Alfie out of his thoughts. "Proceed."

Alfie looked away from the shoe and played his turn, his hand growing stronger as the hourglass ran down. Throughout the game, Rayan would speak a word of magic and make the chairs of the players switch places, zooming around the table, leaving Alfie dizzy in his seat.

"After all," Rayan had explained mischievously, "I can't have you drawing from the same person over and over again, learning their tells and using them to your advantage. What would be the fun in that?"

Alfie wondered if this was just another way to keep them on their toes. He sidestepped charmed card after charmed card, putting them back into the deck once he came across them. One was meant to make him endlessly vomit, one meant to blot out his eyesight for three turns, and when he found the terrible card that had killed the monkey-masked boy in the deck, he took it as his own before discarding it to the bottom of the deck, not wanting to watch someone else cut their own throat.

Without the Monkey, the woman in the dragon mask was to Alfie's right. As the hourglass began to peter out, she plucked the drunkening card from his hand with confident fingers. She'd probably assumed he had no charmed cards because he had yet to react to any. That assumption would usually be right, but not in this case.

As soon as she touched it, a hiccup erupted from her mouth and her whole body relaxed as she gave a slow, syrupy laugh.

"You know what I just realized?" Another hiccup. "I'm wearing a mask on top of a mask. Do you get it? Do you get what I'm trying to tell you pendejos? I'm wearing two masks at the same time!" She threw her head back and laughed, sounding as if she'd drunk a bathtub of sangria.

Rayan massaged his temples. "One of you had to do a drunkening card. Dragon, you took a card from the Fox. Please return a card, as the rules state," Rayan said to the girl, impatient.

"You call these stupid things masks!" She gestured sloppily at her red mask. "I've worn more masks than you idiots can count! I could show you how it's really done!"

"Can we get on with it, missy?" the Bear growled. But the girl just kept laughing.

Rayan gave a long sigh. "Just relinquish a maldito card, Dragon. That or forfeit your hand."

"Fine, fine!" she said. "But the truth is right in your face! In *my* face, actually," she said, chuckling gleefully like a child with a secret. Alfie did not have time for her nonsense. He was so close to securing the books. His fingers itched to turn their pages and all he could do was sit and wait for this girl to stop laughing herself into a stupor.

She finally chose a card to give up, but instead of placing it back in the deck, she flicked it at Alfie. She burst out laughing when it swatted against the nose of his mask. He should've let it drop to the ground. Should've moved out of the way or even stopped the card from touching him with a word of magic. But instead he raised his hand, letting his magic match the red shade he saw swirling in the card, and caught it as it fell from his face.

Perhaps it was fate. Or just fast reflexes. Either way, it was done.

As soon as he touched it, something jolted his finger as if he'd just pricked it on a lightning bolt. He'd been right about her magic being different; it wasn't a trick of the eye. This card was strange. He focused on it. It was a charmed card full of the girl's red magic. Just as when he'd watched it before, the color kept shifting in shade, a complex patchwork of reds that wouldn't settle. He couldn't mimic it at the drop of a hat the way he could the others'.

The magic was lithe and sharp as a whip. If this magic had a face it would be smirking, and Alfie wanted to know why. He pressed the magic further and under the surface he felt a pulse. Each pulse getting faster as if something were coming to a head. It reminded him of something. A moment too late, Alfie thought of it.

A countdown.

From the face of the card exploded a cloud of sweet-smelling smoke. Alfie dropped it on the table and shot out of his chair so fast that it clattered to the floor behind him. He covered his nose and mouth with his hands, sweat rolling down his face. Was it poisonous?

Rayan, a wind twister, pushed the air away, inadvertently saving Alfie from breathing it in too. A fit of coughing erupted in the room. Alfie heard chairs toppling over and bodies hitting the floor. When the air cleared, all the other players were knocked out cold on the ground, their masks askew. Rayan's men had charged into the room but had fallen victim to the smoke as well. Only Rayan and Alfie still stood. Alfie looked at the table and his heart sputtered in his chest.

The prize books were gone.

Everything he'd done was for nothing. He'd lied to his family and come home to the quiet palace full of Dez's memory for nothing.

"Thief!" Rayan screamed, pointing a sausage finger over Alfie's shoulder.

The woman in the dragon mask had dashed out the glass doors to the balcony before clumsily hoisting herself onto the stone rail, nearly falling over the edge in the process.

"Gracias for the game, gentlemen." She gave another loud hiccup, the card's effects far from wearing off. She took off her mask to reveal a round face with full lips and heavy brows. "And don't bother looking for me. I can be a bit hard to find," she warned with a loopy smile.

She ran her hands through her hair and the long, straight tresses turned into bouncy curls. She passed her hand over her face and the bridge of her nose straightened and shortened. Her eyes became wider set—her whole face changing with a quick touch.

Another hiccup sent her reeling, and she windmilled her arms before falling gracelessly backward off the balcony. Alfie could hear her swearing as she landed and took off running. Rayan stood stock-still, his mouth agape.

His fox mask secure, Alfie ran out of the double doors to the balcony and, after a moment's hesitation, leaped over its lip. The fall was five men high.

"Amortiguar!" When he landed in a crouch, his palm against the ground, the cobblestoned road was soft as sand. He braced his hand against the ground and took off at a run, disappearing into the night.

THE FACE THIEF

Alfie pursued the girl through the Bow, his mask secured.

He chased her as she darted through the rows of colorful estates, winging his shoulder on the trunk of a flourishing, well-tended mango tree between homes. He trailed her around a corner toward a square of expensive shops where the wealthy spent their pesos, but when he burst out of a narrow, hacienda-lined road into the shopping square, the girl was nowhere in sight. His chest tightened as he turned in a circle, looking every which way. She had to be here, didn't she? He'd been just behind her. Alfie couldn't lose her, couldn't lose those books. Tonight had to be worth coming home to Dez's absence and lying to his family. He would not go home empty-handed.

Alfie walked through the square, peeking into the narrow spaces between stores where she might hide. During the day, this shopping square would be full of vendors doling out wedges of flan and cones of thick-cut yucca fries. But they'd gone home hours ago. Below a full moon, the square sat dark and silent.

As he darted past a dressmaker's shop, glass crunched beneath his feet. Its window had been broken, but the shop was empty. Strange. He kept going. He didn't want to lose her. Ahead, a woman wearing a yellow dress and a brimmed hat stumbled out of the alley between two shops. He paused. How many people would be out in an empty shopping square in the middle of the night? Her shadow swayed at her feet like a drunken sailor. When he focused on her, he could see that shifting, red magic buzzing within her. Alfie jogged to catch up to her.

"Señorita," Alfie said, stepping in front of her. "The books."

The slurring voice beneath the floppy hat was forcibly high-pitched, as if she were trying to disguise herself. "Young man, I have no idea what you are talking about!"

There were many ways she could have hidden from him, including changing her face. The drunkening card must've been very strong for her to act this ridiculous.

Alfie knocked the hat off her head, and there was the face he'd seen before she'd fallen from the balcony. "I know who you are. The books, if you please."

"Rude," she tutted before shoving him away. "And you don't know me. No one does."

"How drunk are you if you truly thought this absurd disguise would work?" Alfie asked.

"Drunk enough to tell you to go screw yourself," she quipped. Her shadow whipped angrily about her, like a threatened animal. She swayed on her feet and Alfie gripped her by the shoulders to stop her from falling. "Get off me." She pushed him away. Alfie raised his hands in surrender. He didn't know how to go about this. She was drunk, he didn't want to take advan—

He shook his head. She'd been the one to take advantage. He owed her nothing.

"Please don't make this more difficult than it needs to be. I won't report you to the guards. Just give me the books and you can be on your way—whoever you are beneath that illusion spellwork." When her magic settled on a shade for a fleeting moment, Alfie finally got his to match hers. He reached for the magic she used to conceal herself, hoping to disrupt it just as he'd disrupted the charmed cards in the cambió game.

His brow furrowed. He didn't feel the frame of illusion spellwork on her. Strange. It was the equivalent of finding not a single stitch on a piece of clothing. He felt nothing but the red magic that ran through her like a second current of blood, seamlessly. Every *propio* had a limit, a hard restriction on its power. When it came to Alfie's, the only type of magic that was impossible for him to disrupt was someone's *propio*. If he could not dismantle the magic she was using to change her appearance, then it must be her *propio*. Paloma had always told him that one's *propio* was a reflection of who they were, their very soul. What kind of person was she if, underneath it all, she was someone else?

A liar, Alfie thought. *Someone not to be trusted.*

Still, he didn't want to hurt her if he didn't have to.

He stretched out his hand. His shadow curled tight around his feet. "The books, por favor."

She stepped back with a drunken sway. "'Please' isn't an accepted form of payment here. You want the books, you can pay for them or you can give me something of equal value. If not." *Hiccup.* "Then you really can piss off."

"Fine." He gave a sharp sigh. "How much?"

Her eyes roamed over him and he knew she was trying to decide how high he would go. He wished he hadn't worn a cloak made of such rich fabric.

"One million gold pesos," she crowed, her head tilting back as she shouted.

"Qué?"

"You heard me."

Alfie stared at her. "Don't be ridiculous."

She shrugged. "Don't lose card games."

Alfie gritted his teeth. "Señorita, I do not want to hurt you."

"Don't worry," she said with a bubbling laugh. "You won't."

Alfie bristled at the cutting sound of her laugh. "The books are mine. If you hadn't interrupted the game I would have won them honorably."

"You think so?" She smirked. He had a feeling that this expression was her default regardless of what face she wore. She glanced down at his shadow, which writhed in annoyance at his feet. "I'd venture to guess that you were using your *propio*. Not so honorable, if you ask me."

Alfie's eyes narrowed. "Who are you to call me dishonorable? You're a thief."

She threw her hands in the air as if he'd just said the dumbest thing she'd ever heard. "And you're trying to steal from a thief. I'd say that puts you beneath me."

Alfie glared at her before taking a deep breath through his nose. "Look, I don't want to hurt you," he said, his voice rough with annoyance.

She crossed her arms. "That's all well and good because I doubt you can."

Something in her tone rubbed him raw. "Then let me prove it," he said, his voice level and sure. He wanted to feel dangerous, like the players at the cambió game. He was wearing a fox mask, but he was behaving like a maldito doe. This girl had stolen from him, yet he was still hesitating. Tonight, he would be a fox. "We'll play a game for the books."

"Haven't you lost enough games for one night, muchacho?" she asked with a snort.

"Every time I wound you," Alfie pressed on, "I get a book. Every time you wound me—"

"Wounding you will be enough of a prize, thank you very much." She pulled the dress over her head and cursed like a sailor when her arms and head got stuck in it for an awkward moment. Alfie rolled his eyes. This was like dealing with a more violent version of drunk Luka.

She threw the dress over her shoulder. Now she wore the black shirt tucked into her belted trousers that she had worn at the cambió game. Her black bag stretched across her body from one shoulder to the opposite hip.

She sank into a sloppy defensive stance, breaking form to hiccup. "Let's play, then."

There was a moment of silence. That tense moment that must boil over before two people can be at each other's throats. Through the slanted holes of his mask, their eyes locked. With an upward thrust of her wrist, a line of stones the size of his fist rose from the cobbled ground.

Part of his body screamed to attack quickly, desperately. But he waited.

Paciencia, Prince Alfehr. Patience is a magic all its own. Paloma's voice rang in his head. Alfie moved into a defensive stance and waited. The girl looked at him and let out an annoyed puff of air.

"I don't know if you've noticed, but I'm a little sauced. I'd like to be in bed at a decent hour. So let's make this quick." She tilted her head and slowly looked him up and down. "Unless you'd like to skip the fight and join me there?"

Alfie stiffened, breaking his stance slightly.

With a splaying of her fingers, the stones shot forward. Alfie clumsily pulled tendrils of water from the humid air and froze it into a sheet of ice to block. But he hadn't summoned enough. He blocked two of the stones but was pummeled in the chest by the last few. He backed up before pressing a hand to his stinging chest. Blood welled beneath his shirt.

"*Sanar,*" he said, healing the wounds.

"That's one." She grinned. "Let's say three strikes for this game. It's a bit late for a kit like you to be without your mamá. We don't want her to worry, do we?"

Alfie glared at her through the mask.

Elemental magic was visceral, physical. It didn't require as much study or focus as spoken and written magic did. What it required was instinct, which Alfie always seemed to be in short supply of. And because of the noble preference for written and spoken magic, another holdover from Englassen rule, only rudimentary study of the elements was necessary to complete one's bruxo studies. Alfie had never defended against it in a fight.

"Why'd you back up? Scared of me already?" Her smirk sharpened.

Alfie ground his teeth. "Fine, three strikes and the game is over." This time he would be ready. She could barely stand on her own feet. He'd use that to his advantage. He beckoned her with an outstretched hand. "You want to end this fight, then come finish it."

The girl snorted at him. "If you insist."

She dashed forward, her steps fast but clumsy. When she raised her hands, Alfie watched her red magic flow sloppily from her body to the ground to pull three large stones from the cobbled street. She'd expelled so much energy just to grab three stones?

Just as she meant to attack, Alfie looked down at her feet and said, "*Adherir!*"

The girl's feet stuck to the ground as if glued. The momentum she'd built while running worked against her and she fell forward onto her face with a loud *thwack*. The stones clattered to the ground, one hitting her on the back. She shouted a stream of expletives as she pushed herself up onto her hands and knees. Her forehead was bleeding. Alfie let the magic release her feet.

"One to one, then." He crossed his arms in pride. She was a fighter, but she wasn't properly trained. When stone carvers who'd studied magic called upon the earth, Alfie could see their colored magic surge with precision to raise stones. Hers barreled out of her recklessly only to grip three rocks. With an expulsion of that much energy she should have been able to do more, but she had no discipline. She'd soon tire herself out. If he played this right, it would be just like the cambió game—she might be stronger and faster, but he was smarter.

"Of course you're into desk magic," she grumbled, shakily standing. Alfie cocked his head. He'd never heard of spoken and written magic referred to by that term or with such disdain. "Figures, you move like you've been sitting at a desk all your maldito life."

Alfie outstretched his hand. "A book, please."

She glared at him, indignant. "You didn't wound me."

Alfie shot her a look. "You wounded yourself thanks to my magic. It counts."

She sucked her teeth and threw a book at him with such force it slammed into his chest.

"Your first and only win for the night, Fox," she said with a slur. "Cherish it."

A smirk tugged his lips, one that he hoped rivaled hers. "We'll see about that, Dragon."

In a flash of movement, she launched herself at him, fists raised. She threw a messy punch. Alfie shifted sideways, her knuckles clipping his cheek as he caught her arm in his hand.

"*Adormecer!*" Numb.

Her arm fell limply to her side, swinging like a pendulum. She stared at it. "What the—"

Alfie landed a swift kick to her stomach, sending her falling onto her back. It wasn't a rib-breaking hit, but it still would hurt in the morning.

The girl forced herself onto her knees, her arm still limp. A plume of satisfaction caught in his chest when he saw her shocked face. Maybe he was more fox-like than he'd thought.

Alfie closed the distance between them and held his hand out. "I'd numb the other arm too, but then how would you give me another book?"

The girl glowered up at him. On the ground between them their shadows snapped at each other. By the sheer force of her glare alone, he should've known that she was about to cheat. But Alfie was distracted by their shadows sniping at each other. It looked exactly like what happened whenever he and Dez had gotten into arguments as children. His heart ached at the sight.

Just like with her trump card, he guessed her intentions a moment too late. She whipped her hand upward. A stone from the road shot up between Alfie's feet to hit him in the groin.

The pain roiled his stomach, sending him staggering. Then she was on her feet, her fist cloaked in a globe of stone. Before he could say a word of magic, she struck him with a powerful punch. His nose broke under the stone. The chunk of mask around his nose and cheeks shattered, crumbling away. She stepped forward, her palm thrusting up toward the sky. A column of cobblestone-tipped earth rose from the ground and pounded against his stomach like a fist.

He flew back, slamming into the wall of the shop behind him. His bag flew off his shoulder and landed ahead of him, at the midpoint between him and the thief.

Finn let the column of earth fall back into the ground.

For a moment, she thought he was going to walk it off. He pushed off the wall, raising his hand in her direction, but then he fell back against it, crumpling slowly to the ground until he lay pathetically on his side. His mask, now cracked and loose, was hiked up over his bleeding nose.

She swung her numbed arm uselessly. It was beginning to prickle. Hopefully it'd wear off soon. The idiot had numbed it so much that he might as well have chopped it off.

"Pendejo," she muttered, nearly tripping over her own feet as she stumbled toward him. The drunkening card still had her head abuzz. It'd made her so tipsy that she'd tried to steal a dress before realizing she should just change her face. But then she was too drunk to get it to stick. But she'd still bested him. Drunk as hell and still unbeatable. Not too bad, if she said so herself.

She made to dig through his pockets before pausing in surprise. He had a holstered flask at his hip. She wouldn't have expected that from someone so soft. Finn opened it, letting it spill onto the ground. Served him right for being such a pain. She searched his pockets, taking what she found before standing and tipping his head back with the toe of her boot. His head flopped back against the ground, jaw slack, lips parted. The blood from his nose ran into his mouth.

He obviously didn't know how to fight with elemental magic, but he didn't have to carry a water flask; he was talented enough to pull it from the air. A bruxo for sure. He probably spent his days lounging in some sprawling hacienda learning complicated magic instead of working odd jobs in the poorer rings. He definitely knew his way around a desk, but fancy desk magic wasn't enough here. This was the street, not a dueling ground.

"Home advantage," she said to his still body. "Nothing personal."

She thought of unmasking him, but she knew better than

anyone the importance of a good mask. What right did she have to take that comfort from someone else? She turned away from him and stumbled to his bag, which had fallen away from him when he'd flown backward. She rummaged through it. Inside was the book she'd given him and more gold pesos.

She wished the boy's satchel had some tonic to cure the headache hammering behind her eyes. Her shadow swayed like a docked ship. Damn that stupid card and this stupid boy. From behind her, he moaned in pain. She turned to see him pushing himself onto his hands and knees.

"You don't play fair," he grunted, adjusting what remained of his mask before it slipped off his face. She watched him place his hand over his nose, probably doing some healing magic. It'd be nice to be able to do that herself instead of having to pay some back-alley, fake bruxo in the Pinch who swore they'd passed their bruxo examinations to heal her.

"Don't kid yourself. I was never playing," she said, dropping his bag as she stood.

"Aren't you forgetting something?" The boy raised his hand, and between his fingers was the card she'd used to knock out the players at the cambió game.

She shook her head, the movement making her nauseous. "You are a strange little fox."

With a flick of his fingers the card flew through the air to her. She caught it reflexively.

Then she noticed something odd.

She herself had magicked the card, so it could only be controlled by her, no one else. She'd charmed it to expel that knockout smoke once in Rayan's parlor. That was all. Yet she could feel the card pulsing with her own magic, as if she herself had commanded it to release the smoke again, right now, to attack her. But that was impossible; it had to be a trick.

"You said you wanted to be in bed at a decent hour," the boy said. The card sent out a burst of that sweet smoke. Finn's head swam. "Sleep tight."

A fox would have let her hit the ground without intervention. A doe would have carried her somewhere safe. But Alfie was neither of those things, so he would do neither. As she fell, he spoke a word of magic to cushion her fall. He shakily rose to his feet and doubled over to clutch his stomach where she'd knocked the wind out of him. She really hadn't been playing.

He transferred the books from her bag into his own. Then he grasped the thief under her armpits and pulled her into a dark alley between two shops. Alfie propped her against the alley wall. Now if a guard made their rounds they likely would not see her, and if she woke before sunrise she'd have plenty of time to get away. What happened to her would be up to her. He looked up, and the dark of the night sky was muddled with clouds. It looked like it might rain.

Alfie took off his cloak and draped it over her shoulders, fastening it around her neck. Then he was satisfied.

He stepped away from the thief and tossed his doorknob at the wall she leaned against. It sank in. He let the doorknob darken to his royal blue. For his *propio* magic to work for travel, he assigned each location a shade of magic and a special twist of the doorknob.

He turned it once to the right before murmuring, "*Voy.*"

The magic obliged, and the wall opened before him, inviting him into the colorful quiet of its channels. Alfie stole one last glance at the girl, still fast asleep. He thought of waiting for her to wake up. Then he thought of the hit he'd taken to the groin.

Neither a fox nor a doe, but do not be a fool, he thought.

He turned away from the girl and walked into the magic as if it were a road well-traveled.

THE CHEST

The tunnel of magic opened into Alfie's bedroom. He grimaced in pain as he stepped out, then sat on the edge of his bed and took the books out of his bag.

There were five books instead of the four he'd expected. He must have accidentally grabbed something from the thief when he'd taken the books out of her bag. It was a small, palm-sized journal. He was surprised to find that the pages held fine sketches of more faces than he could count. They were drawn with such care that Alfie couldn't imagine them coming from the person who'd punched him with a stone-cloaked fist. She must've stolen it. Alfie shoved it back in his bag and turned his attention to the four books from the game.

All but one were Englassen. The last was a slim, old book in traditional Castallano script.

Alfie thumbed through the pages and smiled at the familiar stories. It was a rare first edition of a famous book of Castallan myths and legends. The book even had his favorite childhood tale— "The Birth of Man and Magic."

His exhaustion aside, Alfie couldn't help but read it, remembering how enthralled he'd been when Paloma had read it to him and Dez when they were boys.

Before there was man and woman, sand and sea, sun and moon, there were only gods. One sunless day, or perhaps it was a moonless night, the gods grew ill. They sneezed, and through the fingers clasped over their noses, stars shot free, spreading through the sky. When they coughed, puffs of cloud pillowed the cosmos. They picked dirt from their nails and land flourished. They wiped the sweat from their brows and the salted puddles became oceans.

The gods decreed that the land they had birthed must be tended to. So, from the light of the stars, the silt of the ocean floor, and the breath in the clouds, they made man and woman to be the guardians of the earth. But creating mankind was not like creating oceans and stars. Men had hearts and the gods could not agree on what to fill their hearts with.

And so Luz took half of mankind in her hands and filled them with light.

Sombra took the rest and threaded them with only darkness.

But both the god and the goddess were wrong.

The tale went on as most children's tales did—with the creation of a monstrous villain. Sombra, the god who created the dark, grew intertwined with the darkness until he and it were one. As

the darkness grew in strength, so did he. He wished to snuff out
the light and drench the world in shadow. The world was said to
be a strange place then, teetering with an imbalance of light and
dark as Luz and Sombra fought for control of man. Rivers ran violet
and flowers grew as tall as castles. Creatures of myth roamed the
land. But before the corrupted god could darken the globe, a man
of dark and a woman of light embraced to become one, the man of
dark falling and stretching at her feet to become her shadow. Their
embrace created mankind as it was always meant to be—a balance
of light and dark. From that balance, magic was born and the world
finally found its footing. Rivers ran blue. Flowers were small enough
to be plucked between a child's soft fingers. Dragons shrank down
into lizards and all beasts of legend disappeared from sight. Then
came Alfie and Dez's favorite part.

> *Sombra demanded that the light be snuffed out. As
> punishment, he was cast out of the heavens, forbidden to
> return. When he fell to earth, the darkness rooted within
> him corrupted all who crossed his path. The world's finest
> bruxos parted the god from the dark power he so loved,
> turning his once immortal body to bones. Learning from
> Sombra's faults, the remaining gods and goddesses turned
> their gazes heavenward. They built the kingdom their
> children would come to after death and left all matters of
> earth to mankind.*

He and Dez had had so many questions for Paloma after hearing
the tale. How did they trap Sombra? Was it true that if Sombra

rose again he would bring about what legends called Nocturna? It was something that Alfie had only ever heard described as a great darkness that Sombra would cast over the world, a dismantling of all things good. But Paloma had shooed those questions away, telling them to pay attention to the moral of the story.

We all carry good and bad within us, light and dark. That is what makes us human. And remember, no matter how far into the darkness we may fall, it is never too late to seek the light.

Alfie stroked the book with his thumb. What was good and bad had been so obvious then. Now, as he stared at the illegal books he'd stolen from a thief, the line was not so clear. Alfie smothered those thoughts. For better or worse, he had the books. He may as well learn from them what he could. With that, Alfie grabbed the one on top. The first two books were on Englassen history, useless to him. The next one was about Englassen folklore and legend—another waste of his time. Alfie looked at the final book.

If this one didn't hold the knowledge he needed to save Dez, he would have to let this go for good. He'd promised himself before attending the game that this would be his last attempt before committing to being Castallan's future king like his parents wanted. Swallowing thickly, Alfie picked up the book, willing it to contain what he needed. The book was so old that the gold letters on the spine had faded to barely legible script, but Alfie's brows shot up as he deciphered the title: *Sealing the Damned.*

"Coño! For gods' sake," Alfie cursed with a roll of his eyes. Still, he opened it and began to read.

It quickly became clear that this was an eccentric book. The spellwork within it appeared to be experimental, almost fantastical.

Alfie's brows crept up his forehead as he read chapters that spoke of monsters of dark power and how to seal them with strange magic techniques.

It spoke of old magic. Magic with soul, magic that colored men with its desires and bent them to its will. Magic born from man's sin.

Alfie snorted. What would be next, spellwork to slay dragons? Halt time? Stop death? Men colored magic, that was a universal truth. Fear of sin coloring magic was just something to say to children to make them think twice before dabbling in troublesome spellwork.

Still, his eyes clung to the crudely drawn images of creatures outlined in black. Monsters made of smoke and darkness that looked as if they'd crept from a child's nightmares to etch themselves upon the old pages of this book. He turned to the next chapter, its title loosely translated as "The Strength in Circles, of Sealing and Banishment of Dark Entities." It was utter nonsense, he knew, but he couldn't stop himself from reading on, couldn't help but hope that somewhere in its pages there might be something useful.

The chapter spoke of the circle as a symbol for eternity before describing spellwork that promised to seal spirits, demons, and entities of dark power in objects with a circle of blood and a word of magic. Written magic was an art he'd done in ink and chalk, but the book spoke of magic written in blood. Blood magic was only ever used in works Paloma called "unsavory."

If the spellwork you seek requires blood, she'd once tutted, *you ought to rethink performing such spellwork in the first place.*

But maybe the magic that could help him find Dez required a little blood and a lot of nerve. Alfie ran his thumb over the dark circle drawn in the book and imagined it splashed red.

Alfie's bedroom doors burst open and Paloma stormed in, her red dueña's robes flowing behind her. When her eyes found him, an anger flared in her that he'd never seen before.

She strode across the room and stood so close they were nearly nose-to-nose. "Where have you been?"

Alfie opened his mouth, but no sound came out. Reflexively, he moved his hand to pull the books closer to him, but Paloma wrenched them away. Her lips disappeared into a hard line when she saw what they were.

"Paloma—I can explain—" Alfie sputtered.

"Luka came to find you and found an empty bed instead," Paloma said, her eyes narrowing. "You're lucky he called upon me first instead of your mother and father."

Even while being caught, Alfie couldn't help but feel a spark of hope knowing that Luka had sought him out. His stomach dropped at the thought of missing it.

"I know what you've been up to. I enlisted a sailor on your ship to report on your doings. I'm glad I did," she said before he could protest.

A flush prickled his neck. She'd collared him like a dog too foolish to find its way home.

"How dare you even think of dabbling in Englassen magic?" she snapped. "I thought you would get it out of your system and return home. But now this! Luka was beside himself—"

Alfie's face reddened further. "You told Luka?"

"He begged me to tell him anything I knew. You hadn't sent word in months!"

Luka was loyal enough not to tell his parents a word about his doings, and Alfie couldn't even send him a letter. Guilt sank into his bones, but he refused to let it smother his anger.

"What I do is not your concern. Or Luka's," he said through gritted teeth.

Paloma looked at him like she would when he threw mid-lesson tantrums as a child. It was infuriating. "The king and queen don't know, but if you put one more toe out of line I will tell them. I will not let you trifle with forbidden magic in some fool's errand to bring back the dead."

Alfie closed the distance between them, anger clawing his insides. "Falling into that void doesn't mean he's dead. You have no proof! *No one* has proof!"

Paloma's eyes widened with a flash of alarm. It was the same look she'd given him one day soon after Dez's disappearance, when he'd grabbed her by the shoulders and shoved her against the wall in a fit of rage. Shame welled up within him and spilled over, embarrassment sticking to his skin in an oily sheet. It was fear of that anger within him that had led him to drowning himself in the flask at his hip. He would not let himself become that person again, the person whose anger would incite fear in those he cared about. He would much rather be numb than feel himself break open from the heat of his fury again.

Alfie took a step back. "Perdóname, I didn't mean—I wasn't going to—"

"Alfie," she said softly. "I know you weren't. But you must listen to me now as you did on that day. Dez is gone. That girl's *propio* was to create voids—endless, dark, empty places with no food, no water, no time, no magic. She disappeared Dez into it. Your father forced her to open that void again under the pain of death, and he sent bruxos into that dark hole to find him. Just as the girl had warned, none of them came back."

Alfie shook his head, not wanting to imagine Dez starving to death in the darkness. Men and magic needed each other to survive. This was an undisputed fact. Magic flowed through the air and men took it in like flowers took in sunlight. Without magic, the human body would wither away. And Alfie remembered what it felt like to stand beside the black void that had swallowed his brother. He'd felt no magic coming from it. Since then, he hadn't been able to even set foot in the Blue Room. It had once been a parlor where they'd played as boys. Now it would forever be the last place Alfie saw Dez. That wing of the palace had since been closed to all, left to sit in the silence of their loss.

But Alfie refused to let what had happened in that room go. He couldn't.

"None of the bruxos my father sent to find him were me. And Dez isn't just anyone," Alfie said, but his confidence was deflating at the look on Paloma's face.

"Dez's *propio* was extraordinary, but it cannot bring him back."

"You don't know that," Alfie seethed. "No one knows that for sure."

If anyone could survive this, it would be Dez. As a child, Dez would carve animal figurines out of wood—web-toed water foxes, quilbears, red-bellied wolves. When he finished a carving and held it in his hand, it came to life. There was no other way to describe it. The wolves would chase their tails, the puffer pigs would puff up to twice their size when startled, the quilbears would raise their hackles. Each figure had its own personality, its own will. He'd kept his figures in a glass cupboard in his room where they roamed and slept, pressing their paws to the glass whenever Dez came near.

The day Dez had been taken from them, all his figurines froze, motionless. Alfie couldn't help but hope that if Dez could breathe life into the lifeless, then he somehow could survive what had happened. He had to be alive, waiting for Alfie to find him.

Alfie didn't notice he was crying until a tear ran down his lip and he tasted salt.

Paloma touched his shoulder with an awkward hand. She was never the sort to initiate touch. Dueños weren't the touching type. So Alfie knew he must look pathetic beyond words. He shook her hand off, and she let it hang in the air for a moment before pulling it back to her side.

"Your mother and father cannot take another loss, Prince Alfehr," she said, her voice quiet. "This is your last warning, entiendes? If you continue down this path, I will tell them."

With that, Paloma took the Englassen books and swept out of his rooms, shutting the doors behind her. Alfie was left with nothing but the bitter taste of anger and pity on his tongue.

He sat at the edge of his bed, rubbing the back of his hand across his eyes. It was over. Those books had given him nothing and now he had to move on, but he couldn't stomach the thought of leaving Dez behind, of moving forward toward a throne that had been Dez's since birth. To do it, he would need to be brave.

Brave. He had something to make him brave.

He walked to the far side of his room where the chest he'd kept on the ship was left in the corner. "*Abrir*," he said. At his word, the lock clicked open. Alfie stared at its contents.

Within it was every book, talisman, and trinket Alfie had acquired while away from home.

The last three months of his grief kept in a box.

Alfie pulled a stub of a violet candle out of the chest. A woman in a marketplace in the winter kingdom of Uppskala had sold it to him and told him that he must burn it at midnight under a waxing moon to speak with a lost loved one. He'd been so desperate that he did for a week before tossing it in the chest, never to be used again. Then he decided to stop looking for things that might call his brother back and start seeking whatever would give him the power to enter the void and find his brother, which led him to Rayan's games.

Alfie had once drunkenly confided in one of the players about looking for magic that could pull *propio* from one body to another. Then he could take that criminal's *propio*, open the void his brother had been spirited into, and go find him himself.

The man had simply said, "Well, if what you're looking for even exists, I'd bet that type of spellwork was cooked up in Englass. Sounds a bit like their style, eh?"

That nameless man had lit a fire in Alfie's mind. It was true. The last time bruxos dabbled in such foul spellwork, Alfie's ancestors had been conquered. By Englass.

Englass believed magic belonged to Englassen nobility and no one else, which was why they'd developed siphoning spellwork to take magical energy from those of Castallan in order to give it to Englassen nobles. If the practice of moving *propio* magic from one body to the other was being studied somewhere, it had to be in Englass.

Back during enslavement, if a Castallano was discovered with a moving shadow, they were killed in fear of being able to resist the siphon spellwork.

Alfie would have been murdered before he could walk.

It was despicable for him, a Castallan prince, to even think of studying Englassen practices. Yet here he was. Alfie kneaded his temples with his fingers. Why was he still doing this? Still looking for solutions when, logically, there was no way anyone could be saved from what had happened to Dez. Still, even if his forays into the illegal led to nothing, every time he added an object to this chest, it was a way of saying, *I'm still looking for you; I will always look for you.*

He hoped that wherever his brother was, he knew that.

Alfie scoured the chest until his hand closed around something small, something to make him brave. He balanced it on his palm. It was a wooden dragon figurine on a gold chain. The dragon had once been a bright silver, but now the paint was chipping.

Dez had given it to him when he was eight years old and nightmares kept sending him crawling into Dez's bed. Dez had told him to be brave, but Alfie had never felt very brave.

"Well, I made you something that'll help you be brave always," Dez had said.

Alfie perked up at that. "Really?"

"Really." Dez reached into his pocket and opened his palm to show Alfie a silver dragon figurine. When Alfie reached to stroke its nose, the dragon nuzzled his knuckles.

"But how will it keep me brave?"

"Well," Dez said. "If you want to be valiente, you need a dragon to protect your bravery for you. Keep it safe." Alfie quirked an eyebrow. "Trust me. I'm going to open the dragon's mouth and when I do, you give me your fiercest, bravest roar, all right? Just like a dragon."

Alfie was skeptical, but if Dez was suggesting it, it was worth a try. Dez tapped the dragon's nose and it stretched its small mouth open. Alfie roared his wildest roar. He laughed when Dez reared back, pretending that the roar had hit him like a physical force. Then Dez tapped the dragon's snout again and it closed its mouth.

"We got it!" Dez said. "The dragon caught your bravery right in its mouth. Safe and sound." The dragon stretched its jaws in a yawn on Dez's palm. "Your bravery will always be here with the dragon. So you can stay brave all night, okay? No more nightmares."

Dez tilted his open palm toward Alfie's. The dragon ambled onto Alfie's hand before curling into a sleepy spiral on his palm. In that moment, Alfie had felt invincible.

On the day Dez had disappeared, the dragon, too, fell still as death.

Alfie had hidden the dragon away because it hurt too much to see it. Tonight he pulled the chain over his neck and let the dragon fall against his chest. He was going to need every ounce of bravery he could muster, because he was going to have to become the king that Castallan needed and hope that Dez would forgive him.

He locked the chest with a word of magic and crawled into bed.

On his bedside table sat a long-necked bottle. Alfie took a swig of the sleeping tonic and chased it with a swig from a bottle of tequila, hoping it would calm him and let him rest easy. The combination left him woozy and heavy-limbed. He held the dragon until, at last, sleep took him.

It was only when sleep whistled its first notes through him that he realized he'd seen one of the faces in the thief's journal somewhere—on a wanted poster.

THE BET

If Finn had a peso for every time she woke up with a sack over her head, she wouldn't need to do the things that led to her waking up with a sack over her head.

She'd jolted awake in an alley wearing a cloak that wasn't hers with her hands and ankles tied together like a trussed-up turkey. She'd expected to see the boy in the fox mask, but instead she woke to the sight of a man she'd never met, a burlap sack in his meaty hand. When she bucked and fought in his arms, he laughed and said, "What? Got plans for the night? You'll have to reschedule. You're expected at family dinner."

Finn froze in his arms. She had no family. Not unless he counted Ignacio. A shiver flitted up her spine. Did this have to do with him? Then the man's fist came down against her temple and there was only darkness.

She woke, for the second time that night, as her center of gravity shifted. She squirmed in the meaty arms that held her, and was dropped into the chair with a plop. The sack was wrenched off her head, pulling a few strands of her hair with it.

As her eyes adjusted to the dark cellar, she trained her expression into one of confidence, as if she were lounging on a throne instead of tied to an uncomfortable stool in a cellar where no one could hear her scream. Her shadow flared out around her, like the wings of a great bird.

"If it isn't the Face Thief," a voice called from the darkness before her. A woman stepped forward and sat in the empty, high-backed chair a few paces ahead of Finn. Her grin revealed a row of yellowed teeth. Finn had a feeling that this wasn't the place where business began, but where it ended with screams and blood.

Beside the woman's feet was a bucket. Her shadow curled around it, predatory. "I've heard of you, the famous face-changing thief making a name for herself in my city. I'd hoped we'd cross paths at some point, but not under such, let's say, unpleasant circumstances."

"Who the hell are you and what do you want with me?"

The woman gave a laugh. "It's refreshing to meet someone who doesn't know me." She leaned forward, her voice tapering down into a whisper, as if they were exchanging secrets. "Someone who doesn't know how afraid they should be when they wake up in this cellar."

Finn glowered at her, a mask to hide the pounding of her heart. "I only know people who are worth knowing. Sorry you didn't make the maldito cut."

"Let's get to the reason we're here, shall we? I'm Kol. Surely you've heard my name. Maybe even seen my work?"

Finn stilled in her chair. She'd only been in the city for the past month, but even she'd heard of Kol and her deadly gang, known as la Familia. Still, Finn wouldn't let the fear show on her face. Kol was a big dog and Finn had every intention of teaching her to sit.

"Now, before I ask you to return the books you stole from a game my men were poised to win, I'd like to show you what happened to the last pendejo to deny me what I asked for."

Kol leaned over in her chair and reached into the bucket with one hand, then pulled out a decapitated head by its mop of dark hair. Blood dropped from the open neck, and the man's tongue slipped out of his dead mouth. Finn's stomach roiled and pitched.

"Now that you know the stakes, that's enough of that!" Kol dropped the head back into the bucket. Finn heard the sound of flesh slapping against something wet and willed herself not to vomit. Kol held up her hands and a woman appeared from behind her to wipe them with a handkerchief. "Thank you, Mija."

"My pleasure, Madre," the woman said obediently, then retreated back into the shadows.

Finn heard Kol's minions shifting in the dark around her— well-muscled men and women trained to snap necks first and ask questions second. "You're disgusting," Finn said to her.

"No, I'm impatient." Kol tapped the bucket with her foot. "And greedy when it comes to what's mine. Those books were already guaranteed to a buyer for a hefty price, worth more than your life." She looked Finn up and down. "Twice over. Now, tell me where you hid them."

The thief swallowed thickly. "I don't have them."

Kol tilted her head, her frighteningly cordial smile wavering. "Don't lie, muchacha."

"I'm not," Finn growled, her cheeks warming. She'd rather lie and say she'd sold them than admit the truth. "They were stolen from me."

A silence stretched through the cellar. Kol stared at her blank-faced before throwing her head back in an uproarious laugh that stretched long and wide like an accordion.

She waved her hands, a signal to her minions that they too could laugh. Then the entire cellar boomed with their guffaws. Finn scowled, her jaw tense.

"Some thief you are! And to think I was the slightest bit threatened by you." She wiped tears from the corners of her eyes. "With you stealing some of my business and all."

"Just let me go and you and your thick-necked goons can laugh all night long."

Kol raised a single hand and her minions fell silent. "I don't think so. You see, you still owe me for those books. And you'll be paying off that debt by working for me." She spread her arms wide as if inviting Finn to embrace her. "Welcome to la Familia, Mija."

Finn's stomach tightened. The last time she was made someone's daughter, things didn't go too well.

After her parents died and Ignacio had taken her as his ward, she'd spent years working with him in circuses all over Castallan. He had a charm that was palpable, hypnotic, making him a talented ringmaster. Ignacio loved the attention, loved to watch people lean forward and heed his words, his commands. She'd grown up working odd jobs at the circuses while he performed, but they never stayed with one show for long. As soon as Finn began to make friends, to fit within the fabric of a mismatched circus family, Ignacio would demand that they leave. It took years for her to realize he didn't want to leave because he was restless. He made them leave because he didn't like to watch her make friends, to see her want to be with anyone but him.

He'd always hated when she left his side without express permission. On most days, she'd been afraid to test him, to show even an ounce of independence. But in her more rebellious moments she'd disobeyed and accepted the beatings, if only to spite him, to prove that she was strong enough to take it. On one such day, she'd disappeared for hours to explore the city their circus was visiting.

When she'd returned, Ignacio closed the distance between them and clapped a hand across her face, jerking her neck with the strength of the slap. When she only stared at him, her cheek stinging, her chin high, and her chest rising and falling with bottled anger, he smiled down at her.

"I'm not angry," he said, his hands finding her shoulders. "I knew you would come back. You always do. Because you know, just as I know, that no one else will have you, that your place is here with me." He pressed a kiss to her forehead then, his hand mussing her hair. "Forever."

That final word poured through her, cold and fast, like an eel slithering through icy water. He'd said it to her before, but on that night, his words smothered her with panic. Would this be her life, forever? That was the night she'd escaped, the night she'd made him feel as powerless as he'd made her feel before running for the dock and sneaking onto the first ship she saw. She would not be pulled into another family again. She wouldn't let Kol secure a new collar around her throat and jerk her into line. She would die first.

"I'm not joining you," Finn snarled.

"You took what was mine, Face Thief. And a thief who gets her own supply stolen off her . . ." Kol made a clucking sound with her tongue. "That's not a thief at all. That's a pretender. You're lucky I'm even offering you a chance to learn from a real thief. I expect you to join ranks without a fuss. But I'm prepared for a fuss. You know of my *propio*, girl. Save yourself the trouble."

She knew fighting was a waste of strength. Kol had a monstrous *propio*—with a look she could stifle anyone's magic at the drop of a hat. There was no chance of getting out of here alive. But Finn never did anything quietly. She sure as hell wasn't going to start now.

"So, what say you?" Kol asked, leaning forward in her chair.

Finn jutted her tied hands upward. Thin shards of rock shot up from the ground to cut through the rope binding her wrists together. She pulled her hands apart.

Kol's minions rushed out of the shadows to grab her. Her ankles still bound, she pummeled one with a volley of rock she pulled from the cellar ground. She encased her fist with stone and punched the next one squarely in the nose. But then, in one terrifying moment, it all stopped. Her hold on the earth was severed, the rock falling from her fist in sad fragments. Kol's minions converged on her in the space of a breath. The last thing she saw before a meaty fist pounded into her jaw was Kol's smiling face. That's how easy it was for her to rob Finn of every ounce of magic that ran through her veins. Just a moment, a look.

She flailed back and forth between the henchmen, who landed kicks and punches on every spot they could reach. There must've been ten of them waiting in the shadows. One unbearable kick to her ribs doubled her over. She watched blood dribble out of her nose and onto the floor.

"Put her down," she heard Kol say. "Some children just need discipline is all."

A broad-shouldered woman shoved her to the ground, right into the puddle of blood from her nose. She forced Finn onto her stomach and pegged her face to the dirt with a foot on her cheek.

Finn panted, taking in dirt with each breath. Her whole body rang with pain. Kol grinned down at her from her seat as if Finn were an honored guest.

"After all that excitement, you know what I'm in the mood for," Kol said, cocking her head as if she were mulling it over. "Sancocho."

Finn froze on the ground, the thud of her heart suddenly louder.

"What was that one pub in the Brim called, the one with the stew everyone talks about? The famous sancocho?"

"The Apple Core Pub and Inn," a voice behind Finn supplied.

A cold pit knotted her stomach. Kol knew where she lived. She must've been watching her for a while. Fear wound around her neck like a vise, choking her from the inside out.

"There is nowhere you can go where we won't follow, Face Thief. You've got two options: join la Familia or die where you stand."

"No," Finn said, her voice splintering.

"'No' is not one of the two options."

"I want a third."

"I want what I'm owed. I want your loyalty, or I want your blood spilled at my feet."

"Pick something you want, and I'll steal it. Something of

equal value for what you lost." Finn's voice was thin and rough, desperation leaking through the fissures and crevices. She hated the sound. "Anything. If I can't get it done, then I'll work for you."

Kol cocked her head sideways. "And exactly what do I get out of this when I already have you right where I want you?"

"Everyone knows you like a good gamble, Kol," she said. "Give me another chance to win my life back, and it'll be that much sweeter when you take it from me."

Silence stretched between them. Finn could taste blood pooling in her mouth.

"Sit her up," Kol said.

They wrenched Finn back up and put her on her knees. Someone pinned her arms painfully behind her, nearly elbow to elbow. Kol stood from her chair and made her way to Finn. She gripped Finn roughly by the chin, running her callused thumb over the line of her jaw. Kol's shadow surged toward Finn, like a beast closing in on its dinner.

Finn refused to give Kol the satisfaction of looking at her smug face. Instead she stared at the tattoo on the inside of Kol's wrist—a bull with flared nostrils, its horns angled as if they might poke through Kol's skin. Finn longed to take her dagger and shove it through the bull's face until the tip of her blade wriggled out the other side.

"What did you do, hmm?" Kol asked. "What did you do that would make you never want to see your own face again? What made you bury it under all this magic?"

Even with a split lip and an eye swelling shut, Finn couldn't stop herself from grinning. "I was born with a face like yours, but the gods were merciful enough to give me the power to hide it."

Kol's lip quirked. "Oh, I'm ugly. That's the truth. And my *propio*, just as ugly. Underneath it all your face might be bonita, but with a gift like that, inside you must be as ugly as me. We're a pair, I think."

Finn hocked a loogie, slow and deliberate, and spat in her face. It dribbled down Kol's cheek. Kol's smile didn't falter. She pressed her thumb on Finn's lips, like a seal on a letter.

"I've dealt with much worse than a little spit, muchacha. When you join me, you'll learn as much," Kol said. Her minions laughed at that. Finn's lips curled back until Kol's rough thumb was pressed against the flat ridge of her teeth instead of the soft of her lips. Kol pulled her thumb away slowly, as if Finn were no danger to her at all. The realization stung her. She really was no danger to Kol. Kol had blocked her stone carving, and her henchmen had Finn on her knees.

"I think I have just the challenge for someone as skilled as you," Kol said. Finn's heart usually raced with excitement just before a job was offered. But this time it wouldn't be a task she chose. It was being shoved down her throat. Her heart slogged in her chest, sore and tired and scared, but painfully alive. Like an injured animal limping away from its hunter.

"I'll be nice—I'll let you keep most of your magic. Your stone carving, you'll have. But you'll be keeping that face of yours for now," Kol said. "No *propio* until you've completed the task. I'm going to ask you to bring me something I've wanted for some time now. . . ."

Finn spat blood at the ground between Kol's feet. "A social life?"

There was a quick dry sound, like snapping a twig over a bent knee, and pain shot through her wrist. She couldn't stop the anguished yelp from slipping past her lips.

"Not quite," Kol said. "What you'll be getting for me is a bit more useful than that."

"I'm on the edge of my seat," Finn said, her words rough with fury.

"The deal is that in exchange for your freedom, you will bring me the vanishing cloak."

One of Kol's men snorted behind her. Finn stared at her incredulously, the pain in her wrist numbed by rage. "The vanishing cloak? Passed from son to son? King to king?"

"That's the one. Bring me the vanishing cloak from the palace in three days' time. If you succeed, you'll get your freedom. But if, for some reason, you should fail . . ." Her minions snickered at that. "You work for me with a smile. Is the deal set, Face Thief?"

Finn glared at Kol, a glower so hot it might singe her brows off. Kol's grin only widened.

"Where I come from, both parties voluntarily agree and shake hands, entiendes?" Kol asked.

With four thugs holding her down and her magic stolen, this was anything but voluntary, but people like Kol changed the definition of that word when it suited. Nos became yeses as they flowed in one ear and out the other.

Someone let go of Finn's hand. She raised it to shake Kol's.

Kol shook her head. "No. I don't want that one."

The goon restraining her paused before pulling the free hand back and letting go of the other. The one with a splintered wrist.

Finn refused to miss a beat. She raised her limp hand to meet Kol's. When the mobster gripped it hard, jarring what was already shattered, Finn let what should've been a pained sob fuel a low, feral growl.

"Set?" Kol asked, a polite lilt in her voice.

"The deal is set," Finn snarled.

Finn tried to unlock the door to her rented room at the Apple Core. It took her three tries because her hands kept shaking.

When it finally creaked open, she rushed in and slammed it shut, upsetting her tender wrist, which she'd just had healed by some back-alley bruxo in the Pinch. She'd paid him with the fox-masked boy's cloak. She wished she could hang him with it—if not for him, Kol's gang wouldn't have caught her. But then again, Kol still would've found her, wouldn't she? She knew she stayed here at this pub, knew her every move. Bile rose in the back of her throat.

She had to leave town, had to change her face, had to get out of this. Finn rushed to the cracked mirror that hung above the small desk beside her narrow bed. Her face was purpling with bruises, as if she'd messily eaten a fistful of berries. Her bottom lip had split.

She passed her hands over her face and thought of a different nose, one that was wider. But when her hand fell from her face, the same one remained. She pounded her fists on the desk, upsetting her wrist again. After letting out a stream of expletives, she took a deep breath and tried again. This time she passed her hands through her hair as she thought of blonde tresses. Nothing happened.

Frustration raked its nails over her bruised skin. Who the hell was Kol to decide if she should be able to use her *propio*? Finn didn't give a damn about her name or the face she was born with—all of that she could toss over her shoulder and never look back—but her *propio* was the only thing she held dear. The only thing she clung to. If she could change her face then she could change her fate, her future, and now that was gone. Stolen.

She felt like a sealed bottle of fizzy drink. Whenever she tried to use her *propio* it was as if she was shaking the bottle instead of removing the stopper. Pressure built inside with nowhere to go. A painful headache bloomed between her brows. Her *propio* was gone unless she got the vanishing cloak, a mission that would surely end with her getting run through by a palace guard.

Run, her mind hissed.

But there was no point in that. If Kol had la Familia watching her, there was no way she'd make it out of the city alive.

Finn grew still, hunched over the desk, her breaths ragged. With a frustrated scream she lifted the husk of the desk, tender wrist and all, and threw it across the room. The ramshackle thing broke against the wall, narrowly missing the small window.

She thought of admitting that she couldn't handle the bet, getting her magic back and working for Kol. She thought of Kol's satisfied smirk, of her thumb pressed against her lips. Finn scrubbed at her bruised mouth, chasing the memory away. She couldn't do that. She wouldn't.

She thought of taking on the bet. Of infiltrating the palace. It was a suicide mission in any circumstance, but to waltz in without being able to change her face? It was absurd.

Her mind fell silent, tying itself in knots trying to come up with an answer.

Her bed gave a familiar yawn of a creak as she sat. She'd slept in this bed for weeks now—just long enough to call it hers. She should've known better. The moment the sheets started to feel comfortable, she should've run and never come back. When you put down roots, you pulled up weaknesses, vulnerabilities, strings. Always strings.

And there was his voice in her head. Ignacio.

Puppet strings, Finny . . . Puppet strings . . .

A cold sweat prickled on her forehead. Kol was just like him, someone else trying to make her their obedient little daughter. Trying to control her. Control her face, who she was, who she worked for. She couldn't help but be pulled by a memory.

During their first days together, Ignacio had treated her to a slice of sweet flan at a marketplace, and she'd kindled the courage to ask him why he'd taken her off the streets.

He'd gazed down at her with that terrifying intensity, a hunched bridge between love and obsession. "To love me," he'd said. "I made you my daughter to love me."

Ignacio's *propio* was compulsion. Like anyone else's *propio*, it had its limitations. In order to control a person, he needed them to reveal their true self to him, to tell him something intimate that gave him a foothold on their spirit to latch onto. Then they were his for the taking. He need only look them in the eyes and speak to make them obey his command. But his *propio* made it difficult to tell who loved him. He'd forget where the real person began and his compulsion ended.

"But the love of one's child," he'd said. "That is real. You're the only one who I know will love me truly. No matter what I say or do to you, little chameleon, I'll know that you love me. That you are mine."

Then he'd held her in his arms the way she'd remembered her

parents had and she'd felt safe and loved. But as she grew older he'd stifled her, demanded all her time, all her love. There could be no other recipient. And if another recipient arose, Ignacio would snuff them out.

Or he would tell her to snuff them out.

Don't act like killing has ever been a problem for you, Finny, his voice purred between her ears. *We both know you're a natural.*

In another searing flash of memory, Finn remembered a little girl standing before her, a girl as young and lost and hungry as Finn had been then. In her mind's eye, Finn watched herself dig her nails into the girl's skin, tackling her until she landed on her back. Her stomach roiled as the sound of rusted nails sinking into skin beat in her mind like a drum.

Finn's panting broke her out of the memory. She pulled her knees to her chest. "I'm safe here," she murmured to herself with shaking breaths. "He'll never recover, never be able to find me. Just calm down."

But her own words couldn't slow her trembling heart. Her palms and face were slick with sweat. She screwed her eyes shut and counted. Counting helped.

By the time she counted down from ten twice over, her pulse had finally calmed, and she'd made her decision.

No one was ever going to own her like that again. Not Kol, not Ignacio, not a maldito soul. She was going to do the unthinkable. She was going to finesse the vanishing cloak right out of the palace. If she died in the process, then that would be that. But if she pulled it off, Kol would never see it coming. She certainly wouldn't expect Finn to use the cloak to catch her unawares and cut her throat. Then she'd have her *propio* back and she'd leave this city for good.

Finn stifled the yawn building in the back of her throat. There was no time for rest when she had a heist to plan. She would sleep when she was dead.

And that, she thought, might be sooner than she'd anticipated.

THE PIG

Finn couldn't help but think that this must be punishment for stealing those pork skewers.

She'd done many strange things in her short career of thievery. She'd changed her face into that of a woman whose family suspected she had been murdered by her husband. Finn had haunted the husband for two whole weeks before he finally cracked. Turned out, the family had been right.

She'd done many odd things, but this was likely the strangest.

Finn was inside a dead pig.

It turned out that there was some fancy dinner at the palace. The occasion gave her an opening: a gargantuan puffer pig to be delivered to the royal kitchens. The chef himself was a stone carver, and he'd constructed a clay box for the hog to be transported and then baked in.

So Finn had snuck into the renowned chef's kitchen and wriggled herself into the great split in the boar's stomach. Surrounded by an array of fragrant herbs and spices, she waited until the guards delivered the pig and the servants carried it into the palace kitchens. There she heard the sizzling of pans and the bubbling of pots brought to a boil. Now she just needed them to leave the crated pig somewhere while she escaped.

"Into the oven, then!" the boy carrying the crate said. Finn's heart sputtered in her chest.

The servants grunted and Finn felt the crate being lifted higher and pushed forward. A sudden wave of heat rushed over her.

Damn, damn, damn!

Should she burst out of the pig and the crate? Would she have to kill them? Where the hell would she hide the bodies?

"Not just yet!" a voice boomed. "Leave it in the pantry for now. Bake it in an hour."

"Sorry, jefe!" Finn heard the boy say. "Right away!"

Finn felt the crate being pulled out of the oven. The stifling heat receded. Sweat poured down her face. She hoped these people liked their pork salty.

With that, the crate was lowered onto the floor. She heard them retreat from the crate, shutting a door behind them. Silence swaddled her. It was now or never.

She got on all fours, her back grazing the pig's cavernous rib cage. Finn rocked sideways, her cheek pressed to the pig's wet, meaty flank. The pig finally rolled onto its side. From within, Finn thrust her hand upward, lifting the lid off the crate and lowering it to the ground. With another swipe, she collapsed one side of the crate to give her space to exit.

She crawled out of the slit in the pig's belly, tearing it even wider in her haste. When she was finally free, she'd never been happier to lie on the dirty, hard floor. Covered in a layer of seasoning and moisture, she smelled like a walking kitchen.

Finn rose from the ground and resettled the boar into its former position. She stepped back and took stock of the damage. The skin was mashed down on the side she'd rolled it onto.

"There goes the dinner presentation," she said. With careful flicks of her hands she reconstructed the crate wall she'd collapsed. She lowered the lid back over it and set to work. The pantry was bigger than her rented room, with wall-to-wall shelves of pickled spices and herbs. She felt around the walls, looking for what Kol had told her to find.

Before sending her off, Kol had provided her with a map and told her how to access the secret passageways of the palace.

"Why are you telling me this?" Finn had asked, her eyes narrowing.

"I want my cloak, Face Thief. I've got no chance of getting it if you're too thick-headed to get around the palace unseen. Find the switches hidden in the walls and you'll get into the secret passages."

She pulled the map out from under her shirt. It was stained with very expensive seasonings, but still good to read.

She checked for the switch behind each bottled spice but found nothing but sandy, stone walls. Finn moved to inspect the wall behind the pantry door. Just when she got behind it, it swung open. She flattened herself against the wall, the open door blocking her from sight. She heard a voice murmuring as bottles of spices pinged against each other. Then they were gone.

That was too close. She needed to find the passageway or she'd be stuck here until someone found her. Then she saw it. There, half obscured by a bottle of pickled garlic, was a statue the size of her little finger jutting from the wall—a bird with outstretched wings.

Finn twisted it to the left and heard a click. Slowly, the spice-laden wall swung inward. Finn hurried into the passage, leaning against the heavy wall of stone to close it.

She'd made it. She sagged against the wall, breathing a long sigh of relief. Her fingers skittered up the wall in the dark, searching for the torch Kol had said would be there. She found it and lit it with a set of sparking stones she'd brought. Light poured down the dark, tight passage.

Now all there was left to do was find the cloak, grab it, and walk out the front doors.

"Easy," Finn said.

She didn't believe herself.

From his bedroom balcony, Alfie watched the fireflies wink in and out of existence across the grounds.

Soon winter would strike and the chill would chase them away until spring came. In Castallan, the weather never got so cold as to see your own breath, as it did in the winter kingdom of Uppskala, but the air grew cooler still and the shimmering lace capes worn by nobles were replaced by weightier cloaks.

"Everything has its season," his father had once told him. Did his mourning have a season? Would it peel away from him, like petals peeled from stems as winter marched ever closer? Alfie's jaw tightened at the thought. His mourning was like the fireflies—there were moments when it disappeared from sight, but it would always spark into existence again, recurring, resilient.

Everything had its season, but seasons always repeated. Though he'd promised himself to let go of his plans to find Dez and commit to becoming king of Castallan, he knew the grief would never leave him.

The clock in his bedroom chimed the hour, and Alfie started before rushing back into his rooms to change into his formal clothes for tonight's dinner.

His shadow zigzagged about his feet, betraying his nerves, as he smoothed his blue double-breasted overcoat. He adjusted the silver circlet before throwing his hands up in exasperation. Did it matter if he looked like a proper prince if everyone at this dinner was going to whisper behind their hands about the validity of his rule? About how unfit for the throne he was compared with Dez? Alfie massaged his temples.

Now would be a great time for a pep talk from Luka, but Luka hadn't spoken to him since Alfie had come home. Alfie could only hope that giving him space would help the situation.

A knock sounded at his door. Alfie dashed to it, hoping to find Luka on the other side. Instead, it was his mother, swathed in a ruffled red gown. A cape of gold lace trailed behind her. Her black hair was pulled back and threaded with scarlet ribbon.

Alfie deflated. "You look lovely, Mamá."

She tilted her head. "You look disappointed."

"That obvious?"

"Nonchalance has never been your strong suit." She squeezed his hand. "Give him some time and do some well-deserved groveling. Things will go back to the way they were, Mijo."

Alfie nodded, but he knew she was wrong. She didn't know

about Luka catching him sneaking out of the palace, or how he knew what Alfie had been up to for the last three months.

"I know," he forced himself to say. "You're right."

"I am always right." She offered him her arm. "Now come with me. You and I are due for some mother-son time."

Alfie smiled and took her arm. She grinned back, giving his hand another comforting squeeze. But as they walked into the hall, she shot him a look, a spark of humor in her eyes. "And if you disappear for so long again, I will break my chancla off on your backside, oíste?"

Alfie could not help but laugh at that. "Yes, Mother."

If I were a prince's bedroom, where would I hide? Finn thought as she stared at the map by the light of the torch. She didn't know if her voice would somehow be heard through the wall, and she wasn't stupid enough to test the theory.

She was still beside the kitchen pantry, on the second lowest level of the palace. Her shadow moved this way and that as she considered which way to go. According to the map, the prince's chambers were, as expected, on the highest floor of the palace.

Naturally, she thought, and rolled the map back up in her hand. Kol had told her that the royal family each had a key to the palace vault, and she'd rather ransack the prince's rooms than the king and queen's.

She walked through the winding passage until she came across a steel ladder. She'd need to climb two floors and walk another long passageway through the fifth floor until she found the next ladder. Then finally she'd be on the prince's floor. As she walked, the torch lighting her way, she could see small, notched slats appearing intermittently in the walls. Her curiosity finally getting the best of her, she grasped a slat by its small notch and slid it sideways. Through the slot she looked into a grand dining room where servants adjusted place settings.

"Peepholes," she murmured. A boy carrying a vase of flowers passed so close that she could smell its petals. She stepped back, holding the torch low. But no one seemed to notice. The guards must've used these passages to spy. Was she going to bump into one of them? Should she even keep the torch lit? Finn stopped herself from stamping out the flame.

She'd take the risk of using the torch to get through the passages faster, and then maybe she'd be less likely to bump into anyone at all. Hopefully. She swallowed hard and listened. She heard no footsteps. She moved on and walked down the winding passage, stopping at the occasional peephole. She looked into a library so vast it could house a village, and then into what appeared to be a training room where the walls were covered in an array of the finest weapons she'd ever seen. She had to stop herself from stealing one of the fancy machetes. But for the most part the palace was what she expected, immaculate and boring.

She walked until she found a ladder. Rung by rung she climbed in the dark, carrying the lit torch in her mouth like a dog would a bone. Sweating, she climbed until she got to the seventh-floor passage. The passage that led to the prince's chambers couldn't be reached directly from where she was. She would need to move through a bathroom to get to the passageway on the far side of the room. Then she'd have a direct route to the prince's quarters.

Finn pulled open the slat and peered in. She saw a grand,

sweeping bathroom with a sunken bathtub of black stone that was more like a pool. Around the rim was an assortment of soaps, lotions, and two bottles of wine. There were five different faucets, as elegant as swans' necks, arching over the lip of the tub. What could you need five faucets for? And who drank while taking a bath? She rolled her eyes. *Royals*.

Warm, perfumed air wafted through the slat, but no one was in the tub. The surface was covered in the sudsy remains of a bubble bath. She waited, counting the seconds to see if someone had gone under. Nobody could hold their breath for that long.

There was no use in waiting any longer. Someone had likely just gotten out of the bath, and she had only a few precious minutes to find the passageway on the far side of the room before a servant came to clean. She twisted the bird on the wall and the passage swung outward. She scurried out and pushed it closed behind her. She felt naked—there was too much space and too little to hide behind. A voice called out from the tub, shattering the silence.

"Rosa, I'm ready."

Finn and her shadow froze where she stood behind the tub faucets. Her eyes darted down. She hadn't seen the boy because his body was hidden by the froth of bubbles. He kept his eyes closed. What a fool—she could kill him right now.

"Rosa!" he called a bit louder. "The hot towel, please!"

Finn nearly ran back to the wall, but whoever was supposed to be serving him had apparently stepped out. If he shouted one more time they might hear him or he might open his stupid eyes and notice a thief standing over him.

Finn clambered to the fine dish of steaming towels beside the lip of the tub where the boy leaned his head. She picked one up and draped it carefully over his eyes.

"Gracias." He luxuriated in the water and breathed a long, dramatic sigh. "I'm trying to get as relaxed as I can, so that I don't wring Alfie's neck when I see him next. The wine's for that too." He reached a soapy hand out of the tub, grabbed the bottle, and took a swig. "He has me so maldito worried about him that I'm tense. *Me!* Do you know how hard it is to get me tense? The palace masseuse could barely work out the knots in my neck." He paused, wrinkling his nose. "Rosa, did you stop by the kitchens? You smell like you've bathed in oregano."

Finn didn't answer him. She dashed across the room and looked for the bird in the tiled walls. Each tile was patterned, making it difficult to see something as small as the bird would be. She wiped her face with the back of her hand. The steam clung to her skin.

"Rosa? You're still there, aren't you?" He raised his hand to take the towel off his eyes.

From the far side of the room, Finn gave a high-pitched "*Mm-hmm!*" The boy dropped his hand back into the water.

"Did you strain your voice?" he asked.

Scouring the wall in a panic, Finn gave a loud cough and said, "*Mm-hmmm.*"

"Something's been going around. The steam will do you good. Clear the passages."

If only she could find the maldito passages.

She heard footsteps beyond the double doors of the bathroom. Rosa was coming! Finn got on all fours, searching the tiles below her waist. There it was! A tiny bird jutted out no higher than her knee. Finn crouched and twisted it. A square of eight tiles pushed outward. She crawled into the darkness of the passage and hurriedly shut the door behind her. With a shuddering breath, she stood up, her hair frizzing from the steam.

She opened the slat, and there was Rosa picking up the boy's clothes.

That was too close. This whole thing was too close.

Finn moved through the passages, peering at the map as she walked. She was passing a room labeled on the map as "Fallen Prince's Rooms" when she paused. Finn had been far from the capital city when the prince had been killed. But she still remembered people weeping in the streets as if they'd known him. She'd been too busy trying to survive to shed a maldito tear.

Still, curiosity gnawed at her. Finn slid aside the slat and stared into the room. The curtains were drawn. Darkness swept through the room. Finn felt around the wall and found the little bird peeking out of the stone, twisting it until the passage swung outward.

Inside the room was a double bed swathed in deep red sheets and a mountain of pillows. Against the wall before the bed was a tall, glass-paned cupboard. It was full of beautifully carved figurines of animals. Whoever had made them must have been truly skilled. One figure of a dog chasing its own tail looked as if it would start spinning in the cabinet at any moment.

In the bottom row of the cabinet was a fox figurine. It sat up, its tail curled forward, a clever look on its face. Finn smiled and caught her reflection in the glass, just as vulpine as the fox. The memory of the boy in the fox mask flashed in her mind. He may have bested her once, but he was too soft to be a fox. Finn had the edge for it.

She opened the case and filched it, dropping it into her pocket. She hadn't stolen a machete, so she'd let herself have this trifle. As she stepped back into the passage, her eyes scanned the room one last time. She knew it belonged to a dead man, but still, there was something particularly sad about the room. As if it were waiting for him to come home to it. But there was no time to think on that. Finn walked into the darkness and moved on.

Finally, she found herself in the passage to the prince's quarters. She opened the slat. The room was empty, but certainly lived in. Clothes were strewn on the bed. Books were left open on a redwood desk. Finn opened the passage door and slid in, pushing it closed behind her.

The room smelled like what Finn guessed was the cologne the prince wore. Or maybe the soap he used. Something clean and soft that lay on the nose, subtle as a feather.

Her brow furrowed. She'd smelled it before.

The sound of servants talking in the hall outside jarred her back to the present. She opened the prince's drawers and carefully fingered through rows of fine clothes with fabric that slid over her fingertips like water. She searched the pockets for the key and found none. She opened his tall armoire and even crawled in to search for hidden compartments. Still nothing.

She moved to the drawers of his bedside table, where a corked bottle of pale, cloudy liquid sat. She looked through the drawers, knocking on them quietly with her fist. She heard a hollow thud. Finn's heart jumped. She pressed on the wood and the panel gave to reveal a hidden compartment beneath. She reached in and her fingers closed around something narrow and cold. She pulled a golden key as long as her hand out of the drawer. This had to be it! Then there was a noise, the quiet twist of the doorknob. Someone was coming.

She pushed the drawer closed, not bothering to close the hidden compartment, and rolled soundlessly beneath the bed. Someone walked into the room. Their steps were quick, almost harried. Finn watched as a simple cream skirt moved quickly around the bed and came to a stop in front of the bedside table, right before Finn's nose. The skirt's hem was torn, the fabric rougher than any noble would deign to wear. Whoever this was, they had to be a servant.

Finn heard the sound of a bottle being uncorked. Then there was sniffling and the telltale swishing of a bottle being shaken. Was the servant crying?

The feet dashed out the door.

THE DINNER PARTY

The palace's banquet room was full of mingling nobles.

Servants moved through the room seamlessly with trays of finger foods and goblets of chilled sangria. The hall felt strangely empty, and Alfie knew he wasn't the only one thinking it. This was the first dinner they'd had since Dezmin had been taken. Not only was Dez gone, but everyone who had been discovered to be connected to the assassination and the failed coup was absent as well—they were either in prison or they'd taken their own lives in shame.

Alfie had nearly been driven mad with suspicion in the first months after Dez's disappearance. There had been no sign of rebellion or tension to signal the attempt on the royal family's lives that ended with the loss of Dez. Alfie had drilled everyone who had questioned the families involved, his parents included. Each one came to the same conclusion—the coup had been attempted by a small group of nobles who wanted more power and were willing to kill for it. That girl with the monstrous *propio* who had disappeared Dez into that dark hole could do nothing but name the ones who had pulled her into the operation—Marco Zelas, Alonso Marquez, and Maria Villanueva. She knew little else about the larger meaning behind it all, but from those names the king had ferreted out the rest of the betrayers.

If there had been a revolt by the poor, the mistreated, then Alfie could more easily rationalize it. But nobles putting their lives on the line for more power when they already held so much? And if those noble families had been willing to spill royal blood, how many more in this room were willing to do the same? A chill rolled up his spine.

Alfie could feel the nobles in the room whispering about it even when their lips were still or when they bowed to him in deference. The echoes of what had happened and what was to come for the kingdom were everywhere. Alfie would give anything to have Luka distract him from it all, but that wasn't an option today.

Luka moved through the party expertly, engaging all he met with sparkling conversation, but whenever Alfie came near him he would find a polite, subtle way to pull away. Luka had been raised in the palace and knew how to put on a good face during important occasions. But Alfie could feel the anger rolling off him in waves each time they made eye contact.

"Prince Alfehr." A soft voice spoke, startling Alfie where he stood.

He was so distracted by wanting to get a chance to speak with Luka that he hadn't noticed Aurora approach him. She'd had to cough lightly to get his attention.

"Aurora!" Alfie said before bowing low. "It's so nice to see you. It's been so long since we've spoken."

To say Aurora was beautiful was a terrible understatement. Her skin was dark and rich, but her eyes were a nearly translucent gray that shone against her complexion like stars against the night sky. But her beauty wasn't why Alfie was so unnerved by her. His heart sputtered whenever he saw her because Aurora might become his wife in a few years' time.

Aurora curtsied, the fabric of her silver gown whispering against the floor. "Yes, we haven't spoken since . . ." Her voice petered out.

"Since the funeral," Alfie said, finishing her sentence. He felt a heavy weight on his chest at the mere thought of that day. Of watching the dueño perform the service, speaking words of Dez's spirit moving on to a place of peace—words that did nothing but rub salt into Alfie's grief. Aurora had been Dez's betrothed before he died. Now her future was up in the air. The king and queen had yet to decide if she was to become Alfie's betrothed or if Alfie should marry a royal from an allying kingdom to strengthen foreign relations in the aftermath of Dez's death. Alfie himself didn't know which option made the most sense, but he didn't think it was right just to pass Aurora from prince to prince as if she were an object. Maybe she'd truly loved Dezmin and wouldn't consider any other; Alfie couldn't say.

After a silence stretched between them, Alfie couldn't stop the apology rising within him. "I'm so sorry that everything that happened has led to . . . that now your life is not what you thought it would . . ." He couldn't get the words right. "I'm just sorry that everything has happened as it did. And I'm sorry that everything is uncertain now." The apology sounded clunky, but he hoped she would understand.

She gave him a small, knowing smile, as if she could read his thoughts. "It's not your fault, Prince Alfehr. And I'm hardly the only one with an uncertain future now. I'm sorry for you and your family too."

Alfie nodded, feeling the awkwardness trickle away. "Thank you, Aurora." He smoothed his tunic and swallowed before posing his next question. "I never asked you this before, and I know I may be overstepping but . . . Did you and Dez . . . ," Alfie began, his voice lowering. "I just want to say that if you and Dez loved each other and you would rather not be considered as my betrothed, I will do everything within my power to guide my parents against matching us. You and I, we don't have to be anything that you're not comfortable with."

Aurora looked down for a moment, and Alfie couldn't tell if he'd gravely disrespected her with such a question. But then she looked up at him, her eyes sympathetic. "I appreciate your concern, Prince Alfehr. Your brother and I were close, but only as friends. We both knew what this was. I was chosen to be a queen, not to be the love of his life," she said lightly, but her eyes bore a sadness that Alfie recognized. "I still miss him though."

"I know." If they were not so obviously being watched by everyone in the ballroom he would've reached to touch her arm. "I do too. Every day."

"And his memory, it's everywhere in the palace, isn't it?" she said, her eyes sweeping over the ballroom. "I've been avoiding coming to speak with you because I was afraid that it would be too . . ." She pressed her lips together in a thin line. "It must be hard."

Alfie felt a lump in his throat. "It is."

She gave him a watery smile. "We should talk about something else, shouldn't we?"

Alfie nodded, his eyes burning. "How is your flame casting? Still as impressive as ever?"

Her smile turned into more of a smirk at that. She raised her hand and flexed her fingers. Alfie watched the beginnings of lightning crackling at her fingertips. It was the most difficult feat for a flame caster to learn and very few ever did. Not even Dezmin had been able to summon lightning. Yet Aurora had a handle on it before the age of twenty. Nobles seldom dabbled in elemental magic, but she was such a prodigy that her family sought to nurture her talent.

"Of course," Aurora said triumphantly as she let the pinpricks of light at her fingertips fade. Then she leaned closer to whisper conspiratorially. "We both know that the king and queen chose me so that they could have a grandchild who would light the palace on fire before they could even walk."

For a moment Alfie was stunned into silence at her bluntness, but then the two burst out laughing. She was right: his mother and father had certainly been keen on her as a future queen not only for her standing and her beauty but also for her talent in both elemental and spoken magic. It was nice to be around someone who knew the smoke and mirrors of his world.

"Well, if that comes to pass, I'm a skilled water charmer, so we won't lose the palace entirely."

"Yes." She laughed before saying to him softly, "No matter what happens, betrothal or no, we'll just fine, you and I."

Alfie found himself nodding. "I think you're right."

A comfortable silence wrapped around them, and for a moment, Alfie felt light.

Then he looked over Aurora's shoulder and saw Tiago Vera approaching Luka. Though Alfie couldn't see his face, he knew by the tightness of Luka's shoulders that Luka was uncomfortable.

"Aurora," Alfie said, "I'm sorry, but I must excuse myself."

"It's all right," she said with a warm smile. She touched his arm, and he was happy for the comfort. "It was nice to speak with you, Prince Alfehr."

"And you." He bowed low to her again, holding it for an extra moment in respect to her. She curtsied before turning to walk to a group of other young noblewomen. As quickly as he could without calling the attention of the guests, Alfie began to dart across the room to Luka's side.

"Luka," Tiago crowed. "So nice to see you."

Tiago and Luka had courted for months before Tiago had left Luka for one of his friends. Luka had spiraled into a sadness that Alfie had never seen on him. He'd only been sixteen, his first heartbreak. That pain was something Alfie never wanted to see marring his spirit again. To this day, Tiago was hell-bent on reminding Luka of how thoroughly he'd crushed him.

Even if Luka refused to speak to him, Alfie wasn't going to let him handle this alone. He sped to Luka's side and cleared his throat. Tiago's triumphant smirk fell away.

"Your Highness," he said, dropping into a low bow. Alfie had to stop himself from rolling his eyes. "Welcome home. It's been so long since I saw you last."

"Tiago," Alfie said, tilting his chin up. "It truly has been too long. I've been far from home and yet, even at sea, I did hear of you squandering half your inheritance gambling over the summer."

An embarrassed flush bloomed on Tiago's face.

Luka's eyebrows rose and with a moment of eye contact they were communicating as seamlessly as they always had.

Take him down, Alfie's eyes said.

Naturally, Luka's replied.

But Tiago beat Luka to the punch. "Prince Alfehr, it's wonderful to see you back, safe and sound, but one must wonder," Tiago said, cocking his head as if in thought. "If you have no future, then what will become of our beloved Castallan when you rule it?"

Alfie froze where he stood, hot anger pooling in his stomach as Tiago's lips unfurled in a satisfied smirk.

At the age of five, all royals were taken to the royal diviner, where she would glimpse their future and speak of what greatness their lives would bring. Dezmin had been told that his legacy would be eternal, a sign that he was to become the king that their parents had hoped for. When Alfie's mother took him to his own divining, he'd hoped to hear the diviner speak of a future of conquests, like the stories he'd been read. He feared that she would say his life would be full of cowardice or bereft of glory, a life his parents would not be proud of, but what she said was much worse.

"I cannot divine him," the diviner had said, snuffing out Alfie's hopes. "There is a piece missing, an important one. Without it I cannot see the prince's future."

How could his parents think he was the one to lead this kingdom when he didn't even have a future to speak of? When he wasn't whole.

If Tiago had thought of this, how many others were tittering about it behind their hands, wondering if Alfie's rule would spell the end of their kingdom? A stunning wave of embarrassment twisted through Alfie as he sputtered for a response in the face of Tiago's sneer.

Alfie was saved when Luka stepped forward, his narrowed eyes on Tiago. "You would do well to hold your maldito tongue. Like your prince said," Luka uttered, reminding Tiago of his station, "you failed in the gambling dens; I wouldn't press your luck with us either. Make yourself scarce, Tiago, like your inheritance."

Tiago gaped at them, his face pinched tight with humiliation before he turned on his heel and walked away. Luka and Alfie looked at each other for a moment before bursting out laughing. But when the laughter died, Luka looked away, as if remembering that he was still angry.

"That doesn't change anything, Prince Alfehr." It was strange hearing his full name and title in Luka's mouth.

Luka's tone aside, Alfie's heart lightened all the same. If Luka had defended him, then maybe they were closer to going back to the way things were. "You know me well enough to call me Alfie."

Luka cut his eyes at him, his practiced smile faltering. "Do I?" Luka plucked a goblet of sangria from a passing servant's tray.

"Yes," Alfie insisted. Luka took a generous gulp of sangria. "Careful," he said, his voice low. "You know you don't do well with the sweet stuff."

Luka raised his eyebrows before motioning for another servant to come his way. Luka downed his sangria goblet and handed the servant his empty glass before taking a fresh one.

"And you don't do well with sneaking in and out of the palace with contraband," Luka hissed over the lip of his glass. "But I'm not lecturing you now, am I?"

Alfie's shadow moved away from Luka warily. "Luka—"

"What?" Luka went on quietly, his polite smile still on. "Are you afraid that if I drink too much I'll tell everyone about your new hobby? How would I even phrase it?" Luka cocked his head and tapped his chin, as if he were thoughtfully contemplating. "I suppose I could start with: 'Did you know that when everyone is asleep, Prince Alfie here gets a doorknob—'"

"Luka," Alfie said, his voice snapping like a whip. He kept his face composed, a careful smile to match Luka's. "I know you're angry with me. You have every right to be." Luka snorted. "We have to talk about it, but that time can't be now."

"I can't promise I won't kill you before then," Luka muttered, sipping his sangria.

"You could," Alfie said, hoping that Luka's joke meant he was a little less angry. "But then you'd be left alone at this boring party."

"Then I'll kill you right afterward," Luka quipped.

Alfie nodded at that. "We'll compromise, then."

Luka's lips quirked up into a genuine smile, and Alfie couldn't help but grin back. Maybe everything really would go back to normal soon. The queen walked toward them, the voluminous skirts of her tiered gown skimming the polished floor.

"And how fares the night for my favorite boys?" She stood between them and gripped them each by the shoulder. "It's so nice to see you both together again, getting along."

Luka stiffened at her words. He stepped away from her touch, and her smile wavered.

"It is nice," Luka said, conjuring a smile so brittle that Alfie could spot the cracks splintering it. "Would you excuse me?" Luka said with a bow.

Mother meant well, Alfie knew, but it had been too soon to say something like that.

"Of course," Queen Amada said, her eyes bright with concern.

She nodded at Alfie, silently telling him to follow as Luka made for the doors.

Alfie followed Luka out of the banquet hall and into the hallway. As soon as the doors shut behind them, Luka let out a growl of anger and ran a hand through his dark hair.

"I know you're angry—" Alfie began, but Luka silenced him with a furious look.

"*Yes!*" he said, nearly shouting. Alfie was thankful that the walls were soundproof. "I know that you know! And I know that you keep pretending that everything's going to be fine now that you're back, even as you're sneaking out of the palace, risking your life on a fool's errand! And you have the gall to think things can just be *nice* again? You left, Alfie. Three months and not a single *maldito* letter!"

Alfie swallowed hard, unsure of what to say. "I know. And I'm sorry. I needed time. Please just listen—"

"No," Luka hissed, closing the space between them, his eyes glassy. "No, you listen. You left me here! You left me here to look at his empty place at the table, *alone!*"

Alfie felt a pang in his chest as Luka wrung his hands in frustration. He'd left because he couldn't take seeing the places where Dez once stood, where he should still be standing, but he hadn't even thought of what his leaving would mean for Luka. He'd thought of no one but himself.

Alfie's shadow stretched forward toward Luka, but Luka only stepped away. "Luka, I'm stopping now, I promise. It's over, all of it." He was telling the truth. He'd promised himself he would stop should those Englassen books lead him nowhere, and not a one of those books had anything to offer to save Dez.

Luka stared at him, his unfocused eyes narrowing. "I'm not a fool. I don't believe you. Why is it that when you choose to be reckless you decide to do something that will get you killed? Why can't you just drink and sleep around like every other rebellious royal?"

Alfie's hands curled into fists. "I handled my grief in my own maldito way, Luka. Not everyone is you."

"Not everyone is next in line to be king, Alfie," Luka shot back.

"Why does everything have to come down to that?" Alfie said, feeling the walls closing in on him. He knew he would have to be king, but the reality of it still weighed too heavily on him, like an anchor dragging him down into unfathomable depths.

"Because it's important! And this is foolish. Dez is gone. You can't bring him back. And the worst thing is you seem to think you're the only one here who lost a brother," he seethed. "Dez was mine too. And you made it feel as if one brother was taken and the other *left*!"

"I didn't mean—"

"I don't care about what you meant," Luka snapped. "And maybe you've forgotten, but you were important to Dez. Your maldito life was important to him! This kingdom, this family's legacy, was important to him too. He wouldn't want you to get yourself killed and throw it all away. And I won't watch you do it."

Alfie's face burned with shame as Luka stormed off without giving him a second glance. He was far too drunk to believe him now. If he needed space, he would give him that. He owed him that much. But the flush in Luka's face and the subtle sway in his steps told Alfie that all the sangria he'd had was hitting him.

"Please just go to your room and sleep it off," Alfie said. "We can talk tomorrow."

Luka waved a hand dismissively over his head without turning around and disappeared around a corner. Alfie wanted to follow, but his mother would have his head if he left the party. If he was to be king, he needed to make an impression at these events. That was what Luka wanted him to do, wasn't it? Commit to his royal duties? Still, he longed to go after him.

Alfie shook away that urge. He walked to the double doors to the ballroom, pasted a smile on his face, and went back in.

Finn counted to one hundred before she rolled out from under the bed, righted the secret compartment in the drawer, and hesitantly stepped back into the passage.

What had just happened?

She thought of the sound of the bottle being shaken and the girl weeping. It felt wrong. Poisoning took malice, and Finn could hear only regret in the girl's cries. Beneath her gnawing curiosity flashed a question—did the prince deserve to die? She peeked into the slat again and saw the neck of the bottle on the prince's bedside drawers. For a moment she considered dumping it out. Then she snorted. What did she possibly owe a prince? She was here to rob him, not save him.

What kind of person are you if you just sit back and let some-one get killed? she thought.

Finn pressed her forehead to the stone wall. Letting someone get poisoned certainly wasn't the worst thing she'd done. What was the point of turning back now?

That thought sat in her stomach like a stone.

You are exactly what I've always said you are, Mija. A monster.

Ignacio's voice rang in her head like a gong. Her fingers itched to dump out the bottle, to prove that voice wrong. But what did one good deed matter? It was foolish of her to even think that one good thing would save her from all the bad. This wasn't some children's story.

She was who she was.

For a moment she sank into that memory once more, the memory of the first time she'd taken a life. She could see the girl bleeding out beneath her, could feel something dark and crooked take root inside of her. Her palms were sweating, her breaths ragged and uneven.

After three countdowns she quieted the part of her mind that echoed with guilt for things long past. She was too far gone to drown in guilt. She'd learned to swim in those waters long ago. She needed to focus.

Finn shut the slat, the key to the vault secure in her pocket. Whatever was going on, it had nothing to do with her. She was here to get the cloak.

Now that she'd retrieved the key, she needed to travel back down to get to the royal vault. It must've taken nearly an hour to go through the tangle of passages and ladders into the depths of the palace. She felt the air shifting, becoming danker. She wondered if the palace really had dungeons like she'd heard. Curious, she checked the map. Yes, it did.

She'd be avoiding those, thank you very much.

Finally, she made it to a passage that opened into the hall where the vault's floor-to-ceiling silver doors stood. Of course, there was no direct passage into the vault. She wasn't that lucky or the palace architect wasn't that stupid. Through the slat she could see two guards sitting at a table before the vault. The table was scattered with playing cards. It looked like they'd been playing a round of cambió. She grimaced. She'd had more than enough of that game.

One of the guards was already nodding off. The other was staring at the ceiling as if he could will himself to float up to the party upstairs.

Out of her bag, Finn pulled a stoppered vial full of five gray quilbear quills as thin as a fingernail and as long as her middle finger. She pulled off the stopper and with a beckoning motion of her hand, the quills rose to her eye level.

Quilbears were massive beasts covered in sharp, venomous quills that they shot at enemies and prey. The quills themselves were strong, threaded with a great deal of metal. And what was metal but a type of stone?

With a flick of her fingers, Finn poised two quills at the slat's opening. She needed to do this right the first time. If she missed, they might spot the quills and realize someone was trying to knock them out. But if she could hit them, she could get into that vault without a hitch.

Finn held her breath and eyed her targets. Neither was moving much. Now was the time. With a purposeful flick of her fingers, the quills zoomed out of the slat.

Don't move, don't move, don't move, Finn thought fervently.

The quills buried themselves in each of the guards' necks, and their heads lolled forward as they fell fast asleep. Finn put her fist in her mouth to stop herself from shouting in victory. Her shadow swirled triumphantly around her.

She exited the passage and plucked the quills out of the guards' necks, then pushed the key into the slot of the great door. The lock gave a resounding click. Finn looked back at the two guards whose heads were resting on the table, still fast asleep. Quilbear venom knocked people out for a good ten minutes. Fifteen, if she was lucky. She needed to find the cloak and get out before then. She pushed open the great doors and closed them behind her. Her jaw dropped.

The vault was bathed in the golden glow that came only from treasures too expensive to comprehend. Everything shined, calling out to her fingers for thieving. There were dummies draped in the most beautiful gowns and headpieces she'd ever laid eyes on. They must've been the wedding clothes of former queens. There were preserved documents that even Finn recognized as historic: Castallan declarations, sacred texts from before Englassen occupation, and marriage contracts between princes and princesses. She opened chests and found more gold pesos than she'd known existed and necklaces so heavy with jewels they might snap her neck. Beside a neatly arranged pile of tapestries was an undressed dummy in a glass case. Something beautiful must've once been kept in it. Finn wondered what, but then her eyes fell back on the gold. Before she could stop herself, she was shoving fistfuls of pesos into her pockets.

"*Stop*," she told herself. She wasn't going to get out of the palace unseen if she was lugging around a chest of gold. She emptied her pockets.

Well, she emptied most of them.

Then she set about finding the vanishing cloak. What the cloak actually looked like, Finn wasn't sure. Every Castallan child had been told the story of the great rebellion that began with a single vanishing cloak. But in every tale it changed in color or description. Some said it was light as a shadow, others said it was weighty with history. Some said it was the rich red of the Castallan flag. Others claimed it shimmered with every color known to man and all the colors that weren't. Finn didn't know what to look for. She figured she'd know it when she saw it. But she tried on fancy cloak after cloak and none made her invisible or looked particularly special.

With a growl of frustration, Finn plopped herself on top of a dark wood chest, her arms crossed. How the hell was she going to find something when she didn't even know what it looked like? She rolled her neck from side to side, feeling the tension cording through it. As she searched the vault in vain, she walked past a pedestal topped with a velvet pillow. On the pillow sat what looked like a severed piece of a statue—two thickly muscled arms and hands carved from dark, smooth stone. The work was so painstakingly detailed that it didn't seem carved at all; it looked as if it'd sprung from some mountain face just as it was.

The stone hands were interlocked, the long fingers laced together. Probably a piece of some famous sculpture she knew nothing about. Finn was hardly one for art, but she couldn't tear her eyes away from it. It even had fine hairs sculpted onto the arms. She'd never seen a statue with that kind of detail. Whatever sculpture the arms came from, Finn knew it was a towering, imposing one.

Finn reached for it, and just before her fingertip grazed it she felt a zap of magic crackle through the air, shooting from her fingertip through her body. She wrenched her hand back.

"Coño! What the hell was that?" she said before rolling her stiff shoulders. The stone arms sat there, unbothered, seemingly unimpressed by her attempt to grab them.

Finn made a crude gesture at them with her hands. "Make a statue out of these," she hissed, catching her angry reflection in the glass case.

In that moment, something clicked into place in her mind. What if what she really needed was a cloak that she couldn't see?

Finn turned back to the glass case with the empty dummy inside. She pulled the glass door open and reached for the dummy's shoulder. Where her fingers should have brushed a bare sturdy frame, she felt something light and textured, a patchwork of tiny scales. With both hands she tugged the invisible garment off the dummy.

She pulled it over her own shoulders and felt for the sleeves. At first it seemed like it would be too big for her, but as her arms slipped through, the sleeves shrank and tightened comfortably. She felt the hem come up so that it wouldn't drag on the floor. But when she looked down at herself, her body was still visible.

"Really?" she said, annoyed. What had she done to make her luck this sour? When she turned back to the glass case, intending to return the cloak, she felt the hood of the cloak swish behind her neck. It was worth a shot. She pulled the hood over her head.

Her body disappeared before her eyes.

She'd done it. She'd found the vanishing cloak.

"Amazing," she breathed.

Everyone knew the story of how this cloak had saved Castallan from enslavement. Englass believed that magic was a privilege that only they should enjoy. All others were seen as primitive, unworthy of the gift of magic. And if a people's mother tongue was wiped out, if their connection to their past, their ancestors, their history, was forgotten, then they could no longer call upon magic.

When Englass invaded Castallan generations ago, they'd sought to snuff Castallan's language, like a candlewick between wet fingertips, destroying their connection to magic along with it.

The Englassen regime destroyed all of Castallan's books of magic, forbidding them from speaking their mother tongue or using spoken and written spellwork. Generations of being forced to speak only Englass's language passed until Castallanos had forgotten their language entirely. Their connection to spoken and written magic had been severed. They knew nothing beyond the little they were allowed to do with elemental magic when doing farmwork for their Englassen masters.

Then a Castallano slave had stolen this very vanishing cloak and used it to sneak into the libraries where he found a secret cache of books of Castallan's language. With each word he learned, he discovered the marvelous breadth of magic once more and taught it to his people in secret. His teachings spread, and Castallan finally rebelled and overthrew their colonizers. This cloak had returned magic to her ancestors and, in turn, had given them their freedom.

She walked in small circles, feeling the cloak swish around her heels. She was wearing history about her shoulders. Her shadow zoomed around her excitedly, visible on the floor. She'd have to keep it curled beneath the cloak to stay out of sight.

With the cloak to keep her hidden, she made her way back to the ornate filigree doors of the vault. She turned back and stared wistfully at the gold that could buy her a maldito ship instead of passage on one. But she needed to get out unnoticed, not alert the guards that someone had ransacked the vault. The pesos in her pockets would have to be enough.

She crept out of the vault and pulled the great doors shut. The two guards were still asleep. Finn had to keep herself from snorting. With the cloak on, she walked away from the guards, not bothering to duck back into the secret passages. She had what she came for, and now she was going to enjoy it. She was going to walk around these royals with her head held high.

And maybe she'd finesse a few things here and there. If the mood struck.

Who was she kidding? The mood always struck.

Luka took another long swig of the bottle as he leaned against a shelf in the wine cellar.

With every gulp he drowned out the memory of Alfie's empty apologies and seeing Tiago looking so characteristically smug at the dinner party. After he'd finished a bottle he grabbed another for his trek to his rooms. He was in a much better mood than he had been when he'd left Alfie standing in the hall looking so lost. So guilty and sorry.

Luka guzzled the wine to blur that thought. After a few loud gulps, it grew murkier and murkier, until he couldn't remember why he'd started downing the wine in the first place. But he was no quitter, so he finished the bottle regardless. As he made his way to the grand staircase, Luka handed the empty bottle to the nearest guard with a wink.

Whenever Luka was drunk, he made a point of looking at the patterned tiles on the stairs as he stumbled up to his rooms. The designs wiggled and escaped the bordered squares they'd been caged in, mingling with each other until new patterns emerged.

Sure, this method of walking made Luka fall multiple times. But it was entertaining, and Luka lived to be entertained.

When what felt like the millionth guard tried to help him to his rooms, Luka stared at him in disbelief. "Gods, how many of you are in this place? I can walk myself to my rooms, guard number three thousand and one. You ought to be guarding something more important, like innocent bystanders from Alfie's awkward dancing."

Then Luka laughed so hard that he almost vomited onto the tiled floor he so admired.

When he made it to the sweeping corridor to his bedchambers, he paused. Alfie's words rang in his head like the most annoying of bells: *Please just go to your room and sleep it off.*

"Pendejo," Luka sniffed before leaning against his door, contemplating. At this moment, it was very important to do the exact opposite of what Alfie said. Very important. He pushed off the door and promptly stumbled to the ground, catching himself with a palm against the floor.

"Opposite, opposite," he mused as he shakily stood. What was the opposite of going to his room and sleeping? Luka snapped his fingers as he cracked the code. "Going to Alfie's room and staying awake!" He stumbled down the corridor and burst into Alfie's room. He flopped onto the bed and watched the canopy spin over his head. On the bedside set of drawers sat a bottle of tonic Alfie drank to calm him when he was nervous. Alfie always seemed to be nervous.

Except when he was disappearing for months at a time without a single word, getting into trouble without asking Luka to come along, or even telling him. He seemed more than calm then.

"Stupid abandoning jerk," Luka muttered before reaching for the bottle. It felt cool in his hand. Luka laid it against his forehead. It rolled onto his nose and balanced precariously on the bridge.

Luka plucked the bottle off his face, twisted the cork free, and took a long swig before throwing the bottle across the room, letting it roll toward the double doors to the balcony.

He rose from the bed, too annoyed to fall asleep. His mind fuzzy from wine and the tonic, Luka stumbled out of Alfie's room. Drunk or not, he would give Alfie a piece of his mind.

THE BLUE ROOM

Her steps as silent as the rest of her was invisible, Finn took a tour of the palace.

She sampled the pork that she'd snuck in through and could confirm that it was worth all the praise. She bet her sweat improved the flavor. She walked in through the banquet hall's open doors and watched the nobles dance, which proved to be less entertaining than expected. She listened in on conversations and mimicked the nobles' scandalized expressions as they traded gossip.

"Did you hear he was caught with his mistress?"

"*No.*"

"Truly! And she gave him an ultimatum."

"Again?"

"*Again.*"

When she grew tired of pantomiming gasps and looks of shock, Finn sauntered out of the banquet hall and went back to exploring. She knew she ought to leave, but she wanted to take her time out of spite. After all, she had nothing to fear, not with the vanishing cloak around her shoulders.

Finn walked through a wing of fine art, the library she'd peeked into earlier, and more parlors than she could count when she found herself in a quiet wing of the castle where there were no guards, no guests.

It was strangely empty and unkempt. Where the tiled floors gleamed throughout the palace, these were dull, as if they hadn't been trod on or scrubbed for months. The curtains were drawn over ceiling-high stained glass windows. At the end of the corridor was a set of double doors. Curiosity gnawed at her. Why was this wing so deserted? What had happened here?

Before she could talk herself out of it, she pushed open the doors, walked in, and shut them behind her. The room was a sweeping parlor with a blue tiled floor and swaths of darker blue fabric draping across the octagonal ceiling. Much of the furniture was covered in white sheets, like petrified ghosts unable to move or speak.

Creepy, she thought, wrapping her arms around herself.

Musty nets of cobwebs hung from the curtains. A thick film of dust lay stagnant on the one table where the white sheet had slid off, like moss over a pond. She ran her fingers over it and marveled at how she could feel her fingertips traveling through the grime, but couldn't see them. She made a tangle of intersecting lines in the dust and a little star with her pinkie. It looked like a phantom trying to scrawl a message. Finn the Phantom. She smiled. She liked that.

With a creak, the doors opened behind her.

Finn jumped, nearly forgetting she was invisible. Standing in the doorway was a boy, tall and a bit nervous-looking. He looked strangely familiar.

"Luka?" he called into the room. "Have you passed out in here?" He hovered at the door, looking too uncomfortable to walk in, as if something within this room had haunted him for far too long. His eyes were shining. He hurriedly rubbed them with the back of his hand.

He took a deep breath in and let it flow slowly from his mouth until his shoulders relaxed. His movements still unsure, he stepped in.

It was well past midnight now. What was he doing here? He was slim built, and from the little she saw of him thus far, she knew that every step he took was weighed and measured twice over in his head. There was a thoughtfulness to him and his furrowed brow. He looked delicate, even. Breakable. He was attractive, she thought, with his large gold eyes and the way his slim body tapered at his waist. He was endearing in his obvious weakness, like a puppy with a limp. Not quite guapo, but he was cute.

He scanned the room before he approached the table Finn was standing at. He ducked his head beneath it as if accustomed to finding someone sleeping under a table. His shadow zigzagged around him searchingly. She nearly snorted at the sight. What could the *propio* of some pampered palace boy be? The ability to make nice flower arrangements?

When the boy stepped closer, Finn held her breath. He was only a step or two away from her and had no idea.

He drummed his fingers on the table, then he paused, his eyes narrowing. Finn followed his gaze. He was staring at the marks she'd made on the table. Finn took a step back. Through the thin cloak, her hip grazed the edge of the table. The pesos in her pocket chimed.

His eyes snapped up, his shadow stilling in suspicion like a dog at the sound of unknown footsteps. Finn held still and willed her heart to stop hammering in her chest. It wasn't as if he could see her. He would decide he'd imagined a noise and move on. It'd be fine.

He reached out and nearly skimmed her nose with his fingertips. Then he dropped his hand and breathed sharply through his nose, clearly chiding himself for thinking someone was there.

That was close.

But then he looked back at the table and suspicion etched itself onto his face once more. His eyes locked on where she was standing. This time he squinted, focusing, as if that would help. She wanted to snort and tell him not to give himself a nosebleed. His gold eyes widened, and his hand shot forward, quick as a cobra, to grip her by the arm.

"What the hell are you doing here?"

THE PRINCE, THE THIEF,
AND THE DRUNK

"Are you following me?" Alfie asked as the somehow-invisible arm struggled in his grip.

He could see magic flowing through her. It was that same shifting wine red that he'd seen at the cambió game. "Who are you?" he demanded. "I can see you—answer me!"

The answer he got was a punch to the jaw. The girl wrenched her arm from his grip. Alfie lunged forward and grabbed her around her middle, holding her so that her back was pressed to his chest. She bucked against him.

"You heard me! Who are you? Take off the invisibility enchantment you've got on."

The girl threw away her elbow, hitting him in the face. He lurched back, his hands clamping over his sore nose. His eyes focused, he watched her figure, outlined in that familiar red magic, make a mad dash for the door.

Alfie locked his eyes on her red silhouette. "*Paralizar!*"

She froze. He could see the magic reverberating through her, buzzing with anger like a kicked beehive. Her shadow still surged around her, snapping at him like a threatened dog. This magic wouldn't hold long. He needed to act fast.

Alfie held her by the arm. When he raised his other hand it brushed against a hood he couldn't see. It fell off her head and she appeared before him, no longer invisible. She was frozen, her body leaning forward, a hand reaching for the doorknob. He knew her immediately—the dark eyes, the curly hair that fell just below her shoulders, the snarl that curved her lips. His *propio* hadn't been wrong. This really was the girl in the dragon mask, the one with the shifting red magic.

Alfie brushed his hand along her arm again and felt the fabric of whatever she was wearing that he couldn't see. His fingers skimmed a patchwork of feather-light scales, and he gasped. His father had let him hold it only a few times, but he would never mistake the feel of it for anything else. Vanishing cloaks were too rare to be owned by a common thief; this had to be the one kept in the palace vault. She'd stolen the single most treasured item in the entire palace, maybe the entire kingdom.

How had she done it? Had she changed her face into a guard's and sauntered in?

Then something else clicked in his mind, the journal of faces that she'd dropped. Of course he'd seen one of them on a wanted poster. The sketches in her journal were of the faces she'd worn while committing crimes.

He looked at her pointedly. "I am going to unfreeze you and you are not going to run. If you run, I will freeze you again and have you thrown in the dungeons, entiendes?"

She couldn't answer, but Alfie watched the magic thrumming through her slow and calm.

Alfie let his magic fall away. The girl's arm dropped. She paused for a long moment, seeming to think of what to say. Then she shrugged, as if giving up the search for a clever retort.

"I'm here to steal this cloak." He must've looked confused at her honesty because she walked back to the table, sat on it, and crossed her arms. "I'm leveling with you. I'm tired. It's been a hell of a week, and I came in here through a maldito pig. I don't have the energy to lie."

Alfie wondered if "coming in through a pig" was some form of slang he had yet to hear.

"You do know what that cloak is, don't you? Vanishing cloaks are extremely rare, but this one is not just any cloak. It's—"

"Sí, I know." She shot him a silencing look, the heat of her gaze a visual swear. "The cloak passed from king to king. The cloak that sparked a rebellion. The cloak that bought us our freedom. Not all of us have to sit at a polished desk to learn things."

"And you still want to take it? You're not at all concerned with what it means to people?"

"No," she said without pause. Alfie cocked his head at her. He didn't want to feel refreshed by how little she cared about the legacy, the weight of history, as his parents called it. But he was. Sore jaw aside, he was.

"I need it to get a job done," she said. She raised her arm and regarded the cloak thoughtfully. "And it'd be useful to have in my line of work."

"And what is that exactly? Your line of work."

She gestured at herself, as if she were wearing a sign. "What do you think?"

"Thieving identities, I would think."

The girl's brows rose. "Among other things. . . . How would you know that?"

Alfie stared at her, annoyed. "You don't recognize me?"

She looked at him blankly. "No."

"You encased your fist with stone and punched me in the face."

"Stone Fist is sort of my signature." She shrugged.

"It happened two days ago." When she only squinted at him, Alfie ground his teeth. Surely she recognized his voice. He couldn't be *that* forgettable. "We've met before."

She looked at him for a long moment. "You've got me confused with someone else."

"I do not," he said. "It's not possible for me to misrecognize you."

She snorted. "That confident in your eyesight?"

"Yes," he said, insistent. "I can see magic. I know yours. You were the one impersonating the woman at Rayan's house. We fought after the cambió game."

Her jaw went slack. Then her face pinched tight with anger. "If you hadn't done whatever the hell you did to knock me out, I wouldn't even be here! You pampered little son of a—"

"You might want to keep your voice down, if you want the cloak," Alfie lied, knowing full well that they were too far into the closed wing of the palace for anyone to hear. Within the space of a breath, she closed the distance between them and held a dagger under his chin.

"How'd you do it?" she asked. "How did you magic my trump card in the alley?" Then she stared at him in disbelief, her shadow stilling. "Wait, you're gonna let me have the cloak?"

Alfie sidestepped the question of his *propio*, raising his chin defiantly over the knife. "I will lend you the cloak—"

"Smartest thing you've said all day, I'm sure." She lowered the dagger slightly. "How do you have the maldito authority to give it to me?"

"Lend," Alfie corrected her tersely, his shadow snapping forward in annoyance. "It's mine to lend." He was lying through his teeth. His parents would have his hide if they knew about this.

She snorted at his words. "Yours to lend." Then she cocked her head and scanned his face. "Wait, you're the maldito prince, aren't you?"

Alfie resisted the urge to press the heels of his hands into his eyes. "Yes."

"I punched a prince in the face," she said, amused. "Never thought I'd say that."

Alfie pressed on, his voice clipped. "I will lend you the cloak under one condition."

The girl rubbed her temples with her free hand, looking too exhausted to appreciate the ease of the situation. "I'm getting really tired of conditions, Prince. Aren't you supposed to be forgiving and obliging to maidens? Isn't that what being a prince is all about?"

"You punched me in the face with a stone fist."

"I repeat, forgiving and obliging to ladies."

"Are you going to let me tell you my condition?"

She threw her hands up. "Yes, fine, what is it? What would

you like, Prince? How may I serve you?" she said with a mocking caricature of a bow.

He'd never heard someone say *prince* in a way that made it sound like such an insult. At least not to his face. "You have the power to change your face and your whole body, yes? You can change everything."

"Yes."

"Can you do that to others?" he asked.

The girl blinked at him. "Sí."

"Then once in a while I would like you to do that to me."

"Change you?"

"Yes," Alfie said. The books from the cambió game had yielded nothing useful, so he would commit to becoming king as he'd promised. But every now and again he would shed the weight of his legacy. He would be free, if only for a moment. Maybe that would be enough.

"You truly are out of a storybook. I expect you want to disguise yourself as a commoner and learn that true wealth is measured in love and friendship and other bullshi—"

"I didn't ask for your commentary, thief," he said, trying to match her wit. But she only gave him a crooked smile and he wished he could wipe it off her face, but getting her help was more important than his wounded pride. "Look, if you promise to help me, you can borrow the cloak to do whatever you need to do. I'll be collecting it afterward."

She crossed her arms, looking annoyed at the prospect of acquiescing to his request without more of a fight. He doubted she did much of anything without a fight.

"And if I just leave with the cloak now?"

"I will subdue you."

When she looked unconvinced, he raised an eyebrow as if to say, *Just watch me.* She pinched the bridge of her nose.

Alfie raised his hand slowly, not wanting to spook her into bringing out her dagger again. "Do we have a deal?"

She looked down at his hand, then up at his face.

"Deal," she said, her lips curving into a grin. All teeth, no heart. A look that told him she thought him a fool and had no intention of returning the cloak. Just as he did with her trump card, Alfie looked forward to catching her unawares. He had her journal; that was all he'd need to find her again. They shook on the deal, her small hand gripping tighter than he expected.

He watched her shadow zigzag excitedly, almost deviously, on the ground. When hers edged too close to his own, his shadow curled around his feet reservedly.

Alfie wondered if she ever worried about what her shadow revealed about her like he did, or if she lived her life so freely that whatever her shadow reflected was already obvious. He looked at the impish smirk that curved her lips and the swagger in her stance.

Probably the latter.

"What is your name?" he asked. This was the strangest conversation he'd ever had, so why not end it the way conversations were supposed to begin?

"Finn Voy," she said, the name short and sharp as the dagger she'd held under his chin.

Alfie's brow furrowed. Her surname was Voy, the word he used to move through the channels of magic that connected the world. Strange coincidence.

She raised a brow at him. "Yours?"

Alfie tilted his head. She didn't know his name. There was something comforting about that.

"Alfehr Reyes," he said.

The doors behind him burst open. Luka stumbled through, his movements shaky and unsure.

"Alfie," he said, his voice quiet. Of course Luka would find him now, at the worst moment.

"Bathtub Boy," Finn muttered.

Alfie stepped in front of her, hoping to block her from Luka's view. By the way Luka swayed on his feet, he looked drunk enough that come tomorrow morning he'd likely think he'd hallucinated. "Luka, you should be in bed. I looked for you everywhere."

"I was in your room. I drank wine and sangria and your tonic. Then I was looking for you and I . . . I don't feel well," Luka said, his voice a sliver of its usual cheery ring. Alfie felt the thief behind him stiffen.

Luka rubbed his ashen face with his hands. "Something's wrong."

He sounded like a sick child looking for his mamá. Alfie couldn't stop himself from stepping forward and pressing a hand to Luka's forehead.

"You're burning up." Luka was a flame caster, so he tended to run hotter than the average person, but this was too much. Alfie looked over his shoulder to check on the girl, but she was out of sight. Using his *propio*, he could see the red silhouette of her body.

When Alfie turned back to Luka, blood was pouring out of his nose and seeping from the corners of his eyes. His eyes rolled back as he fell forward.

"Luka!" Alfie cried out as he caught him. Alfie lowered his cousin to the ground. He knelt beside him. "Qué fue? Tell me what happened!"

Luka's jaw tightened. He shook with such force that it took nearly all Alfie's strength to hold him. Then he fell still, only his chest moving, rising and falling rapidly.

Luka's eyes slowly opened again and Alfie felt his world right itself for a moment.

"Alfie," Luka said, his voice lilting with a drunken ring, his eyes glazed over. When he smiled, Alfie saw blood splashed on his teeth. "I'm sorry . . . I yelled at you. I wanted to help."

Alfie didn't like his tone, how carefully he was putting the words together, as if they were his last.

"Be quiet, Luka! You're not going anywhere. I'm not finished with you yet. Just be quiet." He put his hands on Luka's chest and spoke words of healing magic, over and over again. But Luka's body wouldn't accept it. The channels that carried magic through him were quieting, emptying. Alfie's magic fizzled out on contact.

"When have I ever been quiet?" Luka's voice came out soft, and for a moment Alfie thought the magic was working, that if he could joke then he must be healing. But then Luka fell silent, his heart petering out into a death march under Alfie's hands in the very same room where he'd lost Dez, lost everything.

"Luka," Alfie said, his voice threadbare. "What can I do? Tell me what to do."

Luka's breath came slower and slower. Desperate, Alfie looked over his shoulder, knowing the girl was in the room. "Did you do this?" he shouted when he found her red-lined silhouette again. "Did you hurt him to get the cloak?"

She pulled the hood of the cloak down and lifted her foot to take a step forward, but then she thought better of it. "I didn't—I didn't do anything to anyone. Not like that."

Alfie watched the magic swirling through her. Magic was like a heartbeat; when people lied it moved erratically. Hers didn't, so it wasn't her. He hadn't just made a deal with a girl who had done this to Luka.

"Help me," he said to her, his voice breaking. "*Por favor.*"

For a moment she stood there, frozen. Then she closed the distance between them and knelt beside Luka.

"I don't—I can't help. I don't know much desk magic. Someone taught me to magic the card for the cambió game. I don't know anything else." Her eyes told Alfie exactly what he didn't want to hear.

Luka was dying and there was nothing that could be done.

For a moment, Alfie felt nothing. But chasing that cold numbness was a blistering anger. *No.* This room was not going to take anyone else from him, from his family. Not again.

His eyes darted about the room, looking for anything that could help, but it held nothing but haunting memories. He nearly stood to run and get help, but the thought of leaving Luka here only to return to find a corpse held him fast.

His spiraling mind found Paloma's voice and clung to it.

To perform the most powerful magic, you must stop calling the magic to you. Instead, you must approach it on its own plane.

If he couldn't help Luka with rudimentary healing spellwork, then he would need to reach for more complex magic. He needed to focus, to reach a state where he and the magic were one and the same. If magic were a pool, then he was merely wading in the shallows; the most potent magic was found in its depths.

Luka started to shake again, his body convulsing against the ground, foamy spittle stained pink with blood gathered at the corners of his mouth.

"Please," he said to the thief. "Just keep his head on your lap. I don't want him to hurt himself while he shakes, and I need to concentrate."

She hesitated for a moment before shuffling behind Luka and pulling his head and shoulders onto her lap. Alfie placed his hands on his chest and did as Paloma always told him to do before performing advanced spellwork—ignore his fears, his anxieties, and let himself fall into the magic, reach a state where it was only him and the magic working as one. Alfie calmed his shaking breaths, closed his eyes, and let his mind fall blank and clear.

The noises around him—the girl's fidgeting, Luka's whimpers—disappeared. He couldn't feel his hands on Luka's chest, couldn't feel the tiled floor under his knees.

When he opened his eyes, the Blue Room was gone. Luka and Finn were gone. All around him were colorful streams of magic and the shimmering colorless, free magic that swirled through the air, waiting to be pulled into a body and colored in its image. When bruxos were erudite enough to reach this realm, they could see the color of magic too, but Alfie was the only one who could see it outside this plane. He'd only ever heard of dueños and philosophers being able to reach this place after years of study and meditation. Alfie stood in the ever-present nexus from which everyone drew their magic. One used magic, coloring it with their touch, then let it go back into the ether. It returned here to turn colorless once more for someone else to use.

"*Por favor,*" Alfie heard himself say. "Please help me save him."

But the more he begged the magic, the more he tried to grip it in his shaking hands, the more it bowed away from him, skittering away from his touch.

Alfie knew what this meant.

If magic shies away from your touch, your intentions are not the right ones. You must let it go. Paloma's words echoed in his mind.

But he couldn't leave this place until he found a magic that would help Luka. Against every lesson he'd learned, Alfie concentrated harder, forced himself further into the magic. He moved through it, trying to grasp at streams of free magic that slipped out of his hands like eels. He was swimming against the current of the magic he'd been taught to respect. But he didn't care. He couldn't respect what would not save Luka.

Chasing after the currents of magic, Alfie found himself face-to-face with a wall, a barrier of sorts. It looked like a wall of adobe brick, but each brick was a different color.

Bricks of magic.

Whatever was beyond this wall could help, he knew it.

Alfie banged his fists on the barrier. "Let me in! *Abrir!*" he shouted weakly. Nothing happened. The wall stood silent and un-wavering.

Alfie pressed his forehead against it, his eyes wet. "Please," he begged. "I need help. I'll do anything, *please*."

A glimmer of light caught Alfie's eye. He turned toward it, and there at the center of the wall was a keyhole ringed in white light. The keyhole was the size of his hand and was level with his chest in the brick wall. Something powerful was hidden here. It had to be. Perhaps this was a test. Maybe he needed to prove himself worthy to get to whatever powerful magic lay behind the brick.

Alfie leaned close and ran his finger along the outline of the keyhole built of magic.

A spark lit in Alfie's mind.

The wall was made of magic. It must need a key of magic.

In this realm where magic could be built into a solid wall, then perhaps it could be made into a key too? It was all Alfie could think of. It wasn't as if he had the time to search through this vast network of magic for a key, if it even existed. He would need to press his magic into the keyhole and shape it to fit the lock, which was easier said than done.

Paloma's voice echoed in his head. *The finest bruxos are so intertwined with their magic that it's as if their magic has nerves. As if they can feel the world around them through the flow of their magic. Magic becomes an extension of themselves, their very flesh.*

After much practice, Alfie had felt that level of connection only a few times. He'd spoken a spell and briefly felt his magic zip through the air, as if it were an extension of his own skin. But those moments were few and far between. Now he would need to feel through his magic entirely. He needed to feel every edge of the lock and mold his magic to it before turning the key.

His hands shaking with nerves, Alfie guided a stream of his dark blue magic into the keyhole. He leaned forward and tried to look into it, hoping he might be able to spot its shape. But he was too nervous to feel anything. He let the magic fizzle out. He paced before the keyhole, his palms sweating.

"Focus," he said to himself. Magic needed to be guided with confident hands. Hands that trusted it. He tried twice more, nearly pressing his eye against the wall to try to see the lock's inner machinations, but nothing happened. His magic was moving blindly. They weren't connected. Alfie could not feel the grooves of the lock, couldn't feel anything but his heart pounding in his chest. He let his magic fall away.

Alfie pressed his forehead to the wall once more, his fingers curled against the bricks. Sweat poured down his brow. He wiped his forehead with the back of his hand.

"I can do this," he said. "I will do it. For Luka."

Alfie leaned forward and tried to look into the keyhole again, but then he stepped back. That was the problem. He was still trying to look instead of surrendering his senses to his magic.

Alfie stepped away from the keyhole, leaving a wide space between him and the wall. He closed his eyes and let his magic pool in his hand once more. Alfie focused on the feeling of his magic blooming in his hand like a flower seeking sunlight. He breathed slowly until he felt his magic expanding and contracting in time with his breaths.

For a moment Alfie thought he'd opened his eyes and failed to surrender his senses again, but he hadn't. He could see through the perspective of the magic flowing from his hand to the wall. He'd really done it! His magic zoomed into the keyhole, and within, Alfie could see the dips and arches of the lock. He was so excited that he'd finally connected with his magic at this level that he lost focus and his vision into the keyhole began to blur. Alfie concentrated once more and slowly shaped his magic to fit the keyhole's every drop and rise. Sweat dripping down his temples, Alfie twisted his hand to the right and his magic followed suit. He felt the lock click into place.

He opened his eyes and the colored bricks were rumbling, parting where the lock once stood to leave a doorway of shimmering, free magic.

Without a second thought, Alfie ran forward. He passed through the doorway of magic like a veil of light, only to be plunged into a chamber of darkness.

The familiar patchwork of colored magic and the shimmer of free magic were gone. This place held something else, a darkness he'd never seen before.

Where he walked there was no ground, no color, no sound— only blackness. Though he always felt a spark of warmth when he conversed with magic, here he felt a chill deep in his bones, as if his marrow had been replaced with ice. Goose bumps sprouted on his arms as he stepped deeper and deeper into the darkness. And then a voice was purring, rich and deep.

What brings you here, mi hijo?

It sounded like many voices intertwined, each one branching from the next, a mouth within a mouth within a mouth. Tendrils of smoke curled before the prince appraisingly, winding around each other in a tight circle, as if their space was limited, though

Alfie stood in endless darkness. He swallowed hard. He spoke the language of magic, but it never spoke back. It communicated in a different way. Hearing its will in the silence was something that took years of study. But this magic had a voice. It was strange, unlike anything he'd ever encountered.

Odder still was the magic's color—an inky, all-encompassing black. All his life, Alfie had been taught that magic did not exist in extremes of purity or evil, white or black. There were only the myriad shades in between. But before him stood the undoing of everything he'd known. This magic was darker than a crow's feathers, darker than ink spilled across a fresh roll of parchment. It was impossible, it was terrifying, but he didn't care. Couldn't. Not if Luka was dying.

"I need to save Luka; I need help. *Please.* You are the only magic that didn't turn away from me. Please, help me."

We could help you with that, that would be easy, it said. Alfie's heart raced. The voice was like the hisses of many snakes, hypnotic and terrifying all at once. *But first you must set us free.*

"I don't understand," Alfie said.

Magic *was* free. It flowed through all living things and wasn't something to be caged. Yet he could feel something holding back this black magic. Alfie took a breath to calm his racing heart and focused, letting his *propio* engage. He stumbled back at the sight. Before him, caging the darkness, was ring upon ring of different hues of magic. From pastel blue to gold to magenta to silver and back again. How many bruxos had contributed to this? How many had drawn rings of binding magic around it to keep it at bay? This shadowed magic sat sequestered at its center.

What was so terrible about this magic that it needed to be bound by so many bruxos? A cold tremble flitted down Alfie's spine. Even the idea of caging magic was unlawful, dishonorable. It went against everything he'd been taught about respecting magic as the foundation of the world. To chain magic was to spit on the natural order of things. It made him feel ill to even think about it.

We have waited here for the one who could find us, free us. It is you, my child. Set us free. Then we will save your friend.

Alfie listened and felt himself nodding along. The words echoed around him in silken whispers. This voice almost had a scent to it, something heady and rich.

He shook himself free of his reverie. Something about this was off. It wasn't right. Magic did not bargain or make deals. It did not have desires like men did. This made no sense at all. The words he'd seen in that silly book before Paloma took it from him echoed in his mind: *There exists old magic. Magic with soul, magic that colors men with its wants and bends them to its will.*

Had the book been speaking truth instead of fantasy? It had warned against this kind of magic vehemently. But if this magic could help Luka, did it matter how strange it was? What kind of person would he be if he would rather obey the natural order of things than save his best friend? He was willing to break every rule to try to find Dez. For Luka he should feel the same.

At that, the curls of smoke stopped their rhythmic circling, seemingly offended.

You hesitate? The magic tsked. *If you are not interested in our help, then . . .* With every word the magic's voice grew quieter and quieter, and Alfie felt his chance slipping away.

"Wait! No, wait! Please! I will free you, but—"

Be careful, boy. We are not known to bow to conditions and your time is running out.

Then Alfie could hear Luka's heart beat as if he were in Luka's very chest. The darkness pulsed with slow beats, the space between them stretching far too long.

No. Luka was not going to die. Alfie wouldn't let it happen.

His voice breaking with fear, Alfie said, "Just promise me that Luka will come back as himself and he'll be safe. He'll be him. Make him strong enough to survive this. That's all. If you swear to heal him and never hurt him, I will set you free."

The magic curled about once more. Friendly and purring.

If you free us, the boy will be safe from harm, this we swear. We will not touch him. We will give him the strength to survive this. To him it will be but a nightmare long forgotten.

Alfie hesitated again, the darkness around him foreboding and endless. This was wrong. He shouldn't do it. But then there was the whisper of a thousand voices booming from each direction.

Free us, free us, free us.

Beneath the chant was the slogging beat of Luka's heart. He had to do it. There was no time. But this black magic was bound by rings of different shades of magic. This was stronger than any magic he'd seen. Something old. Something he knew he should not be touching.

Something that would save Luka's life.

Alfie engaged his *propio*. He let his magic match the color of each ring, then he pushed his magic in and felt for a seam to tear it, to ruin it. Ring after ring of colored magic shattered in his hands like glass, the shards pricking his skin until his palms were slick with blood. To reach this state, this realm of magic, was a mental exercise, not a physical one. Why was he bleeding? This wasn't right.

Then a ring of dark green magic stood before him. The shade and its sure, slow movement were as familiar to Alfie as his very own magic. Alfie froze where he stood. This was Paloma's magic. It had to be. To unravel a stranger's spellwork was one thing, but to do it to the magic of someone he knew, someone who'd helped raise him, was something entirely different. The thought alone felt like a betrayal. He didn't know if he could go through with it. And if Paloma had caged this being, then it must be something too terrible for words. What would happen if he released it?

FREE US! FREE US! FREE US!

The shrieking dragged Alfie away from those thoughts. He had to save Luka. Paloma would have to forgive him for this. How could she not? If Luka's life hung in the balance, then nothing else could matter.

With quivering hands, Alfie took Paloma's magic in his hands and broke it. He closed his eyes as he did it, afraid to watch himself do such a thing. It felt worse than the others, as if he'd snapped the neck of an innocent animal. Alfie swallowed thickly and forced himself to move on to the next, and then the next.

Finally, there was only one ring left. A ring that shined silver, a color he'd never seen in all his years of watching magic flow through the air. He let his magic match its shade and threaded his magic into the ring. This one was strong. The ring of magic was so flawlessly drawn that he feared he wouldn't be able to dispel it; he feared that he *would* be able to dispel it just as much.

He found it. The magic's seam, a stitch for him to tug at. He began to pull on it with all his might. At first there was nothing, the strength of the magic unshakable, and Alfie knew it was over. He'd lost Luka, lost everything to this room again. But then the threads of magic begin to pull apart and burst, fraying at the edges. He pulled harder. The magic singed his fingers, fighting him. But he wouldn't stop. Wouldn't take the pain as a warning.

With a great shattering, the magic splintered and broke into countless pieces in his hands. It fell through his fingers in a fine silver sand.

As Alfie lost consciousness and fell tumbling into the darkness, he finally knew the word to describe this magic.

Hungry.

FREEDOM

With a glorious burst of energy, the tangle of magic bloomed into the room as the boy who'd released it fainted.

It twisted in the air, spreading its dark, smoky limbs this way and that, full of an exhilaration it could hardly contain. It had forgotten how large the world truly was.

The magic peered down at the boy passed out on the floor. One mere life had hung in the balance, and that was all it took to trick the fool into opening a cage that had locked it away for centuries.

A strangled sound of shock stole the magic's attention. Before it on the ground sat a girl, her face tight with fear.

She shuffled away from the freed magic, her breaths ragged. The magic watched in amusement as she grabbed a dagger from her belt and threw it. The knife flew through its sinuous form without a sound. Her eyes widened in terror as she realized that she was truly powerless before it.

If the magic had a mouth, it would have stretched into a wide grin. But that was what it needed, wasn't it? A mouth. A body. Its master could not return without one. Maybe this girl would do?

The magic circled the quivering girl like a scavenger would a corpse. How strange it was to finally be free, yet to still feel caged without its master. Without his command.

"Get away from me," the girl snarled through clenched teeth. "Stay away!"

The magic curled closer, running its airy form over her like a breeze burned black. Her shadow quivered about her, drawing the magic's attention. A host with *propio* would be sublime.

The girl gave a strangled whimper at the chill of its touch, as it looked into her soul, into the balance of light and dark within her. The boy who'd freed it had too much light, that much was clear. But this girl had some darkness in her, deep and unyielding. The body that could house this magic best would be one that waded in the dark, not one that basked in the light. Maybe she could be of use.

But then the magic recoiled.

She held a darkness in her that was painfully close to eclipsing her fully, but not close enough.

Her fearful breaths bursting past her lips, the girl's eyes rolled back in her head and she fainted just as the boy had. The magic wasted no time. It passed through the walls of the room and drifted down the halls in search of a proper host. At the sight of the opulent corridors, an awareness struck it like lightning. What its master so needed was here, within these very walls.

It only needed a body to get to it.

The magic darted down the twisting hallways of the palace. A servant woman rounded the corner of the corridor. She caught sight of the black tendril of magic curling through the air like a snake and froze in fear. The woman opened her mouth to scream, but the magic did not let her. It poured itself through her lips, forcing itself into her body, not bothering to gaze at the balance of light and dark within her. It would not be picky when it came to a body now, not when its master's awakening was so close at hand.

It burrowed into her body like a blade into a beating heart, like a row of teeth sunk into a juicy apple. For a magnificent moment, the magic had arms to move, lips to part in a feverish grin, a pair of legs that would take it deep into the palace to retrieve what it so needed.

Then the useless body began to tremble. Fissures of darkness bloomed on her flesh like shattered glass. After a moment, the body burst into black dust, leaving the dark magic homeless once more.

The magic surged through the air angrily. It needed a body. It needed to wake its master and be made whole again. Once more, it flew through the halls until it found another, a young boy. The magic poured itself into him, burning down the child's throat like whiskey. For yet another precious moment it was swaddled in flesh and bone. Then, once more, the body crumbled to ash around it, leaving it exposed and naked in the silent corridor. The magic quaked angrily. The thought of leaving this place without what belonged to its master was painful, but it needed a body and strength. It would not find either in these walls.

The magic poured itself through the walls of the palace like blood gushing from an open wound, and soon it was out in the open air, an entire kingdom before it. The first fledgling peels of sunlight began to lighten the sky.

An endless supply of bodies to wriggle into like fingers into gloves.

It would find what it needed. Then it would return for what belonged to its master.

THE WHY

When Alfie awoke on the floor of the Blue Room, sunlight was pouring through the windows, caressing his face in gentle strokes. Calm. As if what had happened were nothing more than a nightmare.

But Alfie knew better.

He sat up so quickly his head spun. A layer of sweat lay dried on his forehead. His bones rang with an impossible soreness. Alfie looked around the room, focusing until his head ached. Nothing.

The dark magic was gone. He was safe, for now.

Alfie caught his breath, his hand against his chest. His shadow was limp at his feet, dragging behind him like the train of a gown. It was a shade lighter than it ought to be—a sign that the awful thing he'd released had made him sick with effort. What had he done?

A loud, wet snore stole his attention.

Just behind him, Luka was lying on the ground, his limbs splayed out like a starfish. A film of dried drool stained his cheek and his hair was mashed down on one side. His chest rose and fell. There was no blood on the floor. It was as if it had never happened.

Alfie could feel his heart beating in his throat.

Luka was alive. The relief of it draped over him, pulling him under like the tug of sleep. His eyes stinging, Alfie could not help but grab Luka's hand and squeeze it.

A dagger sliced through the air, nearly winging Alfie's ear. He dodged, before throwing himself over Luka like a shield.

Before him stood the thief, looking livid. "What the hell did you do?"

Alfie looked behind him, where the dagger had wedged itself into the wall. "Qué?"

"When you fixed him." She pointed at Luka with a shaking finger. "What did you do?"

Alfie raised his hands in flat-palmed surrender and spoke the truth. "I have no idea."

Her jaw dropped, as if she couldn't believe he was this stupid. "That *thing* circled me like I was its maldito dinner, and you're telling me that you don't even know what it was?"

Alfie could only stare at her uselessly. He truly didn't know what it was, but he was certain that it was something that should never see the light of day. Worst of all, he knew that no matter what it was, he could not regret releasing it when Luka lay before him, alive and well.

The thief glared at him. "Explain," she hissed.

Alfie swallowed. "I'm not sure of what happened. Truly." He didn't know how to even begin to explain what had happened.

"Well, whatever the hell you did, it was big." Her gaze darted down to Luka. "Considering that he's good as new. How has he not woken up with all this noise?"

Alfie whisked a hand over his tearing eyes. "He sleeps like a rock after a night of drinking." He prodded Luka, who rolled onto his side with a grumble, still fast asleep.

Luka was safe. But he could not stay swaddled in the warmth of that fact. He needed to find whatever he'd released before it hurt someone. There was no doubt in his mind that it could hurt someone. Would, if left unchecked.

The thief advanced on him, her steps quick and purposeful. For a moment Alfie thought she might prove her skills with that dagger. Instead, she walked around him and pulled her dagger out of the wall.

"Wait, you were awake when I . . ." He quieted, unsure of how to verbalize what he'd done. "When I did it. What happened?" He watched her move down the wall to pull out a second dagger. "Did you throw that at it?" He had to know everything if he was going to go after it.

She slipped the daggers into the sheaths at her belt. "That information will cost you."

Alfie squinted at her. "Really?"

She pointed at her face. "Do I look like I'm joking?"

A short time ago, she'd held Luka in her lap while Alfie had wept trying to save him. He'd thought that now she'd see him as more than someone to rob. He felt stupid for being so naive. He pulled his coin purse from his pocket and threw it at her with more force than necessary.

She pocketed the purse, shaking out the hand she'd caught it with. "Nice throw. Didn't expect someone like you to throw anything besides temper tantrums."

"Finn," he said, his voice clipped. "Just tell me. Please."

"Fine," she said. "You put your hands on the boy's chest. You went really still, too still. Your shadow too. Then the air started changing. I could see my breath. I wanted to run, but I couldn't move it was so freezing cold. I shouted at you, but you didn't hear me, you just stayed still. Then it got so cold I couldn't shout anymore. And your hands." She fell quiet, her eyes darting to his palms. "They started bleeding, like they'd been torn open."

Alfie's breath caught in his chest. He thought of how every ring of magic he broke sent terrible pain through his hands.

"Then all the blood that came out of the guy rolled back into him, like he was a maldito sponge. It wasn't like healing magic. It was like you'd turned back time, like he'd never gotten sick in the first place. It didn't make any sense." Now she was holding her arms instead of crossing them, almost hugging herself. Her shadow curled protectively around her feet. "And then . . . It's hard to explain."

"You're doing fine," Alfie said, nodding for her to go on though he wished she wouldn't.

"There was a sort of—" Her hands waved through the air as if she were trying to draw him a picture. "A sort of dark tangle floating over you."

"Like thick, black smoke?" Alfie asked.

She nodded fervently, as if she was finally sure that she hadn't gone mad. Magic was visible only to him outside the realm of magic, thanks to his *propio*. How could she see it too? This was all wrong.

"Yeah, like if oil could fly. It got close to me, surrounded me like it was sizing me up." She shivered at that. "Then it flew through the wall. Disappeared."

Alfie swallowed, his throat feeling thick. "I spoke to it," he said, his words hushed. "I spoke to that dark magic. It was trapped. It said it would save Luka if I let it free."

Finn stared at him, brows raised. "You talked to that . . . thing?"

Alfie pressed the heels of his hands into his eyes. "I told it I'd release it if it promised to heal Luka and never hurt him." His hands dropped from his face into his lap, limp and shaking. "It agreed. So I set it free."

Alfie looked away from her stunned face, his mind racing. He had to tell someone who could help. Paloma? His parents? The thought alone made his stomach turn. He'd already disappointed them; he wouldn't shame them again by having them clean up his mess. He'd fix it himself. Somehow.

"Thank you for telling me everything." His body stood in the Blue Room, but his mind was miles ahead. He needed to find what he'd released and stop it before it harmed anyone. But what magic would he use to stop it? Magic was free. To trap it was impossible, unless the magic was your own. Bruxos sealed their own magic into talismans to draw upon later for strength. It was a tactic often used in war should a bruxo run low on energy in battle. But those were wisps of their own magic sealed away. What he'd released was hardly a wisp, and it certainly wasn't Alfie's to control. And he could not replicate the rings of magic that had caged it. He knew nothing of how to subdue it. He'd never seen anything like it. He'd never read about it either.

His swirling thoughts came to a screeching halt. There was one book that came close—the Englassen book Paloma had taken from him. If there was a book that could help him, it was that one.

The thief moved to the chair where he'd draped the vanishing cloak.

"Not so fast," Alfie said, her movement jarring him from his whirlwind of thoughts.

"I'm not a fan of doing things slowly." She reached for the cloak.

Alfie seized it. She looked at him, her eyebrow raised in challenge.

He tugged the cloak around his own shoulders. He would need it for what he had to do. "For your help thus far, I'll do you the favor of letting you go. But our deal is off."

"What the hell do you mean the deal's off? You can't call off a deal once it's set."

"I'm doing it anyway."

Her jaw hung slack. "Aren't you a prince? Aren't you supposed to be all about honor?"

"Today I'm making an exception," he snapped. "Listen, I have more important matters to deal with right now. I'm letting you go when I should be calling for the guardsmen. Leave the palace now before I come to my senses." He didn't have time for this. He needed to put Luka to bed and find that book. The longer that corrupted magic was free, the more damage it could do. Each second he wasted struck him like a blow.

The thief cocked her head. "You're going off to find that thing you set free, aren't you?"

"If you must know, yes," he said as he crouched beside Luka. Why did she care?

"All right," the thief said, rolling her shoulders back. "Let's get going, then."

Alfie stared at her. "What?"

She rolled her eyes as if it were obvious. "Vámonos. Let's go find this thing."

"You want to help me find it?" He would never expect her to be so generous.

"It's got nothing to do with you, Prince." With a flick of her wrist she produced yet another dagger. She picked her nails with its sharp tip. "Nothing makes me feel small without paying the price. That creepy thing owes me a debt for that, and I always get what I'm owed."

Alfie stared at her, wondering how anyone could be so foolish as to chase this magic in the name of pride. Yet he couldn't help but consider the offer. He didn't want to go after this magic at all, let alone by himself, and it wasn't as if he could ask someone else. Admitting what he'd done would be too shameful, but this girl already knew it all. She'd witnessed it with him. Alfie shook his head. This was absurd. Fear was driving him to stupidity.

"As if I would take you with me."

Finn gave a snort. "You'd be maldito lucky to have me."

"A moment ago you threw a dagger at my face—"

She waved her hand at him dismissively. "Just to scare you a bit, don't be a baby."

"—I cannot have someone I don't trust with me while I'm trying to remedy this."

"You don't need to trust me, you need me. Period. You know your way around a library, but this won't have anything to do with that. At least not completely." Alfie looked away from her. "You know I'm right."

"Why do you want to come?" He didn't want to do this alone, but he wasn't foolish enough to depend on a girl who'd leave him in the lurch. If she was coming, he must know why.

"I told you, nothing makes me feel small wi—"

"Yes, I heard that." That brash response was nothing. He wouldn't rely on the promise that her ego would keep her around. That was too much of a gamble. "It isn't enough."

She threw her hands up. "Why do you need to know? You're lucky I'm even offering."

"I won't take you with me unless I know your motives." Alfie watched her magic flow erratically. She did not like this question. "I will know if you are lying. So don't waste my time."

With every moment that she stood before him refusing to tell him, time bore down upon him, begging him to chase what he'd released. He needed to make this decision quickly. The city was full of representatives from every province and major city here for the ball. For months his parents had toiled to instill confidence in them for Alfie's upcoming rule, all their hard work leading up to tomorrow's ball. If it got out that the prince had released something dangerous so carelessly, they certainly would not want him to be king.

His mistake could put an end to the Reyes' reign.

When she only glared at him, Alfie pressed on. "Tell me or I will leave you behind."

Finn would've laughed at how ridiculous the boy looked, demanding an answer from her as if she couldn't beat him to a bloody pulp with her hands tied behind her back. But his question hung heavy in the air, smothering her chuckle.

She should know better than to go after an opponent that she didn't understand, even if it had the gall to make her feel like a scared child. But still, there was something to be gained here and she couldn't grasp the words she needed to explain. Or she didn't want to grasp them, to turn them over in her hands and see them for what they were.

She thought of the moment she'd left the prince's rooms without dumping out the poisoned bottle. Of Bathtub Boy dying of that same poison. She'd done her fair share of terrible things, and she knew that such things would cause others pain, but she'd never been around to witness the aftermath. The prince's face at seeing the boy dying, the terrible hopeless sound that had wrenched through him; these were things she would never forget. They'd crawled into her mind and made a home there. She couldn't help but wonder how many were left to mourn, how many had wept over a corpse that she'd left behind with reckless abandon for survival.

For Ignacio.

A monster, just as I always said you were, Mija.

Finn pushed Ignacio's voice away before it pulled her under. Her stomach twisted into a knot of guilt and a searing desire to be something other than what Ignacio had told her she was. To be better.

Or to at least try. For once.

"Finn." The prince's voice snapped her out of the memory's choke hold.

She sucked her teeth. "I grew up in a world where watching bad things happen to others and not lifting a finger was how you survived, if not doing some bad things yourself. It's how I've lived my life for a long time."

The prince tilted his head. "But not today?"

Finn looked away from him and picked at her nails. "No, not today."

"Why?"

"Because whatever monster you released looks like it could end the maldito world if it feels like it. I need to fix this, so that the world keeps spinning and I have more chances to say, 'Not today.'" She held his gaze. "Understand, Prince?"

She'd spent so much time drowning in her past that she hadn't been able to swim to the surface and see a future for herself that wasn't stained with blood and fear. She wouldn't let memories of Ignacio or some strange magic snuff it out before she had a chance to reach for it. To take it and weigh it in her hands like a freshly filched coin purse.

The prince looked at her for a long moment, as if he were reading a compass. She squared her shoulders, inviting his scrutiny, though she knew that if she were a compass, she would be one that had never pointed north. She wondered if he could see it all through her skin.

"Very well," he said. "I believe you." He seemed a little relieved.

Finn nodded, her face unfazed. But something reverberated through her, as if the taut string that held the broken pieces of her together had been plucked. It took her a moment to realize that was the first time anyone had ever said that to her. At least, that she could remember.

"Fine," she said flatly to fill the silence and quiet that ringing thought. "And I still get to borrow the cloak when this is all done, are we clear?" After this she was going to hunt Kol down with that cloak and get her *propio* back, one way or another. That was really why she had to help the prince, she decided. Not because of the heartbreak on his face as he'd knelt over that boy. No. She was doing this for the cloak. For revenge.

"Fine," he said back.

When the quiet stretched a beat too long for her comfort, Finn looked at him expectantly. "Well? What's the maldito plan?"

Alfie looked up at her from where he knelt beside Bathtub Boy. "First, we get Luka to bed. Then, I need a book."

Finn rolled her eyes as the late morning sun stretched its glowing fingers across the room's tiled floor. "Of course you do."

THE MAN IN THE GRAY CLOAK

The magic soared through the air, hungry for a home of flesh and bone.

In a tangle of black smoke, it moved past the green expanse of the palace grounds and through the sunlit rings of the city, from the immaculate haciendas of the Bow to the swirling marketplace of the Brim, the dirtied alleys of the Bash, and finally the sea-soaked, outer ring of the city—the Pinch. And yet it could not find what it searched for.

It went unnoticed by the men and women who celebrated and drank in the name of tomorrow's holiday, their energy tugging on the magic as if begging it to claim them as its own. But as it drew nearer, making the downy hairs on their necks rise in quiet alarm, the dark magic grew repulsed.

It could hear the thoughts in their simple minds, the hopes for love, for safety, for the health of their children. It could feel the light burning within them, the stench of it stifling.

The magic could not take just any body. Only a body that

could hold a candle to its former master's darkness would do; the rest would crumble to ash, as they had in the palace. It had zoomed through the city several times now, finding nothing but useless bodies. It was like a man dying of thirst surrounded by poisoned waters it could not drink.

Aggravated, the magic made its way, yet again, through the Brim, hoping that it had simply missed its prey when it searched before, hoping that this ring did have what it so desperately sought. It flew down a dank alleyway between rollicking pubs where the air smelled of sweat and spilled tequila. There, leaned pathetically against the alley wall, was a man in a tattered gray cloak taking a long swig from a nearly empty bottle of tequila. He had a scar across his eyes, as if someone had drawn a blade from one temple to the other in a messy slice. The man stank of poverty. His irises were a milky green, and the way he moved down the alley told the darkness that his vision was murky at best, perhaps not fully blind but close. This man should mean nothing to the magic, just another drunk in the Brim, and yet the dark magic felt a pull to the man, like a fierce current hidden beneath calm seas.

It drew close, attracted to the darkness that roiled inside him. Within the man's mind, a single desire beat like a drum.

To kill.

The image of a person sat in his mind, heavy with ire, someone he'd once called his kin. His hands were curled into fists, his chipped, dirtied fingernails biting into his own flesh as he dreamed of the girl's demise over and over again. At his feet curled a graying shadow. The magic pulsed with excitement at the sight. This man had *propio*, a deeper connection to magic that made him stronger, an ideal host. Those two simpletons in the palace had had moving shadows as well, but they were not dark enough. This man was the perfect combination of all that the magic sought.

He was magnificent.

The dark magic drew close to him, making the hairs on the nape of his neck stand on end. He shivered and pulled his cloak closer about him, his cloudy eyes searching for the source of the sudden chill.

We can give you what you seek.... The magic purred around him, its voice a braid of hisses.

The man started where he sat. "Who are you? What do you want?" he croaked.

We want to give you what you desire....

He stiffened at the proposition. "How do you know what I want?"

The dark magic pressed into his mind and played the images the man so desperately wanted to make reality—that girl dying in his hands, begging for forgiveness.

The man gasped, his hands clutching at his head. "What are you?"

We are a power that can give you what you seek, for a price. We can make you what you once were.

Again, the magic pressed into his mind and pulled upon the man's fondest memories. Memories of the time before his eyes had been ruined by the one he so desperately wanted to kill, when his power over others was as unstoppable as the rising sun.

The man's eyes flew wide with hunger, and the dark magic could sense him wondering if this was all a dream.

"Name your price," the man said, his voice cracking with desperation. "Please, I will do whatever you ask."

Give us your body to grow in, help us spread over this city.

To awaken its master, it first must spread its darkness to others. Only then would it have enough to take what belonged to its master from the palace and clear the throne for a true king.

Once we have accomplished this, we will give you the girl. . . .

The man barely seemed to be listening, his mind clinging fervently to the fantasy of what was to come.

"Yes," he said. He spoke the word as if he were saying a prayer. "Please take me."

The dark magic reared back like a cobra of smoke and poured itself into the mouth of the man in the gray cloak. The man wrenched backward against the wall as the magic worked its way down his throat, into his very veins. The further the magic dug into him, the more the man's shadow drew inward, his own darkness moving inward to eclipse whatever smidgen of light he had left.

The man screamed in agony as his body burned from the inside out, filling with a power meant for a god that must instead settle for a man.

For a moment, the dark magic feared the man would burst into ash and it would be homeless once more. But then a calm fell over him. Now that its essence had been given a body, the magic could feel its power fortifying the man, bringing him strength.

That, and a hunger to spread.

The man stood slowly. As he passed a hand over his eyes, the magic heard his unspoken command. His vision was restored. The magic surged with the pleasure of serving a master even if it wasn't his own. It was made to be commanded and this man would do until its master returned.

"Incredible," the man sighed, his head swiveling as he took in his surroundings.

That is only the beginning. . . .

The man flexed his hands and slid his shoulders back. Desires slid from his mind and into the magic's grasp without pause. In the blink of an eye, his shabby clothes were made new. The worn shoes at his feet were replaced with boots of fine leather, his legs draped in soft-clothed trousers and his shirt of rough-hewn fabric transformed into a fine emerald silk that hung loose on his chest. The holes in his gray cloak knitted closed as it returned to its former spotless glory. He was clothed in a gray storm cloud and could not wait to unleash a barrage of lightning.

The dark magic spoke in his mind. *Spread over this city; find those who are dark-hearted and they will become our servants, ours to control.*

The man strode out of the alleyway, his head held high. He moved toward a pub with a bright blue door, as good a place to start as any. Perhaps there were men with dark intentions within, men who would be worthy of their cause, men whose bodies would help awaken their waiting master. The magic stretched its jaws, spreading its own hunger through the man's veins like wildfire. The man shivered.

"I'll do as you ask." His hand on the pub's doorknob, the man paused. "And then I get what I want."

The magic flashed the image of the one he hungered to punish in his mind once more. *You will have exactly what you wish and more.*

"Then let's begin, shall we?"

THE BOOK

Hunched close beneath the cover of the vanishing cloak, Alfie and Finn moved through the tiled corridors of the palace to retrieve the book.

First he'd lugged Luka to his room (a sight that the guards were quite familiar with thanks to Luka's habit of overdrinking and underthinking). Then, while the thief remained hidden, they used the cloak to walk to Paloma's private room unseen by the guards and the servants who rushed about to prepare lunch to be delivered to the doors of the royal family after yesterday's late night.

All the while, Alfie feared that they would turn a corner and the dark magic would be there, lying in wait. But they had yet to encounter it. Whether by luck or because it had truly left the palace, Alfie didn't know, but he was grateful all the same.

Until he found himself stepping into a pile of ash that went over his shoe. He moved backward, giving a short sound of surprise. Thankfully, the corridor was empty.

"What the hell is that?" Finn asked as she pulled the cloak off them.

"I'm not sure," Alfie said, his fingers ghosting over the black ash. But it wasn't black. It was a shade darker than should be possible, so dark that he blinked at it, startled by the depth of the color. This was a part of that foul magic, it could be nothing else. But why would it leave behind a pile of some sort of residue? His finger skated over something small and smooth beneath the surface of the dust. Alfie tentatively pinched it between his fingers and the black sand parted to reveal a silver earring.

His heart caught in his chest.

The servant boy who had nearly dropped a feather duster onto his own head, the boy who had looked at Alfie with such hope and admiration. He'd worn this earring.

Alfie shot up to his feet, his stomach roiling.

"This," Finn said, her eyes wide. "This stuff was a person?"

Alfie could only nod, his throat feeling as if it was closing, leaving him to choke.

Hunger. That was what he'd felt emanating from the magic before he'd freed it from its cage of rings—a desire to feed that left Alfie feeling like a cornered animal. What would happen if the Englassen book didn't have the answers he needed? Would all of Castallan be reduced to this black dust?

"Prince," Finn said. She pointed over his shoulder, her face pale.

On the far end of the hall sat another pile of ash, this one larger than the first.

Alfie leaned against the wall, his hands shaking. He wasn't

fit to be king; he was scarcely fit to live after this. He'd done the very opposite of what his parents had taught him—he'd thought of himself, of his own desires above all else. And now people were suffering because of it. He put his face in his hands and willed his stinging eyes not to spill over.

The sound of rock rumbling quietly brought his attention back. Finn made a parting motion with her hands, and the stone ground beneath the first pile of ash split open. The remains of the boy fell in.

When he stared at her, she shrugged. "You said you want to take care of this without anyone finding out, right?"

She was right; they could hardly leave the piles of ash in the corridor, but his chest ached at the sight. "They deserve a proper burial."

Finn stared at the sunken ashes. "A lot of people deserve a lot of things. But if this thing is destroying people that quick, we don't have time for that."

Guilt aside, he found himself nodding. A thought struck him. "Wait, don't close it."

They would need to track the magic down somehow, and if this dust was what it left in its wake, it was the perfect thing to use for tracking spellwork. If they followed the dust, they were bound to find its source. Alfie reached into the crevice, his throat burning at the thought of the little boy it once was. He pulled a handful of dust from the floor.

"To trace it by?" Finn asked, her eyes on his black-stained fingers. He nodded, glad to not find an ounce of judgment in her eyes. He pushed the black dust into his pocket.

"Rest easy," Alfie said to the pile of remaining ash. There

would be no body for this boy's family to bury, to weep over. Just like Dez.

Finn made a closing motion and the stone pressed together again. They walked to the next pile and she did the same. Alfie watched, trying to swallow the bile crawling up the back of his throat. He couldn't help but be both disgusted by her and grateful she was there. The way she stepped over the remains made him wonder what she'd done in her life to make this so easy. Yet without her resolve he didn't know if he'd still be standing.

"Let's go on, then," she said. They stepped back under the cloak and walked down a twist of corridors, passing the towering doors of the library before they finally stood before Paloma's door. Alfie stared at it, his hand frozen before the knob, his stomach twisting in anxiety.

He'd never been invited into Paloma's rooms, let alone snuck into them unsupervised. To barge into her private quarters felt wrong, but his people were being reduced to ash. He had no time to waste on worrying about breaking rules of decorum.

Alfie opened the door and they darted in. He felt like he should clap a hand over his eyes to stop himself from even looking at the room. A narrow bed sat in the far corner, and shelves of books were neatly organized against the walls, their spines in different shades of leather. There was a dark wood desk where rolls of parchment and quills awaited her attention. He knew Paloma's schedule—she would be in the library at this hour, leaving her room empty.

Finn pulled the cloak off them. "What are we looking for?" Her face was taut, no hint of the usual smirk.

"A black book with gold Englassen script."

The thief turned to the nearest shelf, scanning the spines with keen eyes. Alfie went to the shelf beside the bed and searched. His hands passed over basic books of magic that Paloma had used to teach him as a child. Every book seemed to represent a moment where she'd encouraged him to become a better prince, a better person, and the longer he stayed in this room the more he felt himself disappointing her. Alfie clutched the collar of his shirt and tugged. Finn's movement on the other side of the room caught his eye.

Without looking away from the shelf, he said, "Put it back."

She sighed and put Paloma's small silver mirror back on the shelf. No time for jokes, but still time to steal, it seemed. He was about to chastise her, but then he spotted it. There, wedged between thick volumes of magic.

Alfie's guilt wavered, his fingers itching to turn the pages. He knew they should leave and head back to his room in case Paloma decided to come back, but Alfie could not wait. He needed something to give him hope that he could fix this.

He frantically thumbed through the book until he found the chapter that spoke of sealing magic. He'd been reading it just as Paloma snatched the books from him. He was keenly aware of Finn's bored eyes on him. She was picking her nails as if she'd rather be anywhere else.

He read that the entity needed to be sealed into an object of great value to the sealer, something he hadn't noticed during his first read. He looked down at the dragon on his chest. It was the most precious thing he owned. He did not want to use it to trap the magic in fear that it would break, but he hardly had a choice.

The spellwork needed only a single word of magic; the book

described the spoken magic as the simple word for closing in Englassen. To use it in his own language, the word would be *cer-rar*. It was easy enough to remember.

Just beneath the illustrations came a warning that chilled him to the bone.

> *Sealing an entity with one's blood must be done only in the most dire of circumstances. To seal with one's blood is to tie oneself to the sealed entity. The longer that the being is sealed, the more it will draw upon the sealer's energy, his very life force. The consequences can be lethal.*

The sweat on his palms soaked the spine of the book.

He swallowed the lump in his throat. Was this why the diviner could see no future for him? Because he'd been fated since childhood to give his future away to this vile magic?

"Prince." The thief sighed, leaning against the desk. "We don't have all day."

Alfie wiped the sweat off his forehead, his throat dry. "No, we don't."

Whatever needed to be done, he needed to do it quickly. The ball was tomorrow night and he needed to be here to present himself as the future king of Castallan. Not to mention, his family would certainly notice if he was missing for very long. He would have to handle this today. Now. While his family still slept and relaxed after last night's festivities.

A voice sounded from outside the door. Paloma. Finn and Alfie froze where they stood, their eyes wide. If she walked in now to see him and a stranger in her private rooms, Alfie would be done for.

"Where's the cloak?" he whispered.

Finn swiveled around.

His eyes narrowed. "You lost the cloak?"

"I didn't lose it," she hissed back. "I put it down, is all." She got on her hands and knees and groped at the ground like a blind man searching for his cane.

"You *idiot*," Alfie growled before dropping to his knees and joining her in the search. If they got caught because this fool didn't have the foresight to hold the maldito cloak, then maybe he deserved whatever punishment Paloma doled out.

"Where did you see it last?"

She shot him a look. "It's invisible."

"You know what I mean!"

"Here!" Finn murmured before yanking Alfie up to his feet and tossing the cloak over them. As it had before, it stretched to envelop them both, just barely.

Paloma stepped into the room, shutting the door behind her. She held a book in her hand and leaned against the door for a moment to read on, engrossed. Alfie and Finn stood stock-still. They were in the middle of the small room; if she walked forward she might bump into them. But if they tried to move in this silence she might hear them. Finn made to move sideways; Alfie grabbed her by the shoulders and shook his head.

No, he mouthed, hoping she would listen to him for once.

You wanna get caught? she mouthed back.

He raised a single finger to his lips. They needed some noise to muffle their movements.

Paloma snapped the book closed before walking to her desk. Alfie held his breath and leaned sideways as she moved past them. Her dueña's robes nearly brushed against his leg.

When she reached to pull the chair before her desk back, Alfie looked at Finn and nodded. While the chair scraped against the floor, Alfie pulled Finn close and moved them to the only hiding space he could see in the tight room—the thin bar of space between two bookshelves. They stood chest to chest between the shelves.

Finn glared up at him, her eyes seeming to say, *Really? This is the best you could do?*

But before Alfie could scowl down at her, Paloma was opening a drawer in her desk and pulling out a round mirror the size of a dinner plate.

A scrying mirror. He'd never seen her use one of these before. Paloma was such a private figure that he never imagined her being close enough to someone to have a scrying mirror. Whose mirror did hers pair with? Finn prodded him with her finger and raised her eyebrows as if asking him to explain why he was so interested in an ordinary mirror. He supposed she'd never seen one before. It certainly wasn't the kind of thing found outside the wealthiest parts of the city.

He cocked his head toward Paloma and mouthed, *Watch.*

Paloma sat at her desk and leaned the mirror on an easel before her. Alfie could see it over her shoulder. Finn rose on her tiptoes, her chest pressing against him so she could get a better look. Finn was what some would call generously built. He hadn't accounted for that when he'd chosen this hiding space, not that he could simply conjure up another. In the space of a heartbeat, his senses had narrowed to the place where the soft of her chest met him, pressing further when she took in breath. Alfie's face reddened. He shifted backward, bumping into the bookshelf.

He screwed his eyes shut as the shelf gave a loud, whining *creaaaaaaak*.

Paloma's back tensed. She turned and stared at the bookshelf. Finn was so close to him that Alfie could feel her breath catch in her chest.

Paloma squinted at the shelf before turning back to the mirror.

Alfie glared down at Finn and she raised her hands in surrender as if to say, *Not my fault*.

"*Revelar*," Paloma said to the mirror.

Finn's eyes widened as the mirror began to glow a soft blue. The glass rippled like a pond disturbed by a dropped pebble. It cleared and stilled to reveal the face of a woman Alfie did not recognize. Alfie's eyebrows rose. She had the blonde hair, blue eyes, and delicate features of someone from Uppskala. She wore blue, velvet robes trimmed with brown fur—she was Uppskala's version of a dueña. Why was Paloma calling on a foreign dueña?

"Svana," Paloma said. Alfie could see the top of the woman's face over her shoulder.

"Paloma," she said, her Uppskalan accent flowing thick and slow over the quick syllables of Castallano. "You wished to speak. What is it?"

Paloma took in a breath. "I woke in the night with a terrible feeling in my bones. Something feels wrong." Paloma's hands clasped the edge of the desk, her fingers curled tight. "I cannot explain it. But I just know—I know that it has to do with . . ." She went silent once more.

Tension tightened like a knot between the two dueñas.

"You cannot be serious. Do you think so little of the rings of protection magic that are in place? To free it would require dueños from each of the ruling five kingdoms."

Rings of protection magic. Alfie's hands curled into fists as he was transported back into that endless darkness. He could remember each ring he'd destroyed. He could smell the blood running down his fingers. His palms were slick with sweat, his breath hitching in his chest.

"I don't know, Svana. I feel it," she said. "Something is not right."

Alfie's stomach dropped. He'd never seen Paloma show even an ounce of fear. Anger and disappointment, yes, but never fear.

"Castallan's pieces are safe, yes?"

Paloma nodded. "I checked myself. They are untouched."

Alfie's brow furrowed. What pieces were they talking about?

"You truly have not sensed anything?" Paloma asked, her voice strangely desperate. "Nothing that feels . . . wrong?" Silence. "Svana?"

Svana sputtered. "Perhaps, but that does not mean it has been freed. We have held it at bay for centuries. It will never get back to him. Never." Svana's voice came again, soft and insistent. Intimate. "How does the fable end, Paloma? After shadow and light join. Tell me."

Alfie's spine straightened. They couldn't be talking about *that* fable—the story of how magic and man were made, of the evil god who'd been enamored with the dark.

Paloma gave a shaky sigh and spoke the words that Alfie feared.

"The god who so favored the dark was cast out of the heavens, forbidden to return. The world's finest bruxos worked together and parted him from the dark power he so loved, turning his body to stone. He and his black magic were never seen again." Paloma spoke the words like a prayer, like something that held weight and truth.

Like something that was much more than a mere children's myth.

"Our ancestors splintered him from his power, and so long as we keep it locked away, he cannot return. He will stay a nameless villain in a children's story. This I promise you."

Alfie's teeth ground painfully against one another, the weight of what he'd done falling on him with unbearable pressure. He knew that what he'd released had to be something bad, but he hadn't expected this.

He'd freed the very thing that could revive the god of the dark. According to legend, Sombra would sweep the world into Nocturna—an endless night, an unraveling of mankind into monsters who thrived on hatred, violence, and greed. Alfie's heart sputtered in his chest. This could destroy not only his family's reign, but the entire world.

What have I done?

"You're right. I only needed to hear you say it." Paloma gently touched the mirror with her fingertips. Alfie looked away, knowing this was not for him to see.

The two exchanged goodbyes, and Paloma tenderly wrapped the mirror in velvet before tucking it back into her desk. When she finally left, Alfie opened his mouth to speak but Finn held up her hands, counting down with her fingers.

After a long minute they wriggled out from between the bookshelves and took the cloak off. Alfie leaned over, his hands on his knees as he willed himself not to vomit.

"Prince," Finn said. "Your teacher having a secret girlfriend can't be what's rattling you. People have secret girlfriends all the maldito time."

Her words flowed around him like water around stone, muffled and blunted by the panic racing through his veins. She was blissfully unaware of what he'd just learned. What he'd done.

Alfie looked at her, his mind a tangle of panic. "We're never making it out of this alive."

Finn crossed her arms. "Must you speak in riddles like a troll under a maldito bridge? Tell me what's going on!"

Alfie didn't want to explain what Paloma's conversation had made clear about what he'd released. He told himself it was because there wasn't any time with this foul magic running free in his city, but he knew it was because he feared she would leave him to handle this on his own.

Alfie quickly explained what he'd seen when he'd released the black magic, how it matched with what Paloma had said and how it all related to the legend of "The Birth of Man and Magic." What he'd released was the power that had been severed from that god, turning his body to stone. Her eyes went wide as saucers as he spoke.

"Wait, wait, wait," Finn said, raising a silencing hand. "You released a maldito *god*?"

"No, not exactly," Alfie said quickly, desperate to clarify. "I freed Sombra's power, which could possibly bring him back if not stopped . . . ," he said, his voice quieting as he went on.

"Oh *good*!" Finn glared at him. "I thought I had something to worry about. But it's just an evil god's power! No problem, then!"

Alfie crossed his arms. She'd all but begged to come with him. He knew he'd made a mistake, but he didn't need this judgment when they were about to embark on the most dangerous mission of their lives. "Well, if it's too much for you, you know where the door is."

Finn scowled up at him. "I haven't met a maldito thing that was too much for me. When I do, you'll know it."

Alfie rolled his eyes, though she was probably right. He tried to hide the relief that flooded through him. He wouldn't have to do this alone, after all.

"After spending your whole maldito life in the library, all you can come up with is that you'll try to trap the creepy smoke thing with some desk magic you've never even done before?"

Her words stung, pressing at the sore spot of his uncertainty. "This is not normal magic. It's not as if there are endless tomes about magic that can speak and turn people into dust!"

She opened her mouth to argue but fell silent.

"Well?" Alfie pressed. "Do you have any ideas you'd like to contribute?" This plan was so far from perfect, it was laughable. But it was all they had and he wouldn't have her tearing it down unless she had a better idea.

"So we track it down and trap it," Finn said, shaking her head at the madness of it. "With whatever wild desk magic you learned from that book. Magic you've never performed."

"It's all I know that might work."

Fear of chasing this magic with a half-baked plan raked its claws over him, but Alfie could not let that stop him. A pit curled and hardened in his stomach at the thought of the ball tomorrow. He'd done this terrible thing at the worst possible time—just before his parents would present him as the future of their kingdom at the ball and just after he'd finally promised himself to give up the search for Dez and become a king his family would be proud of. Guilt and shame stung him in turn. His parents' and his kingdom's faith rested on his shoulders. He could not fail them again.

Finn squared her shoulders. "All right, let's get on with it, then," she said, as if she were accustomed to resigning herself to the madness of a half-baked plan. Alfie felt his heart lift, if only for a moment.

If she was agreeing to try, then maybe it could actually work.

Or maybe she was just as wild as she seemed.

Alfie swallowed thickly. He'd released the power of a god, a power dark enough to make dueños the world over come together to trap it. A power that struck fear in even Paloma's heart and, left unchecked, would plunge this world into darkness. Alfie plucked a pinch of black dust from his pocket; the silver earring found in the ash flashed in his mind's eye. He would stop this thing from hurting anyone else, even if it cost him his life. He lay the dust on his palm.

"*Encontrar*," he said.

The black dust in his hand gave a tug eastward toward the outer rings of the city, where the people of Castallan celebrated, unaware of what their foolish prince had done.

THE BLUE THIMBLE

Following the prince's tracking spell was much less convenient than Finn had expected.

Under the vanishing cloak, she and Alfie had snuck out of the palace, hopping onto the back of a carriage that had come to deliver goods for tomorrow's Equinox Ball. According to the prince, it was clear that the black dust they were using to track Sombra's magic was not on the palace grounds because the dust in his hand would heat up as they got closer to it. But once the carriage entered the next ring of the city, the Bow, the dust grew warmer, so she and the prince dismounted and searched on foot. They'd skulked through the Bow's quiet neighborhoods, where noblewomen sauntered out of their brightly colored haciendas in their long, belted skirts and glimmering lace capes, along with noblemen in their freshly polished leather boots. The dust had gotten warmer but not warm enough. They'd moved on to the next ring, the Brim, where the dust grew hotter still. The prince, thinking it might have gone to the Pinch, steered them closer to the gate leading out of the Brim and into the poorer ring, but the dust fell cold as they approached. So they turned back into the maze of the Brim, moving through the nests of shops, searching in vain for that vile, smoky magic. Hours had passed, morning turning to afternoon, before Alfie felt the dust surge with heat in his palm.

"Espérate," Alfie said. "It's getting much warmer now. We're close." He swallowed thickly and Finn couldn't blame him. The thought of Sombra's magic curling close to her, as if it were hunting for something just beneath her flesh, had left her covered in goose bumps since the encounter. They walked on, down a more secluded lane of market stalls, the prince's spell leading them like a compass.

With the Equinox Festival happening tomorrow and the royal family hosting a ball, the city had already broken out in celebration. Tipsy couples danced in tight circles, tossing pesos at the musicians playing quick merengues back to back.

Finn should have been roaming the marketplace, thieving from every drunk she came across and treating herself to some sangria, but instead she followed the prince on his scheme to track this magic and trap it with whatever he'd learned from that weird Englassen book.

Like all Castallano children, Finn had heard the legend of Sombra and Nocturna—the darkness he would bring if awakened. She'd once asked her mother what Nocturna even meant.

"It means the end of all things good," her mother had said as she mashed garlic cloves. Finn had shrugged those words off as a child. Now they rang in her ears, the sound crisp as the snap of a bone.

"There!" Alfie said, drawing her from her thoughts. He pointed at a pub with blue doors tucked into a darkened, quiet corner of the Brim. He walked toward it, the hand holding the black dust outstretched before him. His palm was turning pink from the heat of the dust. "This must be the place."

The end of all things good could be waiting for them inside this very pub. Finn stopped short at the sight of its name—the Blue Thimble.

"This place?" Finn swallowed. The Blue Thimble was where she was supposed to meet Kol to give her the vanishing cloak. Would she even be here tonight? It was too strange a coincidence. And any place Kol owned was not the sort that you simply walked into. No one dared to step into her pubs without an invitation from the boss herself.

Alfie looked down at her from beneath the hood of his cloak. Once they'd reached the Brim, they'd removed the vanishing cloak to move with ease, but the prince still wore his own to keep people from recognizing him. "Sí. Do you have a problem with this specific pub?"

"No," she said, quelling the fear billowing up inside her. She'd meant to kill Kol anyway; might as well kill her and help the prince trap the magic at the same time. Two annoying birds, one stone fist.

The prince squared his shoulders. "Then we ought to get this over with. Quickly."

It was bold of him to think they'd be able to trap this thing at all, let alone quickly. Exchanging a grimace at what was to come, the two opened the blue doors of the pub and stepped in.

The first thing that hit her was the smell. The metallic scent of blood clung to her, coating her tongue. She clapped a hand over her mouth and nose as she took in the horror around her.

There was so much blood. Too much.

The Blue Thimble was large and sweeping, with a serving bar that stretched the length of its left side, and the pub in its entirety was awash with blood. The wood bar was slick with it, as if it had been varnished red. Twenty or so corpses were strewn about the place, like toys tossed by a spoiled child. Limbs had been cut off, throats slashed, and bellies eviscerated to leak rivers of red. The pub's countless tables and chairs were toppled and overturned onto the slippery ground. Her eyes couldn't make sense of what she saw. The red overwhelmed her, dizzying her senses.

Finn bent over and vomited where she stood.

She grabbed the bar for support. Her hand came away wet and crimson. With a strangled gasp she took a step away and slipped on something bony—a dismembered hand splayed on the floor like a spider of flesh and bone. Finn landed on her knees, her trousers stained red. From this angle she could see that the floor was dotted with piles of the same black dust from the palace, as if someone had emptied a chimney into the pub and spread the ash in mounds.

The prince pulled her up gently by the shoulders. He was saying something to her, but his voice was muffled and carried an echo, as if it were coming from the inside of a long-necked bottle.

Two drops of blood splattered on Alfie's forehead. He froze mid-sentence, fear pulling his face taut as the blood rolled down his nose and onto the bow of his lips. His gaze drew up and Finn followed his stare, afraid of what they'd find. A body was pegged to the ceiling with knives, a smile cut into the throat. Blood dripped from it like a leaky faucet.

The corpse dripped three more times, dotting his cheeks with blood before Finn pulled him sideways. He was stunned to silence as he wiped his face, smearing the blood in fat stripes.

For a moment, her fear was eclipsed by a flicker of hope. This was Kol's pub. Maybe she'd been killed in this massacre. If Kol had been killed, then her magic would die with her, and Finn would be free to use her *propio* again.

Finn focused, willing her face to change, but she felt that same stoppered ache building in her head. Her *propio* was still blocked. The ember of hope was snuffed out, replaced by a blinding anger that singed her from the inside out. She wanted to overturn the bloody tables, to add more carnage to the scene. So Kol was alive, but after this massacre, likely done by an enemy mobster, Kol had probably left town. How would Finn find her now?

Then the thought came, crawling from the darkest recesses of her mind: *Will I be stuck like this forever? Trapped with this face?*

That made her sicker than the bloody scene before her.

The prince's eyes widened. He pointed over her shoulder. "Finn."

Finn followed his gaze back to the blood-smeared bar she'd gripped only moments before. At first, she couldn't tell what Alfie pointed at among the broken bottles and unmoving bodies draped over it, but then her eyes found it. A hand with blackened nails rose from behind the bar, curling over the wood, its palm slick with blood. A second hand followed. A man rose slowly from behind the serving bar. He was shaking violently, his eyes black from edge to edge. His veins, raised and dark, squirmed beneath his flesh. He breathed raggedly, the sound sending a shudder through her bones. Finn and Alfie skittered back, stepping on limbs and puddles of blood as they darted away from the man.

"I can see it inside him," the prince said, his face ashen. "He's full of it."

Finn squinted at him. "Full of shit?"

He blinked down at her. "*No.* The dark magic, it's inside him!"

She looked back at the man and grimaced. "Well, that can't be good."

She'd expected the dark magic to reduce people to dust, like the victims in the palace, not to live inside of them, like some sort of parasite. Was an echo of this man still alive and being controlled by the magic? Finn's jaw tensed. She knew too well the agony of being trapped in your body while another pulled the strings. Her hand twitched, wanting to conjure a dagger to put this man out of his misery. But when the man crawled over the bar with a guttural growl, Finn knew she'd been wrong. No. This creature was not a man any longer. He'd become something else entirely, and Finn was afraid to find out what.

He stretched a black-nailed hand toward them, his breaths hoarse, his knees digging into the shards of glass on the bar. Finn flicked her wrist, pulling a dagger into her palm, but as she took aim at the man's throat, his skin began to break open, black fissures spreading over his body like splinters in broken glass. Piece by piece of him began to slough away into black dust, as if his flesh were burning from the inside out. Finn stared, her mouth agape as he fell away into nothing without a sound. Not a cry of pain or surprise came from his lips. All that remained of him were his clothes and the black dust on the bar that sat to be soaked up by the thickening blood.

"What the hell just happened?" Finn said, taking a tentative step toward the bar.

Alfie grabbed her by the arm, his voice thin with fright. "Wait!"

A dark curl of smoke, a smaller version of what she'd seen in the Blue Room, rose from the ashes of the body. The magic had burned the man from the inside out and now it would seek a new body to smolder. She'd be damned if it was hers.

Beside her, the prince stood still, the stink of fear marking him like a dog marks a tree.

She grabbed him, her nails digging into his shoulder. "Do your maldito thing! Trap it!"

Her touch seemed to spur him back to life. The prince pulled a necklace over his neck; hanging off it was a deftly carved dragon figurine. He bit his thumb until the skin broke and messily drew a circle on the dragon's chest.

Alfie took a deep, shaking breath, raised the dragon high, and shouted, *"Cerrar!"*

Finn waited for something, anything.

Nothing.

Not a maldito thing happened. The dark smoke paid the prince no mind. It kept rising slowly from the ashes, collecting in a horrid ball of darkness over the bar.

Alfie looked down at the dragon, his mouth closing and opening uselessly.

Finn glowered up at him. *"Really?"*

His voice a hushed whisper of fear, he said, "It's not working, it's—"

"Yeah, I can see that it's not working! We've got to get out of here!"

"No! I have to keep trying," Alfie shouted. "Or it'll hurt someone else!"

"Yeah," Finn sputtered. "And that someone else will be *you*! Let's go!"

Alfie opened his mouth to protest when a moan of pain rang from farther into the tavern, among the overturned tables and still bodies. A man stood up from the carnage, limping, somehow alive. He'd been so still that they'd mistaken him for a corpse in this scarlet tapestry of death. His eyes weren't blackened; he was still normal. Clutching the bleeding wound on his side he looked at Finn and shouted, "Help, help me, please!"

The coil of dark magic twisted at the sound of the man's voice. It zoomed away from Alfie and Finn and poured itself down the man's throat as he screamed in pain. Alfie cried out, his arm reaching forward as if he could somehow help the man. The stranger fell to his knees, convulsing. Alfie took a step toward him but Finn held him back, her arm outstretched before the prince's chest. Then the man fell still and slack, his head hanging, face hidden. Silent where he knelt among the broken furniture and shattered glass.

"It moves from body to body." Alfie's voice was hushed with horror. "Killing as it goes."

Finn stepped forward and squared her shoulders. "Hey, you!" she shouted at the still, black-eyed man. "I don't care that you're related to some stupid god. You're going to answer my maldito questions. What do you want?" She hated herself for letting a quiver of fear wriggle into her words, but the way the man stood, tremors of excitement running through his body like a child about to receive a sweet, made her stomach roil. "Answer me, or I'll skin you alive!"

He flexed his fingers and smiled at her like a cat would at a limping mouse.

"You've been singing of our master for lifetimes, calling him," he said. Black, raised veins squirmed beneath his skin like worms. He opened his mouth and sang, his cry a crooked twist of countless voices twined as one:

> *The Black King, turned to bone,*
> *In your heart he'll make his home*
> *Your eyes will bleed, your soul burned black,*
> *At his feet, you'll bend your back*
>
> *So hurry little ones, off to bed!*
> *Lest Sombra wake and take your head!*

It was a lilting children's song about that stupid legend. A song one sang to a friend for a scare and some laughs. Now each word rang in Finn's bones like a threat. Like a promise.

"You've been singing his name." The man cocked his head at her, his grin wide. "We will clear this world of false kings and wake him. He will answer your call."

With a laugh that sent spittle flying from his lips, he ran toward her. He moved as if he were unused to being confined in flesh, his body jerking at odd angles. She heard the slip of blood beneath his feet.

Finn never waited to be attacked; it wasn't her style. She liked the power of making the first move, whether it was a good idea or not. In this case, it seemed like a very bad idea. But if Finn was known for anything, it was for jumping headfirst into things that were very bad ideas.

And she'd be maldito if she wasn't going to stay consistent.

She dashed forward to meet him at the center of the pub, pulling stone from the ground to cloak her fists. The man made no move to defend himself; he only grinned. Finn landed a swift punch to his stomach. She felt his ribs crack, but the creature only stumbled back, a laugh bursting from his lips.

"For our cause we need bodies," he crooned in his singsong voice. He stood straight, cracked ribs and all. Ignacio had taught Finn the agony of injured ribs; the man should've been doubled over in pain. "It matters not if they are broken or whole. And yours will do *nicely*."

As he launched himself at her, Finn raised her fists again, but he batted them away easily, and she knew that he'd only been playing with her when he'd let her punch him. The embarrassment stung like the crack of a whip.

In the space of a breath, his black-nailed hand closed around her throat and, with terrifying strength, he lifted her off the ground. She clawed at his wrist, tearing at the delicate flesh there until his blood soaked her fingers, but he only grinned up at her. The grin slipped as he surveyed her, as if smelling a stink on her skin. "You are close, but of no use."

His hand squeezed tighter, and Finn could feel her bones creaking under his strength. How long until they splintered?

Her eyes tearing, she choked out a single word. "*Prince!*"

She heard clumsy footsteps slipping in the blood, and then came the thick thud of something sharp sinking into flesh. The man stilled and dropped her, his eyes wide. Heat returned to her body as her back hit the blood-soaked ground. Her shadow was gray and limp at her feet. Behind the black-eyed man stood the prince, with a dagger of ice poking through the man's chest.

As the black-eyed man fell to the ground, still with death, Alfie didn't know how he'd done it.

How he'd killed someone with his own hands.

Finn had called for him and the desperation in her voice had sent a shock of adrenaline through him, his paralyzing fear replaced with searing energy. He'd run behind the man and stabbed him in the back, right through the heart. Like some sort of coward. And now he stood at the center of the pub in a nest of overturned tables and chairs, a body at his feet and his heart in his throat.

A sound broke past his lips, a mixture of a gasp and a sob.

He'd feared himself on the day he'd attacked Paloma. He'd so deeply feared what he was capable of that he sought to bury it. But who was he if he could kill a man this way? Worst was the nagging inside him that told him he had no time for this, no time to break open and worry that he was losing himself. He had to trap this magic and save his kingdom, even if it meant committing acts that made him a stranger to himself.

Finn rose to her feet slowly and walked to his side, her eyes wide with uncharacteristic fear. Then her hand was on his back, resting stiffly between his shoulder blades.

"One bad thing doesn't undo all the good, Prince," she said, her eyes on the corpse. "It takes more than this to lose yourself, trust me. I've seen it."

Alfie fell silent. How could she see so clearly into his heart as it broke in his chest? It occurred to him that long ago she must have reacted this way to a killing of her own, but over time she'd shed that part of herself like a snake shed its skin. It struck Alfie as a horribly sad way to live. He jerked the flask from his hip and took a long swig. The heat of the tequila settled over him, like a patch placed over a gushing wound. He looked at her, his eyes wet. "Will you stop me if I get too close?"

She met his gaze, the set of her mouth grim. "If you do, I'll tell you and you'll decide to step back or dive in, but I can't stop you."

Alfie could only nod before whisking the back of his hand over his eyes. His shadow curled close around him, his anxiety pooling around his feet. The blood spilling from the man was stretching across the floor. He made to step away but let the blood soak the sole of his shoe instead. This was his fault. He'd freed this dark magic and stained his hands with this man's blood. Why not his shoes too?

"I'm so sorry," Alfie said to the body, his voice thick. He knelt beside it, unsure of what to do. What to say. Paloma had told him never to dabble in unknown magic because it always came with unknown consequences.

He should have listened to her. He should have known his place.

Alfie's hand found the corpse's shoulder. "Please forgive me," he said, his eyes wet. "I never meant to hurt you or anyone. This is my fault."

Finn's hand moved from his back to his shoulder. "Prince, we have to go before it happens again. Come on, get up."

"No," Alfie said. His limbs felt weighted with stone. He was responsible for all of this, for the boy and nothing but his earring left in the ash. He could not leave no matter how afraid he was.

The corpse's shoulder twitched beneath his hand.

Alfie wrenched his hand away and shot to his feet. The magic was going to rise out of the body again. This time he would get it right. He would seal it. The body convulsed against the floor, sloshing in its own blood. It trembled against the shards of glass littered on the ground, sounding like nails scraping a chalkboard

It wasn't the body that was moving but the dark magic within it, fighting to get out, like a parasite caught in a dead host. A body with a still heart was of no use to it. Alfie killing this man was forcing the magic to escape once more, in search of a new home.

The dead man's jaw slackened, easing open. A thick, black smoke oozed out of the bloodied mouth like dark sap from a tree. Alfie's thoughts shaved down to a sliver of panic, and he could barely string a thought together as the corpse seized and belched more and more dark magic, its back arching from the effort.

He had to contain it somehow. There had to be truth in that Englassen book. It was his only hope of ending this.

"It didn't work then, it's not going to work now! We have to go!" Finn shouted beside him as darkness oozed out of the body. She tried to pull him away again, but he remained rooted to the floor. She looked up at him, incredulous. "You'd really give your life for this?"

Alfie's grip on the dragon tightened. When he looked down at her, he didn't try to mask the fear that racked his body. Let at least one person know that fear would not stop him. "Is there nothing you would give yours for?"

Finn looked at him as if he'd grown a second head. "You've lost your maldito mind."

Alfie trained his gaze back on the magic pouring out of the body like pus from an abscess. He was terrified of it, but he was more afraid of who he would become if he let it run free. This was his responsibility. He would die here before he ran away like a coward.

Like a coward who would stab a man in the back.

"You're an idiot." She backed away from him, stepping around a broken bar stool as she pulled daggers from her belt. Alfie could swear he heard respect hidden deep in the insult. "You're brave, but you're an idiot."

The darkness swirled before him. His body grew numb and cold at the sight of it, blacker than any shade he'd ever produced.

An idea flickered to life in Alfie's mind like a struck match.

"Magic of the same color always flows together," he said, conjuring Paloma's calm.

"This isn't the time for a maldito magic lesson!" Finn snapped from behind him.

"Hush!"

Magic of the same color always flowed together. This was a fact he'd seen with his own eyes while watching people's magic permeate the air in ribbons of color. This was how his *propio* worked, how he was able to weave his own magic into someone else's. If this black magic saw a magic of its own shade, it might follow it, try to stick with it, maybe even obey it. It would make sense. Maybe that was what he needed to do to seal it away.

Alfie let his magic deepen to a pitch as black as he could get it. With the dragon held tight in his palm, Alfie let his newly darkened magic envelop it. The black magic that oozed from the body seemed to take notice and moved excitedly at the sight. It slithered through the air, away from the corpse and into the dragon's open mouth as if it had found its brethren. Alfie felt the little dragon grow warm in his hand. The magic stayed in it, as if waiting for Alfie's word. His command.

His magic still black as night, Alfie pressed the bloodied tip of his thumb against the dragon with all his might and shouted again, "*Cerrar!*"

He shut his eyes, expecting the black magic to recognize his trick and swallow him whole. But it didn't. The dragon only hummed in his palm, warm with energy.

Alfie slumped against the bar, pulling the dragon chain around his neck. Somehow, he'd done it. Maybe, just maybe, things would be all right after all. Maybe he could fix this.

As if in answer to that fantasy, the corpse collapsed in on itself, skin blackening and sloughing away until the body was nothing but a pile of ash.

As the ashes flew up his nostrils, Alfie's stomach twisted at the scent of burnt flesh, a life and all its possibilities snuffed out in one fell swoop.

Or maybe nothing would ever be all right again.

Then Finn was crouching at his side, her back leaned against one of the only small round tables left upright in the pub, spared from the chaos that had unfolded here. "It worked?"

Alfie squeezed the dragon that sat warm against his chest. "I—I think so."

"So that's it, then? We caught it?" He heard a lilt of hope in her voice and Alfie couldn't help but cling to it. "We're done?"

His bloodied hand still wrapped tight around the dragon, Alfie took in a shaky breath. He would not have to bear looks of shame from Paloma and his parents. No one else would die because of his foolish mistake. He could present himself at the ball tomorrow night with his head held high, with the promise that he would protect his kingdom's future instead of endangering it. Alfie whisked a hand over his eyes. "We did it."

Now he needed only to figure out where to keep this foul magic so that no one else would find it. But that dilemma sounded like a holiday compared with what they'd just endured.

Finn nodded, her shoulders sagging in relief. "Then let's get the hell out of here."

Alfie stood slowly, grabbing the table behind Finn for leverage. When his shaking hand came away bloody, he couldn't tell if it was from the table or if his palm had already been scarlet from the man he'd killed. Alfie walked close by her side as they stepped over corpses, shattered lamps, and smashed bottles. His shoulder bumped hers, and he couldn't help but savor the moment of contact. To relish the knowledge that he was not alone here, that though this day was a nightmare, it was a shared one.

When they finally stepped out of the pub, Alfie gulped in the cool air. He'd never been so thankful to breathe air that did not taste of clotted blood.

"I've got to say, Prince," she said, "I didn't think you could pull it off."

As they moved deeper into the Brim and farther from the bloodied pub behind them, Alfie stared at the stalls of magical baubles and trinkets, pastries and sangria, with a new appreciation. His people were safe to enjoy all that the marketplace had to offer, all that this kingdom had to offer. He watched his people move merrily from booth to booth, smiles on their faces as they prepared for tomorrow's Equinox Festival.

Alfie's heart still ached at the thought of the man he'd killed and all those who had fallen to dust at the magic's touch, but now there was hope. He'd fixed it.

His mind hazy with exhaustion and adrenaline, he couldn't help but look at Finn, gratitude welling up in his voice. "Finn," he said. "Gracias. I—"

A force he couldn't see thrust Alfie back, sending him flying the length of ten men until he slammed against the door of the Blue Thimble, his head cracking against it, his sentence dying on his lips.

"Prince!" he heard Finn shout as he slid down the door and onto the ground, but it sounded as if she were calling his name from the other end of an endless tunnel.

Then there was only darkness.

A FATHER'S INSTINCT

The man walked through the Brim, power flitting through him like lightning trapped in a bottle.

He'd torn through a pub, letting the magic within him ravage everyone in sight and slaughtering those who dared fight against him. With each body the magic claimed, more power bloomed within him. His senses grew deliriously heightened. Each hair on his skin seemed to be alive. He could sense the currents of air, individual threads of wind that moved in their own right. He could smell the fresh coat of paint swathed on a hacienda miles away, deep in the city.

As he watched the people in the marketplace, he wanted to shout, to laugh in their faces, to tear them limb from limb so they might know how insignificant they were beside him.

He wanted to make them all kneel.

Not yet, the magic hissed. *Those in the pub fall to dust, for they are not worthy. This power you feel will fade as their bodies fade. We must seek those strong enough for—*

"Silence," he said. Something called to him in the air. Something painfully familiar that clawed at his insides for attention, for punishment. There, in this medley of scent and sound and touch, was the girl who had taken everything from him. He could smell the scent of her, of her fear.

Not now. The magic persisted. *You will have the girl and much more after we—*

He shook his head, the magic's words falling on deaf ears. Finn was here. Fate had brought her to this city just as he'd thought. The man turned on his heel and walked back toward the pub he'd left soaked in blood, knowing his daughter would be there awaiting his love, his judgment. It was strange how those two things were often one and the same.

As the magic writhed in annoyance within him, Ignacio pushed its words away. After all, what kind of father would he be if he didn't pay his daughter a visit?

THE PUPPET MASTER

A dagger in her hand, Finn barreled through the crowds of the Brim and ran back to the Blue Thimble, where the prince sat crumpled against its doors. She knelt at his side, her eyes scouring the congested marketplace for an enemy, for whoever had magicked the prince backward as if he were a stick for a dog to fetch.

But there was no one of note around her, just shoppers moving from one brightly colored stand to another, chattering about the festival on their tongues. A few were looking at her and the prince, whispering behind their hands, taking steps forward to help but moving back at the sight of her dagger and her snarling face.

Alfie's chest rose and fell to a steady rhythm, but the back of his head bled against the door where he'd fallen after slamming against it.

"Is your friend all right, señorita?" An old man ambled toward her and Alfie, a cane in his hand. He reached for her shoulder. "Qué pasó—"

The man fell quiet, frozen before her.

Her heart pounding in her throat, she stared up at him and snapped her fingers in front of the man's still face. "Hello?"

It was as if the man had been turned into a statue. He did not blink, but his eyes didn't water from the effort. His fingers didn't cramp and twitch where they hovered above Finn's shoulder, she could feel the heat emanating from his skin, and yet he was still as the dead. Was she somehow imagining all of this? Had she hit her head during the fight in the bar?

It was then that she noticed how strangely silent it had become.

She looked beyond the old man and saw that every soul in the Brim, from the shoppers and the vendors to the dancing couples and the street musicians, had fallen still. Mouths hung open, mid-conversation. Hands were frozen, outstretched to drop pesos into a merchant's palm. Everything and everyone but her had stopped.

"What the hell?" she said. Her words boomed in the silence. She turned around and stared at the marketplace sprawled out behind her. Even a bit of spittle flying from a shouting man's mouth hung in midair. She was swaddled in silence. While everyone was perfectly still, the prince's chest rose and fell, as if since he'd been incapacitated by an injury, he had been spared. Finn had never been so thankful to see him breathe.

"Prince!" She shook his shoulder. "Wake up! Something's going on, wake up!" But he didn't wake, didn't make a sound.

A sound cut through the quiet, a voice on the wind behind her.

"*Little chameleon . . .*"

She heard his voice on the wind, lilting and soft as a lullaby.

Ignacio.

"He's not here," she said to herself. "He's not here. Wake up."

This was all a nightmare. The whole thing. What she'd seen in the palace, Kol taking her *propio*, the Brim freezing. It was all a dream. Soon she'd wake up. She would. She had to.

"You know I don't like it when you make friends with unsavory types. . . ."

She was still crouched beside the bleeding prince, her ears ringing with Ignacio's warning. Her hands shaking, Finn turned, following the pull of the sound. There, in the center of the stillness on the other side of the stretch of market stalls ahead of the Blue Thimble, stood Ignacio. A chilling energy zipped through her, wriggling beneath her skin like a snake slithering through grass. Shock squeezed her heart in a tight vise. She couldn't breathe. The quiet was no longer the absence of sound but a warning of what was to come.

He took a step forward.

That one motion sent a tight knot of fear unspooling within her until she was nothing but flesh full of paralyzing terror. He was here to collar her once more, to drag her back into his arms and under his will. Finn turned away from him and left the prince where he lay, taking off in a sprint around the corner of the Blue Thimble and down a stretch of the Brim that was dedicated to stalls of fine jewelry, silks, gowns, and capes. She dashed by the silent market stalls where the buyers and sellers stood eerily frozen, bolts of fabric petrified in midair. Finn's arms pumped at her sides, her feet carrying her farther and farther from the prince. Staying near Alfie now would only convince Ignacio that she cared for him, and that would be all the motivation Ignacio needed to kill him.

Or to make her kill him.

"No," she said, rejecting that thought with every ounce of

energy she had as she ran deeper into the twists and turns of the
Brim, leaving the prince far behind her. She wouldn't let him make
her do those things anymore.

She wouldn't.

She didn't make it ten paces before string wrapped around her
ankle like a vise and held fast. Her own momentum worked against
her and she fell forward, landing on her stomach beside a stall of
jewel-toned dresses, her mouth open against the dirt. The pull was
so strong it felt as if a hand had sprung from the ground to grip her
ankle. She looked over her shoulder.

Ignacio took another leisurely step forward.

"Puppet strings, my little chameleon. Puppet strings."

His mouth hadn't moved, yet his voice whistled through the
air. Everywhere and nowhere, as if it always had been in her head.
How was he doing this? How had he found her? And his eyes, they'd
changed. Black from edge to edge. Her mind narrowed to a hazy
point of pure panic.

He looked just like the man in the Blue Thimble.

Ignacio was entangled with the dark magic. Finn's throat
thickened and seized with fear. He had been a monster before
when he was only a man. Now he was something else, a creature
who would use every ounce of the dark magic within him to hunt
her down like a dog that had strayed too far from its master. He
didn't titter about a dark god coming to life like the man in the Blue
Thimble did. Ignacio was himself, only made powerful. She didn't
know if this was better or worse.

Finn could hardly breathe as Ignacio took another step forward,
his black eyes glinting.

Adrenaline burning through her, she made to cut the string with her dagger, but it wouldn't break. The thread bent on her blade but would not snap. He was still walking to her. She had to get away. She pulled on the string with her free hand. It sliced into her palm and after a long, painful moment, it broke free from her ankle. She was up and running again.

"Where are you hurrying off to?" he called. "We haven't had the chance to catch up, and I have a gift for you, little chameleon. One I think you'll like."

Don't look back, don't look back. If she didn't look him in the eye, he couldn't do what he'd always done to her.

She'd made it past four market stalls before she heard a whirring sound, like a fisherman casting out a line. Pricks of pain stung her skin as strings cut through her clothes and burrowed themselves in the flesh of her back and the backs of her ankles. He yanked her with such force that she landed faceup and skidded back toward him. Her lungs burning, she got on all fours. She was beside the stalls of dresses again. She sawed at the strings, but this time they wouldn't give, whether by her hand or her dagger's edge. She could feel them burrowing deeper into her skin, as if they were trying to replace her very veins. She clawed her way forward, fighting the pull. A string dragged her violently by the heel, and when it pulled backward she felt her skin rip, as if a seam had come undone. Her leg gave uselessly beneath her weight. Blood didn't drip but gushed from the torn flesh of her heel. She was done for. She would be his again.

Then there was only the sound of his measured walk. Her eyes clung to the ground as his feet came to a stop just beside her head.

"Now look at what you've done." Ignacio tutted with a fatherly click of the tongue, as if she were a child with a scraped knee. "You shouldn't have run. Now you've hurt yourself. That seems to be what you do, doesn't it? Silly things that only end up hurting you in the end."

There was no point in looking away anymore. She looked up and faced him. Finn couldn't hold back a gasp. Up close she could see that he looked exactly as he had when they'd first met a decade ago—young and vibrant, strong brows and dark brown hair, thick and lustrous. His skin was smooth, and there were no marks to show what she'd done to him. No ruined skin around his eyes. No milky pupils. Black, raised veins pulsed beneath his skin, just like the infected men in the pub—a latticework of darkness. Fear pooled in her belly at the sight. She clutched her middle, afraid that she might be sick in front of him.

"You wanted me to run," she spat at him before folding her hands over the wound in her heel. Putting pressure on it wasn't helping. Her hands came away slick with blood. She didn't know the desk magic to heal it. "You don't want anything unless it tries to run from you."

"In your case, limp away. But you're right," he said with a crooked smile. It hurt to remember that she'd learned it from him. How she'd practiced in the mirror, wanting to catch mischief in the curve of her lips just like he did. Even now when she smiled, she could find him in her face. "You know me so well."

Ignacio had a *propio*, but he could control someone only if they revealed their deepest truth to him. He couldn't control her until she'd told him hers, the thing that shamed her the most. Yet now he could make everyone in the Brim freeze? This dark magic had heightened his powers beyond her worst nightmares. The sour taste of fear crawled up her throat like bile.

Though fear curdled in her stomach, a snarl curled her lip. "I can't wait to watch you crumble to maldito dust." Maybe this moment of terror would be a blessing. After all, Ignacio would be destroyed by this magic like that man in the Blue Thimble, wouldn't he?

But Ignacio only smiled at her before tapping her on the nose. "Oh, my dear. I am not those fools. This magic strengthens me, gives me everything I ask." He leaned in close and tipped his forehead against hers. When she tried to move away, he seized her by the back of the neck and held her there. "I told you I would never die, didn't I? You should have believed me."

Finn put her hands on his chest and shoved him away. When he touched her, her skin crawled, as if it would rather fall from her bones than feel his caress. Her body no longer felt like her own; it was a tool for him to wield, to sheathe, to sharpen, to parade as his pride and joy. And if he was right, if this magic sustained him instead of destroyed him, then she would never be free of him. She would be locked in her body again, a puppet dancing to the pull of his strings.

Ignacio straightened and gazed down at her, his vile face outlined in a halo of sunlight. "The gods saw fit to grant me what I needed to find myself again," he said with a flourish of his cloak. It had once been a sign of comfort for her. He'd wrapped her in it when she was small. Now she wondered if he would wrap her corpse in it. "And to find you."

She didn't speak. She buried her dagger in his foot. Ignacio looked down at her, disappointed. He didn't even flinch. He pulled the bloody knife from his shoe, and within moments the boot knitted itself closed. She imagined his skin doing the same beneath.

"Don't think that because I love you, I won't hurt you. I can do both," he said. "I would rather end you now and remember you as you once were, when you were my good little girl."

"I was never good," Finn spat. "You made sure of that."

"I made sure you were clothed and fed and loved!" he thundered. "And you sliced through my eyes, left me with *nothing*! To think I was going to give you a gift."

"I don't want a maldito thing from you, and you never loved me, you filthy liar!" she shouted. The sting of his lies burned her more now that she'd spent so much time without him. She wouldn't let him speak her truths for her. Not this time. "You put your voice in my head and made me whatever you wanted me to be."

Ignacio shook his head as if she were a child lying about sneaking a cookie before dinner when her face was covered in crumbs. "Do you remember when I asked you if you loved me, and you said being with me was like suffocating in the middle of a crowd and no one noticing? Suffocating and not being able to scream. That's what you said, isn't it?"

He spun his fingers in a slow circle. Just like that, every time Finn drew in breath it pulled away from her lips. There was nothing to breathe. She clutched at her throat.

He looked down at her piteously. "Just lie down, Finny. It'll be quicker that way."

"Please," she croaked with her last puff of breath. "Let me go."

He knelt, reaching for her cheek, his face twisted with grief. "Can't you see how hard this is for me? No parent should have to bury their child, and I will never join you in the next life."

She wrenched away from his touch. He was still mad enough to think he couldn't die like he'd told her when they'd first met, but now that he had this power, maybe he was right.

She tried to rise from the ground, but he held her down by the shoulder. She could see her shadow spasming on the ground beside her. The longer she choked, the grayer it became.

"All this time, I thought I wanted to hurt you. But I still want to save you. Just lie down," he said softly. "It'll be just like falling asleep, Mija."

Finn could feel her body giving in. Her sight began to dwindle and blur. Ignacio's mouth was moving, but she couldn't hear him over the roar of her panicked heart.

Since the day she'd run away, part of her knew that this was how she would die. With him standing over her, smiling that maniacal, fatherly smile. Soft and jagged all at once. She'd known it. But her mind couldn't stop protesting. Even at death's door, she held her ground.

I don't want to die. Not today. Not with him.

"*Fuerza!*" a voice called from behind her.

With bloodshot eyes, Finn watched Ignacio fly back into a vendor's wooden shop. The force of the fall collapsed the ramshackle shop on top of him. Finn's breath returned, and she gasped, her eyes tearing. Standing over her was a very haggard-looking prince.

"You were supposed to help me," Alfie said, quickly kneeling beside her, his pulse roaring in his ears, "not leave me to bleed to death."

He did not know if he'd killed the man or just incapacitated him, but he had a feeling that, had he waited a moment longer, Finn would be dead.

Between gasps, she said, "Just now—I was supposed—to be dead—give me—a break."

"We need to get out of here," he said, eyes wide with panic. The Brim was alive again. The gowns and capes in the market stalls swayed in the breeze. Merchants and shoppers loitered about as if a man had not put a stop to their every move with a flick of his hand.

Finn crawled to her feet, slapping his hand away when he reached to help. She staggered five paces before her leg gave. She flopped back onto her stomach with a pained cry. Alfie stared at the blood pooling around her heel.

"Be still!"

"I have to run," she said, her voice hoarse. "*Now.*"

He pointed at her graying shadow. "You will die if you don't stop bleeding."

"I'm already dead," she said, her voice threadbare. But she stopped trying to crawl. She fell still and pliant. He didn't know her well, but it didn't make sense for her to look this way. It was like taking a sip of cocoa only to find spoiled milk rolling down your throat.

The Brim fell silent once again, everyone freezing mid-movement.

Finn's eyes flew wide with fear as she tried to crawl away again. The wooden rubble of the fallen shop exploded outward with a shattering crack. Alfie shielded his eyes from the debris.

"And who is this, Finny?" the man asked, his tone conversational as he emerged from the rubble, spotless. He smiled at Finn, a grin that looked more like a beast showing its teeth. "A resilient one, isn't he? I thought that blow to the head would keep you quiet until I was ready to come for you. No matter, the more the merrier. I'm Ignacio, Finn's fa—"

"Finn's nothing," Finn spat. Panic burning in her eyes, she looked at Alfie and whispered, *"Run."*

Alfie wanted to. His body begged him to turn away from the smothering black magic that was pouring out of this man. But it would not have been released if not for him. If he had to die trying to stop it, then so be it.

"Leave her be." Alfie knew his words would mean nothing to this man, but it was what he wanted to say. These might be his last moments alive, so he was going to say what he wished.

"You know how I feel about you making friends without my approval," Ignacio said, his eyes never leaving Finn's face. As if Alfie wasn't worth a glance.

"Run, stupid," she said again. "Just run."

"Put pressure on the wound," Alfie said to her, his eyes locked on the man in the gray cloak. "You still owe me a favor for the vanishing cloak. Live long enough to fulfill it."

The dragon warmed against his chest. Was it responding to being this close to more black magic, more of itself? Alfie pushed away the thought and focused. He needed to stop this man.

A stall to his left sold blown glass vases, trinkets, and figurines.

"Romper," he said. The glass items shattered. *"Volar."* With a wave of his hand the shards shot toward the man. Alfie wanted to look away. He didn't want to see the glass bury itself in the man's skin. But nothing of the sort happened.

"No," the man said. It was as simple as that. The shards slowed, stopping a hair away from him, suspended in midair. Alfie's jaw fell slack. This man had stopped the glass without uttering a single word of magic. He had just said no. It should not have worked in the same way that breathing in water instead of air should not work. None of this could be possible.

The man smiled at him. "Have you ever felt as if your whole life has led up to a single moment, muchacho?" The glass quivered before shooting back at Alfie. Too shocked to defend himself, Alfie raised his arms uselessly over his face. A wall of rock shot up from the ground to guard him. He looked behind him to see Finn with her hand stretched forward. Their eyes met. He could not bring himself to speak, but he hoped his eyes spoke for him: *Thank you.*

"Finny, come now. Wait your turn, I'm talking to your friend."

Alfie watched Finn's face crease with agony as she fought to keep the wall of earth up. But with only a look from the man, it crumbled to sand. This was not the magic Alfie knew.

He turned his attention back to Alfie, a wicked grin on his face. "As I said, have you ever felt as if your whole life has led up to a single moment? I suppose you wouldn't; you look so young. So untried. Walk to me," he said, beckoning. Alfie moved forward, one step after another. There was no struggle, no fight beyond the one in his mind. This magic was seamless, pulling him forward as if he were an element to be controlled. "Stop, and keep your arms at your sides," he added, an afterthought, as if testing his power.

Ignacio watched with relish as Alfie's arms lowered, palms flat against his sides. He could feel the dragon burning against his chest, as if trying to call his attention to something, but he couldn't afford to be distracted. He thought of stunning spellwork that would give him a few moments to grab Finn and get away. *Paralizar.* Maybe it'd be enough. "*Par—*"

"Don't talk."

Alfie stopped. He couldn't form a sound. If this man told him not to breathe, he would stop. He would stop until he died. He should have listened to the thief.

He should have run.

The man looked down at Alfie's hand. "Let me see," he said. Alfie felt his arm rise up of its own accord. The man hadn't even given the magic a specific instruction or command to raise Alfie's arm. It interpreted his words, his desires, and put them into action. There was no balance here, no rules, nothing. This was not right.

The man took Alfie's hand and ran his fingers along the palm. "Soft as a dove. Don't scream," he said. He looked at Alfie's hand and said, "Break." Alfie's index finger broke with a brittle snap. Alfie wanted to scream but he couldn't, couldn't fuel a roar with his pain, but he could whimper like a child. The man must have wanted to hear it, because the magic allowed it.

He smiled at Alfie as if they were about to play a very fun game.

Ignacio raised his arm and flexed his fingers. Then whirring through the air were fine white strings. They burrowed deep into Alfie's skin at his knees, elbows. The man lifted his hand, made a fist, and pulled backward. Alfie felt as if his bones were going to pull free from his skin. The strings pulled him down onto his knees.

"When you were my little girl, you would only eat your fish if I took the bones out for you. You'd point them out and I would pull, do you remember?" When there was silence his eyes hardened, his light tone gone in a flash. "*Answer me.*"

"I remember," Finn said, her voice quivering.

"Let's play, then! Which bone should I take first?" he mused.

"No," Alfie heard her say quietly behind him.

"What was that?"

"No!" she shouted. "I won't!"

Sweat prickled on Alfie's forehead. The dragon was searing against his chest now, scorching his skin.

"You will," Ignacio said. "If I tell you to. But I won't just yet. I'll start. I say we start small—his little finger."

He flicked his hand. A string whirred and burrowed itself in the tip of Alfie's finger, wriggling under his nail. It sliced through the flesh at the tip of his finger over and over again, then the string nestled into the gash and pushed outward, parting the skin wide until blood poured out. Screams of pain grew and crested inside him, waves with no shore to break on. He could not speak, only endure. With a beckoning finger from Ignacio, the string began to pull and pull until Alfie could feel the bone rising. He could see the white, bloody tip of it bursting through his bleeding skin, like a tooth through gums. He couldn't scream. Couldn't move.

Ignacio cocked his head at Alfie. "Scream, if you like."

Alfie's mouth fell open, scream after scream tearing from his throat. He couldn't tell if he was screaming because the man had told him to or because of the pain. All he wanted was for it to stop, for it all to stop. The pain, this man, the thief whimpering behind him as if she'd seen these horrors far too many times. He needed it to stop. The dragon pulsed rapidly against his chest in sync with his heartbeat. A sudden wave of pain tore through Alfie's body, as if he were being wrung dry of every ounce of energy he had left. This pain was beyond what the man was doing; this was something else. It felt as if the pain had come from within and wriggled out of his skin, maggots bursting out of an abandoned corpse.

Then his wish came true. Everything stopped.

The man in the gray cloak stopped. Alfie could move again. He stood shakily, watching the bloodied strings fall from his body. A pained sob broke past his lips as he closed his hand over his bleeding finger, willing the flesh to close over the visible bone. He looked over his shoulder. Finn had her head tucked between her knees, her hands clapped over her ears, a look of anguish frozen on her face.

How did he do it? How did this happen? Every bone in his body rang with pain, as if a needle had punctured every inch of him simultaneously. What had he done?

The dragon was glowing black against his skin. He could feel the magic buzzing within it with renewed vigor, as if it had just been fed.

Alfie's stomach clenched.

He'd used the magic. It had heard his desire to be free and listened. That must have been where the pain had come from, from using it. Magic usually bloomed from his fingertips, but this one had singed him from the inside out. What had he done? Was he now infected with the magic? He took stock of himself. His veins weren't black and raised like the man before him. He didn't feel different. He was in pain, but otherwise he felt the same.

The dragon warmed on his chest, as if it needed the command

of another to live. As if begging to be mastered. He'd kept his magic black as tar just as it had been when he'd trapped the magic, so maybe the dragon had protected him because it saw Alfie as one of its own—as a being of dark magic.

Still, it made no sense. Magic of the same shade never harmed its own, and yet this magic had frozen the crazed man before him. The only rule this magic seemed to follow was that whoever mastered it could use it in any way, without question.

Alfie looked at the man in front of him. He was still frozen, but pieces of him were beginning to thaw. His eyes were no longer stuck in one position. He watched Alfie intently, his eyes narrowing. The prince didn't have time to think on it any longer. He needed to kill this man and seal the magic within him, put an end to all the trouble he'd caused.

Alfie dashed forward and pulled a blade of ice from the air. He would need to stab the man's heart to free the magic within him. Fear thrilling through him, Alfie made to plunge the ice dagger into his chest. As his arm came forward in an arc toward the man's heart, Ignacio unfroze and snatched him by the wrist.

"Very nice try," he tutted with the tone of an amused teacher. "But not quite."

Without another word he swung Alfie by the arm, throwing him as easily as one would a stick for a dog to fetch. Alfie rolled to a stop on his back beside Finn. The throw had jarred whatever control he'd had on the dark magic sealed in the dragon. Finn stirred to life, the terror written in her body in full motion again as she clapped her hands more tightly around her ears, as if trying to wish the present away into the past.

Alfie rolled onto all fours and crawled in front of Finn, kneeling ahead of her.

"Leave her alone!" he shouted. Ignacio only cocked his head at Alfie in curiosity, as if wondering what foolish request he would make next.

"Just run," Finn whispered behind him. "Go."

Alfie looked at her over his shoulder. She held her bleeding heel in her hands. The hopelessness on her face held him where he stood. She'd stayed with him in the pub when he could hardly breathe from fear; he would not leave her to weather this on her own.

Ignacio gave an annoyed sound. "You've overstayed your welcome, muchacho."

Ignacio raised his hand, his fingers splayed, before squeezing it into a fist, and Alfie mourned the fact that this would be the last thing he ever saw.

Ignacio watched the boy kneel before Finn. His eyes were screwed shut, his face tight with fear as he waited for the inevitable. He could see his daughter over the boy's shoulder, her eyes clinging resolutely to his back as if she were willing him to stay alive.

He smiled.

She was still the same girl, still wishing her father would show mercy when what she truly needed was discipline. He would kill this boy and bring her into line once more.

Ignacio squeezed his hand into a fist, willing his strings to tear through the boy, flaying him from the inside out.

Nothing happened. He tried again. Still nothing. Where had his power gone?

Ignacio . . . The dark magic spoke in his mind, its voice a braided tangle of whispers and hisses. *We promised you the girl. We've allowed you a taste of her pain, but you shall have no more until you do as we asked, do as you promised.*

"No, please just let me—"

No! The hisses came sharp and angry, sending a shock through his body. Ignacio stilled and waited for the blinding pain to pass. *First we work to spread and take what is ours. Then the girl.*

Ignacio gritted his teeth. "Fine."

With a swipe of his hand the Brim filled with life once more. Finn and the boy looked around in shock as festive music sounded around them. Finn scuttled away like a wounded animal and Ignacio clutched the image tight in his mind to savor. "I'll be back for you, Finn. You know how I love to find you."

Ignacio stepped backward into the rushing crowds of the Brim, disappearing from sight.

THE PRINCE AND THE DOOR

The black-eyed man had disappeared.

The Brim surged back to life, shoppers and merchants haggling once more. No one took notice of Alfie kneeling in the dirt when there was tequila to drink and songs to sing.

"He's gone," Alfie said, his voice hoarse. In the face of death, something had clotted his throat. When he stood, his body strained painfully beneath his weight, sore from the dark magic.

Behind him, Finn said nothing. She was too still, as if Ignacio had frozen her once more.

Alfie approached her slowly, his voice hushed. "Finn. Can you hear me?"

She started at that, her eyes finding his before darting away. Her throat was working. "I said I'd help you, but I can't. Not if he's here." Her face twisted with an emotion that didn't seem right for it. "I can't." She turned and dashed through the roaming crowds of the Brim.

"Finn!" Alfie shouted after her, following as she darted through an opening between stalls and burst out the other side into another stretch of the Brim. They had moved from the dress section into a lane of stalls that specialized in hand-carved wood.

"Finn, please," he said as she ducked into a stone alley between two shops. "*Wait!*"

She stopped then but did not turn to look at him. Her back quivered and Alfie could think only of the last time they'd been in an alley, of her smirk as she'd fought him after the cambió game. She might as well have been a different person now.

"I can't." Each word sounded as if it'd been pulled up from a deep well, hand over hand.

Alfie bit the inside of his cheek, unsure of what to say. She was afraid and so was he, but he needed her help to save his kingdom. Ignacio housed the core of magic he'd released, and Finn knew him. She might know his weaknesses. Maybe she could draw him to her so that Alfie could try to trap the magic again? The man promised to find her, so keeping Finn at his side all but guaranteed another chance at trapping the magic within him. He couldn't do this without her.

He stepped closer to her stiff back. "Finn, please listen—"

She spun on him, shoving him hard against the alley wall. With a twist of her hands, coils of rock wrapped about Alfie's wrists, waist, and ankles, securing him tight against the wall.

It all happened so fast that he could not process it. He fell still with shock. Why was she trapping him like this when a moment ago he'd gotten on his knees beside her, prepared to die?

"Finn," he said, betrayal burning his words, curling them at the edges. "Why?"

She looked at him, her dark eyes blown wide with fear. She opened her mouth to speak and he knew what she meant to say—*I'm sorry*. But she pressed her mouth closed in a quivering line instead. Somehow that made the words louder still, as if she'd shouted them. She reached behind her head and pulled the hood of the vanishing cloak up, disappearing from sight.

"Finn! Wait!" Alfie shouted, but she did not reappear. Alfie looked at the stone coils holding him down. "*Romper!*" With each repetition, pieces of rock broke away from him. He pushed off the wall, his body crying out in pain from Ignacio and using the dark magic. He hurried through the Brim. Using his *propio*, he searched the milling crowds for her red magic, but she was nowhere to be found. He didn't know what to do. He needed her. Not only because she knew Ignacio and could help Alfie stop him, but also because she was the only other person who'd seen what he'd seen, who could tell him that the fear surging through him was valid and real. And now she was gone. How would he find her?

Alfie ducked back into the empty alley where she'd trapped him. He healed his broken fingers and the wound on the back of his head. He needed a moment of quiet away from the crowds of the Brim, a moment to calm himself. His stomach knotted in guilt at the thought of using Finn as bait to draw Ignacio, but he had no time for guilt now. He needed to focus. He didn't even know the magic's goal. Did it simply want to reduce Castallan to black dust?

The slap of a skipping rope against the cobbled ground forced him out of his thoughts. A quartet of girls and boys were jumping rope, two of them turning the ropes while the others jumped.

The Black King, turned to bone,
In your heart he'll make his home
Your eyes will bleed, your soul burned black,
At his feet, you'll bend your back

So hurry little ones, off to bed!
Lest Sombra wake and take your head!

They sang it over and over again, spinning the rope faster until it snapped against a boy's ankle, ending the game in a fit of giggles. Alfie's pulse roared in his ears.

The magic's goal was there, in the song that the black-eyed man had sung in the pub. It wanted to bring Sombra back, to find the bones he'd been reduced to and unite them once more. Alfie could hardly breathe. His desperation to save Luka might bring to life the villain that gave him nightmares as a child—Sombra himself. His stomach roiled. He put his hand over his eyes, willing himself not to be sick in this alley.

The legend spoke of bruxos parting the god and his dark magic, thus turning his body to bones, bones spread throughout the world over so that they could never be reunited with the magic, so that Sombra could never be awakened.

This dark magic was working to find Sombra's bones, to restore his body. To bring about Nocturna—an unraveling of all things good.

Svana had asked Paloma if she'd checked on "the pieces" in

Castallan. She must have been talking about pieces of Sombra's body—the body of the dark god of legend.

Alfie's mind spun with possibilities, new fears to consider, new paths to explore. Should he try to find the pieces of Sombra's body and destroy them? Was that even possible? Where would he begin? The bones could be anywhere in the world. There were too many options. No, his best chance was to stop the magic before it found Sombra's bones and awakened him.

A shiver skittered up his spine at the thought.

"Focus," he told himself. He could not let himself spiral into fear now. He was uncertain of many things, but he knew he needed to find Finn. She would be the key to drawing Ignacio to her once he had a plan to trap the magic once more—if he could find her. Then a thought flickered to life in Alfie's mind.

Alfie pulled Finn's journal out of his pocket. Ever since he'd discovered it in his bag after their battle over the books, he'd found himself carrying it around in his pocket, thumbing through the sketched faces, wondering about the girl who'd drawn them and knocked him clean off his feet. Luckily for him, this book was exactly what he needed to find her.

He let his own magic darken into that wine red of hers. With her journal he should be able to get to her, even if it was somewhere he'd never been, but he needed to concentrate. Moving through the channels of magic was tricky, trickier still when using object transport. If he didn't keep a clear head, things could go wrong. As a child, he'd tried to haphazardly transport and found himself stuck in a laundry chute instead of the library. If he wasn't careful, he might find himself stuck between places or worse. He wasn't even sure of all the consequences. He was the only person who could do this, thanks to his *propio*, so he didn't know to what extent he could mess up. He supposed he'd be finding out.

He took his doorknob out of his pocket and dropped it on the ground between his feet. It spun before sinking in. Alfie knelt down and gripped it. "*Voy.*"

The floor broke into its portal of colors, the hues of magic connecting everything and everyone. He stepped into it, hoping the magic would lead him true.

Alfie came to feeling a ring of pressure circling his middle.

He wondered if this was what corsets felt like. His neck hurt as if he'd been sleeping with his head flopping off the bed's edge. He raised his head and saw a small spare room. A bed was tucked in one corner. There was a cracked mirror on the wall and a broken desk lay in pieces on the far side of the room. The room was a mess, clothes strewn on the floor and food left to spoil. There, beside the destroyed desk, stood Finn. She leaned against the room's one small window, glaring at him, her nostrils flared. Her heel was wrapped in a makeshift bandage of dirty cloth.

"Where am I?" Alfie murmured.

"Interesting question," she said, her voice terse. "Half of you is in my room, the other half is in the hall."

"Qué?" Alfie said. His voice was syrup-slow, his mind fuzzy at the edges.

He was so tired that he must've lost control of the magic on the way, and now he was stuck in the middle of her door. His head, arms, and torso hung into the room, his waist was caught in the door, and his legs and backside were hanging outside in the hall. He was lucky he'd maintained enough concentration to get caught in the door instead of split by it.

"Coño," he cursed, exhausted.

"How did you find me?" She hobbled to him, her wounded leg stiff and bleeding. She bent before him, leaning so close that her breath ghosted over his nose. There was real fear in her eyes then and Alfie knew without question who she was afraid would find her. "Tell me how you tracked me or else you can stay where you are and be my royal doorknocker."

The small journal still in his hand, Alfie pressed his palms to the wood and said, "*Ondular.*" The wood rippled as if it were made of water. Finn's jaw dropped as Alfie stood and stepped through it. After he passed through, the wood stilled again. The hole his waist had been stuck in remained, like a peephole in a giant's door. A wave of exhaustion swept through him.

Finn reached behind her and picked up an ax from her bed. "To think I went through all the trouble."

"I found you by using my *propio* and this." Alfie held out the journal. She snatched it from him, her face flushing with anger. When she opened her mouth to insult him, no doubt, he raised his hands in surrender. "I accidentally took it when I got my books back from you." Beneath her fury he could see a fear so palpable that it struck him square in the chest. He couldn't stop himself from adding, "I promise, no one else is coming. Not that I know of."

"Good. Then get the hell out of my room."

"No," Alfie said, and she crossed her arms, an angry surprise crossing her face, as if she couldn't believe he had the audacity to disobey her. "I'm here because I need your help."

"You know, everyone always seems to need my maldito help."
She hobbled away from him to the shabby set of drawers on the far
side of the squat room. She rummaged through, throwing shirts and
trousers over her shoulder and onto her bed, where a bag sat waiting
to be packed. "Kol needed my help getting the cloak, that monster in
the gray cloak needs my help in putting myself into an early grave,
and a few hours ago you needed my help saving Bathtub Boy, a favor
that's brought me nothing but trouble. Now you need more help?"
She gave a sharp laugh. "You won't be getting it. I'm leaving town.
So why don't you do me a maldito favor for once and fix the hole you
put in the door before the landlady sees it and throws her chancla
at me."

"Leaving town?" Alfie stepped forward, only to get hit in the
face by a shirt in desperate need of laundering. He placed it on the
bed. Was she so simple to think that man and the black magic inside
him would stay in this city? "You truly think you can outrun what
we saw?"

"I don't think," Finn said, rifling through her drawers. "I *know*.
And we're only a few maldito blocks from the Blue Thimble, Prince.
I'm not staying here to wait for Ignacio to come knocking down my
door, which you already put a giant maldito hole in. I'm leaving now."

She lived in the Brim, then. He'd traveled only a short distance
to get to her, and he'd still passed out midway. This dark magic
had done a number on him. Alfie forced those thoughts to quiet.
His mind spun trying to find a way to keep her here. He knew he
shouldn't mention it, that this would strike a nerve, but what did he
have to lose? "Was it him you were trapped by?"

The girl froze. Her injured leg aside, she was upon him in a breath. She seized him by the shirt and slammed him against the wall.

"You think you know trapped, Prince? You don't know a maldito thing. You were weeping over being trapped behind walls of money," she snarled. "Trapped is feeling your body move without you saying so. Trapped is living with a man whose *propio* is controlling you with a fistful of words. If you really knew what trapped meant." She let go of his shirt and rubbed her palms on her trousers as if he were filthy. "You would understand why I'm leaving."

Compulsion. Now Ignacio's words made sense, his taunting Finn about her having to obey him. Alfie had thought he'd meant it in a parental sense, not a literal one. He remembered how the man had relished in watching Alfie's body obey his command, as if it were an extension of Ignacio and not Alfie's at all. Guilt combed through him. She was right. He knew nothing about what had happened to her. It wasn't fair of him to ask her to help him, but there was no choice.

Finn winced and leaned sideways, gripping at the wall. The cloth wrapped around her ankle was soaked with blood, the more she moved, the more she bled.

"At least let me heal you."

"I don't want anyone's maldito help!" she spat, her words snapping like a whip.

Alfie's anger flared to match hers, and then they were chest to chest. "You may not want it, but you certainly need it!"

Finn glared up at him for a long moment. He returned her glower with one of his own, unrelenting. Finally, she staggered away and perched on the edge of her bed.

Alfie knelt before her and carefully untied the blood-soaked cloth. She cursed as he pulled it free of her skin. He held his hand over the wound, the word for healing on his tongue.

"*Sanar*," he said. Nothing. His hand was shaking. The reality of what they'd seen in the Brim had shaken him to his core and the magic was slipping through his fingers, responding to his feelings of uncertainty. It didn't feel safe in his hands. Too much arrogance and the magic would flee, too little confidence and the results were the same. Balance. He needed balance.

He cleared his head and thought of his mother bending a hand over his scraped knee when he was a boy. He thought of what she'd said whenever he hurt himself.

"*Sana, sana, colita de rana. Si no sana hoy, sanarás mañana.*" The magic flowed through him. Finn's heel slowly mended under his touch.

"What was that?" she asked.

"Something my mother would sing to me when I was little and hurt."

It was a nonsense song about a baby frog that had lost its tail. Magic had a language, and bruxos were taught that certain words led to certain results, but if you were truly fluent in magic, the use of the language didn't have to be strict. Those words his mother would sing made him think of healing, so they became the words he could use to heal. It was what Alfie found the most fascinating about magic, how it was painted by one's experiences, memories, emotions.

She looked at his left hand, where the two fingers that the man had broken were newly healed before he'd traveled to find her. "What does she say when you get hurt now?"

Alfie pulled that hand back. "I make sure she never knows I am."

Silence spread between them. She touched her heel gingerly.

"Finn." He rose from his kneel to stand before her. "Will you at least let me explain why I need your help? Please." Healing her seemed to have granted him some currency because she gave a barely perceptible nod.

"I need to fix this, stop the magic I released before it hurts more people. To do that, I need help with your *propio*. If I'm away from the palace for much longer, my family and the guardsmen will notice my absence. So first, I need you to come back with me so you can change Luka's appearance to match mine. That way I can leave the palace to fix this without anyone knowing." If he was going to stop this, he needed someone to cover for him in the meantime. The thought of telling Luka what he'd done made his stomach roil, but if he wanted a chance to fix this, he would need Luka's help. "After that—"

Finn looked away from him, her eyes flinty. "There's no point in telling me what's after that when I can't do the first thing. I can't change anyone."

Alfie stared at her. "You lied when I asked if you could?"

"I didn't lie," she said, sounding annoyed. "I just can't do it right now."

Alfie shot her a look. If it was her *propio* she should be able to do it whenever she pleased. Was she just trying to get more out of him? He'd already promised her the maldito cloak. "You can't or you won't?"

She pinched the bridge of her nose. "My *propio* is blocked."

"How is that possible?" Alfie asked, his brow furrowed.

"I tried to steal the cloak because I was forced to by Kol. She's a mobster in the Pinch. Her *propio* is that she can block other people's magic. She blocked mine and refused to free me until I got her this stupid cloak."

"Oh," Alfie said, the word falling heavily from his lips. "That's awful."

"The understatement of the maldito century." She leaned back against the wall.

"Where is she now? Can you find her, make her return your magic?"

She crossed her arms. "Gone. Left town with my magic still locked up inside me. That pub we were at, the Blue Thimble, is Kol's pub. She's certainly not dead because my magic's still gone. But there's no way she stuck around after that massacre. So my *propio's* gone."

"I'm so sorry," Alfie said. *Propio* magic was something so intrinsic, so essential to him that he couldn't imagine losing it. If she didn't find Kol, she might never have her *propio* again.

"Wait," she said, her eyes widening. "Your *propio* is that you do weird stuff with other people's magic, right? Like you did with my trump card after the cambió game."

Alfie resisted the urge to roll his eyes. "In a manner of speaking, yes. I can manipulate other people's magic."

"Then give it a go." When he looked down at her, confused, she added, "Fix me."

He blinked at her. "It's not that easy; I can't do it just like that."

"You seemed to before." She stood, suddenly full of energy, and closed the distance between them. Her shadow surged around her excitedly. His curled closer about his feet.

"You don't understand. When I use my *propio*, it's like . . . It's hard to explain, but I can see magic. Think of it this way: everyone's magic has a color. I can change my magic to any shade. Once I match my magic to someone else's, I can feel around their magic for a seam and I either sew my own thread into it or I rip it, breaking it entirely. But—"

"So you forge it. You forge other people's magic the way I—some people forge signatures."

Alfie's brow furrowed. He didn't like that explanation of it. "In a way, I suppose."

"If everyone's magic is a different color, what color is yours?"

Alfie was surprised into silence. Whenever he told anyone that he could see magic, they always asked about their own, not his. It felt like a secret.

"That's private," he said.

She rolled her eyes. "What's mine, then?"

"Dark, deep red. A bit like sangria."

She grinned triumphantly at that, as if she'd just won a bet with herself, then said, "Okay, well then, do your magic color paint thing on me. You said you thread your magic through and rip seams, right? Then stop talking and rip my *maldito* seams." Alfie felt his face color. Finn's eyes rolled heavenward. "You're such a delicate thing. I mean break Kol's magic."

"You didn't let me finish." He palmed his face as if he could mop up the flush with his hand. "*Propio* magic is different. There is no seam to rip, even if I match my color to it. It's seamless, edgeless.

It'd be like trying to find a corner in a circle. It's not possible. I can manipulate anyone's regular magic, but I cannot touch *propio* magic, entiendes?"

Finn slumped. "You could've gotten to that point faster."

"You could've listened slower." A beat of silence drummed between them before he broke it. "Since the mobster blocked your magic you've tried to change yourself, but have you tried to change someone else?"

Finn shook her head. "Why would I? She blocked my *propio*. I can't access any of it."

"Did Kol know you could change other people?" he asked. *Propio* magic always had a catch of some sort. A limit. Maybe the mobster had to be aware of the ability to block it. Maybe Finn could still help him.

Finn thought for a moment. "No."

"Then try it," Alfie said. She looked at him. "Try it on me."

"Will you shut up and let me go if I try?"

He chewed the inside of his cheek. "Yes."

She stepped closer, pursing her lips before placing a hand on his cheek. It was a gentler touch than he'd expected and he found himself flinching in surprise.

"Stand still."

"I'm sorry," he said through gritted teeth. "I didn't expect you to touch my face."

"What did you expect me to change? Your leg?"

Their shadows moved jaggedly around each other on the ground. Alfie bit his tongue and fell silent. The girl shut her eyes and moved her palm over his nose.

A tingle swept over his nose. Finn's eyes lit up. "Wépa!" she said. "I can still do it!"

Alfie looked over his shoulder at her cracked mirror and recoiled. She'd given him more of a beak than a nose. "So you'll help me, then?"

She turned back to her bag. "Never said that, but glad to know I've still got it."

A sound of frustration parted his lips. "Do you really think you can escape this? Him?"

"When you were barely out of your silk diapers I was escaping, surviving. I can do it again." She sounded as if she were trying to convince herself. "I'll do it again."

"Finn—"

"Prince," she snapped. "No one makes me do what I don't want to do, so stop trying."

He shook his head. "I am not telling you. I'm asking you to help me. Help me end this together. I get rid of this dark magic and you get rid of that man. *Please.*"

That word seemed to sting her. She rounded on him, her eyes shining. "Please? You think please means a maldito thing to me?" With her this close he could see that she was shaking. "You want me to face *him*? Then you'll have to do what he did. Put your hands on me, hold a dagger to my throat! Tell me I am nothing and if I don't do as you say that's what I'll stay till the day I die! Make me do what you want!" She shoved him with both hands as if trying to provoke him, to prove that he was capable of what she claimed. "I'm well past please, Prince. I'm leaving before he finds me; if you're smart you'll do the same."

Her words cracked against him like a slap, and Alfie thought of how the man in the Brim had commanded her, each word from his mouth a crippling blow. A new guilt formed like a stone in his stomach. If it weren't for him releasing the magic, Ignacio wouldn't be able to hurt her the way he could now. He'd brought this upon her and now he was asking her to help him fix it. Shame bubbled within him, and he didn't know what to say to make it right.

Alfie swallowed hard. He didn't know her well enough to delve into these matters, of that he was sure, but even if she refused to help him and they never crossed paths again, he wanted her to know something. "I think please means more to you than you think."

She gave a sharp, angry sound, like a laugh turned inside out, as she stuffed more clothes in her bag, her back to him. "Then you're even more foolish than you look."

"When I said please in the palace, you held Luka in your lap so I could heal him. You helped me." Finn froze, and something in the rigid way she stood called to him for comfort, but it wasn't his place to touch her. He didn't know what she wanted, and she'd already been made to bear so many things she didn't want. He would not add another. "You told me you wanted more time to say 'Not today,' to stop letting terrible things happen without trying to stop them. I believed you then and I believe you now, even if you don't. So I'm asking you one last time to come with me, but the decision is yours. Tell me no again and I will leave and never come back."

Silence stretched between them. Alfie's heart beat in his chest like a bird in a cage.

"No." She did not turn to look at him. She only said the word.

The word sailed through him like a stone through a windowpane.

He wanted to beg her to reconsider, but he'd promised he wouldn't and in this world where all he knew had gone up in smoke, the strength of his word would anchor him to what once was. He would not break it, even if it meant doing this alone. Dying alone.

But he deserved this, didn't he? When he'd met this girl, he'd thought himself above her. He'd thought her *propio* meant she was someone selfish and reckless. But he was wrong. She was a girl who cloaked herself in the lives of others to save her own. It was he who had been the reckless one, he who had put this world in danger. Shame poured through him, thick and slow. Alfie walked to her door and pulled it open.

"Espérate," she said, her voice frayed at the edges.

He turned and she was looking at him with wide eyes that spoke of fear and something more, as if she'd recognized something in him that she could trust. Alfie was struck with the memory of being a frightened little boy and Dez coaxing him to jump into the pool, promising to catch him. He'd looked at Dez just like this when he'd caught him in his arms.

"Fine." She scrubbed a hand across her eyes. "I'll help you. Under one condition. I get the vanishing cloak for good, and a chest of gold at least my weight." She glared up at him, her chin raised high as if daring him to argue. But today, he wouldn't dream of it. His parents would kill him, but at least the kingdom would be saved.

"Deal," he said. Then he turned toward her wall and tossed the doorknob at it. "We've already wasted enough time. We've got to get back to the palace."

She stared at the doorknob. "So this is how you get around? How you got here?"

Alfie nodded. All his life he could carry only himself through his doors of magic, but with the dragon in his hand he was certain it would take both of them. This horrid magic had already done the impossible; why doubt it now?

"*Oye!*" A gruff voice sounded from the hall. "What the hell did you do to my door?"

"That'd be the landlady!" Finn grabbed a fistful of sheathed daggers from beneath her bed and shoved them into her bag. "Hurry up! Open your wall tunnel thing!"

Alfie turned toward the door. "I could fix it—"

Finn pulled him back by the shoulder. "No need, let's go."

"You're behind on rent and then you break the *maldito* door too!" the landlady shouted.

Alfie shot Finn a look.

Finn shrugged. "If I help you stop this magic, then the whole city owes me. Let's go!"

His hand shaking in fear of what was to come from using this magic again, Alfie twisted the doorknob. The tunnel of magic opened just as the gray-haired woman threw the door open behind them. Shouting a stream of obscenities, the elderly woman stormed in with a sandal in hand. It was a testament to the strictness of his mother that even though Alfie had faced a dark magic earlier today, the mere sight of a sandal about to be thrown still struck fear in his heart.

"Shit, go!" Finn cursed.

Alfie held the dragon tight in his hand and asked it to carry Finn with him safely. Pain reverberated through him violently, like the taut string of a guitar plucked until the string snapped free. He stepped into the magic, Finn gripping him like an anchor of flesh and bone.

Over his shoulder, Alfie watched the landlady throw her sandal as the wall began to close behind them.

THE HOURGLASS

When Luka woke late in the afternoon after his night of drinking, he felt strangely bright-eyed. Strong, even.

He stretched his arms over his head before folding the plush blankets over and wriggling out of bed. Luka snorted when he saw that he was still wearing what he'd worn to the dinner party the night before.

"Typical," he said. Drunk Luka was never a fan of changing into sleeping clothes. He was a mess, but at least he was a consistent mess. Luka remembered nothing of last night beyond the dinner party, but maybe that was for the best.

He marveled at how full of energy he felt, like a child who'd gorged himself on sweets. "This is the greatest wine hangover I've ever had," he declared, his voice still rough with sleep.

Then Luka remembered what had driven him to the wine in the first place.

Alfie. Stupid Alfie and his lies. His dangerous games for illegal goods. His dabbling in Englassen magic.

The sudden burst of energy he felt simmered, falling from a roaring flame to a spark.

Luka gritted his teeth. No, he was done letting Alfie's nonsense drag him down into anger and frustration. He and Alfie needed to talk. Now.

Luka burst out of his bedroom doors and darted down the long, winding hall, his bare feet cold against the tiled floor. He nodded at the guards and servants, who scarcely spared him a second glance regardless of his disheveled attire. Luka walking about wearing last night's clothes was hardly a spectacle.

When he reached Alfie's double doors he raised his fist to knock. Then he chided himself with a sharp exhale through his nose. As if Alfie deserved such courtesies! Luka burst into Alfie's room and shut the doors behind him.

"Alfie," Luka began, his voice sounding annoyingly hesitant. He cleared his throat and squared his shoulders. "We need to—"

The room was empty. The bed was made and littered with the overly formal clothes Alfie had no doubt been choosing between for last night's dinner party.

Which meant he hadn't gone to bed last night. Luka's stomach tightened.

With the ball tomorrow, Alfie should be here. He always spent the days before a ball pacing in his room, carving out the time and space to commit to his anxiety. He didn't even go to the library on days like this. If he wasn't here, then he was likely somewhere he shouldn't be.

Luka massaged his temples with his hands. Was this a sign? Did this mean he ought to just tell the king and queen what Alfie had been up to?

He sighed at the thought. He'd never been a maldito snitch and he didn't really want to start now. But if Alfie was still dabbling in dangerous games for illegal goods, telling his parents could save the prince's life; it would be worth it, wouldn't it?

"Coño," Luka cursed the empty room. He didn't want to go to the king and queen without giving Alfie one last chance. That was the trouble with loving one's brother. It made you allow the stupidest things.

An idea sparked in Luka's mind. He darted to Alfie's armoire. Behind layers of finely made clothes was a box of cambió game materials. Luka pulled the hourglass out, balancing it on the soft of his palm. Its base filled his palm and it was scarcely longer than his hand.

He flopped onto Alfie's bed and set the hourglass on the bedside set of drawers.

"If this hourglass runs out before you get here," Luka said, watching the sand pour, "then I alert the guards that you're missing and tell the king and queen everything you've been doing. It's up to you, pendejo."

Now it was a game of chance. If Alfie wasn't home when it ran out, then he would tell the king and queen everything. It was a fair deal, he decided. There was still a chance for Alfie to come home and listen to Luka for once. But as he waited, he couldn't stop himself from dwelling on the tangle of dark questions that slithered like snakes between his ears, hissing the worst. *What if he's at one of those illegal games right now? Is he even alive? What will you tell the king and queen if he isn't?*

He clapped his hands over his ears. The act of it was somehow comforting, though it did nothing to muffle his thoughts. He shot upright and stared at the hourglass, his eyes darting between it and the wall. The wall that Alfie always came home through.

"If you're dead, I'll kill you," Luka said to the wall. He was an optimist, so he usually took silence as affirmation. Alfie always took silence as an opportunity to fill the quiet with self-doubt. Today, Luka found himself doing the latter, his mind overflowing with images of where Alfie could be—somewhere dark fighting for his life or lying still, already having lost it.

Sweat gathering at his temples, Luka watched the hourglass. The sand dribbled slow as honey. There were still so many long minutes to wait.

He got up and paced, his eyes still glued to the hourglass. He strode across the room to Alfie's armoire and thumbed through his clothing to distract himself. With nothing else to do, Luka tried on one of the prince's shirts. As he pulled it over his head, it ripped at the shoulder where Alfie was slimmer. Luka quickly wriggled out of it, rolled the shirt into a ball, and stuffed it in the back of the armoire. As he shoved the torn shirt in, his fingers brushed against something warm and familiar. Behind the rows of clothing was Alfie's fur-lined winter cloak. He'd lent it to Luka when they'd traveled to Uppskala last year. Luka smiled at the memories of going ice rafting in the winter kingdom's rapids and dining on the freshest, most delicious fish that either of them had ever tasted. They'd even watched the famed northern lights while sipping mugs of mulled wine and chatting up the good-looking Uppskalan nobles who came their way. Things had been so different then.

Before Dez had died, Alfie had still been Alfie—a little too sullen for his own good, but his laugh came easy. He could let himself be reckless, be free. Now, to Luka, it felt like Alfie was too cautious to laugh, let alone live his life. Before everything had happened, Alfie had loved going traveling with Luka and trying new things. It was something Luka liked to call adventuring, and though Alfie was hardly as bold as him, he'd tagged along with Luka on more journeys than he could count.

Of course, Luka knew why Alfie was so keen on getting out of the palace after he'd finished his bruxo studies. The prince had always had a hard time watching his father fawn over Dez. Alfie had spent his adolescence training intensely under Paloma in hopes of catching his father's attention, but Dez had always been the apple of the king's eye. Whenever Alfie wanted to escape his feelings of inadequacy by having some fun, Luka saw no harm in lending him a hand. Luka's fingers dropped from the winter cloak, guilt knotting tight in his stomach.

Maybe if he'd just talked to Alfie about all this instead of taking him adventuring every chance he got, then maybe Alfie wouldn't be going out at night looking for trouble instead of facing what was to come. Luka had taught him the bliss of escapism and avoidance and now it was coming back to bite him in the culo.

Luka shut the armoire and turned back to the hourglass. It wasn't even halfway done yet. With every grain of sand Luka felt his breath catch, a grislier scenario of where Alfie could be blooming in his head.

Luka threw his hands up. "This is ridiculous!" he shouted. With long, hurried strides he made his way to the doors and threw them open. The two guards stationed beyond Alfie's doors turned to look at him.

"Are you and the prince in need of something, Master Luka?" one said.

Luka stared at him and looked over his shoulder. The sand poured on. He looked back at the guard. "No. Not yet."

The guard regarded him strangely. "Yes, Master Luka."

Silence stretched between them. "But in a few minutes, yes."

The guard looked even more perplexed. "In a few minutes what, Master Luka?"

"I don't know!" Luka found himself shouting. "But I will know in a few. Damn. Minutes!" He slammed the doors shut in their confused faces, made his way back to Alfie's bed, and threw himself face-first onto it.

"Gods!" he said, his voice muffled by the bedsheets. "Hurry up."

He resolved to not look at the hourglass again until he had counted to one hundred, but by the time he reached eighteen he'd peeked at it before ramming his face back into the dark of the bedsheets. When he reached thirty he began counting by twos. By forty he was counting by fives. By seventy he thought, screw it all to hell and looked. The hourglass still wasn't even close to empty.

He took it in his hands and shook it, urging the sand to flow down.

"Go down, you son of a—" The hourglass shattered in his hands as if it were made of brittle ice. Luka yelped as the glass and sand flowed through his fingers and onto the floor. The glass should've burrowed in his flesh; instead it bounced off his skin, leaving him unharmed. He shook the sand off his hands.

"What the hell kind of cheap hourglass . . . ," he said. He looked at the mess on the floor. "Well, technically the sand's run out now, hasn't it?"

He stared at the wall where Alfie should be stepping through. Nothing happened.

"Screw it."

Luka bolted off the bed, dashed back to the doors, and threw them both open.

"Yes, Master Luka?" one guard said uneasily.

Just when Luka opened his mouth to tell the guards that Alfie was missing and to inform the king and queen, Alfie and a girl tumbled through the wall, landing on the ground in a heap. A lone sandal followed behind them, zooming through the wall and slamming against Alfie's bedside table with a *thwack*. Luka stared at them, eyes wide. Alfie had never traveled with someone else before. He'd thought it was impossible.

"Everything all right in there?" the second guard asked, craning his neck to get a look in the room. But Luka was already closing the doors.

"Perfectly fine! Keep up the good work, boys! Making our kingdom so proud!" He shut the doors and hurried to where Alfie sat beside the girl, his back pressed against the wall as his body curled forward in pain. But worry over Alfie could not blunt Luka's anger.

"Where the hell have you been?" he hissed. "And who is this? Did you just transport with someone?" All his life, Alfie had told him that he couldn't transport with anyone else; it just wasn't done. Luka's mind was too scattered to stop supplying questions. He pointed at the smelly sandal that had flown through the wall. "And whose chancla is that?"

Alfie had used his doorknob for transport more times than he could count, and each time the magic opened its door and invited him in, cutting a path for him in its great expanse, carrying him on its current. There was a sense of gentleness to it, of cordiality between him and the magic.

Using the dark magic was different.

As soon as he and Finn stepped into the magic, it slurped them in through its teeth. It was as if they had been swallowed whole, forced down this magic's twisting throat and into the depths of its belly.

Then for an endless moment he felt as if he were flattening, moving through a corridor of darkness so cramped that only a mouse could hope to squirm out. He couldn't breathe, couldn't think, couldn't scream. As they moved through the magic, terrible pain seared his body, as if his very flesh were being scraped from his bones. As if soon there would be nothing left but marrow. The pain he'd felt when he'd used the magic to stop Ignacio was nothing compared with this. That was a hum of agony; this was a ballad, long and wrenching.

The magic belched them onto his bedroom floor. His body was a bundle of nerves rubbed raw. A scream rose in his throat like bile, but he'd scarcely had time to breathe before Luka stood over him, his face pinched with anger, questions flying from his lips.

"There's a lot to explain," Alfie said breathlessly. The thought that Ignacio was loose in his city with the dark magic at his fingertips turned his mind into a senseless jumble. He didn't know if he even could explain it all to Luka.

"Then start," Luka retorted. And Alfie could not fathom where to begin.

He wanted to keep the grisly reality from his best friend, but he found that he was too tired and too afraid to lie. His throat burning, Alfie told him the truth.

He told him everything—the poisoning, the release of the dark magic, the little servant boy's earring, facing Ignacio, and what he'd learned of the magic's goal to find Sombra's bones from that horrid little song (Finn startled at this information; he had yet to talk to her about it). He hadn't been this honest with Luka in months, and the information flew past his lips as if he were pulling colored scarves from his mouth, hand over hand, like a magician.

When Alfie finally fell quiet, Luka only stared at him, wide-eyed. He was too stunned to speak, which was very much a first for him.

When Alfie couldn't bear the silence any longer he held his hands out, open-palmed. "What has happened is my fault, but I couldn't let you go. I couldn't lose you in that room." Alfie whisked a hand over his eyes. "I know this is my responsibility and for once I don't want to run away from my duties and my kingdom, I want to save it. Por favor, will you help me?"

Silence curdled between them once more and Alfie waited for the shock on Luka's face to settle and change into something else.

Luka stepped forward and pulled Alfie into a fierce hug.

Alfie gripped him back, and the wave of relief that Luka was alive, here to be embraced and argued with, swept him away from his fear of what he'd done, if only for a moment.

"You're a fool," Luka said, his voice thick. He pulled back and took Alfie by the shoulders. "But I'm still here because of your foolishness. Tell me how I can help."

THE PLAN

"So," Luka began, his gaze darting between Alfie and Finn. "You're telling me you two have absolutely no plan for how to stop this?"

Finn eyes rolled heavenward. "You're a perceptive one, aren't you?"

"We don't," Alfie said, before Finn could pull Luka into an argument. "Not quite. Not yet."

Luka stared at him as if the answer were obvious. "Then we must go to Paloma; there's no other choice. She will know what to do. She has to, doesn't she?"

Panic pulled at Alfie's stomach. He couldn't disappoint Paloma again. He couldn't tell her that he'd undone the work of the dueños before her for his own reasons. The thought alone had his palms slick with sweat.

"No, I can come up with a plan to fix this, and it's not as if the dueños had this under control. That method that they used to hide the magic away did not stop me from finding it and setting it free. If I could do that, others will be able to as well. We need to find our own way to trap the magic and put it someplace completely untouchable, unfindable. A place where there is no life for it to feast on, no bodies for it to infect," Alfie said, wringing his hands. "Just give me a moment."

Alfie's mind raced with possibilities, each one building only to burst at the slightest prodding, like a soap bubble. Each idea gave way to doubts, to flaws in his logic, to failure. Luka watched him, his eyes sharp. If Alfie didn't come up with something now, then Luka would tell Paloma for sure.

Finn broke the silence, throwing her hands up in the air with a growl of frustration. "I can't believe I was stupid enough to listen to you. I'm not going to wait here like some sitting duck for Ignacio to find while you come up with another half-baked plan. I should've known that some pampered bruxo like you would just pull me into more trouble without even an inkling of how to clean up your own maldito mess."

The snap of her voice rubbed him raw. He gritted his teeth. "You know nothing about me."

Her eyes swept over him, from head to toe and back again. "I know enough."

Anger zipped through him, moving his feet until he was before her, nearly chest to chest. "Why do you enjoy making people feel small?"

She raised her chin. He couldn't understand how she could be so much shorter than him yet make him feel as if she were looking down her nose at him.

"Don't kid yourself," she said, challenge written in every line of her face. "I didn't make you small; you were small to begin with."

Her words burned through him, pitting his stomach with nothing short of fury. "In my experience, those who do this only do it because they themselves feel small, insignificant."

"Did your mamá tell you that after a long day of servants kissing your ass after they scrubbed it clean—"

"*Hey!*" Luka shouted. "Cállate! Both of you!"

Alfie tore his eyes from Finn's smirking face, the anger inside of him falling to a crackling simmer. If they couldn't even handle a conversation without screaming at one another, how were they going to get through this mess? He internally chided himself. Ignacio was terrorizing his kingdom with Sombra's magic and he was letting himself get distracted by a bout of name-calling. He shuddered to think of what the black-eyed man was doing to his people while Alfie sat safe and sound in his palace. Shame pooled in him.

"Look," Luka said. "I have an idea." He glanced at Alfie then, his eyes skittish. "You're not going to like it."

Luka seldom looked this uncomfortable. A knot drew tight in Alfie's stomach.

"Well, will I like it?" Finn asked.

Alfie shot her a look. She shrugged it off.

"Just let me explain before you say anything. You say you need somewhere to place the magic," Luka began tentatively. "Somewhere no one can go. Somewhere it cannot be touched and cannot infect anybody." He stopped then, mashing his lips into a thin line.

No matter what the suggestion was, Alfie would take it if it would help him rid his kingdom of this magic. From what Alfie had seen in the Brim, Ignacio's power was monstrous, and there couldn't be a valid option to stop it that he would reject. Yet Luka was looking at him as if he would explode upon hearing it.

"Yeah, yeah, yeah," Finn huffed, leaning against a wall with her arms crossed. "We know this. Get on with it."

Luka ignored her instead of flinging witty repartee in her direction. It wasn't like him. A sense of dread descended on Alfie like a veil, blurring everything in sight. Whatever he was going to suggest was going to be bad.

"Luka." Alfie swallowed thickly. "Please just tell me what it is."

"You know that such a place exists," Luka said, his eyes pleading for Alfie to piece it together himself, so that he would not have to say it aloud. "You've seen it yourself." He clasped his hands before him in a tangled knot of fingers. "You saw it in the Blue Room."

The idea sprouted in Alfie's mind then, pricking him with its thorns, drawing blood and grief and an anger so powerful that it numbed him with its heat, cauterized every wound he had.

"No," Alfie heard himself say, his voice a rasp of fury.

"You have to at least consider it. It's the only thing that makes sense—"

"*I don't care if it makes sense!*" he shouted, the words bursting from his mouth before he could temper the heat in them. The mere idea of it made it feel as if his lungs were pinioned flat, as if he couldn't breathe. "I won't do it."

A gusty sigh came from the other side of the room. Finn stared at him as if she were watching a child throw a tantrum. "Can someone please explain what the hell is going on?"

Luka looked at her and opened his mouth to speak before shutting it. He looked at Alfie then, not asking permission but giving warning. "If she's going to help you on this, she has to know the full story."

"No she doesn't," Alfie bit out, his fingers curling into fists. "Because we are not going to go through with this plan."

Luka pinched the bridge of his nose, closing his eyes for a long moment before speaking again. "If you want to handle this on your own, then by all means do it. But if you cannot come up with a plan, then I'm going to Paloma. This is the only plan that makes sense, and you know it. If you reject it, I'm walking out the door to tell her everything."

Alfie held Luka's gaze. He wanted to look resolute, but he could feel the shift inside of him and he knew that he was looking at Luka pleadingly, begging him to not make him do this.

The moment broke. Luka shook his head at him, a wordless apology, and turned toward the door. Alfie opened his mouth to argue, but his words died in his throat.

Luka turned the doorknob.

"Wait," Alfie called, his voice threadbare.

"No," Finn said, pushing off the wall. "Don't wait. Open the maldito door and let me out. If you fools are just gonna yell at each other instead of coming up with a plan, then I'm hopping on the first ship out of this gods-forsaken city."

Finn stormed across his room, pushing Luka out of the way and reaching for the hood of the vanishing cloak that still hung on her shoulders.

"Listen." His throat burning, Alfie spoke. "My brother was taken from me, but not in the way you and the rest of the world were told." Castallan and the rest of the world were told that Dez had been killed by a nameless assassin. The details of how he'd died—the coup and Xiomara's terrible *propio*—had been kept secret. The knowledge of an internal attempt to slaughter the royal family and a woman with the ability to create voids was hardly the sort of thing that would keep the people calm or preserve the international reputation of the kingdom.

Finn paused at the door and looked at him over her shoulder, curiosity flickering in her eyes.

"There was an attempted coup planned by Castallano nobles. A girl broke into the palace, a girl with a *propio* that could create . . ." His breath caught as his lips tried to form the word. "Voids."

Finn raised a brow. "Voids?"

"Empty, vacuous places. Places with no time, no magic, no life." Alfie's voice broke around those final two words and then Luka was beside him, a silent comfort as Alfie's eyes burned. He held them open, not wanting to blink, not wanting to feel the warm slip of tears down his face.

Finn didn't seem to pay attention to how he struggled to speak, and he was thankful for that.

She crossed her arms, considering. "So you want to trap the magic, then get this girl to use her *propio* to open the void and then you toss this magic in there?"

Alfie nodded and folded a hand over his eyes. "It makes sense. No one would be able to get to it there. It would never be able to harm anyone." He dropped his hand and held Finn's gaze. "It would never fall into the wrong hands again."

A silence stretched between them, an understanding folded in the quiet.

Finn gave a single nod. "Fine. I'm in. Where's the girl?"

"That's the tricky bit," Luka said with a grimace, and Alfie was happy to have a break from talking. "She's in the Clock Tower."

Finn stiffened. "*Qué?*"

The Clock Tower was a prison that housed Castallan's most vile criminals. Anyone who was taken was never seen again, and now they would have to break in and sneak this girl out. He would have to ask the girl who had taken Dez from him for help. The mere idea of it tore at his insides and only Luka's hand on his shoulder stopped him from letting the weight of it drag him into its depths.

"Yes, well . . ." Luka rubbed the back of his neck. "It'll require some planning."

Finn chewed her lip, her eyes meeting Alfie's. "You said you wanted me to change you two into each other." Finn pointed at Luka and Alfie. "So that we can leave, then we break the girl out of prison, and I lure Ignacio to us. We kill him, you trap the maldito magic in your dragon thing and toss it in the void."

Alfie nodded, his throat still aching from the effort of keeping everything inside of him at bay. "Yes, that would be the plan." They would have to use Finn to lure Ignacio away from the city, somewhere where others wouldn't be hurt in the crossfire. Then they'd have to try to kill him again and take the magic.

"Wait, I'm not going?" Luka asked, looking offended. "I came up with the maldito plan!"

"Luka," Alfie said. "You nearly died only hours ago."

"So did you," Luka shot back, and Alfie grimaced at the thought of Ignacio trying to debone him like a fish. "And I feel fine now. Stronger than ever, even! I won't let you face this alone."

Alfie shook his head. Having Luka with him on this journey was something he both wished for and feared. On the one hand, there was the comfort of having his best friend with him. On the other was the prospect of putting Luka in danger once more, but not being able to save him this time. "No. Someone needs to stay here and be me so I'm not missed. Her *propio* will do that, so you're covering for me."

"Well, can't she stay here pretending to be you and I go with you instead?" Luka asked.

"It's not an option," Alfie said before quickly explaining how Kol had blocked her *propio*. "And even if it was, she would just rob the palace and leave."

Finn picked her nails with the tip of her dagger. "That's true."

"Fine," Luka huffed.

Alfie relished the sound. Things were still somewhat normal if Luka was huffing, blowing a curl off his forehead with a gusty sigh. The life he knew hadn't been destroyed just yet.

"All right," Finn said. "We know we're headed to the maldito Clock Tower, but how are we getting in and out?" When Alfie fell silent she shot him a look. "Were you planning on knocking and asking politely?"

Alfie didn't take the bait. He walked to his desk and unfurled a roll of parchment. With a quick hand he grabbed a white feathered quill from the drawer and dipped it into the inkwell. With a barely audible *sluuurp*, ink flowed into the quill's stem, the feather darkening to a rich ebony as it filled with ink. On the parchment Alfie drew five circles within one another. Luka and Finn gathered behind him, staring as he etched the inner workings of the Clock Tower on the parchment.

"The Clock Tower is separated into rings, like San Cristóbal. It has five rings within it. The innermost ring." Alfie tapped the smallest circle with his quill tip, a dot of ink sprouting there. "That's where the prisoners are kept. But the prisoner that we need is not held there; she is in a single cell in the second innermost ring, away from the general prisoners in solitary confinement." Alfie drew an X on the east side of the second smallest ring, his memory tugging him to the day he'd been there, standing before that girl's door, his heart pounding in his throat. He swallowed down the adrenaline surging through him, his hand curling tight around the lip of his desk. "And she's heavily guarded."

"Alfie," Luka said slowly, as if he did not want to know the answer. As if he already knew the answer. "How do you know this?"

Alfie looked away from him, but Finn caught his eye then. Her eyebrows rose.

"You've been to the Clock Tower?" she asked, looking un-characteristically impressed. Of course his most shameful moment would be the one to impress her.

Alfie looked intently at the crude map he'd drawn. "Yes."

"*What?*" Luka nearly shouted.

"Look," Alfie said, stopping Luka before he could say more. "There's no time to explain now when we have a plan to hash out. It's not important." Alfie told himself that was why he didn't want to speak of it, not because he was ashamed of what he'd almost done, of the look on Paloma's face when she'd found him at the Clock Tower. Alfie shoved those thoughts away.

Luka stared at Alfie, unblinking. "You broke into the foulest prison in our kingdom and the details of how and why aren't important?"

Finn nodded. "It'd be all I ever talked about."

"No," Alfie insisted. "Not more important than coming up with a plan to stop Sombra's magic from destroying our kingdom."

Luka held his gaze for a long moment before relenting with a glare. "Fine. But this is not the end of this maldito conversation."

"Why don't we get into the prison the way you did last time, then?" Finn asked, and Alfie was thankful for her interruption. "If it worked for you last time, should work now."

Alfie shook his head and looked anywhere but Luka's face. "Last time I went to the prison I did it via tether." Tethers were a form of transportation magic that most bruxos used, but Alfie seldom did, thanks to his *propio*. Tethering spellwork bonded two objects, so that if you touched one and spoke the right word of magic, it transported you to the other. Alfie had tethered two objects and paid a prison guard to take one of the tethers to the prison. But that tether had since been confiscated, by Paloma.

Her face flashed in his mind once more, disappointed and, even worse, afraid for him. Shame roiled his stomach, but there was no time to stew in it now.

Since he'd used a tether before, Alfie hadn't connected his doorknob to the prison, he hadn't assigned the prison a color of magic to travel by with his *propio* magic, so there was no way to use it to travel to the prison now. Using the bit of Sombra's magic he'd caught in the dragon to spirit him and Finn there was out of the question as well. Transporting him and Finn from the Brim to the palace had left him barely able to stand. To use it for such a great distance might kill him.

Alfie looked down at the dragon hanging on his neck. "We can't use this either. The distance . . . I don't think I'll be able to handle it."

"Good," Finn said with a grimace. "I wouldn't do that again if you paid me." She tilted her head then. "Well, depends on how much."

"Good to know your priorities are in order," Luka sniped at her, but he was still staring at Alfie, his face pinched tight and tense. "Then you'll have to get there the old-fashioned way. Horseback."

Alfie nodded at that. The prison was about thirty miles beyond the city, an hour and a half's ride at top speed.

"We've still got the issue of getting in and out of the *maldito* prison unnoticed," Finn said, her voice flat with disinterest, as if planning a heist were part of her everyday schedule. "Along with sneaking out with a third person."

"You and I will use the vanishing cloak to sneak in. But when we get the prisoner, all three of us can't fit beneath it." Alfie looked at Finn. "I'll need you to use your *propio* to disguise me so that I can walk out of the prison while you and the prisoner follow under the vanishing cloak."

Finn chewed on the inside of her cheek. "As what? A guard?"

Alfie shook his head. From what he remembered, the guards at the prison had very specific schedules and duties to attend to. He'd stick out.

"Who else could you disguise yourself as?" Luka asked. "Certainly not a prisoner."

As Alfie thought, Paloma's voice echoed in his mind. *Magic is a gift and as dueños we all must do our penance to thank the gods for such a gift.*

"You'll disguise me as a dueño," Alfie said to Finn. It was the only option. "Dueños perform penance at the Clock Tower all the time. Paloma herself did." Alfie's voice quieted around her name and Luka turned at the sound. For once, Alfie wished Luka didn't know him so well. "If you disguise me as a dueño then it'll be easy for me to move around the prison and to leave when I please. No one will pay attention to me."

Finn nodded slowly at that. "Bien, so now we have a way in and out, but how do we distract the guards so that we can sneak out of the prisoner's cell unnoticed?"

Alfie stared down at the map of concentric circles, his mind falling silent as he grasped for options. "We need a distraction. A big one. Something to pull the guards away from their posts at her door so we can get in, get her under the vanishing cloak, and get out."

Luka tilted his head at that, his dark eyes sparking. It was the same face he made whenever he was about to beat Alfie at cambió. "I've got an idea. Leave it to me." He gave a sigh then. "I come up with the best parts of this maldito plan and I don't even get to participate." He turned on his heel and made for the door. "Wait here."

THE PRINCE OF STRUTTING

Just like that, the plan had been set.

Bathtub Boy had retrieved the perfect distraction to use in the prison while they broke Xiomara out. Then he'd headed off to his quarters, still grousing about not being able to come with them. Now it was only Finn and the prince standing in his rooms.

"We'll leave tomorrow morning. It's too late to try to infiltrate the prison now," he said, his fingers worrying the sleeves of his shirt.

He was right, she knew. They'd lost the day to their hunt for Sombra's magic and their fight with Ignacio. Now the moon was rising. If they were going to break someone out of a prison, it ought to be during the thick of the day when things were busy, when things that would otherwise look suspicious would simply be overlooked. Not at night when the guards were on high alert.

The prince looked frustrated as he chewed the inside of his cheek, and the same impatience coiled tight inside of her. He'd seen Ignacio's power, just as she had, and the idea of waiting even a moment before starting off on this plan was maddening. How much more powerful would Ignacio be come morning? What terrible things would he do with these hours that they would spend waiting for dawn? But if they were going to pull this off, they needed to wait. It wasn't as if dueños just waltzed into this prison in the middle of the maldito night.

"Fine." Finn pushed off the wall she leaned against and walked to the door, raising her arm to pull the hood of the cloak over her head. "Then I'll head out and be back in the morn—"

"No, wait. Stay," Alfie said. His voice always had the quality of a hand outstretched, open to help, to guide. She wondered if he knew how soft and horrifically vulnerable it made him sound.

Finn turned to him, her eyebrows raised. When her eyes darted to the bed, the prince's face reddened.

"I didn't mean—I meant—I—" He put a hand over his eyes and sighed.

Finn couldn't help but laugh. "You're very precious, you know. This is why it was so easy to distract you when we first fought." She shook her head, remembering when she'd jokingly asked if he'd wanted to join her in bed to throw him off his game. His lips had parted when she'd said that, as if her words had laced the air with honey and he hoped to taste it.

He seemed to be remembering it too. Alfie's hand moved from his eyes and up into his curly locks. "And you're very sure in your opinions."

"Only when I'm absolutely right."

Alfie shook his head at that. "I meant to say you can stay here, in my rooms. I'll stay with Luka for the night."

Finn looked at the bed again. Each pillow must've cost a goose every last one of its feathers. The thick sheets of red and gold called to her aching body—a night of comfort instead of wondering how many more days she could afford in an inn almost felt worth the horrors of the day. But with the prince's eyes on her, she stopped the relief from spreading over her, cool and healing as a salve.

Finn turned in a slow circle, surveying the room with its plush bed on its raised dais. The floors and walls lacquered with brightly colored tiles. She'd been here once before and never thought she'd be returning, let alone to sleep in his bed.

"Is that a good idea?" she asked as she stepped forward and leaned against the poster of the bed, its stiff pressure between her shoulder blades. The prince looked at her, concern already tugging his features. "Won't your servants die of shock when they come in and find a girl in your bed?"

Alfie breathed a long sigh through his nose. "I will inform them that they are not to enter my rooms for the time being."

A silence fell between them and she could see him struggling to swallow down a retort. He fought and lost.

"And it's hardly any of your business, but it's not as if I've never had anyone in my bed."

Finn's lips quirked up. Did he know that each time he hurried to defend himself, he tossed a rope down to her that she could use to pull him clean off his high horse?

"Well, did you at least wash the sheets after?"

His face reddened and he sputtered before speaking. "Are you always this rude?"

"Depends on the company." She plopped onto the bed and kicked her shoes off. One boot landed on its side, revealing the sole that was still caked in blood from the pub. The air changed then, and the remnants of her joke sat sour on her tongue.

The silence stretched on. The prince's eyes clung to the shoe, his throat working. If it went any longer she would fill it with thoughts of Ignacio, of his strings, of the pub slick with blood.

"You know, making you look like a dueño won't be enough," she said. "You'll need to embody a dueño, move like one."

He quirked an eyebrow. "You assume I haven't considered this?"

"I'm sure you've considered it." She rolled her eyes. "Considering is different from actually doing something right. You walk like a maldito peacock, and I doubt it's a habit you can kick overnight."

"I walk like a peacock?" he repeated as if he didn't know if he should be insulted or just confused.

Her gaze dropped to his narrow hips. "You strut."

"Qué?" He started where he stood and brought his hands forward, clasping them before him as if he could block her view. "No I don't."

"All I'm saying is that you move like a prince and if you want to move about the prison without drawing attention to yourself, then you'd better do it right."

The prince crossed his arms then, and again she saw the internal battle inside of him. His pride and the desire to get this right clashing in his mind. The latter won out.

"Show me," he said, his face open, asking for answers. "Please."

Finn stood from his bed and worked with him, showing him how to walk, to hobble and hunch instead of strut with the pride of a crown. She taught him how to lower and soften his voice into that rasp that wise bruxos of a certain age seemed to master.

When he had it down he looked at her, impressed. "You truly are knowledgeable about this."

"It's my life," she said. Or it had been, she thought with a frown, before Kol took it from her.

At her words, Alfie held her gaze, his gold eyes round with a concern so genuine that it made her skin crawl.

Finn did not like it when the prince looked at her.

She'd spent her life impersonating others. She was the master of looking past someone's facade to the truth that beat within them, hard and fast. Yet when he looked at her, his head tilted, thoughtful, cautious, it was she who felt laid bare, pages of secrets open at his fingertips.

"Out with it, then." She crossed her arms. "Why are you looking at me like that? Say it."

With a tilt of his head he finally asked, "How do you hold on to yourself?"

She squinted at him. "Qué?"

"If you slip in and out of identities the way I do cloaks, how do you hold on to yourself?"

Finn blew air through her teeth. What a soft life he must lead to not see the freedom in what she could do. In the power of being so many people that you became no one at all. People with one face, one story, have weaknesses, vulnerabilities, things to exploit and dangle over their heads. But to be no one was to have nothing to lose and nothing to gain. That was true freedom, plain and simple.

"That's the best part," she said, her shoulder lifting in a shrug. "If you can trade identities at the drop of a hat, then you're invincible. Thanks to my gift not a man on this earth can touch me."

Alfie fell silent, frowning at her as if she'd said something sad instead of clever. "But then no one can help you either."

Finn bristled, something within her sputtering where it usually ran smooth as honey. She didn't like how easily he did that—with a fistful of words he could turn her strength into weakness. All her repartee, opaque and clever at first, now felt embarrassingly transparent. If she longed to be untouchable, it was because someone had taken her in their hands and broken her. If she wanted to fly from identity to identity, then she'd tarnished the one she'd been born with too much to return to it.

And if the prince could sense this, surely others could too.

What did you do that would make you never want to see your own face again? What made you bury it under all this magic?

Finn shoved Kol's rasping voice from her mind and found the prince's golden eyes still clinging to hers. He looked away from her then. From the discomfort prickling between them, she could tell that he knew he'd overstepped. That he'd spoken to her with the concern of a friend when they were barely acquaintances, on a good day.

The sweeping room suddenly felt small. It seemed to fold in on itself, like those delicate paper flowers sold in the Brim—large swaths of colored tissue creased and curved into something new.

"I should go," he said, his voice unraveling the silence.

"Sí," she said, her words frayed as she lowered herself onto the plush bed. "You should." Finn settled into the bed, pulling the thick blankets about her.

He did not rise to the bait this time. "I'll come for you in the morning," he said.

She watched him open the door, and the sight of his back, of his hand closing on the doorknob, brought her back to earlier today. To when she'd told him she wouldn't help him. And instead of trying to twist her to his will until she gave in, he'd simply reached for the door as he did now. He hadn't seen her as something to bend into whatever shape would better serve him.

He'd seen her as a person. A person who had said no.

Her heart beat in her throat, and inside her rose the urge to define where they stood. The urge to canvas the crevasse between them and see it as she knew it was—insurmountable.

"Prince." The word fell from her lips, soft and pillowed with the sudden rush of exhaustion falling over her as she nestled into the sheets. She raised herself up onto her elbows and stared at him where he stood at the door, his back still to her.

He didn't turn to look at her. "Yes?"

"Did you magic the door and windows to keep me from escaping?"

His hand still on the doorknob, he turned his face slightly, and she could see the delicate sweep of his profile, the way his Adam's apple bobbed in his elegant neck as he swallowed. The tense set of his mouth told her the answer before he spoke it.

"Yes."

The knot in her stomach loosened then. The boundaries had been redrawn, defined in thick sweeps of ink. Her world, his, and the vast space between.

"Good." She sank back into the pillows, a yawn curling her tongue. "Then you're smarter than you look."

THE FAREWELL

As the sun rose, Alfie, Luka, and Finn stood in the palace stables, tension reverberating through them, as if they were the plucked strings of finely tuned instruments. Alfie rubbed his slick palms against his trousers and saddled his horse.

Finn had transformed Luka and Alfie into one another. Luka had scribbled a note to the king and queen saying that after his run-in with Tiago he would rather skip the Equinox Ball tonight and travel with a friend instead. Since Luka had too many friends to count and loved to travel, the king and queen would hardly be surprised by this.

The whuffling of the horses and the warm scent of hay should have calmed Alfie, but his body screamed for rest from using the magic. The few hours of sleep he'd gotten had done him no good. With shaking hands, he readied two horses for their journey to the prison where Xiomara dwelled.

Finn pulled the hood of the cloak off and appeared in the corner of the stable, tucked away from the stable doors where sunlight had begun to pour through, greeting the whickering horses with its warm caress.

She stared up at the horse Alfie had saddled for her, her lips curving into a grimace.

"Do you know how to ride a horse?" Alfie asked, wanting to break the silence instead of filling it with his fearful thoughts of what was to come.

She shot him a look. "I spent years working in traveling circuses. Of course I know how to ride a maldito horse." She shifted uncomfortably beside it, her shoulders tensing when it gave a whinny. "I just don't like to."

"Why's that?" Luka asked before stroking her horse's nose with a practiced hand.

Finn eyed the steed warily. "I don't like things I can't—"

"Thieve?" Alfie supplied as he ran his hand over his own horse's dark mane.

Finn rolled her eyes. "I don't like things I can't communicate with, control. Even the most well-trained, friendly horse can buck you off if it feels like it." Then she looked at Alfie pointedly. "And of course I could thieve a maldito horse. What kind of second-rate thief do you think I am?"

Luka tilted his head. "You mean steal an actual horse or steal from a horse?"

"Both. Obviously."

Luka gave a bark of laughter at that and Alfie was thankful for the sound. He wondered if that would be the last time he heard it, if he would die at Ignacio's hands before he could see Luka again. What was Ignacio doing now? How many had he killed with that poisonous magic? He swallowed thickly, pushing those thoughts away before they swallowed him whole. When Alfie finished readying his horse, he stood still, not wanting to admit that there was nothing left to do but leave.

Luka, wearing Alfie's face (a sight Alfie would never get used to), opened his mouth to speak but fell silent. What could be said now, when death hung heavy over Alfie like a veil.

Lies, Alfie thought. *Comforting lies.*

"I'll be back." Alfie swallowed before his voice could splinter. "I promise."

"I know," Luka said, his throat working. "Here, take this." He handed Alfie a velvet drawstring pouch. Inside were two stoppered vials. "Some healing draughts in case you need them."

Healing draughts were not as specific or helpful as Alfie using healing magic on himself to fix a certain wound. They could not mend a broken bone or stop the blood from gushing from a lesion. What they did was give the body a burst of energy, a bit of help so that one had the strength needed to heal naturally. They might come in handy, but Alfie hoped they wouldn't.

"I will come home," Alfie said, his hand still tight on Luka's shoulder, as if he could leave the impression of the promise on Luka's skin. "But if I fail, if I don't come back, I need you to tell Paloma the truth and try to put a stop to this."

"Cállate. Don't say that nonsense," Luka said, his eyes shining. "If you die, I'll kill you."

Alfie laughed before pulling Luka into a hug and clapping him on the back. He couldn't bring himself to break the embrace, to let go. He gave Luka's shoulder one more squeeze before pulling back, his eyes stinging. Behind them, Finn mounted her horse. When they left the stable she would pull up the hood of the vanishing cloak, and Alfie would lead her horse under the guise that he was bringing the horse for a friend.

Alfie pulled a roll of parchment from his bag. "Take this," he said to Luka. "I've magicked it to match mine," Alfie said, pointing at another roll of parchment in his bag. "Anything that happens to one will happen to the other. What you write, I'll see, and vice versa. So if you need me, we'll have a way to talk."

Luka rolled his eyes before grabbing the parchment. "And to report on my very important research?"

"Yes," Alfie said, his lips quirking up at the sarcasm dripping from Luka's voice. "That too."

Before going to bed, Alfie had tasked Luka with looking into any and all books on Sombra while he and Finn were gone in case Luka could discover any weaknesses that could help them when they had to face Ignacio once more.

Alfie chuckled at Luka's forlorn expression. "Would you really rather infiltrate a prison than read books in the library?"

Luka stared at him. "Yes. Obviously. What do you expect me to find out? That Sombra's magic is allergic to oregano?"

Alfie snorted at that. "To be honest, at this point nothing would surprise me."

"Gods," Finn mumbled from her unseen place on the horse. "No more maldito oregano."

The sound of pounding hooves drew Alfie's gaze out the stable doors. A red-caped guard was leading his horse in a sprint to the stables.

"Quick," Alfie hissed at Finn. "Pull the hood up!"

Finn disappeared before Alfie's eyes just as the rider led his horse into a halt before the stable doors and dismounted in a hurry. At the sight of Luka and Alfie, his spine straightened.

"Buenos días, Prince Alfehr," he said, bowing low to Luka. "And to you as well, Master Luka." He bowed then to Alfie.

Alfie blinked at him for a moment before remembering that he was wearing Luka's face. "Good morning."

The man peered about the stable. "Has the stable boy gone, Your Grace?"

Alfie had asked the boy to leave for a bit, to give him some privacy to say goodbye and so that he, Luka, and Finn could speak freely.

Luka nodded at the man. "Yes, but he'll be returning soon enough."

The man nodded and hurriedly led his horse into the stable and into an empty stall well stocked with hay. He didn't even bother to unsaddle the horse or water it before leaving it in its stall. A froth of sweat had gathered at the horse's neck and the guard looked shaken as he made for the stable doors.

"Are you all right?" Alfie asked.

The man looked at him and Luka silently, as if considering the propriety of the answer to Alfie's question. Then he sighed and seemed to think better of his hesitance. "Alas, you'll surely hear soon enough, from me or otherwise. I have an urgent message for the king and queen. A pub in the Brim was found littered with bodies this morning. The likes of which I have never seen." He swallowed thickly as he shook his head at the thought. "I must be off to deliver this message. If you'll excuse me." He bowed to each of them again and then the man was gone, dashing away from the stables and toward the palace, his red cape rippling behind him. Alfie could only watch, the thought of that pub searing his mind and thickening his throat.

Though Finn was still shrouded by the vanishing cloak, Alfie could feel waves of tension roiling from where she sat.

Luka looked at him, his eyes shining with concern at the mention of the pub. He seemed to want to say something, and Alfie knew Luka was fighting the urge to ask him to stay, to not risk his life. Instead, Luka shook his head and pressed his lips into a tight line. Alfie could not express how grateful he was for that, because he didn't know if he could leave if Luka asked him to stay.

Luka cleared his throat and looked pointedly at the spot where Finn sat atop her horse. "Make sure he comes back in one piece."

A snort came from where she sat atop the saddle, still invisible. "He's too skinny to break into any more pieces."

Luka grinned. "I like her."

Alfie mounted his horse, his head swimming as he pulled himself up. But he kept himself from swaying as he settled on the saddle; he couldn't let Luka know how much this magic had done to him so far. For all he knew, this was the last time they would see each other. He wanted to say goodbye to Luka, but the word wouldn't come. Or if that word came, others would follow and he'd drown in it all. He was relieved when Luka beat him to it.

"Later, sourpuss," he said with a small smile.

Alfie rolled his eyes at the childhood nickname, grinning all the same. "Hasta luego." With a stone in his throat, Alfie took the reins of Finn's horse and led it into a trot beside his own as they rode across the palace grounds.

They rode in silence through horse paths carved through the rings for speedy travelers until Alfie finally led them to the gate out of the Pinch, San Cristóbal's outermost ring, that led out of the city and into the surrounding countryside. Here, fields of sugarcane stretched far into the distance, with only a winding dirt road to interrupt the stretches of green. Luckily, the path was smooth, without climbing hills or rough terrain. It would be an easy enough journey. Until they got there.

In the distance, a little over an hour's ride away, stood the eyesore that they would infiltrate—the Clock Tower.

There, the sugarcane fields gave way to dry, barren dirt. The land had been salted, made inhospitable to even a tendril of life. On the arid stretch of land, the prison was built in a foreboding tower of adobe brick, exposed to the baking sun and surrounded by a thick moat of water enchanted to boil. It housed only the foulest criminals. Their magic was blocked by written magic carved into their wrists and oral suppressants, making them magically impotent. Worst of all was the meaning behind the prison's name. The ceiling of the great tower was a clock, its minute hand as long as five men. The clock ticked and tocked deafeningly to remind the prisoners of the endless time they had left in their cells. It was common for prisoners to be driven mad from the merciless clock that glared down upon them, an unstopping, ticking moon. It was a life that Alfie wouldn't wish on his worst enemy. Then Alfie thought of the girl they were going to release from the prison. On second thought, he would wish it upon her.

As the sun dipped closer and closer to the horizon, Alfie's blood chilled in his veins. They had only six hours to sneak into the prison, get the prisoner out, and trap the magic. It would be an impossible plan if they had days; with only hours it sounded absolutely absurd. Still, they would have to try. The magic's goal of bringing back Sombra was far too horrific for it to be dealt with slowly. It needed to be captured and banished into the void as soon as possible.

With the city gates disappearing far behind them, Finn removed her hood and took the reins of her horse. They rode at top speed down the curving dirt road slithering through the rustling sugarcane fields like a snake. The adobe brick tower loomed in the far distance, looking like a finger jutting up from the sugarcane to reach for the sky and claim it as its own.

For a long hour they rode too fast to speak, their horses dashing down the flat road side by side. Alfie dug his heels into his horse, urging it on, but when a lather of sweat gathered at the horse's neck and mouth, he signaled for Finn to slow to a halt.

They slowed to a stop and Alfie dismounted, stroking his horse's warm nose. The poor thing was exhausted.

"Sorry, Peluche." Alfie uncorked a canteen of water he'd strapped at the horse's side and with a twist of his fingers a long ribbon of water flowed out. He carefully funneled ribbon water into the horse's gasping mouth while Finn watched.

She snorted at him from her saddle. "Of course you would name a horse 'teddy bear.'"

Alfie moved on to her horse, gathering water before it to drink. "I didn't name him. My mother did." His voice softened on *mother*.

He thought of her face when he'd returned to the palace.

"You came home," she'd said. Would he make it home again after this?

A loud munch broke him from his thoughts. Finn was chomping into an apple that he'd packed onto her horse's saddlebag in case they got hungry.

"What's my horse's name, then?"

Alfie scratched her horse behind the ear and it leaned forward, pressing its head against his shoulder. He and Luka had trained with this horse as boys and it always acted like an overgrown kitten around them.

"I named your horse when I was a boy. He's called Gassy." Alfie patted the horse's flank, relishing the sight of Finn's mouth pausing mid-chew. "I'm sure you'll learn why before the journey's up."

Alfie corked the canteen and swiftly mounted Peluche once more. "Let's start slow now, give them a chance to recover before we speed up. We should get to the tower in half an hour, maybe less."

Still grimacing at the horse beneath her, Finn nodded and they eased into a trot.

Finn was silent as they ambled down the path and he was grateful for that. He wanted nothing more than to run through the plan over and over again until they arrived—get to the prison, have Finn lay down the distraction while he waited nearby, then they'd get as close to Xiomara's cell as they could before setting off the distraction. Once the guards around her cell left to investigate all the noise, they'd break in, get Xiomara under the cloak with Finn, and walk out of the prison. After they snuck Xiomara out would come the most difficult part. They would need to draw Ignacio to them, somewhere away from the city, kill him, seal the magic in the toy, and toss it into Xiomara's void.

He repeated it in his mind over and over, like a chant. The only sound around him was the bristle of the breeze-kissed sugarcane lining the road.

Alfie touched his face, startling at the different features under his fingers. He would never get used to wearing Luka's face. He couldn't imagine what Finn's life had been like, darting from identity to identity.

"That's the best part," she'd told him last night, but to Alfie it felt like not quite a nightmare, but a strange dream he couldn't wake from.

"I can take it off you, if you want," Finn said, motioning at his face. He hadn't noticed she'd been watching him. "When I transform you into a dueño, I'll want to start with a blank canvas anyway."

Alfie thought on it. They were far from the city anyway. It wasn't as if he'd be spotted, and if she was going to take this mask off him to change him into a dueño later, why not have a break for a moment and wear his own face? "Yes, please."

As their horses ambled side by side, Finn looked at him intently and waved her hand. Alfie's body tingled then and he felt himself shifting, his torso growing longer and slimmer, his nose drawing up slightly. Then it was over. He put his hands on his face and sighed into them. "Gracias."

She shrugged. Silence reigned for a long moment before she spoke again.

"The way your brother died." Finn gave a low whistle, shattering the silence. She shifted on her saddle, wincing as her backside bumped against it. "That's something."

Alfie's jaw tightened. He was shocked by her ability to bring up exactly what he didn't want to talk about. He looked away from her and focused on the green fields around him, the pound of his horse's hooves on the dirt ground. "Yes," he said through gritted teeth. "It was."

"I remember when I heard the news of the assassination," she said. "I was in a city far from here and people were still weeping in the streets, as if they knew him."

The way she said that crawled under his skin. Whenever anyone spoke of Dez it was always with deep reverence and sorrow, but she said it so flippantly. "This bothered you?"

She shrugged before leaning sideways in her saddle to skim her fingers over the heads of the sugarcane stalks. "It didn't make sense. They didn't know him. I didn't know him. Why cry when his death doesn't affect me?"

Alfie squinted at her. "Of course who becomes king of Castallan affects you. You're Castallano, you live here."

Finn snorted at that. "People like me, we're ants, and rulers are just a big foot looming over us ready to squish us into the dirt. Doesn't matter whose body the foot is attached to, the purpose is still the same. Now it's just your foot hovering over my head instead of his."

"Is that how you really see us?" Alfie asked. "As something to hurt you?"

She gave a dry laugh. "What do you expect me to see you all as? Protectors of the people? Get the stars out of your eyes, Prince. Do you think the kids living with nothing, the ones thieving and begging, see you as a protector? You with your polished desk and your fancy magic." She gave another loud snort. "The rich are born rich and die richer, the rest of us die early. You're no protector. You're just another foot waiting to grind us into the dirt."

Alfie rubbed the back of his neck. He knew that there was poverty and unrest in his kingdom. That was everywhere. He wasn't so naive as to think otherwise. But still, it was hard to swallow. When he heard Finn speak, every glorified idea he had about his kingdom cracked and crumbled—nothing but a gossamer shell to hide the flaws within. The motto of his kingdom, *magia para todos*, magic for all, suddenly rang hollow.

But if he and Finn somehow stopped this dark magic, and he had the chance to become the king his parents wanted him to, then maybe he could change this? Maybe he could be a different king. Not a foot hovering overhead but a hand outstretched to pull his people up. He could make the motto of his kingdom true. If he lived long enough to become king.

They fell into another silence then and he wondered if this was what the whole journey would contain—flares of anger followed by stretches of silence and on and on.

"How exactly does the void thing work—"

"Finn," Alfie said, his voice low with barely suppressed anger. He knew they needed that criminal's help, but he did not want to think about it, didn't want to face it until he really had to. "Please. Leave it be."

She took his warning for bait. "Why?"

"Because I don't want to think about it," he snapped. His fingers twitched on the reins, begging him to reach for the cool flask at his hip, to silence the anger that was rising in him like the tide. The anger that could turn him into someone he wasn't. "It'll only make me angry."

Finn cocked her head. "Why not be angry, then? It's as natural a feeling as anything else."

Alfie sighed through his nose and reached sideways, letting his fingers brush the heads of the sugarcane stalks, the tingle of their touch calming him slightly. Of course she would advocate for anger; it wasn't as if she thought twice before acting on impulse. "I don't like who I become when I give in to anger." An image flashed in his mind of that day, of his hands gripping Paloma by the robes and throwing her against the wall. He bit back his disgust with himself. "That person is not me."

"Yes it is, estúpido," she said. "Who you are when you're angry is still you. It doesn't have to be all of you, but it's a piece of you all the same. If you deny that, you might as well deny your whole maldito self and be done with it."

Alfie bristled at her tone. She spoke as if she were asking him to switch shirts instead of telling him to give in to the part of him that he feared most.

"Some things you can't outrun." Her voice came differently now, not soft, but lacking its usual sharpness—a blunted dagger. "Some things you ought to just run to. Get it over with."

Alfie thought of how she'd run from Ignacio only to be dragged back, reeled in like a fish, but the horror of that memory could not dull his embarrassment. To draw this tone out of her, he must seem pathetic right now. He didn't want her pity or her maldito advice.

"Well," he said. "When I feel like denying my whole identity and running around in a mask instead, I'll be sure to call on you."

"Fine." Her eyes rolled heavenward. "You sure you can trust Bathtub Boy to cover for you?"

Alfie still didn't know where that nickname came from. "He'll cover for me, and his name is Luka." He swallowed thickly, wishing he could turn his horse back and head home. Luka had nearly died, and Alfie wanted nothing more than to protect him, to find whoever had targeted him and punish them as they deserved. His fingers twitching, Alfie reached into his own saddlebag and pulled out a mango and a small knife. His dagger glided over its flesh, peeling the fruit free. He popped a piece into his mouth, focusing on the burst of flavor instead of his desire to turn his horse around and gallop home.

Finn watched him carefully. "You want to know who tried to kill him."

"Yes, obviously," Alfie said, kneading his temples. "But I have to handle the dark magic first." Even if he did somehow get rid of the dark magic, it wasn't as if he could just tell anyone that Luka had nearly been killed without also explaining the release of the dark magic in the first place. He had no idea what his next move ought to be on that front.

"Well, I've got a start for you. It was definitely done by poison," Finn said matter-of-factly. "Poison left for *you.*"

The mango fell from his hand onto the dirt road. "*Me?*"

"Yes, you," she insisted. "I was in your room looking for the key to the vault." She pulled a key out of her pocket, tossing it at him. It was his key. Alfie's mind felt as if it were on the verge of bursting. "While I was searching a servant came in. I heard a bottle of something being shaken up. I wasn't sure if it'd been poisoned or not, but after what happened to Bathtub Boy, I sure as hell am."

His fingers were sticky with mango juice, but he couldn't stop himself from putting his hand over his eyes. "My sleeping tonic."

Luka had said that he'd drunk Alfie's tonic. He hadn't even thought of it. Part of him wanted to shout at Finn, to demand to know why she hadn't dumped out the bottle and stopped all this from happening in the first place. But it felt pointless. It wasn't as if she could be sure of what had happened when it had. She was a thief who owed him nothing. It seemed absurd to expect anything else of her.

His mind buzzed with an endless line of questions, each one nudging the others to be chosen next. Who had tried to poison him? Was it the same person who'd taken Dez from him? Would another assassination attempt happen again while he was away? Was Luka in danger of being poisoned while impersonating him for the day?

"You want to go home." Finn's voice rang quiet but strong. "Protect your family."

Underneath her facade Alfie could see a flash of understanding. As if she'd once had people to protect. "I want to," Alfie said. "But I can't."

His mother's voice rang in his head, clear as a bell: *You never think things through, Alfie. If you're to be a king, you must think of your people before yourself. Always.*

This magic threatened his entire kingdom, not just his family. And so he had to take responsibility for his actions. He must take care of the black magic first. Without delay.

Finn nodded at him, taking his flaring emotions in stride. He couldn't understand how she could be so calm. She'd witnessed what he'd witnessed in the Blue Room. How was she so relaxed when he could barely stop himself from shaking?

"You're not worried about that man?" he asked. "Ignacio?"

She flinched at his name, like a child would at a crack of thunder, but she recovered quickly, smoothing her face into nonchalance. "I don't have much fear in me, Prince. I'm not going to waste it on him," she said, her mouth curling into a snarl around that word.

She tossed him a smirk that almost covered the turmoil churning beneath it. Almost.

"That's enough rest for these beasts," she said before digging her heels into her horse's sides and easing into a sprint, leaving Alfie in her dust.

THE MAN WHO COULD NOT DIE

As yet another body burst into ash before him, Ignacio sucked his teeth in annoyance.

He sat in the Blue Thimble, the blood-caked pub that he'd marked as his own when he'd received his power—when the thrill of it all had slaked a bloodlust in him that every man in the pub had paid dearly for. The corpses had been removed by the guardsmen, but the blood remained, staining every surface with red-tinted proof of his might. The pub had been closed after the massacre, and Ignacio had taken it as his own private sanctuary, a place to draw victims from the Brim to infect.

He'd spent the night prowling the rings of this city, hunting for bodies to claim as his own, but in each ring they merely burst into dust. After hours of failure he'd returned to the Blue Thimble, frustration coiling tight inside him as the morning sun poured through the pub's windows. Though the magic begged him to continue, Ignacio couldn't be bothered, not when her name beat in his mind like a drum.

Finn. Finn. Finn.

He took a swig of spiced rum, toeing his boot through the ashen remains of another imbecile. He'd come all this way for her. His vision nothing but a blur of colors and lines, his pockets empty, he'd charmed his way onto a ship with a story of a long-lost sister he hoped to find in the city, so that he wouldn't die blind and alone. A sailor pitied him enough to offer him a sudden opening on the boat. One of the passengers had disappeared the night before. It was all very curious. Well, not to Ignacio. He'd killed that man. Dragged him into an alley and cut his throat. But to the rest of the world it was all very curious. And Ignacio didn't mind indulging the rest of the world.

He'd come to the capital city because when she was young, baby fat still padding the panes of her face, she'd always said she wanted to be here for the Equinox Festival. So he'd found his way to San Cristóbal and received this power like a gift from the gods themselves. He'd shown her how powerful he'd become, and still she had not fallen into line. She'd slipped through his fingers like water. His hands curled into fists, his blackened nails biting into the flesh of his palms. The dark magic within him healed it immediately, so quick he barely had a moment to savor the pain.

He could remember the day he'd taken her as his own. The memory sat in his mind in brightened shades, colors that spoke of a turning point that would redraw the course of his life. He'd been watching her for a few days then, the shadow moving at her feet calling to him, a mirror of his own. She'd been scavenging for scraps in a garbage heap between pubs. Her bones had shown through her skin like moonlight through glass.

He approached her from behind. She sensed him immediately

even though he hadn't made a sound. Instinct like that was what it took to survive on the street.

She'd glared up at him, her hackles raised. For a skinny little thing she was fearsome.

"Where's your mamá, papá?" Ignacio asked, cocking his head at her.

"Gone." She pulled a small dagger from the dirty sheath at her waist. "Dead and buried a few days now. Worm food. Same as you'll be if you touch me."

Ignacio had only smiled down at her, unfazed. He was sure she'd faced more than her fair share of people with less than savory intentions on the street. He could hardly blame her for flashing the dagger and her teeth.

"I don't think so," Ignacio said, waving her threat away with a smile. "I won't be dying tonight. Not any night, for that matter."

She squinted up at him, unconvinced. "Everyone dies."

She'd said that with a certainty that no child should know.

Ignacio shook his head. "I won't die. My word is law, more powerful than death." He gestured at his moving shadow, which curled on the ground before his feet. "If my body tries to perish, I'll just tell it not to. And I'll do the same for you too." His gaze locked on hers, a promise in his eyes. "If you like."

Finn only looked up at him, as if trying to decide if he was too confident, too stupid, or a bit of both.

Ignacio pulled a red apple out of the pocket of his cloak. He meant to hand it to her, but she snatched it from him without a word and bit into it savagely, juice dripping down her chin.

Ignacio stood, turned on his heel, and strode away. After five long strides he glanced at her over his shoulder.

"Are you coming?"

Finn stood still, her eyes still on the apple core. She tossed it over her shoulder and followed him like a dog after her master, as she always should.

When had she changed from that?

Ignacio. The dark magic purred in his mind insistently.

"What is it?" Ignacio snapped.

We must gain strength, we must spread our touch, only then will we—

"Have the strength to take what is ours from the palace. Yes, I understand," Ignacio interjected, annoyed. The magic insisted upon filling his mind with images of what lay in wait in the palace, and the promise of untold power that would not fade. He need only infect as many as he could first, for each body he infected would in turn give him more strength, strength to storm the palace and take it for himself.

But each time he had spread the magic to another body, that euphoric burst in power had been temporary. Each body he took quickly expired under the weight of the magic, like an oil-soaked match tossed into a roaring hearth. With each loss, his strength dwindled along with them. He'd infected many from this pub before his encounter with Finn, the power blooming in him with frightening intensity as he'd conjured those strings and halted time around him. But it had quickly faded as those bodies burned away to dust, and he'd been left with nothing but exhaustion and a hunger for more. He could not storm a palace full of guards with this fatigue, this feeling of strength finding him only to trickle away in an instant.

You are not listening. We must seek dark hearts, the magic's voice came again, an insistent whisper between his ears. *Those are the ones that will carry our power without falling apart in a mere moment.*

Find them and we will take what is ours from the palace and clear the throne for a true king. And you will be rewarded.

The magic filled his mind's eye with visions of the power that would pour through him when he retrieved what he needed from the palace. Power that would give him the strength to take every throne that this world had to offer.

When we own the world, the magic purred, *there will be no place for her to escape to. Nowhere for her to hide. I will deliver her to you.*

Ignacio watched as the vision showed Finn fleeing from town to town, city to city, continent to continent. Every place she went, she saw Ignacio's face, his reign. With every sight of his power her fear doubled and tripled, crippling her until she fell to her hands and knees, until she could run no more. Finn crawled to Ignacio's throne, bowing, her forehead pressed shamefully to the ground at his feet. She shook with the fear that she wore so well for him. She begged him to take her back, to let her be his daughter again.

Please, she said, tears running down her face. Her begging sounded like prayers. Prayers to him, her only god. She grasped his hands in hers and pressed desperate kisses against his palms. *Por favor, let me come home.*

A ripple of euphoria rolled through him, spreading through his body like fire swallowing a dry twig. His hands shook in anticipation.

"Dark hearts?" he said. Ignacio stepped out of the pub and into the bustling marketplace as the sun dipped ever closer to the horizon. He turned his gaze to the north, where he knew the Clock Tower loomed tall somewhere in the distance—a beacon of blackened hearts, chained and ripe for the taking. "I know just the place."

A PRINCE AND A THIEF
WALK INTO A PRISON

The sight of the Clock Tower a mere mile before them struck Finn like a fist to the belly. Her fingers tight on the reins, she resisted the urge to turn the still horse beneath her and ride away.

This place was a thief's nightmare. The Clock Tower was the prison where you entered and only exited as a corpse. To make it worse, they were going to this prison to find Xiomara—a woman with the power to create voids. Finn had certainly never seen a void, nor had she heard of one before the prince had explained the truth of his brother's death, but she certainly didn't want to see one any time soon. She swallowed thickly. Her horse whickered, seeming to sense the fear rippling through her.

"Can't blame you, Gassy," she mumbled to it.

"Finn."

Alfie's voice drew her out of her thoughts. He'd already dismounted while she'd stared at the prison, wide-eyed. He dragged his gaze away from the tower and cocked his head toward the thicket of sugarcane at his side. "We'll take the horses into the field and hide them there before we head out."

She nodded at that, her throat dry, and dismounted before tugging her horse into the field behind Alfie's. The horses whinnied, only quieting when Alfie hummed at them in hushing sounds. When they'd walked deep enough into the field for the prince's liking, he said, "*Doblar*."

At his word, a wide circle of sugarcane bent to the ground, giving them a clear space to leave the horses comfortably hidden, as well as a space for her to set to work transforming him into an elderly dueño. It was a strange request, to say the least. She'd been asked many times to make someone look younger. This was the first time someone had asked her to age them.

After he watered the horses one more time, he stood before Finn and asked her to get started, his stance stiff and uncomfortable as he waited for her to get to work.

"I have to whiten your hair," Finn said, tilting her chin up to stare at his head. He was so tall that it was inconvenient.

She raised an eyebrow when he didn't move. "Should I levitate up to your head, then?"

"Oh, sorry," he said, sheepish. He bent at the waist in an awkward half bow, his forehead hovering just before hers. The swaying sugarcane stalks made the air sound restless, buzzing with energy.

Finn reached up and passed her hands through his hair, the pads of her fingers making paths through his black curls. It was a shame to make them look limp with age when they were so full of life, springing against her palm at the lightest touch. She worked her way from the front to the back, finishing with her thumb brushing the line at the nape of his neck where thick locks met soft skin. He'd been still at first, but as her hands moved, his body had relaxed, almost leaning into her touch. Was he enjoying this? Her hands paused. Was she?

Finn shook that thought away and flexed her fingers before laying her hands on his cheeks. His eyes flickered down then, showing the dark sweep of his lashes. He looked away as if he wasn't sure of where he was allowed to look at this moment. But then he gave up and his gaze drifted up to claim hers.

"Close your maldito eyes," Finn snapped.

"I didn't know if I should or shouldn't," he sputtered. "You didn't tell me which would be helpful—"

"How would having your giant eyes on me be helpful?"

Alfie glared at her and she could feel him biting the inside of his cheek; the sudden dip of movement against her palm was strangely distracting.

"Well?" Finn said.

After a long, angry sigh through his nose, Alfie closed his eyes. It was only when she felt the heat draining from her face that she realized she'd been blushing.

No, not blushing, her mind argued. *Flushed. With annoyance. Anger.*

Satisfied with that correction, Finn set to work, quickly loosening the skin of his face and molding wrinkles. She lost herself in the practice of transformation, in how much she missed doing this to her own face. Happy with her work, she lowered her hands. "Your face is done."

Alfie stood upright and rubbed at his lower back; the gesture made him look older still. Finn quickly aged his hands before pulling her small mirror out of her bag and holding it in front of his new face.

"Wow. Increíble." He pinched and tugged the loosened skin. Finn felt a plume of pride catch in her chest. The prince was well-versed in desk magic, so he must've at least heard of spellwork that could change one's appearance, but none of that ever worked as well as her *propio* did.

"What is your *propio*'s limit?"

Finn raised an eyebrow. "Why do you want to know?"

His eyes still clung to the mirror, so distracted that his words flew past his lips too quick for him to catch them. "Because the way you change people is so flawless that I wonder what you can't do."

Thrown off by the compliment, Finn fell silent.

The prince looked at her then, his newly aged face looking suddenly uncomfortable. "Though that's a bit of a personal question, I understand. You don't have to answer," he said. "If you don't want."

She shrugged at that, smoothing her face into nonchalance. It wasn't as if the prince could hold the information against her. "When I change myself or someone else, it's like they're made out of clay, and I only have so much clay to use. So if you asked me to make you five feet tall, I couldn't do it. There's too much clay, you'd come out too wide. Likewise, if a child asked me to make them tall as you, it wouldn't be possible either. I'd have to stretch them too much, they'd look like a straw, the sculpture would collapse. So I have to work within the limitations of each body I change."

"Fascinating," he said, and Finn rolled her eyes. He sounded like he longed to write what she'd said down for further study. Though he always seemed to sound like that.

"Remember," she said as she put the mirror away. "Like I told

Bathtub Boy, my magic will stick to you effortlessly for a few hours, but eventually it'll be up to you to keep the disguise up. That's how it works when I change other people. I lay down the framework and—"

"And I power the framework with my magic," Alfie said. "I understand."

"If you exhaust yourself, the disguise will crumble. That's the other restriction. So be careful."

Alfie nodded, his hands kneading his newly wrinkled face with a sense of wonder tinged with fear.

He clearly missed his own face, and Finn wondered what that would feel like. The feeling of wanting to be the same. Of looking at your own face and not recoiling. When she surfaced from that thought, she found the prince's eyes roving over her face, his gaze tinged with concern. Though his gold eyes were paired with a new, older face, they still held the quality of seeing exactly what she was thinking, no matter how she hid it.

"What?" she snapped. "What is it?"

He started at her brusque tone before pointing at her nose. "You've just got some dirt on your face."

Finn blinked. Her face warm, she scrubbed at her nose with the back of her hand.

"The cart will be arriving soon. We should get to the roadside to wait. Are you ready?"

"I just spent the last ten minutes making sure you were ready," she said. "I've *been* ready."

The prince frowned at her. He opened his mouth as if to say something but forced himself to swallow it. She was more comfortable when he looked at her this way—with a contempt that slanted his eyes instead of a worry that rounded them. This look, she understood.

"You're certain that this will work?" Alfie asked her as they huddled under the vanishing cloak, watching as the canopied cart pulled by two horses made its way down the road to them.

Alfie had provided the information about when carts came to deliver supplies to the prison. He'd done his research on the Clock Tower months ago in preparation for the last time he'd come. Finn had come up with the plan to sneak onto the carriage without breaking a sweat. He'd agreed to it but was doubtful. Then again, he didn't have a better idea, and there was no time to waste. The ride to the prison and this cart they'd been waiting for had taken longer than Alfie had expected; soon it would be afternoon. Time seemed to dart onward, leaving them struggling to keep up. The ball would begin tonight and Alfie could only hope that this would all be under control by then, that he'd somehow get back in time to relieve Luka and present himself as Castallan's next king.

"Relax, old man," Finn said, grinning when he glared down at her. "If there's one thing I know, it's that horses don't like snakes." She took the sock she'd borrowed from him and stuffed it with small rocks. She set it on the ground at the edge of the road.

Alfie hoped she was right. They did not have time for mistakes. The ball was five hours away and this magic trapped in Ignacio's body still wreaked havoc wherever it was.

The cart curved through the road between the sugarcane fields, drawing ever closer to the barren land that stood before them, an island of dust in a sea of sugarcane. The cart's horses trotted in unison as the two drivers chatted. Finn raised her hand and curved it back and forth in rolling, serpentine motions. The rocks in the black sock responded as the sock slithered forward across the road toward the horses' stamping feet.

She held up three fingers and counted down. "Tres, dos, uno—"

One horse gave a shrill neigh, rearing back on its hind legs at the sight of the pseudo snake. The other followed suit before stomping on the sock as the drivers shouted in alarm. They pulled the cart to a stop before one hopped off his perch to calm the horses.

"Now!" Finn whispered.

Together beneath the cloak, they dashed to the back of the cart and crawled in. It was full of food for the prison. Sacks of flour, potatoes, and purple onions were piled on the cart's floor. Alfie pulled Finn to the back corner. They crouched against the adjoining walls of the cart. Alfie could hear the drivers arguing as they steadied the horses.

"Check the back," one man said. "Make sure everything's in order."

Alfie pressed his back harder against the corner and hoped the man wouldn't crawl into the cart to investigate.

A man appeared at the rear and eyed its contents, a look of boredom slackening his face. Then his eyes sharpened. His gaze locked on the ground just before Alfie.

Alfie looked down to see that his shoe was sticking out from beneath the cloak. He pulled his foot in, accidentally knocking his knee against a sack of potatoes. The sack fell sideways and hit the ground with a clunk. The man stared, rubbing his eyes in confusion.

Finn reached for a dagger in her belt loop, but Alfie grabbed her hand and shook his head. He would not let this go awry. They had no time for mistakes now, but enough people had been hurt already. His heart in his throat, Alfie grabbed the dragon on his chest. Finn watched him uneasily as he fervently thought, *Forget you saw me. Forget you saw me.*

A wave of pain tore through him, as if needles were slicing through every patch of his skin. His head swam.

The man's eyes glazed over before clearing again. He blinked, as if trying to hold tight to a memory as it slipped through his fingers. He shook his head. "Todo bien back here!"

The man walked back to the head of the cart and the cart rolled on. His mind hazy with pain, Alfie startled at the trickle of something warm flowing over his lip. His nose was bleeding. With shaking fingers he pinched his nose and tilted his head back.

This magic was ravaging him from the inside out.

"That bad, huh?" Finn muttered.

"Worse," he said, his heart beating wildly in his chest.

The pain blooming in his bones aside, Alfie couldn't help but be astounded by the magic's reach. How could it easily erase a single memory from a man's head? There was spellwork that could wipe a man's mind clean, but there was no magic that worked so selectively, plucking one memory like a petal from a stem. The price of that magic tore through Alfie as he blinked away his spotty vision, his hands trembling. If this was a mere echo of the magic, how strong would it be if it reunited with Sombra's body?

Then a thought sprouted in his mind, thorny and prickly. The words of the Englassen book echoed in his mind:

The longer that the being is sealed, the more it will draw upon the sealer's energy, his very life force.

Even if he banished the magic away, it would still be attached to him, drawing upon his life until there was nothing left to feast on. A prickling chill swept over his body. The reality of his death formed, hard and unignorable. Yet there was also something freeing to it. He'd worried about what legacy he would leave behind for his kingdom. Now the answer was simple—his life. The magic would sap him of it with time and when he died the seal would break. But hidden in the void, it would not be able to return and hurt anyone else. His life was worth that, he knew, but the thought of losing it sapped him of hope even more than this foul magic could.

They rode in the cart in silence until the wheels began rumbling on new, uneven ground; they'd crossed from the dirt road surrounded by sugarcane into the prison's clearing, where the ground sat dry and cracked beneath the cart. Then a wave of terrible heat swept over them.

"What the hell is that?" Finn said, wiping her brow.

"We're riding across the drawbridge over the boiling moat." He released his nose and gingerly leaned forward. It had stopped bleeding. Now sweat gathered on his upper lip instead.

Finn's eyebrows rose. "I thought that was just a story."

"I'm afraid not," Alfie said. There were rumors that if a grown man fell in the moat, he would be cooked alive before he even had the chance to scream, steamed from the inside out.

The cart gave a bump as they moved off the bridge and back onto land. The wave of heat abated slightly as the cart rolled to a stop. Alfie and Finn scurried out before the prison guards stepped forward to retrieve the goods. Before them stood the Clock Tower.

Alfie had been here before, yet the prison still looked shockingly wide and impossibly tall, like a stone telescope jutting from the earth, its edges perfectly rounded. Not a single window adorned it. Its adobe bricks baked in the sun. The spit of land between the moat and the tower was minuscule, only a strip of parched dirt between them and a torturous, steaming death.

But there was no time to dwell on that. His head still swimming from using the magic, Alfie nodded toward the prison guards carrying the sacks of food into a side entrance of the tower, a small door to the left of the prison's main entrance—a pair of foreboding double doors that towered over all who entered. They followed quickly behind the guardsmen down a tight hall of sandy stone walls, scarcely lit by enchanted flames hovering in sconces. They were walking toward what Alfie knew to be a food cellar. On the way Alfie spotted a closet door; he cocked his head toward it. They ducked into it as the men walked on.

With the door shut, the closet was dark as night. Alfie was grateful for the cover as he wrenched the cloak off, his body screaming in pain and exhaustion. He slid down the wall and sat against it, his head between his knees.

He heard the scratch of a struck match. A small bud of a flame hovered between them, and Finn's face loomed out of the dark. She was squatting in front of him, scanning him. He was glad they'd decided not to use the dark magic to transport them here. He couldn't imagine the pain if they'd tried to travel such a distance on the back of this magic.

He closed his eyes and focused on taking in breaths instead of choking on them. Finn said nothing, only kept the flame glowing between them. She did not tell him he was a fool. She did not tell him that this magic was going to destroy him and that this was all his fault in the first place. She just let him breathe. It was a comfort he couldn't verbalize.

"Can you stand?" she whispered.

Alfie braced his palms against the cold floor. "Let's find out."

She stepped away to give him room. Alfie slowly rose, his back supported by the wall. He moved forward, righting himself, but as soon as he did his vision swam. It felt as if the world beneath his feet was spinning on its toes. A faraway voice told him that he was falling. Finn extinguished the match. As the closet fell dark she caught him in her arms, his forehead falling to the soft juncture where her neck curved into her shoulder. She leaned him back against the wall, holding him there.

When he raised his head their cheeks brushed past each other, a shock of warmth. The darkness of the closet heightened his senses, and he could feel so keenly the heat of her through his dueño's robes, smell the sweat that trailed down her skin from their journey here. With her fingers splayed against his collarbone, Alfie hoped she couldn't feel his pulse quickening.

"*Luz,*" he murmured, his voice hushed. A globe of white light the size of an apple hovered over his palm, casting a glow over her face. He'd hoped the return of his sight would calm the rest of his senses, but it did no such thing. He saw now that wishing for such a thing would be like coaxing a blooming flower to fall into a tight bud once more. It couldn't be taken back.

"If you faint this often, do you even need to sleep at night?" she asked.

With that insult, his pulse came down easily.

"It's just the magic," he said. Usually magic flowed through him, blooming at his fingertips. But this magic didn't flow, it burned, leaving his whole body singed. It wrung him dry. Just when he thought it had taken everything from him, it only twisted him tighter.

But Alfie refused to let his fear of the magic ruin this accomplishment. He couldn't help but relish the moment. They'd done it. They'd snuck into the Clock Tower.

"We made it," Alfie said.

"We did," she said, her lips quirking at the corners. For a moment that was all there was, their smiles and the soft light that traced them in the dark.

"You do know that getting out is always harder than getting in, right?" she said.

"Just let me have this one victory, thief."

"Fine, Prince."

For a long moment, she let him have it.

"All right," she said. "We should get going."

Alfie nodded, his throat dry. "You're right." He reached for the doorknob, but he couldn't will himself to turn it. He was here again, for almost the same reason, but with the twist of breaking the prisoner out of jail instead of killing her. He didn't know what would've happened if Paloma hadn't stopped him last time. He didn't know if he would be able to stop himself today.

"I'm behind you."

Alfie didn't know if she meant that literally or figuratively, but his shoulders relaxed at those words. He turned to look at her, but she'd disappeared under the cloak again.

Alfie tucked the dragon back beneath his robes and turned to the door. "Thank you, Finn."

"You say that too much."

Alfie shook his head before turning the knob and peering out the door. The tight hall was empty, the men long finished bringing in the food from the cart.

His true face hidden by Finn's magic, he stepped out the door and shut it after he felt Finn move past him beneath the cloak. The corridor was empty, no dueños to look at him and wonder who he might be, no guards to avoid. A stroke of luck.

Alfie lifted a foot to take a step when a voice barked, "You there!"

Alfie froze. Finn cursed under her breath beside him.

The prince turned and regarded the guard with his most dueño-like expression. "Yes."

"Did you get lost? You're the one they sent to perform the service, yes?" he asked.

Alfie stared at him, frozen in panic. Finn elbowed him in the side.

"Sí, of course. The service," Alfie said. "In old age one becomes forgetful."

The guard regarded Alfie strangely before saying, "Follow me."

Alfie swallowed thickly before following the guard down the stone corridor. He would do what this man said quickly, then he and Finn would get back to the plan.

Alfie started when her breath tickled his ear.

"Shall I knock him out and stuff him in a closet?"

"Do. Not," Alfie murmured. "And stay close."

In the silence, Alfie could swear that he heard Finn roll her eyes.

THE SERVICE

Alfie internally cursed as the guard led him down a path of twists and turns through the prison's ground floor. It was difficult to keep track of where they were going.

If only he'd waited an extra moment in the closet with Finn, then maybe this guard wouldn't have spotted him. Now they were wasting time going to whatever "service" this guard thought Alfie was supposed to perform. They were supposed to be headed to the center of the tower to lay the distraction and then to Xiomara's cell on the eighth floor, but now the guard was leading them through the outermost ring of the ground floor. They didn't have time for this.

Alfie walked stiffly, the pain of the magic sinking deeper as the day wore on. He felt Finn following beside him, the vanishing cloak brushing him as she moved. He knew she was doing that on purpose, to remind him that she was still with him. With every flick of the cloak he felt a burst of comfort. He wasn't alone.

The guard led them up a wide flight of stairs, through a pair of double doors and into a sweeping chamber that was well lit with ensconced, enchanted flames. At the chamber's center was a dais. A man was lying on it. A group of people dressed in black stood below the raised dais. Alfie swallowed.

A funeral. He'd agreed to officiate a funeral.

When Alfie stood at the foot of the dais, his shadow fell still at his feet, his whole being coming to a halt at what he saw before him.

He knew this man.

An anger fierce and unyielding singed him from the inside out. He ground his heels into the floor to stop himself from lunging at the corpse.

"Marco Zelas." Alfie stared at the face that he remembered as the young and vibrant son of a noble family. He'd laughed loudly and taught Alfie his first swear word. Then he'd helped plan the coup that had taken Dez from him. Alfie's fingers curled into fists, his nails biting into his skin. The graze of Finn's shoulder against him pulled him back to the present, and he wondered if she'd done that by accident or because she knew he needed someone to remind him to keep himself in check.

"Sí, Marco Zelas," the guard said, impatient. The guard motioned at the group of people standing beyond the dais. Alfie recognized each one. Marco's mother, father, and two brothers. Their faces were drawn and somber. "You're to perform the service for the family, as ordered by Queen Amada."

Alfie flinched at his mother's name. Prisoners did not receive proper blessings, but Marco's mother and his mother had been friends. Alfie could imagine his mother offering her friend this one piece of solace, but he did not want to bless this body and ready it for the afterlife. He wanted to let it rot in the sun. How dare Marco

Zelas lie there peacefully when Alfie was left alive to twist and writhe under the grief of all he'd lost? Alfie was afraid to even open his mouth. He might curse this maldito body and ruin his disguise.

Alfie couldn't look away from Marco's blank, gaunt face. He still couldn't understand why he'd been a part of the coup. What had he had to gain? Marco had been wealthy beyond most people's wildest dreams. Why did he need more power so badly that he would have Dez killed to get it? There had to be something else going on. Something bigger.

As Alfie asked that question over and over again in his mind, and as his desperation to know grew within him, he felt the dragon burn hot beneath his robes. Pain tore through him.

In Alfie's mind's eye flashed the image of a tattoo on the inside of a man's wrist—the menacing face of a bull, its sharp horns jutting forward.

With a sharp intake of breath, Alfie resurfaced, awash with pain. He'd asked, and so the magic began to answer him. What had the black magic shown him? Someone with a tattoo of horns on his inner wrist? Who was he? Why did he want his brother dead?

A pair of gentle hands on his arm startled him. It was Marco Zelas's mother, grief hanging over her like a veil. Her ink-black dress swallowed her spindly frame. Alfie hadn't remembered her being so frail.

"Thank you so much for doing this for our family," she said, her eyes wet at the corners. She bowed and brought Alfie's hands to her forehead, a greeting of respect for dueños. "My boy did things that weren't right. He deserved to die here, but he is still mi hijo. Please, send him on as you would anyone else." Her hands were shaking, and Alfie felt the billowing flame of anger within him flicker and dwindle. He hated when that happened. He wanted so badly to hold on to his fury, to stoke it. Why did it feel like he was betraying Dez whenever he tried to let go?

"Of course, señora," Alfie said, making his voice as low and soft as the dueños he'd heard. She started sobbing outright then. Alfie knew it was inappropriate for a dueño to hug someone, so he stood, stiff backed, his throat burning at the sound of a mother grieving her son. It sounded too much like his own mother. One of her sons stepped forward to the dais and took her by the shoulders.

"Thank you for this," he said, leading his mother back to the seating area.

Alfie's mind spun, not knowing what disaster of the moment to focus on. There was the fact that performing this service was wasting his time, that he and Finn should be carrying out their plan to break out Xiomara instead of being here. Then there was the terrible fury building within him, telling him to curse Marco Zelas's dead body in front of his family. He gritted his teeth, wishing he could release the turmoil burning inside him.

When the guard looked at him pointedly, Alfie cleared his throat and dipped one finger in the bowl of ash on the dais and dipped another into the bowl of chalk. If he wanted to save his kingdom, he needed to get through this ceremony. With a tense finger, he drew a horizontal line of each across Marco's forehead. He hoped he remembered this right. "You were born at the crossroads of light and dark. The gods kindled light in your heart, stretched a shadow at your feet, and put destiny in your hands. You have reached your final destiny, and to the crossroads of light and dark you must return."

Alfie froze upon realizing what was supposed to come next. Cremation. Alfie was no flame caster, but the dueño the guard thought Alfie to be certainly was.

The guard gave a quiet cough behind him, urging him on. Alfie's heart hammered in his chest. He raised an arm, his palm facing the corpse.

Could he tell the guard that he'd run out of strength and couldn't cast a flame? Should he pretend to be ill and excuse himself? Every lie sounded ridiculous. He needed to light the body now before the guard got suspicious. He did not come all this way to be discovered before he could find Xiomara. His mind flailed, trying to think of something, anything.

A gust of pain swept over him, the dragon warming beneath his robes. Then, just beneath his palm, a flame caught on Marco's chest and began to spread. Alfie gripped the dais to stop himself from falling, from crying out at the ache that swelled within him, suspended like a note that never ended.

As the body began to smoke and blaze, the flames licking the oil anointing the dais, the family watched on, faces drawn with pain. The guard, a wind twister, guided the smoke up and into the vents of the chamber ceiling with practiced movements of his arms.

Alfie's body quaked as another wave of exhaustion swept through him. If he let go of the dais he would fall and lose the disguise Finn had given him. Sweat poured down his temples. They were going to get caught, and it would be his fault. Just as this magic was his fault. His hands slipped off the dais. He sagged sideways.

"Steady now," Finn murmured beside him, her voice anchoring

him to the present once more. His head pounding, Alfie righted himself and grasped the dais.

The guard cleared his throat and said, "I'll take you back to your usual duties now."

He led Alfie back into the prison. As he followed, Alfie swayed on his feet. But then Finn was beside him again, letting him lean on her shoulder.

"Keep it together," came her voice in a taut whisper. Together they walked, Alfie using her as a crutch while the guard kept turning back to shoot him strange looks. He must've looked odd walking with such a lean. From what he could tell, the guard was leading them inward on the ground floor, through the tightening rings of the prison and toward the center—where they were already supposed to be planting the distraction if not for the maldito service. His head heavy with exhaustion, he couldn't imagine climbing the eight floors to Xiomara's cell, but they didn't have a choice in the matter. Not with Ignacio running loose with that polluted magic.

Alfie rubbed at his eyes. His face tingled the same way it had when Finn had changed him. His heart leaped in his throat. He was getting too tired, and his face was beginning to shift back. He could feel wrinkles pulling taut with each step they took. He needed to get away from the guard and catch his breath before it was too late.

"Young man," Alfie said, his voice breaking and sounding too young for a moment. "If I might be so bold as to ask that you take me to the nearest baño. My bladder is not what it once was."

The guard grimaced and led him around a corner, pointing to a door. Alfie moved off Finn and walked in slowly to give her time to get in too.

"I'll be just a minute," Alfie said to him. When he shut the door he sped to the water basin and splashed his face. Finn's magic slipped from his hold and the old face in the mirror shifted slowly back to his own.

A coughing fit erupted in his chest. He put a hand over his mouth and took hold of the basin to stop himself from falling. When he pulled his hand away, it was spattered with thickened blood. His breaths came out in sharp wheezes, as if his lungs were pinioned, spread flat and unable to take in a breath. He spat clots of blood into the basin, its metallic taste clinging to his tongue.

This magic was going to kill him.

Finn appeared beside him in the mirror's eye, her hand pulling back the hood of the vanishing cloak. The look on her face told him that he wasn't exaggerating. This was going to be the end of him. Alfie stepped away from the mirror and pressed his back against the cold stone wall, his body quivering as he slid to the ground.

He had some control over the magic and it was hurting him. What would it do to his people if it went on unchecked?

Then there were soft hands on his face, halting the dizzy spiral of thoughts. Finn was crouched before him, her eyes locked on his.

"Hey, hey," Finn was saying over and over again. Her palms were cold. He leaned into her touch, too afraid to stop himself. "Look at me." When he said nothing, she gripped him by the chin. "Mírame. Count." She said it with a calm that spoke of practice, of routine. The surety of her gaze steadied him.

"Diez, nueve," she started, nodding at him to continue. He counted on, his voice feeble.

She took his hand and pressed it to her chest. He could feel her heart beating steady beneath his palm, so controlled compared with his own. "Slow yours down, meet me in the middle."

Her heart thrumming beneath his palm, Alfie closed his eyes and counted. With every count down his pulse slowed and calmed.

"You're okay now," she told him, and somehow her words made it true. He couldn't help but wonder when her words had begun to carry weight that could tether him to life as he felt it slipping so quickly from his hands. Whatever had caused it, he was thankful.

"I'm okay." He opened his eyes and nodded shakily. "Where did you learn to do that?" Alfie asked. When she squinted at him, he said, "Counting."

She stilled, her lips drawing into a tense line, and he knew without asking that this had to do with Ignacio.

"Given enough time," she said, her eyes on the wall behind him instead of his face, "you can learn to survive most anything. You learn to breathe when your lungs are too scared to move and you learn to calm before your heart bursts. You learn." She shrugged. "Or you die."

Her heartbeat was picking up beneath his palm, and Alfie's chest ached at her words. He couldn't help but wonder what else she'd been made to learn to survive. How much of herself had she hollowed out and cut away in that effort?

From the moment he'd gotten stuck in her door, his perception of her had been shifting, sliver by sliver—as if he stood before a painting streaked with dust and he need only brush his fingers through the grime to see more of it and less of what he'd thought it was. And he could not go back, could not replace the dust and see what he'd wanted—a ferocious, heartless thief. Now he only saw some-one who was risking her life for his own foolish mistakes. Someone who bore more scars than he could count, but still rose for another fight. Someone who, if they'd met in different circumstances, might be his friend.

Before he could stop himself, the words spilled past his lips. "There are some things people should not have to learn. At least not so well."

Finn's eyes met his and again he got the impression of some-thing unseen swimming beneath the calm of her face. With his hand splayed over her heart, his thumb had fallen into the soft hollow of her throat. When she looked away from him and swallowed, he felt her throat move with the act of it, sending a thrill through his fingers.

Finn said nothing. With a careful hand, she took his palm from her chest and put it down on his bent knee. Her eyes scanned his sallow, sweating face before looking at the dragon.

"When you were standing over that guy's body, your eyes went wide like you were seeing something I couldn't see. What happened?"

Alfie swallowed thickly, the anger inside him flickering back to life. "That man was involved in my brother's death. He used to be a friend of my family, someone we trusted." Alfie's jaw clenched tight at that. "I never understood why he did what he did. I asked for clarity and the dragon answered."

Finn blinked at that. "It just answered? Just like that?"

Alfie nodded, his head aching from the slight movement. "This magic, it's not like normal magic. . . . It just, it listens. Or it listened to me. It responds to desire without a word, without question."

Her eyes darted back to the dragon, her gaze wary. "What did it show you?"

The image of the strange tattoo flashed in Alfie's mind and he wished he could recall it now and see something in it, something that would give him a clue as to why Dez was taken from him, but he saw nothing new. Only the snarling bull and its sharp horns. "It showed me a tattoo of a bull."

Finn tilted her head at that. "A bull. Like an angry-looking one with its horns thrusting forward?"

Alfie stared at her, his heart beating in his throat. Had she seen some other tattoo of a bull or the same one he'd seen in his vision? He had to know. He reached hurriedly into his bag and pulled out the roll of parchment he'd brought to communicate with Luka. "Could you draw it?"

He unfurled the parchment, laid it flat on the stone ground. At the top of the page Luka had scribbled three lines of messages.

Everything all right?

Alfie?

You had better respond or I will go to Paloma this maldito second.

Alfie could hear the words in Luka's voice and wanted to laugh, but instead what rose in his throat was another wet cough. Blood splattered the parchment.

"Shit," he cursed. Luka would see this and think the worst, which wasn't far from the truth. Alfie quickly scrawled a note.

We're fine, hurt but fine. Don't worry.

Those last two words seemed absurd as he wrote them. With the parchment flecked with blood, worry would be the only thing on Luka's mind. But Alfie pushed that thought away; he needed to know if Finn was thinking of the same tattoo that he was. Maybe she would know more?

"Here." He handed her the black-feathered quill from his bag. "Draw it. Please."

Finn crouched beside him and on the lower corner of the parchment she drew the exact tattoo that the dark magic had shown him, from the black eyes to the froth pooling in the bull's curled lips. As she used the quill, its black feather began to whiten at the tip with the release of the ink.

"Yes," he said, his voice hushed. "That's it. Do you know anything about it?"

"I don't know a thing, but the mobster who blocked my *propio* had it on her arm."

Alfie's mind spun. What could this mean? Was this some sort of organization that was unhappy with the royal family? Those involved had confessed that it was just a group of nobles, but if a mobster was involved, then it must be more than just nobles. He wanted so badly to know more. To call upon the magic and demand that it tell him everything.

The dragon seemed to hear and it warmed on his chest, pulsing as if it had a heartbeat of its own.

"Prince." Finn was staring at him, her eyes flickering between him and the dragon. "Don't."

"I just," Alfie said, stopping before his voice broke. "I just want the truth."

"We all want the truth, but is it worth your maldito life?" she said, and he looked away from her, the answer sitting sour on his tongue.

"I don't like this," she said with a shake of her head.

"Then we finally agree on something," he said.

Finn looked at the dragon for a long moment, then nodded to herself as if she'd decided on something. She outstretched her hand. "Give it here."

"Give you what?"

"You know what." Finn motioned to his neck.

"Qué? No."

"The thing's clearly deadly and you're too easily tempted into using it. If you wear it the whole time you're going to die. You're all shaky." When he didn't budge she gestured at the ground. "Look at your maldito shadow if you don't believe me!"

Even when he'd caught a deadly flu as a child and the fever had left his blood boiling, his shadow had never gotten this pale. It looked like a mere outline now, the shadow of a shadow. She was right, the dragon was drawing too much on him and he kept calling upon it by accident. But still, it was too important to be out of his sight.

"Finn, this is a dangerous thing—"

"*I'm* a dangerous thing," she said, insistent. "Prince, you brought me with you to help, so let me help! We've got to break out this prisoner fast if we want to stop Ignacio from turning this whole maldito city to dust! If you keep letting that magic sap you dry, you won't last long enough to even get to the prisoner."

Everything she was saying made sense. The night before when

he'd gone to bed, he'd taken the necklace off and kept it at his bedside. Being separated from it made him feel better immediately, as if he weren't as connected to it. He was sure he couldn't call upon it unless it was on his person, and since he was the one who could turn his magic black, he felt certain that he was the only one who could command it. He should just give it to her. If she carried it, he wouldn't accidentally call upon the magic anymore. He was entrusting her with his life, whether he liked it or not. He should be able to let her hold it for a little while, shouldn't he?

"Very well," he said, surrendering. Alfie slowly pulled the necklace off his neck and handed it to her. When the dragon fell into her palm he felt a strange sap on his energy, as if a piece of himself was pulled away from his body. He swallowed thickly. The Englassen book had been right; he'd truly bound himself to this magic, body and soul.

With a wary look, Finn pulled the chain over her head, letting the dragon fall against her chest.

Even though she couldn't turn her magic black to call upon the dragon the way he could, Alfie hoped that while it was in her possession it would, somehow, protect her from harm. That it would listen to her if she needed help. That they could both make it out of this prison alive.

"Finn," he said. "Just be careful."

Finn looked down at the dragon on her chest, as if daring it to try something. "I'll be fine, Prince." She extended a hand down to him. "Now get up."

Alfie took her hand and let her pull him up. She quickly reapplied the disguise.

"We let this guard take you wherever he wants, you stay there while I set the distraction, then I'll come back for you and we'll head to the prisoner. Then we'll set it off, get the prisoner, and get the hell out of here," she said.

Alfie shook his head and told himself it was the fact that she was carrying the dragon that made him so desperate to stay by her side. "The plan was for me to stay close while you lay the distraction in the center ring so that after we could head to Xiomara's corridor together."

Finn shot him a look. "Prince, you can barely stand. If we want to make it out of here alive, you need to stay sharp. Go to wherever the guard takes you and wait for me there. Try to catch your maldito breath before we go any further," she said, her eyes darting to his shadow once more. "At this rate, you'll be too exhausted to do anything when the time comes to trap Ignacio." She met his eyes then. "If we make it that far."

Alfie breathed a long sigh through his nose. She was right again, annoyingly so. "Fine. I'll wait for you."

Finn held out her hands expectantly. "Fireworks."

Alfie carefully handed her the shrunken bundles of fireworks from his bag—this was the distraction that Luka had come up with. Once the fireworks went off at the center ring of the tower, the guards would be drawn from their posts, leaving Xiomara's cell unguarded. They fit in her palm like marbles. In their miniature state, no one would be able to see them when they were placed. On the night of the Equinox Festival a grand fireworks show took place over the palace, so the storeroom was full of so many that the ones Luka had stolen would hardly be missed.

"These aren't regular fireworks you can buy in the Brim. These ones were meant to be launched from the palace roof. Be careful." He eyed her warily. "Just lay them throughout the center ring of the tower; do not set them off until you and I are together again, near Xiomara's cell, entiendes?"

If she set them off and he was down here on the lower floor of the prison, waiting for her, then he wouldn't have time to get all the way to Xiomara's cell at the top of the tower to break her out while the guards were distracted by the light show. If the fireworks were triggered early, this whole plan would be for nothing. He worried his lip between his teeth.

She rolled her eyes. "From here on out I'd like five gold pesos every time you tell me to be careful. I'm not an idiot, Prince. I won't set them off until we're in position. Now, are you ready to go?"

Alfie nodded shakily as he rose from the ground and leaned against the wall.

Finn pulled the hood of the cloak over her head, disappearing before Alfie's eyes.

After taking a deep breath, Alfie pushed off the wall, and opened the door. The guard straightened, grumbling about how long Alfie had taken in the bathroom before leading him down the hall. After walking down more twisting corridors, they walked into the center of the tower, where there stood a sweeping circular chamber as big as the palace's grand ballroom. This was where the prisoners were kept. Guards made their rotations, walking in circles on each floor of cells, stone banisters closing off the higher floors from the drop to the ground floor. And, of course, the prison's namesake was also here.

This chamber was full of an incessant ticking. Above this endless pillar of cells was the enormous clock. It took up the entire ceiling, glaring down at the prisoners like a ticking moon.

The groans and cries of prisoners swaddled Alfie in agony. At the sight of him in his dueño disguise, prisoners clawed at their bars, begging for forgiveness, for salvation, until a guard barked at them to keep quiet. Alfie looked away from their dirty, desperate faces. He felt Finn shudder beside him. The guard led them across the ground floor of cells, through yet another nest of twisting corridors and down a staircase. They were now on the lowest floor of the prison, just below the first floor of cells beneath the ticking clock.

The air suddenly grew sweltering. Heat clung to Alfie's face like a mask. He heard the clanging of pots and pans.

The guard led them to the kitchens of the prison, where dueños stood stirring vats of food for the prisoners. Alfie's eyebrows rose. Paloma had told him that to rise in the ranks, one had to do years of penance, but he had imagined them doing something with a bit more gravitas.

"I'll leave you to it," the guard said before turning on his heel and walking away.

Alfie watched the dueños silently cooking and ladling un-appetizing, thick stews into bowls for the guards to deliver to cells.

"I'll be back," Finn whispered beside him, her breath tickling his cheek.

"Be careful," he murmured. "And hurry." It shouldn't take her long to lay the fireworks, but worry still tightened his stomach. They'd already wasted too much time with the funeral and Alfie's rest in the lavatory. The longer they spent here, the more time the magic had to harm his people. He and Finn would need to move quicker than ever to make up the time.

He waited for her to demand five gold pesos for him telling her to be careful, but he heard nothing. She was already gone.

Only in her absence did he realize how part of him yearned for the sound of her voice curving with the punch of a joke—a sound that made her face bright in his mind's eye even when she was hidden by the cloak.

THE REUNION

As the darkness purred within him, hungry for the hearty meal ahead, Ignacio stepped before the bridge that stretched over the Clock Tower's boiling moat, his gray cloak flicking in the steaming breeze.

The two guards posted at the bridge's entrance startled at the sight of him, pulling their blades from their scabbards.

"State your business!" one said, brandishing his blade. "You're not allowed—"

With a flick of his wrist the man flew backward, skipping down the moat like a stone before sinking into the searing hot water.

The remaining guard watched his comrade shriek in agony before sinking silently into the depths, his mouth filling with boiling water. He dropped his sword and raised his hands in surrender. He was young, not yet twenty. Still a boy.

"Please, señor," he begged. "I don't want any trouble."

Ignacio stepped close to the quivering guard. He gripped him by the neck and raised him high off the ground. The boy choked and kicked, his eyes bulging as he struggled for breath. "Whether or not you want trouble is hardly important when trouble wants you."

Ignacio twisted his fingers and a coil of magic bloomed in his palm. He pushed it down the man's throat and watched him convulse in his hand. His shadow drew inward, his eyes blackened, and then he fell still.

Ignacio put him down and felt a sliver of new power squirming through him. He breathed a long sigh of anticipation. There were so many waiting in that prison to feed him. He could hardly wait.

A battalion of ten guards rushed across the bridge to apprehend him, but Ignacio made quick work of the men, forcing his magic down their throats as they thrashed and whimpered only to rise as extensions of himself. Many of them were too weak for his power and crumpled to dust before Ignacio's eyes, but enough of the guards carried the darkness as if they were born for it. They looked to him, awaiting his command. At the sight of them, the magic within Ignacio prowled and paced, yearning for more bodies to claim as its own.

Together, he and his newly minted men walked across the bridge. When they stood before the prison doors, Ignacio raised his hand and the bridge exploded in a burst of wood and smoke behind them. No one would be leaving this place without feeding him first.

The power of the men he'd just taken sent a prickling sensation through his body, leaving his senses sharpened once more. When he touched the handles of the towering double doors of the prison, he felt the resin that sealed the wood. He sensed the mice that ran through tunnels they'd dug in the prison walls. He heard the groans and cries of prisoners deep in the tower, begging for freedom.

Today their prayers would be answered.

He gripped the towering doors of dark wood. In his fingers they felt like curtains waiting to be pulled apart, to open and pour victory over his skin like sunlight. Ignacio tore them off their hinges and tossed them behind him.

He took one step into the dank prison and stopped. As his foot touched the floor it was as if he'd bonded with it, each brick an extension of his flesh. An awareness flitted over him, like fingers through his hair, like a spider over its web.

She was here.

In the tangle of sweat and sorrow that filled the Clock Tower, he could smell her on the breeze as if he were standing in a field of her, a field ripe for a long-awaited harvest. He closed his eyes and he could hear her heartbeat tapping out its stubborn rhythm, a rhythm he wished to conduct.

A smile tugged his lips wide.

Dark hearts, the magic reminded. *We must focus*.

Ignacio stepped into the prison. "I will do as you wish," he said, his smile sharpening.

But who was to say that he couldn't serve the magic and himself all at once?

THE LIBRARY

Luka accidentally tore the thick leather cover off yet another book. He gave a gusty sigh and let his head drop onto the desk before him. The sound echoed in the palace's nearly empty library. "Gods damn it."

All day Luka had been breaking things left and right, leaving a path of destruction in his wake. He wanted to tell Alfie about it, to ask him what it meant, but now seemed like a bad time to write on their shared parchment, *Greetings, it seems I've suddenly gained inhuman strength ever since you saved my life with the help of an evil magic. Thoughts?* He didn't want to distract Alfie, and, truth be told, he was afraid of the answer, afraid that it meant a bit of Sombra's magic lived inside of him, strengthening him.

This morning he'd broken the hourglass and yanked two sets of doors off their hinges. By the afternoon he'd broken a side table in Alfie's room along with an ottoman and an armoire. When a servant had come in with his freshly pressed clothes for the ball and seen the damage he'd done, Luka had said, "Do you ever just walk into your room and hate all the furniture?"

And now, while he tried to research Sombra in the library as Alfie had asked, yet another book suffered by his hand.

The quiet of the library made his skin crawl. On any day, it would bother him, but today, when he so longed for noise and chaos and distraction to keep him from thinking about Alfie, the silent library was the last place he wanted to be. But Alfie had asked him to do research to try to discover if Sombra had any weakness that would help him and Finn, and so he'd called upon the library attendants to pull every book on Castallano mythology that the library had to offer.

Two new books floated down from the shelves behind him to rest on the dark wood desk, sent by the only librarians who remained here instead of celebrating the festival like everyone else. The books opened before him and their pages fluttered open to Sombra's myth. Luka bit back a sigh in frustration as he read. The attendants kept finding more maldito books about Sombra, but each one he read held nothing of value. Nothing that he and Alfie had not heard before. This was pointless. All the while, with every passing minute his fear for Alfie's life hollowed him out, leaving a husk of panic in its place.

He reached for the warm mug of spiced cocoa beside the piles of books he'd stacked for research. When he'd arrived at the library, a servant had asked him if he wanted something to drink. Alfie would never ask for spiced cocoa, he found it too sweet, but Luka needed something comforting to calm his nerves, Alfie's boring taste in drinks be damned. He closed his eyes, letting himself fall into the honeyed taste of it.

"Prince Alfehr, it's been too long," a hushed voice intoned at Luka's side.

Luka choked on his gulp of cocoa at the sudden sound in the

library. He looked up to see the scholar who had taught him and Alfie Castallano history as children. The elderly man bowed and smiled down at Luka, unearthing a maze of wrinkles in his cheeks. He was a kind man but his lessons had put Luka to sleep on a daily basis. Of course he was here, in the library, the most boring room in the whole palace, in the whole kingdom too, probably.

"Hello, Maestro Guillermo, wonderful to see you."

"I am glad to hear that my favorite student has returned home at last."

Luka nearly rolled his eyes. Was there any teacher who didn't see Alfie as their favorite student? He longed to tease Alfie about being every teacher's wildest fantasy. But he wasn't here to be teased and made fun of. To roll his eyes and call Luka every teacher's nightmare. His heart sagged in his chest at the thought of Alfie and the dangerous things he was doing while Luka sat here, safe in the library. Would Alfie ever return to sit here and be boring in the library? To deflect Luka's jokes with a pointed turn of a page?

"I'm surprised to see you here, so late in the day. Should you not be dressing for the ball?"

Luka glanced at the library clock and grimaced at the time. He really should be getting ready, but dressing for the ball hardly felt important in the face of all that had happened.

"Prince Alfehr, estás bien?" Maestro Guillermo said, his face pinched with concern. "You look troubled."

Luka forced a smile. "Not troubled at all, only lost in thought. I'm doing some research on Castallano mythology," Luka said, trying to conjure Alfie's honest enthusiasm for all things book-related. "It's . . . riveting."

Guillermo's eyes scanned the books and their titles. "Ah, and not just any mythology; your and Luka's favorite tale as children."

Luka caught himself before he started at the sound of his name. He looked at the open book and grimaced. "The Birth of Man and Magic" certainly was no longer his favorite.

The elderly man leaned over and tapped the page. "You see that there," he said, pointing at the end of the tale where Sombra was turned into a mere skeleton, his bones spread far around the world over so that his body might never be made whole again. "Many scholars believe that is a mistake."

Luka's brow furrowed. "You're saying he wasn't turned into a skeleton when he was severed from his magic?"

"Well," Maestro Guillermo said as he sank into the plush chair beside Luka's, excitement lighting his eyes. "Most myths were told orally for quite some time before they were preserved with the written word. You remember this from our lessons, of course."

Luka did not. "Of course," Luka said.

"Tales told orally often change with each telling, becoming more ludicrous with each performance. Small, inconsequential arguments become battles of good versus evil, horses become dragons, it's quite fascina—"

"Yes, all fascinating," Luka said hurriedly, hoping to pull Guillermo back to the point. Maybe he knew something useful that would help Alfie. "But what about this legend changed, specifically? What do scholars think actually happened to Sombra's body in the original tale?"

"Many claim that in the original tale, when Sombra was severed from his magic, his body did not turn to bones, but to stone—a statue of sorts. Then the statue was cleaved into stone pieces and spread throughout the world over. In oral tales it's common for words to change into others, particularly words that rhyme. Stone and bone sound quite similar. Understandable that they would become interchangeable, no?"

Luka nodded at his former teacher, a frown tugging his lips. As if that would be useful, but maybe Guillermo knew the information that Alfie needed. Maybe Luka need only ask.

"Maestro Guillermo, in your studies, have you ever heard of Sombra having any weaknesses? Vulnerabilities?" When his former teacher stared at him, an eyebrow raised, Luka added, "Just curious, is all."

The elder man's brow furrowed. "Not that I know of. In every incarnation of the fable he seems quite invincible."

Luka deflated. "Yes, of course."

"He is a god, after all. They don't usually have any weaknesses to speak of."

Luka massaged his temples, resisting the urge to pound his forehead against the desk. "Right."

"But these are all just tales," Guillermo said with a laugh. "Nothing to be taken seriously."

"Sí, nothing but tales," Luka said as he reached for the roll of parchment from his bag. After what Alfie had told him, he would never believe that anything was just a tale again. And though he doubted it was what Alfie wanted or needed to hear, he should probably tell him about what Maestro Guillermo said about Sombra being turned to stone instead of bone, just in case. "One moment, please; I just need to write something down."

Luka unfurled the parchment, turning and angling it away from Guillermo as the man leafed through the books Luka had been studying.

Luka's thoughts fell into a numb silence at the sight of the parchment. It was flecked with blood. His best friend's handwriting was scrawled messily, his fear in every stroke.

We're fine, hurt but all right. Don't worry.

Luka swiftly reached to grab his quill and scrawl a message demanding to know what had happened, but his forearm toppled the mug of spiced cocoa, sending the thick brown liquid spilling across the magicked parchment.

"No!" Luka shouted as he tried to sop up the cocoa with his sleeve.

The librarians scouring the shelves turned to look at him, their eyebrows raised. One nearly fell from his ladder at the sudden sound.

"*Secar!*" Luka shouted at the parchment. He knew that the drying spell would not be able to save it, but he had to try. It was one thing to speak the drying spell to a soaked piece of cloth, a material that was changed but not ruined when wet, but to use it on a piece of parchment that had already begun to disintegrate was quite another. The parchment grew slightly dryer, but it had already crumbled to a mushy mess.

"Are you quite all right, Prince Alfehr?" Guillermo asked. He put a weathered hand on Luka's shoulder, his eyes wide. "It's only a piece of parchment, after all."

Luka stared down at the soaked parchment, his throat thickening with fear. There was a corner of the parchment that was damp with cocoa, but still dry enough to write on if he did so carefully, a sliver left intact. He had only a few moments to write a last message. The parchment's integrity was crumbling and once that happened the spell would break; there would be no way for him to reach Alfie. Luka took up his quill and carefully wrote.

Sombra turned into stone not bones. A statue.

His words cramped and small, the quill shaking in his hand, he added to the dissolving parchment, *Be safe.*

THE FIREWORKS

The giant clock above Finn's head ticked relentlessly.

She imagined herself jumping up and punching it with a stone-cloaked fist, shattering the glass and ripping its hands off. It was close enough that she might reach it if she really leaped for it. Blowing a stray curl out of her face, Finn abandoned that plan and focused on what she was here to do. She placed the final pair of shrunken explosions, which were no longer than her index finger, against the strip of adobe brick between two cells. The fireworks were tiny now, but once the prince set them off, they would pack a big punch.

Nearly half an hour ago she'd left the prince to recover in the basement kitchens and dashed up a steep staircase to get back to the ground floor of this dank tower. Here, stacked floors of prison cells sat beneath the heinous clock. After carefully placing bundles of fireworks on each of the floors, she had finally reached the highest one. Sweat dripped down her temples, her thighs burning from the endless flights of stairs she'd climbed.

Leaving explosives all over a prison should've been more of a fun occasion, but as she moved through the ticking tower, Finn could think of nothing but the prince. It was mostly out of jealousy, she was sure. After all, he was waiting for her eight floors below, stationary and calm instead of sweatily running up flight after flight of stairs. She bet there was a place to get cool water in the kitchens too.

"Lucky pendejo," she murmured.

But the envy withered away at the thought of how he swayed on his feet, his shadow shedding shades like a tree shed its leaves, left bare and vulnerable. How much longer would he last?

Finn blinked at that thought. When had she started giving a damn about the prince? This was his fault anyway; so what if he died? While that thought had once skimmed the surface of her mind and sunk in without a splash, now it clattered like something that no longer belonged there.

That renegade thought gave rise to others, like waves curling up toward the shore in a rush of froth and salt. She thought of the worry etched on his face as he'd given her the dragon. He'd bitten the inside of his cheek, his face falling lopsided as his teeth found purchase. The prince felt too much, too often, and though he tried to keep it locked within him, it always showed up on his face—in a furrowed brow, a flush rising up his neck, the soft indent of a sucked-in cheek. Just before the dragon slipped from his hand to hers, he'd mumbled something, his lips moving as if in prayer. And she'd known without hearing that it was her safety that he'd asked for.

Finn pushed the prince out of her mind and forced herself to concentrate on the task at hand. She needed to get back to the prince so that they could make their way toward the prisoner's cell before setting off the fireworks. They had a dark magic to hunt and this prisoner was the key to it all.

Finn turned on her heel and made to dash for the stairs on the far side of the floor when she slipped on a puddle of something and fell onto her back.

For a moment she saw stars. When her vision cleared there was a guard standing over her. At first she didn't panic; she was wearing the cloak, after all. It wasn't as if he could see her.

But he was looking straight at her. She moved slightly to the left, his eyes followed. She moved to the right, his gaze darted with her. How?

She reached for her head and felt only hair, not the hood. When she'd fallen the hood had slipped from her head. She was visible. Panic reverberated through her, as if a taut string had been plucked inside her.

She was caught.

"Gods," the guard said, "where the hell did you come from, girl?"

As Finn unsheathed a dagger from her belt, the guard grinned down at her and brandished his long blade.

He bent forward, his hands on his knees as if he were addressing a child. "What's a little thing like you gonna do with a little thing like that?"

Finn glared at him before snapping forward into a crouch and thrusting the dagger through his boot and into his foot. The man screamed as she leaned her weight on the dagger.

"I'm sure you know how annoying a little prick can be," she growled before giving the blade a sharp twist.

The man cried out again and tried to swing his sword at her. She ducked, pulling her dagger from his foot and punching him in the nose with the same hand. The yowling guard stumbled back against the bars of a cell. The prisoner within grabbed him, holding him fast against the bars. The other inmates began to cheer and point.

The prisoner choking the guard shouted, "Let me out, muchacha! Let us all out!"

A chant broke out among the cells, growing stronger and stronger as more prisoners caught on.

"LET US OUT! LET US OUT!"

The four guards on the other side of the floor were rushing toward her. The ones on lower floors pointed up at her, leaning over the banisters to get a better look.

"LET US OUT! LET US OUT!"

The guards were closing in from both sides of the circular floor. Even if she pulled the hood up, she wouldn't be able to get away without bumping into them. She needed a distraction. A big one.

The dragon warmed against her chest, pulsing like a second heartbeat.

Every set of fireworks she'd laid exploded in deafening *booms*, filling the tower with bursts of color.

Alfie stood beside one of the many kitchen sinks, slowly drying freshly washed bowls.

Finn had been right. Taking a break in the kitchen while she set the fireworks had made his spotty vision clearer. His head still ached, but the pain was dull now instead of piercing. Though he couldn't help but wonder if Finn was all right. He'd been left with the other dueños in the kitchen for longer than he'd expected. Shouldn't she be back by now? Then again, he reasoned, Finn was laying the fireworks on all eight floors of the central tower above him. No easy task.

Alfie put down his dishrag and worried the long sleeves of his dueño's robes between his fingers. He looked up at the stone ceiling of the kitchen and imagined her at the top of the tower beneath that maddening ticking clock, eight floors above him. He wished he could turn to smoke and float up through the floors until he hovered at her side like a weightless ghost.

Alfie gasped, tipping forward as pain moved through him in widening ripples. With gritted teeth, he braced himself against the sink. Why did his body ring with pain again when he wasn't using the magic? Was this just an echo from the last time he'd called upon it?

The raucous pops and squeals of fireworks rang out from above the kitchen.

Alfie stiffened. The dueños paused in their work, eyeing one another warily.

"Damn it," Alfie cursed under his breath. How could she be so foolish? That thought stumbled in his mind, incorrect. Finn was reckless, but she was also a sleek criminal who could probably nail a fly to a tree with one of her daggers. She wasn't one to make a mistake like this.

Had she set the fireworks off because she was in danger? Did she need help?

Alfie stood paralyzed, unsure of what to do. Should he use the distraction as they planned and go after Xiomara now or try to find Finn and make sure she was all right?

As the dueños began to call for the guards, Alfie dashed out of the kitchens, his mind made up. If the distraction was happening now, he needed to get to Xiomara's cell. Finn was clever enough to know she should meet him there. He worried for her, but it could not trump his worry for his kingdom and this dark magic. There was no choice, he told himself, and yet part of him burned with the thought that he was choosing wrongly.

The sweaty stretch of hallway beyond the kitchen was empty, likely because no guards wanted to spend the day close to the stifling heat. He was on the bottom floor of the prison, and the more dangerous the criminal, the higher the floor—Xiomara's cell was on the highest level of the prison. How was he going to get there before the fireworks stopped and the guards returned to their posts?

But then, there was a way. A risky way, but a way all the same.

Magic was fluid, it always had been. It was why when he'd said the words of a nursery song instead of words of healing magic, it was enough to heal Finn. It was the strength of the memory of his mother singing it to him when he was hurt that made the magic work. He had very strong memories of the hallway of the prisoner's cell where Paloma had stopped him. The memories were potent because they were painful. He'd thrown one of his greatest mentors against a wall like some monster.

He could remember it so clearly it was as if he were standing in that corridor again, his fists shaking at his sides. The guard he'd paid to sneak him in had led him up endless flights of stairs.

When Alfie was finally brought to the prisoner's door, only a pane of wood separating him from the woman who took his brother from him, Paloma was there waiting for him. Alfie's heart had sputtered in his chest at the sight. He'd been so careful. How could she have known about his plans? Then a wave of anger replaced the shock. How could she stand in his way when he needed this so badly?

As soon as they'd met eyes, Alfie felt filthy with shame. What was he doing? What would any of this do? With a dismissive hand from Paloma, the guard was quick to leave, stopping his begging that she not report him for sneaking in a prince. Then there was only silence between the prince and his teacher.

"Let me pass," Alfie had demanded, but beneath his steel resolve he felt a quiver of hesitation.

"If you are here for anything but vengeance," Paloma had said gently, taking Alfie by the shoulders. Alfie shrugged off her touch. "I will step aside."

"I am your prince. You do not give me ultimatums. Let me pass." Alfie stepped toward the door, but Paloma did not move.

"All true, but you are also my student. And a teacher's first duty is to protect their student." Her eyes softened. "Even if it is from themselves."

Alfie gripped her by the robes, pulled her forward, and threw her back against the door.

"I could make you let me pass," he heard himself say. It was as if someone else was in his skin. Someone blisteringly angry. Someone he'd never wanted to be.

"You could," Paloma said. "But I know you too well. I know the difference between 'could' and 'will.' Those words spell the difference between a good man and a bad one. The light and the dark. I know which you turn to."

Alfie slowly let his teacher go and punched the stone wall beside the door, the bones of his knuckles reverberating beneath his skin. He pressed the heels of his hands into his eyes. Why couldn't he hold on to this anger? Why was he so easily swayed? Why couldn't he do what needed to be done to avenge Dez?

Why was he so weak?

Paloma's voice came again, gentle. "I cannot stop you from whatever you seek here." She stepped away from the door, granting him a clear path to the monster inside, and Alfie burned with the need to throw the door open and let his anger run free. "Do what you must, and I'll wait for you here, for when you're ready to go home."

The word home *was what had undone him. His shoulders had sagged. His hands dropped from his face, and all the anger he'd been nurturing within himself for this moment wilted. What would killing this girl do aside from prove that he missed his brother so much it was driving him mad? He was already well aware of that. Though he hated himself for it, he just wanted to go home.*

When Paloma had taken him by the arm, Alfie let her lead him away.

He would have to use that memory to travel to Xiomara's cell.

To use this risky form of magic to travel a vast distance would be asking for death, but since he was transporting from one part of this prison to another, maybe he would survive it.

If he made it to Xiomara's cell, this time there would be no Paloma to stop him. This time he hadn't come for vengeance, but he wondered if he would be able to stop himself from taking it. And if this risky magic even worked, what if there were guards roaming the prisoner's hall? He did not have an escort this time to make sure the hall was clear, or a vanishing cloak. What would he do if they found him? And with his fading shadow, did he even have the strength to do this?

Alfie turned another corner and found a closet. He stepped in, shut the door, and leaned against it. He would risk it. He would try to transfer to the hall on the strength of memory and hope that he could pretend to be a lost dueño if he was caught.

He pulled the doorknob out of his robes and tossed it. It rattled before sinking into the wall. Alfie thought of that day, of Paloma and the door to that cell. Of his anger, his hopelessness.

"*Voy*," he said.

For a long moment, nothing happened. He felt no shift in the magic. Then the doorknob glowed with light. Alfie twisted the doorknob and the wall gave way to the threads of magic that he knew so well.

The magic pulled him in, jostling him painfully before spitting him out exactly where he wanted—the lonely hall with only one door. He landed roughly on his knees on the stone ground. Exhaustion swept through him. His face was tingling. He broke into another fit of coughing, blood splattering the floor. Fear trembled through him as he wiped his mouth with the back of his hand. The transport had been too much for him in this state.

Is this how it ends? he couldn't help but think.

Then he remembered Luka handing him that pouch. Alfie dug into his pocket and pulled out a vial of the healing draught. He tugged the stopper out with his teeth and downed the shimmering liquid in one gulp. A calming tingle rolled down his body, a small boost of energy he so desperately needed. He wanted to drink the other vial, but Finn might need it. If he ever found her again.

Alfie forced himself to rise and lean against the wall, his body in agony just from standing upright. He gritted his teeth and pushed the pain away. He must break this girl out of prison and put a stop to this black magic. Alfie took one staggering step forward. The hall was strangely silent. How had the fireworks stopped so quickly? Something had gone wrong. He knew in his bones that whatever had happened wasn't some silly accident with the fireworks. Finn must be in trouble. But did he have time to go find her when he stood so close to Xiomara's door? Would it be another selfish choice to seek her out instead of moving forward with their plan?

Alfie's warring thoughts quieted when he felt a strange warmth spreading through the pocket of his dueño robes, something wet. He reached into his cloak and pulled out the roll of parchment, but it was soaked to mush with something sticky and sweet.

Spiced cocoa. Luka's favorite. He must have spilled it. Alfie's heart sagged in his chest. The parchment was a sopping mess, and Alfie knew that it was beyond repair—the spell was broken. He and Luka could no longer use the parchment to communicate. But a corner of it had been wet, yet not so soaked that it was impossible to write on. Luka must've scribbled a note on it at the very last minute, before the spellwork fell apart. It was his final message.

Sombra turned into stone, not bones. A statue.
Be safe.

Alfie stared at the words Luka had scrawled into the wedge of parchment no longer than his finger. Sombra had been turned to stone? What did that mean when it came to stopping Ignacio?

"You there! Muchacho!" a guard called from behind him. He dropped the tray of food he'd been carrying for a prisoner. "What are you doing here?"

Alfie's hands flew to his face. There were no more wrinkles, only smooth skin and the features he recognized as his own. He'd lost Finn's magic after transporting.

The guard was running toward him, his hand moving to the machete at his hip.

Alfie raised his hand and shouted, *"Parar!"*

The guard's spine straightened. His body froze before falling to the ground, stiff as a board. Alfie rose off the ground and stepped over the guard.

"Sorry," he muttered, his voice rough with pain. But there was no time to stew in guilt.

Alfie walked to the door. In the Clock Tower, prisoners' magic was stifled and blocked, so there was no need for extreme precautions to lock them in. The door to the cell was simple. Made of wood with a strong, but easily magicked, lock. At least to anyone who was fluent in the language of magic.

Alfie stood at the door to Xiomara's cell. His hands shook at his sides and he couldn't help but reach for the flask at his hip. He could feel the anger bubbling up within him, churning in his stomach like a beast roaring to be freed. He did not want to feel it, did not want to surrender to it again. The tequila sitting cool in the flask would blur the sharp edges of his pain. He need only take a sip. Just one. He pulled the flask from his hip and unscrewed the cap, raising it to his bloodstained lips. The burning scent fell over him with the soothing softness of a blanket.

But before the tequila flowed over his lips, a sharp-tongued voice echoed in his mind.

Who you are when you're angry is still you. It doesn't have to be all of you, but it's a piece of you all the same. If you deny that, you might as well deny your whole maldito self and be done with it.

He could not remember opening a door and inviting the thief in, but she'd somehow nestled into his mind and made a home there. Her face bright in his mind, Alfie pulled the flask away from his nose. With a shaking hand, he put it back in his holster.

For months, he'd had been torn between the anger and hunger for vengeance, and the opposite pull begging him to let go of that anger, to move forward. Each side came with its own brand of shame that brought the flask to his lips to quiet it all. The drink blunted that battle within him, coating his mind in a numbness that removed the guesswork of which part of him was right or wrong. But he would not live that way any longer.

He was a boy who'd let his anger swallow him whole and attacked his own mentor, and he was a boy who'd watched Marco Zelas's mother grieve with the ache of empathy in his chest. These jagged pieces fought within him each day, but they formed him all the same, and he would need all of himself to get through this moment.

Fear coursed through him at the thought of being alone with this girl, with no one to keep him from giving in to a part of him that scared him so deeply. Finn had said she would be there to tell him when he was too close to stepping over the line, but she was nowhere to be found.

But then again, that wasn't what she'd said, was it?

If you do, I'll tell you and you'll decide to step back or dive in, but I can't stop you.

This decision was going to be his either way. He would depend on no drink or no person to hold him accountable. He would have to trust that who he was was enough to withstand this.

Alfie took in a trembling breath and leaned against the door to gather his strength. Then he pressed his palm to the lock. *"Abrir."*

"Coño!" Finn cursed as the fireworks erupted around her in a spray of color and sparks.

The guards looked about in shock as a monstrously huge firework of the great bird on the Castallan flag swooped over their heads in a surge of red, flaming wings. Dragons and other mythical beasts streaked through the air. With a yelp, Finn dodged a shooting star with a shimmering rainbow tail. It hit a guard straight in the stomach, sending him flying over the railing and down the ten-floor drop.

The prisoners were jeering in their cells as the guards ran about in a panic, shouting orders to no avail.

How had this happened?

The dragon pulsed against her chest again, as if in answer to her question.

The prince's voice bloomed in her head, soft with worry and confusion. *This magic, it's not like normal magic . . . It just, it listens. Or it listened to me.*

It made sense that it would listen to him; he was the one who sealed the maldito thing, after all. And he had that kooky *propio* color magic thing. But why would it listen to her?

"He's going to kill me," she muttered as she dropped into a

crouch to dodge a streaming yellow firework. She was supposed to go back to him, then they would set the fireworks off together when they were close to the prisoner's cell, not now when they were eight floors apart. At this rate, the fireworks would end before she even got to the prince, let alone before they got to Xiomara's cell. Without them as a distraction, how would they sneak the girl out of her cell? They needed her to even have a chance at getting rid of the dark magic.

"*Shit*," she cursed again as a guard ran past her screaming, his trousers alight from a firework.

Then all at once, it stopped.

The fireworks, like flaming bolts of colored silk, froze in place. The guards and prisoners too. The clock had fallen silent.

Her breath caught in her lungs as if they'd been sewn closed. She knew before he spoke that he was here, here to claim her once again.

"Little chameleon," Ignacio called from below.

Something within her that he'd broken long ago splintered into even tinier pieces, grinding into dust. This was always how it felt when he found her, as if part of her were crumbling ever smaller. With a lump trembling in her throat, Finn looked down over the banister. There, on the ground floor, stood Ignacio, smiling up at her.

"I knew we would cross paths again," he said. His voice was a whisper, but it echoed throughout the tower, as if birds flew about carrying his words. She could hear the sharp smile in his voice, the grin of a predator closing in on limping prey. Ignacio raised his hand and then he was floating up the open center of the tower to meet her. She couldn't move, couldn't breathe. He hovered before her and gripped the banister, his eyes black as ever.

"Why are you here?" she bit out. "Did you follow me? Why can't you just leave me alone?" She hated the quiver in her voice. Whenever he was around she sounded like a child again.

"I'm not here for you, Finny. Though this is a lovely coincidence." He leaned forward, beseeching. "Come home to me. Don't you see? Together, with this power at my fingertips, the world will be ours. What you saw with the strings, it was only the beginning. That was when I'd only infected weak men. But now, with all the men for me to take in this prison, I will have an army of soldiers, men dark enough, strong enough to carry the magic and not fall to ash. The magic will flourish and my power will multiply. Soon I will be powerful enough to take what is mine. Once I have it, I will wake a sleeping power, Finn—a god that will take the world in his hands and remake it as his own, and he will honor me for all I've done for him. I forgive you for that nonsense in the Brim. Come now, step into our future, Mija. We will wake the god and rule with him forever and always."

Finn gritted her teeth and pushed his black-veined hand away. "The only future I'm interested in is the one where you're dead and left for the scavengers to pick clean."

Ignacio's eyes hardened, all fatherly affection swept away. A silence trembled between them. In a flash of movement, his hand cracked against her face, a slap that sent her head slipping sideways only to have him grab her by the wrists, his blackened nails sinking into her skin. He jerked her forward, leaning so close that his breath ghosted over her nose. "I should've left you to become nothing with those fool parents of yours."

Finn froze, her body brittle.

Ignacio found her days after her parents had been killed. He didn't know anything about them. She wouldn't have him sullying the few memories she had of them by speaking as if he knew them. "Keep my parents out of your maldito mouth," Finn snarled. "What the hell do you know of them? They were dead before you found me. If they'd been alive I would've never been desperate enough to let you take me in."

"As usual, you're so sure of yourself, so sure of what you think you know." His grip on her wrists tightened painfully and Finn refused to wince. "Your parents were dead the day I took you in, yes, but that was not the night I decided you were mine. I was there the night you killed that little girl for the bread, Finn," he said, his eyes alight. "I saw your moving shadow, just like mine. I saw how you took what you needed and left her body in the alley. Then I knew you must be mine, no matter the cost," he said, lifting his shoulder in a shrug. "Your parents were hardly difficult to dispatch."

Finn's blood seemed to stop its flow through her veins, her whole body falling still at his words, at the memory of that night. It unfurled in her mind, like a bolt of silk stained with blood.

She'd been hungry, so hungry, and though they'd tried to hide it, she knew her mother and father were skipping meals so that she could eat what little they had. Her mother's cheeks had begun to sink inward, sharp cuts in her once round face, and Finn had decided that she had to help, do what she could for them.

She hadn't meant to kill the girl as they'd fought over the lone, burnt loaf of bread in the garbage outside of a bakery, but it had happened. She remembered the girl's chipped nails digging into her skin as Finn shoved her by the shoulders. Quicker than a flash of lightning it was over, and Finn stood above the girl's corpse with the bread in her shaking hands.

She'd come home, the bread dusted with dirt, her eyes puffy. When she'd handed the loaf to her mother, she'd knelt before Finn, concern rounding her eyes.

"Finn," she'd said. And when Finn refused to look at her, her mother had taken her chin in her fingers and gently tilted her face up. "Did you steal this?"

She hadn't stolen it, she'd done much worse, but she couldn't bring herself to say it. When Finn remained silent her mother had sighed, her warm hand dropping from Finn's face.

"Nothing good can come of that, oíste? Bad things happen to people who do bad things and I won't have them happen to you," she'd said, warning stiffening her voice. "We'll manage. Don't do it again."

Finn had nodded solemnly at that. "Yes, mamá."

Then her mother had gathered her into her arms and pressed a kiss to her forehead.

When her mother found that a piece of the loaf was soaked red, she froze before carefully cutting it off and toasting the slices for dinner. Only a few days after that terrible night, her parents had been found with their throats slit and Finn's life had been forever changed.

In the end, her mother had been right; bad things did happen to people who did bad things. Ignacio had seen her, he'd seen himself in her, and her parents had paid the price.

"You." She knew the word had come from her own lips, but it was as if she existed in a place outside her body, in a place of absolute numbness, a respite before the anger would rise and crash within her in a frothing wave. "You killed them."

"I did," he said. "I wanted a child of my own with *propio* like me, and I thought you were worthy, so I cut your papá's throat first. While he choked on his blood your mamá begged me to spare her, for her daughter's sake." He cocked his head at that, as if he'd told a clever joke. "How could they know what a waste you would be? How you would come to nothing. I did them a favor when I bled them like pigs."

Finn's teeth were clamped so tightly against each other she feared they would shatter beneath the pressure. Anger singed her insides as her eyes stung. With him standing before her, his lips curved smugly, her fury grew so powerful it snuffed out the sorrow she felt for her parents, cauterized the wounds in her heart until they were sealed shut. She needed to kill him. She needed to feel life pour out of him and leak through her fingers.

She wrenched herself free of Ignacio's grip and made to grab for his neck, to snap it in her hands. She was too furious to think to take her time, to make him suffer. Too angry to think of savoring it. But Ignacio only captured her wrists once more, a laugh on his lips as he dug his nails into her skin.

"There you are," Ignacio said, his eyes roving hungrily over her face. "There's my girl. The killer. You really thought you could just move on and become someone else? You can't change who you are, Finn. And even if you did, who but me will accept you after all you've done. Who would accept a killer? Who will believe that you can be anything else?"

For a moment, Finn faltered. With him standing before her, she didn't want to be anything but a killer. And he was right. Who would believe that she could be anything else?

But then she knew the answer to that question, didn't she?

I believe you, the prince had said to her, his gold eyes sincere and true. *I believed you then and I believe you now, even if you don't.*

If he believed, why couldn't she?

"One person will," Finn said. "And I'll get others. Not a maldito thing will bring me back to you." She gripped the dragon against her chest and it buzzed in her palm. "I'd rather watch the world burn first."

"So be it," Ignacio spat. He released her bleeding wrists and floated away from the banister until he hovered at the center of the circular opening beneath the clock. With a wave of his hand, the still fireworks began exploding outward, pelting colored embers every which way. Finn held her hands over her face to block the spray. They dug into her forearms like tiny, sizzling teeth.

The showering color painted him in harsh light, brought life to the fury burning in his eyes. "If you wish to watch the world burn, then I will burn it for you."

Finn dropped her bleeding arms from her face, barely registering the sting of the burns. "You asked for your own death the day you touched my family." The words curled her lips into a snarl and, for a moment, she could think of nothing but her mother's words. *Bad things happen to bad people.* Finn would make sure Ignacio learned the truth in those words. "I'm going to kill you."

He only looked at her, amused. "Goodbye, Finn." With a snap of his fingers life poured into the prison once more. Guards shouted and ran as the fireworks fell away, raining on them like burning snowflakes. Prisoners jeered in their cells and in the midst of it all, Ignacio hovered like an angel of death readying his scythe. Finn wanted to run, wanted to sink into the floor, but her legs couldn't move. They never did when he looked at her this way, as if a punishment swift and harsh were building within him and she deserved it.

He raised his fist. A knot of dark magic gathered above their heads. The guards and the prisoners alike stopped to stare, finally noticing Ignacio at the center of the chaos. He splayed his fingers, and the tangle of dark magic shot out in countless tendrils.

"Take all the bodies fit for our cause," Ignacio said, his eyes still on Finn.

The streams of darkness poured into the mouths of guards and slithered between bars to take the trapped prisoners as its own. Finn and the two guards who had tried to apprehend her moments ago stood paralyzed, watching as the dark magic curved around them to infect others. The dark magic zoomed past them and a handful of caged prisoners, as if turning up its nose at them. Finn had never been so happy to be snubbed as the prison gave way to the screams of the infected and the dark magic forced itself down their throats and into their hearts.

For a moment, the prison was still, teetering on the edge of total chaos as the fireworks disappeared from the air, coating the floor in smoky shimmers. Finn couldn't help but hope that if she stayed still, stayed quiet enough, the prison wouldn't tip into calamity.

Ignacio looked down at his legion of infected soldiers. A snarl unfurled from his lips. "Kill all who cannot house the dark." His eyes met hers. "Every single one."

The guard who was in the choke hold of a now black-eyed prisoner gave a shrill yelp. "Help me, please!"

Finn turned at the sound. The call was so pitiful that she reached for the same dagger she'd stabbed into his foot moments ago, but with a dry snap, the prisoner twisted his head sideways, breaking his neck.

When Finn turned back, Ignacio was out of sight, gone to muster his army, as if her death weren't worth watching. As if she were worth nothing, just as he'd always said.

The prisoner gripped his bars and pulled them apart with his bare hands before turning to Finn and launching himself in a sprint toward her and the uninfected guards.

"You've been calling his name," the prisoner crooned, just like the infected man in the pub. "Soon we will wake him. Soon he will answer your call."

More were following him, breaking out of their cells and whispering of the god they would wake, their eyes trained on Finn and the uninfected guards. "Those not dark enough to carry his will within them," an infected woman crooned, "stand against him."

Understanding snapped in her head like a whip. Those who weren't dark-hearted enough were turned to ash at the magic's touch, but others were strengthened by it. And with Ignacio's command, if they could not carry the dark magic they were marked for death.

Finn moved to run, but she was trapped. The horde of black-eyed guards and prisoners was closing in from either side of her on the circular floor.

"Shit, shit, shit," Finn said as she pulled another dagger from her belt. She and the two guards stood back to back, turning in slow circles, made sudden allies as the fiends drew nearer and nearer. How would she get out of this?

Then one of the guards grabbed her with his meaty hand.

"Take her! Take her and let us go!"

"Are you serious?" Finn shouted as she squirmed in his grip.

"Ladies first," the other growled as she was thrown forward, sent skidding to a halt before the horde of black-eyed monsters.

When two prisoners reached for her, the raised black veins wriggling beneath the flesh of their arms, Finn crouched down to the dead guard. She pulled the blade from his hand and swung at the infected men, chopping a hand away with a downward swipe. She could hear the guards behind her fighting the other side but could not look over her shoulder to, hopefully, watch them die after throwing her to the dogs. Finn gave another swing of the blade and a black-eyed woman gripped it in her hand, her face blank as the blade sank into her flesh. They felt nothing, knew nothing but the command to spread and discard the bodies that could not carry the magic. Finn's stomach turned as the woman let the blade sink farther without a word. Her hands broken and bleeding, the woman wrenched the blade out of Finn's grasp, letting it clatter to the floor. Arms swung at her, hoping to claim her as they did the dead guard at her feet.

Finn dodged and arched backward until her palms met the ground. She flipped back to stand beside the guards who had left her for dead. They started when she tapped them both on the shoulders.

"Cowards first," she said. With a twist of her wrists, the stone of the ground rose to hold the guards by their ankles. Unable to move and dodge, they were descended on by the black-eyed men in a wave of outstretched hands and whispers of a god to come.

Finn climbed up on the banister and hung off the side, her legs swinging over the long drop to the ground floor. She needed to get out of the way as the black-eyed prisoners pulled tight around the trapped pair of guards. If she was out of sight, they wouldn't come for her.

Finn saw a black-eyed woman grip one by the neck before plunging her hand into his chest, tearing at the skin sealed over his heart as if it were the gauzy wrapping on a gift. Blood burst out of him as he screamed and tried to push away only to find another monster behind him, pulling his arms wide, then back, as if trying to pull them from their sockets.

"Help us!" he shouted at Finn, but then both men disappeared beneath the horde and she could only see blood seeping across the floor from where they stood, as if a wellspring of red had sprouted from the ground.

Finn looked down at the ten-floor drop, her heart pounding in her throat.

She was too high to jump down and the horde before her would be finished with the guards soon enough. She needed to get out of here, and the maldito clock wouldn't stop ticking above her head.

Wait. The clock.

Finn climbed back onto the banister and dashed farther down it to where the minute hand ticked. Her pulse pounding in her ears, she stood on the banister willing herself to jump, but her body would not move. The drop swelled beneath her, dragging her stomach up to meet her throat, but she would rather splatter on the ground than be taken by Ignacio's minions. The faces of her parents flashed in her mind, flush with life—life that he'd snuffed out.

No, if she died it wouldn't be at his hands, it would be at her own, and if it was this jump that delivered her from this life, so be it. At least she might see them again.

With that thought in mind, she swung her arms for momentum and leaped. For a terrifying moment, her legs pumped uselessly over the long drop down to Ignacio, her hands grasping at nothing but air. Then her fingers gripped the wide tip of the minute hand from either side. She swung her legs forward, building momentum that made the hand swing from seven to two, to the other side of the floor where there were no infected waiting. She swung her legs again and jumped from the clock, landing painfully draped over the banister, her legs hanging out over the long drop. She scrambled over it and onto safe ground. The black-eyed monsters had converged on more victims—three prisoners left in their barred cell like lambs awaiting slaughter—but she could see their eyes darting in her direction too. They would come for her. She needed to keep them occupied.

Finn looked around. There were uninfected prisoners trapped in their cells, screaming for release. She didn't want to use the dragon, she knew it would hurt the prince, wherever he was, but she needed to find him and get him out of here. She owed him that. Finn gripped the dragon in her hand and imagined what she wanted.

On all ten floors of the prison, each cell door clattered off its hinges with an earthshaking boom. The remaining prisoners took off running and shouting for help. The black-eyed horde looked about like dogs hearing the feet of new prey, bounding after new bodies to exterminate. Finn watched two black-eyed prisoners leap onto one of the men who'd run out of his cell, pinning him to the ground before snapping his neck with a rough twist. He wasn't dark enough to carry the magic. Finn shuddered at the sight of his still body before shaking herself free of those thoughts. She had to hope that this would distract them long enough to find the prince and escape with the prisoner. She squeezed the dragon again, preparing to ask for its help once more, her stomach twisting with guilt at the thought of the prince curled over in pain, blood pouring from his nose.

"Lead me to him!" she snapped at the dragon, promising herself that this would be the very last time she used it. "Find him!"

The dragon gave a pull that led her forward and to the left, where a small passage took her away from the circular floors of cells down a long corridor. She hoped it would lead her to the prince instead of more trouble. But she'd settle for both.

The lock clicked open. His heart pounding in his chest, Alfie stepped in and shut the door behind him.

Then came a chorus of ticking.

The room was small, with a cot and a grimy waste bucket. There were no windows. Built into every brick of the cell walls were clocks.

She could not be placed under the large clock with the common prisoners, so they had made her cell a terrible reminder of her time left in this prison. There, sitting with her back pressed to the wall farthest from the door, her head tucked between her knees to block the sound, was the girl who had taken his brother from him. Xiomara Santoro. She hadn't even heard him, hadn't looked up. At the sight of her, adrenaline surged through him in a wave, numbing his pain and searing his body with unbridled fury.

His head ringing with the ticking, Alfie shouted, "*Silenciar!*"

The clocks fell silent and Xiomara looked up, shocked. She was smaller than Alfie had remembered. Had his nightmares made her seem bigger? She started at the sight of him before her and he knew she was wondering if he was some sort of illusion. Her face was gaunt and sallow, and her hair was shorn short, as if someone had hacked it off with a razor while she struggled. Her clothes were filthy with grime and dark circles rimmed her eyes. She stared at the prince in shock.

A deafening silence passed between them, one that carried all he felt; he need only tip it and let his anger flow free and rapid.

"Do you know who I am?" Alfie heard himself say, his body shaking with barely contained rage.

She nodded, eyes wide.

"Do you remember what you did? What you took from me?" His voice was teetering on the edge between cold anger and uncontrollable rage. He felt as if he might split in two and whatever crawled out of the tear would be someone else entirely.

She nodded again. Alfie's fingernails bit into his palms.

"Do you know how you ruined my life, my family's lives, in one moment? The future of our whole kingdom was forever changed! All because of what you did." She still said nothing, looking more alarmed than anything else. In three quick strides Alfie was upon her, wrenching her up from the ground and slamming her against the wall. "I don't even know how my father let you live. You shouldn't be here, because he's not here! He was supposed to be king, not me. History had eyes for him, he was born with it. Now everyone is left with me. All of that falls on you, do you understand?" When she still said nothing, Alfie jerked her forward by her dirtied shirt. "Answer me!"

She only looked at Alfie, a procession of emotions marching over her face, from fear to guilt to sorrow and back again. This was not what Alfie had wanted. He wanted someone who had no shame. Someone who he could justify beating to a bloody pulp. This scared husk of a person was so much worse. He couldn't take this. He wouldn't.

"*Say something!*" Alfie shouted. An anger-fueled burst of energy overtook him. He could live just a little longer if he could make this woman answer for her crimes.

But she only looked at Alfie, her dark eyes soft with remorse. She opened her mouth and pointed in. Her tongue had been cut to a stub. She was mute.

Alfie let go of her. She crumpled to the ground, skittering as far from the prince as she could manage. Especially horrible criminals were often made mute so that they could never speak a word of magic again. At the thought of the bite of a blade against her tongue, Alfie felt it welling within him, like sap from a tree—pity. He felt pity for this girl who deserved every punishment that came her way. Why couldn't he hold on to his anger? Why was he so soft that he could look at her and feel sorrow instead of fury? His mind had split in two, butting heads against one another—half of him angry at this girl and all that she'd done, the other half angry at himself for feeling even a drop of sadness for her.

Alfie massaged his temples. "Gods."

His hands were shaking and he wanted so desperately to be home spending a lazy afternoon in the palace with Luka that his heart ached. He didn't know why he ever thought seeing this pitiful woman would make him feel any better. And now he couldn't even exact his revenge. Now he had to sneak this cretin out of prison, away from the punishment she so deserved, to fix a problem that he himself had stupidly unleashed.

Alfie's hand traveled to his chest where the dragon should have been. But it was with the thief. He'd finally cornered the person they needed, but he'd let Finn's magic fade from his face, and he had no way of getting himself and this woman out of the prison.

Alfie dropped his hand from his face. "Listen." She cowered on the ground, knees under her chin and arms wrapped around herself. "I need you to come with me. Out of the Clock Tower."

She shook her head vigorously. Why would she want to stay here?

"You're not allowed to tell me no." There was so much steel in his voice that he almost didn't recognize it. "You owe me, owe this kingdom. And I need your help. If you help me, you'll save countless lives." She stopped shaking her head at that. "You can consider it penance for what you've done. Do you understand?" When she still looked too stunned to respond, Alfie added, "Whether you do or don't, you're coming with me, so you may as well nod."

She nodded. Alfie could see symbols carved into her scarred wrists. Written spellwork to stifle the magic within her. Alfie wondered how many times those markings had been redone. How many times the same wounds were reopened and drawn. The magic could have been written in ink, Alfie knew. It needn't be carved into the skin so painfully. He chided himself for that moment of sympathy. He wouldn't allow himself to feel sorry for this girl.

He still had no idea how he would get them out. All his plans had included using the vanishing cloak and Finn's *propio*. But she was gone. He didn't even know if she was safe. Or alive.

Then a wedge of pain splintered his body, hot and searing. Alfie cried out, gripping the wall as another *boom* blasted beneath his feet— the sound of steel clattering against stone. The sound of trouble.

THE GREAT ESCAPE

Spots of light dotted Alfie's vision as he groaned in pain.

Agony tore through him in three waves that left his legs shaking. Why was this happening? He wasn't using the dragon, yet the pain rippled through him as if he were calling on Sombra's magic over and over again. Had he used it one too many times and now could it sap the life from him whenever it pleased?

Even from within this isolated cell, the prison had suddenly boomed with sound around him. He could hear people shouting in commotion, the pounding of too many feet. If it wasn't absolutely absurd, Alfie would think that all the prisoners had been released from their cells.

Whatever it was, he had a feeling that it had to do with Finn. He turned back to the prisoner, forcing himself to stand tall as a cold sweat seeped down his forehead. The prisoner still stared up at him in fear, but beneath that was a flash of concern as her eyes raked over him, silently asking what was wrong with him. He scowled at her. She was supposed to be heartless, she wasn't supposed to look at him with worry. Whatever worry she had, he did not want it.

"We are leaving," Alfie said, his voice coming out weaker than he wanted. When the prisoner didn't move he leveled her with a glare. "*Now.*" She got to her feet and tentatively stood behind him, but where was Finn?

He couldn't leave without her.

That thought gave rise to others, and he quieted them, telling himself that he had to find her because she had the dragon; without it his plan would fall apart. Yes, that was why he must go after her.

Alfie turned back to Xiomara. "We are going to search for someone before we leave." Alfie opened the door and craned his neck about. There was no one in the hall aside from the guard he'd knocked out, who still lay stiff on the ground down the hall. "Follow me and do not try to run," he said, his voice unrecognizably tight.

Alfie stepped out the door only to collide with a body he could not see. He skidded sideways.

"Prince." Her voice came with a bout of heavy breathing, as if she'd just run up a mountain. Then she appeared, her hand pulling the hood off her head. When her eyes met his they were wide with fear, but beneath that there was something else—relief.

At the sight of her Alfie was drawn forward, as if the world had tilted on its axis to deliver him to her. He didn't know which of them moved first, but in the space of a breath he was opening his arms and she was stepping into them.

"You're all right," he said. Her curly hair tickled his nose.

"That's a matter of opinion," she quipped, her face hidden,

tucked under his chin. He could feel her breath against his neck.

Could she tell that it was her voice he'd clung to only moments before when he faced what he feared most? Her voice calling him a fool and telling him to trust himself, to find the line and choose to stay behind it.

Did she know that she was already in his head? He couldn't help but wonder, was he in her head too?

Finn pulled from his embrace with a jerk, as if remembering herself. "We've got to go!"

He looked at her, his eyes clinging to the worried set of her mouth, then her bleeding wrists. Her face was a shade too pale. "Finn, what happened?"

She squinted up at him. "You let my magic fade already? How has no one caught you?" Finn looked behind him and took a large step backward. "Is that her? Void girl?"

"Her magic is bound. She can't hurt us," he said hurriedly. "What happened to you? Why did you set off the fireworks early? I was . . ."

Worried, his mind supplied.

"Confused," he said instead.

"It all just happened, the maldito dragon!" she said. "A guard caught me and I needed a distraction. And the magic just listened to me, like you said."

"*Qué?* You used it? How?" She shouldn't have been able to use it, but that must have been why he'd felt such pain when she was gone. In a way, it made sense. But how could she wield it? The magic only listened to him because he'd dyed his magic black, made it think he was a part of it. Why would it listen to Finn? The realization clicked into place in the space of a breath. Alfie muttered a curse and kneaded his temples. Of course it had listened to her. He'd asked it to. He'd hoped as long as it was with her it would protect her, listen to her if she needed help. He'd been wishing for the best, not commanding the black magic, but it was connected to him and listened all the same.

"Coño," Alfie cursed into his hands.

"Then I released all the prisoners."

"*What?*"

"It was the dragon again, not me! Ignacio showed up and stopped the fireworks, I didn't have a choice—"

"Wait, Ignacio is here?" His hand fell from his face and found the bend of her arm. "Are you all right?" He looked at the dried blood on her wrists, anger rising in a tidal wave. "Did he do this?"

She looked away from him, her face drawn. "Doesn't matter if I'm okay or not."

"It does," he insisted, and he knew he needn't finish his sentence, needn't say that it mattered to him, because when her eyes found his, he could see her spotting those words on his face; they were clinging to his skin like drops of sweat.

"It doesn't matter, we've got no time!" she said. "Ignacio infected the prisoners and guards with the magic. He came here because the magic gets stronger when he infects people, but it only works on certain kinds of people, ones who can carry the magic without turning to dust. Bad people, I'd wager. So he came here. Once he's got this whole prison under his power, he'll be strong enough to do whatever you fear and worse," she said, her eyes shining with fright. "Did Bathtub Boy find anything out that can help us stop him?"

Alfie's mind sputtered as her words sank in. If Ignacio had already infected the prison, then his power now would make their last encounter in the Brim look like child's play. He'd tried to pull Alfie's bones from his skin then; what would he do now with the magic within him stronger than ever?

"Prince!" Finn said, gripping his shoulder. "Did Bathtub Boy come up with anything?"

His body numb with fear, he fished the sliver of dried parchment from his pocket. "Not anything that will help us. He sent me a message saying that Sombra's body didn't turn to bone, it was turned to stone, like a statue."

Finn stared up at him, her eyes lit with discovery. "Of course," she whispered. "What Ignacio's looking for is in the palace!"

Alfie looked at her, confused that a message he thought so inconsequential could brighten her face with realization. "What do you mean?"

"Sombra's body turned to stone, not bone," she repeated, her words hushed. "Ignacio is after those weird stone hands in the palace vault! Those are pieces of Sombra! We have to get there first and stop him from getting them!"

Alfie's jaw went slack as it all fell into place in his mind. That strange piece of a statue in the vault, the thing he'd always thought to be the least interesting among the palace's treasures, was a piece of the god's body. There were many fragmented pieces of art in the vault, salvaged from when Englass had attempted to destroy all forms of Castallan's culture. Alfie had assumed the stone arms were just another recovered piece of art from a time long past. But instead they were the key to begin to wake Sombra.

"We've got to get to the palace! Stop him from reaching those hands!"

Alfie's mind spun with diverging paths to take. If Ignacio had already infected the prison, he would surely be powerful enough to storm the palace. Should they fight him here, face him now, stop him from getting to the hands? Or should they go to the city and try to warn his people?

He didn't know what path was right—but the thought of Ignacio getting any closer to those stone hands made his stomach tighten.

"If he's here, then we'll face him here. Now."

Finn stared at him. "Are you out of your mind?"

"No," he snapped. "I'm trying to stop a man full of evil magic from getting anywhere near those hands and my family."

She pinched the bridge of her nose with her fingers. "I can't believe I have to be the maldito cautious one right now. Prince, what happens if we die trying to stop him, hmm?" She leaned forward, daring him to ignore her. "If we die, which at this point is very possible, no one will be able to warn your family of what's coming. No one will know to protect the maldito stone hands. I know you don't want everyone to know about what you did, but you've got to go home and tell them! Give them a fighting chance!"

Alfie blinked at her. Was that why he'd avoided the thought of going home? To keep himself from having to admit his mistake? Alfie swallowed down his shame and left it for another time. She was right. They needed to go home.

Already knowing that she was right, Finn took the vanishing cloak off and tossed it at the prisoner. "Put that on! We can't have a guard killing you on sight when we get to the palace." Then Finn turned to Alfie expectantly. "Use the dragon and transport the three of us to the palace. It's our best shot of getting out of here alive!"

Alfie could only look at her in dismay. With his head already swimming from Finn's use of the dragon, he could not imagine what kind of pain would tear through him if he tried to transport just him and Finn, let alone the prisoner too. He didn't know if he would survive it.

"It might kill you if you try, right?" Finn said, voicing his thoughts. Her eyes scanned him and he could see her tallying the signs of his weakness—his unsteady stance, the remnants of a nosebleed staining his sleeve, the flash of blood on his teeth.

Alfie nodded.

"Then we find another way," she said, resolute.

The quickness with which she abandoned that plan for his sake and his sake alone struck him like a blow, but the sound of a barrage of feet pounding closer and closer drew Alfie's attention away.

Finn grabbed his arm and the prisoner's, dragging them forward. "Come on!"

Together they ran down the hall, Alfie's head pounding in exhaustion with every step. Finn's tight grip on his arm was the only thing that tethered him to the present. Behind them a horde of black-eyed prisoners and guards poured into the hall. The tightness of the corridor made them fall over each other, trampling one another in the process. They moved down the hall in a squirming mass of tangled limbs, their black-nailed hands reaching out for them. But this time, some of the hands were stained with fresh blood. Alfie's stomach tightened.

"Don't look back!" Finn barked at him.

With her dragging them forward, they raced down the corridor to a fork in the hall; one way led up a spiral staircase, the other down a curving hall.

"Which way?" Finn asked, her head swiveling between the two options.

Alfie had opened his mouth to speak when a hand gripped him by the ankle and pulled. His face slammed against the stone as he was yanked backward. A black-eyed prisoner had scuttled out of the horde to grab his leg and drag him backward to the mob that swelled behind them.

Panic surging through him, Alfie flipped onto his back and kicked the prisoner in the face. He felt the man's nose break beneath his shoe, but the prisoner wouldn't let go, didn't even seem to take notice. He only pulled Alfie's ankle with his cold fingers.

A hand grabbed Alfie by the wrist. Standing over him was a wide-eyed Xiomara, holding on to him with all her strength. Their eyes met and even in such a chaotic moment, Alfie saw a remorse in her that scorched him from the inside out. He felt sick at the thought that he'd rather have been dragged back into those bloodstained hands than have her save him, touch him. How much of him had this eclipsed if he would rather die than be saved by her?

Finn unsheathed a dagger and leaped over Alfie. With a slash she cut the man's fingers from his grasping hand. Then Finn kicked him hard under the chin, sending him rolling backward.

Alfie stood, unsteady on his feet, when he noticed Xiomara's hand was still tight about his wrist. He wrenched himself free and a flash of hurt flickered in her eyes.

"Come on!" Finn shouted. She grabbed Alfie by the arm and led him back to the fork in the hall. She made the decision without asking this time and pulled him up the stairs, Xiomara lagging behind.

Then the man who'd grabbed Alfie's ankle had closed in on them once more. This time he leaped at Xiomara as she sprinted toward the stairs, sending them both rolling down the hall opposite the staircase.

Xiomara kicked at the man as his bloody hand wrapped around her neck.

"We have to help her!" Alfie heard himself say, annoyed at his own words. But as Alfie made to race back down the stairs, the mob poured into the fork between the stairs and the hallway, their hands reaching for Alfie. For a moment, he could see Xiomara struggling beneath the man who had leaped at her. Her arms were extended, holding him back by the shoulders as he squeezed her neck with his bleeding hand. She met Alfie's eyes, looking as if she desperately wanted to tell him something. Then she quickly gripped at the ground behind her and pulled something up over her head. She disappeared beneath the vanishing cloak.

"Let's go!" Finn shouted, gripping him by his shirt and pulling him up the stairs. "She's done for!"

"No!" he shouted, fighting Finn's pull. What was the point of any of this if they lost her? But Finn would not release him. She dragged him up the stairs as the mob began to squeeze its way into the tight stairwell, their mass squirming forward as they trampled over one another, fighting to get to them first.

Together they reached a wooden door at the top of the stairs. Finn shoved Alfie through it. A sweltering breeze hit Alfie's face. They were on the roof of the towering prison, the hot sun nearly disappearing beneath the horizon. Finn stood before the stairwell's doorway. She spread her arms wide, and with shaking fingers she made a pulling motion, drawing her elbows toward her sides. Then, with a grunt of effort, her hands met before her in a clap. The stone stairwell collapsed in on itself, becoming nothing but a blockade of rock.

Alfie dropped to his knees before it, his chest heaving.

"We have to find her," he heard himself say, his voice frayed, broken. "We can't leave without her, we can't. Finn—"

"No," she said, gripping him hard by the shoulders. "We need to get out of here."

Alfie pushed against her, but her resolute stare stopped him. He hung his head.

"*Prince*. Prince, look at me." Alfie raised his head, his throat burning. What would they do now? How would they trap the magic without that girl?

"Do you think we could use the dragon to transport the two of us?" she asked.

Alfie wasn't sure. The dragon had wrung him dry, taking nearly every drop of strength he had to offer, but they didn't have much of a choice, did they?

"I can try." He held out his hand. It would likely kill him, but he had to try. "Give it to me."

Finn froze, her eyes wide.

The realization struck him square in the chest. "The dragon was in the cloak pocket, wasn't it?"

Finn nodded. Xiomara had it. If she was still alive, that is. In the silence he could hear the rock shifting in the collapsed stairwell.

Those creatures were still coming, and they had no way off this forsaken tower.

Alfie ran a shaking hand through his hair before walking to the edge of the roof. A staggering drop and a boiling moat stared up at him.

He'd been foolish enough to wonder if he could become a king who would change his kingdom for the better, a king who would be different from the way Finn had described them—a foot hovering overhead to stamp her into dust. Instead, he'd destroyed Castallan with his carelessness, and maybe the rest of the world too.

Alfie crouched down and sat at the edge, his legs swinging over the open air. Before him the sky was a spill of pink and orange as the sun set. He would find the view beautiful if not for the circumstances. Soon night would fall, the ball would begin, and he would be here, waiting to die. "Well, that's it, then."

It was over. The horde was going to dig through the rubble Finn had made. It was only a matter of time, and there was no way out of here. No way home. No way to stop the magic from destroying everything he knew.

"I could try to make a bridge of rock to walk down or something, but . . ." Finn plopped herself down next to him. "But collapsing a hall of stone is one thing; holding things up for us to walk on all the way down is another. I don't think I could hold it. And you haven't got the energy to do some fancy magic, do you?"

Alfie shook his head.

"Prince." She looked at him as if she had already resigned herself to her fate, as if the decision had been made ages ago but she was only just letting him know now. He knew what she would say.

He shook his aching head. "No."

"You should try to transport yourself home. The regular way. With your doorknob."

Alfie looked at her, shame welling up inside him like sap from a tree. "You think I would leave you here to die?"

Finn shrugged. "It's the smart thing to do."

Alfie desperately wanted to go home, to run to his family and hide from what he'd done. But his mouth would never move to say those words of magic.

"It's the wrong thing to do. I won't leave you here, Finn."

"People leave each other behind all the time," she said, her gaze pointed ahead at the horizon.

"Not me," Alfie said. If this dark magic took the world and everything he knew, it wouldn't take who he was as well. "Not today."

Finn's eyes flashed at the sound of her own words coming from his mouth. "I give you permission to go. I absolve you of whatever guilt you're building in your head. Ignacio wants me, then he's going to head to the palace for the stone hands. I can stall him. You've got to go warn them. You have to go home, with or without me."

There was truth in her words, but still, Alfie could not move. "I won't leave you."

"I'm not your family!" Finn shouted at him, her eyes shining as she rounded on him. "Don't be stupid. Protect them while you still can! If I had mine, if they were still here, if Ignacio hadn't—" She turned away from him then, her chest heaving. They'd never spoken about her family, about who beyond Ignacio had called her their kin, and Alfie had a feeling that she'd lost them in the worst way—early and painfully. His heart ached at the thought. He'd lost Dez and he still couldn't fathom losing more. "Just go. Leave me here."

He knew not to reach for her even though her body seemed to beg for comfort. So he hoped his words could replace touch, could double as a warm arm about the shoulders, a hand cradling the back of her head. "I love my family with all my heart," he said. "But they would scarcely forgive me for leaving someone behind for my own gain. For leaving behind a friend," he corrected himself. "I'm not going anywhere."

First her face held nothing but confusion and surprise, as if she'd stepped outside expecting a summer day only to find a snowstorm, but swimming beneath the surface was something more.

"You're an idiot." The sharpness of her words clashed with the softness of her voice.

He couldn't help but smile at that. "So you've said."

Silence fell between them, smooth as silk, but Alfie did not want his final moments to be spent in silence, inside his own head. He'd spent too much of his life there, wrapped up in tangles of worries.

Instead, he asked the first question that popped into his head. "Is your last name really Voy?"

She gave a snort. "No. I used to be Finn Santiago. After my parents died I wanted a fresh start. And I wanted to go everywhere, see everything. So I settled on Voy."

Voy, the very word for travel in magic's tongue. The word he used to move through the magic that bound this world.

It was strange to think that he'd been saying her name each time he used his *propio*. As if he'd been carrying her with him, or maybe she'd been carrying him forward, the same way she did today when her words had spurred him on when he stood before Xiomara's door.

It felt as if there was a strange string of destiny that had been tugging him toward her. He was only sorry that it would end this way.

"You still have that flask on you?" she asked, her eyes back on the horizon.

Alfie grabbed the flask from his hip and took a stinging sip of the tequila before passing it to her. She took a swig, and his eyes were drawn to the subtle movement of her throat as she swallowed. He remembered when she'd held his palm to her chest, just over her beating heart, and how his thumb fell to the soft dip at the base of her throat. Drops spilled when she pulled the flask away.

Alfie told himself that it was the alcohol and the inevitability of their deaths that made him do it, but when a drop of tequila clung to her upper lip, Alfie reached out and swiped his thumb across it, his finger skimming the soft of her lip. He brought his thumb to his lips, tasting that final lingering drop of tequila. She watched him with a look that tracked heat down his body to chase the burn of the alcohol. It stung his tongue and for a fleeting moment he wished it was the taste of her on his lips instead of the drink.

That sudden bravery dissipated in a puff of smoke. His face grew warm. "Tequila mustache," he joked. "Waste not, want not."

She tilted her head. Her eyes spoke of mischief, of knowing exactly what he hoped to hide and shining a beam of sunlight on it. Alfie knew that from now on, the taste of tequila would not simply be a drink or a salve to rub over his wounds. It would forever be colored by the sharp intake of breath she took when his thumb grazed her lip.

A shrill whistle rang out beneath them, startling them both.

They jumped apart at the sound. It was only then that Alfie realized how close they'd gotten in the first place. They stared out over the prison grounds and there, across the boiling moat, was one of the horse-drawn carriages that ferried dueños to and from the prison. A lone figure stood behind it, waving both hands.

Alfie squinted, shock zipping through him. "Is that—"

"The prisoner!"

Xiomara had somehow made it out. The vanishing cloak must've saved her. Like bile rising up his throat, Alfie felt a sour, unclean version of gratitude well up within him. She could've just left, taken her freedom and started a new life elsewhere, but instead she'd stayed. His mind battled within him once more, sharp tugs pulling him taut between hatred and compassion, gratitude and fury.

"We've got to find a way down to her." Finn grimaced as she stared down the drop. "You don't suppose we could survive that jump, do you?"

Alfie shot her a look. "Define 'survive.'"

"Well!" Finn threw up her hands. "Have you got any bright ideas, then?" The rubble of the stairwell shifted and rumbled behind them. She winced at the sound. "And make it quick."

Alfie looked around the roof. There were a few swords and other weapons discarded on the ground along with old bottles of cerveza and tequila. The roof must've been a training ground for the guards that, apparently, was also used for social purposes. A thick coil of rope sat at the far end of the roof, collecting dust in the blistering sun.

"I've got one, but I'm not sure I would call it bright."

As the prince explained quickly, Finn nodded along, chewing on her fingernail.

This could work. Maybe.

On his knees, the prince tied one end of the rope tight around the hilt of one blade. He handed it up to her.

"Drive it into the ground with all your strength. Use your stone carving to make it secure. It'll have to hold our weight."

Finn nodded and raised the sword high, her fingers twitching to manipulate the steel of the blade and the stone of the ceiling. With both hands, she plunged the blade downward, and at her command the stone ceiling parted to accept it before closing tight around the blade. With a curl of her wrist, the adobe brick of the ceiling rose in a mound to encompass the hilt of the blade, looking much like an oversized anthill. The knot of rope was beneath the stone now. She tugged on the rope with all her might, leaning back on her heels. It didn't budge.

"Done," she said.

The prince had already tied the other end of the rope to the hilt of the second blade. He handed it to her with a nod.

Finn gripped the blade and stepped to the very edge of the roof. She would control the blade's descent just as she controlled those quilbear quills in the palace. But instead of sending fine quills to burrow into the necks of guards, she would be guiding the blade to the waiting carriage and driving it through the roof. Then they would each use part of Alfie's dueño costume to slide down the rope and to safety.

If she drove the blade into the ground beside the carriage, there was a chance that they would dip too close to the water as they zipped down and be boiled bloody before they could make it to land. The carriage would have to do. Finn just hoped the prisoner stayed out of the way. Finn could see her standing beside the carriage, still waving at them with both hands.

"Here goes nothing," she muttered. With a pull of her hand, the blade rose. She punched her fist forward and the blade sailed through the air, the rope tied at its hilt zooming with it. She curled her fingers forward and the blade followed her command, flying in a sharp arc before burying itself in the roof of the carriage with a distant thud.

"Wépa!" Finn punched the air in victory. The prisoner jumped in fright next to the carriage, but then she seemed to understand. She climbed onto the carriage roof and Finn could see her gripping the hilt of the blade, keeping it secure. Finn turned to look at Alfie triumphantly, but his eyes were half closed. A new trickle of blood oozed from his nose. Guilt wormed through her and she thought of each time she'd called upon the dark magic, how each time had struck him like a blow, and yet when they'd reunited and she'd explained herself, his face had changed, as if the pain from the magic had been worth it because it brought her back to him, safe.

Finn felt a spark of something within her, something that had been there for some time, but was only just waking from its slumber—something lush that raised its head and asked to be seen.

Finn buried it deep inside her and vowed to forget its face.

She crouched beside him. "Prince, we're ready to go."

Alfie nodded before wiping at his nose and slowly standing.

When he met her gaze he murmured, "I'm fine."

She didn't know what bothered her more, the fact that she'd looked concerned enough to warrant that sentence or that he was clearly lying through his teeth.

"You first."

Alfie shuffled to the edge of the roof where the rope flew down over the edge in a steep slope, taut with tension. He took a layer of his dueño disguise and wrapped it around the rope, holding it on either side.

He gulped as he peered at the sharp drop. The steam from the boiling moat sizzled beneath them. "If this fails, we'll be boiled alive."

Finn stared down at the bubbling water, a trickle of sweat rolling down her temple to hang on her chin. "Well, I've always been a fan of dumplings."

That stopped him short. After a beat of silence, a broken laugh parted his lips, and Finn was glad to hear it.

He did it so rarely that it felt hard-earned, sending a surge of pride through her. With her crouching beside him, she could feel his breath ghosting over her face and she was drawn back to the swipe of his thumb across her skin, of how such a quick touch had stopped her cold.

He tilted his face up to look at her, his gold eyes glinting. "That joke was so bad that now I actually want to jump."

Behind them the blockade of collapsed rock burst outward, pelting them with gravel. The black-eyed prisoners poured through its opening, crawling over one another to try to reach them.

"Then I've got great comic timing! *Go!*"

The prince pushed off from the roof and zoomed down the rope. They were supposed to go one at a time in case the rope couldn't take their combined weight, but there was no time now. No time to even sit and push off like the prince had done.

Finn leaped after him, her legs pumping through the air as if she could run the distance if she tried hard enough. Her stomach twisted as her feet left the safety of the roof. She raised the cloth from the prince's robes over her head, a flood of doubt pouring through her mind.

What if the cloth rips?

What if the rope isn't secure enough to hold the two of us?

Am I about to be boiled alive?

Time sped up. Finn fell forward, looping the cloth of the robes over the rope at the last possible moment. The cloth held, her wrists twinging with pain as the rope brought her fall to a jerking halt. She slid down the rope, following after the prince, relief running through her.

An unnatural shriek tore through the air behind her. Finn looked over her shoulder in time to see a black-eyed woman leap from the roof toward her at terrifying speed, her outstretched hands clawing through the air.

The prisoner wrapped her arms around Finn's waist, dragging the rope down.

"Shit!" Finn wriggled, trying to shake the woman off, but her grip was too tight. Her hands were slipping on the cloth as they zoomed on, picking up speed thanks to the extra weight.

"*Fuerza!*" she heard the prince shout.

The infected woman at her waist was blown back, nearly taking Finn with her. With a grimace Finn watched the woman careen down, slamming into the ground just beside the moat. She didn't have time to shout a thank-you to the prince. That woman's weight had done its damage. She could feel the rope dipping and sagging;

the extra weight had likely pulled too much on the sword embedded in the carriage roof. Finn could see Xiomara leaning all her weight on it to keep it still, but it wasn't working. The rope was still sagging.

"Shit, shit, shit!" Finn cursed. The rope was going to dip too low and send them straight into the boiling water just before landing.

The prince seemed to notice the problem. Before her, he swung his legs forward, like a child on a swing, and just before the rope dipped too close to the water, he let go of his cloth and let the momentum carry him that final distance to safe, solid ground. He rolled onto the ground in a heap of red dueño's robes.

Finn followed his lead, swinging herself forward with all her might and letting go just before her toes skimmed the water.

She flew through the air, but she didn't have the prince's long limbs. She didn't know if her momentum would be enough.

It wasn't.

As her flying leap began to arc downward, she knew she would be a hair short. She would fall into the boiling water just a few steps away from solid land. But then Alfie scrambled to his feet and leaned over the edge of the moat, snatching her from the air just before she fell to her death.

Together they tumbled down onto the dirt ground, rolling to a stop with Finn on top of him, her face buried in the crook of his neck, his arms tight around her back.

Pressing her palms against the ground on either side of his head, she pushed herself up and peered down at him, her heart pounding in her chest. "Prince, are you all right?"

His eyes still closed, Alfie's lips quirked up. "I'm not a dumpling. That'll do for now."

He looked up at her, his eyes crinkling at the corners. Finn felt the rumble of the laugh in his chest before she heard it. It struck her that right now, even with his skin made sallow from Sombra's magic and dirt in his hair from their fall, he still looked better than when she'd first met him in his clean cloak and mask. He looked best when he laughed.

Finn pulled out of his arms and stood, holding her hand out for him to take.

He took her hand and let her help him up. "At least I got to do the saving for once."

She reached up to brush the dirt off his shoulders. "Don't get used to it."

Xiomara dashed to their side, pointing back at the Clock Tower.

Black-eyed prisoners and guards were surging out of the prison to give chase. With no bridge, they leaped recklessly into the water and tried to swim through, their skin bleeding and boiling. The infected on the roof threw themselves off foolishly only to fall into the moat or splatter on the ground below.

"Let's go!" Finn said. "You two in the back." She shoved Alfie toward the carriage door when he went to man the head of the carriage instead.

"What? But I—"

"Prince, you're half dead. Get in the back and rest. And keep an eye on her." Finn looked pointedly at Xiomara as she scrambled into the back of the carriage.

Alfie opened his mouth to protest, but then Ignacio's voice boomed around them.

"*Stop!*" Ignacio shouted. He stood on the roof, his eyes locked on Finn's. Each of the black-eyed monsters pouring out of the prison stopped mid-run, awaiting their master's word.

"Let them go," Ignacio said, his voice echoing around them. "Let them warn the pretender rulers of what is to come. Let them tell the people that their true king will soon rise."

He cocked his head at Finn, a chilling gesture that she knew too well. Then his voice whispered in her ear alone. She could feel his hot breath on her ear though he did not move from the tower roof, *Run all you like, Finn. You know I love to hunt you.*

A shudder rolled up Finn's spine.

"Finn—" Alfie began, his voice tight with a concern that made her eyes want to search for the ground. Her throat burning, she shoved him into the carriage and shut the door behind him. She climbed up to the head of the carriage, jerked the reins, and guided the horses forward. She didn't dare look back, but she knew that Ignacio was watching her.

And smiling.

WORDS CARVED IN WOOD

As Finn took the reins and sent the horses galloping back to San Cristóbal, Alfie sat inside the carriage, his eyes trained on Xiomara. She squirmed uncomfortably beneath his gaze.

Xiomara had saved his life. She could have let that infected man drag him away, but instead she'd grabbed his wrist, her hooded eyes full of fear for him.

To add insult to injury, when they'd been separated she could have run away with the vanishing cloak, absolving herself of any responsibility, but she'd stayed and helped them escape.

She had saved his life. Twice. And Alfie had never felt so fiercely angry and confused.

More than anything he'd wanted her to be a monster, to be worth all the nightmares, all the anxiety, all the what-ifs. He'd wanted her to be uncooperative. And yet she'd proven the opposite. She'd been scared of Alfie but not averse to helping him, saving him.

Alfie hated her for it.

He wanted to fall asleep in the shaking carriage, to regain his strength for the fight ahead, but the turmoil twisting his insides kept him awake. He stared at the girl, his gaze hardening. She looked away from him, her face tight.

Alfie wanted to shake her into anger, into anything but this guilty and inexplicably helpful person. The sorrowful look on her face made him feel guilty for hating her.

Why feel guilt when she took Dez from us? he thought. *The only thing I should feel guilty about is letting her take another maldito breath.*

Alfie's hands curled into fists as his anger swelled. He should exact his revenge for what she'd done to him. What she'd done to his family. She deserved it, didn't she?

A bump in the road lifted the carriage off the ground, turning his stomach as it sped on with loud creaks. Finn's shrill curse tore him away from the whispers in his mind.

Alfie took a deep breath. He could kill her, he knew he could. But that wasn't who he was. And it never would be. He thought of Paloma stopping him from hurting this girl before.

Her voice echoed loud in his head, drowning out his thoughts: *I know the difference between "could" and "will." Those words spell the difference between a good man and a bad one. The light and the dark. I know which you turn to.*

He hadn't lost himself to the dark yet, and he wouldn't do it now.

Alfie's fists unclenched. The prisoner stared up at him, fear in her eyes.

"I want to make something abundantly clear," Alfie began, the steel in his voice barely recognizable to his ears. "Just because I broke you out of the Clock Tower does not mean I forgive you.

It does not mean I will ask for you to be granted clemency. It does not mean anything aside from the fact that something very bad has been released, and I need your power to get rid of it, entiendes?" She nodded shakily. Her fear only made him angrier. "Maybe if years had passed instead of months, I wouldn't be saying this. But I need to know why you did it. I need that question answered, because until it is I don't think I'll be able to go on with my life, whatever little of it I have left. I'm afraid that I might just kill you myself before we even leave. I need to know the truth."

Xiomara only looked at him, her mouth opening and closing silently.

He had no paper or quills for her to write with, but they would have to make do. Alfie pulled the sheathed dagger that Finn had lent him from his pocket. Xiomara skittered away, her back against the carriage door.

He held it out to her. "Here."

She took it in her hands gingerly, confused.

He pointed at the wood of the carriage interior walls. "You could carve it in the wood. Just try." He couldn't help but add a fervent, "Please."

Xiomara wished the girl hadn't left her with the angry prince.

The sun had set as they tore away from the prison, and now fledgling moonlight poured through the windows of the carriage, lighting Xiomara's pallid face with an eerie glow. She looked at the dagger in her hand. She hadn't written in so long, and even if she had, she wouldn't know where to begin, and she knew that whatever she said wouldn't be enough.

Should she begin with how she had gotten her *propio*? She'd grown up in a home where her father beat her mother bloody. Xiomara would sit in her room with her hands over her ears, a poor attempt to block out the sounds of her mother begging, then whimpering, then silence.

It was on the day that her father killed her mother that Xiomara gained her *propio*. She'd found her mother lying facedown in a pool of her own blood. She'd turned her over and felt all the broken things shifting inside of her, like a bag of shattered glass. Something within her tore open and never closed, something dark and empty, all-encompassing.

She'd spent all her life wanting to block out the noise, the violence, imagining that she could send it somewhere else. Her *propio* took that feeling and made it real. She'd waited until her father had fallen into a drunken sleep and beat him until he stopped breathing, then the house was full of still, bloodied bodies. She'd wanted it all to go away, to just disappear.

That's exactly what happened.

The vacuum within her became physical. A void of blackness opened in the floor, swallowed her parents whole. At her command, it closed.

Should she tell the prince about the months she'd spent on the streets, parentless and afraid of herself? Scared that she would swallow herself and the whole world if she wasn't careful?

Should she tell him about when her *propio* was discovered and suddenly some very powerful people wanted to take care of her, be her new family. How kind Marco Zelas's smile had looked when he'd wrapped an arm around her shoulder and promised to keep her safe.

So long as she did something for them.

So long as she helped him get rid of the royal family.

Should she tell the prince that her nerves had made it impossible to eat for weeks ahead of the planned day? That she'd been a teenager on her own and had let her desire for family and protection cloud her judgment?

These thoughts ran through Xiomara's mind in a matter of seconds. The prince was still staring down at her expectantly, his chest rising and falling rapidly as if he'd been chasing these answers his entire life.

Xiomara didn't know where to begin, but she knew one thing.

She took the dagger and slowly carved into the wood wall: *I want to make it right.*

The prince looked down at her words, his face inscrutable for a moment. Then he breathed deeply through his nose and gave one stiff nod as if that were enough. For now.

"Just answer me this," he said. "And please, please don't lie. I'll know if you lie."

Xiomara nodded at him, a lump growing in her throat. The prince took a deep breath. His voice still shook. "Did you want to kill him? Did you want to take him from us?"

The question made her chest ache. It took her back to that terrible moment. She wanted so badly to refute it that she opened her mouth to speak, but only a strangled cry came out. She shook her head with such force that her neck hurt. She felt her eyes burning.

"All right," the prince said. His expression was hard, but his gold eyes were tinged with sympathy. "All right."

A long silence stretched between them. The prince stared at the words she'd written, his gold eyes clouded.

"I know someone else who's been made to do things she didn't want to do," he said softly. Xiomara looked up at him, but he wasn't looking at her. He leaned his head against the carriage window and stared up at the sky as if he were searching for answers in the stars.

Finn had imagined her own death more times than anyone her age should have.

As the carriage zoomed down the sugarcane-lined road, whipping the stalks forward in forced bows, the scenarios played in her mind. Each one had the common thread of Ignacio standing over her, watching her take her last breaths. Even after she'd slashed his eyes, she'd always assumed that he'd be the last thing she saw. Now it seemed that she would be right about that, no surprises there.

But she'd never expected her death to be entangled with the fate of a prince who had more book recommendations than sense, and the fate of a kingdom she'd told herself meant nothing to her. Yet here she was, steering a careening carriage in hopes of getting to the palace in time to stop Ignacio from retrieving those eerie stone hands.

But she supposed these things were supposed to be a surprise anyway.

And then there was the surprise of the prince himself.

She would never forget the way he looked at her when she'd found him in Xiomara's cell, as if the world had been swathed in darkness and in her eyes she carried the light. His face had softened and he'd bowed his head, as if embarrassed by something he thought. Or felt. She was afraid to know what he was thinking and afraid not to know, afraid of the answers that her mind was supplying.

His voice echoed again in her head, soft and insistent. *I believe you.*

His words had formed into flesh and bone—a hand held out to pull her to her feet and out of Ignacio's grasp. Even when the despair of what had happened to her parents had razed her to the ground, his words had found her, promising that she could break free of the fate that Ignacio had sewn into her skin years ago. His voice in her head pushing her forward had felt more intimate than anything she'd ever experienced, and he didn't even know it.

He never would. She was never going to tell him.

But the fact that she knew it was enough to make her face burn hot under the cool moonlight pouring over her.

The carriage rocked as the prince climbed carefully from the back into the seat beside her at the carriage's head. Finn didn't turn to look at him. She stared ahead at the winding dirt road, willing her face to cool. She didn't want to see how drawn and sallow his face had become from using the magic. They were already dashing toward death; no need to speed the process further.

"I told her . . ." Alfie's words ground to a halt. He seemed to struggle with something. "I told Xiomara the plan."

Finn raised an eyebrow. She'd never heard him use the girl's name, and from the way his nostrils flared, it took a toll on him to utter it even once.

"Which is?" she asked.

"We get to the palace and warn them of what's to come, and ask the dueños to set up protections to stall Ignacio and his soldiers from getting to the hands. When he comes for the hands, you and I will take him on. If we're lucky, we kill him, and I successfully trick the magic into the toy dragon. Xiomara will stay hidden under the vanishing cloak until the time is right and then open the void for me. I'll toss it in there and there will be no bodies for it to infect, no way for it to use its power again."

"And if we're not lucky?" Finn asked, her voice worn thin.

A silence spread thick between them.

"If we're not lucky." Alfie tilted his head back, his eyes closed. "Then we'll have nothing to worry about any longer."

"A sweet way to say we'll be dead," Finn said.

"Would you rather I say it the sour way?" he murmured to the moon.

The prince's face was bathed in moonlight as he bit the inside of his cheek. Her mother had always told her that keeping one's softness in the face of a world that was tough and callous was a strength unto itself. It struck her that her mother would've liked Alfie very much. "No," she said. "Sweet's all right for now."

Silence reigned for a long moment, and Finn wondered if he'd fallen asleep.

"Did you really kill someone when you were eight years old?" Alfie asked, his voice soft. His eyes were closed and his head leaned sideways. The dragon sat against his chest. He must have made Xiomara give it back to him when they'd spoken in the carriage. If he leaned a hair more, his forehead would press against her shoulder.

The moonlight silvered him, tracing the delicate cut of his features in its cool light. Finn wondered if this was what magic looked like to him, lush color licking the skin. Or was it a softer glow, trapped beneath the flesh like a flush blooming up the neck to claim cheeks and lips. Maybe a shimmer, like sweat.

"Why are you asking me that now?"

"Because I don't believe you," he said, his eyes meeting hers. The gold of his gaze took on a new life, the brightness pronounced and dazzling. "And if we're going to die together tonight, I want to know who I'm dying with."

Silence stretched between them.

After what Ignacio had done to her, a fear of him had taken root, black and crooked inside of her. Finn decided that if she feared one man that much, she couldn't afford to fear anything else. So then, when she was afraid of something, she chased it down, taught it that it ought to be afraid of her instead.

But still, she could never stop fearing the truths that lived inside of her. She'd told Ignacio about what she'd done to that little girl when she was eight, her darkest secret, and he'd used it against her. He'd taken her words and fashioned them into a collar to choke her with. No matter how many wild heists she'd pulled off, knife fights she'd won, or encounters with this dark magic she'd survived, she could never stop fearing herself—the parts of her that made her wish she could tear open her own skin and crawl out. The parts that made her hide herself under face after face. The parts of her that had killed that little girl and, in turn, killed her parents too. Her throat thickened at that thought.

She'd never stopped believing that if she spoke that secret to someone else, she would find nothing but looks of disgust—or worse, pity.

But she didn't want to die with that fear festering inside her, corrupting her like the dark magic did its victims. Even if she had only a few hours left before Ignacio found her again, she wanted those hours to be hers, weightless, without a secret pulling her down as she tried desperately to swim up.

Alfie raised his head and looked at her, his eyes soft with concern. If she was going to try, why not try with him?

Why not try with a friend?

"Yes, I did," she said, her grip on the reins tightening. "It wasn't on purpose, though."

"What happened?"

"My parents and I lived in a small, poor barrio where there were too many people and too little food. They pretended that things were fine, but I knew they weren't eating so that I could." Finn swallowed, her throat burning. "I decided to try to help. I snuck out to look for food. One night I was wandering in the alley beside a bakery where sometimes they'd toss out old bread. And I saw a loaf, burnt black as hell but a loaf all the same. When I rushed over to pick it up someone shoved me out of the way."

Finn could see the little girl's eyes in her mind. She couldn't have been much older than Finn had been. One of her front teeth had been missing and she'd been covered in a layer of street grime just as Finn had—a particular coating of filth that could only come from sleeping in alleyways and rummaging through garbage for food. There was a look of absolute ferocity in the girl's eyes as she lunged for the bread. It scared Finn to see it. Not because of the intensity of her stare, but because Finn had known that her own eyes had looked the same—scorched with desperation and fear.

"And then?" Alfie said quietly. Finn didn't know how long she'd been quiet.

"We both were fighting over the bread, shoving each other around, scratching at each other and yanking at each other's filthy clothes. Then I just . . ." Finn shook her head and mashed her lips together. If they'd just been standing in a different position, then maybe it all would have ended differently. "I tackled her. She fell onto her back with me on top of her. I didn't know that there was a wooden plank on the floor behind her, one with sharp nails sticking up out of the wood . . ." For a moment Finn lost her words, but Alfie knew better than to say anything. "Someone must've been building something and threw that plank away in the alley." Finn took in a breath and tried to make her voice run smooth, but failed. "When I knocked her to the ground, I could hear it happen. I swear I could hear the nails sink into her. She went silent, died in a moment. One went through her neck, through the back of her head." Then her words were coming too rapidly to control. "There was blood every-where, the bread was wet with it. Worst part is that when we were fighting over that maldito bread, I'd thought to myself, *I don't care if she dies as long as I can just get something in my stomach. Just a bite.*" She blinked to keep her stinging eyes from spilling over. "My wish came true, it seems."

There was a beat of silence before Alfie's voice came, warm as a child's blanket. "I'm so sorry."

She forced herself to shrug nonchalantly, though her eyes kept darting to his face. The prince was so expressive that she knew the moment he felt disgust toward her, she would see it on his face, clear as day. She couldn't help but search for it as she spoke. There would be a strange comfort in confirming what she already knew to be true—that she was as much a monster as Ignacio had always said.

His voice was feather soft. "But that . . . that wasn't your fault at all." She could hear every ounce of kindness pouring into his voice. She hated him for it.

"You weren't there," she snapped. "You wouldn't know whose *maldito* fault it was." She didn't want to tell him about her parents, about what Ignacio had done to them, thanks to her. The wound was too fresh to speak of. She couldn't bear to say it aloud. "Before this dark magic, the restriction on Ignacio's *propio* was that he needed to know something about you to control you with his *propio*. Something you would share with hardly anyone." Finn swallowed, her throat working. "When I told him about that little girl, he had all he needed to own me. He wanted to be the only person in my life. When I reached for anyone else, tried to make a connection, he commanded me to kill them." The prince stilled, and she couldn't bear the thought of looking at his face and seeing disgust there. Still, she couldn't stop the words from parting her lips. "And the deaths were never merciful. With Ignacio it was always slow, personal. My hands wrapped around someone's neck and him telling me to squeeze." In a flash of searing memory Finn could remember the boy struggling beneath her, how he'd clawed at her fingers and scraped his heels against the ground as she'd closed her fingers tighter and tighter around his throat. "A stabbing and a slow bleed. Poison slipped into a goblet." Finn couldn't help but think of Bathtub Boy dying on the floor, his eyes weeping blood, the prince crying out.

"Finn," Alfie said. "It wasn't your fault." He sat up then and looked at her. She turned away, her eyes trained on the road. "Look at me please." With a ragged breath Finn met his eyes. There she saw concern and something else that she refused to name—an emotion that met her eyes without fear, yet she was afraid of it still. Afraid that seeing such a thing in his eyes would unspool something she'd kept coiled tight inside of her for so long. "You are no monster. Even if you've been made to think so." His voice was quiet but strong. "I won't let you die thinking it. I won't."

Finn's breath caught in her throat. Ignacio had spent years hammering his words into her head about who she was and who she could be, all of it starting with that night in the alley. But the prince didn't speak to her with disgust or pity. He spoke as if she could still be saved. As if she weren't as broken and monstrous as Ignacio made her feel.

Maybe she wasn't.

"That night with the bread, that was the night my face changed for the first time." She'd never told anyone else about the moment that triggered her *propio*. But she didn't want to die with that secret locked in her chest too.

"You just wanted to be someone else after that night," he said.

Finn could only nod at that, her throat burning. Alfie sat back and stared forward again.

"My *propio* came for the first time at a moment that would look so insignificant to anyone but me," Alfie said.

"What happened?" Finn said, more than glad to move away from her own memories. When he didn't speak, she asked again, "Qué fue?"

"It really was a day like any other," he said, but his voice carried a current of barely masked pain, like a river meant to gush held back by a flimsy dam. "I was nine. I walked into the library to find Dez.

When I got there, he and my father were sitting together, laughing and smiling at each other." Alfie's voice quieted to a pained murmur. "They didn't even notice that I was approaching. And I just, I saw this look on my father's face. It was a look of such love for Dez. Such pride. And I'd never seen him look at me like that. I knew he never would. Never like that. That day was the first time I began to see magic and change my magic to match someone else's. The first thing I did was change my magic to match Dez's shade of gold." Alfie cleared his throat, his voice thick. "Dez gained his *propio* after holding me as an infant for the first time, because he loved me. I got mine because I was jealous of him. Some brother I was." He fell quiet for a long moment. "I just mean to say, you're not the only person who wished you were someone else. You weren't alone in that, even if it felt that way."

His words dusted her skin and clung there, like fallen snow. To share one's faults was a weakness; this had been clear to her for most of her life. Your faults could be used against you, used to control you, hurt you. If she'd known this as a child, she would've kept her secrets to herself instead of entrusting them to Ignacio. But Finn always prided herself on being a fast learner. Since then, she'd known that her scars and the stories that came with them were to be suffered in silence. They were something to be carried on the skin and the soul as a map of her most wretched moments. But it had never occurred to her that scars could be shared, the burden slung across two pairs of shoulders instead of one. It was a stunning feeling that sprouted and grew from the boy beside her and the soft cast of his eyes when he regarded her, as he tucked her secrets into his pocket for safekeeping instead of unsheathing them like a dagger to hold beneath her chin.

"Blue," he said suddenly.

Finn tilted her head. "Blue?"

"The color of my magic, it's blue," he said. "You asked me before. It's dark blue. When I showed Luka what it looked like with paint, he said it looked like the color of the night sky in a children's book."

She could imagine that. Something clean and soothing, calm, but a bit sad too. It was his color. "That makes sense."

"And your magic isn't one color," he said, his words hurried, as if they didn't have much time left. She supposed they didn't.

"It isn't?"

"No, it's a deep red but it's constantly shifting shades. Constantly changing."

Finn smirked. "Just like me."

"Just like you. I have never met—seen anything like it." Alfie cleared his throat.

Finn was glad to have an excuse to keep her eyes forward, the wind cooling the flush warming her cheeks. She gripped the reins tight as the horses moved with a curve in the road. "Why were you going after Englassen books?" she asked.

"Why do you want to know?" he asked, his voice hushed.

"You get to know who you're dying with, but I don't?"

The prince was silent for a moment before he heaved a sigh. "I thought something in those books might help me bring my brother back. Or that's how it began. It continued for much stupider reasons."

"Like what?"

"To be reckless. To do something, anything, that would prove

I'm just as wrong for the throne as I've always felt." From the corner of her eye she saw him rubbing the back of his neck, a gesture that would be forever paired with him in her head. "My parents call it the weight of history. They tell me that I am the product, the progress of our ancestors—people who were enslaved by Englass, disconnected from their magic, their culture. And I believe them, I believe in our history and I'm grateful," he said, his words hurried as if he feared she'd think him spoiled. "But when I think about all that was sacrificed for me to be who I am, have what I have, I get so paralyzed with nerves, I can't think. Can't do anything. It sounds stupid, but if I can't handle the weight of history, how can I ever hope to become king? I'm wrong for it, I know it. Sometimes, I suspect my parents know it too. Especially Father. I know he wishes it were me, not Dez, who'd been taken."

Finn shook her head. "No, it's not you who's wrong."

"Hmmm?"

"It's not you who's wrong for the throne. It's how you're looking at it."

"You're an expert on ruling now?" he said dryly.

She shook her head again. "No, but I'm an expert on people, breaking them down so that I can mimic them."

"So you're an expert on me, then?"

She thought for a moment. "Sí."

His laugh rang hollow and sad. "Well, that makes one of us."

Finn remembered how he'd draped his cloak on her after they'd fought on the night of the cambió game. As if she were someone to be protected instead of a stranger who'd robbed him and knocked him flat on his back.

"You're the kind of person who sees everything as something precious, something fragile. You're afraid that you'll break it."

"Yes," he said quietly.

"You can't see things that way. I'm not saying that Castallan isn't great. It is. But it isn't perfect. It never has been, never will be. Forget history. Forget legacy," she said, and she wished she'd spent more time taking her own advice. She should've lived her life instead of running from the past. "If what you actually want to do is rule, gods help you, then just accept that your kingdom is a giant cesspool of shit like everywhere else. Then you won't be afraid to take risks to make it better. And then maybe you'll fix some things. If you walk around acting like you're ruling over something perfect and fragile as glass, you're gonna do nothing but polish it up and admire it. If you want to be a half-decent king, forget about everything that came before you, look at this place as it is, and deal with what you see."

Alfie looked at her then and his eyes held her in a way that no one else's had—as if beneath the grime of everything she'd done, the lives she'd ended, the pain she'd caused, there was someone worth knowing.

"I wish I'd met you earlier." Something in the way he said it made her eyes sting.

"Right now, I wish for a lot of things." More time would be the first, and she could hear the same feeling in his silence. The fear of death creeping behind them, following their footsteps.

But maybe this was as good as it could be. The moment she'd met Ignacio, she'd been on borrowed time. Still, her heart hammered in her chest, speeding up its rhythm to match how quickly her life was winding down, ending.

"Finn?"

"Yeah," she said, her throat burning.

"You'll never have to go back to him. We'll kill him or we'll die trying. And if we should die tonight," he said, "I'm glad we will go together."

"I don't want to go at all." She hated how small she sounded. Finn let go of the reins with one hand to rub her eyes before gripping the fabric of her trousers.

"Neither do I, but at least we won't be alone," he said. "I'll introduce you to Dez when we get there. You'd like him."

Finn had never bothered to think about the afterlife. She'd assumed that if there was some paradise of eternal rest she wouldn't qualify. But maybe with a prince to vouch for her, she'd make it through.

"My parents died when I was really young," she said. She remembered so little of them. Some of her most cherished memories were of how they would look down at her tenderly and swing her by the arms while they walked. How they'd called her Mija and pressed kisses to her cheeks. "I won't know anyone in the next world."

"You'll know me," he said. His hand grazed hers tentatively, a question in his touch. Only when she moved hers closer did he interlace their fingers, a touch of softness cutting through the wind blowing past the carriage. "And now I know you."

She'd always imagined the weight of someone's hand in her own to feel like an anchor, tugging her into a forced stasis when she only wanted to run, to be free. Yet now, she wanted nothing more than to stay. She felt more freedom in this moment than all her years combined.

Freedom, she was coming to understand, could be found in a person instead of a place.

The road straight and clear ahead of her, Finn turned and looked at the prince. In his gold eyes was the same unguarded fear that she felt in her bones, a vulnerability that left her raw and exposed to all that was to come. But there was power in the fear that surged between them, power in knowing that death was coming and that there wasn't time to pretend, to be anyone but who you were, to feel anything but what you felt. She cast her eyes back on the road.

"All right," she said. "Then we'll go together."

The thief and the prince rode on, the lacework of their fingers a promise that where one of them went, the other would surely follow.

THE SUBSTITUTE PRINCE

Luka was nervous.

The last time he'd been nervous at a ball he was—well, he couldn't remember. Social functions were more his element than fire was. This was all very out of character and annoying. Needing to do something with his hands, he worried the collar of his deep blue overcoat that Alfie himself would have worn to the ball, if he were here to attend it. But he was not.

Instead, Luka was sitting on Alfie's gilded throne beside the king's and queen's on the far side of the ballroom, opposite the grand marble staircase. Guests were announced, sauntered down the stairs, and strode across the ballroom to bow before the royal family with practiced smiles as the ball unfolded before them. Luka cursed himself for destroying the parchment Alfie had given him. Now he had no way of knowing if Alfie was okay. The worry pounded between his ears, its rhythm steady and fierce.

Castallan's noblest danced and mingled on the glimmering, tiled floor. The ballroom was dressed in curtains magicked to darken and brighten throughout the night. Candles floated throughout as if stars had been charmed down from the heavens. The Equinox Festival was about the balance of dark and light, and the ball's decor never ceased to reflect that. The domed ceiling of the ballroom was a patchwork of stained glass that, during the day, cast shadows in every color imaginable. But today he could only see the outline of the moon looming overhead, as if blocked by sheer, colored tissue paper, but Luka couldn't let himself get lost in the tequila and the opulence of the ball as he usually would. Not with Alfie's words echoing in his mind in an endless chant.

But if I fail, if I don't come back, I need you to tell Paloma the truth and try to put a stop to this.

Was now the time? Had he failed? The world had yet to come crashing down around him, but still, Alfie had been gone for so long. He would not miss such an important night unless something terrible was happening.

If he was still alive, that is.

At that thought, Luka stood from the throne and started across the ballroom, his gold cape swishing at his ankles as he moved. He stepped around the nobleman who had come to greet him without a word. He pretended not to hear the queen ask where he was rushing to. He ignored the faces confused at his rudeness. There was no time for that anymore. Not now. Paloma stood in her formal dueña robes, trimmed in gold, at the far side of the ballroom, always preferring to keep out of the social politics of royal balls.

"Paloma," Luka said, gripping her by the shoulder. She raised her brows, glancing at where his hand gripped her shoulder before looking at his face.

"Prince Alfehr," she said, her eyes searching his face. "What is it?"

It was wholly improper to touch a dueña in such a way, but Luka was done with propriety. "I'm not Prince Alfie," he admitted. He thought saying that aloud would be freeing, but instead he felt as if he'd been stripped of his coat in the dead of winter, exposing himself to the elements, to the consequences of this foolish lie he'd agreed to.

"I beg your pardon?" Paloma said, pulling from his grip. Her voice dropped to a murmur, conscious of the nobles looking their way. "Have you been drinking?"

He swallowed thickly, his fear that Alfie was already dead crawling up his throat like bile. "There's something I need to tell you."

THE TWO PRINCES OF CASTALLAN

The carriage rolled down the stone bridge across the lake and onto the palace grounds, where guests walked daintily up the castle's stairs to be announced at the ball.

"Out of the maldito way!" Alfie shouted as a pair of nobles yelped, picked up their skirts, and dashed away as Finn pulled the carriage to a screeching halt at the palace stairs. The ride had given him the rest he needed and though his body still ached from Sombra's magic, he felt renewed, ready to fight for his kingdom.

He stepped off the carriage, and the guards were upon them in a moment.

Alfie raised his hands in a flat-palmed defense. "I am Prince Alfehr, heir to the throne of Castallan. I have urgent news."

A guard gave a bark of laughter, his eyes sliding over Alfie's tattered dueño's robes. "Are you drunk, muchacho? Prince Alfehr is inside enjoying the festivities."

The guards surrounded their carriage in a wide ring, hands on the hilts of their swords.

One guard stared up at Finn where she sat at the head of his carriage, his brows raised. "May I see your invitation?"

"Sure." Finn raised her foot and kicked the man in the face. He fell onto his back and swore, his hands flying to his bleeding nose.

The nobles hurried inside, scandalized at the sight as the guards pulled closer.

"Listen to me!" Alfie shouted. "We're not here to hurt anyone."

"Speak for yourself," Finn murmured from her seat. Alfie shot her a look.

"I am Prince Alfehr and I'm here to warn of an attack. Let me into the palace at once!"

"Not likely, chico." A guard raised his sword, but a column of rock rose between his legs, knocking him in the groin. Alfie needn't look over his shoulder to know Finn had done it.

Another guard surged into his place, his fist raised, and before Alfie knew it, he'd pulled a coil of water from the lake and frozen it into a globe about his fist. He landed a punch to the man's cheek, sending him staggering away.

Then Finn was at his side, her brows raised as she looked at his ice-coated fist.

Alfie relished the bit of pride he saw curving her lips. "Learned from the best."

In that moment of distraction, a guard sent a stone pounding into Alfie's stomach. He doubled over, clutching at his knees as he tried to draw breath.

Finn stood before him, pelting the approaching guards with stones, nailing two right in the nose and parting the ground to swallow another until only his head was visible.

"Get up, Prince!" she barked. "If we're dying tonight, we're dying in a big dramatic battle, not in some skirmish with your *maldito* guards."

Alfie got to his feet as yet another wave of guards moved to surround them. He met her gaze and couldn't help but smile, his heart curling around the pain of Dez's memory.

In the books you always have to have a sword fight in a big, dramatic place. And when you shout the whole room echoes. . . . You always need a good echo.

"You're right," he said. "We'll die somewhere with a good echo."

Finn cocked her head to one side before nodding with an understanding that made Alfie feel as if she'd been there with him in the palace library, brandishing her own practice sword beside him and Dez. "Exactly."

Alfie raised his hand and shouted, *"Fuerza!"* A guardsman was thrown back against the wall of a noblewoman's carriage.

"Stop this at once!"

Alfie froze. He recognized that voice—Maria, the head of the palace guard. She unsheathed her sword and rushed forward, her eyes narrowed.

Finn stepped forward, spoiling for a fight, but Alfie grabbed her by the shoulder and pushed her behind him as the guardswoman raised her sword in an arc toward his neck.

"Maria!" Alfie shouted. The guard stopped cold at the sound of her name, the steel of her blade pressed against his throat. He tilted his chin up and met her gaze. "When I was eight years old I fell down the ballroom stairs and you carried me to the infirmary. I wept so much that it soaked the collar of your cape. You sang me a lullaby to calm me. Look at me! I am no impostor, I am your prince!"

Maria stood stock-still, her eyes sweeping over him. She pulled the sword back from his neck before dropping into a low bow. "My apologies, Prince Alfehr. I did not—"

Alfie waved a hand. "There is no time, just let us pass. And tell the guardsmen to prepare themselves for an attack. The palace is about to be stormed! And protect the palace vault at all costs, do you understand me?"

Maria needed no other preamble.

"Let the prince pass!" she shouted at the guardsmen. They drew back, sheathing their swords, confusion painting their faces. "You!" Maria shouted at a young guard. "Escort the prince and his guest to the ballroom. *Now!* Let no one stand in their path!"

"No, I pick this one," Finn said, pointing at the guard she'd kicked in the nose. He glared up at her, his hand still clamped over his bleeding face. "Come on, glass nose."

With a glower, the guard stood and followed as Alfie, Finn, and the still hidden Xiomara ran through the palace's open doors and made for the ballroom. Shedding his years of propriety, Alfie barreled through nobles who leisurely walked the grand hallways.

"Move!" he shouted, startling a group of older noblemen as they skittered out of his path. Finn knocked a servant onto his backside as they dashed. Alfie could feel Xiomara's presence beside them as they ran through the twist of hallways. Guards moved to stop them, but after a nod from their red-caped, bleeding escort, they let them pass.

Finally, they reached the open, towering doors to the ballroom. Alfie dashed down the tiled stairs, nearly tripping over his dirtied dueño's robes. He stopped at the foot of the stairwell, panting as the ballroom grew silent around him, scandalized whispers curling through the air like smoke.

"Is that the prince?"

"Is he wearing . . . dueño's robes?"

Alfie tapped his throat. "*Amplificar.*" He could feel a tingle beneath his chin, the touch of magic that would magnify his voice for all to hear. "Everyone!" Alfie shouted, his voice sonorous, echoing throughout the ballroom. The musicians stopped their strumming to stare at him. "Listen to me! You must evacuate the palace at once! An enemy attack is—"

"What is the meaning of this?" On the far side of the ballroom, the king stood from his throne and the queen followed suit, their guards curled tight around them in a wall of brawn.

Alfie's heart ached. He had thought he never would see them again. He wanted to throw himself into their arms like he'd done as a child. He wanted to weep and promise that he would never make a mistake like this again. But there was no time for such things.

Alfie ran clear across the sweeping ballroom and stopped before the ring of guards. The nobles scattered, wanting no part of what they no doubt suspected was some ridiculous social faux pas. Alfie undid the magnifying spell before speaking once more. "Mother, Father—"

Upon seeing his face up close, the queen's anger melted for a moment only to freeze solid once more. "You are not our son; our son is here. You are an impostor to the crown. Seize him at once!"

"Wait!" a voice cried out from the crowd. Luka, still wearing Alfie's face, moved through the crowd to them. Paloma was at his heels, looking at Alfie with such anger that the glare of it made him want to raise a hand to shield himself. His stomach knotted. She knew. Luka had told her.

"Qué tal, Bathtub Boy," Finn said.

Alfie's arms were already open when Luka reached him and pulled him into a fierce embrace.

"You're late," Luka said as they parted.

"Better late than never," Alfie joked, though his throat burned with the relief of seeing his best friend once more.

"Alfie," the queen said, her eyes darting between Alfie and Luka. Alfie didn't know which of them she was addressing. "Explain this."

"I've got it." Finn waved her hand and Luka transformed back into himself. "There you go," Finn said as the king and queen stared, wide-eyed. Alfie had never seen the king's jaw fall slack like this.

In the space of a breath, Paloma had pushed Luka out of the way and stood before Alfie. She drew her hand back and slapped him, sending his head swiveling sideways.

The sting of it was nothing compared with the shame that carved him hollow. Paloma's face was flushed with anger as a guard moved to restrain her, but Alfie raised a hand to stop him. He'd earned this.

"You foolish boy," she said. "How could you be so thoughtless—"

Alfie hadn't the time to utter a single word before Finn moved in front of him, a dagger pressed to Paloma's throat. "Use your words, not your hands, like a big girl."

Paloma towered over Finn, regarding her like an insect to be squashed under her shoe.

"*Paloma!*" Queen Amada thundered. With a wave of her hand the guards parted and she stood before Alfie, the king close behind her. Finn had the good sense to lower the dagger and move back to

Alfie's side. Then, through gritted teeth, the queen said, "Touch my son again and you will regret it for the rest of your days."

Silence roiled between them.

Her searing gaze still locked on Alfie's, Paloma stepped away, fury trembling on her skin.

"Alfie," Queen Amada said, her voice shaking as she took his face in her hands. "Where have you been? What is going on?"

Alfie swallowed, sweat trickling down his temples. What would she do when he told her? Would his mother slap him like Paloma had? Or worse, would she recoil from him, lost to him forever? Whatever the outcome, he would have to take it. "We must prepare for an attack—"

A great splintering sound tore through the ballroom. The floor-to-ceiling stained glass windows were cracking open, fissures spider-webbing through the pains. Bursts of colored glass sprayed into the ballroom as the black-eyed infected crawled through the gaps. Their flesh broke on the shards of glass as they pawed their way into the ballroom. A group of noblewomen standing by the windows tried to run, but they scarcely made it a few paces before the black-eyed creatures seized them by their gowns like scavengers searching for corpses to pick clean. Alfie looked away as the shadows of the guests were torn up from the ground and forced into their convulsing bodies. The guards reacted without hesitation, pulling Alfie, Finn, Paloma, and Luka behind them to be protected, but Alfie knew that he could not stay there. It was he who must do the protecting today.

"Mother, Father," Alfie said, as screams overtook the ballroom. "Run. Hide. *Please*."

"Prince," Finn said, pointing over his shoulder, her finger

shaking. There at the top of the stairs, with a battalion of black-eyed minions behind him, stood Ignacio, smiling down at them.

Alfie turned to Paloma, his heart quaking in his chest. "You know what I've done. What needs to be kept safe. I won't ask you to forgive me, but please protect the vault. Finn and I will hold him off."

Paloma's eyes were still hard when she nodded.

Alfie looked at the guardsmen crowding close around them, their swords drawn. "Protect the king and queen! Protect the vault!"

The king, ashen-faced and struck silent, opened his mouth to protest, and the guardsmen refused to let Alfie and Finn step out of their circle of protection.

"I am your crown prince! I caused this," Alfie said to the guards before meeting his parents' eyes. "Let me take care of it."

A moment of tense silence passed between the prince and his parents. His father's chest heaved before he looked at the queen. After a moment's hesitation, she gave a tacit nod. The guardsmen parted, letting Alfie and Finn run into the chaos of the ballroom.

THE HANDS OF A GOD

"Luka! Come with me!" Paloma shouted, grabbing him by the arm as Alfie and the thief dashed away.

Luka fought against her pull. "Let me go!" He wrenched his arm free of Paloma's grasp and burst through the guardsmen that surrounded them. Behind Luka was the far wall of the ballroom and the royal thrones; before him the ballroom stretched in a chaos of fleeing guests and shrieks of fear. He ran forward in the direction Alfie had gone in but could not spot him. As he dashed against the current of fleeing guests, black-eyed monsters leaped on people like rabid dogs, either killing them where they stood or forcing darkness down their throats. Luka could only stare, his hearing muffled to a dull roar.

Fear wriggled through him, stitching its jagged patterns onto his skin. He turned in a circle, searching for Alfie in the screaming crowds. Had these monsters already taken him? Had fate been cruel enough to let him see Alfie again for a moment, only to have him taken again?

A hand gripped his shoulder and Luka started. The shrieks of the ballroom tore through him once more.

"Master Luka!" a palace guard shouted. "Come with me, the royal family—"

A black-eyed woman tackled the guard to the ground with a growl.

"*No!*" Luka shouted. Forgetting his newfound strength, he gripped the woman by the shoulder and threw her clear across the ballroom. She slammed against the opposite wall. Luka winced as her twitching body slid from the wall to the ground. Broken bones aside, she was already trying to drag herself forward on all fours. He hadn't meant to hurt her, hadn't wanted to. But he had to do something.

Still splayed on the ground, the guard was breathing heavily, his eyes closed.

"Are you all right?" Luka knelt and shook his shoulder. "We've got to help Alfie, we—"

The guard opened his eyes and they were black as night from edge to edge. His veins were raised and dark as eels. Luka shot up out of his crouch. The guard rose off the ground with a terrifying grace. He rose chest first, as if a string tied to his clavicle were tugging him up.

This is really it, Luka thought, his mind skidding to a halt. *This is when I die.*

The guard looked at him for a moment before turning away, seeming to lose interest. Without pause he launched himself at another screaming victim. Luka stared after him, somehow alive. He'd be offended if he wasn't so afraid.

What the hell was going on?

Running bodies, some black-eyed, some not, tore past him as he wheeled around, looking for Alfie in the pandemonium. Bruxos flung their elements at the black-eyed to no avail. They surged forward even as their bodies burned, even as they were pelted with stone, drowned with ice, and flayed with gales of wind. Words of magic could not hold them for long either; they shook it off like dogs did rain.

"Luka!"

He turned to see Paloma running toward him again. A black-eyed woman was trailing her from behind in a ruby gown—a party guest turned monster.

Luka dashed to Paloma and pulled her behind him before opening his palm, setting the woman alight with a stream of fire. Then, with a punch, he sent her flaming body skidding across the ballroom floor.

Paloma stared at him, her mouth agape.

"Don't ask, I have no clue," Luka said, motioning at himself.

Paloma shook her head. "I need your help. What the dark magic searches for—the pieces of his body—they are in the vault."

There were pieces of Sombra's body in the palace? He'd lived here all his life and he'd somehow missed that? Though he supposed the few times he'd been in the vault, he'd paid attention to nothing but the jewels. His adrenaline was burning through him with too much fervor to dwell on his surprise further.

"I can't leave Alfie here. I can't—"

"If you want to help him, you'll protect the vault. If these monsters reach the vault then all are lost, not just Alfie."

The naked fear on her face was chilling. Luka had never thought Paloma even carried fear in her emotional range. He'd thought that decades of study had reduced her emotions to nonchalance, wizened dueña-ness, and rigidity, but as the look in her eyes stole into his heart, he knew he must help her.

Luka swallowed, his throat dry. His eyes scanned the crowd, searching for Alfie once more to no avail. He would help him in whatever way he could. "Lead the way."

Paloma grabbed Luka and pulled him toward a wall. Embedded in the tiled wall was a tiny statue of a bird that Luka had never noticed. Paloma twisted it and a square of the wall swung inward. She pulled Luka in and shut it behind her.

Luka looked around the dark passage, a globe of flame lit above his palm. He was almost insulted that he hadn't known about these passages.

"What about the others?" he asked. The screams of the ballroom still echoed beyond the wall.

Paloma shook her head. "We need that man distracted while we get to the vault." Luka opened his mouth to protest. "There's no time!" She grabbed his arm and then they were running down the winding passage before exiting into the nest of halls that led to the vault. The halls were empty and silent, a deafening quiet compared with the shrieks of the ballroom.

Finally they were speeding down the hall leading to the vault. Luka nearly tripped over his feet at the sight. The filigreed door to the vault had been torn from its hinges.

"No, no, no," Paloma whispered as she ran faster.

At least twenty guards lay crumpled on the ground. Some with necks that sat twisted at broken angles, others with their throats slashed, their bellies torn open. Luka put his hand over his mouth at the sight of the blood, but Paloma didn't even pause. She dashed into the gaping maw in the wall where the doors once stood. Luka followed her in and nearly bumped into her back.

"Paloma, wha—"

A crackling sound, like a strike of lightning, silenced him. At the far end of the vault a trio of black-eyed women wearing colorful ball gowns were surrounding a glass case. Inside was a pair of stone hands. Each time they tried to touch the case, a spark of energy shocked them. With every shock Luka saw the translucent silhouette of a barrier blocking them. The more they touched it, the more the barrier attacked them, peeling the flesh from their arms as they reached forward. But they didn't scream, didn't move away. They leaned into it. Black shadows spread over the barrier, eating away at it like acid.

"*No!*" Paloma shouted, but it was too late. The darkness poured over the barrier until it winked out of existence. One of the women punched through the glass, her hands bleeding and covered in shards. She gathered the stone hands in her arms.

"We have to stop them," Paloma said.

Luka blinked at her. "From taking a statue?" Then it struck him. Sombra turned to stone, not bone. These were the hands of a god.

"*Fuerza!*" Paloma shouted, and two of the black-eyed women were thrown back against the stone wall. Then with a turn of her wrists, thick coils of stone from the walls pinned the women down as they writhed and fought. Luka could see the stone already beginning to crumble. They were strong.

The last black-eyed woman standing turned to them, the stone arms in her possession and her eyes blank.

She ran at them, her speed beguiling.

"Don't let her get out the door!" Paloma shouted.

Unsure of what else to do, Luka ran at the woman and tackled her. He held her down by the shoulders. Just like the other monsters, she didn't try to hurt him, but she tried to break free from his hold, wriggling and bucking beneath him.

"Where are they? Where are the hands?" Paloma stood over him, breathless. The woman didn't have them anymore.

"I don't know, she was just holding them when I grabbed her!"

A quick tapping sound from behind drew Luka's attention. The stone hands were skittering on their fingers like spiders across the floor of the vault toward the door.

"You failed to mention that the hands are *alive*!" Luka shouted.

"They haven't been for centuries," Paloma shot back, her usual monotone voice clipped with annoyance. She focused on the stone hands. "*Parar!*" But the hands didn't listen to the magic, didn't freeze. They kept going. "*Parar!* They're too close to the magic; it's woken them."

Luka had no time to ask her for clarification on that, because the hands were darting out of the vault and down the hall. Paloma made a messy gesture with her hand and a band of stone curled around the black-eyed woman's waist. It wouldn't hold for long, but it would keep her down. She jerked Luka away from the writhing woman and dragged him out of the vault.

"Those hands cannot get to the ballroom, do you understand?" she said as they ran, trailing behind as the hands turned a corner. Luka had thought the day that Alfie had brought the thief into the palace had been the weirdest day of his life. But chasing some stone hands down the palace halls with Paloma left that day in the dust.

With quick gestures, Paloma raised blockades of stone from the ground to corral the hands into a corner. She dove forward and landed on them.

She gripped them to her chest by their forearms, the hands stretching up toward her neck like a morbid bouquet of flowers. Luka crouched in front of her, watching them wriggle against her chest. Paloma got on her knees and opened her mouth to speak, but the hands wrapped tight around her throat like a vise. Eyes wide, Paloma choked, gasping for breath.

"Shit!" Luka cursed. He tugged at the disembodied forearms, but the fingers wouldn't unwrap from Paloma's neck. Luka only dragged her forward with every pull. "I'm sorry!" he said as she wheezed helplessly. Luka grabbed the fingers and with all his might, pulled each digit back one by one. Finally he pulled the hands free of her. Paloma collapsed forward, gasping for breath.

The hands fought in Luka's arms and he could only think to say, "Bad hands! Very bad hands!"

Calling upon every ounce of his baffling strength, Luka forced the hands to knit their fingers together and held them with each of his palms pressing the hands flush against one another.

"Are you all right?" Luka asked her as he held the writhing statue.

Paloma slowly rose to her feet, her voice raspy. "It doesn't matter. We've got to get to my quarters. I've got to get them far away from here, from that man in the ballroom." Paloma's eyes shifted to look just over Luka's shoulder. Her face tightened.

At the far end of the hall were the three women from the vault, and they'd brought friends. A horde of black-eyed monsters stood impossibly still, staring at the statue Luka held.

"Uh-oh," Luka said. Then the monsters were running to them at a breakneck speed. Luka dropped to his knees before Paloma. "Hop on my back!"

Paloma threw her arms around his neck and Luka took off down the hall as fast as his legs could carry him.

"*Fuerza!*" Paloma shouted from his back. "*Parar!*"

He could hear the bodies of the black-eyed falling to the ground, being thrown backward or pelted with Paloma's stone carving. But he knew she couldn't keep this up for long; there were too many of them and magic didn't seem to affect them for long. The stone hands were wrestling between his palms, fighting to break free.

"Luka!" Paloma shouted. Luka looked over his shoulder just in time to see a black-eyed woman launch herself toward them. The force of the collision sent Luka rolling onto the ground. The stone hands flew out of his grasp. Luka made to run after them, but a yelp of pain drew him back. Behind him Paloma wrestled with the black-eyed woman. The dueña's ankle was bent at an awkward angle, twisted from the fall. The woman pegged her to the ground like a cat would a mouse.

"Go!" Paloma shouted. "Get the hands! Leave me!"

Luka's eyes darted between her and the hands scuttling farther down the hallway. He and Paloma had never quite seen eye to eye— after all, he was always pulling Alfie out of lessons and into trouble. But he couldn't leave her in the grips of these monsters.

Her face tightened; she seemed to know what he was thinking. "Luka, do as I say!"

Luka bounded forward and knocked the black-veined woman off Paloma. With his inexplicable strength he sent the woman skipping across the corridor floor like a stone across a lake, back toward the rest of the black-eyed monsters rushing toward them. He flexed his fingers and summoned a globe of flame, readying himself for a fight. These monsters couldn't harm him for some reason, but he could certainly harm them.

He shot Paloma a tight grin. "Since when have I ever done as you asked?"

THE DRAGON

Finn had expected complete bedlam, but the ballroom was beyond that.

Guests were searching for escape only to be savagely tackled by the black-eyed monsters who crashed in through the ballroom's floor-to-ceiling windows. The guards still stood on the far side of the ballroom in a circle of brawn around the king and queen.

Together they'd left the king and queen behind and dashed into the fray, barreling through screaming nobles. As they ran, Alfie's eyes darted over her shoulder, a look of panic on his face. He gripped her close, pulled water from the air, and froze it in a globe of ice around his fist. Then he punched the black-eyed man running toward them in the face, sending him stumbling backward.

An infected woman was rushing at the prince from behind. With a quick movement, Finn made the woman's feet sink into the stone ballroom floor. She fell onto all fours, silently trying to crawl forward. Her eyes were glued to their shadows. Behind Alfie, another woman was running toward them. Alfie turned around and threw out his hand.

"*Parar!*" he said. For a moment the woman's body froze against the ground, halted by his magic. But Finn could see her slowly breaking free. Was there anything this black magic couldn't resist?

A thought struck her and her heart froze in her chest. "Where's Xiomara?" she hissed at Alfie. Was the prisoner even still alive? Had she been taken down by Ignacio's monsters?

Alfie's eyes narrowed in focus, something Finn now recognized as him engaging his *propio*. "I can see her magic," he said hurriedly before shouting another spell to force a black-eyed man away from them. "She's all right, staying close to the walls, out of the way like we discussed."

"Well, what do we do now? We can't keep trying to stop them all!" Finn said. "We've got to find Ignacio!" Ignacio had stood at the top of the stairs and in the blink of an eye, he'd disappeared, taunting them with his presence only to disappear from sight once more. Bodies littered the floor. Some lay still with death while others convulsed, their skin marred with black veins, their eyes darkening.

"Prince Alfehr!" A guard appeared out of the fray and moved to stand before him, shouting. "Protect the crown prince!"

"No!" Alfie shouted at him while Finn raised a wall of stone from the ballroom floor to block an infected woman's path to them. She shoved back the wall of stone, sending the monster careening backward with it. "Protect my family, and everyone else who hasn't been touched yet. Do not kill any of the rest, that's how it spreads.

Subdue them any way you can! But don't kill them. Do you understand? Go tell the other guards!"

The guard looked perplexed. "But, Prince Alfehr, I have to—"

"I am your future king; what you must do is follow my orders," Alfie said, and Finn had to sneak a glance at him. The boy sounded like a king. "Protect everyone, my friend, and I will do the rest."

The guard nodded, still looking confused, before darting back into the fray.

"Do you see him?" Alfie asked Finn, his eyes scanning the cavernous expanse of the ballroom. Ignacio had been at the top of the stairs for a moment, then he was gone.

"No!" she said, annoyed. He always liked to make her wait. For praise, for punishment. It didn't matter. There was always a wait.

"Stop," a voice as rich as velvet said, cutting through the chaos like a knife. The infected halted where they stood. The nobles stopped as well. Only Finn and Alfie could move. Finn turned toward the voice, and there he was, lounging on the throne of the king as if he were born to sit in it.

A knot of fury unspooled inside of her, searing hot. This man had cut her parents' throats and yet he looked at her as if she owed him—an apology, her life, her love, everything she had. She wanted nothing more than to pull that smile off his face and send him straight to his grave. She would do it or die trying.

"What a nice surprise to see you here, Mija. To think I assumed I would have to hunt you down only to find that you've delivered yourself to me, like a gift," he said, his dark eyes alight. "Are you so eager to join your lovely parents where I put them?"

Finn's breath caught in her chest before rising up her throat in a growl. For a moment she was nothing but fury again, only gnashed teeth and a hunger for vengeance that left her hollow.

Alfie straightened and his eyes flickered between Ignacio and Finn. She could tell from the prince's look that he knew Ignacio had killed them. The heartbreak in his eyes, heartbreak for her, pulled her out of her fury. The sorrow in his gaze stiffened into resolve. He squared his shoulders beside her and faced Ignacio. "You're disgusting."

Ignacio ignored the prince. He stood from the throne and strode to the center of the ballroom. She knew him. He intended to have her walk the rest of the way to him. "Let's make this between you and me, as it should be. And I let both your amigos go." Finn looked at him, feigning confusion. Ignacio rolled his eyes. He raised his hand and Finn turned to see Xiomara slam against a wall, the hood of the vanishing cloak flying off on impact.

"You must know by now that this magic is nothing to be trifled with," Ignacio said, cocking his head at her. "Here, I'll even be nice. I'll give you a peace offering." He snapped his fingers and in a flash of light a body appeared at his feet, tied by the ankles and wrists. Finn gasped. It was Kol.

She struggled against her binds, a gag corking her mouth.

Days ago, Finn had wanted nothing but cold, bloody vengeance after Kol had stolen her *propio*, but Ignacio and the dark magic had claimed her focus. Seeing the mobster now was strange, pulling her back to when her life seemed much less complicated. Finn shook her head. She never thought that her life would get so difficult that the prospect of a mobster thieving her *propio* would seem simple in comparison.

With Kol here and her *propio* well within reach, Finn couldn't stop her fingers from twitching toward the dagger at her hip. One quick slice and she'd have her *propio* back. Ignacio's eyes lit up as he watched her hand move, and his delight was enough to stop her.

"We crossed paths at the Blue Thimble. When I learned what she'd done to you, I decided to keep her as a gift for you."

Ignacio had told her he had a gift for her when they'd fought in the Brim. She'd never imagined that it would be Kol.

The mobster stared at Finn, her eyes wide with fear. Finn could only imagine the horrors she'd withstood at Ignacio's hands.

"Let her go," she found herself saying. No one deserved Ignacio's cruelty, not even Kol.

Ignacio looked at Finn, disgust written in every pane of his face. "Have I taught you nothing? Has this fool boy made you soft?" He leveled Alfie with a glare. "She took something from you, Mija, and after I spent a bit of time with her, I learned what else she had planned for you. Don't you want to know?"

"I don't want a *maldito* thing from you, just let her go," Finn said. Beside her the prince was stock-still, staring at Kol, his gold eyes round and desperate. In the prison, when Alfie had asked the dark magic to show him why his brother had been killed, the dark magic had shown him a tattoo—a tattoo that Kol herself had. The mobster would know more about the tattoo he'd seen in his vision; she might know about his brother's assassination. Though Finn had no love for Kol, she wanted the prince to find what he needed. She glanced at the prince, but his eyes were focused in front of him. His hand beside hers shifted with minute movements, and she knew what he was doing.

Wine and blood had been spilled all over the floor in the chaos. The prince curled his fingers, and a frozen spike of wine rose from the puddle just behind Ignacio. With barely perceptible movements of his fingers, he moved the frozen blade and pointed it at Ignacio's back, at his heart.

Sweat gathered at her temples. Could they really end this?

Then Ignacio cocked his head and flexed his fingers. Alfie gave a sound of protest, as if something had been snatched from his hand. The frozen blade shot around Ignacio so quickly that Finn had no time to react. Alfie jerked sideways, pushing Finn away as he tried to dodge the blade poised for his heart, but he moved too slowly. It buried itself just below the prince's collarbone with a *thunk*.

Alfie curled forward with a shout of pain, his hand closing around the spike of ice as he willed it to melt.

"That was an adorable attempt, but I'm afraid you'll have to try a bit harder," Ignacio said.

With a hiss, Alfie put pressure on the wound to stop the gush of blood. He spoke a quick word of magic to heal it as Ignacio's eyes found Finn once more.

"She meant to frame you," Ignacio went on. He flexed his fingers and Kol writhed against the ground, her eyes rolling back from the pain until Ignacio dropped his hand back to his side. She fell still, her chest rising and falling rapidly. "She blackmailed a servant girl into poisoning the prince's tonic and used your bet to place you in the palace to be framed for the murder. She even had guards in her pocket who were paid to report seeing you skulking around the palace, but you were too clever, just as I raised you to be. You did what she thought you couldn't. You got the cloak and slipped away before they could find you." A spark of pride lit his eyes.

Finn's head spun, these new details buzzing between her ears. Kol had set her up to take the fall for Alfie's death. That must've been why she'd given Finn a map of the palace passages, because she'd wanted her to get caught in them. If Kol's plan had succeeded, she would've ended up spending the rest of her days in the Clock Tower, and Alfie would've been killed.

"Why did she do it?" Alfie demanded from beside Finn. "Why did she try to kill me? Was she part of my brother's assassination too?" When Ignacio only stared at Alfie, amused, the prince stepped forward, his face twisted with anger. "*Tell me!*"

"Ah, wouldn't you like to know," Ignacio said, a laugh booming from his lips. "I'm sure Kol would love to tell you; it's an interesting story, particularly where your dead brother is concerned."

Alfie's body turned rigid at that, and Finn had to grip him by the arm to stop him from dashing forward to meet Ignacio.

"But, alas, Kol's time has come to an end. My children come first and those who hurt them," he said, leaning over Kol's trembling body, "pay the price."

Finn's heart pounded in her throat. "Don't—"

Ignacio gave a swish of his hand. Kol's neck twisted sharply to the left and flopped back to the ground at an awkward angle, like a snapped branch clinging desperately to a tree.

Finn gasped as she felt Kol's hold on her lift like a veil. It was as if a river within her had been blocked, walled off by a thick dam, and now it flowed once more, its current cooling her from the inside out. She was whole again. A feeling she could not explain darted through her—the sudden absence of pain, the rush of sleep coming to claim you after a long day. She was free; her *propio* was back.

Ignacio smiled at her. "You see how much your father loves you?"

Finn shook her head at him. He only loved what he owned, and he never would own her again.

With another wave of his hand the three sets of doorways out of the ballroom swung open. "I'll even let the rest go. How's that?"

He snapped his fingers and the ballroom guests came to life again, while his black-eyed minions stayed still. The deafening screams of the nobles echoed around Finn once more and she resisted the urge to clap a hand over her ears.

"*Get out!*" Ignacio roared, the magic making his voice boom throughout the ballroom like a crack of thunder. The guests fell still and quiet at his command, as if a god had spoken and they wondered if they should pray. "Or stay and die. The choice is yours."

At the sight of the open doors, the royals and guards began to escape, running with reckless abandon. The shadowless stood still, awaiting Ignacio's command but looking hungrily at the running nobles.

Finn watched as the king and queen were rushed out of the room by a group of guards. They shouted Alfie's name, but the prince looked away from them, his eyes shining as they were ushered out of the ballroom.

Now it was only Alfie and her against Ignacio. Xiomara was still out cold on the far side of the ballroom.

Ignacio glanced at the shadowless noncommittally. "Feast on whoever you like, but the three in this room are mine."

At that, his servants loped out of the room, running after the scent of prey.

The ballroom was swaddled in silence. Ignacio cocked his head at Finn, amused. A shiver rolled up her spine, and she didn't know if she'd be able to move. But then the prince's voice sounded at her side.

"I'm right behind you," he said.

She looked at him. His face was resolute. Fear burned beneath it all, but it wasn't enough to stop him from stepping forward. She wouldn't let it stop her either.

"Give me some cover," she said to him.

He nodded. "It's yours."

Then she was running forward, straight for Ignacio. The prince pulled water from every vase, every glass of wine, every bead of sweat in the room. With a wave of his hands the water turned into a heavy, thick mist. Finn closed the distance to Ignacio and pulled stones from the palace ground, sending them at the spot where he had stood as the mist closed around him. She could hear him gasp as the stones made contact. Had she done it? Had she somehow landed a blow?

The mist cleared around her. Ignacio stood before her, his chest bleeding through his shirt from the stones. He grinned at her before disappearing in a puff of black mist. Some sort of illusion?

He was toying with them.

Frustration twisted through her, painful and familiar. Why were things always like this when it came to him? She was forever a step behind, thinking she'd finally rid herself of him only to find him smiling down at her once more, readying to strike her with another blow, another command, another collar around her neck. Why was she even fighting anymore? What was the point?

"Prince!" she called, turning to find him. But Alfie was not there.

Behind her stood a little girl. She looked exactly as Finn remembered, just as Finn saw her in her nightmares.

It was the girl she'd killed—the very first life she'd ever taken.

The ballroom was empty. It was just her and the girl. The girl's eyes softened as she gazed at her, her hair ruffled by a warm, heady breeze that passed between them.

Then the air turned cold as her brown eyes darkened. Her veins thickened and grew black, standing out against her skin like spiderwebs spun from shadows. She lunged forward, and tackled Finn to the ground. She wrapped her callused hands around Finn's throat and squeezed with all her might. Finn couldn't take in a wisp of a breath. Her eyes watered. Her heart beat wildly in her throat.

"You deserve this," the girl was saying over and over. Her voice carried like an echo, eerie and resonant. "You deserve to die for what you did."

And though Finn clawed at the girl's hands, trying desperately to break free, part of her still believed that her words were true. A life for a life.

Then the face changed. One dimple became two, dark eyes became gold. It wasn't the little girl choking her.

It was Alfie.

He snapped out of it just after she did. Alfie wrenched backward, panic in his eyes.

"I don't know how—I—I wasn't hurting you it was—I—" he sputtered.

She rubbed her throat, breathing deep through her mouth. "It's okay," she croaked. "It's okay. You haven't crossed the line, Prince. It wasn't you."

His eyes wet, Alfie nodded at her words, clinging to them as he looked down at his hands in unabashed fear. She looked at him and wanted to say what she'd wished someone had said to her each time Ignacio had made her end a life with her bare hands.

It wasn't you, it was never you, she wanted to shout. *It was your body, but it wasn't your own. It was your hands, but they aren't stained. His are.*

Without asking, she knew who Alfie had been imagining— Xiomara. Guilt written in his features, the prince pressed the heels of his hands into his eyes. Why did Ignacio have the power to cultivate darkness in everyone and everything?

"So this is the muchacho you left me for?" Ignacio tutted from behind them. Finn and Alfie started, scrambling to their feet. "This boy who would wrap his hands around your throat? You know I'm the only one who knows the real you and still loves you. How many times do I have to tell you that? The only person you have is me."

Alfie stepped forward, eyes aflame. "That's not true, she—"

Ignacio raised a hand and Alfie's mouth shut, his lips mashing together as he struggled to open his mouth.

"I know who you are, boy. I can see into your head the way this magic did when you set it free." When Alfie raised a hand to charm water, Ignacio gave another cutting gesture and Alfie's hands fell still.

"Leave him be!" Finn made to stand in front of the prince, but Ignacio shot her a dark look.

"You move and he dies, do you understand me?"

Finn froze where she stood; when he spoke to her that way she was a helpless child again. She could barely breathe.

From behind her came a skittering sound and Finn feared that he would bind her with his strings once more, but it wasn't strings. A pair of stone hands scuttled across the ground on their fingers—Sombra's hands, the ones she'd seen in the palace vault. Once Ignacio had them he would become stronger than ever and they could barely handle him now. And where was the prince's teacher? Alfie had asked her to protect the hands. Had Ignacio's minions killed her before she had the chance?

"Prince!" Finn shouted as she made to dash for the hands. Alfie opened his mouth to speak a word of magic.

"Ah, ah, ah," Ignacio tutted, and with a swipe of his hand Alfie and Finn were flung sideways against the nearest wall. Her ribs rang with pain as her side hit the wall. She heard the prince cry out beside her as they slid down to the ground.

"Not so fast. This is what I've come for, Finny. This is the beginning of my reign. Our reign, if you choose. If you listen to your father."

Ignacio knelt down and the stone hands aligned themselves with his, opening and curling around his flesh, like sleeves and gloves of rock. Ignacio hunched over, his eyes flying wide as the stone encased his arms. His whole body shook in what looked like rapture and Finn could feel a prickle of power in the air. This, she thought, must be how the air felt just before one was struck by lightning—charged with an energy so palpable that it felt like it was pressing down on her shoulders. For a moment, there was only the sound of Ignacio's ragged breaths.

Finn reached to her side and gripped the prince's shirt, her fingers shaking on his sleeve. She didn't know what else to do or say.

They'd lost. He pinned her gaze beneath his and she knew he was thinking the same thing.

Ignacio straightened. With a twist of his fingers Alfie and Finn were pulled up from the ground and made to stand before him once more. A shudder skittered down Finn's spine as he puppeted them. She would never forget the pure violation of these moments. Of feeling his will crawl under her skin and claim her as her own. He released them from his hold then, as if daring them to try to run. Neither did. What use would it be to run now?

"Now," Ignacio said. "Where was I?" But his voice was no longer fully his own; beneath it was a timbre, low and strong, that made the hairs on Finn's neck raise.

There beneath Ignacio's voice, she knew, was the echo of a god.

Ignacio circled the prince predatorily. "You may look like a king, but you certainly aren't. We both know that, don't we? Pathetic and simpering, clinging to that little dragon like a child." He looked at Finn with a feral grin. "Perhaps you'd like to see a real one."

Before their eyes Ignacio began to shift. Finn could hear his bones cracking and rearranging, lengthening. He hunched his back and fell forward on all fours with a growl that belonged to a beast, not a man. His body began to stretch. In the blink of an eye the empty ballroom was taken up by the hulking body of a black dragon. Tendrils of smoke streamed from its nose, the promise of a barrage of fire to come.

"Coño," Finn breathed.

THE ULTIMATUM

Finn flung her arms forward, and a wall of earth shot up from the ground to guard them, but the dragon's tail swung down and cut through the rock wall as if it were warm butter, whacking them in the process. Finn and Alfie skidded down the tiled floor to the far side of the ballroom.

"We've got to use the dragon!" Finn shouted at him. There was no choice. Before them the black dragon inhaled, smoke surging from its flared nostrils. A wound over Alfie's left eye was gushing with blood. He must've been hit by debris.

"Every time we use it things get worse!" he said back as they scrambled to their feet. "We try our best to hold him off. If we can't manage, then we use it."

Finn tackled him out of the way as the dragon blew a blistering stream of blue fire, scorching the spot they stood at.

"*If!*" Finn shouted at him as she pulled him to his feet. "You still think this is an 'if' situation?!"

Alfie's eyes flew wide with panic as he looked over her shoulder at the dragon. Finn looked behind her to see another stream of fire surging their way. She raised another wall of earth and Alfie pulled her against it. Fire rushed all around them, singeing the rock. It felt like they were in an oven, the gargantuan ballroom filling with an oppressive heat.

"Charm water!" Finn shouted over the roar of the flames. She pulled more and more stone from the ground to replace the pieces that were melting from the dragon's heat.

Alfie skimmed his fingers through the sweltering air. Only a dribble of water trailed his fingers. "The air is too dry!"

"Then use the dragon! Make some!"

The fire stopped surging around them, and the dragon's hulking footsteps shook the palace to its bones. The rock shield Finn had pulled up collapsed into smoking rubble.

"Prince! We have to!" she said. Alfie gave her a sober look before finally pulling the figurine out from beneath his shirt.

The beast reared its head back and blew another blue jet of fire so hot that it felt as if it'd caught the sun in its mouth. Alfie held the silver dragon high, and a gargantuan wave of water rose out of thin air around him to counter the flame. It was a wave that could swallow the palace whole.

Finn looked at him. There was blood pouring from his nose and the corners of his lips now. His face was ashen. His shadow was lightening at a terrible speed. She shouldn't have asked him to use the dragon. What he was doing was too much.

And yet it wasn't enough.

The dragon's flames intensified, turning nearly white. Alfie's wave rushed forward to encompass the creature, but in an explosion of mist, the fire evaporated the wave in a mere moment.

As the prince swayed on his feet, Ignacio's voice boomed all around them. *This is a family affair, muchacho. Perhaps you ought to sit this one out.*

Finn heard the whirring of strings before she saw them. They soared through the air, wrapping around Alfie's wrists and ankles. They lurched him backward, slamming him against the wall. His body hit the wall with such a force that she feared for his life. The strings held him against the wall suspended, his feet dangling over the tiled floor.

"Stop!" she shouted at Ignacio. "Stop it."

The dragon only swung its tail back and forth, excited. More strings flew in from every direction until the prince was trapped in a spiderweb of sharp twine.

The dragon sat comfortably, wrapping its tail about itself. Ignacio's voice sounded once again.

I could pull him apart, you know. It would take only a moment. Unless you'd like to convince me otherwise. . . .

Sweat trickled down her temples. Ignacio had taken her parents from her, had taken her life into his hands and broken it. She would rather die where she stood than beg Ignacio for his mercy, than bargain with him. She had no life anymore, only this anger to hold on to; it burned and sustained her all at once and she could not let it go.

But then the prince's voice sounded in her head, just as it had before. When they'd faced the first infected man in the pub, she'd asked him if he was foolish enough to give his life to stop Sombra's magic, and with fear trembling through his words, he'd said:

Is there nothing you would give yours for?

She'd had no answer to his question then, but now she did. If her anger for Ignacio was her life, she would give it for a moment, for the prince, for hope of ending this. With her jaw working, Finn raised her hands in surrender to the monster before her.

"Don't hurt him," she said. "Let's keep this between you and me." The dragon gave a content purr.

Good girl.

Slowly the dragon shrank and turned back into the man she'd once called Father. He sauntered across the ballroom.

From behind her, the prince groaned in pain.

"No," Alfie said, his voice quiet but resolute. "Let me go."

Anger sparked in Ignacio's eyes. He raised a hand and all the strings wrapped around the prince's extremities began to pull in opposite directions, jerking his legs and arms as he screamed in agony.

Finn held her hands up in surrender again; it was a motion she knew he loved to see her do. "Let him go and I stay. I'll do whatever you want. We'll do this your way."

"Finn, don't." Alfie's broken voice sounded from behind, but she couldn't turn to look at him when his face might make her change her mind.

Ignacio cocked his head. "You do what I want and I'll think of letting him go, how's that?"

The prince started another protest but Finn had already nodded. If he had her he might lose interest in the prince. Maybe. What else could she do?

She stole a glance behind her and met Alfie's gold-eyed gaze. The heartbreak on his face struck her like a blow. She looked away. "Tell me what you want."

Ignacio smiled at that and she knew that what he asked would be much worse than what she imagined. "I want the prince to take the magic he's trapped in that little toy of his and give it a new home—you."

Her blood froze in her veins. Ignacio wanted the prince to infect her with the magic.

Alfie made a sound of protest behind her and then his voice was rough, strained with an anger unleashed. "You'll have to kill me first, you monster!"

Finn's heart sputtered in her chest. She knew Ignacio wanted her to fall into line. He wanted to remind her that the only friend and family she could have was him. Yet she hadn't expected this. It was so typical of Ignacio to use those close to her to hurt her. Still, his words cracked across her face like a slap.

"I'm not dark-hearted enough for the magic, Ignacio," she said, trying to keep her voice level. The magic had avoided taking her before. She certainly wasn't the type to properly house it. It would just burn her to ash. To kill her so quickly hardly seemed his style. Maybe she could talk him out of it. "It'll only kill me. Is that what you want?"

Ignacio shook his head at her with the look of a parent helping a child with her schoolwork. "You need only accept yourself as the killer that you are, Mija. Then you will be the finest home this dark magic could find. I wonder if perhaps you require the proper motivation to embrace your truth." He pointed at the prince. "He will pass the magic into your body, and you will either turn to the darkness within yourself or you will cling to this foolish idea of who you wish you were and the magic will singe you into nothing. Either

I'll have you as my own or you perish. And if the boy refuses to do it, he dies."

Finn could barely hear the prince swearing behind her. All sounds were muffled. This was it, then. Live as a dark-eyed demon or die at his hands. The choices ahead of her weren't choices at all, but the very same fate dressed as differing options—whether she became one of Ignacio's black-eyed minions or turned to dust, either way she'd be dead.

The only real choice left was to end her life believing what the prince had believed—that she could be better, if given the chance.

"I'll do it," Finn heard herself say.

The look of sheer satisfaction on Ignacio's face made her stomach twist. "Very good girl."

Finn walked to where Alfie was pinned to the wall, each step tearing at her heart. When she stood before him, the prince looked like he could barely breathe.

"Finn, I don't know what will happen to you if—"

"I don't know either," she said. "But he might let you go and maybe you'll have the chance to end this." It was a silly hope, but hope was all they had left now.

"No." His whole body was rigid with refusal. "I'm the one who started this. We'll fight him, we'll die together. But I won't let you take this alone." His eyes met hers, and they were such a rich gold that you would expect them to leak honey instead of tears. "You don't have to do this," he pleaded. "You don't owe me, or anyone."

For a moment, Finn could only look at him. A smile curved her lips. "Alfie," she said. It was the first time she'd said his name, and she was struck by the wish that she'd spent the last day saying it over and over again. "All my life I've been made to do things I didn't want to do. This isn't one of them. I'm doing this because a friend got stuck in my door and asked for help."

A sound parted his lips, one that spoke of something already broken shattering even smaller. He fought against his restraints and leaned closer to her. His warm breath ghosted across her face as he tipped his forehead against hers. "I won't be able to save you if you do this."

She offered him a wry smile, a meager gift in the face of what was to come. "We've already almost died a couple of times today. What's one more?"

Alfie closed his eyes. "One more could be all that's left."

Ignacio sighed. "You know I'm not a patient man, Finny."

Finn wished she would never have to hear his voice again. One way or another, tonight that wish would come true.

Alfie looked at her, his eyes moving over her face the way a child's fingers ran over a flower's petals, slow and careful. He looked at her as if to memorize Finn as she was now, as she would no longer be as soon as this magic took her. With the dragon figurine around his neck, he needed only give the command.

"Take her," he said, his voice breaking around the words. The magic poured out of the dragon in a tendril of black.

The stream of obsidian magic reared back like a snake before darting forward at her chest, pouring into her heart. She felt it surging through her veins, singeing her inside and out. It was as if she were housing the sun itself. As it lanced through her, Finn refused to do what Ignacio had said. She refused to turn to the part of her who had killed for him, who left others behind without a thought, the part of her who believed she was monstrous enough to house this magic. Instead, she clung to the look on the prince's face—a look of anguish that could only come from losing someone worth having. Someone too good to carry this evil inside of her.

There was no doubt in her mind that she would die in a mere moment, extinguished by the dark magic like a candlewick between wet fingertips. But if you could die in a moment, then maybe you could live in one too. And if she could choose a moment to suspend, to hold gently between her palms, she thought, it might be this one: with the prince's eyes on hers and the knowledge that she was not who Ignacio had said she was. She was herself.

She bit back a scream, maddeningly full of power. Finn hunched forward, her hands on the ground, her fingers curling against the ballroom floor as she waited to shatter, to burn into nothing, to finally live in a world where Ignacio could not find her. Then she went still. The pain stopped and there was only immense power.

"Finn?" she heard the prince say, his voice thick with hope and fear.

She opened her eyes and by the look on his face, she knew her eyes had blackened. Yet, somehow, she still was of her own mind. Shock and relief burst inside of her, flowing under her skin like a cool stream. She was still herself. She didn't know how long that would last, but she was still here.

"Try to get free and wake up Xiomara. Stay out of the way," she said before turning her back on his surprised face and striding down the ballroom to meet Ignacio at its center. No matter how much time she had left, she would use it to take Ignacio down with her. For herself and for her parents, she would put him in his grave.

"Finally," Ignacio sighed as his black eyes found hers. "Like father, like daughter. You're mine to guide once more. Now, kill the boy."

His words were the pull of a weak current. She walked through them.

Ignacio's eyes narrowed. "I said kill the boy, Finn."

She was tired of listening. She took off in a run toward him, her fists raised.

Ignacio gave a sharp laugh—half delighted joy and half fury. "Of course. You've always been a maldito fighter, but I've always been able to break you."

Finn swallowed his words and made them fuel her, stoke the unbearable anger within her. With a swipe of her hands, twin boulders rose from the ground and hurtled at him. Ignacio waved a hand, and the boulders exploded into pebbles at his feet.

"Come now, Finn," he tutted. "What's the point in this? Why not join me? Forget the boy, forget the world. You were most yourself when you were with me."

"You made me whoever you wanted me to be. You made me forget who I was. You took them from me." She closed the distance between them and with one powerful swing her fist met his jaw, sending him flying backward. He collided with the king's and queen's thrones, shattering them in an explosion of sound and dust. But he rose from the rubble laughing. For a moment his jaw bled profusely, but before her eyes it healed shut.

"No," he said. His steps were slow and unbothered. "I showed you who you are. I freed you from a mediocre family, a medio-cre life. It's not my fault you didn't like what you saw when you learned who you truly were. That under all of those faces you're just like me."

She closed the distance between them, gripped him by his cloak, and slammed him into the ground. The stone of the ballroom floor cracked under the force of her strength. She landed another punch to his jaw. "You took my family from me and told me what to see." Another punch. "You lying." Another. "Manipulative." Another. "Pendejo!"

But he was laughing at her, his broken face further split by his smile. It healed in moments. Finn pulled him up from the ground roughly and landed punch after punch, kick after kick. With an angry cry, she pelted him with a boulder that she pulled from the ballroom floor. She sent him flying across the room again, blasting him against the stone wall. He slid off the wall, landing on his knees before standing sinuously, as if nothing had happened.

"I already told you," he growled, his patience running thin. "Don't think I can't love you *and* hurt you. I can do both."

He dropped into a low stance and with a quick round of jabs, stones as large as the prince flew toward Finn at lightning speed. She dodged the first volley and broke another boulder into pieces with a punch. But the last stone came too fast. She raised her arms against it, and it hit her full force in the chest, throwing her backward, skidding on the palace floor.

"How long are we going to do this, Mija?" Ignacio asked, flexing his fingers. He pulled water from the air, freezing it into spikes. She felt them burrow into the flesh of her arms; one tore through her collarbone and she couldn't stop herself from crying out. "Why not let me be your father?" he said, beseeching. She hated how good he was at sounding like everything he did was for her. Out of love. It wasn't. It never was.

"Stop it." She rose shakily as he closed the distance between them.

"You have to do what you must to teach your children respect. Even if it hurts."

She moved to break through the rock, but Ignacio's voice cut through the air like a knife. "Don't move," he commanded, engaging his *propio*.

She froze.

Then he was in front of her. He gripped her gently by the jaw, his fingers rubbing slow circles against her skin. "Look at me."

Her head rose slowly. Her body shook as she tried to resist. Not even the black magic in her was enough to fully resist him.

"Love me like you used to. When you were little. Think the world of me like you did back then," he said, his voice soft and desperate.

Finn smiled softly up at him, a look of wonder on her face.

Ignacio's face softened. "You love me now? You truly do?"

Finn nodded, her eyes wide and blank. "I always have."

Tears gathered in his eyes. "You're mine again." With a wave of his hand the stones holding her to the ground fell away. He pulled her into a crushing embrace. "Today is the beginning of our new life. Things are going to be good again. Perfect. The world is ou—"

His breath caught in his throat and Finn felt blood gush over her hand as she drove her dagger deeper into his back, through to his heart. She gave the dagger a sharp twist.

"You loved me . . . ," she heard him whisper, his voice dwindling to nothing.

She pulled back and looked in his wide eyes. "Don't think I can't love you and hurt you. I can do both," she said, parroting his words. He'd commanded her to love him as she once did. But she never had. Her love for him had never been real. The command had meant nothing.

His blackened eyes found hers one last time, wide and vulnerable as if, for once, he was going to beg her forgiveness. He reached a hand out to her, his fingers grazing her cheek, the touch sending a chill down her spine, as he fell backward onto the stone ground. His eyes stared unseeing at the ceiling. Ignacio was still with death, but the tension curled tight inside Finn would not loosen. She couldn't let herself believe that she was finally free of him. That he'd finally paid for what he'd done to her, and who he'd taken from her.

With a shaking breath Finn watched the corpse, fearing that he would rise again with that smile on his face. But he didn't. He was finally dead. Finn had always feared that part of her would be saddened at the loss of Ignacio, that she'd regret ending his life if she ever got the chance to, but she felt nothing but freedom running through her, like wind through her hair. She didn't care if enjoying a kill made her a monster; any monster who put an end to Ignacio was a saint in their own right.

Finn looked over her shoulder for the prince and made to shout for him to hurry and use the dragon to seal whatever was about to burst from Ignacio, but Alfie was no longer alone. She started at the sight of Bathtub Boy beside him. Luka looked strangely untouched, as if the battle in the palace had never happened. There wasn't a scratch on him.

The realization stunned her. An idea flickered into existence in Finn's mind.

She knew how to stop this magic.

Before she could shout for the prince, the black magic that had been growing in Ignacio's body surged out of his corpse, his body crumbling to nothing as it escaped. The stone hands peeled away from his skin, re-forming into their original shape.

Her heart sputtered as the magic rose in a curling black wave before her, poised to swallow her whole. She wanted to run, to close her eyes and wish it away, but she couldn't let this magic escape. She thought of Alfie, staring at his hands in horror after he'd been made to hurt her. There was too much at stake in this room and beyond for her to let it go.

She'd told the prince that she'd spent her life watching bad things happen without lifting a finger to stop them and that she'd wanted to end that. She'd asked him to believe in her and he had, the very same way her parents once had and would have now if they were still here.

Now it was time to prove it.

She could carry the echo of magic from Alfie's dragon. Maybe she could contain this. Give him some time to trap it.

"Take me," she said to it. She'd never been more afraid in her life. "Take me."

The magic curled around her like a great snake before forcing itself into her mouth. Her mind clouded with the power. What was in the dragon figurine was a terrifying boost in strength, but it was nothing compared to this. This was the source of it all. This was too much. This . . .

You are so close to the dark, my child, so close. The black magic purred in her ears, soft as velvet. She felt the cold of the stone hands as they skittered up her body like spiders to lie over her arms. *Turn to it. Let it take you. You and I will rule over an earth scorched black. There will be no more fear, no more sadness, for there will be no more hearts to feel, only you and I. Surrender, my child. Surrender to who you are.*

She ground her heels into the floor, trying to fight its control, but as the stone hands wrapped around her skin, it eclipsed her.

You asked me to take you. You will hold to that promise.

Then she could think of nothing but the hunger. Nothing but the need to stretch over this kingdom like a wave of darkness.

With Ignacio gone, the strings fell away and Alfie dropped to the ground like a stone. She'd done it. She'd done the impossible before his eyes. She'd beat Ignacio at his own game. But the magic. The magic would fly free. And the hands too, those needed to be contained! Alfie struggled to his feet, his eyes on Finn. He needed to get to her, to seal it before— A loud creaking pulled Alfie's gaze upward. A huge chunk of stone framing the ballroom's glass ceiling had come loose, swinging like a baby tooth. Then it was falling, careening toward him.

Alfie threw his hands uselessly over his face but the rock never hit. He dropped his arms, and looked up to see Luka holding the gargantuan boulder in his hands like an avocado at breakfast.

"Miss me, sourpuss?" Luka said before hurling the stone to the far side of the ballroom.

Alfie's mouth hung open in shock. "What just . . ." He gestured wildly at the fallen stone.

Luka looked uncharacteristically sheepish. "Well, it appears that I have superstrength?" His voice lilted at the end of the statement, as if Luka were asking himself if it were true.

Alfie blinked up at him before pulling him into a fierce hug. When they parted he asked, "How?"

"No clue." Luka shrugged. "I have to assume that it developed naturally. Like my good looks and sense of humor."

Alfie grinned up at his best friend before remembering that he still needed to get to Finn and use Xiomara's void to get rid of the magic for good. He didn't know if he could save Finn from the magic she had taken in. But he would try.

Luka looked away from Alfie and blanched. "Alfie, something's wrong." Luka pointed forward.

Finn stood before them. She looked hungry.

"Finn," Alfie said hesitantly. She cocked her head at him, then grinned and began a slow walk to them.

Alfie rose to his feet. "Luka," he whispered, his voice taut. "Run."

Luka shook his head. "I won't leave you."

"I need you to do something else for me," Alfie said, his voice shaking from the pain of standing with the bruised ribs he'd gotten from being thrown against the wall. "Wake up Xiomara. We need her to banish this magic, do you understand? Wake her, otherwise we'll both die." He pushed Luka behind him.

"All right," Luka said, worry in his eyes. "Be safe." Alfie felt a little less afraid when he heard Luka's footsteps dashing toward Xiomara.

"Finn," he said, walking toward her. "You know me. I know you can hear me, I know you're a fighter. Break free of it."

This was different from when she'd taken in the magic of the silver dragon. Now there wasn't a semblance of her left. She'd taken the magic that had been inside of Ignacio. She'd made the sacrifice to contain it. But she had to break free. He couldn't kill her to get control of the magic. He wouldn't.

She said nothing, approaching him with measured steps before she thrust her arm out and a pillar of stone jutted from the ground in front of Alfie, pelting him in the stomach with such force that he fell to his knees, clutching his middle.

"Alfie!" Luka cried out from Xiomara's side. Alfie gasped in pain as he forced himself upright.

"Stay back, Luka!" he shouted. "Stay away."

Finn didn't even seem to notice Luka. She kept advancing on the prince. Alfie felt his heart leap when he looked down and saw a sliver of her shadow still clinging to her feet, dragging behind her. She had to be fighting it. Part of her was still there.

Finn thrust her arms forward and a barrage of flame followed. Alfie leaped out of the way, deflecting the flame with a weak wave of water. She followed him, still moving slowly. Almost hesitantly. She was fighting. Trying.

There had to be a way to pull the magic from her and back into the dragon without killing her. He would subdue her and try to pull it out of her somehow. If that didn't work, he would have to go for her heart.

With a word of magic, Alfie raised sharp shards of glass from the shattered windows and grimaced at where he'd have to hit her— the places that would slow her down. Her knees, her stomach.

"*Volar!*" he said. The glass shot forward and dug into her skin. But they dislodged and fell away as she moved, her flesh closing over the wounds.

She was finally upon him, an arm's reach away. For a moment she paused, her body shuddering.

"Finn," Alfie said, his heart breaking. Her black eyes narrowed as her hand shot out and gripped him by the neck, raising him off the ground with ease. Alfie swung his legs forward and kicked her in the chest, sending her stumbling. She dropped the dragon necklace as she fell.

Alfie fell to the ground with a grunt of pain, and as she tried to rise, he tackled her and held her down. He grabbed the dragon where it fell beside her and put his hands on her chest, feeling the magic coursing through her, beating out of her heart. He focused and tried to pull it out. But the magic resisted, coiling itself tighter within her. His *propio* wasn't helping. The core of this black magic couldn't be tricked into listening to him just because he'd dyed his magic black.

He would have to kill her, there was no choice. His heart ached at the thought, but he knew it was right. For his people, for the world, he couldn't afford to be selfish again the way he'd been when he'd saved Luka. He couldn't afford to not think of the consequences of his actions. His eyes burning, Alfie wrenched the dagger from Finn's own belt and made to plunge it into her chest.

Her black eyes leveled him with a glare as she gripped his wrist, stopping the dagger just before it grazed her chest. With her other hand she shot a stone at his chest. Alfie flew backward again, skidding to a halt a few strides away from her. His ribs burned with pain. He couldn't help but scream in agony, his fingers curling with pain against the stone floor.

She stood up and walked to him slowly.

As she closed the distance between them, he formed a spike of ice in his hand. Now was the time, now he had a perfect shot. He had to do it. For his family, for his people.

Then Alfie heard fast footsteps. Luka stood between them, a globe of flame hovering in his hand.

"Keep away from him!" he shouted.

"Luka, no!" Alfie cried.

"Run, Alfie," Luka said over his shoulder. "Get out now!"

Finn didn't hesitate. She grabbed Luka's arm with both hands, her eyes narrowed to slits.

"No!" Alfie screamed. Finn gave his arm a sharp twist and Luka screamed in pain. Alfie could only think that this was how he would die—at the hands of a friend while his best friend died beside him.

But death didn't come. Finn stood frozen, then she dropped to her knees, and the black magic poured out of her open mouth like a thick, syrupy smoke. The dragon trembled in Alfie's hand. He held it up and watched in disbelief as the magic flowed like a river of black into the silver dragon. And not just the core of the magic that had infected Finn but all its echoes. The black magic that had been plaguing the rings of the city crashed through the windows and domed ceiling of the palace. Shattered glass rained on them as the black magic flowed into the toy. In a mere moment it was all over and the magic was locked tight in the palm of Alfie's hand. Finn fell onto her back, the magic wrung out of her. Alfie gasped with relief. Somehow, she was still breathing.

The stone hands lay beside her, completely still. With the magic trapped again without a host, without so many bodies to bolster its cause, the hands had fallen still once more.

And Alfie hadn't even had to use his blood to do the sealing magic or use his *propio* to trick the black magic into the figurine. It stayed in the little dragon without a fight. His heart leaped in his chest. The magic was trapped in the dragon, but he was no longer connected to it. It would no longer be able to hurt him, drain his life into it.

He was free.

But how had it happened?

A groan of pain from Luka pulled Alfie back to the present. The prince bent over Luka and grimaced. His arm had been pulled out of its socket. "I'm sorry, this is going to hurt." With a sharp twist, he shoved Luka's shoulder back into place. Luka cried out. "I know, I know. You're fine now."

"Speak for yourself! That hurt like *hell*."

"You'll live," Alfie said. Luka opened his mouth to ask another question, but Alfie knew that now wasn't the time for explanations. He had dark magic to get rid of. "Wait here. Look after Finn. I have to take care of this first."

Luka nodded and knelt beside Finn. Alfie rose to his feet to find Xiomara, but she was already standing, moving toward him with a pained hobble. Luka must have woken her up before rushing to Alfie's aid.

When she stood before him, waiting for his word, Alfie's throat thickened. He didn't want to look into this black abyss again unless it was to see his brother step out, alive and well. But life had led him here for different, darker reasons and he could not delay no matter how much his stomach twisted and his eyes stung.

"Can you open the void?" he finally asked, his voice strained.

Xiomara nodded firmly before she took the vanishing cloak off and handed it to Alfie. She raised her hand in a fist, then splayed her fingers open. Before Alfie bloomed an opening into absolute darkness. The very darkness that had swallowed Dez whole.

Alfie held the dragon figurine out; it sat warm in his palm against the sudden chill emanating from the void. His hand shook. He had never been parted from it since Dez had died. He'd squeezed it between his fingers when he missed his brother the most. To place the dragon in the void was to promise to never open it again. To promise to never try to seek Dez in its depths.

To accept that his brother was never coming home.

While drowning in the depths of his grief, part of him had always held out hope that one day he'd wade out. One day he would open this door of darkness and find his brother. Now the grief faced him with its open maw, endless and swift and harsh.

But he could not let there be even the slightest chance of this magic running free once more, even if it snuffed out the light of his greatest wish. His people must come first. In that moment, he promised himself that he would never open this void again.

"Goodbye, Dez." Hot tears slipped down his cheeks and nose. He ran his fingers over the figurine one last time. "I love you. Rest easy."

With a ragged breath, he dropped the silver dragon into the abyss and it disappeared, careening into the endless dark.

It was finally over.

For a moment there was only Alfie, Xiomara, and the past that stretched its jaws between them. Though Xiomara couldn't speak, Alfie could see the question in her eyes: *What now?*

Alfie felt the weight of that silence. This woman, this murderer's life, sat neatly in his hands; Alfie didn't know if he could stop himself from closing his fist over it and crushing it.

"I still want to hurt you," Alfie heard himself say. "I always will." Xiomara pressed her lips into a quivering line. "But I won't." He would never let himself become that monster who'd choked Finn earlier. Ignacio and the black magic had shown him exactly what he would become if he let his hatred for Xiomara consume him. He refused to be darkened by vengeance, even if it meant letting go of the girl who'd taken his brother from him.

Xiomara curled forward, her hands on her knees, a grimace pulling her face taut.

"What is it? What's wrong?" Had opening the void hurt her?

Xiomara shifted her shirt up. A thick shard of stone jutted from her lower belly, the blood soaking her trousers. He hadn't been able to see the blood against the dark brown color of her prisoner's uniform.

"You're hurt," Alfie said, taking another step forward to heal her, but Xiomara held a hand up to stop him. She shook her head.

"Don't be ridiculous," Alfie said. "You'll die if I don't heal you." She looked at him with eyes that said, *I know.*

And Alfie knew what she was thinking. She was the only one who could open this void. So long as she lived, there would be a danger of this magic coming back. Someone could force Xiomara to open it, or maybe she would open it herself, accidentally or otherwise. The only way to truly stop this magic from ever returning was for her to die.

After months of wishing she were dead, Alfie couldn't find any pleasure in this moment.

"There are other ways," he said weakly, not able to stop himself. "You don't have to."

But Xiomara shook her head again, silencing him. She shakily knelt down, a hand pressed to her sopping wound. Using her blood as ink, she wrote a message on the ballroom floor.

I want to make things right.

Alfie's heart ached. He closed the space between them and helped her stand. She winced, gripping his arm.

"All right," he said, his throat burning. "If that's what you want."

Alfie didn't want to watch her bleed out. She didn't deserve that slow agony. No one did. Alfie pulled a ribbon of water from the air and shaped it into a thick, sharp dagger. She seemed to understand and took it from his hand.

Xiomara moved before the void, the dagger poised at her chest. She closed her eyes.

"Xiomara," Alfie found himself saying. She looked at him, her eyes widening in surprise at the sound of her name. "Gracias."

She gave him a nod before closing her eyes once more. For a moment, she stood still, her throat working as tears rolled down her cheeks. She pushed the dagger into her chest and without a sound, the silent prisoner of the Clock Tower staggered backward and fell into the void she'd opened. It closed behind her, never to be summoned by her hand again.

Alfie didn't know if letting Xiomara die was the right thing to do. He didn't know if he should feel angry or elated. He doubted he ever would, but there was no time to twist and writhe under the gravity of it all. There was still one more person to save. Alfie dashed back to where Finn lay on the ground. Luka scooted away to give him room to work, his face grave.

"I've been trying," Luka said hopelessly. "She's not responding."

Alfie laid his hand on Finn's chest and ran his magic through her. Sombra's magic had battered her. Her pulse was slow, her shadow a sliver of gray curled at her feet. He might lose her. Even Luka had the good sense to stay quiet and let him work.

Alfie leaned forward and healed a pair of bruised ribs. Had the magic violently flying out of her done this? She'd been healing naturally when they were fighting, but now he could see bruises blooming on her skin. The black magic had left her to fend for herself.

He touched her forehead. It was burning with fever. He laid his hands on her stomach and poured his magic into the wounds that peppered her midsection, then her face and arms. Every wound he found he healed or tried to. Then he remembered the healing draught he'd saved for her.

Alfie hurriedly pulled the vial out of the pouch in his pocket, unstoppered it, and slowly poured it into her mouth. He tilted her head and gently rubbed her throat, hoping she would swallow it.

He'd done what he could. Now all they could do was wait.

"Will she be all right?" Luka asked, his voice quiet.

"I don't know," Alfie said. But if anyone could survive this, it would be her.

As if in answer to his worries, Finn gave a groggy groan. She opened her eyes slowly. He could feel his heart pounding in his throat.

"Prince," she said.

At the sound of her voice, something within him healed so quickly that it felt exactly like breaking.

"Thief," he said, his voice hushed.

She looked up at him, her eyes searching. "Did you—is it—"

"It's gone, in the void," he assured her. Her body relaxed, but she still stared at him, questions brewing between her ears. All at once the answer came to Alfie's mind. Of course Luka was safe and strangely powerful. Before Alfie had released it, Sombra's magic had agreed to make Luka strong and not to harm him. How could he not have seen it before? "When I released the magic, I made it promise to never hurt Luka. When you did, the deal was broken."

Finn nodded, looking characteristically unfazed. "I figured as much."

Alfie stared at her, amused. Nothing shocked her. She pressed her palms to the ground and, with a grunt of pain, forced herself up slowly so that she was sitting with her legs stretched out before her. Alfie had to stop himself from helping her up.

"Before the magic took me over, I saw Bathtub Boy next to you, and he didn't have a maldito scratch on him. I remembered what you said, about making the magic promise to never hurt him. Hurting him seemed like a good bet. So I gave his arm a twist for good measure." She shot Luka a glance, her eyes darting to his arm. "Sorry about that."

Luka waved the hand dismissively. "None taken. Worse ways to die, but no better way to live if you ask me."

Finn's lips slanted into her crooked grin.

"You were amazing," Alfie said to her. "Really."

For a long moment they only looked at each other. Their faces were peppered with grime and wounds from battle, but they smiled all the same.

Then Luka gave a high-pitched, "*Ah-hem!*"

"You were good too, Luka," Alfie said.

"I was, wasn't I?" Luka said with a sage nod, as if he were perched on a throne instead of sitting on the rubble-littered ground.

Then Alfie couldn't stop himself from laughing, and Luka joined in.

"Don't make me laugh," Finn said with a grin, her voice tight with pain. "It hurts when I laugh."

For years, Alfie would wonder how they'd found the energy to laugh after all they'd been through. But later he'd come to realize that they'd laughed simply because there was time.

After days of death and rebirth, of shadow and light, of fear and courage, there was finally time to laugh.

THE THIEF, THE PRINCE,
AND THE END

If days ago someone had asked Alfie how he would feel about saying goodbye to Finn, he imagined he would have a myriad of answers.

All those answers would share the common thread of relief. Of a burden unloaded, a headache massaged away.

The last thing he'd expected was an ache in his chest and a lump in his throat.

He was so at a loss that he'd brought Luka with him to the port to say goodbye, if only to do what Luka did best—lighten the mood. Though he stood straight as they waited for her, Alfie knew he was leaning on Luka like a crutch.

After the disastrous Equinox Ball, Finn had rested in the palace for five days. She'd slept through two of them while Alfie sat at her bedside, pretending to read a book when he could only stare at the same sentence over and over again. He left her side only to speak to his parents, who'd thankfully survived the night, though many others had not.

When she'd finally awoken, her shadow darkening to a healthy shade, Paloma had insisted on meeting with Alfie and her to discuss what had happened, from the very beginning.

After Alfie explained everything up to their meeting at the cambió game, Finn took over, describing the circumstances that led her to the palace and all that came afterward. Paloma watched her silently while she spoke. Alfie nodded along, filling in his own details.

When their story was finally over, Alfie expected a harsh reprimand for his recklessness when it came to releasing the magic and Finn's crime of breaking into the palace. But instead, Paloma did something she seldom did.

She smiled.

It was an almost imperceptible upturn of the lips that Alfie had seen only a handful of times. How was now the time for smiling? They'd just told her the whole story of releasing a black magic that had ravaged their kingdom. Yet there she sat, smiling.

"What?" Finn finally asked, looking as unnerved as Alfie. "What's that grin about?"

Alfie's eyebrows rose. He'd never heard anyone talk to Paloma that way. But the dueña only looked amused.

"You asked the black magic to enter your body. Why?"

Her brow furrowed. She crossed her arms defensively. "I don't know. It seemed like the right idea at the time." She drummed her fingers against her forearms. "To buy more time. To—"

"To protect Alfie," Paloma said. When she fell silent, the dueña inclined her head as if daring Finn to disagree.

Alfie watched a flush spread up Finn's neck and cheeks. She turned her head to look out the window. Alfie decided he ought to look down at his lap.

"You invited darkness into your heart, not once but twice. A dangerously foolish decision." Finn leveled the dueña with a sharp glare, likely coming up with a retort to blast Paloma out of her seat. "The magic was dark, but your intentions, they came from a place of light. Pure and true. Even though you invited it in, it could not influence you and take your shadow as it would someone who sought greed or vengeance or hate. Your body could not be burned as others were. You were protected by the light of your intentions, and your intentions, I would say, were quite different from hate."

Silence cut through the room like a blade. Alfie rubbed the back of his neck.

"And you, Prince Alfehr," Paloma said, her voice stern. Alfie straightened in his seat. "You made a selfish, thoughtless choice. You thought of yourself before your people when you chose to release that magic to save Luka."

Alfie hung his head in shame.

"But," Paloma said. Alfie felt hope catch in his chest. "At the very least, you learned. You did not want to hurt your friend to stop the magic, but instead of letting your own desires rule you as you did when it came to Luka, you were willing to take her life for the good of your kingdom. It was only sheer, dumb luck that Luka's interruption saved you from having to kill this girl. But I am certain that you would have made that sacrifice for your people. That leads me to believe that with time, you may become the king we need you to be."

Alfie felt a weight slide off his shoulders, if only for a moment. He would feel guilty for what he'd done for the rest of his days, but for a moment he would give himself a break.

Paloma rose from her seat. "I should think that is sufficient for today. Prince Alfehr, you and I will speak more of this later. For now, your and Señorita Finn's time would be better spent resting and recuperating."

"Yes, thank you, Paloma," Alfie said, bowing his head in respect.

"And it's Finn," the thief said from the bed, picking at her fingernails. "Drop the 'señorita.'"

Paloma chuckled at that, and Alfie had to stop himself from gawking at the dueña. He hadn't heard her laugh like that in some time. Without another word, she walked out of the room and left the prince and the thief to themselves.

Alfie wrung his hands in his lap for a long moment before finally looking up at Finn. She was picking at her blankets as if she wanted to find loose threads. Or make some.

"Do you . . . ," Alfie began, but his voice came out too soft, betraying something within him that he was not yet ready to face. He cleared his throat. "Do you need anything? The cook should have lunch ready. Or I could get you more pillows."

She held up a silencing hand and motioned at the cushions surrounding her. "Prince, I have enough pillows here to build a palace of my own. I'm fine."

"Very well," Alfie said, relenting. Another silence stretched between them. "Do you want me to leave?"

She sucked her teeth. "Did I say I wanted you to leave?"

Alfie's eyes narrowed. "You didn't say you wanted me to stay either."

"You're a grown man, I don't have to tell you where to be."

"Right," he said, his voice strained. Why did she have to be so difficult? "Then I'll just go."

One foot was out the door when he heard her voice again.

"Wait." Alfie watched her tuck a stray curl behind her ear. "You mentioned lunch. Are you hungry?"

He wasn't. "Yes."

She turned to the window, looking away from him. "You could get food and bring it here."

Alfie smiled at the back of her head. "All right."

"If you want. Doesn't matter to me."

Alfie nodded, forgetting that she wasn't looking at him. She shifted uncomfortably in the silence.

"Very well," he said. He watched her shoulders relax. "I'll be back, then."

"Prince," she called again just as his hand closed around the doorknob.

"Yes?" He looked at her over his shoulder. Her eyes found his, searching for an answer she had not yet asked for.

"Did you magic the door and windows to keep me from escaping?"

Alfie shook his head, his gaze never leaving hers. "No."

He watched the corners of her lips tug up before walking out the door, his heart light in his chest.

They'd spent nearly a week that way. On most days, he'd ended up falling asleep in a chair at her bedside when they'd both gotten too tired to speak. Once or twice he'd woken to Luka poking him and waggling his eyebrows suggestively. She'd even drawn a sketch of the horned tattoo he'd seen at the prison so that he would have a picture to reference. He would become king, he'd accepted that, but that did not mean he would give up on finding out the truth behind Dez's death.

On the fifth morning, after a breakfast of eggs, avocado wedges sprinkled with sea salt, thick-cut slices of fried salami, and mangú, Finn drummed her fingers on her empty plate before admitting, "I stole something else when I was here to thieve the cloak."

Alfie snorted. "Obviously."

"I mean something besides pesos." She fished something small out of her pocket. In her palm sat the fox figurine that Dez had carved. Alfie's heart clenched at the sight of it. He remembered asking Dez why he'd carved a fox. Especially since foxes tended to be mischievous characters in the fables and myths they'd been raised on.

"Everyone needs a troublemaker in their life," Dez had said with a wink.

Alfie's eyes drifted from the deftly carved fox to Finn's face. He hadn't really understood what Dez had meant by that until now.

"Keep it," Alfie said, his throat burning. "It suits you, and Dez would have liked you." He couldn't help but smile at that. Dez would've laughed until his sides ached at Finn's crackling wit and brusque attitude. "I don't think he'd mind you having it."

Finn pocketed the fox once more. She could've said something pitying, like she was "sorry for his loss" or another one of those neatly wrapped, sad little phrases that rang hollow in his ears. Instead she smirked up at him, her eyes alight.

"Of course he would've liked me. I'm a maldito delight."

On the sixth morning, Alfie carried a tray of breakfast to her room only to find the bed messy as ever, but empty.

She'd left without saying goodbye.

A note was left on her pillow that said she had to "get her affairs in order," which Alfie took to mean that she was on her way out of the city and maybe Castallan entirely. Out of his life. The note had also told him to meet her in the Pinch one last time. Now that note sat in his pocket heavy as a stone as he and Luka waited for her to appear.

"You look like you're about to turn into a rain cloud," Luka said while munching on freshly buttered corn on the cob sprinkled with cheese and chili flakes.

"I'm just thinking," Alfie said.

"I wonder about what . . . Or *who*?" Luka said, his voice meandering playfully. Alfie shot him a quelling look, but Luka only laughed. "You know, you've got to admit. Fate was really at work when it came to you two."

"Luka—"

"It's like those old, epic love stories. Good versus evil and a bickering pair that end up falli—"

"Luka," Alfie snapped.

Luka raised his hands in surrender, his corn cob leaning crooked. "All I mean to say is that the gods seem to have been conspiring to put you two in the same room."

"And in the end you nearly had to die for it to happen."

Luka made a face at Alfie that said, *Must you make everything so dreary?*

Alfie shot him a look that said, *Yes*.

Luka glanced over Alfie's shoulder, a smile curving his lips.

"Better make it count, then. My life is worth quite a lot, maybe even a goodbye kiss or two."

He inclined his head over Alfie's shoulder. Alfie turned to see Finn approaching them. A hood was drawn over her face, but he knew her by her walk, by how she slipped through the crowd like water. When Alfie turned back, Luka was gone. He was already speeding away into the crowd, giving Alfie two boisterous thumbs-up.

Finn came to a stop before him and because neither could think of what to say, she simply walked past him. He followed.

"You left before I could give you your chest of gold," Alfie said, breaking the silence. "I never took you as the type to forget a payment."

"I didn't," Finn said, her lips curving into a smirk. "I stopped by the vault on my way out. We're square. For now."

Alfie's brows rose and a surprised chuckle rumbled in his chest, as if he was chiding himself for not guessing as much.

"You could've said goodbye." His voice was softer now. "Instead of disappearing—"

"Like a thief in the night," Finn supplied with a mischievous grin.

Alfie only looked at her then, the hurt in his gold eyes making her joke feel almost cruel.

She shrugged and looked anywhere but his face, a string of guilt pulling tight within her. "I felt like a house cat in there; I had to get out. It's not as if I up and left the city."

"Yet," he said. The word sat heavy between them.

"Yet." She nodded.

She wasn't exactly lying to him, but not quite telling the truth either. On her fifth night in the palace she'd been thinking about when to leave when a loud knock rapped at her door. She knew it wasn't Alfie. His knocks were quiet, hesitant, thoughtful, as if worried she might be asleep regardless of the time. Annoyed at herself for being able to distinguish his knocks, Finn had barked, "Enter if you must."

In strode Bathtub Boy. Without preamble he perched on the edge of her bed and stared at her, assessing her with a sweep of his dark eyes.

Finn cocked her head at him. "Is this about the whole breaking your arm thing?"

Luka waved his hand. "No, no, that's all forgiven. However," he said, "I have a favor to ask of you."

"Is that so?" Finn said, amused.

Luka nodded. "Alfie says your trade is thieving goods, but you seem just as adept at thieving hearts."

Finn stared at him blankly. "Was that as embarrassing to say as it was to hear?"

"I was going for charming and clever, but I'll take that."

Finn rolled her eyes. "What are you really trying to ask me?"

Luka leaned forward. "I know your type."

"My type?" She snorted. "I'm afraid there's only one of me. I'm a bit too original to warrant a type."

Luka rolled his eyes. "You're the type that doesn't stick around for long. One of my favorite types to chase, actually," he said with a far-off smile, as if he were reliving memories that Finn hoped he wouldn't say aloud.

"Well, you're right about that." Finn shrugged. "What about it?"

Luka tilted his head and shot her a look. "You must know."

"Know what?"

Luka pinched the bridge of his nose. "It's just like your type to pretend not to know."

She sucked her teeth. "Know what?"

"Just—" Luka began, waving his hands as if trying to fish the words he needed from the air. "Just let him down easy when you go. Be nice about it, or as nice as your type allows you to be. It's not going to be easy for him to lose you."

Finn felt heat rush to her cheeks. Before she could sputter a response, Luka rose from the bed and walked to the door. "Oh, and if you tell him I spoke to you about this, I will deny it. I've courted eight actors and I learned much, I assure you. My lies will be convincing." He wagged a finger at her as she watched, amused. "Don't test me."

With that he was out the door. Bathtub Boy was right. Those days in the palace had begun to soften her. She'd even been thinking about staying in the city. It'd suddenly felt like there were things worth staying for. But she should know better than to get too comfortable here. When she stayed in one place, trouble always followed. She was meant to keep going, moving on. Finn was the type to leave a poisoned bottle to be drunk by someone innocent. She wasn't the type to befriend a prince, or anyone for that matter. So she'd scrawled the prince a note and crept out of the palace.

Alfie's voice drew her back to the present.

"Where will you go?" he asked, his voice soft and desperate. Finn wanted to bottle the sound so that she might uncork it and listen to it whenever she needed a reason to smile. Or frown. He cleared his throat.

"If I told you that, it wouldn't be much of a getaway, would it?"

"I suppose not," Alfie said.

"I can't just go around telling people where I'll be. I'm still a wanted woman! Many wanted women, actually. And some men too."

"I know." Alfie regarded her with a sad sliver of a smile. "You are very much wanted. More than you know."

They looked at each other for a long moment before Alfie tore his eyes away to open his bag. For a moment it looked as if he were pulling nothing but air out of it. But then she realized what it was. The vanishing cloak.

"Take it," he said.

"I shouldn't." The words sounded strange coming from her mouth. She was usually more interested in whether she could, not if she should. And the cloak would be a useful thing to own for anyone, let alone a thief. But the cloak was what connected them and what nearly unraveled the world in the process. The weight of it was too much. She knew it would draw her back here.

Back to him.

His eyes softened. "I gave it to you days ago. It's already yours."

Finn wondered if he was talking about the cloak or something else entirely.

She watched him pinch the invisible cloak by the shoulders. The wind unfurled it, letting it sway in her direction. She could feel it flick against her chest. Then he stepped closer and reached around her to place it on her shoulders.

"No thieving necessary," he said.

For so long, Finn had placed value on the things she owned based on the difficulty of taking them from someone else, how long it took her to plan, how much the owner would miss it, how much she might be able to get should she pawn it off. Though the cloak was a gift, she knew it would be the most cherished thing she'd ever call hers. Alfie smoothed the shoulders of the cloak and smiled down at her.

She was astounded by how he could smile and still look heartbroken, grin and still draw her toward him as if he'd cried out in pain.

"I have something for you too, then," she said. Alfie raised an eyebrow. "It's only fair."

"You're not usually one for fair."

"So you don't want it, then, Prince?"

He gave a bark of laughter, a short, wonderful sound. "Of course I want it, thief."

"Then quiet down so I can give it to you."

She stood still, and Alfie watched her, his head cocked to the side. She would miss the way he felt things with his entire body, his whole being shifting into a question mark when he was confused, and the way his grin unfurled slowly, like a cat stretching after a nap.

She dashed those thoughts away, exhaled a long, deep breath, and placed her hands over her face. A long moment passed. If she were anyone else, it would've looked like she was trying to hide her tears.

"Finn, wha—"

"A moment, Prince!" she snapped, looking through her fingers to watch his reaction. He rolled his eyes but grinned all the same.

Finally, the work done, Finn let her hands drop. Beneath lay a face he'd never seen her wear. The eyes were large and brown with a thick fringe of lashes. There was a dot of a birthmark under the left eye and a thin slash through the right eyebrow, a scar that stopped the hair from growing. The top lip was fuller than the lower and the face was heart-shaped, the forehead wide while the jawline tapered to a soft point of a chin.

Finn watched it dawn on him, watched him realize that this was her face, the one she'd been born with. She'd peeled the magic away and stripped herself of her armor.

She'd let him truly see her.

She tilted her chin up and held his gaze stubbornly, the same way she did anything else. She tried to assess his reaction, daring him to say something stupid. Something that would give her the excuse she needed to go back to cloaking herself in a mask of magic for the rest of her days. But the prince only smiled, his face filling with light.

"Thank you," he said. Then again. "Thank you."

"You're welcome," she muttered. Another phrase she wasn't used to, but it felt right when the words were for his ears.

Alfie raised his arms slightly, looking as if he wasn't sure if he was overstepping his bounds. Finn's body moved before her mind could signal. She embraced him with such force that he stumbled back before wrapping his arms around her.

In that moment, there was only the two of them and the knowledge that a door between them was about to close and lock, the key lost somewhere in the sea that would soon sweep them apart.

The chimes of the two-faced clock rang out to signal sunset, shattering the moment.

People rushed by as if this day were any other. The sea sloshed and roiled, pulling ships toward the dock just as easily as it carried them worlds away. Finn pulled free of the embrace, turned on her heel, and walked away.

Goodbye seemed too final a word. She refused to say it. He must have felt the same way, because she'd made it only a few strides when she heard his voice again.

"I'll see you around," the prince called.

She turned to face him, walking backward.

"No," she said with a vulpine grin. "You won't."

The thief pulled the hood of the vanishing cloak over her head and disappeared.

ACKNOWLEDGMENTS

Books are messy things.

I thought I knew this after working as an editorial assistant for two years, but I understand it more clearly now that I've written my own book. I know now more than ever that writing is a team sport, and without my team, there would be no book in your hands and nothing but the tangles of a story in my head.

First, I want to thank Hillary Jacobson and Alexandra Machinist. You two are an amazing duo of dream agents, and I can't believe how lucky I am to have both of you in my corner. You've been my champions from day one. This book exists because you two believed in me first.

Thank you to my amazing editor, Kristin Rens, who challenged me to push myself and, most importantly, to trust myself. Writing books is never easy but writing a first novel feels like a singular sort of challenge. I could not have asked for a better editor or a better person to lead me and ask me all the tough questions. Thank you so much for everything, and I can't wait to write the rest of this series with you.

And thank you to Kelsey Murphy for all your hard work on this book. From one former editorial assistant to another, I truly appreciate all that you do.

I also want to thank the HarperCollins team, from editorial to marketing to sales to production and onward. Thank you for taking my story and turning it into a book.

To Lauren Pires, Ari Romano, and Thalia Ertman, my indestructible high school squad (aka The Fantastic 4). Thank you for supporting me since I was an awkward teenager who shyly admitted I wanted to write books and cheering me on now that I'm a slightly less awkward adult who shrugs and says "Yeah, I write books I guess" when people ask me what I do.

To Taylor Lewis, Codi Guggliuzza, Norine Mckee, Ashley Delaney, Andrew Lim, and Marlena Chertok, my college crew. We met in a creative writing program, but during those years I learned more about friendship and trusting myself than I did writing, and that's thanks to each of you. A special thank-you to Norine, who read the book first in its earliest draft and told me that it, in fact, only sucked a little. And another thanks to Codi who repeatedly said "*Just do it already!*" when I was sitting in her apartment, too scared to send my manuscript out to agents.

Thank you, Hannah Milton. You've supported me since the day we became roommates at Columbia University and spent our first night in NYC reading each other's stories while everyone else went barhopping. I couldn't have done this without you.

A big thanks to Marisa Dinovis, who pushed me to try #DVpit; Kristina Forest, who was always there to listen to me panic about writing; Kate Sullivan, who constantly assured me that I wasn't a total idiot; and Grace Weatherall, who sent me what I consider my very first piece of fan mail. Your encouragement really changed my life.

The internet once sagely told me that you've got to get roasted if you ever wanna get toasted. Thank you, Whitley Birks, for being an amazing beta-reader and effectively roasting me within an inch of my life. Both the book and I grew from the critiques you gave me. I can't thank you enough.

Thank you, Sandy Liang. You taught me to do a push-up and so much more. I am stronger, inside and out, because of you.

To Margot Levin, thank you for listening to me and helping me remember why I love to write in the first place.

Thank you to the University of Maryland's Jiménez-Porter Writers' House for giving me the resources I needed to become the author I am today. I hope you get all the funding you and your students so deserve. (I'm looking at you, ever-shrinking UMD arts budget!)

Thank you to Eva Freeman, who was my very first creative writing teacher in college. You encouraged me to put my words on paper even when I was afraid to, and I am forever grateful for that. Having a woman of color as my first creative writing teacher was an amazing experience, and I hope I can give other writers half the inspiration you gave me. I'm so happy that we've reunited in NYC, and I can't wait to share this book with Jonah and Micah when they're old enough!

To Carlea Holl-Jensen and Keke Kusumaatmadja, thank you for all the long, after-class meetings and for believing in my work. You both were amazing teachers who pushed me to see myself as a writer in the present tense instead of someone trying to become a writer in the distant, inconceivable future. I am forever in your debt for that. I hope we can meet up at Busboys and Poets again soon!

A big thank-you to Sweetleaf LIC and its entire staff for giving me a place to write, and a special thanks to Andrea Garcia, Kevin Burgos, and Desiree Camacho. Thank you for all the brownie bites and guidance on which Spanish curse words to use, and for watching me make funny faces at my laptop for a year straight without kicking me out.

Another thank-you to the Hungarian Pastry Shop, where I spent a year and a half writing my very first draft and devouring slice after slice of your amazing cakes. I can't wait to give you a photo of my cover so it can be featured on your wall of amazing books that have been written in your legendary shop.

To my family—my mom and dad and stepmom, my sisters, my wild band of cousins (LFAM for life!), and my aunts and uncles—thank you for patiently waiting after hearing me ramble about wanting to write books since I was four years old. It only took twenty-two years, so I think I made it right on time.

And, of course, thank you to you too. Thank you for giving me, Alfie, and Finn a spot on your bookshelf, under your bed, on your desk, or in your heart. Wherever you keep your books, we're honored to be there.

Finn and Alfie saved Castallan—but now they face a brand-new threat.

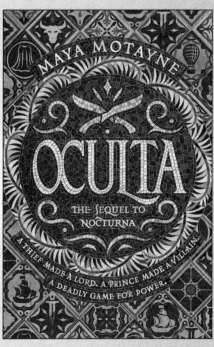

Don't miss *Oculta*, the exhilarating sequel to *Nocturna*!

JOIN THE

Epic Reads
COMMUNITY

THE ULTIMATE YA DESTINATION

◀ **DISCOVER** ▶
your next favorite read

◀ **MEET** ▶
new authors to love

◀ **WIN** ▶
free books

◀ **SHARE** ▶
infographics, playlists, quizzes, and more

◀ **WATCH** ▶
the latest videos

www.epicreads.com